HELLO TO THE CANNIBALS

ALSO BY RICHARD BAUSCH

Real Presence (1980)

Take Me Back (1981)

The Last Good Time (1984)

Spirits, and Other Stories (1987)

Mr. Field's Daughter (1989)

The Fireman's Wife, and Other Stories (1990)

Violence (1992)

Rebel Powers (1993)

Rare & Endangered Species: Stories and a Novella (1994)

Selected Stories of Richard Bausch
(The Modern Library, 1996)

Good Evening Mr. and Mrs. America,
and All the Ships at Sea (1996)

In the Night Season (1998)

Someone to Watch Over Me: Stories (1999)

HELLO TO THE CANNIBALS

A Novel

RICHARD BAUSCH

HarperCollins*Publishers*

Quotations from "Various Tourists," an essay from *The Aztec Treasure House* by Evan S. Connell. Reprinted by permission of Don Congdon Associates, Inc., and Counterpoint Press. © 1979 by Evan S. Connell.

FIRST EDITION

Designed by Nancy B. Field

Library of Congress Cataloging-in-Publication Data

Bausch, Richard
  Hello to the cannibals : a novel / Richard Bausch.—1st ed.
      p. cm.
  ISBN 0-06-019295-X
  1. Kingsley, Mary Henrietta, 1862-1900—Influence—Fiction. 2. Adult child abuse victims—Fiction. 3. Women dramatists—Fiction. 4. Married women—Fiction. 5. Young women—Fiction. 6. Playwriting—Fiction.
  7. Virginia—Fiction. I. Title.
  PS3552.A846 H45 2002
  813'.54—dc21   200202370

02 03 04 05 06 ❖/RRD 10 9 8 7 6 5 4 3 2 1

For Karen, with the long and inexpressible love

In loving memory of my mother and my father:

Helen Simmons Bausch
September 25, 1918–August 4, 1985

Robert Carl Bausch
March 15, 1917–June 30, 1995

and

Also in tribute to the life and work of R. S. Jones,
friend, editor, and artist

ACKNOWLEDGMENTS

Along with having large sections of the work read to her while I was composing the novel, Karen printed it out and read it, and was, as always, indispensable as a reader, friend, advisor, editor, and loving accomplice. The same goes for my eldest daughter, Emily Chiles, my son Paul, and his companion Merrill Feitell, who read portions of the book in manuscript. Also, I want to thank George and Susan Garrett for too many things to list, including strength, and of course the other dear friends who encouraged and stood with me during this arduous labor, and the months of delay: Cary and Karen Kimble, Allen and Donny Wier, Charles and Martha Baxter, Thomas Mallon, Andrea Barrett, Mary Lee Settle, Alan Shapiro, Allan Gurganus, Harriet Wasserman, and Michelle Fields. I am grateful to Dan Conaway for his labor and his great insight in the editing of an enormous manuscript, which he inherited.

The writer Nolde Alexius provided important details about New Orleans and Mardi Gras for me. I have incorporated them almost as she gave them to me. I am very grateful for her help. Two other writers, Tania Nyman and Richard Ford, at different times, took me on walking tours of the Quarter, as did Ms. Alexius and her brother Fritz. I send them all John Berryman's lovely poem/prayer: "Lord, bless everyone in the world, especially some, thou knowest whom."

RB
Broad Run, Virginia
December 2001

The past isn't ever dead. It isn't even past.

—WILLIAM FAULKNER

To the north lay a belt of forest inhabited by the Fans, a tribe known to eat human flesh not merely on special occasions but rather often. She had met some of them, she admired their virility and thought she should know more about them. So, in July, accompanied by an Igalwa interpreter and four nervous Ajumba armed with flintlocks, she started upriver to say hello to the cannibals.

—EVAN S. CONNELL,
  writing about Mary Kingsley in *The Aztec Treasure House*

PROLOGUE

December 21, 1982

Opening night of the Washington Theater production of King Lear. *A cold, blowing mist, one massive cloud trailing over the world. Lily Austin, sitting in the backseat of her father's car on the way to the theater, imagines that this could be part of the gathering elements that will produce the artificial weather onstage, the storm on the heath. She's watched it in rehearsal for weeks. Her father has the role of Edmund in this production, and of course the real weather has him worried. Nothing at all cheerful about it, in this most cheerful of seasons. And now that the sun is down, there's been talk of freezing. An ice storm—the whole city will be paralyzed, he says, fretting, muttering at the closed window on the passenger side in the front seat. It will all look as though it has been encased inside glass, and no one will venture out to go to a play, if the play isn't, in fact, canceled.*

There have been two such storms already this winter, and the bare trees on either side of Pennsylvania Avenue look burdened with ice; the branches bend heavily with each gust. Traffic signals sway and toss and then are still. People hurry along the sidewalks, holding on to their hats and packages. Christmas shoppers.

The voice on the car radio says there's no telling for sure what will happen. It says reassuringly that the storm should move in a more northerly direction, which will mean rising temperatures and a lot of rain. But there are already patches of slickness on the bridges over the Potomac. No question about it; it's a bad night. And even so, the festive storefronts on the wide avenues give a sparkle to the city, a shiny vista of brightness and color, lampposts gar-

landed with sprigs of pine and strands of winking illumination. The asphalt ahead, not quite treacherous yet, shimmers red and soft white with the headlamps and taillights of cars, and you can't see the cars themselves until they are upon you, polished by the weather, and reflecting everything in shiny distortion. To Lily, the pools of misting radiance in the lamps along the street look like cones set under dishes that pour out a million beads of water every second. A shower of diamonds. Brightness inside gloom, so strange. She's fourteen years old today. She gazes out the window, thinking of how to describe the quality of the light. Lately, they call her "chatterbox," as a joke. Yet when she's quiet, they want to know what's going on in her mind. "What are you thinking?" her mother seems always to be asking. Lily answers, "Everything," and it feels true. In the nights, she lies awake, waiting for her parents to close their door, so she can put a light on and read, or write in her notebooks. Nothing is ever quite real to her until she turns it into words.

Tonight, she's holding a wrapped present on her lap—the first volume of The Lord of the Rings—and thinking about how, for all her father's anxiety about it, this night is perfect for Lear. She's also reflecting about how things have been more tense than usual, not just because this is opening night and there's a storm, but because her mother has announced that she wishes to quit the company, where she and Lily's father have been actors as long as Lily can remember. The child is used to gauging the moods and affections of her parents, who are volatile and romantic and the envy of everyone. It's almost like a game she plays, guessing their mood and their temper. She's never taken their quarrels at all seriously because they never do.

Just now, it's true, though her father muses aloud about his anxieties and his woeful expectations, they're not speaking. Her mother, driving the car, gives no hint of having heard any of it.

Up on the left, through the watery gloom and twinkle, is the theater, with its bright marquee, and her father's name, with three others, under the title. People are already lined up in front, clutching umbrellas and leaning into each other in the cold. Lily's father will get out here, and she and her mother will go on into the darker streets north and east of the theater, and the house of Ronda Seiver, a school friend whose birthday is also this week. Ronda is having a mutual birthday party. Something Lily has agreed to. Lily's "real" party will be Sunday afternoon, after the matinee. The cast party. It is all what you expect of the life—growing up, as her mother has said many times, with show people.

They come to a stop in front of the theater. "Not enough to pack the house," says Lily's father. "Certainly not enough. This is a disaster in the making."

Silence.

"Watch. They'll cancel the damn thing. The ice will form and they'll cancel it."

Still, no response.

"Should I file for the divorce, or do you want to?" He looks at Lily's mother, and smiles. "Come on, Doris."

"Well, you're the one who got quiet."

"I spoke just now. You didn't hear me? I've been speaking. Yes, I'm sure that was the sound of my voice. I talked about the bad weather and the ice storm and the small crowd and our chances of being canceled."

" 'If it be now,' " Lily's mother says, " 'tis not to come; if it be not to come, it will be now; if it be not now, yet it will come—' "

"Okay, okay. I still say it looks bad."

"Poor baby. It'll be a packed house. It's still early."

"Huddled masses," Lily says. "They look so miserable."

"Where did you get that?" her father asks. " 'Huddled masses'?" He looks at her mother. "Some kid we've got."

"That's your side of the family," says Doris.

"All my life, I've had a recurring nightmare that I'm in a play and can't remember my lines. And here I am with a kid who has nightmares that she's the only one in the play who does know them."

"I think it's on the Statue of Liberty, isn't it?" Lily says.

"What?"

" 'Huddled masses.' "

"Jesus."

"Scott," says Doris. "Watch your language." She kisses his cheek. The two of them are happy again. They've made up now. The night is gloriously murky, magnificent with shadows and shapes of light, and there's the feeling of wonderful possibility—wild, happy life, unlike everyone else's. The wet, cold air comes in when her father opens the door, but it's bracing. It's going to be fine, as it always eventually is when they argue. They come back together and are friends again, playful and exaggerated, bigger than love, and teasing her.

He likes having the part of Edmund, though he says he's too old for it, almost forty. He has been joking about his age all year. "I'm an old, old man," he'll say to Lily, making his voice tremble with the word old. *"You're not old yet," Lily always tells him, believing him to be ancient.*

"See you, my darling," *her mother says to him now. "And you're not mad at me anymore."*

"We'll discuss it," *he says. "It's not over."*

"You know I haven't enjoyed it this last few years, Scott."

"Maybe I just don't like it that now is when you tell me."

She kisses him again. "It's cold. Go."

He looks back at Lily, shakes his head. "'Huddled masses.'"

"Go," *Doris tells him.* "I'm freezing." *She isn't in this production, but has important duties, anyway. She'll drop Lily at Ronda's house, and then come back to the theater. Scott leans into the car and kisses Lily on the forehead.*

"Well?" *he says to her.*

"Break a leg," *Lily tells him.*

Her father was in a couple of movies before she was old enough to know. She has never seen the movies, and he doesn't talk about them much. Yet she has received the impression that his retirement from being a movie actor must have had something to do with her.

He has said it's a thing he doesn't mind, staying in one place.

But Lily wonders. There are times when he says he doesn't mind something, and he clearly does mind it. She can nearly always tell. Something in his voice and his eyes, and the way he carries himself, even the movement of his hands—they're quicker; they have a nervous, hectic way of moving to his face and then to the front of his shirt, and into his pockets and out again.

"Why don't you want to act anymore," *Lily asks her mother.*

"It's just as I said, sweetie. It's not fun anymore. I'd rather be home with you. Tonight, for instance. It's your birthday and I'm carting you over to Ronda Seiver's house. That doesn't feel right. It's not fair to you and it's not right."

"I don't mind," *Lily tells her. But she hasn't spoken very loud.*

Her mother turns on East Capitol Street, heads past the Folger Shakespeare Library and on, into the flying mist, which is turning to rain. Lily gazes out at the big square building with its tall, dark doors.

Something's going on there, too, people lining up to go inside. Her mother's quiet, somewhere off in her own thoughts. Lately, she does this a lot, and Lily knows it's because she's been deciding about quitting.

"So what did you get for Ronda?"

"I don't think you should quit because of me," Lily says.

"Tell me what you got her."

"Lord of the Rings."

"I thought you didn't like that much."

"Ronda will."

The street opens out into lawns and houses set back in the murk, among drooping pine branches and the jagged arms of heavy, gnarled oaks and maples. Several of the houses are outlined with winking lights. There are candles in some of the windows, behind curtains, a warm glow, which in this moving distance seems intricately laced, tissue thin in the rain, as if the next gust will certainly blow it out.

"You seem a little low for someone going to a birthday party."

"I'd rather go to the show."

"You'll have a good time at Ronda's. And she was so set on this party."

Ronda told Lily that the only way she could get a party thrown at all was to suggest that it be for Lily, too. Ronda's parents are busy people—both lawyers—and while they are in fact mostly innocent of the things Ronda usually has to say about them, it is true that they are gone a lot, always running from one event to another. Sometimes when they travel they take Ronda with them, and she's gone from school for days at a time. There's always some makeup work Ronda has to do to catch up. But this is all right with Ronda. She likes to be considered an object of sympathy; it's a part she plays. She and Lily have on occasion performed little scenes for both sets of parents—bits from Shakespeare, mostly, and a few musical numbers, and Ronda, who overplays everything, says she's humoring Lily because Lily's the one who wants to be an actor when she grows up. Yet her fascination with Lily's parents is boundless, and her indifference to her own parents borders on disrespect. She makes fun of their busy social life, and says she's certain they no longer love each other, are frantically searching for something to do to keep from having to be alone together in the same house.

Tonight, for instance, the night of Ronda's party, they are not there when Lily and her mother arrive. Instead, Ronda's grandfather greets them: Mr. Thomas Stapleton, a tall, narrow-faced, graying man, with gray tufts over each eye and strands of gray hair standing out on top of his head. You can see his balding scalp in the light. He talks with a slight Irish accent, explaining that Ronda's parents will return within the hour. He's here visiting from Syracuse. Lily's mother says that, yes, she remembers Ronda's mother saying something about a visit, and she murmurs to Lily in the confusion that she wishes someone had told her about tonight. Lily whispers back that she didn't know about it. Ronda, standing in the Seivers' hallway, plays the part of the hostess, her straw-colored hair done up in a chignon, wearing a bright red dress and black high-heeled shoes. "Where have you been? We've been dying of worry. Is that for me? Oh, you shouldn't have."

"We agreed on it, didn't we?" Lily says, and laughs.

"We won't be too late," says Lily's mother to Mr. Stapleton. "Eleven or so."

"I'll tell them that."

Lily watches her mother head down the walk. Mr. Stapleton holds the door. Part of his back pocket is sticking out oddly, as if someone has just removed his wallet. He's in his stocking feet. Lily decides that he looks indigent. She repeats the word to herself.

"Come on," Ronda says, already tearing at her present. "What're you waiting for?"

Lily follows her and the trail of torn wrapping paper she leaves, walking down the long hallway and into the living room, where the other guests wait. Two boys and two girls. They're standing by the Seivers' artificial Christmas tree, with its rotating light filter. On the coffee table is a flat cake with slices out of it, a small stack of paper plates, a plastic cup with plastic knives and forks in it, and several opened presents. Someone has sprayed the tree with a pine scent stronger than any fragrance a real tree would ever give off. It smells like cleanser, and causes Lily to cough. She puts one hand over her mouth. Ronda introduces her to the others as a best girlfriend from school, and then apologizes to Lily for not making it clear to them that this is a joint birthday party. There's only Ronda's gift for Lily.

"These guys go to the Catholic school," Ronda says. The boys bow politely, the taller one holding his left hand across his waist, the other at his back. His name is Dominic. The girls' names are Christine and Drinda. The other boy is Brian. Drinda has long, stringy black hair, a white, white face, and is appallingly skinny. She offers a bony white hand with black fingernail polish. She's sixteen. Christine's ruddy, with auburn hair and deep-socketed light brown eyes, and she still has all her baby fat. She actually curtsies. So Lily curtsies back, smiling, amused.

"We started on the cake," Ronda says, still tearing at the wrapping paper. "My mother and father wanted a piece before they left." She holds the book up and shows it around. "This is great."

"The cake smells good," Lily says. "I didn't think I was hungry."

Mr. Stapleton comes in, bending repeatedly to pick up the wrapping paper Ronda has dropped. "Sloppy," he says, shaking his head. "Sloppy." He puts the pieces into a plastic bag and then sits on the couch, puts a pair of glasses on, and opens a magazine. Newsweek.

"Aren't we going to sing happy birthday to Lily?" Christine asks.

"Well," says Lily, "I haven't sung it to Ronda." She begins to sing, facing the other girl, who joins in, with Christine and the boy Brian, while the others stare. Mr. Stapleton looks over the top of his glasses, holding the magazine open on his knees, smiling tolerantly. Finally the boy named Dominic takes up the song, on the last line. They get the names mixed up. Lily sings Ronda's name and Ronda sings Lily's. The other girl sings Ronda's. Dominic sings a mumbled combination of both names and then laughs. Drinda says, "Okay. Now. Are we finished? Jeez."

"When's your birthday?" Lily asks her.

"A thousand years ago. I'm a witch."

"She's a witch," Ronda repeats, laughing.

"It's a sin to believe in witches," says Christine.

"Who said anything about belief?" Drinda asks her.

"That's a bad thing to say," Mr. Stapleton puts in. "Your parents ought to know you talk like that."

"Hey," Drinda says. "They talk like that. Somebody cut the cake. Jeez."

"I'll cut it," Lily says. "I want some. It's my birthday, too." She picks up a plastic knife and makes a wide swath through the left side of the cake, then lifts the piece, most of that side, as it begins to crumble, onto one of the paper plates. She hands the plate to Drinda.

"You don't think I'll eat it," Drinda says.

"You'll make it disappear," says Lily, grinning out of one side of her mouth, as her father has said she does so charmingly.

"*Here,*" Ronda says, handing her a wrapped book. Her one present. She opens it while the others watch. It is one of those serial books, written for young teens. Lily reads the title: Great Explorers. She flips through the pages to the picture section. A woman catches her eye, among all the faces of men. The face is narrow, the eyes dark, the hair wispy and dark-looking under a bonnet. The picture must have been taken just before, or just after, the woman smiled. It shows in the dark eyes and in the lines of shadow bordering the eyes—the suggestion of a smile, a ghost smile. Lily stares. The name under the photograph is Mary Kingsley.

"*Thanks, Ronda,*" Lily says, and puts the book down on the table, next to the cake.

They go down to the basement to listen to music. It's low-ceilinged and dark, with pictures on the walls of the Beatles, and Bob Dylan—Ronda's parents' pictures and this is her parents' recreation room. There is a pool table, a large-screen television, and a sound system, complete with tall speakers and amplifiers. There are bookcases all around, and a big desk stacked with papers in apparent disorder. Ronda turns music on—The Bee Gees—and then decides to make out with Dominic. They sit on the sofa and do this, while the others stand around in the noise. It's as if they're playing a love scene in a movie. Lily sits next to Christine at the other end of the sofa, and the two of them begin to laugh at their own awkwardness, their own inability to keep from attending to what's going on. Across the room, Brian is looking through the books. Then he selects a pool cue and begins to shoot pool. Drinda, who has been standing off to one side, hands folded at her waist and looking very uncomfortable, joins him.

Mr. Stapleton comes partway down the stairs, clearing his throat loudly. It's clear he doesn't want to come in on anything. He leans down and looks at them. Ronda and Dominic have separated and are sitting apart. The music stops, the end of a song.

"*Everything okay down here?*"

"*We're shooting pool,*" Lily says, rising from the sofa.

"*All right. Be good, you-all.*" He turns on the stairs and ascends, slowly, clearing his throat and coughing once, deep.

"*He'll be asleep in five minutes,*" Ronda says.

"*It's a bet,*" says Dominic.

For a time everyone takes turns shooting pool, and then they are all sitting in the shifting light of the television. Nothing good is on, but they

*watch anyway. Lily walks upstairs and retrieves her book from the coffee
table, and has another bite of cake. Mr. Stapleton is dozing on the couch.
He wakes and looks at her. "What?"*

"Just had a piece of cake."

*He closes his eyes, seems to sigh, and then is gone in sleep again, mak-
ing a raw, scratchy, bronchial sound with each inhalation. She backs
away and returns to the basement, carrying her book. Dominic is sitting
on the bottom step, reading the back of a record album. He's smoking a
cigarette, blowing the smoke into the heat vent.*

"Old man's asleep, isn't he," he says to Lily.

"Yep."

"I can hear him. He sounds like a lung patient."

A second later, she says, "Aren't you afraid of getting caught?"

*"Hey, he smokes. Smokes like a train. I see him sitting out on their
front porch, blowing smoke like a chimney."*

*She sits on the step next to him and opens her book. In the room,
there's the sound of television gunfire and car chasing, brakes squealing,
sirens. It's a repeat of* The Dukes of Hazzard. *Lily can tell by the music,
and the voiceover.*

"Want a drag?" Dominic asks her.

"No, thanks."

"Ever try it?"

"Yes," she lies.

"Ever smoke weed?"

She shakes her head.

*"Bet your folks have. Bet they have a lot. You know how it's defined in
the dictionary in my father's library? 'A mild hallucinogenic smoked by
jazz musicians in the United States.' Isn't that great?"*

"My parents aren't jazz musicians."

"They're actors. Next closest thing."

"What about you?"

"I'm clean. Mean and keen."

"Not stuck on yourself or anything."

*He laughs. The reaction surprises her. Soon they're talking about
their schools and the teachers they have, and she discovers that she likes
him. There's something sharp-edged about him that interests her, and,
like her, he has done more reading than most adolescents, and isn't afraid*

to talk about it. He's not doing well in school, but this doesn't worry him. Together, they look through her book of explorers. He stops on the photograph of Mary Kingsley. "Looks like she just laughed."

"I had the same thought," Lily says. "Like she just did or is about to."

"Exactly."

She feels relaxed with him, and wonders how it would be to have a brother. This is more comfortable than anything she has experienced at her school, where the other children often treat her cruelly: because she's bookish, and is faintly secretive-seeming at times; because she prefers Ella Fitzgerald to Pat Benatar; because she has a large vocabulary and on occasion uses it to talk about whatever excites her, or interests her; because she's an only child; because she's more developed in the chest, or wears the wrong clothes, or too many of the right ones; because she has freckles over her nose; because she doesn't watch much television; because her parents are actors and therefore merit either envy or suspicion; and so on and so on—for any of the thousand unfathomable reasons a group of children, forming a pecking order, decide that one among them is strange, not like them, or not enough like them.

The party ends with the parents of the others coming. They talk of the fact that the roads are indeed icing over. Ronda's parents haven't returned, and neither have Lily's. The boy Dominic Martinez stays on for a time, and then wanders on out across the street, hands in his pockets against the cold. Lily watches him go, and sees that he slips several times.

"Where are your parents?" Ronda wants to know. "It's past eleven."

"Where are yours?"

She yawns. "They're always late."

"Well." Lily looks around the room. The old man is drowsing again on the couch, making that asthmatic sound with each breath. The remains of the cake are on the table, the plates, all the debris of the party. Ronda's collecting her presents.

"I'm really exhausted," she says.

"You're not going to bed, Ronda. Come on."

"I'll just fall asleep right here. Where are your parents? Aren't you worried?"

Mr. Stapleton sits up, mumbling, glassy-eyed. "What the hell. I went out again. What time is it?"

Lily tells him. He rises, scratches his head, and moves to the hallway, and the front door. "Where is everybody?"

"They should be here any minute," Lily says, beginning to worry.

At midnight, there's no answer at the theater, and he calls the police. Lily sits on the couch listening to his side of the conversation, and she hears car doors outside. She tells herself that if she looks, it will be Ronda's parents, so she waits, listening to the footsteps, and allowing her imagination to present her with Scott and Doris, invincible, as usual, arm in arm, coming carefully up the walk, to the front door. But it must be neighbors, someone on the other side of the street. No one comes. As the minutes go by, Lily begins to feel an unreasoning terror. It clutches at her heart: it is only a little more than thirty minutes past the time Scott and Doris would ordinarily arrive; yet she can't undo the strands of conviction in her soul that both of them are dead, now. That this night has taken them away from her. She keeps seeing the image of her father, dying as Edmund, sprawled out on the stage. She can't get it out of her mind—the whole violent wrack and turmoil of the play, even as she understands that none of it is like life as life is, now. Sitting in Ronda Seiver's living room, she experiences a terrible dread of the particulars of existence: the world outside, with its glitter of ice and roar of wind, is too big, too immense, a darkness she can't get her mind around.

There isn't anything to do but wait.

They sit in the living room. Lily and Ronda and Mr. Stapleton, who says he's sure it's all right, a simple explanation, and nothing to worry about. Lily forces herself to smile, barely holding on, being polite.

"It's only a little past midnight." Ronda holds Lily's hand.

"Would you like something to eat?" Mr. Stapleton asks.

"No, thank you, sir." Lily begins to tremble, deep down, where she can't reach with will or determination. It comes over her like a fever, but she says nothing, sitting in the false light, looking at Mr. Stapleton and waiting for the phone to ring. She can't draw in air, and then when she does manage to do so, she can't quite let it out. The shaking begins to cause the muscles of her back to seize up.

When the phone finally does ring, all three of them jump. Mr. Stapleton actually emits a sound like a gasp. He's the one who answers.

Lily feels the cold on the inside of her skin, and realizes that she has put her hands to her face. The calm in Mr. Stapleton's voice makes her give way a little, and in the next moment it's clear that her father is on the other end. They've had a slight accident—no one hurt. Lily hears the words. No one hurt. She stands, and then sits down, and then stands again, and Ronda embraces her so forcefully that both of them fall back onto the couch. Ronda's crying. And then they're all standing, and Mr. Stapleton says, "He wants to talk to you. You're welcome to spend the night."

"Hello?" she says into the phone, trying not to cry.

"We're fine, everything's fine. The play went fine."

"Daddy?" she says.

"We're fine, sweetie. Really. We hit the curb and we couldn't shake loose. It's too icy. We're at the Willard. Can you stay there tonight?"

"Yes."

"And on your birthday, too. We'll make it up to you. Promise."

"It's okay." She can't keep the tears from her voice. But she's happy—relieved—and yet oddly still frightened. It has never before entered her mind in such a palpable way that anything might ever happen to her parents.

"We'll come over there as soon as the weather clears up in the morning," he says.

A little later, Ronda's parents call to say that they are stuck at the house of the couple with whom they had dinner. The streets are too treacherous for anyone to take a chance. Ronda lends Lily a nightgown, and Mr. Stapleton makes himself a whiskey to celebrate that everyone's all right. He pours Cokes for Ronda and Lily, and asks them to sit up with him awhile. Ronda yawns, and says, "Okay," clearly reluctant. Lily, still feeling the fright along her nerves, is glad to stay up.

They sit in the living room and watch late news reports about the storm, and the old man sips his whiskey. Between sighs of satisfaction, he talks about how bad the winters are in Syracuse, where Ronda's mother grew up, how the snow can pile up to the windows with a single storm, and how it stays on the ground until the spring. "You've heard the stories of parents saying they walked five miles in the snow—well, Ronda, your mother did just that. No kidding about it." He drinks, looking happy.

"I've heard," Ronda says.

He laughs softly, to himself, and drinks again. After a time, he says, "Well, no sense keeping you girls up. You go on to bed. But don't keep me up, either. This is no pajama party or anything like that."

In Ronda's room, they lie side by side in Ronda's bed in the light from her reading lamp, and she whispers stories about her parents—the arguments she hears between them concerning her grandfather's presence in this house. It's not such a big house that you can get out of someone's way, and the old man watches too much television. Also, he drinks. Tonight, he broke a rule—he's not supposed to have anything when he's baby-sitting. Sometimes he sits up late and you can hear the tip of the bottle touching the lip of the glass as he pours. He's a bad sleeper. Ronda often wakes in the middle of the night to hear him moving around. "Once he wandered in here by mistake. Scared me to pieces. He's had heart trouble for years, and I never go into any room where he's at that I don't expect to find him dead."

"Oh, come on," Lily says. "He's not that old. How old is he?"

"He's sixty-two."

"That's not that old anymore, Ronda. You're being silly."

"You try living with someone like that."

"I think he's nice," Lily says.

Ronda stares dreamily at the ceiling. "I want to be a movie star when I grow up. If I was your father, I never would've stopped."

Lily says, "He likes what he's doing."

"Are you going to be an actor? Mother says you're gonna be a writer. I mean, she says you already are."

"It's just a—a journal."

Ronda turns the light off. "Will you write novels, do you think? Maybe I'll write them. I can write, you know. I just don't find it easy."

"Well, neither do I," Lily says.

"I think you should write plays. And your parents can act in them."

They're quiet for a time. Lily's still feeling the residue of the fright, and she entertains a waking dream of her parents acting in a play of hers; she sees herself, grown, no longer afraid, standing in the wings while they take their bows. She murmers a prayer she has said each night as long as she can remember: "Bless everyone I've laid eyes on, and everyone they've laid eyes on."

"That's nice," Ronda says. "I shouldn't talk about Grandpa Stapleton. But he's old and he drinks, and I worry about him." She sighs. "I can't sleep."

Yet in the next moment, Lily hears her breathing become slow; it deepens, and there's a small snoring sound issuing from the back of her throat.

The house grows quiet. She listens, tries to sleep, and her mind is too restless, still turning on the images of her father as Edmund, dying in rehearsal. It's as if she has never thought of death, the fact of it in the world—its irremediable remorseless power over her and everybody she loves—before now. Her heart races. She sits up, hearing sounds downstairs. Mr. Stapleton walking into the kitchen. She thinks of the book of explorers, something to read. When Mr. Stapleton goes to his room, she'll sneak downstairs and sit reading until she gets sleepy. The time crawls by, while Ronda emits her little sleep sound, and sighs. Lily moves from the bed, and stands at the door of the room, trying to hear. Silence. Finally she opens the door a crack. There's a light on downstairs, but no sound. She waits, listening. Nothing stirs. She steps out into the darkened hallway and moves to the top of the stairs and down, along the downstairs hall to the living room, where one lamp is on, and the television, without sound. Mr. Stapleton sits up from the couch and sees her, a look of startlement on his face. He reaches for his eyeglasses, and nearly falls to the floor, righting himself with an extended hand, and then working to sit up. On the table before him is a bottle of whiskey, and a cocktail glass. He peers at her. "Hey."

"I didn't mean to disturb you," Lily says.

"Can't sleep?"

"I thought if I could read . . ."

"I leave the TV on without sound," he says. "Isn't that something? It's like watching a painting get made because I can't see shit without my glasses. Just colors. It—it lulls me to sleep at night. I'm sorry for the language." He puts the glasses on.

"Well," she says. "Sleep well." She starts back toward the hallway.

"Don't go. Where you going?"

"Upstairs."

"Why?" He moves over. "Sit down. Watch a little TV. Maybe that'll make you sleepy."

"TV keeps me awake."

"We'll talk. Talking to me will make a person sleepy, believe me." He gives a little crooked, pained smile. It's sad. She remembers Ronda's talk, and abruptly feels sorry for him, wonders if he might've heard some of it. Her own sense of avoidance causes her to walk over to him; she wants to

show him that she's not afraid, not leery of him. She stands close, and looks directly down at him.

For a long time, he simply looks back. At last, he reaches to the coffee table behind her and takes a small piece of the cake, and holds it up to her mouth.

"No thank you," she says.

He puts it in his own mouth, and chews it, still staring. "You're not hungry?" he says. His eyes are glassy in the light.

"No," she says.

He swallows, then reaches for some more. "Sit."

She does so.

"Tell me about yourself." He eats the bite of cake. "Are you going to be in the theater, like your parents?"

"Maybe," she says. "But maybe I'll be a writer."

"Oh, a writer. That's a nice thing to be. Will you write about, say, loneliness? That's what most of them end up writing about, I think. Loneliness. Or maybe you'll write about old men living on their married children."

She smiles at him. "No."

"Ah, hell. Of course I'm just being silly. Never mind me."

She's aware that a line has been crossed, and sees that he's aware of it, too. She feels almost as if she should try to console him, watching the shaky way he reaches for more cake.

"Well," he says. "You're so nice to come keep me company. I don't often have anybody to talk to in this house."

She can't think of anything to tell him. It's as if he can see what Ronda said about him in her face. She looks at the television, where there's an image of a red car on a mountain road.

"What do you want to talk about? Tell me—let's see. If you could have any wish in the world, what would it be?"

"I'd be a writer and an actor."

"Wow. And you'd travel and be rich?"

"I don't really care if I'm rich or not." She begins telling him about her love of books and music and her excitement at getting to see her parents onstage, all her enthusiasms. She explains that her father told her about the Greek root for the word entheos, "the God within," and before very long, she's surprised to find herself describing how the image of her father playing Edmund's death in rehearsals got fixed in her head while they were waiting for some word to come through.

"You're very expressive," he says, reaching for the bottle. She watches him pour more for himself. "Your parents must be awful proud of you."

"Yes," she says, enjoying his attention. "But it's kind of rough at school sometimes."

He sips the drink. "Tell me."

"Well, you know. I think they think I talk too much in class. I'm too grown-up, you know, because I like Ella Fitzgerald."

"You know more than they do."

"I know I'm talking your ear off."

"No, go ahead. It makes an old man happy to hear a young, pretty girl talk about herself. The world's an ugly place a lot of the time. We need all the pretty girls we can get."

"Well, I'm not pretty," Lily says.

"Oh, yes you are."

"Aren't you nice to say so." She gives a little nod of her head.

"Go on, talk to me." He pours more of the whiskey. "This doesn't bother you, does it?" He's seen her watching him.

"Not at all."

"You ever tasted whiskey?"

"Once. My father let me have a sip. I didn't like it. He says he used to put it on my gums, when I was a baby. You know, teething."

"Yeah, I did that with my kids, too. Back in the dark ages, when they were young, and I was younger."

"You're not so old," she tells him, thinking again of Ronda's talk about him and also of her own father's teasing complaints about being almost forty.

"Life's gone by me, missy," he says, swallowing the whiskey. He pours still more of it. "I hope you'll forgive me if I get just a little plastered tonight."

"It's fine," she says, because she can't think of what else is expected.

He sits back. "So, tell me more about yourself. It's tough 'n school." He gives a little wave of his hand.

She tells him that, at school, she feels singled out, different. Like some sort of freak. Because she likes Ella, for instance. She says the name again, proud of her mature taste, as her mother has put it, and certain that it will impress him. It does.

"That's someth'n, that you know that music."

"I know all of her music. And Louis Armstrong, too. And Benny Goodman. Glenn Miller."

"Damn," he says, staring.

"I know Chet Baker, too. I have a record of his."

He says nothing, gazing at her, and then down into his glass. He sighs, and takes another swallow.

"I read a lot of plays, too," she says. "Not just books."

"Well, you would. With your folks."

"Yes. They encourage me quite a lot."

"I'll bet they do." He pours still more of the whiskey. "Yes, you're a—you're quite a young woman."

"Not really."

"No—you are." Again, he pours whiskey, and his hands are unsteady now. He spills some of it. He's quite drunk now, and she's fascinated, watching him. She sees that his tremor makes him move more slowly, more deliberately.

"What're you thinking about?" he says.

"Oh," she tells him. "Nothing. Just—this is nice. Talking to you."

"Do you like that?"

"Yes, I do. It's calming."

"Calming."

"Comfortable."

"Yes. You're 'bout as expressive a girl as I've seen in my life. Very grown-up."

"I'm just—I don't know. Lucky. My parents encourage me."

"It's character, too, though. Don' ever underestimate th' power of character. Char-ac-ter." He says the word slowly, as if repeating it for himself. "That's what I mos'ly lack. An' always have, too."

"I bet you do have it," she says.

"How old are you?" he says.

She smiles. "It's my birthday, remember? I'm fourteen."

"Fourteen." He takes another piece of the cake, and eats it slowly, thinking, looking down. His glass is empty, listing to one side in his limp hand. She thinks he might be going to sleep. But then he lifts it, drains the last drop out of it, and puts it down, carefully.

She can smell the cake, and abruptly she can smell the whiskey, too. She says, "Or, really, it's the day after, now. I was fourteen yest—"

He has turned and taken hold of her arms, tight. A small sound comes from her, like a sigh. A lost cry, gone on her breath, as now he buries his *face in her chest, pleading with her in garbled words. She knows it's pleading, and she can't pull away, isn't quite sure how this is supposed to be, this strange, caught moment. But then his hands go in under her night-gown, under what she remembers, as it is happening, is Ronda's night-gown. His hands are all over her, and she's falling, the two of them are tumbling off the couch onto the floor. "No," he says. "No. I'm sorry. Please. Please forgive me."*

But his hands are still working, still holding her. She tries to scream, can't get her breath. He's moving on her, pulling at her panties, raking at her thighs. His weight is suffocating her, and she can't find the air to make any sound but the struggle to breathe; she flails at him, strikes the top of his head, in utter disbelief that this is taking place; and at last she's able to find her voice, a long, low cry, and then something like a shriek. His hand comes to her mouth, the fingers tasting of salt. She bites down, pulls at his hair.

He stops. She's still pulling, trying to shout.

"No," he says, breathless. "Forgive me. You—please. You must, please." He pushes off of her, lifting himself from her, and falters away, coughing, crying, standing over her, then reaching down to take her hand, actually helping her rise. She's quiet, her hair has fallen across her face. She watches him stagger to the other side of the room, both hands held to his head. "I didn't—I didn't do it. Didn't—it—this—I'm sorry. I'm so sorry. Jesus Christ." He's crying, sobbing into his hands. "I don't believe, I don't believe . . ."

It amazes her. With her own trembling fingers she pushes the hair from her face, rearranges the nightgown, still wary, backing toward the door. And now he comes at her in a rush, taking hold of her arms so that she gives forth another little cry. He holds her so strongly that again it's hard to breathe.

"Listen to me," he says. "You can't say anything about this. Do you understand? Never, never say anything about this. You've got to believe me, I never did anything like this."

She starts crying, and her gorge rises; she's afraid she'll be sick.

"Jesus—oh, Jesus. I wish I was dead. Promise me—please."

"I promise," she says, crying, shaking. "I promise."

"Stop it. Stop crying. Control yourself. I swear I'll do something to hurt you."

She looks directly into his eyes. "No," she manages, between sobs.

"*You*," she gets out. And then: "*Won't*." She breathes the words into his face one by one with little gasps of rage and fright and confusion.

"I'll kill you, I swear."

She doesn't answer him this time.

"It—it couldn't be helped. I had too much to drink. Do you understand? Nothing happened. It didn't—"

Again, she says nothing.

He straightens, and his grip loosens slightly. "You came down here and tempted me. You should've stayed where you belong."

"Let me go," Lily says. "Please."

"No one will believe you. Nothing happened. A little groping. Nothing."

"Will you please, please let me go, now."

He does so, and moves again to the other side of the room, that asthmatic sound coming from him. She leaves him there, and makes her way unsteadily up the stairs. She hurts along her arms, and in her chest and back. She's woozy with terror, and with a sickeningly confused mixture of revulsion and guilt—something about all of it seeping into her consciousness as inexpressibly a matter of her own will, something she can't put into words, but a visceral sense of the whole ugly episode being an event over which she had possessed some kind of control, something she sensed and then invited. For wasn't she pleased to sit there under his admiring adult gaze? Didn't she luxuriate in his appreciation of her?

She stops outside the bedroom, hearing him drop the bottle into the trash. He's still weeping. Leaning against the frame of the door, she tries to think. Pulling the sleeves of the nightgown back, she looks for bruises, and is surprised to find none. She moves into the upstairs bathroom, closes and locks the door, and then puts the light on.

She sits on the edge of the tub, and runs water, then stands, and, after checking again that the door is locked, pulls the nightgown over her head, shuddering, sobbing silently, and half choking.

The small knock at the door causes her to gasp out a tiny shriek.

His voice: "You okay in there?"

"Don't come in," she says.

"Good night."

Silence. She waits for more sounds, but nothing comes. When she turns the water off, there's only the quiet of a house at night, in the middle *of a winter storm: the heat kicking on; the infinitesimal crackle of ice and sleet hitting the skylight. Darkness up there, and a reflection of Lily, standing naked in the light, looking up. "Good night," he said, as if nothing had happened. He, the grown-up, the adult, the one who knows how things are supposed to be.*

She bathes quietly but with a feverish pressure on her skin, rubbing herself clean, sobbing softly, thinking with a burning in her stomach of the night ahead, and the morning. She dries herself off, waits until the water drains from the tub, then washes away all traces of herself in it—the ring of dirtiness, the sign of this thing that has happened, that part of her almost disbelieves. "Good night," he said.

After a long wait, in which she thinks she hears him breathing, she opens the door and steps out into the hall. Nothing. He's fluting and sighing and suffering a nightmare in his bed, uttering little terrified sighs, and then blubbering and breathing again. She enters the dark of Ronda's bedroom, where Ronda lies sleeping, stupid with sleep, mouth agape, snoring.

She doesn't sleep. And she knows from the sounds, coming from the hallway and the downstairs, that he's now awake, too. Several times, she hears him coughing and sighing on the other side of the door. Once, she thinks she hears the television. She lies very still, hands over her mouth and nose, breathing into the little warm space of her palms, her own heart beating in her ear on the pillow. She watches light come to the room, the shape of Ronda in the bed next to her, coming into outline.

Ronda wakes, yawns, gets up and moves to the window. Lily pretends to be asleep. Ronda goes out and down the hall, and is gone for a time. Someone coughs downstairs; Lily can't be sure. There are other noises—a radio, water running, doors opening and closing. She gets up and struggles out of the nightgown, and dresses hurriedly, standing in a corner of the room, away from the door.

She hears him at the foot of the stairs. "Lily? Are you awake? Your father is here."

"Yes," she calls. "I'll be right down."

They're talking. She hears the ordinary tone; it's the calm, friendly chatter of adults down in that room, with its low hum of music from the radio, and now here is Ronda coming back from the bathroom. "How did you sleep?" she says.

Lily watches her lift her nightgown over her body, which is still a girl's body, no breasts, no hair under the arms, lean, bony legs.

"Well?"

"Fine," she says.

"I tossed and turned," Ronda says.

"I didn't see."

"You didn't see. That's a weird thing to say. Of course you didn't see if you slept fine."

"My father's here."

Ronda walks over and hugs her. "It was fun. See you at school?"

Downstairs, her father is sitting in the kitchen, drinking a cup of coffee. Mr. Stapleton is seated across from him. He doesn't look at Lily, pouring more of the coffee; and then he does look at her. There is nothing at all in his face, his tired gray flat lightless eyes, the eyes, she thinks, of a statue. There are little forked red veins showing in the whites, which have a faintly yellow cast to them. The eyes see her without taking her in. "How did you sleep, young lady?"

She can't answer him. She moves to her father's side, and takes hold of his upper arm.

"Still groggy?" her father asks.

"I slept fine," she tells him, looking down.

"Are we shy this morning?" her father says.

She glances at him, and then over at Mr. Stapleton, who smiles and nods, holding the coffee cup to his lips; his hand trembles only slightly. "I slept so heavily last night, I'm afraid I might've sleepwalked. Ever do that?"

"Had a cousin who did," Scott says.

"I never did until lately. Don't know where I am or what I'm doing. It's a little scary at my age."

"I want to go home," Lily says.

Her father puts his coffee down and his arm comes around her middle. She almost draws away from him, feels a sinking at heart that he has noticed nothing—and, awfully, that there doesn't seem to be anything to notice. They conduct themselves as cordial strangers, Mr. Stapleton rising now and going to the entrance of the hallway, calling Ronda, who comes down still wearing slippers, though she's put a skirt on, and a white blouse with a frill in front. She hugs Lily's father, and kisses her grandfather on the side of the face. Everything is lightness and warmth. Lily reiterates that she wishes to go home. Mr. Stapleton says that, poor thing, she must not have slept very well. "I bet I sleepwalked last night. I bet I was bumping around in the halls and kept you awake. You do look a little tired. Didn't you—didn't you sleep well, there, young lady?"

Lily can't look at him. "No."

"You said you slept fine," Ronda says.

"Well, we'd better get you home," says Lily's father.

"I hope I didn't keep you awake with my wandering around at night. I—I don't even—don't even know I'm doing it." He laughs, a picture of exasperation with himself, shaking his head.

Just as Lily and her father are leaving the house, Ronda's parents arrive, talking breathlessly about what a terrible night it was, trying to get home in the ice. Lily's father tells about the accident, the long minute of realizing he had no control over the car and that it would not stop until it hit something. "We were only going about ten miles an hour," he says. "We hit the curb and the bumper caught on the street lamp in some way and we couldn't get loose. We ended up walking very slow down to the Willard. Everything was ice. Everything. You couldn't even grab on to anything."

Ronda's parents ask how the opening night was. And he takes time to describe for them the way things went: packed house, in spite of the weather. Lily looks around and sees that Mr. Stapleton is not in the room. She leans a little to one side, to see along the hallway, and there he is, waiting there, gazing back at her. His eyes are empty, and cold. He nods, and moves out of her view.

She pulls at her father's sleeve. "Let's go. Please."

"All right. Hey, don't be rude. These nice people put you up."

"Well, we weren't here for it," Ronda's mother says. She turns to Lily: "You'll have to come back and do it again, when we're here."

"Yes."

"You know, you could spend the night tonight, if you'd like. We don't have any plans."

"Do," Ronda says. "Oh, that would be so cool."

Lily shakes her head. "I'm tired. Please, Daddy. I want to go now."

Her father seems puzzled, shakes his head, shrugging at the adults. They go out to the car, another car. Confused, she hesitates.

"It's a rental," he says. "Silly. Get in."

There are still patches of ice in the yard, whitening crescents at the edges of pools that ripple softly when the chilly breeze moves on them. The air stings her face and neck. As she gets into the car and sits down in it, she sees that Ronda has run out onto the walk, waving her book about the explorers. Lily looks at her friend and understands in the nerves that line her stomach that she will not want to see Ronda anymore. She accepts the book, holds it on her lap, and Ronda leans in and kisses her on the cheek. "See you Monday, right?"

"Right," Lily says. Ronda walks back to the house and Lily sinks down in the seat so that her head is almost below the level of the window. When her father gets in, she glances back. The door of Ronda's house is closed; they're all inside.

"What's wrong?" her father says.

She turns to him, and finds that she can't speak.

"Hey," he says. "What is it, sweetie? Don't you feel right?"

"I'm okay," she says.

After a time, he says: "Tell me what's wrong."

She waits a moment, holding on, something collapsing under her heart. Yet when she turns to speak to him, she hears a lie come, or a truth that makes up a lie: "I didn't sleep well." And she goes on, adding to it, "I had a nightmare." Abruptly, it's as if the whole experience of the previous night, beginning with the panic over the prospect of harm coming to her parents, is being called forth now, a threat. Life as she has always known it hangs in precarious balance: if it comes to trouble, it will be all her doing. She senses this without words, and recalls the feeling of luxuriating in Mr. Stapleton's admiring gaze. "I had a nightmare that you were gone. You and Mother."

He reaches over and touches her hand. She gazes at the black hairs on the backs of his fingers.

At the cast party on Sunday, Ronda and her parents are guests. Ronda explains that her grandfather is not feeling well, and Lily hears Ronda's mother tell Doris that she fears he's sinking into another depression. He's had a couple of episodes, Ronda's father says to Scott. Nothing serious. Just goes to sleep, you know. Lily goes into the storeroom off the main stage entrance. It has always been a favorite place: clothes from every period of *the world's history of wearing clothes are hung in rows, on steel racks, one after another; boxes in ranks and stacked like bricks in a wall, boxes filled with props, with fake telephones and bottles and pistols and knives with retractable blades; fake furniture lying about, decked with glass figurines and delicate china lamps, porcelain busts of fictional people and leather-bound books, ashtrays and doilies and dinnerware. On one side, a bed, with a comforter, as if it's been made up for someone to sleep there. And, piled haphazardly behind the bed, war gear—helmets, breastplates, shields, swords, and, incongruous even in this incompatible array, a microphone hanging from wire hooked to the blade end of a propped spear. She stands here among these things, in this beloved room, this place where she has always felt safe—no, invincible—fortified by the memory of the fantastic and the magical, the truth in her deepest heart, that if the world gets bad, you simply imagine it otherwise, you take hold of it and shake its rust off and make it something bright again. Behind her comes the voice of her mother and Ronda, calling her name. "Lily," Ronda says. "Where are you hiding?" And quite suddenly, standing here, Lily has the urge to begin breaking everything into pieces.*

She experiences a strange non-feeling chill at her heart about the whole rest of the world.

But she turns and smiles at Ronda and says what she knows will be acceptable under the circumstances; she imagines her own soul to be an expanse of drifting sand under an empty sky.

Later, she paints this picture for herself, using acrylics, in her room in the afternoons after school. But it isn't her soul, it's the world. This is how she sees it, now.

During the next few months, she watches her mother sit at her dressing table, putting makeup on, heightening the color and shape of her lips, her eyebrows—a lovely woman, making herself look her best. Lily stops wanting to wear makeup, though she doesn't show this to her parents. She keeps appearances, and soon the fright of Mr. Stapleton starts to fade a little. She begins reading whatever she can find about Mary Kingsley, and by Mary Kingsley. She makes a drawing of her, and then feels it isn't good enough, and destroys it. She stops painting and drawing pictures altogether, and when her mother questions her about it, she says drawing simply no longer interests her. She keeps her journal, sometimes writing into the small hours of the night, and she goes with her father to his work. She soaks everything up, and people begin to decide that she's an oversensitive child, quiet, perhaps even a bit secretive: a girl who has turned inward. Her mother worries about her.

"Where's the Lily I used to know?" she says. "What's wrong? Is it because I quit the company?"

"I don't know what you mean," Lily tells her. "Can we please stop treating me like I've grown another head?"

"You've pushed Ronda away. Why is that? What is it between you two?"

"Nothing. She's got new friends. I got tired of her talk. Didn't you ever notice that all she ever does is talk?"

"That was you," Doris says. "Darling, that was you."

Summer comes, and another winter, and spring. She dreads the night coming, every day, and finds a way to hide this from everyone. Her father is in three other productions. Her mother is true to her word about the company, staying home, sometimes not even attending performances. Lily spends a lot of time at the theater; it engrosses her, and its flow and ruckus fill her mind, quell the turmoil, when she feels as if she might float out of her own body and dissolve. Her father allows her to stay up late on summer nights, to be with him, to watch the rehearsals. It's a blessing, knowing that she can put off lying in the dark, alone. She takes everything of the theater into herself, like a form of nourishment. She imagines a scene: a young woman all in black, posing for a photograph with others, on the veranda of a station house in Freetown, West Africa, circa 1895. She puts down the words that, in her private world, she can hear them speak; it's as if she's ghost-visited.

One night, she hears a tussle in the living room, and steps out of her room to see her father and mother grappling with each other in the entrance to the hall. Her mother's head is turned to one side, where her father's hand holds it, and he's leaning into her, his face a blank, almost bland mask, the muscles of his arms flexed. Her face is white, her lips bloodless. Her eyes are closed, and then they open and look at her. "Oh, Christ," she says. "Scott."

He steps back. "What are you doing awake now?" he says.

Lily says, "I heard noise."

"Go back to bed."

They're both breathing heavily, and her mother moves out of view, holding her hands to her face.

"It's an argument," her father says. "People argue. Go to bed."

She goes back to her room, and lies down, quiet, hands on her chest, thinking, without the words to express it yet, that people are such strange mixtures of tenderness and violence, anger and laughter and grief, and all of it too frightening to bear. The night goes on, quiet, threatening and empty as the distances between the stars. Nothing so terrible happens. In the morning her parents are themselves again, full of kindness and merriment, glad of the very air.

As time goes on, her father seems less and less comfortable with anything as a subject for meaningful conversation with her. She knows that he thinks this new distance between them is probably natural for a man and his maturing young daughter. As best she can, she buries the memory of Mr. Stapleton.

She never tells anyone about him.

ONE

1

Toward the end of her junior year of college, her parents separated, and that summer, the hottest summer anyone could remember, she heard them discuss their dissolving marriage individually, to different people, in distressingly composed, matter-of-fact voices. They might as well have been talking about refinancing a mortgage. With her, they were mutually reserved, polite, careful not to criticize each other. They spoke of reciprocal respect, of what was best for everyone; and it seemed that no rancor existed between them. Indeed, once it came to the final arrangements, they both appeared rather self-satisfied for having accomplished everything with a minimum of pathological scenes. Even the lawyers called it amicable.

In Lily Austin's mind, there was nothing about splitting a household in two that could be called anything of the sort.

Her roommate, Sheri Galatierre, attempted to divert her, asking her along to parties and other social events. Lily mostly demurred. As it had been for years, now, she was troubled by the company of strangers, though she didn't express it that way. She didn't know, really, how to say what she wanted.

Sheri had a way of getting down into her sorrow with her that made her feel worse, though the other woman obviously meant to help. Dominic Martinez also tried to distract her, being goofy and chattering, clowning for her. He had come to the university that year, having transferred in from North Carolina. He'd walked up to her after one of the performances of the drama department, and said, "Ronda Seiver's party." It had startled Lily, and for a moment she hadn't recognized him. "You got the book that had the lady explorer in it."

"Dominic?" she said.

He bowed, exactly as he had that night at Ronda's house.

They had become rather like brother and sister, since then. Dominic sometimes refused to indulge her. He would tell her to grow up and stop twisting her own knife in herself. Strangely, that helped some.

Yet in the hours when she was alone, nothing quite reached the place where she was hurting. The facts hurt; the knowledge of what had lately transpired between her parents caused a deep, unreachable, continual ache. She couldn't shake the old, terrible, familiar sense of having been betrayed. And so while everyone around her spoke in terms of romance, and while it was in all the books and the plays she was reading—and last spring she had played the most romantic of parts, Rosalind, in *As You Like It*—Lily had decided that the whole thing was a lie and a cheat.

Her father, completely serious, and without a trace of irony, had an affair with someone he worked with. He spoke about falling in love. He used the phrase, telling Lily's mother about it, confessing to her that it had been going on for more than a year, crying idiotically and begging her to forgive him. Lily's mother, who had felt the weight of her own increasing estrangement from him, went into an almost surreptitious six-week-long depression, then gathered strength and called a lawyer. Everything was decided with an efficiency, a courtesy, that Lily deplored. It was as if her parents had decided to close a long-running play in which they had performed the lead roles.

This was in 1988. Bush and Dukakis were running for Reagan's soon-to-be vacated office, and Lily, entering her last year of college, found that she couldn't care less. In the fall, back at school, she went through the strangeness of writing to and communicating with her parents separately, and of having to speak to the young woman, a set designer, to whom her father was now married (a civil ceremony in Maryland, three days after the divorce was final, in late July). The strain worked on her in unexpected ways: she had experienced episodes of panic and sleeplessness. And when she could sleep at all she had nightmares—one, quite recently, about her fourteenth birthday. She was more upset about how it made her feel than she was about the nightmare itself; inexplicably, it was worse waking from it than being in it.

She had registered for double the normal hours, having lost a semester when she switched majors, and wanting to graduate on time.

Her teachers liked her ability to lose herself in whatever role she tried, and others commented favorably on her performances. When she had played Rosalind, there was a certain pleasure in being recognized. But she was already discovering that she had no taste for being in front of people. There was something in herself that she defied by continuing to perform, though her sense of this was visceral, flying in the face of her own increasingly introverted feelings. Her discomfiture after the performances, her absence at most of the celebrations and cast parties and social gatherings, had become the subject of talk among the other members of the drama school. She went her own way; and people began to leave her alone. Even Dominic and Sheri kept a certain respectful distance at times.

The panic she managed mostly to keep at bay, though trying to decide what she might do after college, after all this relentless work, was cause for anxiety, too. The anxiety, whatever its source, plagued her. When one was suffering through this kind of distraction, it was nearly impossible to concentrate on memorizing large masses of text. It was difficult enough just getting through assigned reading.

On one of the last football weekends of her senior year—a crisp, breezy Saturday with the smell of burning leaves in the air and a pleasant coolness that seemed a kind of mingling of the fading summer and the coming winter—Sheri cajoled and begged her into accompanying her to the game. The Cavaliers won big, though since she didn't know anything about football she couldn't make much out of the confusion of sun-reflecting, bright-clad, helmeted bodies slamming into each other on the earth-churned grass. But she discovered that she liked the spectacle, and spent much of the game watching everyone else's happy reactions, surprised by how pleasing that was. "What an amazing thing," she said to Sheri, as the game ended. "That was fun."

Sheri, whose speech was punctuated by what Lily thought of as a sort of aural italics, said, "You know, a couple of these boys might end up *rich*. Does Dominic like football?"

"We don't talk about it, but maybe that's me."

"I don't much like it, but I go."

They strolled over to one of the post-game celebrations, at a small apartment in the center of the campus. People talked too loud, trying to be heard over each other, recounting the high points of the victory.

Their enthusiasm made Lily conscious, by contrast, of her own lack of school spirit.

Sheri said, "That's the first game you ever saw? You never even saw a game in *high* school?"

No.

She turned and, with a wave of her bony, hard-knuckled little hand, addressed the others in the room. "Everybody, this girl has *never* been to a damn football game. Today was the first game in her whole damn life. I mean, can yew *imagine?*"

Lily, feeling caught out, raised her eyes against the urge to look down.

And out of the group, a young man emerged, stepping forward to say that he could imagine it: he had never been to a football game, either, including today's game; the truth was, he didn't like the sport. Several people hooted good-naturedly at him, and a girl in an athletic-lettered sweater that hung on her like a robe put a paper party blower in his face and blew it.

He was built like someone who could play football—broad across the chest, with beautifully defined musculature in his arms and shoulders. Lily gazed into his hazel eyes and her embarrassment changed; she saw in them an incitement to stand with him, separate from these others, with their banners and their noisemakers and their letter jackets and sweaters.

Sheri started to say something, and Lily interrupted her, speaking only to him. "My name is Lily."

He extended his hand. "Tyler."

On an impulse, she stepped inside his offered handshake, stood on her toes, and kissed him full on the mouth. He seemed surprised, then kissed back. Everyone was watching them.

"Well," Sheri said, "can yew *believe* this country? Happiness just walks up and says howdy."

"Let's go out on the balcony," he said with a grin.

Lily took his hand, and there were whoops from the others. It was an exhibition; she felt the color rising to her face and neck, walking with him toward the sliding glass door leading out of the room. She told herself, as they stepped onto the balcony overlooking Rugby Drive, that in the morning he would be elsewhere, and so would she.

He said, "We've got them all talking now."

"I guess so." She felt a little stab of embarrassment at the dullness of her answer, and she tried to smile at him, feeling the gesture as a kind of spasm in her face.

"Are you cold?"

She pulled her sweater up from her waist, where it had been tied, and put it on, accidentally striking him on the side of the face with her elbow.

He said, "Whoops."

"Oh, God—did I hurt you?"

"I think I'll make it," he said, with a soft, good laugh. A murmurous baritone music was in it; it calmed her.

From where they stood, looking beyond the grass field, they could see cars waiting at a light, turn signals flashing. He gazed at her, and she was aware of the boniness of her body under her jeans. She had felt skinny and unattractive, yet just now, for a brief few seconds, it didn't seem to matter.

As though something in her thought produced it, there came Sheri's voice on the other side of the curtain: "'Oh, Romeo, wherefore art thou?' Thou silly son of a bitch." The whole room laughed. And Tyler laughed, too, in a murmur, staring. Lily looked out at the stars beyond the rooftops across the way. The moment had turned again; she felt the nerves of her stomach. She wished to seem experienced, adventurous, even alluring, without being cheap—wished, in short, to be the kind of young woman she had so recently played: someone who could get away with taking the small step across a room full of strangers to kiss full on the mouth a man she had just met.

They were alone. She saw the lights from other parties in other buildings winking into the night. Behind them, the noise of the celebration went on, Sheri rattling about her plans for altering reality, her emphatic alto coming to them over music: something from Paul Simon's African album with its wonderful close harmonies.

"I should get us something to drink," Tyler said. "What'll you have?"

"I'll have a beer."

He left her there. She put her hands on the railing, and felt the chill of the coming winter, looking out at the wide, fading glow of the city on the October sky. Yellow leaves littered the lawn below. A fragrance lifted to her from there, earth and pine, and the leaves, pungent with the quick decay of fall. She heard other music coming from another apartment, guitar and pounding bass, but couldn't distinguish what it was. She had the thought that he might not return. How foolish, standing out on the balcony, abandoned by him. In another minute, she would quietly step back inside.

But then he returned, with her beer, and a glass of wine for himself. He had lighted a cigarette, too, and he offered her one.

"Thanks anyway." She sipped the beer. He drank the wine, and smoked. Perhaps he was thinking about how to extricate himself from her.

"They're smoking wacky tobaccy in there," he said. "Ever try it?"

She had, once, with Sheri. She nodded. "I didn't like it much."

"It made me sick," he said. "It was cool at first, and I thought—well, hey. And then I got sick as a dog."

"I didn't feel anything, really. But maybe I didn't do it right."

He nodded. "I sure didn't."

"What're you studying?" she ventured.

He told her he had started college late, that he had been a biology major, premed, and that he had done the first year of med school, but that he had lost interest in it. "I'm in, um, the philosophy department now." He drew in the smoke, and breathed it out. "I know you're in drama."

She stared.

"You were very good in that play."

For a second, she could only smile at him, as if simply appreciating the sight of him. "That's the best thing anybody's said to me in a long time," she said.

He took a drag of the cigarette, and held it up. "This is my last one, you know."

"Congratulations."

He asked about the drama school, and his expression took her in, appeared so welcoming and interested that to her surprise she began telling him details: the circuitous path of barely passed courses and bad advice she had taken on the way to her discovery, so late in her college career, that she wasn't cut out for the study of law. She told him of her decision to change course, to study drama in the hope of teaching it someday.

"What about being an actor?" he said. "You have talent."

"I don't really like doing it much. I don't know. I like to write."

"If you write, what would you write?"

"A play."

"What would it be about?"

She had been fascinated about Keats's last days, spent partly on a boat in the waters off the coast of Italy. "I think someday I'd like to try something about Keats. I'd call it *Lone Splendor*."

"'Bright star! would I were steadfast as thou art.'" He smiled wonderfully. "Keats is a favorite."

"In my first year of high school," she told him, "I carried a book of his odes around with me, like a prayer book."

"So you'd write a play about Keats—wouldn't you almost have to make yourself as good as he was to do it?"

"I haven't thought it out. That's way in the future. There's someone else I've been—well, really sort of obsessed with since I was a little girl—Mary Kingsley."

"Never heard of her."

"She died in 1900. She was an explorer—travel writer. I've been writing some things—she had only about seven active years in the world. I mean, until she was thirty all she did was take care of her mother and her brother. Her father was gone for years at a time. And when he was home, she took care of him, too. But then when both her parents died within a couple of months of each other, she went down to West Africa and ended up traveling to parts of it where no other European ever had. She climbed Mount Cameroon, went to the peak, alone. And she wrote a best-selling book and was world famous for a time. Kipling said she had no ability to feel fear. She's a very strange, fascinating woman."

"You talk about her like she's alive."

They were quiet again, and Lily wondered if she hadn't said too much.

"A woman explorer," Tyler said. "Cool. Why haven't they made a movie?"

She merely returned his look. His tone was patronizing, now, and she caught herself inwardly seeking a pretext to excuse this. It was as if she might spoil the moment if she allowed herself to dwell on such things. But there was something else, something more troubling, just under the flow of her thoughts. She went on: "Well, anyway, I've done a lot of reading about her."

"I've been reading only tomes," he said. "Doorstops. I'll end up being some kind of double major. I'll qualify soon as a career student. I'll be twenty-six years old in December."

"What will you do with a philosophy degree? Teach?"

"I should be thinking about all that, but I haven't been."

Another commotion started inside the apartment: someone had broken a glass. She was waiting for him to say more, and he appeared to realize this with a little awkward turn of his head.

"I don't think I have the patience to teach."

She kept her smile. And again, she felt rather surprisingly calm. It came over her like a sweet warmth. She could fully exhale, now. The tension in her chest had lessened. "Well," she sighed. "We both hate football."

"Oh, I don't hate football," he told her. "I love football. I lied about that."

There was something attractively unselfconscious about him, as though his thoughts were far from himself. She wanted to return this form of, well, *consideration*. In the next instant, she was certain that she had produced the whole thing in her head—he put one hand up to his hairline, and pushed the brown hair back. Highlights of auburn shone in it from the lamp in the window behind them. He drank from his glass of wine, and looked back into the room. "I came here with someone. She went out to get some mixers."

"I came with someone, too," Lily said in an affectionately exasperated tone. "Miss Sheri Galatierre. My roomie."

He said, "Sheri's my sister."

Lily was at a loss.

"She never told you she has an older brother?"

"I think—I guess she must've. I assumed back in Mississippi."

"No, if she mentioned me, she would definitely not have said anything about Mississippi."

Lily waited for him to go on.

He said, "We have the same mother. I'm her half brother. I stayed with Dad. Sheri's from the second marriage. Her father owns a car dealership."

"And your father?"

He looked down. "My father died two years ago."

"I'm sorry to hear that."

"Well," he said. Then: "What about you?"

"Oh, my parents are both alive. Divorced, but alive." She took a long drink of the beer.

"Do your parents live nearby?" he asked.

"My mother lives in Point Royal. That's about seventy miles north."

He said, "I come from near there. My father and I lived there. Do you know where Steel Run is?"

She experienced an odd little thrill. "I do, yes." There was a monthly flea market in Steel Run that she and her mother had frequently visited. Often they would eat lunch in a little café on a side street, nearby. She almost stammered, asking him if he knew it.

"Sure," he said. "I worked behind the counter two summers ago."

"Then we must have already met at some time."

"No, I'd remember meeting you," he said, smiling, putting emphasis on the last word. There was something confiding about it, and gentle.

"Well, Tyler Galatierre," she said. "Who did you come to this party with?"

"Harrison," he said.

"Excuse me?"

"It's Harrison. My last name. Galatierre is the dealership guy. Galatierre Ford and Mercury in Oxford, Mississippi."

"Oh," Lily said. "God, of course."

"You haven't done anything wrong." His teeth were white, small and even; she thought of a child's mouth. "I came here with a date, though," he said. "A friend. I'd like to see more of you. Is it—would it be okay if I called you?"

"If you'd like. I mean—yes. Yes, it would be fine. I'd like that a lot."

He was peering into the room. "She's looking for me. I'd better go back inside."

Lily followed him. His date was someone she recognized from a literature class she'd taken—a tall, dark-haired, big-boned woman with small round blue eyes and a way of pronouncing her words with a nasal elongation of the vowels, something she must have assumed made her sound scholarly. Lily could not remember her name, and when Tyler introduced her as Deirdre, it was clear that Deirdre didn't remember Lily's name, either. They acknowledged that they had seen each other before, and then Lily moved off, with the conviction that this was the last time she would lay eyes on Tyler Harrison. Deirdre took his arm, and stayed at his side for the rest of the hour before they left. Lily, watching from the other end of the room, decided that they were indeed a couple, and felt irritated for entertaining, even for a little while, the idea that there had been anything at all portentous about the evening. This was, after all, only a party after a football game.

2

SHE WENT BACK to the dorm alone, and was in her bed when Sheri came in, drunk and disheveled—wanting, as usual, to talk. Lily heated water in a pot on the hot plate they shared, and fixed some strong instant coffee while her roommate undressed and got into a nightgown with big blue flowers on it. She watched the slow, unsteady way Sheri moved, putting one arm into the nightgown and then pausing, faltering. "Damn," Sheri said, staring at the other sleeve as though it contained instructions in another language. She put her arm into it, then sat on the bed again, suddenly, her eyes widening with surprise. "I fell. I absolutely fell."

"You sat down." Lily felt almost parental toward her.

"Can yew *imagine?*" This was Sheri's phrase. She used it about almost anything, and on occasion Lily failed to hear it, or respond to it. Sheri was all energy and talk, someone for whom stillness, repose, seemed unnatural. There were aspects of life with her that required some tolerance—her presence sometimes made it difficult to study—but Lily was fond of her, and felt a kind of world-weary gratitude in her heart, just for the diversion Sheri provided, her chatter, her energy, her way of not hearing anything *depressing*. "I know I'm just a *big mouth* and you're trying to read," she would say, in that charming drawl, "but I've just got to tell somebody." And she would go on talking, unscrolling the most recent excitement of her affections, or the latest affront to her sensibilities, whatever presently claimed her interest or her astonishment or her appreciation.

Now, Sheri seemed to list one way and then the other, but then she straightened herself and stared. "I had too much to *eat*."

"You had too much to *drink*."

"Whatever."

"Did you have something to smoke, too?"

"I had some, sure. Kind bud."

"At the party?"

"They had it at the party, too?"

On the wall over Sheri's bed were pennants and banners from her high school in Oxford, Mississippi. She looked rather sad now, sitting there in disarray, beneath such vivid colors and shapes, ashen-faced in that bright-flowered nightgown, suggesting the counterfeit gaiety of an older woman trying to seem younger. She rested her elbows on her knees, hands supporting her head, and stared at the space between her feet. "I'm so dizzy."

"I bet that's normal," Lily said. "Don't you think?"

Sheri's eyes narrowed slightly. "Have you ever been *drunk*? I mean, totally, really *drunk*?"

"Yes."

"Swear to God?"

Lily nodded, but felt how unconvincing it was. Oddly, she felt as if she ought to provide some kind of proof. "I've been drunk, okay? I was alone, and I locked the doors and got shitty all on my own, just to see how it felt." She put a trash can down at the other's feet.

"What's this?"

"Just in case."

"I already did that," Sheri said. She looked down into the can, then leaned forward slightly and seemed nervously expectant and sorrowful. "I wish you hadn't made me think of it."

"Forgive me," Lily said.

Sheri pushed the can aside, then regarded her, tilting her head slightly to one side. "That was something at the party. That was romantic."

Lily held out a cup of coffee. "Why didn't you tell me that was your brother?"

"I don't know, honey—that might hurt my stomach. You think it'll hurt my stomach? I don't feel very normal. You made coffee?"

"I made it for you."

"Yeah, that's cool, honey—but that dutn't mean it won't hurt my *stomach*." Sheri took the cup and looked down into it, as though she were searching for something floating there. Finally she put it to her lips and took a small, loud sip. "It's hot."

Lily pulled a chair over and sat down. "Did you tell me you had a brother?"

The other woman held up two fingers, looked at them, and then held them toward her. "Twice. At least. I told you twice that I'm sure of."

"But you didn't say he was here in Charlottesville."

Sheri thought a moment. "Did, too."

"Did you think I knew him at the party?"

She frowned more deeply. "Party. No. I was *about* to introduce you, honey. But you walked up and *kissed* him. I thought you were down on romance and falling in love." She sipped the coffee again. "This is too hot."

"Let it cool." Lily stood, put the chair back, then got a paper cup and went out and along the narrow hallway to the water fountain, where the water was coldest. When she came back to the room, Sheri was lying on the floor next to her bed, holding one of the banners from her wall.

"Sheri."

"I'm sorry," Sheri said, waving the banner. She sat up, reached for her coffee, which she had set in the windowsill.

Lily poured some of the cold water into the coffee, then drank the rest of the water and got into her own bed.

Sheri sat there holding the coffee cup, staring into it. "I'm drunk."

"Drink the coffee. It's cooled down now."

"That Deirdre—she was mad at him when she heard about it. Can yew *imagine*? He didn't do the kissing."

"Are they together?"

Sheri gave a little emphatic wave of the hand that held the coffee, and some of it lipped over the edge of the cup. "You'd think they were *married* or something."

"Do they live together?"

"No."

A moment later, Sheri said, "You thought they *lived* together?"

"No, I was reacting to what you said."

"Why're you so curious about it?"

"I'm just making conversation," Lily said. She lay back and closed her eyes. It troubled her to feel so oddly crestfallen, and she tried to shake it off.

Her roommate went on: "Tyler and I don't really know each other that well. I never saw him face-to-face until I got here, and my mother was totally all out for him and me to get together. Anyway, we haven't done more than say hello a few times, really. The whole thing's been a little hard to—get used to."

Lily decided to wait until morning to say more, or ask more—if she ever asked anything.

"I knew about it, you know," Sheri said.

Lily waited.

"I'll tell you, I come from one seriously fucked-up family. My mother and father had an *affair* while she was still married to Tyler's father. I was the result of that. And she ran away from him, too, pregnant with *me*. All my life I heard it, this *other child* my mother left behind, by this first husband. And a few times my daddy helped her keep tabs on the kid, too. Actually hired people to check up, see what he was doing and all that. Real detective stuff. Every few years pictures would turn up of him going to middle school, or graduating from high school—that kind of stuff. Just so she could see his face. And when Tyler's daddy died, she actually wrote him. He was already going to school here. Where, of course, they sent *me*." Sheri finished her coffee, then lay back with the empty cup on her stomach. "My guess is, I was supposed to be the ambassador of goodwill. But I don't know about Tyler. I don't know if he likes me much. I like him fine."

"Why don't you get into bed?"

Sheri set the cup on the window ledge and crawled up into her bunk, groaning with the effort.

"Why'd your mother leave Tyler behind?"

She had lain over on her back, and she stared at the ceiling, without speaking, for a time. Then she sighed. "Well, think about it—pregnant with me. From another man. Figure it out. Sounds like a soap opera. I was born the year before the summer of love, and my parents had it going before the rest of the country did, I guess."

Lily was quiet.

"This could be kind of cool," Sheri said. "Are you guys gonna start *dating* or something?"

"Don't be ridiculous," said Lily.

"It'd be *cool* as far as I'm concerned. What if we got to be sisters-in-law? I wonder what they'd call us. *Half* sisters-in-law?"

Lily said nothing.

"Don't you think it'd be cool? Oh, that's right—you hate the whole romance thing now. It's just gotta be platonic little geeky pal stuff, like you and Dominic."

She let this go by, and soon the other was snoring. Listening to it, she allowed herself to imagine for a while what it might be like, seeing Tyler Harrison, the little chain of events playing out in her mind—until she caught herself and began working to concentrate on other matters: her studies, the reading she had to do.

3

It's odd to be writing to you, as if you were not dead but in another city, another country far away. I wish we could actually speak to one another, and having said this I admit that this feels like actual communication of a kind. Are the dead so neglectful of us? Your voice is so vibrant in the books, I cannot make my mind believe that you aren't whispering somewhere close to my ear, on the air, not a ghost, but a presence, if that can be separated out from the world of wandering shades. I don't mean it that way. I don't mean it that way at all. Not a ghost, but a soul.

You were hemmed in for so long. It must've been so hard, no matter how cheerfully you spoke of it, and now I set myself the task of trying to understand you well enough to imagine you. Somehow, though you never experienced it yourself, I think you would understand what is happening to me. I have come this far, and all I do now is study. I have no life, really, outside this room. I'm so strange with others, and I know you felt this, too. Outside my window, people move past in groups. Couples. Music comes from the other rooms. I stare at the pages of my textbooks, and nothing seems to get through to my mind. It's all surface. I eat out of cans, and drink coffee to stay awake. There are too many things to worry over, and I want only to find my way to imagining you, in your own time. What that must've been. The disappointment I feel over Tyler Harrison is in how I built him up in my own mind, having come to the conviction that romance is lying. I know you did that once, too, built someone up in your mind. Well, I've begun the play about you, though it's very rough. I don't have time to work on it, and that causes a pressure. I'm thinking of not graduating. Can't concentrate as I'd like, and I have to go home for Thanksgiving and face them, with their polite distance from each other, and him with his new love, his whole new different life. Do you hear resentment? It's just hurt. I'm only twenty, and the ache won't quit. I've begun to think about Tyler Harrison in an abstract way, as if he were an idea I indulged in for a time, like a daydream.

☙

HELLO TO THE CANNIBALS
A play
by
Lily A. Austin

Dark stage. A single point of light in an apparent distance. Enter a man, dressed in the clothes of the late nineteenth century. This is Henry Guillemard. He holds a sheaf of papers, and walks to the edge of the stage and peers out. He looks at the papers, then peers out again, folds the papers in his pocket, and puts his hands on his hips, an almost impatient gesture.

GUILLEMARD

I'm supposed to try and render West Africa in a little space like this? More to the point, I'm supposed to give you what it was like for her, in such a place.

He paces to one side of the stage and then hunches down. There's something conspiratorial about it.

She was beautiful. The first thing you ever thought about her, even when she was an awkward, gawky little girl with no social skills at all, was that she was beautiful. The features were fine, not extraordinary. But there was something in the eyes, those eyes of hers.

4

$\mathcal{T}$HE WEEK BEFORE THANKSGIVING, Lily traveled on a chartered bus to New York with her theater-art class. While she was gone, Sheri developed an abscess in a molar, and ended up in the hospital. Lily came back that Monday to find the room in a terrible mess, and no sign of Sheri. It was the housing administrator, Mrs. Edgeworth, who told her, in a voice that was stretched thin with disapproval, where Ms. Galatierre was. Lily cleaned the room, and then sat at the window, watching the snow fall on the square of lawn below and on the reddish, white-lined university buildings across the way. The snow came with a slow steadiness that made her long for home. She was leaving Wednesday for Thanksgiving.

She trudged over to the hospital to visit Sheri, who seemed not at all surprised to see her. "I'm sick as a *dog*," Sheri said. "Damn infection went crazy. I damn near *died*."

Lily sat by her bed, feeling wrong for not having brought her anything.

"Tyler came to visit me twice. He asked where you were."

The little thrill she experienced was surprising; it left her feeling disagreeably exposed.

Sheri seemed to look right through her. "I thought it was kind of strange, myself."

"Why?" Lily said. "I *am* your roomie, after all."

"I guess so." Sheri appeared doubtful.

"When're you getting out of here?" Lily asked. "Would you like to come home for Thanksgiving with me?"

"I don't know—I don't think I'll be out of here before, like, next week. You think you have a little *dental* problem, and then the next thing you know it's fuck'n *critical*."

"Can I bring you something to read?"

"I got the TV. You know what, Lily? I almost checked out. I had organ trouble from the infection. My fuck'n *organs* got involved. I hope I never hear the fuck'n word *systemic* again ever."

"You look fine now," Lily told her. "It's going to be all right now."

But she did not look fine. Lily went to see her Tuesday, and again Wednesday, in the morning, before driving north. The color had returned to her cheeks, but it was apparent that Sheri's college career was in serious jeopardy. Tyler had not come back. Sheri talked about him—what little she knew. He hadn't ever expressed any curiosity about his mother, their mother. She found this disturbing. "Oh, he's been nice and all that. We've even had a few laughs, you know, just kind of teasing around with each other. But he won't talk about her. His own *mother*. He gets funny—nervous—at the mention of her."

"Well," Lily said, "she left him, after all."

"You're interested in him. I see it in your eyes."

"Can we change the subject, please?"

"What do you see in Dominic, anyway? I mean he's a funny guy, I guess—"

"Dominic and I are friends," Lily said.

"You can't be just friends with a guy. That just doesn't work. Unless you're gay. Are you gay, sister?"

"Oh, could we please not talk about this," Lily said.

The hospital room was gray, with lighter gray trim, and dark blue curtains on the windows. The wintry day outside was the same color as the room. The two of them ended up watching television for an hour. There was always the sense that Tyler might appear in the doorway. Lily saw Sheri glancing that way, and knew that she, too, was waiting.

But no one came.

"I swear," Sheri said, "you'd think I was dead and *buried*."

"I'm here," Lily said.

"My own *brother*. I thought this might be the way we got to know each other."

"Do you think it's because I'm here?" Lily wondered.

"Why would that bother him?"

She could think of no response.

"I swear, you've got a case of weirdness about this guy."

Lily changed the subject. "Will you ask for incompletes in all your courses?"

"I don't want to think about that now."

"Is there anything I can do about it for you?"

"You're sweet," Sheri said. "But I'm screwed, blued, and tattooed."

TWO

1

*T*HANKSGIVING, she had a quiet dinner with her mother and her mother's neighbor and two friends from the neighbor's church. Her father called to say he missed her. It was an awkward minute. She hated the sensation of forced affability, the sense of insincerity on both sides. The following day she drove into Washington, where he lived with his new wife in a small apartment off Wisconsin Avenue, to pay a short call on him. The new wife's name was also Lily, though she went by the name Peggy, her middle name. Peggy explained that her parents had called her Lily-Margaret, and when she reached twenty-one (only four years ago, Lily reflected), she took the shorter name—an act of defiance against the social pretensions of her Southern parents, both of whom had grown up in Nashville society. That was their phrase, Peggy said, and they used it without sarcasm, or a sliver of understanding about how foolish they sounded using it. She said this with an air of tolerant bemusement, as if her own parents were children, and of course she was nervous. Lily found it difficult to look at her, and kept having to force herself not to avert her eyes. Peggy sounded distinctly unsouthern when she talked. She had gone to school in Chicago, and her speech was shaded with what Lily thought of as the flat, hard sound of the Midwest.

Her father and his young wife were working in the new production at the Washington Theater, a revival of *Death of a Salesman*.

They drafted Lily into going to the play, and then out to dinner with them. She didn't take the play in very well, her mind kept wandering away from it, though the audience loved it. Her father played the title role, Willy Loman, coming undone. Lily sat with Peggy in the fourth row of a packed house, and she was forced to smile and nod at various people who worked at the theater: her father's colleagues and friends, friends of both of her parents, and now Peggy's friends, too. Peggy waved, and blew kisses, and twice, before the opening curtain, she excused herself to go speak to somebody.

Lily saw the sets—the painted apartment buildings, the hollow walls of Willy Loman's house—and she was too aware of it all as the practical matter of production. She looked at others in front and to the side of her as the action of the play unfolded. Peggy had done a good job on the sets. In the last scenes, many in the audience were weeping, men and women. The young man who played Biff was too frenetic, Lily thought, and it was during his scenes that Peggy showed some restlessness. At one point Lily leaned toward her and whispered, "Is he trying to be James Dean?" But Peggy gave her an uncomprehending look, so she returned to gazing at the others in the audience. When she could bring her mind back to the action on the stage, she saw that her father was playing Willy with a kind of professional's restraint, as if to say that everyone in the house was in on the sources of Willy's trouble and this was a playing out of what they all already understood to be true. It was an almost off-handed performance: he did not play Willy as losing his mind, he said later, but only as losing his way.

Afterward, he took them to a place where he used to meet Peggy, he said, before they were first involved. He spoke those words and then appeared to want to retract them, or at least temper them, for Lily. His hand went to his mouth, as if to wipe the words away. And then he looked down, clasping and unclasping his hands. Lily knew their affair had started out as a friendship; neither of them had seen it coming. It was strange to be the subject of his attempt now to behave as though nothing was different.

She sought to change the subject, and could only think of saying that he appeared to have lost some weight.

Predictably enough, given his chosen profession, he was a man who spent a lot of time working to keep his appearance. He had kept his waistline, and he spent two hours every day on the treadmill. His hair was dyed dark brown. Lily had once looked upon these remedial actions with a kind of proprietary ache for him. Now, it was hard not to feel ill-tempered about it. He seemed so comfortably settled into his new life that it was as though all the years with her mother had never happened at all.

There was a smudge of makeup still in the corner of his left eye, and along the underside of that ear. She couldn't stop seeing it.

A moment later, he said, "Are you planning to do graduate work?"

"No."

"What then? A job? Want to try out here?"

She hesitated a little, returning his gaze. "I don't want to be an actor. I don't get much joy out of it and I'm not that good at it, in fact."

Peggy touched his arm, then took her hand away. "You've still got makeup on you, honey."

"I never do get all of it. How does it feel seeing me even older than I am?"

"Oh, stop it," Peggy said.

He turned to Lily. "What about the writing?"

She shrugged, knowing that she seemed sullen, and feeling unable to do anything about it. The subject was too personal.

"Well?" he said.

Now, she simply wanted to deflect him. "I haven't written much of anything but schoolwork for four years."

The three of them were sitting in a booth, in the restaurant, in the soft, romantic music that seemed to breathe out of the walls.

"Well, that's writing, isn't it?" He turned to Peggy. "She wrote poems back in high school and won a couple of prizes for it."

"I wrote poems in high school," Peggy said.

Lily glanced at her. "Like everybody, right?" She had meant to include herself in this remark, but she could see that the other woman had taken it to be dismissive. "I think I was one of about four hundred teenage girls in my school who wrote it," she added.

Peggy nodded. "I'm not a poet, that's for sure. And what I was writing was decidedly not poetry, though I thought it was. But I'll bet, from what your father says, you were really writing poetry."

Lily realized her father had been talking about her. The thought both pleased and unnerved her. "No," she said with a laugh. "Mine was the plain old teenage-girl variety. Like everybody else's. Nothing remotely memorable about it."

She drove home in a mood of irritable confusion. Her mother greeted her at the door, looking too heavy in the legs and several years older than she was; she wore a housecoat, and her hair was pulled back in a gray knot. She'd stopped dyeing it. On the coffee table were several days' worth of newspapers and a lot of magazines, none of which she had found the time to read, or even to page through. The television blared. On the ottoman were a box of tissues, a glass of orange juice, and a paper plate on which part of a sandwich lay. Since the divorce, Doris had relaxed into a kind of sedentary existence that was disturbing to her daughter. She liked living alone.

"How's the love of his life?" she asked Lily.

Lily, who called her mother by name, like a sister or a friend, said, "Doris, I wish I understood you better."

"Well, I was curious. She must be something else in bed."

"Oh, for God's sake."

Doris laughed. "It's the eighties, darling."

2

$\mathcal{I}$T'S THE EIGHTIES, DARLING.

Lily had a half-dreaming vision in the night, lying in the bed in the room where she had been a child, and then not a child. She heard her mother's voice, and felt herself slowly drift toward the blur of motion in her mind, the edge of sleep. One hundred years ago, in 1888, Mary Kingsley would have been twenty-six years old. Lily lay in her own childhood bed and did the math, thinking of a girl of twenty-six, living in the household of a world traveler, a scientist, a physician to wealthy noblemen, with a deeply divided nature, whose interest in his one female child included considerations of her use to him.

No, not a girl—a woman.

Someone who, at twenty-six, could say that her entire life had been spent caring for her invalid mother. Lily imagined her, and began to think of her in terms of childhood. She seemed to see her in the light-muted way of dreams, a thin, tall girl with dark-blond hair, closed up in a house in Highgate.

Scene: Guillemard at stage center, as before. Takes out the papers, and rifles through them. His notes.

Let's start with, say, 1874. Here they are in the spring of that year, let us say. Mary and her wandering father, George Kingsley. He has been home for a little more than a week. It's an extended stay this time, two months. You'll notice that his stride is still long; he still walks with a kind of bounce, a spring in his step she admires without quite recognizing it as admiration. He's a man with no fear of dangers, not of war, or travel to distant and exotic places, or even of sickness—his heroism during the cholera epidemic in northern Wales, the year Mary was born, is a family story; her uncle Charles Kingsley wrote about it in a novel she has read through several times, though she's only twelve years old. For her strange, bold father, the parameters of his own island country are too close. He's restless, even in the comforts of his own house, with its chiming clocks, its books, whose pages Mary spends so much of her time with, its artifacts from around the world. But then there is also, always by now, the sickroom, with its odors of camphor and salts, and the stale breathing of closed spaces. He's seen so much of everything, seen things in the world far away. When he turns those eyes upon her, she feels their brilliance.

At times she believes she can feel his terror of what her little life might come to, feels it as a kind of weight. She understands that she must keep him from the knowledge of what she's aware of as an unruly nature, a clutch of unanswerable passions, the secret rages and hungers of her own heart. She shields him from this as certainly as she might stand in front of him to block the sunlight. Her mother is mostly too ill to do much of anything but lie still, and Mary's job is caring for her. She has learned to pay the strictest attention to the smallest details. Lately George has been spending mornings trying to revive a project he had already abandoned once, before Mary was born, a novel set in the time of Charles II. Having two brothers who in their lives achieved fame for their novels, he has begun to feel the work as a sort of gentlemanly obligation. He is not quite aware of this. It's made him cross. She wonders if the urge to be away is settling in again, the longing to be elsewhere.

Light fades. Darkness for several beats, and then lights up on a transformed stage: a lane, winding off in the near distance, bordered by trees. Light of a late afternoon in spring. Stage right, the facade of the

Kingsley house, a porch and a small garden, a high fence. Mary and her father walk slowly downstage, toward the lane, arm in arm. They pause.

GEORGE

The transport, internally, of metabolic matter within an organism.

MARY

Left aorta, right aorta. Left ventricle, right ventricle. It starts there.

GEORGE

The word?

MARY

Circulation.

GEORGE

An easy one. Where on the globe was the city of Tenochtitlán located?

MARY

South America, specifically, Peru.

GEORGE

Bright girl, bright girl. Still easy. Now, translate: *Die Fenster des hauses gingen zur Strafs hinaus.*

MARY

The windows of the 'ouse looked out on the street.

GEORGE

The windows of the hhhhhouse looked out on the street. Say it. Hah. Hah. House.

MARY

Hhhouse.

GEORGE

You sound too much like your mother. I won't count it unless you pronounce it properly. Now, explain for me, please, what a brachistochrone is.

MARY

It's the idealized path a body will take. The curve of fastest descent. Developed by Johann Bernoulli, his brother Jakob, Gottfried Leibniz, and Isaac Newton.

They have come back to stage right. A gold cast to the light, now. They gaze at the house, and after a moment's hesitation, he puts his hand on the door latch. When he speaks, it's with a dispirited lack of conviction. He looks off.

GEORGE

She was somewhat better this morning, did you notice it?

MARY

Not really, Father.

They enter the house. Enter Guillemard, wearing a cape now. He still has the papers in his hand. He holds them up as if to show them.

GUILLEMARD

Great mountainous clouds in the eastern sky, bruised-looking in places, and showing snowy heights where the sun reaches them. Kingsley might as well be staring out at the perspective of tropical forests. From Mary's earliest memory, her mother has had to do with illness—Mary can recall sitting out on the lawn with Uncle Henry, who smelled of gin and whose features were always ringed with smoke from his tobacco, while her mother cared for a sick family across the street, cooking for them and washing out their soiled clothing, and bathing them in their fevers—her mother was always going among the sick, caring for those who were suffering, nursing the dying. Mary has no direct recollection of when her mother took to her own bed. She has been nurse to her since before she was old enough to understand that there was any other way to be with people. She has become very proficient at caring for all the members of the household. And she still manages to keep to her own habits—warm cereal in the mornings, with spiced apples, when available. And the hours of reading, and study, poring through the books in her father's enormous library: *Solar Physics* and *The Anatomy of Melancholy*; Charles Darwin; Dickens; the marvelous book, her favorite, about the robberies and murders of the notorious pirates. The thousand travel books, and papers from lectures given at learned societies, accounts of explorers of the Arctic, the Antarctic, the Himalayas, the Amazon, the South Seas, Australia, Africa. The writings and remembrances of adventurers.

3

ONE HUNDRED YEARS, *one hundred years . . .*

Lily put herself there, walking a sunny street in a suburb of London, having never been to England.

There was only Dominic to talk to about it. And he was mostly a cheerleader; he didn't seem able to see through to her doubts. She felt presumptuous, writing scenes, a child pretending to be a writer, since in fact it had all begun in childhood; it felt like an indulgence. She was a person prying into things, a detective, searching through files and histories for a name, the traces of a life that had ended tragically early, at thirty-seven years of age, a life lived in what would seem to anyone to be a kind of prison, until the last seven years of it. . . .

How does a person become someone wholly different, in seven little years?

Back at school, she busied herself finishing the semester's work. She wanted so badly to be done with all of it—the classes, the crowds, the snippets of academic talk you heard crossing the quad, the people all so tied up with their own concerns, their own bundles of paper and books, the weight of what was left to do. There would be only the one semester left, and she worried herself sleepless about that, about courses she hadn't even signed up to take yet. The final project for her degree, she had decided, would be a monologue, from the point of view of Mary Kingsley. Or a series of voices and scenes about her; or a full-length play about her. Why not?

How about because you haven't got the slightest idea of how to do it?

"You've got big *shadows* under your eyes," Sheri said. "You're studying too much. Come on out with me."

"Aren't you even going to study for your final exams?" Lily asked her.

And Sheri began to cry. "I don't stand a *chance*. I'm not gonna lie to myself."

"But you've come this far."

"Honey, I've been on and off probation every other semester here, and now it's check-out time. I got sick just when I needed to *bury* myself, and it's gone past everything." She stood by her bed with the bright banners from her high school in Oxford and cried, letting the tears drop down her cheeks. It struck Lily that the other girl envied her—she, Lily, with her books and her scribbling and her supposed talent, though Lily knew it was more a talent for being alone than for anything else.

She went home to her mother's house for Christmas with a sense of increasing unease. Christmas morning, her father and Peggy visited (*Baby, we're a family, and it's Christmas and I'm fine with it and I want you on your best behavior about it. Please?*), and Lily watched her mother bustle around, trying to keep everything smooth. It galled her; it made her heartsore and angry. Scott gave her a scarf, and a recording of the songs of Nat King Cole; from Peggy she received a Chet Baker CD. They had apparently talked about her love of jazz. Her mother had made a sweater for her, and a shawl, and also bought music—a boxed set of Ella Fitzgerald. Everyone wanted to spend time with her, and her mother invited cousins and aunts and uncles, some of whom Lily hadn't seen in years. It came to her that they were all worried about her. She worked to reassure her mother, and strove to behave as though she were carefree, happy.

4

She saw Tyler again early in the spring semester, shortly after a snowstorm swept down out of the mountains, covering the town. It went on for a day and a night, then turned to a fine rain, and the rain had frozen over the crust of what had accumulated. It was as though the world were encased in milky glass. And then it was snowing again. People were sliding around on the new layer, which blew across the hardened surface like dust across a table. Sheri had dropped out of school, and gone back home to Mississippi. She called to say that she was getting married. The young man was someone she had never mentioned or talked about in the time Lily had known her, but Lily was not really very surprised. In any case, she supposed she would probably never see her or her half brother again.

One day in the worst part of this second snowfall, while trying to make her way to an improvisation class, she fell on the sidewalk, and had to be helped by two elderly gentlemen to a bench near the corner. From out of the whiteness surrounding the men, a shadow moved, and Tyler Harrison leaned in to look at her. "Lily, is that you?" he said.

"Does she belong to you?" one of the men asked.

"Come on." Tyler leaned down to give her his arm.

She thanked the men for their help, holding on to Tyler's arm.

"Where were you headed?" he asked her.

"Caball Hall," she said.

He walked with her to the building, and when she thanked him, he said, "What time is the class?"

"Two-thirty."

He looked at his watch. "That's forty minutes from now. Let me buy you a cup of coffee."

They went along the walk to a set of brick stairs, which led down to a wide patio in front of the student union. There was a path shoveled through, but it was snow-covered and uneven, and they had to hold on to each other to get to the doors. They went into the cafeteria to a table against the wall. He held a chair for her, and then asked how she wanted her coffee.

"Black," Lily said, showing him a little smile. "With lots of cream and sugar in it."

She watched him cross to the counter, to order. The room was large, and only a few people had braved the weather to come here. They sat separately and in small groups, and there wasn't much talk. Several people were studying. Someone had put INXS on the juke box. But the sound was low. You could barely hear it.

Tyler came back with the coffee, and sat down next to her. She breathed the leather odor of his coat, and there was something else, too: talcum powder or shaving cream, pleasantly sweet. He turned in his chair, leaning one elbow on the back of it and the other on the table, sipping the coffee, gazing at the room.

"You came to my rescue," Lily said. "I looked up and there you were."

"I fell this morning, going down my stairs," he said. "And there wasn't even any ice. Just clumsy and stupid, I guess."

"Did you hurt yourself?"

"A little."

"I'm sorry."

He shook his head, sipped the coffee, then shifted in the chair, resting both elbows on the table and looking over at her with a ruminative, but faintly amused expression. "I've noticed something about girls—um, women—and I wonder if you have any thoughts on it. It's begun to seem to me that girls feel responsible for stuff that has nothing whatever to do with them. There's an earthquake on the other side of the world, and women all over the world—or maybe only American women—feel responsible for it. What do you think?"

"I never discuss sociology before dark," she said.

"Well, see, I fell like an idiot on my stairs this morning and when I told you about it, more than seven hours later, you apologized."

"That's the way you heard it," she said. "Maybe when a man falls down he starts to think some woman must be responsible for it. Maybe we're all conditioned by these kinds of expectations. But that's sociology again, and I can't go into it."

"It's an interesting theory." He smiled.

A moment later, he said, "You were just great as Rosalind. I know I already said this. But I couldn't take my eyes off you. I don't think anyone else could, either."

She told him that saying the lines of the play felt more natural the more you got into the part, and that every time you performed the part, it seemed to come more naturally. Yet it wasn't ever exhaustible; you were always learning more about the character. It was always opening out, and you knew more, felt more, every time you went through it. But the lines. You felt the antique lines as perfectly made for you as breathing. And they weren't antique anymore.

He gave her a little sidelong grin. "So this Shakespeare, he's pretty good then?"

"He can write," she said, laughing. "I think he has some talent."

"Tell me about your class."

She waved this away.

"No, really. Is it an acting class?"

"Improvisation. They give us situations, and we have to act them out. No script."

"A life class. Let's do one."

She said, "Okay. You start."

This caught him off guard, and his embarrassed groping to come up with something made them both laugh.

"I think it's better if some third party gives you the scene," she said.

He put the coffee cup down and cradled it with his hands. She had a sudden urge to reach over and touch his wrist, and then, to her surprise, she acted on it. There was an element of admiration about the gesture, as though she were appreciating the fine curvature of an artist's work in stone. He turned and a light came to his eyes.

"I'm glad I saw you again," she said.

They were sitting there gazing at each other, and then he looked down at the table. The music was Van Halen now, and someone had turned it up.

"How's your writing going?" he said, speaking louder over the music.

"Fits and starts."

"Are you working on the Keats or the Kingsley?"

The fact that he remembered this made her abruptly quite happy. "The Kingsley," she said.

"I wish I could write."

"Maybe you can."

He shook his head, laughing. "No, I think we have it pretty well established by now that I'm not a writer."

"Well, I'm probably not a writer, either."

They were having to shout to be heard now. They went on a little, talking about that, amused by the absurdity of it. When they got up and went outside, the cold and the quiet provided a small shock. They held on to each other again, crossing the open patio and making their way back to Caball Hall. At the entrance of the building, they paused.

"Don't I get a kiss on the cheek?"

She was too anxiously seeking some words to extend the moment, some pretext for them to get together again. She thought of cutting the class. But his lighthearted tone stopped her. "Some other time," she got out.

"Listen," he said. There was something tentative and nervous about his eyes, now. "I never called you because Sheri said you didn't want it."

She said, "Sheri—what—"

He took her by the shoulders, pulled her to him, and kissed her. It was a long kiss. Then he was simply holding her.

She didn't want to move. But others were filing by them, and finally he stepped away, slipping a little on the ice, and laughing. He righted himself and stood there with his hands in his pockets. She saw his breath on the air. "Maybe I ought to wait here and walk you home after the class."

"See you?" she said.

"Count on it," he told her.

When she came out of the class, she thought he might be waiting for her, but he was gone.

5

$\mathscr{S}$HE MADE HER WAY across the ice, home to the silence of her room, and sat in the light by the window, thinking of him out there in the dark. She could call him. She reached for the phone book on the desk and looked up the name. There was a listing for Harrison, but with only the letter L before the name. The address was not a university address. She dialed the number anyway. She let it ring twice, then hung up. This was absurd. It had been a kiss, and probably meant little to him. They had sat in the student union and chatted and tried to be smart for each other. She closed the blind on the window, and took up her study of dramatic monologue and social context in theater. There were examinations to study for. She geared herself up, and began to concentrate. Nothing would stay in her mind. She went out in the hallway to the water fountain and drank. Then walked up and down the hall. The building had an abandoned, run-down feeling.

Finally, back in the room, she sat at her desk, trying to study. She stared out the window at the bleak landscape, hoping to see someone come walking out of the night. Often, when she let herself dream it through, she saw herself in a tall house on a London street, and she could almost believe the smell of coal was on the air. When she was a little girl, her father read stories to her—*Peter Pan,* and Dr. Seuss; Laura Ingalls Wilder and others—and his voice had been so gentle and enveloping. There were always hopes, from everyone, father and mother, uncles, cousins, that she would go out into the world and make her mark. No, there had always been the *assumption* that this would be so. She thought of her fourteenth birthday, and stood abruptly, as if having come upon a spider in the papers before her. Sometimes, the memory of it could still move in her blood with a sudden heat, as if she had only now come from the confined space of that icebound house.

Her mouth was dry. She stood there breathing in small panting gasps, then realized the sound she was making and stopped.

When the knock at the door came, a little cry rose from the back of her throat. She looked with alarm at the mess of the room, and realized her own state of slovenliness. Running her hands through her hair, she said, "One minute." She fixed her blouse, tucked it in, glancing at herself in the mirror beside the door before she opened it.

Standing in the light of the hall was Dominic. She had to work to keep her sense of disappointment from showing.

"I saw your light," he said. "I was on my way home from a humiliating date."

"Well, at least you *had* a date," she said.

"Sometimes these things happen," he told her. "Now and then I can get one of the lady wrestlers, or someone on the bowling team, or occasionally somebody from the nursing home to feel sorry for me." He gazed at her as if at something exotic. But then his familiar smile came back. There was the doughy, open-faced look of high school about him. "Come out and have some coffee with me?"

"I wish I could," she said. "I've got all this studying to do."

He ran his hand nervously through his straw-colored hair. "Here's how I see it happening. This is a vision—a dream of the common man, like a proletarian soap opera, sort of, you know—sun coming up over a hill, Copland's *Fanfare* playing. And, like, I'm the man you're talking to in your dreams when the man of your dreams comes along. He beats me up, and the two of you walk away."

She laughed. "You've got my dream pretty well worked out."

"How're you gonna meet the man of your dreams if I'm not there for him to beat me up?"

"Dom, really—some other time?" she said.

"You won't mind my getting beat up. As long as it's some other time."

"You know what I mean."

"Okay," he said. Then he made a gesture, tipping a nonexistent hat. "And don't think I'm not humiliated."

"It's not that," she said, laughing. "We'll go later. Come on, Dom."

"Cool. I can tell that this really isn't rejection because you're not hitting me or throwing anything at me or screaming at me."

She shook her head. "Poor baby."

"Something's going on," he said. "Tell me."

She leaned against the door frame. "It's silly."

He seemed discouraged. His shoulders sagged. "Jesus. The man of your dreams *has* come along."

She said nothing.

"Really?" he said.

"Dom, I've got to study."

"I'll be goddamned."

"Come see me tomorrow," she said. "And I'll tell you all about it."

"You sure it's not puppy love?"

"I'm not sure of anything. I told you it's silly. We'll talk."

"But there's somebody quivering on the horizon."

She laughed. "Will you stop?"

"Jesus," he said. "Do I feel like an idiot."

"Good night, Dom." She sang the words.

He went off with a sidling gate, looking like Chaplin in all the films.

6

𝒯YLER WAS NOWHERE. And Dominic was full of questions about him. When she told him the name, he said, "I know the guy, I think. Yeah. I thought he was—"

Lily said, "You thought he was what, Dom?"

"Nothing."

"Tell me, please."

"Well, I thought he was sort of attached to somebody else."

Days, weeks passed. The ice melted, and it snowed again, and partly melted again, and there was a slushy dark mess along the street, black boulders she had to walk around when she crossed to the other side. Her classes kept her busy. She saw Dominic, and other friends in the bars across from the Rotunda, but she kept lonely hours, mostly, the routine of trying to study through difficulty concentrating. The books she was reading for her one literature course were filled with romance, the adventures of the world's lovers. Her history texts cataloged the long record of human slaughter and migration. She had once felt herself to be separated from it all by her own capacity to remain detached, to analyze. She had not allowed herself a pause to reflect on much of anything but the next task before her. And the truth was that if she kept working through her own distractedness, she forgot Tyler, and even managed the occasional recurring spells of panic. She slept better, or at least she went to sleep. Her dreams were hectic, full of strands of speech she couldn't fathom. The lovers in the stories she read either broke their own hearts with romantic expectations, or had their expectations answered beyond their wildest dreams. The antique poets sang of love. She dreamed of Mary Kingsley arguing with a boat captain about the draw of water on a craft, in the middle of some African river. She woke with a sense of having been close to her, and during that day she felt rather pleasantly watched over. It was a happy surprise, one afternoon, to discover that she hadn't thought of Tyler at all that day.

Her mother called to ask after her, and to ask why she hadn't called her father. Lily said she would make the call, but she kept putting it off, knowing that each passing day meant another increment of awkwardness she would feel whenever she finally *did* make it.

Hello, Dad? How are you?

Fine. Great to hear from you, kid. I'm sleeping with somebody only a couple of years older than you are, and I've added immeasurably to your sense of the untrustworthiness of the world, but try not to pay any attention to it, okay? Let's just be like we always were when you believed I was going to keep all those promises I made to you and your mother.

One afternoon, she gazed out her window at the couples making their way along the snow-driven street, and had the barren thought that all love ended in estrangement, that it *does* alter when it alteration finds. There was a sour and empty solace in the thought, as if she could let go now that the worst apprehension had been realized.

She had the room to herself, at least for the time being, and she had spread out, her books and papers lying across the other bed, her clothes strewn everywhere. She developed an agreeably heavy feeling in her mind from all the reading; it felt weighty, full. No distractions quite touched her anymore, and friends teased her about her weird, distant look.

7

Were you so terrified of intimacy? Did you have this same expectation, all the time, that things were not going to work out? That something bad was just on the other side of every minute? Why is it that when I look out a window and see lovely green mountains, I immediately think of the killing frost, or the insect hives and the animals hunting each other? That scene out this window in my first months here—the hawk raiding the starlings' nest, and there was utterly nothing they could do. I watched it with a terrible fascination and sick-heartedness, as if it were offered to me by some force as an illustration of the world. I will have love. I will love, and it will be more than romance. It will be stronger, and truer. Yet I'm always fighting the thing in me that wants to deny it all, all the time. That shoulders aside every lighthearted feeling and insists that something will ruin it, bring it down to earth, shake it out of its lovely nest. It's like a form of spiritual arthritis, and I'm always trying to beat it back, having to act to beat it back. I know that this is a product of my history; and even knowing it, I'm discouraged by how often I'm unable entirely to escape its effects. People say I can act. But my whole life is acting, it seems. My impulse, when these doubts and negations plague me, is to fly in the face of them, stare them down, pretend my way beyond the fright they cause, deny them a single increment of my allegiance. They're patient; they wait.

It helps me sometimes, imagining you at my age, living in that time: in a society with such a fixed idea of women and what was expected, and you with your own fixed, steely determination anyway to do what you would. It helps to keep this little journal by addressing you, like this. A secret friend, behind the diary, the spirit of the burning lamp in my mind: you.

8

"*You* NEED TO GET OUT," Dominic said. "And I'm clearly not the man to do it." He had followed her out of the literature class, and they were standing in the archway near the entrance to the colonnade. "I guess I could be drafted to take you out, if it came to that," he continued, not quite looking at her. "I'm no draft dodger. I mean, if I had to, I could make the sacrifice. Oh, I know. You're afraid of hurting my feelings by rejecting me later on."

"I've got studying, Dom. I'm not even doing the spring play. If I do one other thing, it means something else drops off the screen. Why aren't you studying, anyway?"

He was. He had also tried out for and gotten the part of Bottom in *A Midsummer Night's Dream*. "If you really loved me, you'd give up studying and come be in Willy's fanciful love fable with me."

"I'd end up in the hospital with exhaustion. As it is, I'm going on two hours' sleep."

"I've almost charmed you into it. I can tell by the green, nauseated cast of your lovely face."

She kissed his cheek, and walked away from him.

She felt no sense, really, that she was missing anything. Dominic was there, uncomplicatedly, as her friend. She told him that she was in her senior year of college, and was, at last, serious. She had begun to consider the possibility that upon graduation she might find a way to get to London, where she could write her play.

"You're sick with love, and you can't even see it," Dominic said.

"Go away," she told him. "I'm sick with work."

Her mother called on Sunday evenings, usually. For several weeks they hadn't talked about her father. But then the questions started again: had Lily heard from him? No. Had Lily called him? No.

"Don't you think it would be nice if you called him?"

Lily said, "Why doesn't he give *me* a call?"

"He tells me he has—he says there's never any answer in your room during the days and he's afraid of waking you or disturbing you at night."

"Well," Lily said. "That's how I feel."

"If he were a friend, you'd take the trouble to get through to him."

"You'd be surprised. Ask my friends. Besides, he's not a friend."

"No, he's your father."

"Okay," Lily said, her voice shaking. "I'll call him."

"And so now you're mad at *me*."

"No." She sat forward and put one hand on her head, closing her eyes.

"Lily, do you want to hurt him, is that it?"

She couldn't answer this. She sighed into the phone, and realized that under the circumstances, this was an answer of its own.

"Stop being so angry about it. If I'm not angry, why should you be? He was my husband."

"I don't want to talk about this anymore, Doris."

Conversations like this upset her, and made it difficult to concentrate, and for hours afterward she watched television, or went out and walked the streets of the campus, alone.

THREE

1

She went home for a visit during spring break. When her mother requested that she go on into town to see her father and Peggy, she declined.

"Oh, come on," Doris said. "What're you going to do, disown him? He's your father. I've never known you to be so conventional."

"I don't want to talk about it," Lily said. "I need a little time. Do you think you could leave me alone about it? Do you think you could stop seeming so cosmopolitan about it all, as if it's just *so* all right with you?"

Her mother said nothing, then. She got up after a few minutes and went on into her bedroom. Lily watched her go, looked at the roundness of her, the way her small feet seemed to mince along the carpet in the hallway. A former dancer. It was hard to believe. There was something of the crank about her, now, a subtle zaniness that worked on Lily's nerves. She went down the hall, and knocked on the bedroom door. No answer. "Mom?"

Silence.

"Mom, I'm sorry. Please?"

"Nothing to be sorry for," said Doris. "Good night, dear."

"Good night." Lily waited, listening, but the quiet went on, and then she could discern the sounds of the other woman readying herself for bed. Doris coughed, cleared her throat. Lily heard her running water in the bathroom. When the water stopped, she said, "Doris? Want some coffee?"

"I'm going to bed, honey."

Lily didn't move.

"Go on to bed," said her mother from the other side of the door.

They had a tense two days, during which they both avoided the subject of marriage or divorce, or men in general. They worked crosswords together, and went out to browse in the thrift shops and flea markets in the valley, and they spent one afternoon painting a set of antique chairs, working in the family room, in the middle of an island of spread-out newspapers. Toward the end of this project, the tension relaxed slightly, and Doris talked about the little plays Lily would put on for her parents when she was small. "Do you remember?" Doris said. "Of course you spent so much time over at that theater—I worried about it a little. Thought it had warped you. You got so quiet."

A moment later, she said, "Are you seeing anyone, honey?"

"Are you?"

"Don't be aggressive."

"There's my friend Dom."

"Is he more than a friend?"

"He's a friend. He makes me laugh. We tell each other things. I'm not interested in him that way."

"And there's no one you're interested in that way?"

"This is ridiculous, Doris. What exactly are you seeking to know?"

"All right," Doris said. "I can't answer for where we ended, your father and I. And, honey, I *can't* answer for it. But it was love. Just because it didn't end there doesn't mean it wasn't real. And I want you to have that."

"Do you think I'm—" Lily began. Then stopped. "What're you worrying about?"

"The world isn't all symmetry and order, you know. People have fallen in love over a lot less than friendship."

Neither of them spoke for a time.

"You think you can run your life solely on the basis of intellect?" Doris said.

"I'd like not to be governed wholly by heartthrobs and hormones. I suppose you could say that, yes."

"Is that how you see me? Your father?"

"I wouldn't presume like that, Doris. But I have my own thoughts on this for me."

"It's how you see your father."

"I don't want to talk about this," Lily said. "It just leads in circles."

Perhaps a full minute went by. There was just the sound of their paintbrushes and the crinkling of the newspapers they were sitting on as they shifted their weight, working.

"It's more than friendship on Dom's side, isn't it?"

"Doris, give it a rest—please." A moment later, trying for a lighter tone, she said, "He jokes about it."

"They are *never* joking when they joke about it, sweetie."

2

At school, now, the last of her undergraduate work and the complications of applying to various graduate schools were all the more stressful. She had begun to entertain the idea of taking a break from school. She went to see Dominic in the play, and afterward she went out with him and several members of the cast. He had been good, everyone had done well enough, yet the play had seemed long, and Dominic felt that it had been a disaster, especially where he was concerned. They all talked back and forth about what had gone right or wrong, and though Lily knew most of them, she felt out of place. Dominic was not himself, sitting back in his chair with his leg jumping in that nervous way he had, chewing the cuticles of his fingers and watching everyone. Something was worrying him.

"I'd better leave," Lily said to him. "I've got a mountain of work. I thought you were wonderful."

"I sucked."

"Shut up, Dominic," one of the others said—the young man who had played Lysander. Lily didn't know him.

"You were fine," she said to Dominic.

"Oh, hey, I've slipped from wonderful to fine." He shook his head. "We don't lie to each other about a thing like that, do we?"

"I thought you were wonderful. And fine. And we don't lie to each other and that means we believe each other, okay?"

"There's no 'fine' with Shakespeare, Lily. Come on—either you strike the notes that are in the role or you miss them. It's like hitting the wrong keys on the piano."

"Now you're arguing over my choice of words."

"Who wants Bottom to shut up?" the one who had played Lysander said.

"Well," Dominic said to Lily, "thanks for coming, anyway."

She felt dismissed. But she hesitated about leaving, and ended up staying to the end of the evening. As they were all going out of the place, he hugged her, and asked if she would come to another performance. "I think I can do better," he said.

"You always outdo yourself," she told him.

He held up both hands. "Don't say another word. I'll take that as a yes."

She hugged him, and excused herself.

3

SHE SAW TYLER AGAIN on a warm March afternoon, from the other side of the colonnade. He was standing in the shade of a column, listening to some young woman talk, one hand clasping the other arm at the elbow. Lily felt that if she were to walk over there, she would have to explain who she was. She started off in the other direction, but then he called out to her, and when she turned he was running to catch up with her.

"Hey," he said. "I thought that was you." He walked along beside her. The sidewalk was crowded with other students, and there was a lot of traffic in the street.

"Have you eaten?" he asked. "Will you let me buy you lunch?"

She stopped and looked at him. The sun was bright here, and he was holding one hand up to shade his eyes. "I don't want to be inside," she told him.

He knew of a deli nearby, and they went there and he bought sandwiches, which they carried, with two bottles of iced tea, across to the quad in front of the Rotunda. They sat in the shade of a big oak, and ate the sandwiches, talking about the balmy weather, the pretty sky, the outlandish dress of some of the people strolling past them. He spoke of a professor he knew who made passes at his students, and was about to be fired for it. "He's never had an attractive female student he didn't make a pass at."

"How do you mean that?" she chided him. "'Attractive.'"

He took a large bite of his sandwich, and then held it up, as if that would be a more fitting subject of conversation. "Just meant it's—you know—the—the pretty ones he goes for."

"Do you know anyone who goes for the ugly ones?"

He was chewing, and his expression was of a kind of cagey avoidance. He shook his head, and smiled. At last, he said, "Allow me to change the subject before I get into any more trouble than I already am."

"Hey," she said. "Though it might not seem so to you now, I'm really not one of those people who's always looking for something to be offended by. I was making a joke. I hate people who sit around waiting for the chance to catch somebody up. Really. That's an ego game and I hate it."

He nodded, having taken another bite of the sandwich. There was a smear of mayonnaise on the side of his lip, and she reached over and took it off with her napkin. He grasped her wrist, and then let his hand glide into hers.

"Oh, hell," she said. "What're we doing, anyway?"

"You're beautiful, you know."

"Don't."

"You are."

She waited for him to let go, and when he did, she put the sandwich down in its crown of waxed paper, and kissed him. She kissed his neck, and his ear, and then his mouth. He tasted of the sandwich, and of something else—the faintest trace of tobacco. His chin was rough; he hadn't shaved that morning. When she let go, and sat back on the grass, he leaned with her, and the kiss went on. Finally they were apart, attending to the mess they had made of lunch—the sandwiches were knocked off the paper, lying in the grass. She picked hers up and put it in its wraping, and closed it tight.

"Tyler," she said, "what do we do now?"

He was sitting there, hugging his knees. "I can't stop thinking about you. But I'm—it scares me, Lily."

After a moment, she said, "Oh." And she gathered the refuse from lunch, including his, and stood. He got to his feet and seemed to shift from one leg to the other, looking at her and then looking away. He ran one hand through his rich brown hair, which shone in the mottled sunlight.

"I didn't mean that the way it sounded," he said.

"Well, you know where I live." She smiled. "I have to go."

She walked to the edge of the grass, the sidewalk, where there was a trash can, and looked back at him, perhaps fifty yards away, standing under the spotted shade of the tree. Lifting the trash can lid, she held the remains of their lunch over the opening. Then she released them with suddenness, spreading her fingers wide, as if to express her exact feeling. The wrapped parts of half-eaten sandwiches dropped out of sight. Slowly she replaced the lid, raised one hand slightly to wave at him, then turned and walked away.

4

She began combining her nonclass days and weekends to visit colleges in the Carolinas and Tennessee; she had received news that she was accepted into graduate programs in drama at four of them: the Universities of North and South Carolina, Duke, and Tennessee at Knoxville. These were applications she had sent out early in the fall, and now, because it was expected, she wrote the representatives of each to say that she would reach a decision soon. The truth was, she couldn't bring herself to think of committing to any of them. A kind of inertia had set in, a growing, nameless apathy.

In early May, just before graduation, Sheri called her from Oxford, Mississippi, to say that she was thinking of getting a divorce.

Lily thought she must be joking, and said so.

"Does this sound like I'm *joking*?" Sheri said, in a level voice, sniffling into the static of long distance. "I'm sorry," she said. "Damn, you don't need me whining at you now."

"I'd be hurt if you didn't call me with something like this," Lily said.

The other sobbed, and took a moment getting hold of herself. Then: "I think every last one of the sons of bitches is fucking *crazy*. I mean I *dated* the son of a bitch off and on for five *years*. And he comes home one night drunk and wants me to look at a damn sex *video* with him. We're supposed to go to his parents' house for dinner and he comes in drunk, with this *tape*. We're living with *my* parents, for God's sake. I mean, he's in so tight with my *parents*—"

"Do your parents know about the—the sex video?"

"Hell, my father *drinks* with him. It's not just the movie. It's everything. My father's offered him a damn *job*. You know, wanting to be the good father-in-law, and all that stuff. And Nick's parents treated us like

shit at the wedding. Two really screwy people like that picture Grant
Wood did. You know the one? So I was thinking maybe if we could
move in somewhere—you and me—you're not *doing* anything after you
graduate, are you?"

Lily was surprised to hear herself say, "Actually, no, I'm not."

"Why don't you come down and at least *visit*? There's a good community theater group down here."

They spent the next few moments talking about the possibility,
Sheri would take her for a tour of the delta, and they would go down to
New Orleans, where she had some friends. They could use up the
whole month of July, just having fun and not thinking about troubles
with members of the opposite sex.

Talking about it made the possibility seem already accomplished. It
was a pleasant thought. Lily entertained it with an enjoyable sort of drifting in her soul, listening to her friend go on about warm days and the
Gulf.

When she got off the phone and looked out over the green acre of
grass—the people out there, two young men tossing a Frisbee, a couple
sitting on a blanket, sunning themselves, a girl jogging, wearing a white
bandanna and listening to a Walkman—she suddenly felt a terrible chill.
It raked through her, an inward blast, a tossing. Something in her mind
seemed to buckle. She looked at the room with its sprawl of books, and
then she began trying to put everything in order, working on in spite of
an increasing sense of suffocating exhaustion and emptiness. This was
not panic; this was the abyssal non-feeling of death. The dead freeze
inside kept up, and finally she lay down on her bed. She had been
putting off thoughts about leaving here, and it came to her now that what
her life had become—this repetition of classes and study and work and
aloneness—was unbearable, and that it had been that way most of the
time, for most of the year. How could she not have perceived that the
routine she had fallen into—no, worked out, carefully and meticulously
planned—was really a withdrawal, a pulling into herself so profound that
her two brief interludes with Tyler were no more than surfacing for air in
a process of drowning. Now, understanding it, there was no one she
could call, no one she could feel comfortable calling.

Home.

The word had no meaning. She saw herself as having gone out from a shoreline. Yet it was a paltry kind of going, she realized, and this contributed to her sense of suffocating apathy; this wasn't West Africa, or some group of uncharted islands in wild seas. It wasn't even the Gulf of Mexico. This was her own little protected existence, in a college dormitory that she was afraid to leave. She couldn't shake the sense of catastrophe that clung to every surface of the life around her.

The evening sky reddened, and made strands of fire out of the long clouds near the edges of the hills beyond the square. Against her rising despair, she left the room, and went out into the cooling spring dusk. In a little pub across from the Rotunda, she saw some people she knew, but they were in couples, and so she sat at the bar and ordered a Coke. No one else was alone. Even the bartender had a waitress to talk to. Lily drank the Coke, and watched them. She had not even taken the trouble to ask where Tyler Harrison lived. Her own thought of him, in this aloneness, made her angry with herself. She finished the Coke, paid for it, and went out. It was growing dark. She walked along the street and looked into the windows of the shops. At another bar, she ordered a whiskey, and when the bartender carded her, they joked about it a little. For less than a year, she had been old enough to order the drink. But then she changed her mind, and had a soda water. He brought it to her, and she couldn't finish it. She left this bar, and walked back in the direction of her building. The strains of music reached her from somewhere, and she heard scraps of conversation and laughter.

5

Scene:
Open stage. Mary Kingsley at a desk, at center. A girl, twelve years old. Light on her. She is writing. As she writes, we hear her voice, but it is the voice of the grown woman:

MARY

There was always merriment when Uncle Henry was around. Uncle Henry never announced himself, but would walk right into a room, as though he was perfectly confident that the people he had come to see would be engaged in some worthy pursuit, would not be talking evilly about anyone or doing anything they would not do in the light of his

presence. And his presence was like light, because he was full of stories, and liked to make up rhymes, and he read to me from the
Brownings, and from Dickens, too, when I could get Mother to rest
comfortably. And when Father was in the house, the two men talked
into the hours before dawn, and I loved to lie awake in the sound of
those voices.

*She looks up, and now gets up and strides across the stage, hands
clasped behind her, speaking above us, past us.*

How old was I? Six, and seven. Very small. The fragrance of the tobacco
pleased me, as did the sense that I might be carried by those voices to
faraway places. My father spoke of the side of the family he was not
speaking to, Uncle Charles with his aristocratic wife, and his airs. There
was something between them, troubling them, and I was too young to be
able to decide how I felt about it. I liked it when my mother closed the
shutters on the windows that looked out into the garden behind that
house, liked the sense of cool dark it gave me, moving through the
rooms. This was Highgate. Father had moved us there when I was a baby.
Charley had been born there, in 1866, when I was four. It was a gloomy
place. The Baptist bells tolled periodically, counting time. I lost the sense
of minutes or hours. Days and months and years, turning the pages of
books, looking at the pictures, waiting for the next communication from
the world, from the great distances . . .

6

*I*N THE ROOM, Lily lay dry-eyed on the bed and watched the darkness
lessen with the car lights moving in the street, then grow deeper again
as the cars went on. She had written Sheri's number on a little piece of
torn paper. She got up, closed the window, and changed her clothes.
She wished she could get the panic to stir in her; that had been something to feel, at least. She couldn't stand up to this negation; it was like
an awful storm, a wall of blinding wind, and she felt again the urge to
get out, to move. All the reading and study, the harmony of those hours,
taking everything in as though it would be of some use to her—it was all
nothing, now. Annulled. She had come to a dead stop, and she couldn't

decide why this should have come to pass now, with classes about to end, and everything accomplished. *I am not in love with anybody. Fuck romance. Fuck it all.* Putting the paper with Sheri's number on it into her purse, she opened the door to the room and stepped out.

Here was Dominic.

She experienced a wave of gratitude, and almost walked into his arms. In the next instant, she thought of how awful it would be to afflict him with herself as she felt now. This friend, especially this one, whom she had first met on what turned out to be the last day of her childhood.

"Wouldn't it be nice," Dominic said, "if somebody cut Siskel and Ebert's thumbs off? Then they'd have to say, 'Two stumps up. Way up.'"

She laughed in a bitter, helpless, hysterical spasm.

"Hey, girl," he said, reaching to take her arm. "What's the matter?"

"Nothing. Nothing—exactly." She walked past him, but he followed, keeping a little behind her, and leaning forward when he spoke.

"Lily, hey. Come on—this is me. What is it? What's happened?"

She stopped, put her hand on his chest, and took it away. "I'm a little sick of myself, Dom. And you don't want my company right now, believe me."

They went down the stairs and out into the square together. She had no idea where she was headed.

"Hey," he said. "I've had a revelation about Frank Capra. You remember the scene in *It's a Wonderful Life,* when the angel's given George Bailey his wish and made it so he was never born? And he's running in the snow and it isn't Bedford Falls, it's Pottersville? The town and the world are complete *hell,* right, because George was never born. And there he is, running madly in the snow, in hell, except that it's *jazz* coming from the joints on either side of the street. Great jazz, too. And people are all having a high old time on it. Jazz. Great lively American music. Nightclubs. Fun. Think of it, in Capra's vision, that's *hell.* What do you think? If he wasn't a prig, then he pandered to prigs, right? It's the most fucking ubiquitous movie ever made and so the whole country's full of prigs."

It was the kind of thing he had said to divert her before. She stopped again. "I didn't go see the play again. Where have you been, anyway? I haven't seen you anywhere since that night."

"I've been in the play," he said. "I've been attending to my own cav-ing-in reality. Hey, I know. Why don't you officially designate me your 'listens-to-her-troubles' person? We could go on one of those talk shows. I can see the heading flash on the screen: 'Listens to her troubles, but gets no love from her,' sort of thing. Huh?"

She gave him a smile, but kept on.

"Where are we going?"

She stopped at the corner, where there was traffic. He stood with his hands in his jeans pockets and whistled, and when she glanced at him, he pretended not to be watching her. "Dom," she said. "God, I'm sorry. I'm not fit company now."

"Hey, don't apologize. I wasn't expecting company on this corner, but there's plenty of room." He turned from her and whistled again, then stopped and stared. "Why don't you tell me about your Mary Kingsley play? You still working on it?"

"Not much."

"Stuck, huh. Me, too."

She looked at him. "Are you writing something?"

"A novel?" He said it with an expression of doubtful questioning, as if it were a flimsy excuse that he didn't expect her to believe. "I'm writ-ing about this guy who follows a girl around and gets her to show him how much he annoys her."

They went across the street and on, toward the Rotunda. Down from this was a row of bars and restaurants, and without planning to do so, they went into the Mexican Café. The waitress who seated them knew him. He ordered a burrito, and Lily ordered a salad. They ate qui-etly. It occurred to her that one worked hard and hoped for some kind of respect and admiration from others, but that the admiration itself was not very comforting to have; there was something cloying about it. Dominic lit a cigarette. His skinny hands shook.

"Dom," she said. "You really were wonderful in the play."

"Ask anyone," he said.

"Well, it's the truth. And you've been such a good friend."

"Aw, shucks, you turn my head."

"I *do* mean it," she said, sounding more irritated than she was.

"Okay." And for the first time his expression was serious. He blew smoke at the ceiling, and sat back. There was a nervous energy, almost a jumpiness, about him. His left leg was moving, a pumping motion, up and down. He drummed his fingers on the table.

"Are you going on to graduate school?" she asked him.

"I stopped going to class about a month ago." He had been majoring in history as well as drama, and had been keeping a high average in both. He had often flashed the papers he'd done, with the marks on them. It was a point of pride with him.

"For God's sake," she said. "Why?"

He blew more smoke. "The whole thing started to look rather, uh, what is that word. English word. *Fu-tile*. Yes, that's the one."

She waited for him to go on, but he just sat there smoking the cigarette. "I have this—this awful blankness," she heard herself say. "I can't feel anything."

"Senior syndrome," he said.

"Oh, Christ, don't belittle it with psychobabble."

"I'm not belittling it," he said, amiably. "I'm reducing it to size."

They were quiet. Other people came into the restaurant, and Dominic waved at them. "Guys from the newspaper office," he said to her. "I know them."

"Friends?" she said.

"Well, not as such." He smiled, but there was something rather broken and unhappy about it.

"Tell me what you mean," she said.

"Nothing. You're the one who's depressed."

"Is that what this is? The word is utterly useless to describe this."

"Well, and I am your friend and I'm worried about you. A little worried." He put money down to pay for the food, insisting on it, and when he looked at her, she thought she saw something both hopeful and sad in his eyes.

She touched his hand, meaning it as simple friendly affection, but realizing as she did so that it would be interpreted differently.

He stood. "Lily, if you could think of me—" His face froze. She had never seen him so serious. It came to her that she would only make her way out of the dark by getting out of herself; she wanted surcease from herself, from the trackless emptiness under her skin.

"Walk me back?" she said.

7

$\mathscr{T}$HEY STRODE BACK past the Rotunda, and on to her dormitory. On the stairs he fell, and barked his shin. He kept apologizing.

She was thinking how strange it was that she would end her virginity with Dominic of all people, a friend for whom she felt no sexual attraction at all. At her door, while she fumbled with the keys, he bent over and massaged the hurt place on his leg. The door opened, and he straightened himself, seemed to attempt standing taller. He was as pale as the walls.

"Are you okay?" she said.

"Yeah. I'm flying, can't you tell?" He sounded frightened to her. His eyes were wide. His expression could have been surprise, or even wonder.

"Hey," she said. "This is new to me, too."

She hesitated only a moment. In the little space of darkness inside, with the door closed, she put her arms around his neck and kissed him. He was surprisingly soft to the touch—his shoulders and back were fleshy, as though not quite formed. His mouth tasted of cigarettes and garlic. She let go, and reached for the light switch. He was somewhere behind her. The light came on, too brightly illuminating the disorder of the room. He had moved to the other side, against the wall. He was wringing his hands, looking at everything.

"Hey," she said. "Are you all right? Look." She held out her hands, which trembled slightly. "I'm scared, too."

"Oh, God—I think you're the most wonderful thing on earth."

"It doesn't have to be love, Dom."

He seemed disheartened. "You don't love me?"

"You're my dearest friend," she said.

"It's just—" he began. "I do love you. I do. I know I do because I'm shaking like a fucking leaf."

She turned the light off and moved toward him. The clutter of the room was a problem—there were books and papers strewn across the floor, and clothes on both beds. She tried to get this all out of the way, and he stood frozen at her side in the dark. When she had cleared her bed, she turned to him again.

He said, "Do you want me to take my clothes off?"

"Okay," she said.

He didn't move.

"Dominic?"

"Are you going to take yours off?" he said.

She removed her blouse, her bra. It was too cool in the room. She got in under the blanket and removed her jeans and panties. She felt him near her, removing his own clothes, and she thought of married couples, her parents, the quality of light in the living room of Ronda Seiver's house. It stopped her.

"What?" he said.

"Come close," she said. "Hold me." There was a spinning sensation at the pit of her stomach. Dominic sat down on the bed, and she reached and felt the fleshy skin just above his hip. He was all goose bumps, shivering.

"I have rubbers," he said, with enormous urgency in his voice. "I bought them a month ago." She waited for him to put one on. "Jesus," he said. "It's cold."

She moved in the bed, and he lay next to her under the blanket, and they were not quite touching. Leaning up on one elbow, a shadow-shape in the darkness, he tried to kiss her, and missed her mouth. His lips were cold; they pressed her nose, and quickly he moved down. His body seemed to fall against hers. The first sensation was of a kind of sorrow. She realized how little she knew, for all the movies she had seen and the books she had read. She thought again of Mr. Stapleton. Everything was null inside. Dom moved, and was on top of her, his arms on either side of her head, the surprisingly light weight of him along her abdomen and chest. Nothing was happening. He was soft, the rubber had come off, and he lay back over, sighing. She went with him, still kissing his mouth, reaching down to caress him. His prick felt like a formless, furry pod. The shaft was smaller than she had thought it might be, and when she moved her hand along it, there was a slight change. "Come on," she said. "It's okay. It's really okay."

"I have to put another one on."

She waited again, while he worked at it. He couldn't stay erect, and the prophylactics wouldn't work.

"Forget them," she said. "Come on."

"You don't want a baby."

"You can pull out. Just pull out, Dom. Come on." She had reached a moment of determining that she could go through with this, and make it good; she could put the badness in her mind away, and concentrate on him.

There was reluctance in his voice. "Okay."

"Don't you want to?"

"I feel so lame with these freaking rubbers lying around. Christ, I can't even get a rubber on."

"Come here." She took his arms and pulled him to her, lying back, and finally she guided him into her. For a few moments there was discomfort as he pushed, and then it felt good, it was fine, it was gliding and smooth and good, and she could let go of thinking; he kept thrusting, and slowly it seemed to play itself out, even as he strove to increase it. He had gone flaccid again, sliding out of her. He put his hand there, his finger, working into her, and manipulating the flesh. She stared into the dark, above the faint outline of him, and tried to allow herself the pleasure of the touch, the tactile warm otherness of him, there in the bed with her. But she was worried; she couldn't concentrate. He lay over on her once more and pushed, and entered, and moved, and for a while she felt him going deep inside her again, let herself go toward the enjoyment of it for itself, almost separate from him. She strove not to think of anything but this; she whispered his name aloud, opening her legs wider, reaching up to his face. But then he lost it again, dying out of her, so that she moaned with frustration and reached for him, trying to put him back.

"Ow," he said.

They moved apart. For a few seconds they were just breathing, and outside there was the sound of wind sweeping across the world, thunder drumming in the distances beyond the city. She reached for the lamp by the bed and turned it on, and looked at him.

"Jesus Christ, I'm sorry," he said, running his hands through his hair.

"Did I do something wrong? What did I do?"

"Nothing. It pinched a little. I'm fine." He had his back to her.

"What do you want me to do."

"Get me a doctor?" he said.

"Did I hurt you that bad?"

"Not that kind of doctor."

She was quiet.

"I've been hoping if I could just get talked to by the right person. You know?"

"Tell me what you're feeling."

"Not *that*," he said. "Jesus Christ."

"I'm sorry."

He put his hands behind his head, and stared at the ceiling. "Talk to me."

"Okay," she said. But she could think of nothing whatever to say.

"Well?"

"Pick a subject." She tried to sound casual.

"Nuclear war's really a scary prospect, isn't it?"

"That's keeping it light."

"Something we agree on."

"Dominic, do you want to talk about—" She halted.

"Not about this. No. This. You mean this—as in, *this*?"

"I don't know what I mean."

"Tell me what you're reading."

"I can't read anything, lately. I can't concentrate."

"I'm reading about Torquemada. The Inquisition. And *Bleak House*, for the literature final I'm not going to take. I'm reading the *Kama-sutra*, too. And I still can't get it right."

"Something's been happening to me," Lily told him. "I can't explain it. I have this awful space opening out in my soul."

"I have this big need to get inside something," he said. "Soon."

She pulled the blankets back and moved to take him into her mouth. He tasted badly of the latex and lubricant of the rubbers, and so she got up and went quickly, wrapped in the blanket from the bed, across the dorm hall to the bathroom, where she filled a paper cup with warm water and hand soap, then came back and closed the door, ranged herself over him in the bed, and with her hands and the warm soapy water, washed him. She got a towel from the bureau and dried him off, and he was erect again.

"Good," he said.

Very gently she put everything aside, came back to the bed, and knelt to take him into her mouth. Now he tasted of the soap; she kept going. He lay very still while she worked over him. The shaft went soft once more. His hand caressed the back of her head, so she kept at it for a while, but then her gag reflex started, and she trailed her lips back up his body, to his mouth. His eyes were open and he seemed to be looking at her for some reaction. She stopped.

"Aw, God," he said, and began to cry.

She wrapped herself in her part of the blanket and waited for him to speak. But he just lay there, quietly crying.

"I'm sorry, Dom," she said. "Is it something I'm doing wrong?"

"It's not you." He sniffled, then covered his face with his hands.

"Tell me what you want me to do," she said.

"Shut up. I want you to shut up."

She lay back, legs together, arms at her sides. They were not touching now. Her mind was racing.

"Look," he said, sitting up. "I'm sorry."

"There's nothing to be sorry for. Can't I do anything?"

"I don't know."

"It's supposed to be fairly common the first time," she told him. "Isn't it? Nerves and the strangeness of it. I mean, the strange place. This terrible little room—" She halted.

"This isn't the first time," he said, low.

She waited.

"Or the second."

"Well, the first few times. I'm sure—"

He broke in, rising from the bed. "Oh, come on." He had stood. But then he sat down, hands folded in his lap.

She saw the buttonlike row of bones in the center of his back. "Tell me one of your fantasies. I'll try and do whatever it is," she said.

"You don't understand."

She thought perhaps she did. "Let's just lie here and be close," she said. "We've got all night."

"I've got stuff to do." He had stood, and was putting his clothes back on.

"Dominic, you don't have to go."

When he faced her—half in, half out of his pants—she saw that he had clenched his jaw, and there was a resistance in his eyes, a kind of opaqueness that intended itself, keeping her out. He finished getting into the pants, then put the shirt on and buttoned it, without quite returning her look. When he had put his coat on, he walked over and leaned down to kiss her on the cheek.

"I don't want to see anybody for a while," he said. Then he turned and strode to the door.

She sat up. "What're you going to do?"

"Think of it," he said. "I get to be the one you tell about. I get to be the fumbling virginal boy in your movie or your poem or your play or whatever the fuck it is that you're writing."

"I'm not going to tell anybody anything," she told him. "How can you—how can you say that? It's not fair of you to say that."

"I'm sorry," he said. "Okay?"

"You don't have to be sorry."

"Oh," he said. "Are you one of those people who thinks we actually have a choice about what we feel?"

"I mean," she said, "you don't have to say it."

He opened the door, and the light in the hall made it hard to see his face clearly; he was only shadow, standing there, facing the dim lamp-light, with the shower of brightness pouring down on him from the hall. "God," he said. Then he closed the door and was gone.

She got up, wrapped in the blanket, and went to the window to look out. She saw him cross the grassy lawn, slow, hands in his pockets, appearing casual enough, going on with that faintly Chaplinesque gait. When he disappeared beyond the bend in the road across the way, she closed the curtain, and went out into the hall and across to the shower. She spent the better part of an hour washing herself, over and over, standing under the needlelike spray, watching the rivulets of soap trail down the small bulge of her lower abdomen. It had happened now, and she could never take it back, but it had been accomplished in such a strange, unsatisfying, guilty, not-quite-actual way. She was fairly certain of the reasons for his trouble, yet couldn't shake the sense that *she* was his trouble; that something in her makeup, something stemming from her first terrifying experience, and something of her present inner lassi-tude, had stopped him. She had a moment of what she knew to be self-ish concentration on the fact that he had said it was not the first time he'd had the trouble. Then she went about the practical business of dry-ing off and brushing her teeth, trying not to think at all.

As she came out of the bathroom, three girls from across the hall strolled in, drunk, reeling, from the elevator. They looked down the long perspective of the hallway and regarded her. "Lily," one said. "I saw your boyfriend leave."

"Did he look happy?" Lily called back. "What do you think?" She entered her room and shut the door, then leaned against it, listening for them. They were laughing, struggling with their own door. She went to the phone and picked it up, dialed the first five digits of the number at home, then hung up, and reached down and unplugged the phone with a violent pull of the cord. She got into her nightgown, started to lie down, then stopped. For a time she just stood there gazing upon the rumpled white field of the sheets where she had so recently been with Dominic. She wanted to cry, and couldn't.

In the corridor, the others were laughing and wrestling with each other, saying the name of a professor of psychology everyone hated, a tall, heavy, gloomy older man whose scowl everyone was afraid of. "I'm having an affair with the hulk," one shrieked, laughing. "That's why I flunked psych 102!"

Lily changed the bed, and lay down. It was quiet now. She turned the bedside lamp off and folded her arms across her chest. She could still feel a kind of burning between her thighs, as though Dominic were still working at her. She might have dipped toward sleep, but then she was aware of it again, a ghost pressure there, and she wondered at the fact that she would take this night with her, as she had already been doing with another night, through the years, into old age, all the way to her grave, without ever breathing a word of it to anyone, lover or friend.

FOUR

1

$\mathcal{A}$LL THE NEXT DAY, a Saturday, she wandered the streets of the city, looking for Dominic. It was sunny and cool and felt more like fall than spring. Gusty breezes sounded a repeated murmur in the trees, and tossed the upper branches so the undersides of the leaves showed a lighter shade of green. There was a floral perfume in the air, a sweet freshness of blossoming; even the bus exhaust couldn't dispel it. People wore sweaters and light jackets and caps, and they looked happy, or else too busy to think about questions of happiness and discontent. The wind whipped around in no predictable direction, erratically kicking up grit and dust from the street.

That evening, Sheri called again, and asked her to come to Oxford. "We'd have so much fun and there's lots to do down here."

"I don't know what I'm going to do," Lily told her. "I can't really do anything right now but study."

But she put her coat on and went out again. The air was calmer, and some of the chill had gone. She went into the Mexican Café. There wasn't anyone she knew. Even the waitress who knew Dominic was gone, her day off. Lily went along the sidewalk, muttering low, and realized, too late, that others were turning their heads to watch her. When she returned to the room, she stayed there for the better part of two days. She did not go to her last classes.

She ate little. It was impossible to read or think. When her mother phoned and wondered what school she had settled on for graduate work, she was evasive, and they argued. Lily hung up on her, and then called her back. They reconciled with a complex little series of exchanges about the practical matter of looking for summer work, paying the bills, and when Doris said she had to get off, Lily kept the tears back and let her go. Everything felt like a weight on her mind, and she moved through the hours in a slow, half-drowsing stillness, though she couldn't sleep. The nights were endless. She lay in the bed and tried to read, saying the same line over and over, drifting, nearly dropping off, and then waking with a start.

During the morning of the third day, the telephone rang several times. She didn't answer it; but then it rang and kept ringing—twenty, thirty times, insistent, her mother, she was certain. Finally she picked up.

"It's about time there, girl." Her father's voice.

"Oh," Lily said. "It's you. Hi."

"I'm glad you're so happy to hear from me. I have called before, you know. Lily, are you all right?"

"I'm fine. I thought you were Mother."

"If you think it's your mother, you're not answering the phone?"

"I just got here and the phone was ringing. I thought you would—I thought Doris was calling, and it turned out to be you. I was explaining what I said when I answered, Daddy, okay?"

"I was teasing you, sweetie. Why don't you call me Scott? You call your mom by her name."

She said nothing.

"I'm calling about graduation. Doris says she's worried—"

Lily interrupted him: "I don't know what my plans are."

"Well, can we talk about that? You're finishing up—are you gonna go to the graduation ceremony? We've got some planning to do, don't we?"

"I'm not going to any ceremonies."

Silence. Then, a small sigh of exasperation. "Talk to me, Lily."

"There's nothing to say. I'm not graduating. I'm not going on."

"You mean you're not going to finish the work?"

"Not right now, no. I need a break and I'm taking it."

"Do you want to come up here and do some work at the theater? Maybe I could arrange some understudy work."

"I don't want to do that, Daddy, no."

"Are you coming home?"

"I don't think so."

"Is there—are you in some kind of trouble? How's your life, darling?"

"I have to go now," she said. "Scott." Then, after a pause: "I'm fine, really."

"I think you'd better keep calling me Daddy. And you don't sound fine. Please tell me what this is, Lily. I can't do anything if I don't know anything."

"I'm *okay*. It's the end of the semester. Look, I'd like the chance to lead my own life a little."

He left a pause. Then: "All right, you know where we are, each of us. Let us know if you need anything. And stay in touch—you know, the way you would with, say, an acquaintance you don't much like."

"I'm sorry," she said to him. "Really, Daddy. Please. I'm okay, and I'm not in any trouble I can't handle. It's school stuff. Stress and studying and not getting enough sleep, you know? And I haven't made any plans. I'll let you both know, I promise."

"Your mother doesn't know you're not graduating. I think you ought to be the one to tell her that. I think it would hurt her if that came from me. And I'd sure like to know what we put all this money into if you were going to chuck the whole thing in the last semester. Now, Lily, you've got to explain a thing like that. Don't you think you owe us that much?"

"There's no dark reason. I'll finish next year. Okay? I'd like to get off on my own a little. Please."

He sighed again. "Just let us know what your plans are."

When he broke the connection, she sat there holding the receiver, listening to her own breathing. At last, she put the receiver in its cradle, reclined on the bed, and tried to sleep. Nothing. Her mind wandered over the terrain of her unhappiness. She was ashamed of herself, yet couldn't bring herself to rise or move. Perhaps an hour went by, perhaps more.

When she called her mother, she was fairly certain that Scott had already spilled everything: it was as if Doris were following some prearranged script; Lily could almost hear her father's voice saying, *Don't let on that you know anything.* Her mother said, "Well, are you coming home, then?"

"I don't know," Lily told her. "Sheri wants me to come down to Oxford."

"Mississippi? What's in Mississippi?"

"Sheri's in Mississippi."

"Honey, I don't understand."

"I just mean for a visit," Lily told her. "I'm thinking of spending part of the summer down there. See some things. Maybe New Orleans. She said there was a community theater in Oxford that was looking for people. Maybe I'll see about that, try out or something. I'd like not to get into anything because I'm Daddy's girl. And that's how it would feel getting into something at the Washington, everybody knowing who I am and why I got in."

"What would you do at this community theater in Oxford? I thought I remembered you talking about not wanting go on with the acting."

"Maybe I'd write. I don't know. I'm looking to find out what I want to do. And I don't think I'll find that staying in my old room at home, you know?"

For a few seconds, they were both quiet, and they heard the unearthly sound of long distance humming between them.

"Seems a shame to come this far and then not graduate," Doris said.

"It's just for *now*," Lily said. "It's not like I'm quitting altogether. I've just decided to take some pressure off myself."

"I don't mean to nag—but this all sounds so—so *final*. Maybe it's me."

"I have to go now," Lily said. "I've got an appointment."

"Call me?" Doris said, and began to cry.

Lily stood by the rumpled bed in her dorm room and listened, saying nothing. A sorrow rose up in her, that just as her mother seemed to need something from her in the way of solace, she had no solace to give. "Of course I'll call you," she got out.

"'Bye," Doris said.

"Love you," Lily said.

"Me, too, baby."

The line clicked. She put the receiver down and walked to the window. The sky was banded with pink-streaked clouds, thin as jet trails. The quad below her was empty, not a soul out. A beautiful windless dusk, in spring. She watched as a couple came from the crest of the far hill and crossed toward the Rotunda. An older man went along the street pedaling a ten-speed bike, one pant leg rolled up. She closed the curtain and lay down on the bed again, and began trying to read. But there was no sense in pretending that she would go to any of the remaining functions of the last year of her college career. It made no difference at all to her, and the book she held was all words words words. None of it took the slightest shape of meaning for her.

She tried writing a few pages, sketching toward the play. Dreaming life a hundred years back felt like refuge of a kind. But then she saw it as being just that—a form of escape—and ultimately she couldn't even put her mind on that. She put the pencil down, lay her head on her arms and slept, and woke, and slept again. She lost track of time. A day passed like this, and a night, and another day. She had a dream in which someone said to her the word *anorexia*, and she sat bolt upright in the bed. It seemed impossible to remember the last time she had eaten anything. The thought of food made her nauseous. In the common room of the dorm there was a vending machine, and she tried to buy some crackers. The machine wouldn't work. It took three quarters, and the return slot would not give them back. She pounded on the glass, and a package of chewing gum dropped from its little corralled row. She hit the machine again. Then put another fifty cents in, and it yielded up a small bag of M&M's. She ate them, standing right there at the machine, and then felt as though she might be sick. She went into the bathroom and washed her face, and after a pause, waiting for something to develop, she returned to the room, still light-headed.

Outside, the world went on. There were sirens, sounds of traffic, music, voices. The days had become brilliant with spring sun, bright with blooms, whispery with winds from the green mountains in the near distance, the blue ones beyond. She sat near the window and took her pencil and tried to make something come.

2

Early April 1875
The downstairs hallway of a house. Stairs to the left. Door leading to other rooms on the right. Stage center is an open entrance giving onto a room lined with books. The same girl stands in this entrance. It's as if she's appreciating the room for its contents, the riches there. Now she seems to peer out into the dark beyond the end of the stage. Mary's accent is cockney in all her speeches with others; but in her monologues to the audience, she speaks without accent; her voice is strong, and sonorously alto.

MARY

My mother used to sleep through the night after the evening meal, but lately she's been calling out for me. I'm thirteen years old in this memory. Highgate again; the house is closed up, the one window facing onto the street, the others facing the garden in back. All closed. The bells sound periodically, and there are gamecocks out in the garden, but mostly the noises of the street are kept out. In the mornings the gamecocks are up with the sun, crowing, as if trying to signal someone faraway. They belong to me. I've been raising them for a little more than a year now. They will never fight, though they squabble in what looks like a deadly enough fury with each other—I've had to wade into them with a broom more than once. I confess I've shown a talent for getting into mischief. Recently, out in the garden, I conducted an experiment with some of the gunpowder my father brought back with him from Canada.

She curtsies.

It caused an explosion, which splattered the sheets hanging on the line with manure and alarmed the whole household. When he came into the garden and shook me, I'm afraid I uttered an oath. That is, I quoted him. He did not find the experience salutary. He picked me up, carried me like a package under his arm, and climbed the three flights of stairs to Mother's dim room. He rammed through the partly open door and stood there.

She lowers her chin and speaks deep in her throat.

Who has been teaching this girl such language? Do you know what she said to me?

Raising her voice to a level of pleading softness.

Leave me in peace, can't you? I'm dying of the 'eadache.

She returns to character, pages desultorily through the book, then closes it and stares out again.

In the afternoons, the light in the top of the door falls on the upper part of the stairwell, a shaft with motes in it. You can almost tell the hour by its shifting up the wall, until it goes thin, and is finally extinguished. I've learned by degrees to tell every inch along the wall of that shadow.

Light comes to the top of the stairs. She hears the sound, and turns slightly.

So much of my time is spent in this, well, rather complicated silence, this house with its thousand creaking sounds, the flicker of the gas lamps. Charley's at school; the gardener's somewhere out behind the house; Mrs. Barrett, our housekeeper, is occupied in the downstairs kitchen, addressing the Lord, in her definite little voice, about all of her various needs. The Lord, to Mrs. Barrett, resembles nothing so much as a sort of celestial footman. When my father's letters arrive from afar, I read them before taking them upstairs to Mother's room. One of my cousins, also named Mary (this is a family of Marys, Georges, and Henrys: my middle name is Henrietta), Mary writes sweet, interesting little letters— she wants, like Uncle Charles and Uncle Henry, to write romances and novels (Uncle Charles wrote the famous children's book *Water Babies*)— and I read her letters aloud. Sometimes it's just for the sound of a voice. Even if it's my own. Mother likes to hear them read out, too, but that's different, reading them to her. She's quite good company, actually. Rather witty, though one would never guess it from her troubles; and the rest of the family—Father's side of the family—will have nothing to do with her. Hearing my voice calms her, she tells me. Our Mrs. Barrett comes and goes with an imperiousness born of her place as Father's secretary. But I'm getting old enough to take these tasks for myself, and poor, threatened, pious Mrs. Barrett knows it. But there's no drama here, really. The drama is to come. This is my faithful drudgery, some of which you should see. When I walk up these stairs, to care for my mother, imagine me climbing to the top of a mountain in Cameroon, just to see it all from there. No one in my family dreams that I am the one who inherited the daring and the strength. I am not speaking only about my father and uncles, either.

She turns and crosses to the stairs, climbs them, and stands outside the entrance to her mother's room. She opens the door, letting the light in from the gas lamps in the hall. The light falls across her mother's bed. Her mother is not old, yet her bearing and her voice sound it. She's clearly someone who has not seen fresh air and the outdoors in a long time.

MOTHER

Mary, I've been calling you. The light 'urts me eyes, Mary.

Mary closes the door, turns and moves downstage, stands there look-
ing out, then heaves a deep sigh.

MARY

As you can see, I'm growing tall, growing out of my clothes, and this house is not the world; the world is where Father is, making his investigations, gathering his specimens. The great mystery, out there.

Lights down.

3

ONE AFTERNOON a little more than a week after the failure with Dominic, Lily heard footsteps out in the hall, and then silence, someone hesitating just on the other side of her door. She had been sitting under the window, book open in her lap, staring at the pattern of sunlight and leaf shadow on the opposite wall, and, in her mind, wandering through the gaslit halls of a house she had never been in or seen. There was someone outside her door—a friend of one of the girls who lived across the hall, perhaps? The girls had gone to Pennsylvania for the week, to visit with the family of one of them. Lily had heard them talking about it.

The someone out in the hall moved—shuffling feet, a creaking floorboard. She sat very still, not even breathing. When Sheri lived here with her, there had been a couple of episodes of drunken boys coming to their corridor, calling names out and lurching against the wall. The thump and clatter of them had enraged Lily. But this someone was quiet—too quite, as if listening, waiting.

Or had she imagined it?

The knock on her door almost made her cry out. She closed the book, slowly, and kept quiet. The footsteps went off. She heard the sound of them on the stairs. She leaned into the screen of the window to see down to the entrance of the building, thinking that if it was Dominic, she would follow him. She did not want to be in this room with him again.

It was Tyler. She saw him step out to the lawn and start away, toward the road on the other side of the quad. She called out: "Hey!"

He stopped, turned, and then smiled. It struck Lily absurdly that this was like a scene in a movie. She waved at him, pushed the hair back from either side of her face. She hadn't brushed it in days; she must look like a witch. "Wait for me?" she called, and hated the sound of the question in her voice.

He sat down right there on the grass, folding his arms and crossing his legs. She rushed to the bathroom down the hall and brushed her teeth, ran a brush through the knotted tangle of her hair, and fumbled with her makeup. She couldn't get the lipstick right—her hand shook. She kept going outside the line of her lips. When she stood back and regarded herself, she saw, for perhaps the first time, what a catastrophe she had made of her appearance over the past few days. She washed all the makeup off and reapplied it, with still-trembling fingers, remembering, in a roil of embarrassment, her mother's first lessons in the use of it—light touches, never too much of anything, just enough to highlight her best features and appear not to be wearing it at all. But here was the uneven border of foundation along her hairline, and seeing this she almost washed it all off again. Instead she daubed at it with a piece of toilet paper, like a house painter trying to remove the unevenness in the trim of a windowpane. Finally she got herself to some sort of semblance of being presentable.

But it seemed that so much time had gone by.

He hadn't moved. And he stayed seated as she approached. "I'm a mess," she said. "I've been studying."

"I think you look great." He sat there smiling, gazing up at her. "Are you eating enough? Sleeping enough? You do look a little dark around the eyes." He stood, slapped at the back of his jeans. "I've got one more exam."

She had lost the sense of time; she had been under the impression that exam week was still several days off. So she had been missing exams, too.

"What about you?" he said.

"Oh," she managed to say. "Right. I'm through."

"I thought maybe we'd go have dinner or something."

She had been so happy to see him out the window of her prison room. But now, abruptly, the last time she'd seen him came rushing back.

"Are you cold? You're shivering." He wore a light blue sports jacket over a T-shirt. He took the jacket off and draped it over her shoulders. "I should've called or something. Just walking up like this—it's rude. I didn't think."

"Don't think," she said. It was good to see him. There was no complication in it, and no denying it, either. She didn't care anymore. "Now you're going to be cold," she said.

"I'll take it back if I get cold. We'll be like a couple of people taking turns on a joint."

They went down to the row of shops and restaurants along University Drive. At the street corner, Tyler stood closer to her, and put his arm around her. The surprise of it, the gratification in it, was startling; she drew a quick breath.

He didn't seem to notice. "What do you feel like eating?" he said.

"I don't have a preference." The thought of food gave her a small tremor below her heart. The light changed and they crossed.

He stepped into the corner doorway of a place advertising Bavarian food, a variety of beers. "This all right?"

She nodded. There were several groups of people in the dimness beyond the long bar on the left-hand side. Others sat at the bar, most of them drinking. Tyler knew the waiter, a barrel-chested red-haired man with a lot of blond hair on his arms. They shook hands. The waiter's name was Thornton. Tyler introduced Lily, and Thornton took her hand, then let go with a small bow. He led them with his ambling, big-man's gait to a booth against the far wall, past the last group of people, a gathering of middle-aged men belonging to a group whose purpose it was to preserve barbershop quartet singing. Now and again these men broke into song, elaborate harmonies that were very pleasing to the ear, but faintly annoying, too, for their antique and rather too cute arrangements. Lily and Tyler listened to them, then applauded when they finished, and they politely acknowledged the applause, then launched into another song.

"Now we're stuck," Tyler said.

The singers were performing "Let Me Call You Sweetheart." There were all sorts of harmonies inside harmonies, and repeated phrasings, intricately designed to complement each other.

"I guess I picked the wrong place," Tyler said.

"Was this where we were going all along?"

He nodded, watching the singers. "I'd've gone wherever you wanted—but, yeah, I was headed here. I like the food. Do you like sauerkraut?"

"Sure," she said, keeping her tone as light as she could. "What else do they have?"

4

 $\mathcal{T}$ HE BARBERSHOP SINGERS sang four or five other songs, and Lily was grateful for it, because it drew the two of them together in silent agreement about it. The arrangements were so elaborate that the songs began to blur. Thornton, waiting on them, rolled his eyes as they ordered, and the harmonizing went on. Tyler ordered a full meal: Polish sausage and sauerkraut, with steak fries and salad, and a small pitcher of lager. Lily asked for a chicken sandwich, the only thing she felt she could keep down. She sat with her hands folded in her lap and tried to calm her own mind. She had ordered a dark beer, because she had read somewhere that dark beer soothed the stomach. And when Thornton brought it, Tyler offered a toast.

"To philosophy," he said. "And to what it will buy me on the open market."

They drank. The beer seemed to burn all the way down. She drank again, and the burn was blessedly gone.

He said, "I've got the oddest news. My mother's, um, husband, has offered me a job, down in Oxford. Selling Oldsmobiles. I don't know if this is Sheri's doing or not."

Lily said nothing. It came to her with a pang that he had wanted to see her only to tell her he was leaving.

"Sheri told you about us, right? About what happened. You know all that."

Lily nodded.

"Well, I've gotten these things, you know, from my mother. A couple of little cards. Small communications through Sheri when she was here, and a couple of letters after Sheri went south. I think with my father being gone—I think my mother wants to—"

"You're going to Oxford." Lily had said this with a note of alarm that she now tried to cover with a smile.

"I haven't laid eyes on her since I was about five years old," he continued. "And I don't have much memory of her. But I think I'd like to see her on her own territory. There isn't really anything waiting for me anywhere else, you know. So why not?" He shook his head. "I think they'd like to draw me into the family circle." He looked down at his hands, which rested on either side of the glass of beer.

"Well, she *is* your mother," Lily said. "And they are your family now."

"So I'm told."

She sipped the beer and stared at him.

"I guess I sound bitter. I'm only a little bitter. More than anything else, I'm curious. Of course I'm also curious about *him*. And scared, too. It scares me. The idea of going down there and spending time with them like that."

"I heard from Sheri," Lily told him. "She wants me to go down there and visit."

"Why don't we go together?" he said.

She shrugged. "Right." She couldn't return his look.

"I'm serious, Lily."

She didn't answer. The singing had grown loud again, a woven strand of melodies and harmonies around the tune of rowing the boat gently down the stream.

He drank from his beer, and turned to watch the men singing. It seemed that there were more of them now.

"I'm not going to graduate," she told him.

He nodded. "I'm not going, either."

"I don't mean the ceremony. I stopped going to classes."

"But that seems like such a waste, to come this far and then stop."

"You mean like, say, taking a philosophy degree so you can sell cars?"

He held his beer glass up, as if to offer a toast. "That's different. That's exploration. That's family and blood and all that."

After a pause, she said, "Sheri's talking about getting a divorce."

He nodded, and drank, and said nothing.

The singers went on, working two separate parts of the same song. Lily drank the beer, and wondered how she had landed in this place. Tyler was watching the singers, tapping his fingers on the table.

Finally he turned to her. "I don't know a thing about my own mother. But I think she's got something to do with how I feel about the world."

"How do you feel about it?"

He smiled. "I wish I knew. From one minute to the next. I have to say there's a lot of anger sometimes. The kind you can't do anything with. And then there's fear, too. That bedrock kind that clutches at you inside, and makes it hard to imagine there won't be some terrible catastrophe on the other side of the next minute."

"Believe it or not," Lily said, "I know exactly what you're talking about."

The singing was loud again, a single note with all its attendant related notes on the harmonic scale.

"She left my father," he said. "But she left me, too, and I don't know how many levels of my personality that sank into. I think I was like the consolation prize for the old man." He sighed, and seemed to ponder this, slightly shaking his head. "Anyway, I don't have any reason to stay in this part of the country—"

Lily had the thought that she would be a reason to stay, and suddenly she felt lost. "I try never to think about my parents these days," she said, trying to find anything else to talk about. "I'm not going home, I know that."

"Where *are* you going?"

She didn't look at him, aware that he had leaned toward her. "I don't know." This struck through her as miserable truth. Her heart raced. Taking a long drink of the beer, she fought to get it to stay down, coughing. The voices rose around her, a lambent, oversweet harmony, and Tyler had come around the table and put his hand on her shoulder.

"Hey," he said.

She leaned into him, and he held her, and the singing went on. She had been unable to cry for so long, and now, abruptly, she could. It seemed so simple. A part of her attended in wonder. He had put one hand along the side of her face, and he ran it over her hair, rocking her gently. She kept crying. The singing had stopped. The men were standing, talking; one or two of them had looked over at her and then looked away. She took paper napkins from the table and blew her nose and tried to speak.

Tyler said, "Let's go down there together, Lily."

"I don't know if that's such a good idea," she told him, sniffling. The words felt obligatory, merely what she should say out of politeness.

He kissed her. She had half-expected it, hoped for it. She relaxed in his arms and let it happen, experiencing an exquisite sense of letting go, an internal avalanche. The men were moving past, several of them humming something again. There was an element of unreality in the moment.

Then they had gone, and Tyler was holding her by her arms. "Let's get married, Lily. I've wanted you since that first minute at the party after the football game."

"You—but you—" she began.

"I know about all that—but Sheri got in the way and I was seeing someone else. And—and I've got a lot of—I've got a lot of psychological baggage, you know. But that's all beside the point. The point is, I love you. Couldn't you tell how I felt?"

"How was I supposed to know?" she said. "We seemed so perfect, and then I didn't see you and I didn't see you."

He let go of her, and folded his hands on the table. Thornton had brought the food. She picked up her sandwich and bit into it, and all the glands around her jaw seemed to protest. Yet it was luscious, the flavors of grilled chicken and fresh lettuce and tomato reaching up into all her nasal passages. She thought she had never tasted anything quite so delectable.

"You—you feel something for me, don't you?" Tyler said. "I mean—how do you feel? I know you feel the same."

She had to wait until she could swallow. "Yes. Yes. But let's not talk about it here." She took another bite of the sandwich.

"I'm in love with you," he told her. "Stop eating for a minute."

"You don't understand." She took still another bite. Her stomach hurt. She could feel every bite entering it, and she washed it down with more of the beer. He kept staring. "I haven't really eaten anything for days."

"Days."

He watched her. Presently, he said, "I've been thinking of nothing else but you since I first laid eyes on you, Lily. I—I didn't come after you because you seemed—because—well, because I was so nervous around you. You were so self-possessed."

Dear Daddy,
I don't know how to tell you this

She swept everything from the table where she sat—the lamp, the books and papers, the glass of water she had been drinking. It all went flying. Then she overturned the table itself, and stood there alone, with a cut on her little finger. She stared at it, a bead of blood. The glass hadn't broken. She couldn't decide how it had happened that she had cut herself. She went out and down the hall to the bathroom, and washed it. Then she regarded herself in the mirror. Her own face looked rather deranged in the light. Back in the room, she worked to clean up the mess, throwing the pages away, wiping up the water. The bulb in the lamp had come loose, and the lamp wouldn't work now, so she wrapped the cord around it tight, and put it in the closet. She spent most of the night packing books, records, and tapes. Several times, she stopped to dial her mother's number, but hung up before Doris answered. She did not call her father.

Sheri called, and was cheering in her enthusiasm. Tyler had called down there to say that he and Lily were coming. Her voice squeaked over long distance, sounding as though she were speaking from the other end of a long tunnel. "Just think, we're gonna be sisters-in-law."

Later, Tyler brought roses and perfume, and he picked her up in his arms and carried her to the bed, where she had a dark little fright of remembering what had happened with Dominic. Tyler kissed her, and lay close, but went no further. "We'll do this right," he said. "We'll wait."

She didn't want to wait. She wished to start, desired to get on with everything, feeling the old sense of flying in the face of what she was afraid of. She kissed him, long and slow, and put her hand on him.

"Honey, please," he said. "I really want it to be right."

"It is right," she murmured, kissing him. "I want to."

In a little while they were undressed. He rolled onto her, pushed in—it thrilled her, so easy, so right—but then he stopped. He was supporting himself on his hands, looking down at her. "God," he said. "You're so beautiful." He was holding still.

"Come on," she said, and moved her hips.

"Do you—" he began. "Wait."

She lay still. His presence inside her was a warm, solid feeling: completeness. She said, "What?"

"Aren't you even a little worried about what might happen?" There was something guilty in his voice, almost apologetic.

"I don't care about anything," she heard herself say. And abruptly it was true. She could forget everything, the whole long, troubled, complicated past, and concentrate on this, just this, because it was natural and right and not a lie.

"Maybe." His voice shook. Neither of them had moved.

"I'm very regular," she told him. "So I know when I'm ovulating. There's nothing to worry about."

"Do you want a baby, eventually?" he said. "Is it important?"

"Tyler, this is nothing to worry about *now*. I don't want to think about it now. I told you how I felt."

"You said you don't know if you want children."

"What a time to bring that up. Let's talk about prenuptial agreements."

And they were both laughing again. It was such a strange, wonderful sensation, laughing with him inside her.

He let his weight down, and spoke in her ear. "Tell me. Please."

"I don't know. Do you?"

"No." He moved. It was a glorious feeling.

"Do that again."

"It doesn't matter to you?"

"Tyler. We're making love. Or we *were*."

"But—you aren't worried about getting pregnant?"

She lowered her hips, and raised them, and he sighed, softly, supporting himself on his hands again. She ran her own hands up the tight muscles of his arms. "Come on. I've planned everything I ever did. I don't want to plan anymore."

"Yes," he said, and began to move with a quickness that surprised her. It was almost rough, but it felt good. She raised her hips each time to meet him, and went soft inside, silk on all the inner surfaces. Rightness. "Oh," he said, and came in a burst of liquid heat that she felt as a deep melting.

Afterward, they lay there, and the light failed at the window. There was still so much to do.

"I think we ought to go north and meet your parents tomorrow," he said.

He was far from understanding her. "I don't want to see them. Not my father, anyway. And if we go see my mother, we'll have to see my father."

"I think we ought to." He got up and put his pants on, and went out to the bathroom across the hall.

When he came back, he said, "You're tremendously mad at your father."

"Dr. Freud." She rose from the bed, with the cover sheet around her, and went out to the bathroom. As she crossed the open hallway, a part of her wanted the other girls on that hall to be home, and to see her.

"Now you're mad at me," he called.

"I can't hear you," she yelled, though she had heard him. When she came out, he had dressed. It made her feel exposed. She closed the door to the room and sat on the bed, still wrapped in the sheet.

"Let's drive up there tomorrow," he said. "It's only an hour and a half."

6

WHEN HE HAD GONE, she picked up the phone to dial her mother. There wasn't any answer, but her mother had recently bought an answering machine. A bodiless electronic voice, a machine voice so devoid of any human feeling that it frightened her, spoke: "Hel-lo," it said. "Please . . . leave . . . a . . . mes-sage af-ter . . . the . . . beep." The beep came, longer than she expected, so that she began to speak before it quit, then had to stop and wait, then start again in the silence that followed.

She said, "Doris, I'm coming into town tomorrow morning. Driving up to see you with—with a friend. I don't know when we'll get in. Probably mid-morning. It's so strange talking to these things. Do I say *sincerely* now? 'Bye."

She hung up. She had, she supposed, sounded all right.

Outside, the sun was shining. There were people enjoying the shade, lying or sitting in the grass. She didn't see anyone she knew. She had decided that she would go to a shop and use some of her father's most recent check to buy a new dress. She would wear it to the wedding. The wedding. She walked along the sidewalk, edging past small groups of others, thinking of this thing she was about to do. Get married. It seemed to her now that this was probably how it happened for almost everyone, stumbling into the years, the future. She saw herself being pulled on into time, looking back and pining for her girlhood—that time before the world, and then her family, came apart. But the world was what it was. She wanted to stop brooding, and get on with life. She desired Tyler, of that she was as certain as anyone could be; it was tangible and as aching in her body as hunger.

At the corner of Rugby Avenue and University Drive, she waited for the light, staring at the little window opposite with the words DON'T WALK in it. Another young woman stood at her shoulder and coughed. Lily glanced at her, saw the dark features of the face and the look of pre-occupation. She almost spoke: *I'm getting married this week.* The light changed, and the other woman stepped off the curb. Lily followed. There was an entire world of associations for this stranger who walked along next to her. Lily received the impression of how odd it was to imagine the other's personal life. She felt sorry for whatever this stranger's sorrows might be. Across the street was a dress shop, and leaning against the lamppost opposite the entrance, she saw Dominic. He had his arms folded. When she reached the curb, he straightened and held out his arms, and she walked into them. All the weight seemed to go out of her legs.

"Kid," he said.

"Where have you been?" She was close to crying. She had so much to tell him.

"I've been around." He stepped back, still holding her hands, appraising her with an expression that was almost proprietary. "You look a little wired."

"Where did you go, Dominic?" Now she was crying. She wiped the tears away with the back of her hands, and the mascara stung her eyes.

They worked together to get the mascara off her cheeks, standing very close in the sunlight on the sidewalk. Their reflection showed brokenly in the angle of glass from the window of the dress shop. She saw the sun in their hair in the reflection. He thought she was crying from her old despair.

"I go away for a few days, and look what happens—somebody steals my girlfriend away from me." He dropped her hands, and when she started walking, stepped to her side and kept pace. "My dear Miss Scarlett—this is so sudden."

"Dominic, I didn't see you—"

"Are you gonna say you're sorry you didn't ask my permission?"

She stopped. They had come to an antique shop. There were dolls and dollhouses in the window. "How did you find out?"

"I know Tyler, a little. He's very excited. A little too serious for me sometimes, old Tyler. But that's just when he's preoccupied with the categorical imperative. I like him. Have you done much talking to him?"

"I'm in love, Dom. Completely totally madly utterly out of my mind in love."

"You look bright as a new dime, except for the mascara." He reached to take a little smudge from her cheek. "I've been making a few discoveries myself, love, and I feel tremendously relieved and happy, and I'm happy for you, too."

She saw the complexity in his smile, the slightest shadow crossing it. But then his expression changed again, and he indicated the entrance to the store. "Is this where you were headed?"

"I was going to buy a dress," she said. "I didn't have a specific place in mind."

"After you, kiddo."

She walked into the little opening that led to the entrance, and he casually put his arm around her.

"Still pals?" he said.

She said, "Oh, Dominic. Always and all our lives."

"Promise never to tell anybody I was your first—well, half of your first—the failed first."

"Stop it," she told him. "You're demeaning it. Don't, Dominic. Nothing that ever happened between us was bad, except that I didn't see you for how many days."

"A little self-deprecating humor," he told her. "All the books say it's charming."

"It's not funny, Dom. I thought I'd done something to upset you."

"I'm sorry," he said. "Jesus, really. I told you I wasn't upset with you."

She moved from him to a row of dresses on a rack, and began looking through them. He stood at her side. She held one up. "What do you think?"

He shook his head, and she put it back. She held another up, and he shook his head again. She took out still another. "It steenks," he said.

She laughed, and then hugged him again. "Let's go. I don't see anything you like."

They went out into the sunlight, and walked along the street. He had taken her hand, but then dropped it and hung back a little, just at her shoulder. It was as if he were worried about how it would look. At the corner they stopped, and he put his hands deep in his pockets, looking off. Finally he turned to her. After a slight pause, he said, "I guess you've figured out that I'm queer."

"It's none of my business, is it?" she said.

"Of course it is. You're my closest friend—Lily, of course."

"Okay." She put her arms around him and held tight, and they remained that way for a few moments.

"An enormous weight has been lifted. As they say."

"I'm glad," Lily told him. "Me, too."

"My parents are making plans to leave for foreign shores. I think my father wants to see about volunteering for the next space shuttle."

She laughed, and put both hands on his chest. "Dom."

He reached into his jacket pocket and brought out a folded piece of paper. "This has my address, and my parents' address. I can always be reached through them if this one changes. Or you can send it to my father, care of NASA."

7

That evening her mother called and wanted to know who she was bringing north with her. "Is this a woman friend or a man friend, Lily? And I hope it won't upset you if I say that I think it's a little rude not to let me know even that much about it."

"I'm sorry, Doris. A man friend."

"A *boy*friend man friend?"

Lily paused. "We're getting married, Mother."

Doris coughed, and cleared her throat. "This *is* serious, if you're calling me *Mother*."

After a pause, which she filled with a very long sigh, she said, "When?"

"We just decided about it, this week. Oh, Doris—I'm so happy."

"When are you getting married?"

"This week. We don't want any to-do about it. No ceremony. We're just going to a justice of the peace. It's my idea, too." Lily told her the rest of it— moving South, the job in Mississippi, Tyler's peculiar history with that side of his family—and then waited for a response. She had spoken into a profound silence, and for a second she thought her mother might've broken the connection.

"You're bringing your fiancé north, with twenty-four hours' notice."

"Well, I know it's happening fast," she said. "I never would've believed it. I won't be hurt if you—I mean, I'd understand if you needed more time."

Silence.

"Doris, do you want us not to come?"

"Don't be absurd. I would've liked a little more notice that my daughter is making such a decision. And it wouldn't have hurt if I'd been given some time to prepare for such a visit, either. This place is a wreck. I don't even know that I can get hold of your father."

"You don't have to—don't—don't do that. Don't call him, Doris—please."

"He's your father. Of course I'm going to call him. You haven't called him?"

"I called *you*."

"I'll see what I can arrange," Doris said with another sigh. "And you'll have to live with whatever it is. This is getting married, sweetie. This isn't choosing not to graduate. I know you're all excited and everything, but there are matters—social aspects of it that you can't ignore without seriously hurting people you love. You don't want to do that—surely that's not what you have in mind. Do you know how much it would hurt your father if you just went ahead and did this without telling him?"

Lily felt a rush near her heart. "I was going to tell him."

There was another long pause. "I *wanted* him to leave, Lily. Okay?"

Outside her window, the dark had come. She saw the moon above the lovely stirring of the trees in the soft breeze that blew. You could see the other side of the quad almost as clear as in daylight.

"Did you hear me? I was *relieved.*"

Another pause, and then her mother's voice again, level and low. "The end of love hurts more terribly inside than anything I can name. *That* was what hurt us both. I'm not being philosophical, Lily. I was angry with him, yes. But when he had been out of the house for a few weeks I felt for the first time in years that I could be myself. Really let everything out and relax. Do you understand me?"

"There's nothing vague about that, Doris," Lily said. "I do understand."

"I'm sorry it hurt you, sweetie."

She didn't want to talk about what hurt, now. She kept still.

"It hurts everybody," her mother went on. "I wish there was something for it."

Then there wasn't any sound at all for a time, not even of their breathing. The line was emptiness, the farthest reaches of space.

"Welcome to adulthood, little girl," her mother said in a very small voice, from far, far away, beginning to cry. "Oh, Lily—your father and I were done, my darling, long before Peggy happened."

"Don't," she said. "I don't—you're right, it's none of my business."

"Well, we're on each other's minds, who care about each other. I know that. I expect it."

She told her mother she loved her, acceded to all her suggestions about a small family gathering—she and Tyler, Doris and Scott and Peggy—and got off the phone.

8

$\mathcal{D}$RIVING NORTH in the misty, raining morning, she mentioned to Tyler that she had run into Dominic, and Tyler did not know whom she meant. "Dominic Martinez," she said. "He told me he knew you slightly."

"You mean Dom? The guy in my philosophy classes? Tall, skinny guy?"

"That's him."

They rode along in silence for a few minutes. You couldn't see the mountains at all for the mist and ground fog, or much of the road ahead.

"How do you know Dom?"

"He's been my best friend here. I met him when I was fourteen."

Tyler drove in silence, and when she glanced at him she noted the fine shape of his jaw. His brow was creased, and he was concentrating on the road. She sat back and was happy. She saw the green hills rolling by in the grayness, the farmhouses under the lowering sky. It looked like March, not May. They drove past several trucks whose tires blurred the windshield. The speedometer was at seventy-five miles an hour.

"Aren't you going a little fast?" she said.

He touched the brakes. "I've made this drive a thousand times, sorry."

She patted his elbow.

A moment later, he said, "So you've known Dom all these years?"

"He was at my fourteenth birthday party. He offered me a puff off a cigarette and we talked. I didn't see him again until last year."

She stared at the dashboard, and at the shiny wheel with his hands gripping it, the smooth flesh of his wrists.

"Wish I could've met you when you were fourteen," he said.

There was a smoldering look to the heavy sky ahead. The sun was trying to break through. By the time they got to Steel Run, they could see areas of blue beyond the breaking up of the cloud cover. The road was dry. They went through Steel Run, and he drove down a side street, past shops and an Episcopal church, to a redbrick Victorian with white trim on the porch and around the windows, and dormers in the roof. He slowed, then stopped.

"That's where I grew up." He made a small tsking sound with his tongue, shaking his head. "Some fun."

She waited for him to go on, and when he didn't, she said, "Tell me."

He appeared to come to himself, out of the musing gaze. "Oh, hey, it—there isn't a lot else to say."

"Why does that sound not so good?"

He kept gazing at the house, shaking his head. "Toward the end there, we had some good times, I guess—we could talk a little without it being a life lesson. My father was interested in morality. He was very heavily into it. He didn't drink, didn't smoke, didn't cuss. He was a straight-arrow who knew the woods and wilderness and hunting and fishing, and certain practical matters connected to that, and he worked thirty years for the census bureau. And he wanted me to be a doctor."

The house looked empty. There was a jagged hole in the glass of one of the top windows, a shard of the sky showing in what was left. The tree next to the house was in full bloom, pink blossoms spreading along the side and on, over the broken fence that bordered the lawn.

"Developers are going to tear it down," he said. "I sold it to some people who want to open a Kmart. That and my father's small insurance benefit paid for my lengthy college career." He shook his head, pulling away, and she turned in the seat to watch the house recede in the distance. That side of it, through the pink blossoms, was already broken, a part of the wall having been knocked out. Seeing this caused an inexplicable shiver to run through her, and she brought her gaze around to the road, the other houses they were passing. "Do you know anyone in these places?"

"Some. My dad moved to Miami a couple of years after I left home. That's where he died, and where he's buried. Miami. Christ."

Toys lay in one yard—a bicycle and a doll, a play stove, a rocking horse. A small white dog was tied to the rocking horse, and was dragging it around in the yard. "Did you know these people?"

"No."

They drove on. The houses gave way to fields again, and the road descended, crossed a bridge over the highway, then wound around and merged with it. Route 29 North. Point Royal was eight miles farther on. On one side of the road there was a new outlet mall, an ugly row of facades crowned with royal-blue signs, all of it so new that it shone. She read the names of the stores; it was something to occupy her mind. The closer they came to home, the more unsure she felt, as if her mother or father might discern a clearly mistaken aspect of the whole thing, and point it out in some incontrovertible way.

Her mother was nothing like this, of course, but now Lily could not erase the thought of some pathological eruption rising out of Doris's conviction that this marriage was happening too fast.

"You seem a little nervous," he said.

"I am, I guess. I'm worried about what everyone will say. I mean, we're moving so fast."

"Hey, I'm twenty-six. I've given it a lot of thought. And if you look at it, so have you."

PART·2

Mary and Lily

FIVE

1

February 8, 1876
Dear—

    I name no one. I will not say "diary." I imagine you. I create you some-
where far past the boundaries of my life. Lately I have been thinking about
marriage. What marriage is ever quite rational? I will marry someone my
father brings home, no doubt. The prospect of it disgusts me. I don't want
to think about it. Knowing a stranger and having that stranger know me. I
have sought ways to explain to myself my father's absences. But then the
absences are all I have known. . . .

Mary Henrietta Kingsley wakes one morning to feel a hard, sharp
pain, low in her abdomen, and thinks of her mother's lingering illness. It
is starting for her, she thinks, whatever it is that keeps her mother lying
down through the days. But she makes herself get up, and then remembers what she has read about the female body and its changes. *That* is
happening. She goes and locks her door and examines herself. Uses the
chamber pot and sees blood. Her heart clamors in her chest. There are
the narratives of the habits and customs of the tribes of Africa and the
Americas, letters from her father describing the way the women behave,
and the powerful lure of flesh, and she knows enough already, even at
this young age, to understand in some nonverbal way that every custom
of the primitive tribes is aimed at controlling this force, this very creaturely thing that is happening inside her. She's horrified. And fascinated, too. She attends to the problem, the mess of her own body and its
demands. She looks out the window in the sound of the church bells
and sees men passing on the street. A dog barks nearby. Her own gamecocks set up a racket. For the rest of the day she works in a daze, and
when she tries to read she can't concentrate. Her mother is unusually

demanding, and there's no letter from her father. In the night, she sits in the light of her bedside candle and thinks of the natural process taking place in her. She takes off her nightdress and lies back in the flickering light and tries to appreciate her own almost womanly shape—but she's too thin: the bones of her hips jut out; her breastbone is visible. Her breasts are small, as they should be, but her arms are too long. Stretched out at her sides they reach to below her hips. She thinks of herself in a detached way, oddly more so than ever before in her life.

—I am strange, she says, low. I am strange. I am not like anyone else.

She begins a search through the books for all those passages about sex and sexual practices. She reads about a tribe of Africans whose custom, upon the birth of a child, is to have the father of that child hung upside down in a tree. He hangs there as long as his wife is in labor, and when the child is delivered, if the child is delivered, he is cut down. If the child dies, or the mother dies—if the delivery can't take place, for whatever reason—the man is left to die in the tree. She reads about the custom of sex with brothers and sisters in some tribes of the South Pacific.

At dinner she watches her brother's face, a ten-year-old boy interested in American dime novels. There is really no one she can speak to about any of this. She depends on the books, which are disturbingly silent about it where they ought to be eloquent. She begins to put on the attitude of someone for whom these passions and night-sweating urges have no reality or pull. She takes two months reading only novels and romances, and it seems that there's nothing but strife and pain in the worldly love that comes of sex. She cares for her mother, and feels the uncomplicated nature of this love; she senses that the other love, the love that had produced her and Charley, is the reason for her mother's lingering sorrow and illness.

And now she sees, without wanting to, how her mother is periodically swaddled in that particular way, something she had never quite noted before. She believes, horribly, that she can smell it. And there is something about the monthly rhythm of it that makes all her mother's symptoms worse, each month—the recurring weakness and ongoing pain seems related to this event in her mother's body, the older woman's very femininity: something is wrong with the process in her mother. Mary's own periods make her vaguely queasy—a sick fascination rises in her, and she moves through her duties in a frantic daze, growing more efficient in the care of the invalid: her purpose, she begins to feel. Surely something other than the awful commotion of bodies in contact. And could it have been the birth of two children that made the continual physical frailty and suffering she sees in her mother? She retreats entirely into the books, now, in this eerie solitude of her physical nature.

2

July 1876

 I have decided to keep this journal in the hope that one day someone might find use in it—even, as it may indeed be, some later version of myself, as I like to think. I will soon be fourteen. I have no formal education, and will have none. That is as I guess it should be. Charley, at ten years old, can decipher things and parse sentences and write practically and he has even learned some Latin and Greek or is learning them and he's begun correcting me—making me sound my h's, and I still feel that a lot of everything else is unfair.

 I shall not mention this other matter, which has so concerned me of late. It is a female matter.

 I would like to have a friend that I can be my utter self with, my bumpy, scared, terrible self. Someone I can enjoy the freedom of not having to be charming with all the time. I sometimes lie awake in the nights and imagine someone, another girl, perhaps someone slightly older than I, who understands me. You.

She remarks the changes in her body. She keeps the little notebook, like a diary. It is secreted away in her things, for a privacy she craves, even as so many of the days go by in solitude.

 My life that I live in secret. I offer it to you, in your world, wherever you are.

 Yesterday there was a letter from her father, from America, where he is traveling with Lord Dunraven—the wild, wide spaces of that continent, with its wonderful names, made of the Indian languages: Colorado, Dakota, Salt Lake, Yellowstone, Wyoming. In his letters, he has spoken of the depredations the U.S. government is visiting upon the native tribes, the systematic slaughter and displacement. The railroad has come, is being laid across Indian lands, hunting grounds: *one cannot be surprised at the poor wretches fighting; they depend wholly on the buffalo for food, and the railway and its consequent settlers will soon drive them away for ever. Quite lately these grand rolling plains were black with buffalo and the Indians lived in abundance, now we are considered lucky to have killed two!*

This morning a fine mist is falling as she walks out to the back, to feed the game cocks. She watches the wattles in the necks, the eyes, so piercing, looking anything but stupid, taking her in, glossy little facetless beads, below brows that look like those of old angry men. It strikes her that they are the picture and manifest image of the thing with which she's so preoccupied: passion, animal need. They are slaves to it, and have no understanding of it. They cannot even derive a conscious sense of the pleasure available in it. This is hell. She has the thought that people come back, are made to return in the shape of their former appetites. Embodied in them without the capability of speech. She has touched herself now in the nights, and felt the rising in her blood. She believes it is stronger with her than with anyone she knows, and she's aware that this is tied up in the reading, the fact that she is always living in her mind, even when she's fixing something in the house, performing tasks usually reserved for men—shoveling coal into the furnace downstairs, for instance, or emptying the dustbin. She has a mind full of lurid images.

She feeds the gamecocks, and in the distance there is the sound of horses. Several riders go by in the muddy street. The air smells of horses and coal ash, from the chimney pots; she's wet to the skin when she gets back to the house. Mrs. Barrett is waiting for her.

—You'll catch your death.

—Leave me be, please.

—I shall tell Mr. Kingsley, me.

—Do. When you see 'im again. Or shall I write 'im?

Mrs. Barrett, who can neither read nor write, looks her up and down.

—You're getting to be quite the lady, aren't you?

—Did you require something of me?

—Don't think I don't know what's in that head of yours, girl.

Mary stares back at her.

—Will there be anything else?

—Reading them books. Too much of books is unhealthy.

—Rot.

Mary moves by her, to the stairs.

—Don't you disturb your mother, you.

—Bugger.

—What did you say?

Mary turns on the stairs and says, in a voice scarcely controlling her rage:

—Mrs. Barrett, if I 'ave to contend with you every day in this manner I shall ask Father to discharge you.

—You are a spoiled little girl, and I'm keeping track of the words, me. Mark you.

They hear Mary's mother coughing upstairs.

—There. You've wakened her.

—Excuse me, please, Mary says, and curtsies.

She ascends the stairs and opens her mother's bedroom door, peering into the dimness. Her mother lies very still with her eyes closed. She's capable of lying that way for hours at a time, though she's far from sleep. Mary waits a moment, and her mother, without opening her eyes, speaks:

—Yeh'll drive 'er crazy, she says.

Mary laughs.

—Did you 'ear all that, Mum?

—I wasn't coughing up 'ere, my darling. I was laughing.

Her mother puts one arm over her eyes, turning slightly in the bed.

—I wonder if she'll report it to Father, Mary says.

—Oh, well, of course. English intrigue, you know.

She laughs again. There is such a rapport with her mother; the two of them have become so good at entertaining each other.

—Mrs. Barrett remains a bit exercised.

—Oh, Mary says. Quite.

—Well, that'll keep her off me, a' least.

—Can I get you something from her clutches?

—Nothing now, my darling. I'm going to try sleeping again.

Mary closes the door. She descends the stairs with a feeling of having been strengthened and refreshed. Mrs. Barrett is in the kitchen area, chopping vegetables. Mary takes a carrot and bites the end off of it, and Mrs. Barrett reaches over and grabs the carrot from her.

—Go busy yourself, girl.

—In some cultures girls are married and with child by my age.

—I won't have you speak of these heathen practices in my presence, you. That tree in the Garden of Eden was a tree of knowledge, and you know too much already.

—If you need me, Mrs. Barrett, I'll be in the library, committing Adam's sin all over again.

—I will not listen to blaspheming.

Mary goes into her father's library, and sits in the gray light of the window, reading about a ship that sailed around the Cape of Good Hope. Mrs. Barrett works on furiously in the kitchen, a woman nursing a resentment, energetic in her outrage. Mary thinks of other young women out in the afternoon preening themselves, romantic fools without a thought in their heads but romantic fantasies and games. None of them would have the slightest idea where the Cape of Good Hope is. But then they wouldn't suppose it was knowledge a young woman ought to have, and of course Mary, reclusive, strange Mary, as the family and friends see her, Mary has it. She has come to know a good deal about the ship that sailed so bravely down the world. She's been teaching herself the terminology, not because she has any sense that she will one day use the knowledge, but because it delights her to know the words and their uses: *bowsprit, bobstay, bulwark, davit, mizzen sail, halyard.* These matters keep her from thinking about her body, the bodies of others, their secrets.

She entertains no hope of ever leaving London, and sometimes little hope of ever leaving this house. She doesn't feel wronged by the facts. It is the world she has inherited, and, as she has said to her mother more than once, she respects the opinion of the Human Race. One doesn't live in the world of books without gaining a sense of that respect.

This is what she says to the little world she lives in.

When Charley comes in from school, she meets him in the hallway. Church bells toll in the distance. A vicar has died in the town, no one they knew. Charley reports this, and she follows him into the parlor. He's tall for his age, taller than Mary now, and from a distance looks to be in his teens.

—Did we hear from Father today? he asks, assuming his late demeanor: the man of the house. School has made him proud.

—No, Mary says.

—Please see that I have some juice to drink. I've got a devilish lot of reading to do.

—Do you 'ave greetings for Mrs. Barrett?

—Are you vexing her again?

—I believe she would testify to it.

—Priceless. I'm fortunate to have such an ill-tempered older sister.

—When your voice changes, Charley, that might work.

—Just see that I get what I asked for.

She leaves him there, strides into the kitchen, and tells Mrs. Barrett that Master Charley is home and requires a glass of juice. Then she climbs the stairs to her room, closes the door, and is alone with the sense of having been petulant, shallow. What must others say about her? What is the talk among the lordly Kingsleys about Mary with her solitary existence, and her invalid mother? It seems to Mary that there is a high wall between herself and everyone else, a line of demarcation that no one crosses, not even her father when he's home.

At night, now, listening to the sounds of the house—her mother's fitful groans in the other room, the slow creaks and protests of the old wood settling in the changing temperatures of the dark—she feels a depthless dread, a shiver at the very core of her heart, that spreads through her, and makes it difficult to breathe. Alone. She is alone. She imagines that she has died and is lying in a casket. She crosses her arms over her small breasts. She knows—without understanding quite how she knows—that she will never bear a child, never have a normal life, the life she has only received fragmentary impressions of in her relations with other members of the family—the Kingsleys and the Baileys (her mother's people). She remains skeptical about the visceral sense that she is marked for an early death, yet while she has no trouble imagining far-flung parts of the world, she cannot begin to picture herself having reached the age of her mother, who is not yet thirty-five. She tries to picture it—a husband and children. Perhaps a scientist, or a writer. Someone—a young assistant, or protégé of her father. Someone who shares his love of knowledge and travel. But then what she sees is her own mother—sees herself as this woman lying in bed in a room with drawn curtains, surrounded by the smells of several kinds of physic, and half asleep on laudanum. The vision is confusing and upsetting, and so she stares at the dark and lies very still, thinking of her life as a small waking bordered by two endless sleeps. And sleep won't come. She doesn't feel deprived of it. But she experiences such horrors of thought and half dreaming. On many nights she rises and goes downstairs to read. The only sound is the pages turning, her small breathing. She sometimes murmurs the words, for the sound of them, so there is her voice in the little room, a hedge against the blackness outside. And when day comes she drifts off in the chair, or with her head down on one of the books. The sounds of the others moving in the house brings her out of a sleep that is peopled with ghosts and spirits.

—Do you remember your dreams? she asks Charley one evening.

—What a stupid question, he says.

—Well, do you?

—No. He smiles.

—I mean the question, she says. I 'aven't spoken figuratively.

He stares, chewing.

—Sound your aitches, Mary. You sound like Mother.

—You sound like Father, and you're not old enough to carry it.

—I'm old enough.

They are silent for a time. There's a preening sort of self-satisfaction in his face, but then he smiles at her, a boy again.

—I 'ave a lot of dreams, Charles. Almost constantly when I sleep. And I remember them all.

—Nightmares? he asks.

—I don't know. All my dreams are bizarre.

—Well, but do they frighten you?

She nods.

—Then they must be nightmares.

—Do you 'ave them, Charley?

He leans toward her across the table.

—Every night.

—And are they bizarre?

—They're bloody terrible.

—I don't think you quite know 'ow I mean all this, Charley.

She feels wrong for seeking some kind of reassurance from him, this child for whom she is more mother than sister. Yet she hopes he will say something that reveals a similar experience with his own dreams. In the next moment, she understands the absurdity of speaking seriously to him about anything—he's still so much a baby, though he already has a sharp tongue, and not much patience.

—I wonder if we'll hear from Father today, he says.

—Not for at least another three weeks.

—I wish you weren't so sure all the time, Mary. You don't even go to school. You keep house.

—I was guessing.

—Well stop.

—Leave me be, can't you?

She opens the newspaper, which Mrs. Barrett has brought in, and reads an item on the left-hand side of the page:

MASSACRE

American General George Armstrong Custer Lost!

Entire expedition slaughtered in ambush at Little Big Horn

She looks across the table at her brother, who is absorbed in his own reading, chewing part of a chicken leg.

—Charley. Who was it Father and Dunraven were traveling to join?

—What?

—Father, in his last letter. They were going on an expedition with . . .

He stares.

Mary holds the paper toward him, coming to her feet so suddenly that she nearly upsets the table.

—My God, Charley! Look.

He squints, hands mincing with a napkin, touching his lips with it. Then he looks at her.

—It was this one, Mary says. Custer. General George Armstrong Custer. It was. Oh, God it was, wasn't it.

He rises, moves toward the stairs, and then halts.

—Oh, Charley don't go up there!

He bolts up the stairs, and she starts to follow. But Mrs. Barrett has come into the hall, and they face each other.

—You're as white as death, you. What is it, what's happened?

Charley comes slow back down the stairs, his face blotched with violet patches, his eyes wide and strangely unseeing.

—I can't.

—For God's sake, what is it? Mrs. Barrett says. Tell me.

The boy turns to her but doesn't seem to take her in. Then he faces Mary.

—We have to tell. Don't we. We have to tell Mother.

—Somebody please tell me what this is, Mrs. Barrett says.

Mary retrieves the newspaper and hands it to her.

—We believe Father was with them.

—My God, Charley breaks forth. And Father felt sorry for them! He felt for them! And the bastards! The bastards!

Mary goes into the small parlor and sinks down in one of the chairs. The quiet in the room is astonishing. There is a clock on the mantel, ticking.

Charley paces a little, then stumbles into the dining room and sits at the table there. Mrs. Barrett mutters the words of a hymn.

There has never been such a silence.

And then her mother calls from the top of the stairs:

—Children. Mary, Charles, what is it? What's wrong?

The boy knocks his chair over, standing, and moves to the bottom of the stairs. Mary hears their mother emit a terrible long gasp. Charley starts slowly up the stairs, and Mary follows, taking the newspaper from Mrs. Barrett. She tears the important page out, and puts it in the pocket of her dress. She lets the rest of the newspaper fall from her fingers. Their mother has dropped to her knees in the upstairs hall, and is cringing there as against a gigantic something swooping toward her. Charley tries to lift her. Tears stream down his pale cheeks.

—No! their mother says. No! You stop this! I won't 'ave it!

They work together to get her back into the bedroom, and the bed, where she curls up like a baby and lies there whimpering.

—I won't 'ave it, children. I won't 'ave it.

—Mother, Charley says, something terrible . . .

Mary interrupts him.

—For God's sake, Charley.

Her mother says:

—Tell me, Mary. You tell me.

—Father said in the last letter that they were going to join this man Custer on an expedition.

—It's all right, isn't it, Mary. It's all right.

—Mother, I'm frightened, Charley says.

—No, says their mother, addressing Mary. No. No.

And Mary presses on, holding the page of the newspaper toward her:

—It says here, Mother. Look.

Her mother stares at it, stupefied. Her expression is horrifyingly aghast, the eyes wide, the mouth open, completely without sound, not even the sound of breathing.

Mary touches the side of her face, then draws her hand away.

Charley mutters:

—No it isn't, no it isn't.

—Be quiet, Mary says.

—Father felt sorry for them, he says.

—Please leave me, says their mother.

—Mother, Mary says to her, leaning down close. Mother, it's not right to assume anything at all, is it?

—I'm frightened, Charley says.

—Leave me. Please, children.

—We must wait to know. Please? Mary says. Isn't that right?

—Oh, God! Charley says. It's right there in print! The entire lot of them lost!

—We do not know for certain that Father is dead, Charley!

—Please, their mother says. I can't stand it. Let me be, please. Please.

Mary walks out and down the stairs, past the litter of the newspaper, where it fell. Mrs. Barrett is standing in the hall murmuring the Lord's Prayer over and over. Mary goes out to the garden in back of the house. It's dark. The day's heat is still rising from the ground. The sky is clear, starry, and moonless. She walks to the end of the garden and back, and then she's pacing. *If this is the end of the world,* she thinks, *the end of the world, the end of the world.*

3

July 30, 1876
    Priestley and Lavoisier, among others, the first to identify oxygen. How must it have been to come to the knowledge that we live in gases.
    No. Unable to think or write anything. Pure pretending. Writing this down for some stranger I will never know.
    Father is in North America. Father is. Is. The Indians of North America: wars. Warring factions. Tribes. Hunter-gatherers, raiders. Thousands of them banding together to fight the white men. They would not distinguish an observer. Oh, friend, faraway. They would not distinguish a peaceful observer, whose sympathy they have.

Their mother is up in the nights, sitting on the edge of her bed, wringing her hands. She refuses to lie down, or get up. She cannot be compelled to move. She rocks back and forth, slow, murmuring part of a song she used to sing to Mary, when Mary couldn't sleep. Mary sits with her, and sings the little song herself. But nothing has any effect.

—Mother, Mary tells her, I think the news would've reached us, wouldn't it? If father 'ad been with them.

Her mother turns her head and stares, vacantly, still wringing her hands. Her expression says it all: the news is on its way to them. Her body cringes, precisely as if she can see the physical embodiment of the words heading toward her from the world. Mary tries to soothe her, and feels the sense of the remorseless truth closing around them. There will come a knock at the door. And someone will be standing there, with the final, dire word. Except that she knows it's entirely possible they'll never hear anything else at all. What sort of efforts can the Americans make toward the identification of the dead? How awfully will the savages have disfigured or burned the corpses?

When morning comes, her mother rises, and moves to the entrance of her closet, and without having performed her toilet or removed her nightgown, begins trying to put on her stays, trying to dress herself, distractedly, slowly.

—I must go tell the rest of the family, she mutters.

—That's been taken care of. Days ago, Mary says.

A friend of her father, Henry Guillemard, has been to see the relatives on her father's side. Mary sent word to him the day they learned of the massacre. There has been no word from the Kingsleys. The Bailey side of the family live down in Liverpool. They have sent cards, expressing their concern.

—Your brother said he would leave school.

—No one should do anything yet.

—My Charles is being quite the little man.

—Yes.

—Where are they? Where is the family?

Mary has no answer for this. The Kingsley haughtiness toward her mother has been a source of rage for her father for years. She helps her mother back to the bed.

—A family pulls together at such a time, Mary. Don't it?

—Some families, Mary cannot help saying.

Mrs. Barrett comes to the entrance of the room and asks for the morning off, to go be with her own family. Her son is ill with a fever, and there is worry. The truth is, she fears the proximity of misfortune, fears that it is like contagion, and might spread. Mary dismisses her, and spends the day in her mother's bedchambers. Her mother is too restless and frightened to lie down. She sits at the edge of the bed, moving with that small, involuntary rocking motion, still wringing her hands. Now and then she murmurs:

—What will become of us?

Mary tries to calm her, but the question has entered her mind as well. There is no will or testament, as far as she or her mother know, and she has no understanding of the law as it relates to this. She has read enough to know that, until Charley reaches his majority, all of them are hopelessly at the mercy of the law courts, if the family will do nothing.

Charley returns from school, accompanied by Guillemard, who has again spoken with the Kingsley side of the family, the uncles and aunts. He's gloomy. Charley is sullen. Charley sits in the big wing chair in the parlor, looking too small for it, even being big for his age, and bites the cuticles of his nails.

—What are they thinking? Mary asks Guillemard.

—They simply wish to wait until some certainty . . .

Guillemard stops himself. He's a very large, round man, with a shiny, bald pate and great side whiskers and a beard. His bulk always looks as if it is about to burst out of the clothes he wears, and about his clothes he's quite fastidious. He is a physician, like their father. Now he retrieves a small handkerchief from his coat pocket, takes off his glasses, and begins to wipe the lenses. He sniffles, and says nothing.

—They're bloody sorry, says Charley. They wish there was something they could do. They're sure we'll hear any day now. The bloody, sodding bastards.

—Language, young man, Guillemard says.

—Do you know what 'appens to us if there is no will? Mary asks him.

—You will be taken care of, Henry Guillemard says. I'll see to it, young lady.

—Where will we go?

Charley stirs in his chair suddenly. He draws in air, and attempts to contain himself, and then with a gesture that seems almost dismissive, mutters:

—You sound exactly like *her*. They don't want anything to do with us because of *her*.

—I will pretend you did not speak, she tells him.

—Charles, Guillemard says. There's a good chap.

Charley rises and makes his way upstairs to their mother's room. Mary excuses herself and follows. Here, the only sound is the small, animal whimper of the woman lying in the bed. But then she stirs, and says:

—Mary, they 'ave to be told.

—Dr. Guillemard already went 'round to see them, Mother. They know. They have known for a week.

—I should make ready.

—You needn't bother, Charley says. They're not coming.

—Of course they are.

—With Father gone, they don't have to do anything at all. And so they won't.

—Charley, Mary says.

—I look a mess, their mother says.

—Did you hear me? Charley says. They're not coming. No one is coming.

—There must be someone we can send for, says Mary. Some way of finding out for certain.

—You're still on about that?

—It's the truth, Charley. We don't know anything for certain until word comes.

—Oh bugger this. I'm going out.

—Where are you going? their mother says.

—I'm going out.

They let him go. Mary goes down and invites Guillemard to stay for tea. He demurs, evidently understanding from the exhaustion in her voice that she's not up to company—even family company. When he's gone, she makes the tea, and then drinks it alone, in her mother's room. Her mother hasn't moved from her position on the bed. Mary sits at her side and pats her hip, an automatic motion that neither of them quite feels. Her mother drifts into a fitful sleep. Mary watches this, then goes to the window and looks out at the garden.

She works in the house, and feeds the gamecocks. It is so humid outside that she's soaked in the five minutes it takes to scatter the seed on the bare ground. In the house again, she stands in the doorway of her father's library, and begins to experience the pain of his loss. It's nearly insupportable. Upstairs, her mother is awake, and has begun to whimper again.

—Mother, she says. We don't know for certain.

—I can't stand it, Mary.

—No, nor I.

That afternoon, Charley comes home and locks himself in his room. He wants nothing to eat, nothing to do with anyone. He remains there all night and into the morning. Mrs. Barrett arrives in the forenoon, but won't stay until something is certain. There is no sense working days for which she will not be paid. Mary sends her off, and then returns to her mother's room, where she reads to her, and tries to soothe her. Her mother likes Dickens, and so Mary reads from *The Old Curiosity Shop*. It occurs to her that they are learning to be accustomed to the idea that her father is never going to come home again. Yet they have done nothing toward accepting that. She's begun to believe that they will never know any more than they do at present; there will never be any final word, and no remains, no sign, forever.

Charley comes out of his room and walks down the stairs, into the kitchen. She hurries down to catch him before he can leave, as she is sure he will.

—You look dreadful, he says to her. Why don't you brush your hair at least.

—Charley, what if we never learn anything about it at all?

—Why are you asking me? I don't know anything.

—I'm sorry, she says.

—Why don't you take care of it, Mary. You're the one who's always taking charge of everything. Why don't you find out?

—Why are you angry with me, Charley?

He hesitates, puts one hand to his head, then lets down and begins to cry.

—I don't mean it. I don't. I'm so scared.

She moves to embrace him, but he steps back. It is as if she meant to strike him.

—Don't do that, he says.

—I only wanted to comfort you.

—Well, I don't want it from you. I want my father.

—There must be someone in the family who'll help us.

—They hate her, he says, and so do I.

She slaps him, a blow that sends him reeling across the room. He falls against the stove and stands there, holding the side of his face. When he takes his hand down, she sees the red welt, the print of her hand.

—Don't you ever say such a thing again in my presence, she tells him.

—It's the bloody truth. We've had it spelled out for us.

—Tell me, she says. Which of them would say such a thing?

—*All* of them!

She can't speak for a moment. He straightens, brushes the sleeves of his shirt, looking down.

—If you want to know. Guillemard said. They're so sorry. Nothing they can do, nothing. Nothing. Didn't you listen to him?

—We'll go along then, Mary says. Without them.

—We're going to end up in bloody Newgate, in the workhouse.

He leaves her there, and returns to his room. She makes soup and takes it upstairs to her mother, who is not willing to eat or do much of anything for herself, now. Everything is in this awful hiatus, this static province, the country of waiting: for the knock on the door, the arrival of the wire, the messenger, the one who will carry to them the official, dreaded word. But nothing comes. The nights pass, the days, one after another. Mary begins to fear for her mother's sanity. She can't get her to eat, or take any sustenance. Mrs. Barrett comes calling every day, and every day she turns and makes her way back down the street. Mary keeps the house. No one else comes. There is no mail to speak of. There are not even any further newspaper accounts of the disaster at Little Big Horn.

One afternoon, Mary gets Charley to stay with Mother, and makes her way alone down Highgate Street to the corner, and on, to where Cousin Rose lives with her family. It is a miserably hot day, without a breath of air stirring anywhere, and the sun glares on every surface. Her cousin's house is shut tight, curtains drawn against the heat. Rose receives her, looking beyond her for a companion, and then leading her, doubtfully, into the dim side parlor, where there are chairs ranged along the wall as if for a party. Rose is three years older, and steeped in the proprieties. Her face is elongated and sallow, and because she's nearsighted she has a perpetual squinting expression.

—There's news? she says.

—Nothing, Mary tells her.

Rose's mother enters the room. Gray, small-eyed, stout, dressed in frills and silks, a scarf draped over her shoulders, and tied at her neck to hide a goiter.

—Well, and don't you look the young lady, so grown up and straight, she says.

—This is not the bleedin' time for that sort of silliness, says Mary.

Rose's mother gasps, and then gathers herself.

—Miss Mary Henrietta Kingsley, you will please watch your tongue. And you will conduct yourself according to your station and age, young lady.

Rose says:

—It's been so long since any of us have seen you, Mary. Do you never go out?

—'ere I am, she says.

—I want what I said understood, says Rose's mother.

—Understood, Mary says.

—Everyone wonders about you, says Rose, as if the annoyance of the interruption is a burden that can be borne with patience and diligence. You haven't been to a single gathering this year. And you missed my birthday celebration.

—I wonder if I could speak to Uncle.

—He's in America, actually, says Rose's mother. It was a dreadful fright for us hearing the news about your father and that American general.

—Father is in a place called Chicago, Rose says. I believe it's hundreds of miles away from any savages.

—Yes, it is. I know where it is.

—And there's no news? Rose's mother says.

Mary stands.

—Good afternoon.

—That's all? What did you want here? Why did you come?

—I wanted to see something for myself.

—Oh, and what was that?

—That would be the reason I don't come to anything anymore. Good day.

4

*N*EWS ARRIVES that afternoon, finally, in the form of another letter from her father in which he explains, quite blithely, that he and Dunraven, by providence, were spared the massacre at Little Big Horn, having failed to reach the expedition at all. Bad weather kept them away; it saved their lives.

—Bad weather, Charley says. Weather.

Their mother seems unready or afraid to allow herself the belief that her husband is not slaughtered thousands of miles away. But her appetite, the next morning, is slightly better; she eats the egg that Mary brings her. And something of her humor has returned: she makes a dry little joke about Mrs. Barrett being willing to return to the once-cursed house of Kingsley.

They all settle slowly into the old patterns, though Mary finds that she has moments when she cannot believe her father to be alive. The experience is like a premonition. During the period of terrible waiting, she was plagued by the fact that if her father was indeed dead, she had gone on for days—the days it took for his letter to arrive, and the days it took for the news of the massacre to arrive—in the belief that he was alive in his part of the world. It had never occurred to her that if something were to happen to him, there would be this lag of time before she would know it. The thought is perfectly obvious, of course, but now it carries the weight of experience; it troubles her in the nights, along with everything else that troubles her.

One rainy morning a week later, sitting across from Charley, she alludes to it.

—I'm wondering what Father is going through at this minute. This instant.

—You're strange.

She watches him eat.

—You're as gloomy as Mother, he says.

Mary goes upstairs to check on her. Still asleep. Back in her own room, she changes her dress, her undergarments. The day stretches before her.

In the glass, she looks upon her gangly, long body and is strangely heartsick. A resignation comes over her like a spell of nausea. She wishes her father would come home, and in the same instant experiences a flutter of unease at the thought of a change, any change. How odd, to be in the middle of a state of perpetual alarm and worry, inexpressible anguish, and the sense of being caught in a trap, and still to abhor any alteration of it.

She feels altered inside, and the length of time opens out in front of her like a desert. She experiences an overpowering restlessness. Aftershock. She understands, without the words to express it, quite. The concentrated perception that comes with crisis, and remains when the crisis is past.

On the door frame, she has made several marks, keeping track of her growth over the last year. It's appalling—more than two inches. She sometimes imagines that she can feel it happening, the extremities elongating, the ends of the fingers stretching. She cannot quite place in memory when it was that she began to fear madness. She remembers a phrase from *King Lear*—the one work of Shakespeare that she has read over and over. The phrase troubles her, and still she repeats it, like a prayer:

Oh, let me not be mad, not mad, sweet Heaven!
Keep me in temper. I would not be mad!

The makings of imagination, of fancy—plays, poems, songs, tales, and novels—contain ambushes, matters to haunt her in the blackness. She confines her reading now entirely to the sciences—mathematics, biology, social customs, physics, and chemistry. The world of facts. Especially the facts of chemistry. She wades through all her father's books on the subject: *solids, liquids, gases, compounds.* In the dark of the sleepless nights, she can repeat to herself the names of elements, the theories of Robert Hooke, *the law of extension and compression of elastic bodies;* Huygens and the undulatory theory of light; Fahrenheit, Ampère, and Robert Boyle. She can recite studies of Volta on the properties of heat and gases, and the work of Evangelista Torricelli and his principles of hydromechanics. And of course Isaac Newton. There are no emotions attached to these things, and so there is a solace in them, in knowing them. A protection. She doesn't fully understand much of what she reads—so much of it is foundational—but she has developed the faith that reading other things will teach her, that she can come back to what she doesn't understand, and see it with new eyes. This faith never disappoints her. And there is nothing of the *girl* in it, none of the weakness she has learned is expected of her, even by other girls, like Rose and the other cousins, who are so much concerned with their appearance.

They are readers of romances, gothic tales, stories of supernatural transformations and horrors, and their talk about it all is freighted with a kind of zeal, as if the whole aspect of darkness were something delicious and alluring. Yet she wonders if they are visited by ghosts and terrors in sleep, and she has entertained a desire to ask them. Nothing in their chatter or their behavior has ever left the slightest opening for the discussion of anything serious. She has wanted to say to them, *Are you frightened of losing your mind? Do you have dreams that you are being ravished by wild animals? Are you not afraid to put these books down and face back into the world, or to examine the reasons they stimulate your senses so?*

SIX

1

$\mathcal{L}$ILY SAW THE FAMILIAR HOUSES, trees, and lawns of her street with mingled excitement and unease. She gave Tyler the directions, and he followed them, driving slow. The sun had broken through an opening in the cloud cover, and there was a wide band of stippled shade on the road surface. Reflected leaves rode up the smooth, shiny hood of the car. She remembered watching the same kind of reflection in the polished hood of her father's Ford when they came down this road. How long ago? She had been a little girl. It felt like earlier today. She thought of remarking on this to Tyler, since he was probably nervous, too. "It's gonna be a good time," she said to him.

He reached over and touched her knee. The mist had lifted, burned off by the sun. It would be a hot day. Everything had a washed, fresh look. The grass sparkled with beaded water, as if each blade contained pieces of the flaming sun itself. The shade was blue, the green of the leaves a darker, richer green. The tree branches were wet and black.

They came out of the canopy of leaves and approached the house.

Doris had grown neglectful about the lawn in stages—she still kept the flower bed that stretched across the length of the porch, but the bushes were badly in need of trimming, and the driveway had been narrowed by the thick growth. A trash can lay on its side by the woodpile, which had collapsed at one end. Sunflowers stood up out of the fallow garden in the yard.

Doris came out on the porch to greet them, wearing a halter and dark shorts and sandals. She had let her hair down; it framed her face. She looked healthy, pink-cheeked and well fed. Her lined face glowed in the light.

The introduction was awkward. Tyler held out a hand, but Doris wanted an embrace. She put her arms around his neck and kissed his cheek. "I'm so glad to meet you," she said, stepping back and then reaching for Lily. "How happy I am."

Lily saw that she was forcing it a little, and took hold of her elbow. "You look wonderful," she said.

Doris led them into the house, where she had prepared lemonade, and she talked about the evening's plans—Lily's father and his new wife were coming to dinner, and she'd put a roast in the oven; she hoped Tyler liked roast beef. She'd made an apple pie from scratch, though she couldn't remember the last time she had baked something from scratch, and the crust would probably taste like leather. But she was a person who believed in doing things with special care for special occasions, and this was a very special occasion indeed. She didn't want to cause any discomfiture, but she did wish there was going to be a real wedding, a church wedding with a choir and a lot of people and a priest, a cake with a little bride and groom on top. Tyler and Lily must forgive her for bringing it up, but she couldn't help herself. She went on with a kind of breathless jollity, and Tyler was gracious, the perfect gentleman, nodding and smiling and agreeing, sipping his lemonade.

"I know I'm rattling on," Doris said. "And of course, these days people don't even bother getting married before they move in with each other. You two are doing the right thing."

"The house smells just like Thanksgiving," Tyler said.

"Thank you, dear." Doris turned to Lily. "Your father and Peggy ought to be here by now."

"Can I show Tyler the backyard?" Lily asked.

"There's nothing out there anymore, sweetie. I had your old swing set removed."

Lily smiled. "Well, it sat out there for ten years rusting in the rain. It was starting to look like a fossilized skeleton."

They were all outside, in the wet grass, when Lily's father pulled in, with Peggy, who wore a black, shapeless cotton dress and had her hair in two pigtails one on each side of her head. She looked like someone trying to appear girlish, though she had a cigarette in her mouth and wore dark-red lipstick. Lily noticed the polite way her mother offered her hand to Peggy, and then kissed Lily's father on the cheek. Tyler seemed rather wonderfully at home with them, looking from one person to another, and talking about having grown up in Steel Run, so close.

They were all standing out in the hot sun, being gracious, and getting along better than Lily could have hoped.

She excused herself and went into the house and upstairs to her room. It was essentially as it had been when she was in high school—pictures from productions her father and mother had been in, a row of books, including the book of explorers. She opened it and gazed at Mary Kingsley, then gently closed it and put it back.

The others had come in downstairs. Her father was opening a bottle of red wine. Peggy chattered about the humidity, which was almost as bad as the humidity along Lake Michigan, maybe worse. Tyler said he'd never been to the Midwest.

Lily started down the stairs and they all stopped. They were in the living room, where her mother had set the silver tray—tall glasses, the ice bucket, and the pitcher of lemonade—on the coffee table. No one had taken any of it, though now Doris was offering it. Peggy said she would have a glass, and Doris poured it for her. Lily's father had one arm lightly across the top of Peggy's back. Doris sat in the love seat, legs crossed, the one leg swinging slightly. No one spoke. Lily abruptly had the thought that this might be the longest afternoon of her life.

Her father said, "Where will you have the ceremony?"

"We're leaving for Mississippi, Daddy. We'll probably wait until we get down there. We haven't decided anything, really, except that I don't want a ceremony."

"I never knew you to be such an enemy of ritual," he said.

They were all quiet again. The strangeness was now palpable, like a stirring of overheated air.

Abruptly, Doris began to cry. She excused herself and went into the other room. Lily saw Peggy exchange a look with her father.

Above the mantel of the fireplace were paintings Doris had done years ago, and Tyler began admiring them. Doris had stopped painting because the oils made her allergies act up, and caused her to get skin rashes. The paintings were quite good. Doris had even had a few shows in her youth, back when she was still dancing, and when Lily was a baby. She occasionally taught painting and sketching at the local junior college.

When she returned to the room, wiping her eyes with a napkin and apologizing for what she called her silliness, Tyler remarked that he would like to have anything she might paint to decorate the living room of the place he and Lily would live in. Doris took the napkin away from her face and said, "I haven't painted in years. The oils give me eczema. And I never was any good at watercolor."

"Sure you are," Lily's father said.

"Oh, Scott. You were never very interested in it, even when I was doing it."

"Excuse me—but I think I hung these."

"Only because I asked you to. Do you remember that day, dear?"

They all fell silent. Peggy had paused in her clattering of ice, and swallowed once. She looked at Scott, and then concentrated hard on the drink.

"I think they're wonderful paintings," Tyler said.

2

THE AFTERNOON AND EVENING were better than Lily had feared, everybody finding neutral things to say. She was impressed by the fact that Peggy helped prepare and dish out the food. The conversation at dinner was assiduously superficial, mostly about the verbal incompetence of the Bush administration. Finally Doris, apologizing for changing the subject, asked what the young couple's plans were for the next few days. Lily explained that they would pack everything up and send it south, and they would head there themselves within the week.

"When and where it's going to take place," Scott said. "That's all your mother wants to know, and I want to know. You know me and weddings, but we'd like to be there."

"This is Lily's call," Tyler put in.

"You'll all have to understand," said Lily, putting her hand over Tyler's. She had an image of a wedding in which her family was on one side of the church—the grandparents and all the aunts and uncles and cousins—and Tyler's on the other: she saw it in her mind, the vacant seats on his side. "I just don't want a big fuss."

"No presents?" Scott said. "No cake?"

"We just want to get on with life, Daddy."

For a moment, no one spoke.

"I've never been to Mississippi," Peggy said. "In fact, I've never been farther south than Tennessee. But I almost went there to college. Mississippi, I mean. I had a boyfriend who went down there on a football scholarship."

"Peggy almost married a football player," Scott said. "What saved you, honey?"

"He was majoring in socket wrenches or something. Dumb as a wall."

"But pretty, right?"

"Handsome, sure."

"Would anyone like some coffee?" Doris asked.

After dinner, Tyler and Scott went out on the porch and smoked cigars. They each had a small glass of whiskey, and they looked like the cliché of the about-to-be father-in-law counseling the younger man about women. Lily stood behind the screen door and listened to them, and she was surprised to find that they were actually exchanging jokes about honeymoons.

"Well," Scott said. "On my first honeymoon, the damn room service guy brings the champagne, and he winks at me. I've never seen this fellow before in my life and we're in this—this collusion with each other. I wanted to go out and walk up and down in the halls, denying the whole thing, the whole *concept*."

Lily went to the kitchen, which still smelled of the roast, and out to the patio in back, where Peggy sat alone with her glass, which was empty. Doris had excused herself and gone upstairs when the dishes were done.

"Hello," Peggy said. "I'm incredibly thirsty."

"Let me fix you something," Lily told her.

"I'll come in while you do—it's lonesome out here."

Holding the door for her, Lily realized as if for the first time that this young woman was her stepmother. It was a wildly bizarre moment. Peggy sat in the breakfast nook, quite at home it seemed, while Lily made herself a glass of whiskey with ice.

Lily took a place across from her, deciding that it would be rude to leave her sitting there.

"What are the men talking about?" Peggy asked.

Lily lied. "Politics."

"Tyler's nice."

"Thank you."

Peggy swallowed the lemonade. Above them was the sound of Doris moving around; the floor creaked. "I have news."

Lily waited.

"I don't know that this is the right time," Peggy said.

Lily felt heat rising along her spine, and into her cheeks. She said, "You're pregnant."

The other woman nodded, then smiled and gave her a confiding look. "Scott doesn't know it yet."

You couldn't have thought that this would make me happy, Lily wanted to say. She could only bring herself to murmur, "When do you plan to tell him?"

"I guess now isn't the time." Peggy frowned a little, then forced a level expression. You could see the effort she had made. "It's an accident." She nodded, as if Lily had expressed some surprise. "I don't know how I feel about it, yet. I always swore I'd never have any, you know."

"Cheer up," Lily said, rising. "Maybe something will happen." She was appalled at her own words. She hadn't been able to hold them back.

Peggy stared, holding the glass at her lips. It was as if both women had heard some inexplicable and shocking sound. Lily walked away from her, since there was now nothing else she could think of to do. She went through the living room, out to the porch, where the men were still smoking their cigars. Her father was talking about the month he had spent in Biloxi, Mississippi, when he was in the air force. He saw Lily and stopped. "Where are your mother and Peggy?"

Lily sat on the top step, put her elbows on her knees, and rested her head on her arms. "I don't know."

"What's wrong?"

"You okay, love?" Tyler said.

"I'm a little tired."

"Listen," Scott said. "I'm going to make you-all out a small check. I want you to take it as a wedding present from us."

"You don't have to do that, Daddy."

"Of course I do," Scott said. "Christ almighty. Of course I do."

"It's kind of you," Tyler said to him. The two of them went on talking a little about the future; Tyler said he wasn't sure how long he might remain in the car-sales business. "I'm just going to try it for a while, and see."

Lily ran her hands through her hair and looked at him, and when he looked back, she forced a smile.

"You're awful quiet," he said.

Peggy had come to the front door and was watching through the screen. Lilly saw Peggy out of the corner of her eye.

"Premarital jitters," Scott said lightly. "Hey, kiddo. Don't be nervous." It was his old, teasing tone with her, from when he had lived here and she was small.

It made her want to go through the house and look at all the rooms.

Peggy walked out onto the porch, and along it to the other end, away from them all. She stood with arms folded, looking out at the lawn. "Grass needs cutting," she said.

Lily heard tears in her voice.

The men went on talking; they had gotten onto the subject of single malt scotches, and hadn't noticed. Doris came downstairs and walked into the kitchen, and Lily heard her put ice in a glass. She stood and moved to where Peggy was. Peggy did not look at her. They were side by side, Lily leaning on the railing, looking out at the dusky light on the lawn. Some stars shone in the sky now, through a thin haze. The crickets had started. Fireflies flickered in the deep shadows of the other side of the street. You could still see light in the sky, and nearly transparent striations of cloud in what was visible of the horizon.

"I'm sorry," Lily said, low.

"Forget it." Peggy ran the back of one hand over her eyes, then glanced at the men and kept herself turned from them, arms folded again.

"What're you two talking about?" Scott asked.

Doris had come to the screen. "It looks so blue out there," she said. "From in here."

SEVEN

1

$\mathscr{T}$YLER HAD ARRANGED for the sale of the car before they left to visit Lily's parents, and when they returned to Charlottesville, he completed the deal. He used the money to send their books and clothes to Oxford, along with a few items of furniture that had belonged to his father, and that he had kept in storage for the months he was finishing college: a cedar chest from the old man's boyhood, a wooden nightstand he had fashioned out of pine planks when Tyler was a baby, a big leather reclining chair, and several heads of animals and fish trophies—big game from land and sea, as Tyler described it. He wanted their house, wherever it would be, decorated with these things. He liked to hunt. His father had been an avid hunter. One of his earliest memories was of being out in the cold, in the woods, hunting rabbits, listening to his father's bitch beagle Mina sounding in the distance. "My dad was a hard man," he said. "Old school."

"You mean about hunting?"

"About everything. When I was five, I couldn't catch a ball. No matter how hard I tried. And I tried. So he threw it at my face. He hit me with it three, four times, and finally I learned to put my hands up."

"God," Lily said.

"I learned to catch a ball. And when he wanted to take me hunting, I went with him. And I learned to like it. He took me everywhere."

"How'd he teach you to hunt—by shooting at you?"

Tyler smiled and shook his head. "I got so I loved going out with him."

He had a couple of trophies of his own, including the head of an elk, from a hunting trip the year before his father died. Lily was surprised to find that he owned two high-caliber hunting rifles, a double-barreled shotgun, and several antique pistols. He shipped everything to Oxford.

They were married by a justice of the peace, on May seventeenth, and Tyler, meaning it as a surprise for her, got Dominic to come to the ceremony as a witness. Dominic hugged them both, and seemed happy to be a part of it all. He kissed Lily on the cheek, calling it a "chaste peck, for good luck." Lily saw Tyler's face take on a fleeting expression of curiosity. But then the talk went on, with Dominic making everyone laugh, describing the way his aunt Rosemary, for her fourth marriage, had a drunken priest at the ceremony, and how this priest toppled over at the moment of pronouncing her the wife of a Buick dealer, also drunk. "The priest, when they revived him, got into a crying jag, and said he was helplessly in love with Rosemary and couldn't something be done about it? Rosemary said he should go to confession and we all just stared."

"Was Rosemary widowed three times?" Tyler asked.

"Um, annulled," Dominic said. "Technicalities."

They all went to the Flaming Wok for an early dinner, and at one point, when Tyler had gone to the rest room, Dominic took Lily's hand and said, "How are you?"

"I never dreamed how happy," she told him. "What about you, Dom?"

"Oh, hey, you know. I'm always the same."

She turned her hand in his, and squeezed. "I'm going to miss you."

"I won't let that happen," he said.

She let go and he leaned back.

"I feel very good," he told her. "I'm so happy that I feel completely kind. That's somewhere in Tolstoy, I think."

Tyler came back to the table and sat down, and Dominic offered a toast to the new couple. They drank, and then they were quiet for a few moments, as if out of respect for their own warm feeling. When the waiter brought the check, the two men argued jovially over who should pay it. Dominic had grabbed it, and wouldn't let go. He paid with a credit card, joking that this was one his father had forgotten to cancel. They went out into the dusk, and Dominic hugged them both. Lily promised to stay in touch; Tyler said Dominic should come south for a visit before the summer ended.

"That's a real possibility," Dominic said. "I mean that."

Even so, Lily had for a dark instant the sense that it was just talk. She took his hands and said, "We mean it, too, Dom."

"I know you do. Well, be good to each other for me." He turned and walked away, toward the Rotunda, the college, the new life he was leading in the city.

2

They took the train south, a sleeper. There were two very small beds, one that pulled down from the wall. It was a tiny room, and when they had made love, they decided it was more comfortable to sleep separately; there really wasn't enough room on one bed. She lay in the shifting dimness, the passing lights of stations south, the slow going by of the cities in the night. The ride was surprisingly rough, the train jolting and rattling on the curves, and there was the rhythmic clacking of the seams in the rails, like a counting out of seconds. She couldn't sleep. Tyler was very still in the cot above her, and once she leaned up on her elbow and said his name. Nothing. She lay back, and a string of light poles shot past, a flicker that startled her. Finally she turned in the cot so that she saw only the line of light around the closed door of the room.

Sometime near dawn, when the light from the window had grown steadily and the other lights made less of an impression on her, she drifted into a half sleep that was disturbed by voices in the vestibule. Tyler turned in the cot above her and moaned, and uttered an indecipherable phrase. There was the perceptible coming of morning through the window. A rush of elation went through her, hearing it. She was a married lady. She lay over on her back and luxuriated in the idea.

Perhaps she drifted again. She couldn't tell. Finally she turned to the wall, and was gone for a time, and then, after a space of vague dreaming, she lay over on her back again. Here was Tyler, who had climbed down, and was standing in the sunlight, naked, hands on his hips, completely comfortable and relaxed.

"Hello, world," he said. He saw that she was watching him. "Move over."

She did so. His breath was stale, as, she knew, was her own. It didn't matter. It was deliciously part of their intimacy When he moved inside her she marveled at the ease of it, how well it seemed designed, all of it: their motions, the way her own flesh seemed to pull at him as he withdrew partly, and the way she seemed to divide, with such a lovely relenting, as he pushed back in. She stretched her arms straight up, and then closed them around his neck, raising her hips to take him deeper, then arching her back, moving her hips downward, putting a wonderful-feeling pressure on him. He came with the low utterance of a word she didn't hear, moving so fast now she thought about the noise they were making. He kept going, and she held him, letting go inside, falling through. He had let himself rest on her, so that she was looking over his shoulder at the springs of the bed above. When he stopped, he raised his upper body and looked down at her.

"Oh, baby."

"Good morning," she said.

He withdrew, and lay beside her, but he was partway off the bed. It wasn't going to be possible to hold each other. He got up and went uncertainly, with the motion of the train, into the little cubicle of a bathroom. "Help," he said in mock alarm, pitching forward and laughing. "Oh, God, I pity the poor sailors out at sea on a rocky day like this." The door closed. She lay quite still, laughing, feeling the moistness between her legs and marveling at the fact that she was here.

The train slowed. They were coming into a town. There were other tracks now, and a station platform, and beyond that a clutch of tall buildings drenched in sun.

The sun hurt her eyes. She put one hand up to shade them, and felt the heat of it through the glass. A station platform glided by, and gave way to rows of tenement houses with porches and balconies, adorned with greenery and flowers, and draped, some of them, with laundry. There were laundry lines in the little fenced-in spaces, and a litter of toys, broken-down cars, bicycles, household goods. She saw a refrigerator with its door off and, a few yards farther on, a claw-footed bathtub with copper-colored stains on it.

Tyler came out of the bathroom, toweling off. "Better hurry," he said. "They'll be serving breakfast in a few minutes."

"Peggy's pregnant," she said. She had not even been thinking about it.

"Peggy—" He seemed puzzled for a beat. "Oh, right. Peggy. Really?"

"She hasn't told my father."

"Jesus." He stared.

She stood up with the blanket around her. The room was so small that they had to negotiate her moving around him. He took her by the upper arms and kissed her, and his mouth tasted minty from the toothpaste.

"I'm sorry. I should've told you about it before now."

"I feel sorry for your mom," he said.

"I didn't tell her, either. She doesn't know yet."

"Lily—" he said, and seemed to hesitate.

"Tell me," she said.

He kissed her again, and then held her face in his hands. "I love you."

She dropped the blanket and put her arms around his neck. She had the thought: *We're a match for anything. We're going to be so good.*

He touched her hips, and she moved farther around him, to the doorway of the bathroom. "I'll be right out," she said.

In the dining car, they sat across from each other in a booth, and he reached across the table and took her hands. He looked at the other people in the car, then took a breath and squeezed her hands. "I slept wonderfully. How about you?"

She smiled. "I'm too excited to sleep."

He sat back, and she watched the way his eyes took in everything.

"Tell me about your father. Would I have liked him?"

Tyler frowned, concentrating. "He was kind of hard to figure sometimes. What some people call a man's man from the outside, but then in close—well. There was a soft spot, like a flaw in a piece of metal. I don't mean that as harshly as it sounds." He looked down at where his fingers were folding and refolding the edge of the doily in the center of the table. "He was moody. He had some strange aspects, like anyone. Well, maybe more than just anyone."

"The business about the baseball."

"That and some other things." He kept toying with the doily. "We got along all right." He sat back. "What's the line from Hamlet? 'He was a man, take him for all in all. I shall not look upon his like again.' He wasn't for everybody—including my mother, apparently."

3

$\mathcal{T}$HE TRAIN RUMBLED into Oxford in mid-morning. It was bright and hot in the station, and there was a smell of oil and tar in the air. Beyond the confines of the building, everything was blooming. Lily saw a high green hill dotted with white flowers, a million flecks of snow. Across the top of the hill, houses were ranged, dark-wood balconies festooned with potted plants and wild ivy, splashes of red, violet, and saffron. There wasn't a cloud in the sky. Sheri was waiting for them at the far end of the platform. She wore a soft-blue dress and a wide-brimmed straw hat that she held on her head with one hand in the blustery warm wind.

"If you two don't look as fresh as new money," she said, embracing Lily. "I'm so ecstatic."

"You look like you ought to be in *Gone With the Wind,* wearing that hat," said Tyler.

"Listen, this hat's about to *be* gone with the wind." She took it off as the wind gusted, and her hair covered her face. She stood there before them, arms at her sides, humorously resigned. It was charming. When the wind stopped, each soft blond strand slid in a lovely languidness back into place. "I can see again," she said.

They waited for the porter to unload the bags. It surprised Lily, how good she felt seeing Sheri, whose eyes were so welcoming and friendly.

The porter loaded their bags onto a cart, and Tyler tipped him, then pushed the cart along the platform, through the station, and out to Sheri's car. The station was all brown surfaces—polished oak wainscoting, wooden benches, and a wooden wall with a ticket window in it. Lily saw the young, long-faced man behind the bars of the window, and the man followed her with his gaze, as though he were waiting for her to say something. She smiled slightly and took her eyes away, and when she looked back, he was concentrating on something in front of him, below the sill of the window. She had the sense of wanting to record everything; it was what she always felt upon her arrival in a new city.

"Mama can't wait to see you," Sheri said. She nodded at Tyler. "Both of you."

"We're looking forward to it," he said.

"How was the ride down? It's supposed to be nice sleeping on a train."

"I lost consciousness, and poor Lily was awake all night."

"Well, anyway, you're here and it'll be fun," said Sheri. "Don't you worry about a thing."

Tyler stopped, yawned, and stretched. The muscles of his arms were lean and veined and hard; Lily experienced a little thrill of realizing again how burly and solid he was. He pushed the cart forward, and they walked along with him. A group of Girl Scouts came running past them. Some of them held ice-cream cones.

"Millicent's so excited," Sheri said. Then, to Tyler: "No matter what you came here thinking." She seemed to stop herself. "I mean, she's not like you might expect."

"What did you suppose I might expect?" he asked her.

Sheri pressed on. "She's nervous about it, of course. But it's mostly excitement. She spent all this week cleaning and polishing and dusting and rearranging furniture. Everything's got to be *perfect*. She drove Buddy about out of his little mind this week. You wouldn't *believe* it."

"Buddy?" Tyler said.

Sheri turned to him. "That's what he wants to be called. I keep calling him Daddy, of course. He doesn't like that."

They reached the car. Sheri opened the trunk and stepped back. Tyler started putting the bags in, arranging them neatly, in rows, pushing on them to get them all in. She helped to close the trunk, then turned and leaned against it and regarded him, holding the big hat over her abdomen. "You're not here to cause any trouble, right?" Her smile was playful, but there was a trace of something in her eyes.

"Hey," he said. "I'm bringing my new wife to the only family I have left, strange as that family is. And I'm starting a new job, remember?"

"I guess we are pretty strange," Sheri said. She put her arm over Lily's shoulder, a confiding gesture. "But I've got my roomie back, right?"

They got into the car, Tyler insisting on getting in the back. It was very close and hot in the cramped space, and Sheri turned the air conditioner on high. They had to talk loud over the noise of it. Lily sat with eyes closed for a time, enjoying the cooling rush of air. They rode into the streets of the city, the most decayed parts of it—run-down shacks, sagging porches, and broken or boarded-up windows. It all looked abandoned. There were dirt lawns, and now and again a shady patch of grass under a single tree. Lily saw houses that at first glance appeared prosperous, but then something would undercut the impression: the hull of a washing machine in a side yard; tar paper nailed to the panel of a door.

"Hey, you guys—do you know the difference between a Republican woman and a Democratic one?" Tyler asked. "A Republican woman gives her heart to Bush."

"I don't get it."

"Think about it," Tyler said.

"Lily, do *you* get it?"

"Senator Hart," Lily said. "The Democrat. Remember what happened with him and the girlfriend?"

There was a pause, and then Sheri broke into a high-pitched, trilling laugh with several lovely notes in it. "Damn, I think I get dumber as time goes on."

"That's all right," Tyler said. "We don't love you for your mind."

"Good thing." Sheri's eyes were bright, and she stared ahead, still laughing.

Lily experienced a wave of affection for her. Tyler leaned forward and said, "A joke is like a live thing. Dissecting it kills it."

"That one arrived dead," Lily told him.

"I thought it was funny."

They were waiting at a light. Down the street was a series of shops, fronting on a narrow patch of asphalt. Beyond this was a theater complex and a mall, a white-brick facade that looked like fortification.

"This could be anywhere, USA," Tyler said.

The light changed, and Sheri put the car in gear. "So what're you-all's plans?"

"I'm going to work for your father. That's all we know for sure right now."

"No honeymoon?"

"We haven't given much thought to anything," said Tyler. "Except getting here."

"Lily, are you gonna let me introduce you to the theater people, down here?"

"Sure."

"I bet they'd put on an original play if you'd write one. I remember you were always writing."

"It's a pretty big *if*," Lily said.

Tyler asked to stop at a store, so he could buy some shaving things and maybe something to take his mother. Sheri pulled into a small shopping mall and turned the engine off. He got out without saying anything, and made his way in. For a few moments, the two women sat silently.

"I had a feeling about you and Tyler," Sheri said. "I swear."

"I'm still dazed," said Lily.

"So he told you that I tried to head it all off?"

Lily nodded slightly. "He said you told him I wasn't interested."

"If I did, I don't remember it."

"He's apologized for the—the lapse in time."

"It worries me," Sheri said, "that he's here."

"Why?"

"It's this situation with my mother. I mean—if you knew your mother left you when you were little because she was pregnant with another man's baby, how would you feel about her?"

Lily shook her head. "He seems—curious, I guess. I thought they'd been in touch."

Sheri rolled down her window, then opened her door and sat around with her feet outside the car. She brought a napkin out of her purse and wiped her neck with it, gingerly. Then she folded it and offered it to Lily. "I'm glad you're here and everything and I'm happy it all worked out, but actually it would've been okay with me if he went his way and we went ours."

"Have you spoken to him seriously about any of this?" Lily asked.

"Oh, yeah, right."

"You wanted us to come down here, Sheri."

"I wanted *you* to come down. I was thinking of splitting up with Nick, remember?"

Lily said nothing.

The other patted her own cheeks, then pulled the door toward her and leaned up to look at herself in the side-view mirror. "Well, I hope things work out better for you than they have for me. I'm already seeing someone else. Nick doesn't know it, of course. I mean, it's just platonic, you know."

"You're what?" In the reactive instant she asked the question, Lily realized that this was unwelcome information and that she did not want to talk about it.

"A little," said Sheri, with a small quaver in her voice. "But I mean I'm—Nick and I are together. His father's, like, disowned him. A fuck'n oil tycoon, and won't have a thing to do with him. We're living with Mama and Daddy because Nick lost his job and we ran out of money—" She halted, shook her head, appeared for a few seconds to be thinking of something else, faraway. "He's selling cars at Daddy's dealership, too, now. And I don't have the slightest idea where it's all gonna end up. It's day to day—no kidding."

Lily remembered the impression she'd had of the other young woman's appetite for reporting all her indiscretions and troubles like a kind of ongoing serial or drama. She said, "I'm a little worried about coming in on everyone like this."

"*You're* not what worries me, honey. Believe me."

"What worries you?" Lily said. "You think Tyler's—what—come to get some kind of—I don't understand."

"Forget it. Mother's *excited* about it, don't get me wrong. And there's *plenty* of room. The damn house has, like, *nine* bathrooms."

Tyler had come from the mall, with a plastic bag. Glass clanked in it. He leaned into the passenger-side window. "Anybody want a Coke or something else cold to drink?"

"Not me," Sheri said. Lily shook her head.

He got in and closed the door. "I assume Galatierre Ford isn't far from here."

"I could take you by it," Sheri said.

"That's all right," said Tyler. "I bought a little music b—" He made a small gulping sound that cut the word off. Then he took a breath and repeated himself: "Music box." He reached into the bag and brought it out and opened it. It gave forth a tinkling, unrecognizable music. "Oh, well," he said. "Maybe I'll get her something else when I have more time."

"Are you nervous?" Sheri said.

"Not me." He gave her a placid, smiling look.

Lily reached back and touched his knee. "I love you," she said. "Mr. Man."

He concentrated on putting the music box back in the bag, and she saw that his hands shook. She patted the knee, and faced front, not wanting him to know that she had seen it.

The road wound through farm fields—corn, soybeans, what looked like tobacco, and cotton. Beyond it all, the sky was a clear, pelagic blue. He brought a couple of bottles of RC out of the bag, and offered one to Sheri, and one to Lily.

"Aw, ain't he sweet," Sheri said.

He opened his own and drank most of it down in one gulp. "Where's your father on the subject of last fall's election? Is he happy with the result? I bet he votes Republican. Without ever having met him, I'm willing to bet he never even voted for Truman."

"He's not old enough to have voted for Truman. He was only— what—six years old when Roosevelt died."

"You have it figured out?"

"That's right," Sheri said with mock contentiousness. "I do, yes. You want to make something out of it?"

"You want to step outside?" Tyler asked.

"You first," said Sheri. "I'll speed up so you can get a nice flying start."

"Oh, I'm a lover, not a f—" Again, there was the little gulp. And again, he took a breath and repeated himself: "Not a fighter."

"You're my lover," Lily told him, only glancing back. Her heart ached for what he must be feeling.

The countryside grew uneven and wild—low hills, with stands of skinny pines, and expanses of empty brown pasture. The sun had burned the grass to a dry, flammable dust. They passed through a broken-down wooden gate, and Lily saw a row of fence posts going off to the vanishing point, into the woods, with strands of sagging barbed wire attached to them. The wire was a burned-red color, and it had left stains, like the scars of a whip, on the wooden posts. Beyond one field, under a clutch of heavy trees, was a faded yellow house with a veranda, a double porch. She watched it recede into the distance. The road was gravel now, and a column of blue dust rose behind the car.

"This used to be a plantation," Sheri said.

They came around a slow bend, and the yellow house came into view again. It was not as imposing as it had seemed from a distance. Sheri pulled in front of it and parked next to a big station wagon, blaring on the horn. "Home," she said.

Lily felt suddenly a little shaky herself. She opened her door; Tyler had come around the car. Her husband, standing there holding a bottle of cola, and the paper bag. He handed the bag to her. "This is from both of us—will you give it to her?"

She took it. Her nerves were jangling. Sheri's mother stood out on the veranda—a small, thin-boned woman with chiseled, intelligent features. Dark-brown hair without a trace of gray framing a tan, lined face. She approached, and with an offhand sort of gracefulness extended her hand to Lily, smiling. "Welcome," she said. "Welcome to Mississippi." Her cheekbones were prominent, her eyes deep set, their color such a bottomless shade of green that you lost the black iris at the center. She wore a white blouse, jeans, and sandals. The blouse accentuated the bronze hue of her skin, her brown hair. She was quite beautiful.

She turned to Tyler, who had given his bottle of cola to Sheri and was taking the bags out of the trunk of the car, as though to delay the moment of having to face her. She offered the same hand—a natural gesture of greeting, no more than one might expect from an affable and gracious stranger. "Tyler," she said. "Look how tall you are, and handsome." He stared at her, the smile never leaving his face. He took her hands and held them for a moment, and she gazed up at him without the slightest sign of what must have been playing across the surface of her mind.

"My wife, Lily," he said, in a little, shaken voice. "We brought you this—this small gift here. Kind of—kind of silly."

Lily handed it over.

"Oh," Sheri's mother said with a soft laugh. "I love music boxes."

"I remembered," Tyler said.

Sheri called into the house, "Hey!"

"Nick went with your father into town," Mrs. Galatierre said.

There followed a moment of awkward silence, during which Sheri walked out to the car and closed the trunk. Tyler and Lily began bringing in their bags; Sheri held the door for them. Mrs. Galatierre had melted back into the rooms of the house. It was spacious and cool inside, and dim. There were rooms off rooms, hallways leading to small stairs, which opened onto other hallways, and more rooms. The large picture window at the back of the house provided a view of a patio and a swimming pool, a small garden. Beyond this was a wide field, bordered on the far side by a river or a stream, the winding of it going away, in and out of the folds of green hills, as far as you could see. The sun shone in a blinding replication of itself in the farthest curve of the stream. There was a highway overpass at the most distant point of the horizon. Lily saw shimmering movement there.

"That's the highway to Memphis," Sheri said. She led them downstairs, along a hallway to a room opening out onto the patio. "This is my old room. I hope you guys enjoy it."

It was low-ceilinged, with beams, and on one wall there were built-in bookshelves, a large library. Lily went there and looked at some of the titles. There were a lot of the kind of books one purchased from those mail-order houses whose appeal was to the prospective customer's pretensions to culture—gilt-edged, leather-bound editions that were often only decor. But when she took one out to look at it, she saw that the pages had been thumbed through, and there were small pencil marks in the margins.

"I was supposed to take what I needed of these books when I left for college," Sheri said. "Never got around to it."

There was a double bed, a dressing table and mirror, a bureau, two nightstands—all of this at a remove from the books. A rather wide space occupied the center of the room. It was as if the bed and the other furniture were being stored here, under the big window. The whole rest of the house was above them. You could see the flagstone walk just outside, which led up and around to entrances to the other floors. A breeze played across the surface of the water in the swimming pool. To the left of the bed, through an arched doorway, there was a small laundry room, and a door leading up into the kitchen.

"This is your own private entrance to the pool," Sheri said, indicating the sliding glass doors in the back wall. "We use the French doors off the family room."

"I've been married a little more than two days. I don't swim very well, and I don't know if my wife can." He stopped, and his eyes widened slightly, a look of wonderment coming to his face. "God, listen to that. *My wife*. What a strange, wonderful feeling that is, saying that out like that."

"Your wife can swim," Lily told him.

"*She'll* enjoy the pool, then," Sheri said. "Why don't y'all get freshened up and then come on upstairs."

"Where're you and—" Tyler paused. The strangeness of their relation seemed abruptly too evident. "I don't recall that you told me your husband's name."

"His name is Nick." She laughed softly. "Mama said his name not five minutes ago." She gave him an evaluating look. "Are you nervous?"

He shrugged. "Frazzled."

"Well," Sheri said. "The phone's there by the bed. Lily, you can call your folks and tell them you've arrived, if you want. Just dial one and the number. Y'all've got your own bathroom, off that little hallway there." She indicated a space to the right of the bookcase. "I'm gonna head upstairs. There's nothing doing right away, so take your time."

4

WHEN SHE HAD GONE, and the door had clicked shut, the whole feel of the room changed; it was private, now. Theirs. Lily looked out the window at the water rippling lightly in the pool. More than anything else at the moment, she wanted sleep, and she remembered the days of being alone in the little dorm room in Charlottesville, that long sinking. It had been Tyler who had called her out of it. She reached for him, and kissed the side of his face.

"We're actually here," she said. "How does it feel?"

"I'll let you know when I know."

"You *are* nervous."

He nodded, reaching for her. "I am, Lily. Terrified, all of a sudden. Way down. I got in this room and this thing passed over me, like something awful is going to happen, like a premonition. This clammy fear around my heart. I wonder what I was thinking of, coming here."

"You wanted to know your family. And they wanted to know you. It's going to be sweet, Tyler, you'll see."

"Do you love me, Lily?" he said. It was almost plaintive.

She put her arms around him. "So much," she said. They stood there, and she felt little tremors going through him. She held tight. "And they'll love you, too."

"I can't believe I—I never thought I'd feel like such a coward. Or that I'd worry so much about whether or not they'll like me or want me here. It's stupid—they *asked* me here. But, Lily, why did she just disappear like that, back into the house?"

"She probably went to put her music box away, or something like that. She must be nervous, too, don't you think?"

He pondered this, and when his face broke into a smile, the relief was bright in his eyes. "You're very smart, aren't you, about people."

"We're a match for anything," she told him.

"Not me." He kissed her, then went into the bathroom and washed his face. He had opened his suitcase and taken out a shirt, a pair of pants.

She sat on the bed, and ran her hand over the surface of the comforter. Smooth, soft silk, padded thickly. She took the handset from the phone, put it to her ear, with some trepidation that she might overhear someone else's conversation, and was relieved to hear the dial tone. She dialed her mother's number, and Tyler, drying his face, looked at her from the entrance to the bathroom.

The machine answered. "We're here, Doris. I'll give you a call in a couple of days. Please call Daddy and tell him. Love you, 'bye." She put the receiver down.

He came out. "They weren't there?"

"That infernal machine." She took her blouse off, her bra, and then slipped out of her jeans and panties. He sat on the bed and watched. Naked, she felt wonderfully cool and drowsy, and she walked to him, rested her arms on his shoulders. As he kissed her nipples, one and then the other, she ran her hands through his hair. Then he lay back, and she helped him out of his undershorts. They lay crosswise on the bed, and she kissed him. For a soft moment, she was off in some quarter of her being that was separate from anyone, everyone. She made herself look straight into his eyes as he pushed into her, and strove to think herself back to him. Him alone. He murmured her name. She heard it from a long way off, though his mouth was by her ear. She moved her hips, taking him in and in, her hands over his shoulders, holding him close to her.

"God," he said.

She felt him pulse inside her, little spasms. She let go, and something dropped in her, a delicious falling. It went on, and he lay still. She raised her legs, opened wider, and he had stopped. Soon, she let her legs down, and then he pulled out, and rolled over on his back. She lay with her hands at her sides, legs slightly spread.

"My God," he said.

She touched his hip, then took her hand away. "I'm sleepy now."

He said, "Sleep, baby."

But she couldn't sleep. Her ears thrummed with it when she closed her eyes, and yet it wouldn't come. She watched him put his clothes into the bureau and the closet. Her own suitcases were on the floor near the one chair. He threw his empty bags into the bottom of the closet, then turned and flopped down in the chair, still naked.

"Aren't you going to sleep?" she said.

"You sleep. I'm too jittery."

"I'm sleepy, but I can't drop off."

"I'm making noise."

"That wouldn't stop me."

He looked at her. "You're amazingly beautiful."

She smiled, and opened her legs a little more.

"Jesus," he said.

"Want to come back to bed?"

"Aren't you worried about getting pregnant?"

She spoke through a small shiver, thinking of her mother. "I think maybe I just did."

He said nothing.

"Come back to bed," she murmured.

"Do you want kids, Lily?"

"I already told you how I felt about it."

"But do you want kids," he said again.

"What about you?"

He frowned. "Do you think you'll change your mind?"

"How can I know a thing like that? Would it bother you if I got pregnant?"

"A lot depends on what you *want*," he said.

"Well, I guess what I want depends on what *you* want."

"Lily—" he said, then stopped.

"What?"

"Nothing."

"Well—come take me, sir," she said.

5

A LITTLE LATER, she murmured, "I guess we should go upstairs."

"It's awful quiet."

"Shouldn't we go on up?" she asked.

He said, "I'm sorry—but I don't really feel like facing Mrs. Galatierre just now."

"If you don't mind, I *am* going to try and sleep some, then."

"Let's both do."

She turned to her side and closed her eyes. There was the rushing sound in her ears; the sheets were fresh and cool. He sat up, and when she looked at him over her shoulder, she saw that while his expression was that of someone calmly awaiting whatever would happen next, his hands shook—the slightest trembling. He looked back at her and smiled, and she smiled back. She closed her eyes again, and listened to the sounds of movement in the rooms above. The rushing came to her ears again, a deep whoosh. And she was asleep, dreaming of Dominic; she was wandering the streets of Charlottesville, looking for him. Then she was being looked for, trying to hide. Dominic was somewhere behind her, trailing along in her wake. It was a game. And then it was bad, and it was a heavy, drumming force, weighing her down. She opened her eyes and saw Tyler rearranging his socks in the top of the bureau. He was setting them in by color, folding each into its mate in exactly the same shape. She watched him meticulously fold all his undershirts and shorts. Then he moved to the closet and arranged his slacks, his sport shirts, jackets, and ties, attending to everything with a fussiness that made him seem rather absurd. It endeared him to her, with his boyish expression of intent concentration.

"What're you doing?" she said, or thought she said. He hadn't heard her. She closed her eyes, and he kept working, and she felt sleep come on once more, and when she woke up, two hours later, she wasn't sure she hadn't dreamed the whole thing.

He was gone. The house was quiet. She came to a sitting position in the bed and was momentarily dizzy. She stood, reached for her suitcase, feeling abruptly naked, exposed in the bigness of the room, in this strange house. She carried clean clothes into the bathroom, then stepped back out and opened his bureau drawer. There it all was, arranged, set in a tidiness that filled her with a proprietary affection, and then a little wave of guilt, because, she realized, it was as if she had spied on him in some private foible.

6

*Up*STAIRS, she found an empty house. She padded from room to room on the first level—a large dining room with dark-cherry furniture, cabinets filled with crystal and china; a long, low-ceilinged living room with another wide window overlooking the pool and the fields, the low hills through which the river ran. She felt like an intruder. When she entered the living room, she had a fleeting, unbidden sense that someone would sit up from the sofa there and look at her. Out the window, beyond the hills, the sky was red, now. There were wet patches on the flagstones surrounding the pool. It must have rained. She went down a hallway that opened onto the kitchen, and there a young black woman sat at a small round table, breaking off the ends of string beans and dropping them into an aluminum bowl. When she saw Lily, she gave forth a little startled cry.

"Oh, good God—but you frightened me."

"Me, too," Lily said. "I didn't expect to see anyone."

The other woman shook her head, and ran one hand across her forehead. The other hand she had rested, just the tips of the fingers, on her chest.

"I'm awfully sorry," said Lily, catching her own breath.

"You must be the young prodigal's bride."

Lily nodded. "He's not exactly prodigal, is he?"

"That's what he called himself, not ten minutes ago."

"Where are they?" Lily asked.

"Town. They thought you'd sleep all day."

She looked at the clock. Almost twenty minutes to six. The other young woman had resumed methodically breaking off the ends of the beans and tossing them into the bowl. For a moment Lily felt that she must have trespassed, that she should make her way back to another part of the house. But then the other paused, and smiled. "My name's Rosa." She stood and wiped her hands on her apron, and extended a hand. "Forgive my rudeness. I'm still trying to get over my fright."

Lily said her own name, then: "Need help?"

"With this? No." Rosa sat down and began breaking off the ends of the beans again.

There seemed nothing left to say.

"Sit down, why don't you."

Lily took the chair across from her. The smell of the beans was strong; they carried the fragrance of earth, and grass.

"Where you from?" Rose said.

"Virginia."

"Spent part of my childhood there. In Richmond. Ever been to Richmond?"

"A few times. I have some family there—cousins of my mother."

"We moved here when I was ten," Rosa said. "My parents, two sisters, and me. I'm putting myself through Ole Miss."

"What're you studying?"

"Domestic service."

"Pardon me?"

The other woman laughed, a whispery sound deep in her throat. "Just checking to see how close you're listening to me. A lot of people they bring in here don't see anybody but the black lady maid when they look at me, you know?"

"I'm sorry," Lily said, without quite understanding why she felt the necessity of apologizing.

"You didn't do a thing to be sorry for. I'm sorry for putting you to the test."

A moment later, Lily said, "What *are* you studying?" And they both laughed.

"I'm a history major. I'd like to teach it."

"What period?"

"Nineteenth century, mostly. The Victorians. I have an interest in the Cold War, too. Russian history, and the Industrial Revolution. A little of the Civil War, of course."

"You must know about Mary Kingsley," Lily said.

The other woman's face seemed to brighten. "I read her book—

Travels in West Africa. My family comes from there—way back, of course. The Gabon River. More than two hundred years back. I traced it when I was in high school. Roots, you know?" This was said with an abashed, small smile. "My parents were pretty big on all that. I'm named after Ms. Parks."

"I can't explain it," Lily said. "But the very first time I ever looked at a photograph of her, something happened to me. It was as if I recognized her from somewhere. Does that make any sense?"

"Maybe you knew her in another life."

"I don't mean it like that, though. I'm not doing a very good job of expressing it."

The other woman left a pause, tossing the beans into the bowl, working along. Lily absently reached across and started doing it, too. "Do your parents still live here in Oxford?" she asked.

"My daddy lives in Bakersfield, California, now and my mama lives in Italy. They're separated but not divorced. That's how they describe it. They haven't been in the same room for about three years. Different interests."

Lily heard herself say, "My father had an affair with someone who worked with him. He divorced my mother and married her. A woman my age, who's pregnant now."

"Damn," Rosa said.

Now there was an embarrassed silence. "I must still be half asleep, blurting all that out at you like that. I wouldn't blame you if you felt a little put upon by it."

"Hey, it's okay with me if it's okay with you."

"Well," Lily said. "Nice meeting you."

"Folks'll be home any second," said Rosa.

In the other rooms there were trophies in cases—hunting, shooting, baseball, track and field—and photographs of a big, barrel-chested man standing with other, smaller men in various amateur sporting groups: baseball teams, basketball teams, football teams. There were other photographs of this same man holding up a stringer of fish, or standing next to the strung-up sleekness of a marlin; or kneeling, rifle in hand, over the carcass of a bear. This bear was no doubt the same one that now was a rug in the middle of the floor in the den, a wide room containing heavy leather chairs, oak side tables, carousels of books, and a big glass trophy case. At the center of one pine-paneled wall hung the head of an elk. Opposite that was a flagstone fireplace, flanked by still another large window overlooking the pool, the field, and the far stream beyond. The stream showed its glimmer of reflected sky. Lily read the inscription below the marlin that was mounted above the mantel: "Caught by Millicent Galatierre in the Gulf Stream, July 12, 1981. Fought him for three hours, forty-seven minutes. Presented by her husband, Brendan, August 1, 1981."

There was sound now, on the porch. She heard Rosa come through the kitchen, and saw her cross the hall. They were all arriving. There was the familiar uproar of Sheri's arrival anywhere, her voice carrying down the hall. Lily waited. Tyler walked in, carrying a paper bag full of bottles of gin and whiskey and brandy. "You're up," he said, going on into the kitchen. Sheri entered then, followed by her mother. "You look rested," Mrs. Galatierre said. Her voice was low, supple. She walked across the small span of floor to embrace Lily. There was a youthful leanness in her arms. "I hope you already feel at home, dear."

Tyler stood in the entrance of the room, holding a bottle of whiskey and a glass with ice in it. "Anybody want a drink?" he said.

EIGHT

1

*T*HEY SAT OUT ON THE PATIO, next to the pool. The sun had gone to the other side of the house. Tyler went into the shallow end for a few minutes. Sheri dove in and swam underwater across the length, and came up next to her half brother. "Boo."

"Hey, I want my inflatable water wings," Tyler said, reaching for the side. She went under again, swimming away from him. "I've been deep-sea fishing and I like being on boats," Tyler said. "But I never really liked being in the water." He got down, so that only his head showed above the surface. His movements were uncoordinated and slow. He stood finally and came out, and dried off. Sheri dove from the board. She had been trained to do different dives. Her mother remarked to Lily that she had won prizes in high school competitions.

"She's very good," Lily said, marveling to herself at the fact that Sheri, with her way of telling things about herself, had never mentioned that she had this skill.

After a long interval of diving and swimming to the ladder and diving again, Sheri came out of the water and flopped down on the glider next to her mother. Tyler assumed the role of bartender. There was something faintly hectic about his demeanor, and Lily watched him with an ache. He made a whiskey sour for Sheri. Lily had a glass of wine, as did Millicent Galatierre. Rosa asked when they wanted dinner, and was told that it would have to wait until Buddy and Nick returned from town. "Join us," Mrs. Galatierre said. "Tyler's fixing drinks."

"Got studying to do, thanks," said Rosa.

They all watched her go back into the house.

"How long has she been with you?" Tyler said.

His mother smiled. "Three years—a little more than three years."

Then they seemed all to be waiting for something to occur to them as a subject for conversation. Sheri remarked on the chlorine content of the water, and Tyler spoke about new alternatives to the chemical. Mrs. Galatierre said they had a regular pool person who maintained things, and Sheri teased about how handsome and sexy the pool person was. Mrs. Galatierre looked at Lily and in an amused voice said the pool person was a woman. The talk went on for a while in this vein. It was oddly without any context, seemed to slip from subject to subject, banter between friends, except that it was also uneasy. Sheri told stories about growing up in a place like Oxford, with its ugly past. She talked about high school and about college, too. It was a strange hour. Lily watched Tyler, who spoke about the look of the house, the beautiful, shallow valley that surrounded them, and she thought about Sheri's worry that he had made this journey to cause trouble. He was so obviously trying to be casual and friendly, and so visibly—at least to Lily, anyway—worried about what they might be thinking. He got up to make himself another whiskey. For a little space there was the sound of his voice and Rosa's, exchanging pleasantries in the kitchen.

Sheri sipped her drink, rattled the ice in her glass, and without looking at Mrs. Galatierre said, "You'd think he'd say something."

Mrs. Galatierre glanced at Lily.

Sheri rattled the ice again. "You'd think *you'd* say something."

Millicent Galatierre turned to Lily. "My daughter lacks a sense of propriety about certain things. Perhaps you've noticed."

"Well, it's like you lived a fuck'n *soap opera*," Sheri said, low. The drink had gone to her head.

"Sheri, please," Millicent said. "Remember yourself."

"Was the pool here when you bought the house?" Lily asked.

"No. Buddy had it built."

"I was thirteen before I even knew Tyler existed," Sheri said to Lily. "Can yew *imagine*?"

"I think I might ask for another glass of wine," Lily said to her. "So I can catch up with you." She touched the other woman's arm, meaning to reassure her that this was a joke.

"I'd sure like to know what he's thinking," Sheri said.

"He's an adult. He wants to establish ties with his family. He's going to be working for Buddy. He doesn't have to be thinking anything else. Can't you see that he's nervous about what you-all think?"

"Well, you'd think he'd *say* something about it."

They were quiet for a time. Tyler's laugh came to them from the kitchen; they couldn't hear Rosa.

"I'm gonna ask him myself," Sheri said.

"You will stop," said Millicent, reaching across the small space to take hold of Sheri's wrist. "That is enough. You're embarrassing me."

Sheri looked at her, then looked at where her wrist was held. When her mother let go, she sat back and took the last of her drink, then began to chew an ice cube with a cracking, jaw-breaking sound.

"How did you ever stand this girl as a roommate," Mrs. Galatierre said to Lily.

"We got along great," Sheri said with her mouthful of ice. "I don't mean anything bad. I'm just worried, that's all."

Tyler returned from the kitchen with another glass of whiskey. He sat down at the edge of the shade.

"Did Buddy kill that bear in there on the floor?" he asked quietly.

"Yes."

"Wow. We never hunted anything as big or as dangerous as a bear."

Lily realized that he was talking about his father.

"Buddy only did it that once—when he was a boy. That bear is thirty years old."

"Oh, Jesus Christ," Sheri said. She got up and moved unsteadily toward the house. "I'm gonna take a nap." She went inside, letting the screen door slap to behind her.

"Is she all right?" Tyler asked.

2

Buddy Galatierre arrived after dark, with his son-in-law. He was a tall man, with a muscular chest and powerful shoulders and arms. He had a full head of gray hair, combed back, and bushy grayish eyebrows that gave his ruddy face a look of perpetual questioning. Nick Green was not as tall as his father-in-law, but lanky and thin-faced, with sharp features, thick blue-black hair, and a sallow complexion. There were shadows under his deep-set gray eyes, giving him a dour, brooding expression. Both men had been drinking. You could smell it on them, and Sheri's husband was a little loud with it, rocking on his heels. His hand when Lily shook it was cold and limp, unpleasantly clammy. She thought in the same instant of sex videos and of some other man, the platonic friend of his wife. She regretted knowing anything about him at all, and worried that it might show in her demeanor. Mr. Galatierre bowed to her in perfect eighteenth-century fashion and then took the same hand that she had withdrawn from Nick Green and kissed the back of it. His expression seemed to say that he understood how unlikable the experience of Green's damp handshake had been. When he spoke, he addressed the other man. "That's how it's done around here, Nickie." Then he turned to Tyler. "Well, young man. How good to see you."

"Sir," Tyler said, his voice a tiny increment higher than normal. Lily stood at his side and put her hand inside his elbow.

Tyler and Buddy shook hands. "You ready to go to work?" Buddy said.

"Yes, sir."

"We need an infusion of youth," Mr. Galatierre said.

Tyler nodded, and appeared a little confused, and shy. Lily squeezed his arm.

"You know, I was premed for a time, too," Mr. Galatierre said.

"No, sir, I didn't know that."

"Well, no, of course."

"Jesus Christ," Sheri said. "Can we eat dinner now?"

Rosa had set the table, and Mrs. Galatierre had said to go ahead and serve it. They had all been seated at the table when the two men came in.

"We'll be right back down," Sheri's husband said. "I've got to go wash up."

"How much have you had to drink, tonight, Nick?" said Sheri.

Mrs. Galatierre said, "Sheri."

"It's all right," Nick said, "Mama."

"And please don't call her *Mama*," Sheri said. But Nick had gone out of the room and was already on the stairs. Buddy Galatierre followed, shambling unsteadily, calling to Rosa to fix him a Tom Collins, please, if it wasn't too much of a bother.

Tyler was standing by the table, holding his own drink, staring after him with all the open-faced curiosity of a child. Then he turned and regarded his mother. "I bet," Sheri said, "you'd like to have the whole story." She rested both elbows on the table, hands up to support her head on either side, grinning at him.

"I think I—that is—I know the story, Sheri."

Their mother sighed, and said, low, "Sheri, you've had too much to drink."

Rosa brought in the dinner—roast beef and gravy, mashed potatoes, green beans, corn bread, and salad. She had cut the beef into thin slices. Mrs. Galatierre took two, and passed the plate to Sheri, who passed it on to Tyler without taking any.

"Sheri," Mrs. Galatierre said. "You should put something on your stomach."

"I'm not hungry anymore."

"Well, then perhaps you should leave the table."

Sheri did nothing. Tyler held the plate of meat and waited. Sheri remained as she was. And then her husband came to the entrance of the room.

"I'm afraid Mr. Galatierre will not be down for supper," Nick Green said. "Mr. Galatierre is sleeping in his clothes across the foot of his bed. I just left him there."

Millicent came to her feet. "All right, Nick. Sit down and have something to eat, please." She looked at Tyler and at Lily. "I hope you can forgive us for this." She left the table and went upstairs. Rosa called to her from the hallway, "You want me to keep it warm?"

The answer was lost in the clatter of Sheri's husband pulling a chair out and sitting down, folding his arms on the table and staring across at his wife. "What's wrong with Missy, here?" he said.

"Don't call me that," said Sheri. "I've told you a thousand times."

"Ah, the fever of love is on her."

Sheri got up and left the room, evading his reach. He got shakily to his feet and made as if to follow her, then seemed to think better of it. He sat down and smiled, then reached across the table, offering his hand to Lily. "Don't believe we've met."

"We've met," Lily said. "You were quite gallant and it was very pleasant."

"Really? I don't seem to recall. But then I'm blitzed. Did we shake hands?"

"You kissed my hand." She gave Tyler a look, and he grinned.

"Wait a minute," Nick said. "No, no—you don't fool me. Hey, Buddy kissed your hand. I *shook* your hand. And I'm truly contrite about that because I know my hands get clammy when I've had too much to drink. So my esteemed wife has told me."

For a few moments, no one said anything. Rosa walked in and put portions of everything on Mrs. Galatierre's plate, then took it back into the kitchen. Sheri's husband had helped himself, and was eating wolfishly, as if alone. Tyler and Lily began slowly to eat, watching him, and occasionally sending each other a sidelong glance. Nick stuffed his mouth with corn bread that he had dipped in the gravy. His cheeks bulged, and he seemed to be communing with himself, nodding and muttering under his breath. Then he stopped and looked at Lily.

"You're absolutely sure we met before?"

"About fifteen minutes ago. We were being held prisoner by the evil duke. You released us."

He smiled, nodding. Then he frowned, and seemed to be thinking something over. "And we shook hands."

"You shook hands," Tyler said. "Right."

"God, I'm sorry. Forgive the handshake."

"It's forgiven," Lily said, and folded her arms. It was, she realized, a gesture he might interpret to mean she didn't want to shake hands again.

He did exactly that, nodding, and saying, "I don't blame you." Then he turned to Tyler. "And you? Did I shake hands with you?"

"No," Tyler said. "You kissed my hand."

"Damn." Nick laughed, pointing.

"You're forgiven."

Lily broke forth with a laugh, and then suppressed it. Nick shrugged, and kept on eating, shaking his head now. He took a long drink of the water that Rosa had poured for everyone, then leaned forward in his chair and called out, "Rosa, how 'bout some beer?"

There was no answer from the kitchen. He waited a moment, staring at the door, then picked his napkin out of his lap, threw it down, and stood. "Service around this place leaves something to be desired, you may have noticed." Carefully, he made his way to the kitchen door and, pushing it open, held it. "Rosa?" He went on through, and the door swung shut. Lily and Tyler were alone in the dining room, and the whole house seemed to be breathing with the collective vexations, tensions, and absurdities they had just witnessed.

"Christ," Tyler said, shaking his head. "Nothing like a little pathology to help me relax into things."

"I wonder if it's like this all the time," Lily murmured. "Are you sure you want to stay here?"

Sheri walked back in from the foyer, moved slowly to her chair, and sat down. She didn't look at them.

"Hey, Sheri," Tyler said. "What is it? You were so happy to see us this morning."

Sheri said nothing.

Nick Green came out of the kitchen carrying a six-pack of sixteen-ounce cans of beer by the elastic strap that held them together. One can was missing from it; he held that one in his other hand, and took a long drink, putting his head back, before he settled into his chair. The cans clattered on the table when he set them down. "Well," he said to Sheri. "You do look sexy. If I was a drinking man, I might be forced to make a pass at you." He finished the one beer and opened another, laughing softly to himself.

"Oh please shut up, Nick."

He went on laughing for a time, turning his head from side to side in time with it all, then he drank from the new can, and began to eat again, soaking more corn bread in the beef gravy.

"Sheri," Tyler said. "Did I say or do something to offend you?"

"We're all grown up," Sheri said sadly. "And now we can all be friends. Is that it?"

"You tell me," Tyler said quietly. "I really don't understand."

She said nothing.

"Your father offered me a job and I took it. And I'm here."

Lily said, "Your mother seems all right about it. Just as you said she was." Sheri looked at her as if her presence was surprising.

"I'm worried about everything," Sheri muttered. "It's my nature lately—don't take it too seriously." She hiccupped.

Nick Green looked at her and laughed, opening another of the cans of beer. "I sold five cars today, sugar. I'm bad, bad, double bad. Five in one day." He drank. "I believe I just may have a future in sales, yes indeed. A big future in sales. Is there anything sexier than a salesman on a roll?"

"You mean a drunk salesman on a roll?" Sheri said.

"Hey." He held up the beer. "I sold five cars. It's a record."

"Is that what you were celebrating?" Sheri said. "This time?"

"Hey, you unhappy, sugar?"

She looked down.

"Your excellent father and I were celebrating everything tonight. The arrival of new family, the fixing up of you and me, as it were, the sale of five units in one day, and—and—" He stopped, wavered slightly, took another drink of the beer. "Hell, we were celebrating just being alive in this particular summer of our Lord."

Rosa came in from the kitchen and began, with a certain abruptness, to clear the dishes away. Lily stood up to help, and the other woman said, "That won't be necessary."

"I'm not finished eating yet," Nick said. "As the great Irish poet Mr. Yeats said so well, 'Don't fuck with me when I'm eating.'"

Rosa didn't answer him, but went on clearing away the other places, cleaning around him as he continued to eat. Lily watched this and suddenly felt hemmed in, no place to go in the house for fear that she might come upon a scene. She sat still, not eating, and when Rosa came to her and hesitated, she said, "Oh, I'm through."

"You never got started," Rosa said gently, taking her plate away.

Nick settled back in his chair and ran his hands over his stomach, then emitted a long, low belch.

Sheri said, "For God's sweet sake."

"I apologize from the bottom of my heart."

"So," Tyler said. "How did you and Sheri meet?"

"Met in high school," the other man said. He clasped his hands on top of his head and gazed across the table at Sheri, who was running her hands through her hair and not looking at anyone. "There I was, the school's budding high achiever—running the school newspaper, writing stories and poems for the literary journal, all in the mistaken belief that it would make Missy fall into my arms. But Sheri wouldn't have anything to do with me. Felt she was above me. Which, of course, as we can all very plainly see, she, um, *is*." He sighed, and reached over to touch her shoulder. She pulled away, but there was a faint smile on her face, as if she were being bothered by a child. "Nothing worked," Nick went on. "Until she came home from the University of Virginia, having learned that living in the Upper South causes abscessed teeth and infections and systemic bad grades. Isn't that right, Missy?"

"Oh, Nick, why don't you please go to bed and sleep it off," Sheri said.

Casually, Tyler reached across the table and tore one of the beers out of the plastic ring. "Do you mind?"

"Hell no. I'm happy to share it. There's more in the kitchen."

Lily took one, too, and opened it. She and Tyler drank.

"Now we're getting the right start," Nick said. He turned to Sheri. "Come on, sugar. You have one, too."

She took the last one, muttering, "If I have one, it's one less for you."

"The spirit of sacrifice. That's my sugar cookie. God bless her." He held his can up as if to toast Sheri, who ignored him, drinking hers. He touched her arm, then folded his hands in his lap and looked at Tyler. "You ever notice, women never forget a thing. Not one single goddamn thing."

"No, I never did notice that," Tyler said.

"Well, you'll learn it." He smiled, and shook his head. "Heh. Boy, you will soon learn that." He looked at Sheri. "Won't he learn that, sugar?"

"Please go sleep it off," Sheri said.

"I ain't got a thing to sleep off, sugar. I'm sober as an elementary school teacher on Monday. How much have you had to drink today?"

"I knew it when Mama said you and Daddy had gone into town. I knew exactly what this night would be."

"Well, you're something. You're—what's the word? *Prescient.* I believe that is the word. It's a word, by the way, that I would never use on a customer."

Tyler gulped beer from his can, then yawned. "I'm beat."

"Shit," said Nick. "It's not even nine o'clock. Don't you people watch television?"

"We're both tired," Lily said.

"Sheri won't watch it, either. Will you, Sheri?"

Sheri didn't answer.

"I said, 'Will you,' sugar?"

Lily wanted to scream at him. But then it seemed that the house itself, the walls, contained some form of unspoken mischief; everyone baiting everyone else because of something tainted in the air that seeped through the joists and beams, the cornices and lintels and wainscoting of the place. Nick Green, apparently watching her gaze wander over the walls of the room, now explained that this very old and drafty house had been built by a slave owner way back in 1842. He sat back in his chair and regarded the angles of ceiling and molding, entrance hall and windows, with a sodden, appreciative sigh. "There's a small crookedness in the fireplace, that you can see if you look for it—the angle of the mantel lists slightly to one side, and we don't know if it settled this way over time, or if the original builder got it wrong—you know, miscalculated in some way, exactly as he, uh, miscalculated so many other things: the future, for instance, and the inevitable death of the institution through which he, ah, this distant somebody, achieved the wealth to build such a house in the first place. His name—we know—was Thomas Bilbain. He built the house and lived in it until he died, in 1858. Think of it—guy never saw the end of slavery. His son Joshua fought with Forrest, came out unscathed, and then died with Custer, believe that or not. Guy went to observe. Imagine it. He paid a big price for his curiosity. Anyway, his younger brother Percival kept the house into old age, and then sold it in 1903, to a watchmaker named—hell, honey, what was the name of the watchmaker? Shit. Millhausen, or Munchausen, some German guy who died here after about forty years of solitude and letting everything go. Place was empty for almost twenty years. Somebody tried to make a run at it selling antiques, but that didn't last long. And then Sheri's daddy bought it for a song the year Sheri was born. This luxury is what Sheri grew up with. And people of my daddy's generation used to bring girl-friends here when it was empty. Think of that. Hell, I might've been conceived here if it'd been anybody else than my daddy."

"Nick," Sheri said. "Please. That's enough now."

He laughed. "Someday I'd like to go into the county offices and find out more about the first guy. Bilbain. If I wasn't so damn good at selling cars, I might could be a literary figure. Write a book about the slave owner Bilbain. Who came into life and lived it with slaves and went out of it with slaves. We're all so used to the cataclysm of the Civil War and the dividing line and all that, and thousands of people lived and died in the old system and never really knew they were perpetuating a crime against humanity."

"You don't think they knew?" Lily said.

"Well, it was Washington who said 'I tremble to think that God is Just.'"

"It was Jefferson," said Lily.

"No."

"I think it was Jefferson," Tyler said. "It doesn't sound like Washington."

Nick looked at Sheri. "Your vote?"

"I don't care," she said, rising.

"Hell," said Nick. "I'm always getting the founding fathers and mothers mixed up. Yesterday I thought Martha Washington was Jefferson."

"I'm going to bed," Sheri said. She looked at Lily and mouthed the words, "I'm sorry."

Mrs. Galatierre came into the room looking composed, but with effort. One strand of her hair had come loose, and trailed down the left side of her face. She said, "I'm so sorry for all this. I meant us to have a nice welcome-home dinner." Her expression was impassive, almost serene—but there was the slight disarray of her hair.

"I'm gonna go watch some television," Nick said. "If I said or did anything that offended anybody, I apologize." He left the table. Before he went out of the room he turned. "Sheri, want to join me?"

She stood, without speaking, and followed him out.

"I'm sure it's been a strange evening for you both," Millicent Galatierre said, without quite looking at either Lily or Tyler. "I know it has been for me. We aren't usually so close to the surface with our emotions around here."

NINE

1

November 1878

Dear—someone,

A cow wandered into the lane in back this morning. I call this lane *"the sporting region"* because of what is likely to wander in there—it's even bandied about here that burglars use it. Mother is slightly less ill these days. Father will be home soon from his American expedition, and so she won't have to worry about him. I couldn't get the cow to move. It stared at me and blinked, and looked stubbornly calm.

—Shoo! I said. I didn't want to get too close. Shoo! My gamecocks strolled under its hooves and it stood there and tolerated this. Nothing ordinary in life, but that it achieves an exotic cast when set in incongruous circumstances—this bovine, chewing and staring in the lane, blocking egress. Mother saw it from the window and was frantic, worried that it might damage the garden, such as it is. I went inside and took the broom from Mrs. Barrett, who thought it was a sign from God, since the church bells were ringing again—somebody's wedding. I swatted the cow across the backside with the broom and it lumbered into the fence, almost took it down, then advanced farther into the yard, Mother screaming from the window.

—It's just a cow, I said. For God's sake, darling. Close your window and draw the curtain. There were people stopping in the street. She kept ̣elling. Then she was laughing, and I laughed, too. Our own hysteria ̣uses us sometimes. It's a predicament we share. We look and feel silly to ̣other and we laugh.

̣nally I convinced our ruminant friend that it wasn't such a good ̣ccupy the Kingsley yard, and off the poor thing went, stupid and ̣d as a very big barrel, and crook-legged and aimless. Mother ̣th her steadiest self and closed the window, and I was alone in ̣ ̣ my weapon, my broomstick, like the witches in all the old sto- ̣ mud on the hem of my dress, which Mrs. Barrett bothered to

—Thank you ever so much, Mrs. Barrett.

Oh, silent friend, if you ever come to read this, I am writing you from a gray day at the end of a cold, rainy fall in a country called Britain, and I am sequestered in my room, looking out over Highgate. I am presently six-teen years old. I do not know where my life will end. I have no sense that it leads anywhere but here, and I have such desires, friend.

2

*M*ARY'S FATHER is set to arrive from America, and she and Charley travel by coach, south, through Surrey and Hants, to Southampton, to meet him. They spend the night in an inn at the edge of a small village above Winchester. There are revelers in the tavern below, and their songs rise through the loose floorboards. Mary lies awake, hearing it, and then realizes that for some time she has been listening to silence. She must have slept. She goes to the window and sees that it has snowed in the night. The sky's clear now, and starry, and there's a bright moon. The fields are white, pristine. One black horse stands near the crest of the nearest hill. She watches it walk out of view, then reappear farther along, toward where a body of water shimmers with silver light. It takes her breath away. It's so different from the confines of Highgate.

In the morning, they have bread-and-butter pudding for breakfast, and Charley drinks a cup of strong coffee. It's a bright, freezing, early December day, and the sky is a rich, dark, cloudless winter blue. An unreal blue. Where it snowed, last night, and the road was slogged with mud and slush, there are now heavy, dry, frozen ruts in the surface. Even though the wheels of this coach are equipped with springs, the ride is rough. Charley feels sick to his stomach, and sits back against the padded seat with his hat over his face. He wants air. Mary's cold, but she opens the curtain, and the chilly wind rushes in. They pass Guildford, and ride through the lovely countryside north of Winchester, and Mary takes in the icy air, thinking of the miles gliding away slowly under the wheels, the distance opening from London. She thinks of her father approaching the channel from the vast reaches of the sea, coming home.

Southampton's brittle-looking in the sunlight—old, and intricately laced with white borders of snow—snow still on the window frames and doorways, still stacked atop the towers and dormers—and the narrow streets are rutted even more deeply than the country roads. Mary sees the shop fronts, and the signs rattling and swinging in the bright wind. Crooked columns of coal smoke rise from chimneys, above brick buildings so dark with soot they look charred. The houses on the outskirts are tightly surrounded by the winter brown of shrubs and the dark green of pines, and the gray-blue splendor of spruces. The outbuildings look like afterthoughts. They ride through the busy streets, toward land's end, where the darker line of the ocean makes the sky seem almost pale by comparison. But for this, the town might as well be London.

The harbor's a thicket of masts. A thousand smaller boats rock in the tide, up close. Rats scurry among the piles of refuse on the dock. The coachman stops the horses, and Mary gets out alone, even as Charley scolds her for it. He looks really very much the worse for wear, his eyes glazed over, his skin pale, with a greenish cast.

—Please wait here, Mary says to the coachman, who gets down from his perch and turns his back on them, tending to the horses. The coachman had wanted a half sovereign, and Mary has given him only a crown.

—Are you about to be sick? Mary asks Charley.

—Shut it, he says.

They're standing in a crowd of others. There's already a ship at anchor, but it isn't *The Mercury*. An old man tells Charley that it's a merchant vessel, bound for India, *The Aria*. You can't quite make out the letters on the bow for the algae attached to it. Some men are slung in ropes, working at it all with rags and brushes. Mary and Charley go into a small dram house, and sit at a table in the window, which looks out at the bustle and confusion of the harbor.

Charley orders spiced tea, and drinks it down fast, as if worried that the potboy might change his mind and ask for it back.

—I wonder if Dunraven will come with him to the 'ouse, Mary says.

Charley gives her a look.

—Sound your aitches.

—What's got into you?

Charley puts his hands up to his face.

—I don't want conversation, now, please, he says.

She waits a moment. Out the window, she sees a sail on the narrow band of horizon visible through the slowly rocking vessels.

—Is that *The Mercury?*

Charley squints.

—No.

Mary stares at one of the docked ships, and then reaches across the table to take his hand.

—What?

—It's already in. Already 'ere. *The Mercury.* See it? The fourth one down. I can see the letters on the bow.

Charley stares, then sits back and looks around them.

—He's already come in? Then where is he?

Mary stands, pays the proprietor, and goes back outside. Charley steps up behind her. They cross to the edge of the dock and walk along it, toward the ship.

—Mary, wait for me, he says.

There are too many people. They have to jostle and push their way along. When they reach the quay ramp with its docked tug, they see George Kingsley standing with Lord Dunraven and several other passengers, all looking pale and shaken. Mary approaches, hurrying ahead of Charley, who reaches for her arm to detain her. Their father sees them in that instant, and his face changes, becomes more starkly itself. Mary sees the bones of his cheeks, the gray in his hair. He looks played out, spent. Charley shoulders in front of Mary, proud of his new height, and gives their father a manly handshake. Mary, forgetting herself, throws her arms around his neck.

—Father! It strikes her again, disturbingly, that he's mortal, and that even if he has escaped slaughter on the savage, faraway plains of America, he will eventually be taken from her. She tries to hold tight, and he takes her wrists, forcing them down to her sides. He gazes at her in obvious disbelief.

—These, he says to Lord Dunraven, are my children.

Dunraven bows chivalrously, though there is also about his expression the dim appearance of someone who has discharged a necessary but not altogether pleasant duty. He's a big, heavy man with dark-red hair and thick red side-whiskers. His face has an odd slung-forward appearance, and Mary realizes after the first few moments that he has an overbite, which he is at some pains to conceal—with his hands, with a sort of forced jutting of his jaw, and with talk. When he talks, the overbite is not so obvious. His teeth are squarish and yellow, and seem too large for his mouth. His eyes are so deep set that he appears to have a permanent squint.

Mary is quite certain that she has never seen anyone uglier than Lord Dunraven.

—We had a death onboard, George Kingsley says in a somber voice to Mary. The ship's captain died of apoplexy. The first mate brought us in. The chap was leading us in the Sunday prayer, and dropped over dead in mid-sentence. He didn't even look surprised. No expression on his face at all, nothing on the other side of the eyes. They emptied out, reflected light, and he went over like a sack of feed.

—Look here, Kingsley, let me take you people to London in my carriage, Dunraven says. I have some business to transact there. You can have all your specimens and your artifacts brought up in a wagon, correct? Come along with me, why don't you.

George Kingsley turns to him with something of the air of an excited boy. He stammers:

—Why, that would be wonderful, sir.

—We've already paid for a coach and four, Mary says, low.

Mr. Kingsley stares at his daughter for a moment.

—Well, dismiss it. Why didn't you bring the brougham? We have a perfectly workable carriage, Mary. He faces Lord Dunraven again, and seems ill at ease.

—We discharged Mr. Bethwaite, Father. And the horses have been sold to pay for Charley's school.

—Enough, girl, their father says. Such details are tedious. We shall hire a new hostler and there's an end of it.

Mary walks over and dismisses the hired coach, while George Kingsley arranges with the harbormaster to have everything taken up to London in a wagon. This takes some time. Mary joins Charley, and Dunraven, who stands waiting, one hand on his hip, the other in the side pocket of his coat. The coat is a shade of reddish brown out of which his hair seems to grow, as if sprung from the cloth of the collar. He sees Mary gazing at him, and turns slightly away, evidently impatient at having to wait. Then he looks back, and sees that she's still watching him.

—Look here, he says.

But then her father walks up, and they all make their way out of the dock area, past the public house and on, to a long line of wagons and carriages at the entrance to the harbor. Dunraven's black coach is there, attended to by a pair of young men. Mary and Charley climb in first, followed by their father. Dunraven gives some instructions to the two coachmen, then climbs in himself. He and George Kingsley sit across from Mary and her brother.

—You've gotten to be quite a tall girl, Mary's father says.

She nods politely, but doesn't speak. And then she senses Charley's bruised feelings, not to have been noticed.

—Charley, too, she says.

—Yes, I did see that, too.

Charley prods her surreptitiously with his elbow, and when she turns to him, he gives her a look that expresses his disaffection with her for saying anything.

The coach seems even more unstable on its springs than the one she hired for the journey down here.

They ride along in the jarring quiet. Dunraven has a distinct line running across his forehead where a hat had shaded that part of his head from the sun. Below the line, he's ruddy and healthy-looking; above it he's paste-white, and the contrast, along with his deep-set eyes, makes him appear to be frowning deeply.

—What are you staring at, young miss? You've been staring at me all along.

—Forgive me, Mary says.

Dunraven lifts his chin slightly, a gesture of dismissal. He begins to talk about Disraeli. The Jew, he calls him.

—Really, Kingsley, the entire matter of Victoria being named empress of India. Do we call her empress? This is the British Empire, is it not? I fail to see the benefit of calling our queen the empress of India. The thing sounds wrong. Why, it's as if we have a wog on the throne of England.

—I quite agree, sir.

They go on to talk about the fighting in the Balkans. The Russians have declared war on Turkey, and invaded Rumania. They've crossed the Danube. The trade routes to India are threatened. In Lord Dunraven's opinion, everything is Benjamin Disraeli's fault. Disraeli has recently been named Earl of Beaconsfield by the queen.

—The man's a fool. A foppish dilettante and a writer of silly romances and novels. I have heard people referring in conversation to articles about his books, and they sound to me to be quite absurd.

—I've read the books themselves, Mary says. Did you read *Lothair*? Do you know *Sybil*, or the *Two Nations*?

Dunraven stares, but doesn't answer.

—Well, 'ave you read them or not? Mary says.

George Kingsley reaches across the small space of the closed coach and slaps her. The blow is delivered with very little force, but Mary feels it, like an imprint of his hand, for miles, burning. She says nothing more. The carriage pitches and tilts along the rutted country roads, heading northeast. They go past Winchester and on, to a country inn she hadn't seen on the journey south. The day's clouding over, threatening more snow. The carriage stops in the rattle of wheels on paving stones, and the sneezing of the horses, the clatter of their hooves. The land surrounding the inn is all brown grass and naked trees, a desolate field bordered by a low brown hedge. Lord Dunraven makes a fuss about the care of his horses and coachmen and it's clear that, as in everything else, he expects the preferential treatment to which he's accustomed. Mary, with her burning cheek, has noticed that there's a curious familiarity between the two men: when Dunraven speaks to her father, his tone is less imperious, not as loftily detached. She hears the difference when he asks Charley about his interests at school, and Charley explains that he enjoys studying Greek less than reading translations of the Greek poets and tragedians.

—It's all better in English, Dunraven says. If you ask me.

—Yes, sir, says Charley. I've been reading Browning's translation of *The Iliad*.

—Never understood what all the fuss was about, says Dunraven. Literature. It's for women, if you ask me.

—I don't like it much, Charley says.

It's clear that he's trying to please his father.

Dunraven seems momentarily confused, but then he forces a hard little laugh and says:

—There's a chap. The whole bloody business.

He looks at Mary, and nods.

—Forgive my speech. We have been in wild places, and far from the society of young women.

Mary nods back, glancing at her father.

Dunraven goes on, talking now about the savages of North America, and by savages, he's careful to point out, he does not confine his meaning to the naked killers of the plains. The two men go on to recount to Charley, looking only at Charley, some of what they've seen. Dunraven speaks in the sure tones of someone who's possessed of the conviction that his opinions will be supported. And yet on two occasions Mary's father actually contradicts him, both times about the customs and habits of the North American Cheyenne Indians. In each instance, Dunraven retreats, as if in deference to the expert, the anthropologist and the physician. But these concessions do not, finally, have the sound of agreement in them: it's as though such concerns, anthropology and science, are not worthy of his attention. He's a world traveler, an adventurer. He's sorry to be home. He says so.

At the inn, Mary excuses herself, pleading a headache, and goes to her room. She eats no evening meal, and when her father comes to the door of the room to ask after her, she calls to him that she is abed, and, though not hungry, feeling better.

—Can you open the door for a moment, Mary?

She rises, gathers her robe around herself, unlatches the door, and opens it a crack. Her father is so tall and handsome, standing there in the flickering gaslight, and there's something about his eyes that makes her feel sorry for him—a quality of being beset, of struggling against some powerful anguish.

—I'm all right, she says to him. Really, Father.

—I'm sorry for today, he says.

—Please forget about it, Mary tells him. She has always loved his directness. It occurs to her that witnessing his deference toward Dunraven has been more painful than the blow to her cheek.

—I caused your headache, didn't I, he says.

—No, Father.

—I'm quite proud of you, you know.

She doesn't know what to say to this. He lifts his hand to her face, without touching it, then lets the hand drop to his side.

—I'm unable to believe how much you've grown.

She nods, a gesture of shy acceptance.

—I was upset, Mary. That business on board. I've seen such things.

Never get used to it, of course. In Kansas, I saw a man shot dead in the street. They let him lie there the whole afternoon. This was . . . well.

—We thought you were dead, she says.

—I know. I have the letters from you and your mother.

—We were so frightened.

—There's a brave girl.

—No, she says.

—Well, good night, Mary.

—Good night, Father.

She watches him go down the corridor, then returns to her bed. Outside, the wind howls in the eaves, and she thinks of snow. She imagines it accumulating on the roof, the windowsill, and the branches of the trees. She has a dream that it covers the horses, the carriage, the building itself, collecting in the hollows of her own closed eyes.

The morning is bright, clear, and cold, and it hasn't snowed at all. Dunraven wants an early start. They have biscuits and tea, and by seven o'clock they're jouncing along toward London. Dunraven explains that he feels much better today, and that the upsetting business on board is quite behind him now. He wishes to express his gratitude for the pleasant company he has enjoyed during his ride back to London. He nods at Mary again, and then concentrates on Charley, the adventurer thrilling the heart of a boy, talking about the harrowing experiences his party had in the great mountainous Wyoming territory—the extremes of weather, and the strange behavior of the savages, some of whom were peaceful, nearly docile, in fact, and some of whom preyed on everything around them, man and beast. Raiders, they were. He postulates the theory, which he has spent considerable time developing, that all the darker-skinned races are inferior. But he has a great store of sympathy and understanding for them all, and they respond to him.

—I have a way with them, he says. They love me. They positively fawn over me, do they not, Kingsley?

—Yes, they do, George Kingsley says.

When they stop to rest, Dunraven tells them he wishes to clear his lungs, and walks a few paces into a field.

—The air parts for him, Mary says, low. She can't help herself.

—Don't be impertinent, says her father. He's actually rather an amazing chap. I've seen him face down nine Blackfoot warriors without so much as a twitch. He takes hardship wonderfully. He's missing the small toe of his left foot, and do you know why? He cut it off. Himself. Because it was frostbitten. I saw him do it.

—My God, Charley says, impressed.

Mary looks at the figure in the distance. Dunraven coughs and spits, and walks in a small circle, taking deep breaths and slapping his own trunk with the flat of both hands. It's almost a gesture of someone indicating a hearty appetite, except that the hands move to the face to cover the mouth as another cough comes forth.

—Consumption? she says to her father.

—Not every cough is dire, Mary. He's coughed since I've known him.

Dunraven returns to them, clearing his throat and regarding them with an expression of benevolent sufferance. They climb into the carriage, and ride along for a time in silence.

—Nothing like a little bracing cold air to clear the lungs, he says. Best thing in the world for rejuvenating one's spirits. I'm thankful for the company, Kingsley.

—We thank you for your hospitality.

—Indeed, it's you who will be extending the hospitality. That is, if it isn't too much of a presumption to suppose that I might dine with you at your home?

For a bad few seconds, no one says anything. George Kingsley seems not to have understood him.

—Oh, of course, he says finally, with an enthusiasm that doesn't quite cover his embarrassment.

—That is, I mean, if I wouldn't be in your way.

Mary sees that her father is utterly unprepared, and seeks for something good to say, wanting to soften the effect. She sits forward slightly and murmurs:

—We'd be delighted to 'ave you, sir.

—Yes, her father says quickly. Delighted.

The house in Highgate is lighted up like a Christmas candle, every window. The carriage pulls up, and they get out, and Mary sees Dunraven's face at the sight of the lighted windows.

—Mrs. Kingsley doesn't like to be alone, George Kingsley says.

—I like a lot of light, says Dunraven.

They go to the gate and Charley opens it and holds it for the rest of them. The air is heavy with cold. He gives Mary a look as she goes through. In the front lawn, two of the gamecocks are wandering in the yard.

—I say, Dunraven says.

Mary shoos them around to the back and shuts the inner gate. It is starting to cloud up again, and the coal smoke in the air stings her eyes. There are also the several odors of London's streets—raw sewage and refuse and rotting garbage, the effluvium of the dirty river, the dung of thousands of horses. After the country, the long ride, these odors are fairly overpowering. In the house, her father and Dunraven have gone to the parlor for a drink of brandy and a cigar. Mrs. Barrett is bustling about, picking up her things. This is the room she has made her own in George Kingsley's absence. Mary is surprised to find her mother crossing the hall from the stairs, wearing her flannel nightgown and a sleeping cap. She's carrying a lantern, though the tongues of flame are bright in every light in the house. Charley has begun moving from lamp to lamp, turning them down or off.

—Mother, he says, surprise and consternation in his voice.

—I couldn't eat today, Mrs. Kingsley says. Mary, 'ow could you leave me alone in that fashion?

—Mrs. Barrett was here, Mary says. You were not entirely alone.

—That is a rationaliz-eye-shun and an exagger-eye-shun of enormous proportions, her mother says, in the tone they use with each other when they are alone, and entertaining each other. Mary touches her arm and smiles, and feels a thrill of happiness. She wants to see what a man like Dunraven will find to say or do when confronted with the frank, funny gaze of her mother when she is in this sort of mood.

But George Kingsley steps over to his wife and gently takes the lantern from her.

—Mrs. Kingsley, perhaps you ought to go upstairs, he says.

Mary's mother stares at her.

—Mary?

—Perhaps you ought to go upstairs, George Kingsley repeats, with an insistence.

—I don't 'ave to, his wife says, glancing in the direction of Lord

Dunraven, who clears his throat and looks around the room with an expression of morbid curiosity. Then he steps forward and offers his hand to Mrs. Kingsley.

—Lord Dunraven, madam. It is my distinct pleasure to make your acquaintance.

Mrs. Kingsley looks at him from under her brows, a look of suspicion and wariness.

—Pleased to meet yeh.

—Yes, mum. Very good. I have been enjoying the society of your husband and children.

He lets go of her hand, then reaches for it again and raises it to his lips. Mary's mother seems astonished, then slyly ironical.

—It's a claw, she says to him. Ain't it? Can I boil you an egg?

Dunraven seems momentarily dazed.

Mary's father says:

—Isn't it a good idea now that you go back upstairs.

He turns to Dunraven.

—She's not been well. Female troubles, you know.

Dunraven merely stares at her.

Mary comes forward.

—Mother, let's go upstairs, and I'll read to you.

—I don't want to miss everything, Mary. I don't want to miss boiling 'is egg.

—I'm not a bit hungry, madam. Thank you so very much for your consideration.

Mary's mother winks at her.

—Never knew them not to be 'ungry for a boiled egg.

—They're just going to smoke tobacco and talk about the Indian wars in America.

—I would like to know about all that, I would.

—You ought to go upstairs now, George Kingsley says firmly.

—I fought in the Crimean War, Dunraven says, then seems mildly confused at his own statement.

—Go on upstairs, please.

—I don't 'ave to, Mary's mother says.

George Kingsley looks at Mary.

—Take your mother upstairs, please, Mary.

—Don't 'ave to, Mrs. Kingsley mutters.

Mary leads her up the stairs and puts her gently to bed. Her mother cries softly, like a little girl, and for a time Mary holds her, rocking her gently.

—It was joking at first, Mary.

—I know. And it couldn't've been more appropriate. I was very glad to see it.

—Well, you liked it anyway.

Mary rocks her until she falls asleep.

Downstairs, the men have dined on cold roast lamb, and biscuits prepared by Mrs. Barrett. They're drinking cognac, smoking American cigarettes, which they've brought over on the sea journey. Lord Dunraven holds forth about his exploits in the uncivilized world, and speaks with great confidence on his opinions concerning the reasons for drought and famine in the primitive parts of the globe, especially in Africa, with its tribal wars and internecine slaughter. He goes on to evaluate, with some acrimony, the self-aggrandizement of men like Speke, and Stanley, and Sir Richard Burton, and all the others who apparently fail to see anything but terrain. The source of the Nile River is an absurd thing to search for when there are thousands of benighted human souls occupying those lands.

—I would think much was to be gained from speaking with these people, Mary says.

—Speaking with them? Dunraven says. They'll cut you into pieces and eat you.

—Not according to Mr. Burton's recollections of them.

—Burton is a vain, self-promoting fool, George Kingsley said. I don't wish to talk about him.

—Your daughter has ideas of her own, Kingsley.

—I have left her alone in my library too long. Mary is possessed of a quick mind. I have taken steps to train her.

Dunraven is gazing at Mary.

—Are you aware of the writings of Sir Richard Burton?

—Some, yes, she says. I am interested in science and anthropology.

—And what is your schooling?

—I 'ave none, Mary tells him. But what I can glean on my own.

Dunraven takes a long pull on his cigarette and then looks at her father.

—A little education is a dangerous thing, Kingsley.

—I think I must have mentioned that she's quite able to hold her own in any company, says her father. And she has a sharp tongue, for which I apologize.

—No apology necessary, I'm sure.

Charley is watching them, chewing on a biscuit. Mary clears some of the dishes away, and Mrs. Barrett hurries in to take over. Mary sits down again, hands folded in her lap.

—I guess it's the price of coming from a literary family? Dunraven asks.

—I suppose.

—Charles, here, will write books, no doubt.

—I should like to be a poet, Charley says.

This is the first that Mary has heard of it.

—Tosh! Dunraven says. A lot of emotions, poetry. Again, as I remarked earlier, I should think literature the province, mostly, of women.

—Do you know the work of Lord Tennyson? Mary asks him. It occurs to her with a little start that she means it as a challenge. She can feel the blood coursing through the veins of her face.

—I have some acquaintance with it, yes.

—And Shakespeare?

—I believe Shakespeare has been judged to be overrated, somewhat. I believe I read something to that effect.

—Do you know the sonnets and the plays? Mary says.

—Well, of course.

—And you get nothing out of them?

—I prefer the world of action, young miss.

Dunraven clears his throat, puffs on his rolled tobacco, and looks at her father.

—See here, Kingsley, I wonder if we couldn't speak alone for a few moments. I really must be leaving soon.

—Excuse me, Mary says, rising.

She looks at Charley, in his shadowed corner of the room.

—Charley?

He accompanies her, across to the living room, and the window looking out on Highgate Street. They sit in tall-backed chairs on either side of the window. The two men are muttering in the other room, and Mrs. Barrett is clanging around in the kitchen. It is snowing again, the flakes dropping down through the gathering mist. Finally Dunraven comes out into the hall, and in a harumphing, formal tone of voice takes his leave. They watch him go down the walk, bark orders at the coachmen, get in, and close the door. The carriage pulls away.

—Why do you suppose? Mary says, to no one in particular.

—He's frightened, comes their father's voice.

He has entered the room and stands at Charley's shoulder.

—All the things we've seen in our travels, and nothing quite upset him as much as that chap dropping over dead yesterday morning. Quite shaken, he was. I think he may be curtailing some of his wanderlust.

—So you'll 'ave to find someone else, Mary says.

—Young woman, I do not need your sharpened sense of irony this evening. Now I would like some quiet before I go to bed. Will you please tend to your mother.

—She's asleep.

—Very well, then, just leave me in peace, he says. I have some work to do. Both of you, please.

They leave him there, and go to their separate rooms. Mary undresses and puts on her nightgown, then sits at her window. She can see the rhomboid of light on the lawn, from his study below. The bare trees make skinny, crossing shadows. She watches the snow build up, and is glad of his presence in the house, though she's also troubled by the complications of feeling he has always caused—restlessness and sleeplessness, worry, fear, and exhilaration. She's obscurely sick at heart and happy, all at the same time and with the same degree of intensity. In the distance, the lights from the east end of the city make the snowy sky look like a smoldering wall.

TEN

1

$\mathcal{B}$UDDY GALATIERRE started the clock for Tyler's first paycheck, and then gave him his first week off. Lily wanted badly to find a place for them to live, but Tyler said he liked being in the house with what was left of his family. He had relaxed into it, and seemed so happy to be there. The intense quality of his attention to their every word and movement convinced her to go along, at least for a time. Besides, the novelty of being with them became something she rather enjoyed. She hadn't had much of a family life, she realized, with Scott gone so much. Every evening, they all gathered around the dinner table and talked and played word games and were, well, silly with each other. And Buddy Galatierre seemed to preside over it all. He had a way of leaning on one elbow and raising the other arm to indicate someone at the table, asking for a story, or a comment, or an answer. Lily thought of a conductor in the orchestra pit, encouraging the notes along.

Once night, late, after making love in the dark—surreptitiously, because someone was outside in the pool—she said to Tyler, "You know, I think I wondered if you came here hoping to cause some trouble."

"What an odd thing to say," he said with a little laugh.

"I just mean that I must've bought into Sheri's paranoia."

Though she couldn't see his face, she knew from the faint sigh at the mention of his half sister's name that he had rolled his eyes. "I wanted to get to know this side of my family. That was my dark purpose."

He caressed her arm, a light trailing of his fingers down to the bones of her wrist, but left a moment's pause. "I had resentments. My father was a shit sometimes and he had a way of reminding me when I disappointed him, and everybody thought I was Daddy's boy because I was just desperate to please him, frantic to keep it all smooth every day. So, yeah, I had a lot of time, growing up, to build resentments. And I wasn't ready to like Buddy as much as I do. And Sheri and Millicent—well, they're all I've got left. I don't have any other family."

The following morning Sheri and Lily went shopping in town, and Sheri talked about her platonic friend, whose name she withheld, she said, because Lily might one day run into him, or blurt out his name to Nick.

Lily didn't want to know any of it, but Sheri wasn't hearing any objections. It was as though they had regressed to their old relationship as roommates.

"He teaches. At the university. He's older than Nick, and sometimes I think he understands me in a way—well, in ways no one else does. I want it to be okay, you know. I don't want to hurt anybody." Sheri frowned, and then sighed. Lily already felt duplicitous around Nick, and she desired to be elsewhere. It was a source of wonder to her that her feelings for Sheri could go through such wide swings of affection and aversion.

When they had finished with the shopping, Sheri took her to the community theater in Oxford, a place called The Loft. It was up a flight of stairs alongside a tall wooden structure that had once been a combination pharmacy and dwelling, and was now cut into offices and the theater. There were white lace curtains over the windows on the second floor. It looked like a small hotel. A young woman was seated behind the desk inside. Sheri had known her in high school, and introduced her as Brandi. The two of them talked a little about their respective lives in and out of college. Brandi told them that she was engaged, then turned to Lily and explained that she knew Sheri's Nick, of course, because Nick had taken part in a couple of productions two years ago. One was a failure called *Too Much Food and Too Much Drink*, by a local writer, a man who had taken a graduate degree in creative writing at Stanford, but had gone on to law school and become an attorney. When Brandi met him, the company was already working on producing his play. "I never met a bigger jerk," she said. "He told me he had 'jettisoned' the wife and kids, and his lucrative law practice, to pursue literary fame. Unquote. Then he asked me out. Oh, and guess what the play was about? Nick had the lead role, too—playing a local writer who has, um, spent his life practicing law." Sheri spoke the last phrase with her, nodding, and they both laughed.

Brandi was slight of build, with long, straight, dishwater blond hair, and elliptical dark eyes. She showed them around the place. Lily saw the flyers for the next production, a comedy called *Twelve Thousand and Change*. It had been produced with some success off Broadway several years ago. Brandi spoke about a large cast.

"Lily's a writer," Sheri said. "She's working on a play, too."

Lily stepped in. "I don't have anything like a full play."

"But you are working on one."

"It's probably years away, Sheri."

"Her father's Scott Austin. He's been in movies."

"Actually, I think I know that name," Brandi said.

"I'd be very surprised if you did," Lily told her.

"We'd be glad to have you come read for us."

They walked out onto the landing, in the warm afternoon light, and Brandi Muller offered her hand. "We can always use more talent."

After they had returned to the car, Lily said, "Sheri, don't tell people about the play. I don't have a play. I have some scribblings, some partial scenes. And a journal that anybody would think was—well, weird."

"I thought I was helping," Sheri said.

"I know, and I appreciate it. But there's no sense getting ahead of things."

2

I've been reading in your first book, again, admiring your humor. And your astonishing descriptive powers. I would love to capture that quality in the speeches I write for you. Though lately I'm beginning to think that I'm not cut out to be a playwright.

Also I love how you could go away from yourself, from worries about yourself. I don't remember who said that hell is other people, but sometimes, although I have no trouble being alone for writing, I find it quite the opposite: hell can turn out to be one's self, without the mitigating, roomy promise and comfort of others.

Tyler has started work, and Buddy gave him a new sedan to drive as a demo. I teased him about his fast car, and a fast car is something I know you would like. The other morning, we were all in a parking lot where

Buddy plays softball with a group of men from the dealership. A big gravel lot. The tires made their popping noise, that pleasant crackling sound, and I thought how it is a sound you never heard in your short life. There you are, in the last years of your century; and here I am in mine. So much has changed. And so much hasn't.

For instance, the longing you felt for experience. That is the same, here. But you wanted to go away from home; I realize that I've yearned to find home.

Tyler sold his first car yesterday, so long after starting work. They came home drunk, the three of them; they'd been celebrating. Tyler got sick, poor thing, and I tended to him, and thought of you, with your practical medical knowledge gleaned almost entirely out of books.

I haven't had any luck finding work, and it's been three months. There isn't anything to do at The Loft until they finish with this run. I try to stay out of Millicent's way—but I want to be of help, too. She seldom seems to want any—and of course there's Rosa. They're both perfectly kind, and yet I feel as if my presence may be a strain on them sometimes. How could it not be? I'm what Doris used to call "stay-in company." I hope I can find something soon. Sheri has a job at a real estate office, and she tried to get me something there, with no luck. I'm spending a lot of time going through books—yours and others, and thinking about how I might find some way to travel to some of the places you knew. I get up in the mornings with Tyler, and we play and laugh and tease, and then we have breakfast with Nick and Buddy, and I stand in the doorway and wave good-bye. I cleared the breakfast dishes that first morning and Rosa let me know with sugar-soft sarcasm how much this displeased her. So now I leave the breakfast dishes and return to the downstairs room to read and try to write—and sometimes when Sheri lets me take her to work, I have the car, and go on into town to apply for work. I've had several interviews, and thought a couple of times I'd gotten the job; but nothing's come through. I've visited the university library, which is a pretty good one. They actually have a rare first printing of your Travels.

I've tried to write home, but it's just easier to call. So we've talked a couple of times. A bit clumsily. My father finally told Doris Peggy's news. Doris says she's happy. I can't fathom the least aspect of that. But it's their life. If they can explain it to each other, I can leave it alone. Or try to.

Everyone in the house, thanks to Tyler and Sheri, knows I'm trying to write this play. Nick is especially avid to know about it, and inclined to grin at me when I don't have an answer for him—which I often don't. He said he wants a part in it, and I laughed and told him I hadn't thought I would put a jackass in. It's sometimes a little difficult teasing with him, knowing what I know about Sheri's "platonic friend." I can't help but feel that there's an element of betrayal about it. But you can't be with Nick without making light of things—that's how he is with people; he tends to make everything into a joke, and I've noticed that a lot of the jokes are at his own expense. Except that his continual joking references to the play are making me feel almost sullen around him. Sometimes, he calls me Shakespeare, and I can see that he means it to be affectionate; there isn't the slightest malice in it, and yet it grates on my nerves and I look for excuses to be quiet, or, better yet, away from him.

I wish I could get Tyler to move. But then there we all are at the dinner hour, laughing and telling stories, and it's all so vibrant and I laugh so hard that I don't want it to change. I've joked with Tyler that we could find a place of our own, but still come to the Galatierre house for dinner each night. We have such sweet times together, and I feel wrong for worrying so much. But Tyler and I will be so wonderful when we get off on our own. Last night we talked for a long time in the dark, and he told me that he has always had a terror of intimacy—that it's all tied up in an overwrought sense of worry about what people think of him. And that's a function of the daily moral attention he had to be in all the time with his father. For him, these evening dinner-table rounds of talk and laughter are like the richest nourishment. I said that telling me about a fear of intimacy is a pretty big admission, and very confiding, for someone with those feelings. "Well," he said. "This is you. This is here." My heart changed its rhythm when he said it. I put my arms around him and snuggled close and said I thought that was how most people are in company, anyway. But then he said the idea of getting our own place made him anxious, as if it would be a matter of responsibility he isn't ready for. And it is as if we're all playing at a game of being out of the ordinary flow of living.

Sometimes when we're all together I see him watching them, and he has the most wondering and avid look on his face.

Something is happening to me that I won't put in writing just yet.

3

$\mathcal{E}$ACH DAWN she awakened first, and she would wait for the dark to recede from the windows, feeling faintly sick to her stomach. There were episodes in the night, where she had to get up to pee. She would get back into the bed, the sheets still warm from where she had lain, and Tyler would move closer. The warmth of him, the smell of him, so close, calmed her, made the usual nervousness of being up in the middle of the night give way, and she would lie there thinking of the talk at the previous evening's dinner.

Buddy, Nick, and Tyler had discovered that they shared a love of the woods. They talked about it a lot. They were going to go hunting in the fall, in deer season. Twice already they had gone into the north woods to hunt squirrels and other small game. There was a big land preserve north of town, a farm with several thousand acres of unused wilderness, and Buddy knew the man who owned it. He took Tyler and Nick with him, and when they all returned he made jokes about how the other two had lost their feel for wild nature, tramping around in their boots, afraid of snakes. The boys, as he called them, talked about having to go slow, to compensate for the great age of their companion.

That evening, Tyler told a story about being eleven years old and allowed to carry a shotgun for the first time. On that hunting trip, he was supposed to remain behind and observe. But a rabbit, flushed by the dogs, circled in the brush and high grass, and came right past him, within inches of his feet. He shot both barrels of the gun out of sheer panic, almost wounding himself and all but obliterating the rabbit. As he told the story, he did the sound of the gun, both barrels, standing at the table to demonstrate, and then sitting down, pantomiming the eating of that same ragged, cooked carcass, his father having made him prepare it with the scattershot still in it. Tyler acted out the surprise and difficulty of coming upon the pellets as he chewed, and he leaned forward and mimed spitting them onto his plate. He described the clanking sound they made. And then he portrayed his father, carrying on a regular dinner conversation with a woman he was seeing, evidently oblivious to the occasional clatter of the metal pellets, as if it were perfectly normal to have a boy at the table spitting out shot, and a woman sitting across from him with a look of horror and perplexity on her face. He even briefly acted out the woman, with her startlement and horror at each clanking pellet. It was quite a performance. No one could do anything for a time except laugh. Sheri had put her head down on her folded arms and gasped for air, pleading with her half brother to stop.

"That's harsh," Nick said, wiping his eyes. "Man, that is extreme."

"That's my father," said Tyler, leaning back in his chair.

"You know what, honey, you're the one with the acting talent," Lily said, delighting in him. "That was so wonderful to watch. You did all three characters."

"Man, but is that ever harsh," Nick went on.

Tyler looked down the table at Buddy. "It's a hunter's justice, though, isn't it?"

"I think I have to agree with Nick," Buddy Galatierre said, still laughing.

One morning after the men had gone off to work, Lily worked for an hour in the downstairs room, and then started upstairs into the kitchen, to get a cup of coffee. She heard voices, a man and a woman. Something made her stop, and she heard Millicent say, "You're sweet." There was a suppleness of tone, an affection in her voice, tinged with another note— a disquiet.

"You're such a zany lady, you know it? It's all I can do to keep from making a pass at you. I don't know if I can resist the urge."

"Well, maybe you shouldn't try so hard."

"Oh, yeah?"

"I should've said maybe you'll keep trying."

"How do you mean that?"

"I mean, I'm sure you'll manage not to make a pass, Roger."

"But you don't want me to try so hard, huh."

"Roger."

"What if we both said exactly what's on our minds?"

"Don't stand so close. Someone might come in."

"We're alone."

There was a long silence. Lily turned and began, as soundlessly as she could, descending the stairs. But she heard the hurried clacking of Millicent's heels on the kitchen floor, and now Millicent called to her from the top of the steps, "Hey."

She turned. Millicent's white blouse was rumpled, and her face gleamed with the heat, and with a breathless, anxious, fixed straining to smile. "I want you to meet someone."

She made her way there, and Millicent introduced her to a trim, middle-aged, balding but very darkly handsome man named Roger Gault. Lily looked straight at him, her old habit asserting itself, of going against the grain of her own impulse, which was to avert her eyes. He was a contractor, a friend of the family. He had built the kitchen. Millicent indicated the fine cabinets and the woodwork. Gault leaned against the counter with a bottle of beer, and smiled at both of them. Millicent was agitated, but controlled, and she talked rapidly about plans to knock the west wall down and expand the room into the small den that Buddy never used, and to construct a solarium for all her plants. The work would begin sometime after the weather turned cold. Gault finished his beer and shook Lily's hand, then turned to Millicent and said, with an unmistakable air of familiarity, "I'm a bad influence." He leaned over and kissed her on the temple, and he had to lean farther than he had intended because of the way she pulled back from him, glancing over at Lily.

"Roger, really."

" 'Bye, girls," he said.

They watched him go out along the edge of the pool and on, through the wooden fence, to his car. Millicent had her arms wrapped around herself. She cleared her throat, and then noticed that her blouse had come out at the waist. She tucked it in, while making an awkward few steps toward the entrance of the living room, as though she meant to run away. "That Roger," she said. "He's such a flirt."

Lily remained silent. The remark did not really permit any response other than a nod.

"It's perfectly harmless, of course. I tease with him, you know. But I think he goes too far. I think he needs to have his jets cooled a little."

She felt as though the other woman's mortification was almost palpable in the air between them, like a gauze through which they could barely see each other. She recalled, without wanting to, that Millicent had left Tyler's father for Buddy Galatierre, and had been pregnant with Sheri at the time. The fact went through her and caused a tightening of the nerves in her throat. She feared that Millicent would glean something of what she was thinking from the discomfiture that must certainly be showing in her face. So she busied herself with pouring a glass of ice water.

"I'm afraid if I tell Buddy about him, Buddy'll do something awful, and get himself in trouble."

Lily drank the water to keep from having to speak. She simply nodded, thinking, without wanting to, of Sheri and her married "friend."

"You know—he—he put his arms around me. You might've heard us. He—he tried to kiss me."

Lily frowned, pretending surprise. "Some men don't know where the line is. Or even that there is a line."

The other woman appeared relieved to have this note struck. "Isn't it the truth. I just don't see the good of saying anything about it, though."

"No, of course not."

"I hope you'll—" Millicent seemed momentarily to have lost the thread of her thought. "I hope you'll forgive me for the awkwardness of it."

"There's nothing to forgive," Lily told her. "Don't be silly."

4

*Y*ET THROUGH the rest of the week, she felt the tension of having Millicent's watchful interest in her when the others were gathered. A solicitousness had surfaced in the older woman's behavior toward her, and it made everything seem freighted with significance, and with the possibility of some kind of unlooked-for eruption or failure. It put an unspoken pall on the good times. It was as though both Millicent and her daughter had involved her in their lives in ways that should be reserved for the psychiatrist and the marriage counselor.

When, after a week or so, Millicent asked, in the overly casual tone of someone who had been planning the question for a long time, if she had mentioned anything to Tyler about "that silly business in the kitchen with Roger," she experienced a wave of irritability, turned, and demanded, "What silly business?"

Millicent stared at her for a moment, but then her face softened, and she nodded, touching Lily's shoulder. "Well, you don't need my stupid concerns, of course. I worry all the time over nothing, you know. Buddy's always after me about it. I worry over the silliest things."

"I'm like that, too," Lily told her, relieved at being able to say something completely true. "And it's usually over nothing."

"Oh, isn't that just how it is."

Later, she found herself brooding over the fact that she could not tell Tyler about any of this: it bothered her that she should have knowledge about his half sister and his mother that she could not impart to him, about which she was barred from speaking to him, not so much by the two people involved as by her own sense of what would be right or wrong in their relation. It felt wrong to speak of these things with him; she could not bring herself to begin. So she held them to herself, and carried her worries about all of it.

On a warm evening in mid-June, the whole family went out to dinner and a movie. Everyone was lighthearted. Lily thought the movie was terrible, a bad remake of what had been a bad movie to begin with, and she was surprised to find that the others had liked it, and liked the original, too. They teased her about it, and Millicent's teasing was relaxed, affectionate and friendly, and Lily thought perhaps the tension was over.

That night, getting into bed with Tyler in the basement room, she heard someone jump into the swimming pool outside, and experienced an unexpected thrill, realizing that she was at that moment completely happy. She hadn't thought of her parents—the situation at home—very much in all these weeks. Remembering this abruptly troubled her; it was something undone, which would make a pressure to be set right the longer it was left undone. Except that she didn't actually know what it might be that required doing.

"I have to call home," she said, into the dark.

"Why don't they call you?"

She turned to her side, facing him. "Come here."

In the morning, with the weekend approaching, he wanted to take a day off and drive out in the country. They explored the surrounding little towns, and the Natchez Trace, and then on an impulse drove down to New Orleans for the weekend. It was a honeymoon. They went to the jazz clubs, and sampled the food, and stayed up late making love. They slept wonderfully and were aimless and lazy in the mornings. The weather was perfect, far cooler than usual, they were told. They walked along the Mississippi, basking in mild sun; they saw children playing in a park, and sat on a stone bench to watch ships roll into the harbor.

"You know this river was once the size of a small ocean," he said. "It separated two very large land masses that came together, and formed this, er, continent." He smiled a little apologetically. "Sorry."

"I didn't know that, Tyler. Really."

He leaned over and kissed her, and took her hands. "I usually feel like I can say anything to you. Now I'm nervous. Like this is a date."

They rose, and walked on along the bank of the river, the water of which was lined with little eddies and currents, a muddy design in a smooth, glassy, brown surface.

"Well, you already proposed," she said. "Mr. Man."

"You're a delicious and marvelous mystery to me, Lily."

She thought of the things she had been keeping from him. She determined to try confiding in him more. She said, "I like this. I like being alone here together."

He kissed her ear, and they strolled on, jostling each other pleasantly.

Later, they went up a side street that opened out onto a small lake. The water looked black, and the houses of the street on that side were reflected in it. They sat at the edge and had cold sandwiches and iced tea in big paper cups. Nearby, two straw-hatted old ladies were fishing off a pier. Lily remembered that she had meant to call home, and resolved to do so when they got back. But for now she and Tyler couldn't be reached, and she felt happy in the knowledge of it, enjoyed the sense of being truly alone with him in this exotic place.

"You are glad we came," he said. "Aren't you?"

"Oh," she said. "Yes."

"I meant to Mississippi."

"I know," she said. But she had thought he meant New Orleans. She took a drink of the iced tea and thought about finding a place to live. It would have to be soon, in any case. There were other concerns, now. The time for her period had come and passed; it was two months now. She had felt surprised by her own excitement.

"I could live here," Tyler said.

Had he been reading her thoughts? "Do you mean New Orleans?"

"Yep."

"I think it might be that we have to move out soon anyway," she told him. "As much fun as it's been."

He smiled. "It's been so nice to have the feeling of being in a real family. I never had much of that, growing up. I think I understand perfectly now why Millicent left the old man. But we'll find a place. It's time."

"I'll say it is," she told him. "We're going to need it now."

"Oh?" He stared at her uncomprehendingly.

She remembered that he'd told her once how much he disliked puzzles or games. Yet for some reason she couldn't bring herself to say it out loud. She ran her hand lightly over her lower abdomen, smiling at him.

He looked out at the water, tore at the grass, and put a blade of it into his mouth. "You're—are you—" He stopped and turned to her.

She reached over and touched his chest. "Thanks for playing, and you win the lucky jackpot."

After a pause, he said, "For sure?"

"Well, I haven't seen a doctor, but I'm pretty sure."

He kept working the blade of grass in his mouth, and now it seemed to her that his eyes had grown narrow. The muscles of his jaw were working. She saw a little forking blue vein standing out on the side of his head, above the temple. She'd never noticed it before.

"Tyler."

"Well, if you haven't seen the doctor yet."

"Don't you want it?" She couldn't keep the hurt out of her voice.

He looked off, then reached down and tore at the grass again. "Of course, a baby. Lily—of course. But I—I thought you didn't want any children."

"I thought so, too. But when this began to make itself known—when I started to think maybe it was—oh, Tyler, it's made me so happy. Something of you. Us. It's—it's more, don't you see? It's us together in a deeper way than I thought possible. I know it's sentimental and a cliché and all that, but I'm so happy about it."

He said nothing for a moment, then gave a little deprecating laugh. "It's my upbringing. I've always had trouble believing in happiness." A little breeze lifted a lock of his hair, then let it down again.

She could feel the blood flowing to the bones of her face. "Honey, if you didn't want me to be pregnant—we didn't have to be. Right? We could've taken precautions."

"But you don't know for sure that you are."

"I said—no, I don't."

"Okay."

"Tyler, what is this?"

"Nothing." He stood. "I'm being stupid. It just—it caught me by surprise." He tossed the grass into the wind, and walked off a few paces, then turned and gazed at her, one hand held up over his eyes to blot out the sun. "You're a beautiful picture, sitting there. Like one of those French paintings in the museums." He came back and loomed over her. When she tried to stand, he knelt and took her face in his hands and looked at her. "Listen," he said. "I love you so much."

"Yes," she said. "I love you, too. And we're going to be so happy."

"You haven't said anything to anyone yet, right?"

"Not yet, no."

"Don't say anything yet. Okay?" Something crossed over them both—the shadow of a hawk.

"Tyler?"

He got to his feet again, and stepped back, and when she stood, swiping the crumbs of what they'd had to eat from her lap, he simply gazed at her. His smile somehow failed to include his eyes.

"Tyler, I *want* this. This is learning to *trust* happiness. This is being brave enough for it. I believe that. I know it's a surprise, but can't you feel it, just a little, how right it is?"

"I do. It's just—you know—it's thrown me off a little, that's all. But yes, of course. If you are—we'll—that'll—I mean, that'll be wonderful."

"*Terrific* answer, Tyler." Something moved in her soul, like leaves blown out of a tree. She started away from him, in the direction of the street.

He caught her by the arm and said, "I'm sorry, baby. It *will* be wonderful. We'll make it wonderful. How could it be otherwise with you."

She put her arms around him and held on, her ear against his chest, where she could hear the thrumming of his heart.

"I love you," he said again. "I'm such a clod. Can you forgive me?"

She lifted her head and kissed him. Then: "I thought you'd be so proud."

"I am. I'm very proud. Please—"

She thought he might begin to cry. His eyes swam, and he ran the back of his hand across his mouth. She took that hand, and kissed it, gazing at him.

"Can we keep it a secret for a while?" he said. "Until we're absolutely sure? I want it to be perfect when we tell them."

They walked away from the lake. People sat out on porches, men, women, and children, watching the young couple as they passed. The breeze carried the sound of a clarinet—somebody practicing scales. They went back into the French Quarter, and walked along Chartres Street, looking at the tall verandas and balconies, the skinny-columned porches with the ornate scrollwork and the high, arched windows, the cherry and cream facades and doorways. They remarked on the distant towers of the rest of the city, and how the light made them look insubstantial, like mountains in a mist. They had checked out of the hotel, and packed the car, and when they came to it, they got in and headed north again.

Tyler drove fast, both hands on the wheel. She began to fear that she would in fact find that she wasn't pregnant; she almost wished she hadn't said anything about it until she was sure. He was quiet, daydreaming, musing to himself. She watched a cloud sail across the sunniest part of the sky.

"I love New Orleans," she said. "I'll always love it, now."

He nodded, watching the road.

"Such a beautiful memory."

"'We'll always have Paris,'" he said, and moved the corners of his mouth, badly imitating Bogart.

She laughed, and sat back in the seat, watching the countryside for a few minutes. It was getting gray, clouds rolling in. The white line of the highway kept coming in and in under the shiny hood. "I wonder what it was like traveling around in America back in the 1870s, when Mary Kingsley's father was here. Imagine it—no highways, nothing but dirt roads and paths."

"I'm not much company," he said. "Sorry."

She kissed the side of his face. "It's all right." The sun was again bright in the windows, and she rested her head on his shoulder and began to grow sleepy. "Do you mind if I fall asleep?"

"No."

Perhaps she drifted once or twice, she couldn't tell. When he moved slightly, shifting his weight, she sat straight again. "Mr. Man," she said. "My husband."

"That's me," he said.

"You know, I thought I'd probably never get married. My parents' divorce made me so mistrustful and unromantic. And then there you were, so handsome, that day after the football game."

"You wanted to jump right into bed with me."

She looked at him. "Hey."

"You didn't?"

"Tyler."

"I'm sorry," he said. "You were telling me about being unromantic."

"I was going to say that you made me feel romantic anyway—and I didn't see you all those weeks, and then there you were that day I fell on the ice. You had me, right then, I think. And I got so miserable after that, thinking I wouldn't see you again. Unromantic me. That afternoon you came to the dorm, I'd been holed up in my room for days, and you were so sweet—"

"And *then* you wanted to jump right into bed with me."

She said, "You're doing that on purpose."

"Doing what?" He turned to her with a look of non-understanding. "It's a joke."

She sank down in the seat and folded her arms across her chest. "I don't think it's funny. So cut it the fuck out." She looked out at the land gliding by the window, farm fields, and side roads going off into the flat distances of the delta. They passed a little country store with two men sitting in the shade and a third standing in the sunlight, talking to them. Then they were riding along a weed-choked creek bank, flanked by tall magnolias covered in kudzu.

"I'm sorry," he said. "Hey—I was just kidding you."

"Don't kid that way. I don't like it. There's a brutality in it."

"Hey, I'm sorry. Really. Okay? I didn't mean it like that. My father used to—" He halted. "No, I won't use the old man as an excuse. I didn't mean to be harsh. I just meant to joke about being unromantic, Lily."

She shook her head, but gave him a look she meant as both acceptance of the apology, and loving exasperation with him.

ELEVEN

1

$\mathscr{A}$T THE HOUSE, they found everyone in the pool area, even Rosa, whose white bathing suit made her dark legs look all the more lovely. Nick Green was floating in a multicolored inner tube, with a can of beer in a Styrofoam holder. He held it up and called to them, "The return of the missing! Tyler, you fearful Jesuit! Where the hell did you go? How was New Orleans?"

"How do you know we went there?" Lily said. "In fact, we flew to Italy and back."

Buddy Galatierre was sitting on the steps, with only his feet in the water. He held a glass of whiskey, which he also lifted, as if to offer a toast. "Welcome. Help yourselves to the bar."

Millicent, treading water in the deep end, said, "Lily, your father called. He wants you to call him."

Lily went into the kitchen, where plates of fruit and vegetables and cheeses were laid out. It had all been picked over. She stood with the handset at her ear, punching in the numbers. She inhaled deeply, and let the air out slowly, listening to the call go through, the circuits buzzing and clicking. The ring, and her father's voice.

"It's me," she said to him.

"I have some news, sweetie." He gave forth a small sigh, and when he spoke again his voice broke. "Peg-ah, uh, sweetie—I'm sorry, Jesus. Peg—Peg lost the baby today."

The words went through her, a sharp pang across her chest and abdomen. She leaned against the counter and couldn't speak, seeing in her mind's eye the look on Peggy's face at the remark: *Cheer up, maybe something will happen.*

"Oh, I'm so— Oh, my God, Daddy. Please tell her I'm so, so sorry."

"I know, sweetie. I know." There was a rush of something like relief in his voice, as if he hadn't expected her to respond nearly as strongly as she had. "It's been pretty hard on her," he went on. "We had to take her in for a D and C. There was some necrosis, and they had to clean her out pretty good."

Lily began to cry. "I'm so terribly sorry," she said. "Please tell her how sorry I am. Should I come home? I'll come home."

"No, baby." Her father's voice shook. "She doesn't want any fuss made. Really. There's nothing you can do."

"I want to see her." The truth of this caused a strange pang under her breastbone.

"She really wants to put it behind her, Lily. It's her wish. She didn't even want me to mention it to you. We're going to try again. That's what she wants—to try again."

At this, Lily sobbed, and for a few moments was unable to speak. Her father's voice continued, murmuring. She couldn't hear the words. She felt as if her own recent happiness had been selfish, and the fact that she herself was pregnant made everything worse. It rode over her in waves, and at last her father was simply quiet, breathing on the other end, waiting for her to subside.

"God, I'm sorry," she got out.

"Is everything else all right?" he said, and she heard the doubt in his voice. It was clear that her reaction had surprised him. "Your mother's here," he went on.

And she heard her mother's voice, tearful, faintly raspy with cigarettes. "We hated to call you with this."

Lily wanted to explain everything to them beginning with the cruel remark she'd made. She wanted to make sure Peggy would know how bad she felt. Of course, this wasn't the time. Her mother went on about the hospital, and how she wished Lily would stay in closer touch.

"Sorry," Lily said again. She couldn't manage more. She said it still again when her father came back on the line.

"I'll tell Peggy," he said. "I'll give her your love."

"Yes," Lily said. "Do."

When she had hung up, she went to the room downstairs, with its cement floor and its set-off-to-the-side bookshelf, and lay down. She could hear everyone in the pool, splashing and talking loudly to be heard. Tyler came to the outside door, opened it, and leaned in to look at her. "Is everything all right?"

"No."

He came into the room and closed the door. He hadn't gotten into the water yet. He sat on the edge of the bed and took her hands in his own. "Tell me, Lily," he said. "Is it your mother?"

"Peggy lost her baby."

He said nothing, and there was nothing in his face. He merely returned her look. Then, very low, he said: "Jesus."

"I said a terrible thing to her, Tyler. And it happened."

"There's no connection, Lily."

"I know but I feel awful. I need to be alone a little, Tyler, please."

"Come on outside and be with everybody. Don't be in here by yourself with that."

"In a while," she said. "Please?"

"You want me to stay here with you?"

"No, please."

After he had gone, she rose and went into the bathroom and was ill, nearly retching, holding her abdomen and trying to breathe. Looking at herself in the mirror, she saw the blotched look of her skin, the redness around her eyes. She washed her face, then stepped out, and to the door of the room and on, along the corridor to the stairs up into the kitchen, where she found Millicent, who had put on a light linen blouse over her dark bathing suit, and was standing at the refrigerator, pouring orange juice into a glass half filled with vodka. The small portable television was on. Lily saw a weather map in front of which a man stood smiling.

"Hello," Millicent said. "I was just catching up on the weather."

They watched in silence.

"You look a little under the weather," Millicent said, "speaking of weather." Then: "You've been crying." She put the backs of her fingers on Lily's forehead. "No fever." She tilted her head to one side. "Sugar— Tyler told us, about Peggy. Is there anything we can do?"

"Oh, thank you—but no."

The newscaster was now talking about a special report on the recent violence in Beijing, the gathering of forces to stop the popular revolt. The voice was grave, deep, and fake. Millicent turned the television off.

"Do you need to get home?"

"They don't want me to come home. Peggy didn't want a fuss."

"That happens sometimes. And sometimes it goes the other way. I have a friend who wanted a funeral, a coffin, all of it, for a three-month fetus. It helped her, too. The hard thing is always the assumptions people make about it. Someone said to this woman, this friend of mine, 'Why don't you adopt a baby?' It appalled her. As if it had been a commodity she'd lost. Something simply replaceable, like a car or an appliance. But the person who said it was sincerely trying to help." She touched Lily's forehead again. "You're a little warm. Have you been feeling all right?"

Lily cast her eyes down and said, "Yes."

The older woman took her chin and lifted it, so that they were eye to eye. "You know, I hear it whenever anyone uses the bathrooms in this big old house—I'm a light sleeper and I hear the plumbing working. Someone has been getting up at all hours to use the bathroom down there."

"I'm not sure," Lily said, unable to believe the turn things had taken. She wanted to step into the other's arms and cry. She felt something of an invitation to do so in the gentle pressure of the hand on her chin.

"But you think so," Millicent said.

Lily nodded. Millicent's expression was of a kind of acknowledgment of what had already transpired between them. They were women together, navigating the cares and complications of life in the world. Lily felt it almost as a caress.

"You don't want anyone else to know yet."

"I told Tyler. He—he—I said it wasn't sure."

"But you're pretty sure."

"Yes," she said, beginning to let down again.

Millicent embraced her, a wonderful sheltering gesture that brought forth a long sigh. "You come with me." She led her into the living room. The dark shapes on the wall were like listening, staring presences. "You didn't plan this, sweetie, is that right?"

Lily had the feeling that the older woman was reading her mind, looking through all the layers of her soul to the place where she was most uncertain. She couldn't stop crying. "I wasn't supposed to say anything. Tyler didn't want me to say anything."

"Sometimes young men have a little trouble adjusting to the idea. They usually come around. And I've never seen anybody as in love as you two."

Lily put her head on the other woman's shoulder, sniffling.

"This'll be our secret, for a while," Millicent said.

"I'm sorry," said Lily, not quite understanding why she felt the need to say it. Partly it was from the sense that she had been privy to something the older woman would have preferred no one else see, or know. She took the Kleenex Millicent offered and dabbed at her eyes, and went on to tell about what had happened between her and Peggy.

"You mustn't trouble yourself about it, now, sweetie, given the circumstances, and from what you say, Peggy knew you felt bad about it."

They heard sounds in the kitchen, Buddy's voice, calling Millicent.

"Do you want me to say you've got a headache?"

"No," Lily said. "I'll come out."

"Sweetie, you look awful."

"Hey," came Buddy's voice. "Where are you?" He came to the door of the room. He filled the doorway. Lily saw his friendly face with the continual questioning expression in it. "What're you two doing sitting here in the dark?"

"It's not dark, Buddy."

"Whyn't you open a curtain or something. Let some sun in." He walked to the windows and drew the drapes aside. The sudden brightness hurt Lily's eyes, and abruptly she did have a headache.

"Go away, Buddy," Millicent said.

Buddy walked over and sat down across from them, hands on his knees. He leaned toward Lily and said, in the gentlest voice, "I'm sorry to hear about what happened, kid."

His confiding tone troubled her, and she realized that it was because of what she had seen and heard of Millicent with the contractor. She couldn't get control of the crying. It seemed that everything was in question now, and all her happiness of the morning had fallen away into the darkness of herself. It occurred to her that in the middle of all the good talk and the stories and the convivial evenings, she had been making judgments about these two people; they had broken the rules and prospered, had sundered a family and left a lone boy without a mother, and they seemed to feel no regret about anything. She had allowed these thoughts, however unacknowledged, into her consideration of them. And here was their kindliness, like a reproach.

"I'll be all right," she told them, without quite believing it.

"You go lie down for a while," Millicent said. "You need some rest."

She thanked them and went downstairs to the room. It was gloomy, here, with the single thin slot of light along the sliding door, where Tyler had pushed the closed curtain aside to step in. The others were still in the pool, though they were all quieter now. She heard only the sound of the water and their motions through it. If they talked, it was in tones so low that no words reached her. Everyone knew what had happened. She undressed and got into the bed, and closed her eyes. She wouldn't sleep. She replayed those minutes in her mother's kitchen with Peggy, and remembered with a shock that she herself was pregnant. She knew it, now. There is a moment when rational thought gives way to the truth of experience; her whole being was different, and she knew what it meant. There was no doubt at all in her mind.

2

July 2, 1989
   Surprise!
   I've been meaning to write you lo these months, and not getting around to it, and feeling guilty, and wondering how you are and if you've forgotten me, and if you remember that I said I would come visit you and Tyler. And I'm writing you now to assuage these guilty feelings and to ask how things are with you, how you like it there in the old magnolia-blossomed southern climes, living in the bosom of your husband's family and being married. I have, as it happens, some good news about myself. I am living with a wonderful person named Manny, whose family disowned him ten years ago when he decided he couldn't take over the family business, which he will only describe as "imperialistic" and "exploitative," not to say "colonial" (I supplied that last), and he's very kind and loving, and we are not lovers either, though I think I would. (I know I would.) Instead of availing himself of the protection I've suggested, he's decided on celibacy, and of course that decision stands because of the terrible obvious reason. But we don't dwell on this. We keep a good attitude, and he manages his worry and his knowledge with amazing grace (that has become our song). He's always and in all instances thinking about everyone else. Sometimes, I can't help myself, and I come back here with someone, and when I do, he's like a great roomie who understands,

and is fun to be with, too. He's perfectly and naturally gracious, as if it isn't in his makeup to be otherwise, and I suppose that's true. Lily, he even forgives my petty anger at his choosing to be noble. I love him. I know I have the power to hurt him and that what I sometimes do hurts him, and he never gives a hint of it, and sometimes I get mad at him for that. But then I resolve to do better as a friend and companion. The fact is, I have never known anyone kinder than he, though you, dear girlie, are in all ways his peer in that rare quality. Conversation with him can be a bit halting at times because he's from Chile (the name is Manuel, but he has Americanized it, and insists on that). I met him at the bar where you and Tyler and I had dinner that time. That strange time that is so recent and feels so faraway and long ago.

I wonder how you're doing as a married lady and I think you were in love with Tyler all along, and now I'll bet you know this, too. You didn't like to be romantic, and of course you're the most romantic of souls. Nobody else could be so bereft at its absence.

Tyler, I'm working in a bookstore called The Portico—it has a restaurant attached to it. Some movie stars bought a farm in Ivy, and they come in regularly. They have lunch, and they're so good-looking and somehow so ordinary, too. Everybody leaves them alone, and you can feel everybody leaving them alone. It's so cool. You get the feeling it's not a courtesy so much as it's a kind of snub. Also, writers come in. I think of you, Lily, when I see them.

Anyway, both of you, I expect that you're thriving in your new environs, and I'm tenderly hoping to be asked for a visit. In November, if things go all right here, Manny and I are supposed to go to New Orleans to see his greataunt Violet Beaumont—he calls her "Great-aunt," but there's no blood relation actually. She's ninety-one years old, a former schoolteacher—and still drives a pickup truck. When you are ninety-one, you make plans tentatively, as she put it to Manny on the telephone last week. She calls her own death "the big exit" and seems not the least bit worried about it or frightened. That is, after almost a century alive, she seems to have no particular quarrel with life. Anyway, Manny and I could leave a week early and stop in Oxford for a couple of days. What I'm saying is that we could be talked into making Oxford one of our stops along the way. This would be in the second week of November (I'm guessing you'll have a place of your own by then, if you don't already have one). I hope we can see you both. And of course I understand if we can't.

I like working in a bookstore. I'm trying to sample everything. It's a good thing I don't sell liquor. I'd be drunk every day. Lily, assuming you're still pursuing your work on Mary Kingsley, I'm sending along something I found in a rare-books catalog we have here. Also, I actually read it before packing it up for you. What a marvelously humorous and bright intelligence. I'm betting that you have already read it, of course, but wanted you to have it anyway, on the chance that being a married lady may have carried you away from your maidenly interests. Does that last sentence sound like me? You see I've been immersed in Victorian prose. In any case, please note the address on the envelope and act accordingly. I'd love to hear from you and I would love for you and Tyler to meet Manny.

Love,

and ever your friend,

Dom

"It's written to both of us," Lily said. "Here."

"I'll read it later," Tyler said. "I'm beat just now."

They were standing in the hallway just inside the front door. Lily had brought the mail in and found the letter and opened it, while he watched. He had come in from the dealership, holding his sport coat draped over his shoulder, looking happy and relaxed, though for the past three days, after it had become generally known that Lily was expecting, and that the baby was due in mid-February, he had been anything but relaxed. That first day he had bought toys for both sexes, provisionally favoring toys for boys. And he talked about the future, even speculating on what colleges the child might attend. The others in the house teased him for being so much the cliché of the expectant father. But the coming change had worked in him, of that she was certain.

He was more quiet when they were alone. He would lose track of their conversation, his mind wandering away, or he would sit staring at what he was reading, obviously far removed from it. Sometimes it was as if there was a shadow on his soul, though he denied that anything was wrong, and deflected her questions about it by acting silly, or claiming not to understand what was worrying her. And it was worrying her, even as she was concerned that her own mood might be influencing his. It was possible that he wished simply to avoid aggravating her, and she did notice that things she used to ride over with ease now unnerved her. She wished for one moment's clarity, a way to cut through the fog that seemed to have settled over their lives.

"Tyler," she said now. "Dom wants to come visit. He's got a new—a friend. It won't be until November. And we should have our own place by then."

"Who's his new friend?"

"Read the letter," she said. "It's all in there."

He took it, kissed her, and strolled into the house with his sport coat still slung over his shoulder. She saw him stop at the dining room table and take an orange from the fruit dish there. Then he went on into the kitchen, where Rosa was preparing dinner.

Buddy Galatierre came up the walk, followed by Nick Green. They were both still in their jackets, looking tired and hot. Buddy stopped and put one hand on Lily's shoulder and said, "Hello there, you fragrant darling. Was that mail from home?"

"It's from a friend of ours," Lily said, patting his hand. "He was the witness at our wedding."

"Tell him to come visit. And tell him no hotel."

"It won't be until November, and he'll have a friend with him."

"A woman?"

She shook her head, and supposed that her facial expression told him everything. He showed no sign of having fully understood her, but then when he spoke it was clear that he had. "I had an uncle who was gay," he said to her. "Wonderful company. And people put him through a lot of unnecessary misery, too."

"'Wonderful company,'" she said. "That's exactly what I'd say about Dom."

"You tell him he spends no money on a place to stay in my town. And he stays here. You guys probably won't have as much room, right?"

She kissed him on the cheek.

"Riches," he said.

Nick Green came by her and smiled, but said nothing.

3

*I*N THE NIGHT, she turned to Tyler and put her hand on his hip, moving it slowly around to the front of him. He took her wrist and stopped her. "Not now, baby," he murmured. "I don't feel very good. My stomach's bothering me."

"You've been so quiet. Are you coming down with something?"

"I'll be all right."

She moved close. "Does this bother you?"

"Never," he said.

After a pause, she murmured, "Is something else—is anything else wrong?"

"No. Just my stomach."

"If you're nervous about the responsibility of a baby, let's talk about it. I'm nervous about it, too."

"I'm okay," he said. "I thought being nervous was sort of normal."

"But you've been so pensive."

He was quiet for a long time—long enough for her to wonder if he might have gone to sleep. But then he moved closer, and kissed her ear, the side of her face. "Lily, you keep *looking* at me all the time. It's like you're gauging me or something."

"It's new to me, too," she said. "I think I'm gauging everybody."

"Me, too," he murmured.

She waited a little, then reached over and put her hand on top of his hand. They lay like that for a few quiet moments, and finally she took her hand away.

That Sunday, while the others were outside by the pool, she sat in the living room and made the call home. She spoke to her mother, and found that she couldn't say the words right away. Doris asked how she was, then talked about Peggy, the doctors said she was fine for getting pregnant again when she wanted to. Her spirits were good. She and Scott were indeed going to try again soon. Lily said she was happy to hear it, then took a breath and got it out. It came out baldly, and felt heartless.

Her mother was silent on the other end. She took an audible breath. Then: "Are you happy about it, darling?"

"Yes. I'm ecstatic about it." She saw Tyler fidgeting on the couch, biting the cuticle of his thumbnail and looking off into space. He rose, finally, held his hands out, palms up, as if to ask if she needed him to say something. She waved him away, and blew a kiss.

Doris said, "I'm thrilled for you, sweetie. I'm out of breath."

Lily thought she heard tears in Doris's voice. She thought of her living alone in that house with its rooms that were being repainted and redecorated, her husband married to someone else, planning another family, her daughter pregnant now, too. How terrible if happiness were available only at the cost of it to others. She said, "I'm pretty breathless, too."

When her mother spoke again, the strength had returned to her voice. "You've called your father, right? You absolutely have to do that, you know."

"I'm worried about Peggy. I don't want to get Peggy on the phone."

"Do you want me to tell him to call you?"

So her mother had understood. "Could you?"

"I'll call him right now. I know he's home because I just spoke to him. Stay by the phone—if for some reason I don't get him, I'll call you back."

After her mother broke the connection, Lily went to the sliding glass doors that opened onto the pool and looked out. Tyler was sitting in one of the canvas chairs, hands folded in his lap, gazing off at the distant sparkle of the river, the moving gleam of the highway overpass. It was a bright, hot, still day. The others were ranged in various parts of the pool, tossing a foam football back and forth.

The phone rang, and she jumped. She walked over and answered it. Her father said, "Doris tells us you have news?"

She said the words, a deadpan statement of fact, emotionless as the recital of a street address. She heard it, and couldn't alter it, or muster any lightness of tone. Her father already knew. It was in the way he said how happy he was to hear it, and she sensed, too, that his joy for her was rehearsed—that at heart he was a little taken aback. He had most likely been warned off expressing any kind of surprise. She said, "Thanks, Daddy," though she hadn't quite heard the last of what he said.

"Anyway," he continued, "so Peggy'd like to say hello."

She waited. Her abdomen seized up, a cramp.

"Hello, Lily?" Peggy's voice. "Congratulations." It was full of unfelt brightness, a striving for affectionate cheer.

"Thanks," Lily said. "I—I know you'll be calling us soon—" She couldn't get the rest of it out.

"It's such good news. I'm very happy for you."

"Thanks. Thank you so much." She had to work to keep the stress she felt out of her voice.

"Well, here's your father," Peggy said.

Scott came back on the line and was enthusiastic again, repeating his congratulations and telling her to take care of herself, and give Tyler his best. Lily said she would.

When they had broken the connection, she turned to see that Tyler had come in. "It's too hot out there if you're not swimming."

"That was harder than I thought it would be," she said to him. "I should've had you call them for me." She smiled. "After all, this is your doing."

He took a step toward her, and then seemed to hesitate. Something changed in his eyes, like the memory of something dark. He said, "My stomach still hurts." He put his arms around her.

When she kissed his neck, his breathing quickened; he shuddered. She leaned back to look into his eyes, and felt a little shiver of alarm at the strange blankness in his face. For an instant it was as though she were staring into the cold, lifeless eyes of a statue. But then his expression relaxed into a smile, and he shook his head. "I know it's just nerves," he said. "But my stomach is in knots right now."

TWELVE

1

May 20, 1880

Dear Friend—

Yesterday I earned my father's displeasure again, quite by my own will, I'm afraid. I have hidden away a copy of Locklar's Physics, *because I haven't finished with it, and I heard Father promise it to Bishop Mayhew on the morrow. Well, it is to be a morrow several morrows hence, by my lights. Father raged, and threw the* Geography of Antarctica *at me, which I managed to duck. He chased me out the door of this house, but Bexley Heath is not Highgate, and, skirts and all, I easily outdistanced him. What a wonderful wide lawn is this! Perfect for racing and leaving angry oaths in the far distance. I wandered for an hour through the graveyard, while the sun sailed toward the horizon and the trees became a darker green. You will be happy to know that I have a new friend, for which I thank providence we dragged ourselves to the country. His name is C. F. Varley, an electrical engineer. He comes to see me in the afternoons, and we talk about what he has given me to read. We met in an unusual way: Charley and I were in the town together, to purchase some flour, and I saw some men I knew to be chemists, and I decided to try my knowledge with them. I entered their conversation, told them of my interest, and when asked to go on, espoused something which made them laugh.*

—And are you able to produce gold yet? one of them said.

I went out and stood crying in the street, furious with myself, and furious with Charley, who refused to stop badgering me about it all. And C. F. Varley walked up to me, kindly and calm, and introduced himself. When it became clear, through Charley, not me, what had happened, he averred that he was a friend of Father, and that he would gladly teach me what he knows about chemistry.

I don't know what he says to Father about me. But in this latest instance involving the Locklar's Physics, *he walked over from his cottage while I was camping out among the gravestones. There I was reading the dates, marking*

the lives long and short, and he came to within twelve feet of me before I saw
him, and it took all I had to keep my startlement from showing.

—What have we here? he said.

—We have a diplomatic vigil, said I. A wait for the storm clouds to pass.

—Be these fatherly storm clouds?

—Of a kind, I said.

—Explain.

—A conflict of wills over a book, sir.

—Then are we to put off our talk?

There is such humor in his face: a round, whiskered red face with big
bushy gray eyebrows and a wonderfully wide forehead.

—We could talk here, I told him.

—In a graveyard?

—No one will interrupt us, I said.

—True. But academic.

—Nevertheless, I said.

—You're determined.

—The word comes close.

—Aye, he said. And would there be repercussions concerning the mas-
ter of your house?

—There might be, I said. In truth, sir.

—Thank you for your honesty, he said. I believe I'll delay our visit if
you don't mind.

—I understand completely, sir, I said.

And I watched him walk away, shaking his head and chuckling to
himself. I watched him for a good long time, since there were no buildings
or fences for him to disappear behind, and when he got to the far side of the
field, he turned, a wonderfully crooked old shape there in the descending
darkness, in the fading shade of those tall trees, and waved to me.

The move from Highgate was for Mother's health, and seems to have
had an effect. Though this house is full of what I can only call mistakes in
construction—doors hung all wrong, lintels faltering as if under too much
weight, window frames that don't fit the spaces, breezy as open doors, the
whole house drafty as a barn; and the plumbing is perversely unpre-
dictable. I have been forced to take things in hand. I have been allowed to
receive regularly by post a copy of The English Mechanic, *which I am*
putting to good use. Varley has helped a little, and there is, of course, the
spur of his appreciation: I am unused to that sort of encouragement,
though I must say Mother and Father did purchase The Pursuit of

Knowledge Under Difficulties *for me, a gift whose application seems to have put me at a strange remove from them, at least by turns.*

In any event, I fixed the pump, which at first coughed up copper-stained sludge, and then receded into a stubborn refusal to yield even that, coughing like an old, old horse whenever I worked the handle and belching nothing but earth-smelling air. I supposed the well to be empty, but I fixed it; it took me all of an afternoon. Me. I wrestled with it until it blessed me, and there was a surfeit of water, clear and cold and wonderfully free of secondary flavors. I had the use of the Mechanic *as an assistant. Instructions not terribly well written but clear enough. I fixed it, and when Father saw that I had fixed it he stood up tall and looked at me with new eyes, a grudgingly proud man. He began to talk of my getting about more, out in the world. I'm to leave for a holiday in Wales, with Cousin Rose, in less than a week. There is even talk of a brief foray to Paris. How I would love to be on the waters of the channel, on my way to the Eternal City!*

But all of this is in jeopardy, of course, now that we have run upon these rough waters regarding the Physics.

I stayed out in the air, in the cemetery, for a good hour, walking about and observing the phenomena, and then I ventured back to the entrance of the house. He was seated in the library, still in his waistcoat, and perusing one of the big volumes of natural history he had brought only recently from London. He turned and saw me, and shook his head.

—I suppose you're proud of yourself.

—No, I said. But I will not bend. And no punishment will make me. I shall not relinquish the book until I have done with it myself. Not for you, not for anyone.

He stared at me for quite a long time, then.

—Do I frighten you at all? he asked.

—Yes, you do, said I.

—When do I frighten you?

—When you yell, and throw things.

—Yet there is no change in your behavior. Why is that?

I had no answer for him, so I simply lifted my shoulders slightly in what I suppose passes in most cultures as a shrug.

—Where do you get it? he said.

—Where do I get what?

—Never mind. Will you please try to hurry yourself with my book?

—I will do that, I said.

That was yesterday. And all day today he has glowered and won't speak to me, and I haven't ever let him know how much more I dread that than all his bluster and his noise. I spent the afternoon in Mother's room, reading to her from the newspapers and wishing I could do something to cause a riot in the house, something to make the silence in his part of the house go away. If only he would have someone over for cigars and brandy; if only he would forget that he's angry with me. When he speaks to Mother he tells her to communicate with me:

—Tell "the learned one" I would like to have my book before the end of the week if that is at all within her range of expectations and allowances.

He moves by me without so much as a look, and Mother repeats the message exactly as if I have not been standing there all the while. We both have to suppress our laughter.

I am almost finished with the book, and then he can have it, and not until then.

The environs of Bexley Heath are open and rural compared to Highgate, and the tall, surrounding trees make a lovely shade in the summer afternoons. Mary's father has gone on another journey, and she is the one now who gets the longest letters from him. She understands that he has respect for her, that in some odd way, for all their conflicts and her stubborn refusal to be governed entirely by him, he has learned to favor her. It is true that all the money is spent on Charley's education; yet there is something unfocused and almost frivolous about Charley, and rather overly delicate, too. Her father has perceived this. It's even possible that he wants to use her to shake Charley into a deeper concentration on his studies.

Charley is often too much like his uncle Henry. He's frequently in trouble at school, and can't seem to spend five minutes together on the same subject. Even so, Mary is only allowed German lessons, to help with her father's planned study of religious practices and rites among the primitive tribes of the world—he has said on more than one occasion, with exactly the complacent unfocused casualness of Charley's talk, that it will be definitive. He's been talking about it for years, and some part of Mary has begun to know, without quite admitting it to herself, that her father's plans are like Charley's plans.

She takes the lessons each Friday, and on most Mondays. The instructor, Mr. Meuller, is sometimes called into the city to perform in his other profession, as a taxidermist. His cottage is crowded with animals in a hundred different frozen poses: lions and bears and various equine species, a few sea creatures. Because her father used to quiz her in the language, it comes readily to her, and Mr. Meuller keeps remarking on her quickness of mind.

In the evenings, when not going over the thickets of knowledge about electricity and chemistry with Mr. Varley, she pores over her father's medical books. She needs much of it for her work upstairs, with her mother, who in the first days after the move from Highgate seemed slightly better, but has taken a turn for the worse. Mary has observed blood in the sputum her mother produces, and this has alarmed her. The sick woman insists it is nothing to worry about unduly; she has produced blood before.

—It's an irritation of the throat, she says.

Mary looks into her throat and sees white blisters on the back of it—small round sore places. These grow still smaller and heal, and then appear again. Mary wonders if something in the food her mother's eating produces it, and she works to change the diet—more soups, fewer spices. Since the move to Bexley Heath, they've had to depend on another charwoman, Mrs. Craig, who's a disaster in the kitchen, and so Mary has taught herself to cook, too. She isn't half bad at it, and her mother compliments her. The blisters in the older woman's throat disappear and do not come back, but the cough persists, as does the pain in her lower extremities. It hurts to walk. She's incessantly anxious about her husband's welfare. She tells Mary that with each journey she expects never to see him again; the world is so dangerous. Mary has begun to read about Africa again, roaming through the work of Mr. Burton, his description of his search for the source of the Nile.

When Charley comes home from school, he expects to be served, too. His sister does so cheerfully, with wonderful efficiency and with humor. The household runs smoothly, with all the work Mary has done on it. She finds comfort in the daily tasks she sets herself, and she learns a kind of concentration that shuts away doubt, or uneasiness. She spends each day in a steady labor to keep order and to advance her own growing knowledge of the world, and her reward for all the hard work is what she calls "little hours" with Mr. Varley. She has begun to realize a talent for friendship with men—especially older men, with whom she feels most at ease. Her night sweats and panics have been put down, tamped into the folds of her dark garments, and tied tightly as the knots in her hair: when she looks into the mirror in the mornings, she sees plain, drawn features, unadorned, and she never looks at her own body anymore. She's a grown woman and others are beginning to remark on it.

One, a vicar who accompanied her father back from London one afternoon, looked straight into Mary's face and spoke about her in the third person to her father.

—This young woman would be striking if she took the least care to adorn herself.

Mary, who had been caring for her mother all day and had come down to see what her father might need, had looked at the vicar and said, quite pleasantly:

—Oh, it's not nearly as bad as you think, Vicar. For I do speak our mother tongue.

For this, she was rebuked by her father, who demanded that she apologize. She did so, through her teeth, and later she took the opportunity of spilling some tea on the vicar, an act for which she hoped that God (if he was at all as he was mostly supposed by the civilized populations of the world to be) would forgive her.

She tells all of this to Mr. Varley, who laughs.

—Well, he says, still laughing. From the sound of it, you're a modern lady now, I promise you.

—I'd like to run into the bugger again, Mary says, and then catches herself. Sorry.

He goes deeper into the laugh, coughing.

—No, Mary. Bugger it is. You don't remember his name?

—I never got 'is name. A vicar.

—Delicious.

—I'm certain I could get the name from Father.

—We'll just refer to him as the bugger.

They are both laughing now, and are such good company together, Mary and her elderly male friend. How she loves the time with him. The sun seems brighter, the colors of the world more vivid, when she's with him. He tells her, sputtering and giggling, that he never knew anyone, man or woman, quite like her.

—And tell me, Mary, why is it that you've taken to wearing only black? You aren't in mourning, are you?

—I like black, she tells him. Black favors me. I like my own color in it.

—You're not slightly funereal, though, as a *personality*. I don't believe I've ever been with a more delightful creature.

—Well, you must get out and about more.

She smiles at him and nods, her hands folded tightly at her middle.

He shakes his head, tilts it slightly as if to get a better angle from which to appreciate her.

—I 'ave to get 'ome now and save Mother from a terrible fate: Mrs. Craig's pudding.

Again, he laughs.

—Mary, I'm afraid I must leave Bexley Heath for a time. I'm off for Glasgow tomorrow on business—a lectureship there. I accepted it last year. I'm sorry to say I'll be gone most of the winter.

She wants to reach for him, beg him not to go, but she keeps the humorous expression on her face, standing ramrod straight.

—Well, she finds the strength to say, I guess you will be getting out and about more. The smile she bestows on him shows no trace of the desolation she feels. She wants to kiss his cheek, but then decides against it, and turns from him, strolling away.

—It's going to be a very long and dull winter, she says.

—I'll write you, he says. Will you write me back?

—If there's time in my desperately busy social life. Perhaps we should sign a treaty to the effect that we will acknowledge communications from each other no matter 'ow entangled in the affairs of the world we are.

—Mary, he says seriously. You will make your place in this world. Mark my words. The world will hear of you, young woman.

His eyes well up, and he lifts one arm to wave.

—I'll see you in the spring, she tells him.

—Yes, my friend. Farewell.

2

*S*HE DOESN'T SEE HIM again for years. Her father moves them all to Cambridge, to a narrow house with windows that make it look like a beetle-browed angry face, overlooking a prospect of wide lawns called Parker's Piece. There are cricket games there every afternoon in the summer. Her father, home early from his latest journey, is sixty now, and looking older than that. He's had an attack of rheumatic fever, and is seriously weakened. It has taken him through the winter and spring months, recovering, gaining his strength back. Mary nurses him and her mother, and cares for Charley, who seems to have inherited his mother's propensity for neurasthenic troubles. Mary has no time to think. She spends nights tossing, feeling as if something is undone that needs doing. But there are no other forms of tossing: she sleeps without dreams. Her father decides it's time to settle down and write his book, but the days go by and nothing gets done. Mary works with him, sits at his side, pencil ready, and when he speaks she tries to write it all down. She has little use for the German she's learned, but she keeps taking the lessons. Her father starts to talk, then stalls, then changes his mind. He can get up now, and go out. He takes long walks and sometimes she accompanies him. But her mother doesn't want her to get too far away. He spends days watching university cricket over at Fenner's, or lolling around on a blanket in the grass of Parker's Piece, watching those games. He tells Mary that sitting there in the midst of cricket balls flying through the air gives him a sense of the danger he misses. That fall, feeling fully recovered, he wanders down to the towpath beside the river, and watches the college eights rowing and practicing. He stays too long, and receives a chill. Mary finds herself scolding him, saying that if he has no regard for his own health and well-being, he might remember that there are those in the world who do. He might think of his family a little, and of his rheumatism. He smiles charmingly and tells her that where he's concerned, he would rather she keep her medical opinions to herself.

More and more, she's the only one who can soothe her mother. They still make each other laugh. The sick woman can do a perfectly wicked imitation of Henry Guillemard's glottal voice.

In December, Mr. Varley visits from Bexley Heath, having returned from Glasgow some weeks ago. He looks changed, smaller, and there's a gauntness about his features. He sits with Mary in the front room of the house and remarks on the peaceful look of the fields outside the window. His hands tremble, and he never lets go of his hat.

—I'm so sorry I didn't get back to Bexley Heath sooner, he tells her, looking down at where his fingers work the brim of the hat. The world has a way of interfering with our best intentions.

Mary remarks that this is something she quite understands. Abruptly, she feels the pull of her own desire to confide in him—to tell him about that morning so long ago when she wasn't yet six years old and she had stood in the fresh snow of a winter morning, believing so completely in the delight of the world. She sits forward slightly and starts to speak, but then her father comes into the room and shakes Varley's hand and behaves as if Varley's visit is to him and not to Mary, and of course in one narrow way, in the form of the times, that is all it can be or should be. She sits and attends to their talk, her father going on about plans for one more journey around the world, if he can ever get his full strength back.

—Did you know that Lord Dunraven has gone to Australia?

Varley shakes his head.

—No, I didn't.

—Gone to climb Ayers Rock, Mary's father says. I've heard from him. Capital man, Lord Dunraven.

—Well, says Varley, I haven't had the pleasure of much time with him.

They go on to talk about the murders in Cheapside. Four women, horribly slain, and the newspapers have been full of speculation. There has been a letter from the killer, sent to the chief inspector of police, signed "Jack the Ripper."

—It isn't any Englishman, George Kingsley says.

—Surely you don't agree with those who want to pin it on the Jewish immigrant population, says Varley.

—I heard of something chalked on a wall. "Jews won't be blamed for nothing," in the killer's hand. Or words to that effect.

—Surely you don't take that as being serious, Kingsley. The killer's hand? I read nothing about that.

—I've read that the killer understands anatomy.

Mary's father glances at her, as if uncertain what he might be able to add, without violating the veneer of polite conversation in the presence of a woman. She says:

—I've read the accounts, Father. He slit their throats, disemboweled them, and removed their organs of generation, except for the first victim on the night of the double event, as they call it. The night he killed two.

—I think we will not discuss this further, says her father. The whole thing is too hideous.

Varley leans forward, gazing at her with a severe expression on his face that surprises and disconcerts her. But when he speaks, his tone is merely horrified curiosity:

—Have you read that there's a second letter?

—No, she says.

—The second letter is not signed. It was sent with part of a human kidney, to a man named Lusk.

Mary hasn't seen this among the lurid accounts in the newspapers. But she recalls that at a recent afternoon tea given by her cousin Mary, the other girls were speaking with furtive, excited, giggling silliness about the removed kidney of the latest victim. They posed the theory of cannibalism, and were all the more excited to talk about the crimes. Think of it: a cannibal wandering Cheapside in the darkness.

—I think I did see something to the effect of a second letter, George Kingsley says.

—Well, they're selling newspapers fast as Dickens, if you know what I mean.

—There is an appetite for it, I agree. In my own house apparently.

Mary's mother calls her to the sickroom. She stands and excuses herself, and bows to Varley.

—Very pleasant to see you again, he says.

She bestows her best smile on him, smiling with her mind as well as her face. She hopes he can see it in her eyes. Then she bows to her father and leaves them there. She makes the climb up to her mother, and sits with her, and when she hears the door open and close, she has the sense that she will not see Mr. Varley again soon.

—Poor Varley doesn't have long, I'm afraid, says her father later that evening.

She broods on this, and suffers quietly the gloom of the ending day, like something settling over her mind. Her father seems to feel it, too.

But his low spirits never last. His natural buoyancy takes over. He's a Kingsley, after all. As in earlier times, he makes up games for her, challenges her knowledge of geography and chemistry and the other subjects of their mutual interest. He draws her out of her black mood. Charley takes part, too, but he's getting ready to read for his degree now, and there's a new seriousness between him and his father, almost like a competition.

3

*L*ATE THAT MARCH, when the weather is finally warm again and she can open the windows of the house—windows she herself has recalked and resealed—her father revisits the idea that she should go to Paris. The idea resurfaces one afternoon when a family friend is visiting, a woman who has kept a special fondness for George Kingsley's gangly, awkward, but bright daughter. The lady's name is Lucy, a middle-aged person of accomplishment and strong intellect, with a hyphenated last name: Toulmin-Smith. Mary enjoys her company, because the lady has wide knowledge of the world—she's a medievalist with a good reputation in the field—and she treats Mary as an equal. This friend will accompany her across the channel.

—It's time, her father says. We've been talking about it for years. Mary should see some of civilization if she's ever to be anything but strange.

He says this, and grins; it's a joke between them. And Mary wonders if he means Paris as a joke. Yet things are running smoothly in the house on Parker's Piece. Her mother's feeling stronger—has even gotten out of bed and dressed herself, and walked a little in the shaded lane in front of the house, leaning on George Kingsley's arm, just as they had, Mary imagines, when they were young. They tottered a little; the sun was bright on her father's brown hair, and it made the gray in her mother's more pronounced. They looked sweet, and watching them at the time, Mary couldn't help wondering what their secrets must be. Her mother has never spoken about him as a wooer or romantic companion. There are no stories, no fond memories spun out in the lonely nights, while the two women wait for Mrs. Kingsley to grow sleepy. The connection between Mary's parents is an iron-strong family tie: Mrs. Kingsley's feeling about her husband is almost that of a daughter; indeed there are times when it's exactly as if Mary and her mother are sisters. The idea, the reality, of Paris arises like a change in the look of the sky, far off. She can't quite believe it, even as the arrangements are made and the day of departure approaches.

4

*T*HEY SAIL on a bright Saturday morning in early May. The channel is smooth and calm and lovely, and they watch the cliffs of England recede on the horizon, to the west. Lucy's American by birth, though she'll never claim it; her father was a historian. She's been a friend of the family for as long as Mary can remember. They stand on the boat deck and gaze out at the placid-seeming waters of the channel and talk. Lucy relates the story of her first time in Paris, where she met her husband, twenty-odd years ago.

—Paris is truly the city for love, she says.

It's clear that her hopes for this journey, and about Mary, go too far. For all her involvement with the world of ideas, Lucy seems to be thinking of Paris as an invitation to romance, not for herself, but for her young companion. It strikes Mary that this might well be the reason for the excursion in the first place: her father's hope that she'll meet some suitable someone. A moment later, the idea seems absurd; he has never shown himself to be quite capable of thinking that far beyond himself and his own concerns. She has this thought without bitterness. That is the man as he is, so deeply concentrating on his own affairs, so absent-minded about everything else.

It's not beyond Lucy Toulmin-Smith to think of it, though. Lucy has spoken before, in an oblique way, of her worry over the fact that at twenty-six, Mary is still unmarried. These gentle asides were directed at Mary's father, mostly concerning the unfairness of requiring Mary to care for her mother, and usually wedded to the suggestion that George Kingsley hire a professional nurse.

On the short sail across the channel, Lucy can't help falling into the pattern of mentally trying to put Mary with one or another of the young men they are traveling among, all of whom Mary looks past and around as if they were no more animate than the mizzen mast. She watches a squall on the far horizon, and wonders if it will reach the boat before they tack in toward France, which is visible now, a line of dark green in the bluish distance.

Paris is surprisingly small, and rather sedate compared to her memories of London. She and Lucy take a room in a little hotel off the rue de la Paix. Their window overlooks the Seine and the prospect of the Left Bank, the city crowding to the edge of the river. It seems always crowded with people,

putting his hands on her shoulders and firmly holding her in place. It comes to her that she has never been handled in this way—not since she was a little girl in her father's house.

—Please take your 'ands off me, she says.

—*Excusez-moi*, says the older man, and then rattles on in the other language. *Je vous rend nerveuse? Mademoiselle, je ne suis pas digne de recevoir, mais dis seulement une parole et je serai gueri.*

—I wish to be let go, Mary says firmly.

He drops his hands to his sides, steps back a little, laughing softly, regarding her, one hand up to his chin. It's as if he is showing pride in her. As if he has created her out of the refuse littering the alley.

—What do you want with me? she says, by some means managing to keep the evenness of her voice.

The younger man moves to the door and indicates the room beyond it. There are tables, with bottles of wine on them.

—No, thank you, she says. No.

—*Elle est Anglaise,* the older man says to the younger.

They let her pass, and stare after her. As she makes her way down the street, she looks back twice, and each time they are as she left them, standing in the thrown light of the door, watching her. She turns a corner finally, and then another, and still another. She passes a closed street market, and a dance hall, where three couples turn under a Chinese lantern. At last she finds a café that is open, six separate people sitting in the garishness of an electric light, drinking wine, or ale, or brandy. The waiter is a sallow, pale man with bad skin, but lovely expressive hands. She watches the hands as he wipes the table and asks, in English, what the young miss would care to eat or drink.

—'ow did you know I was English? she says.

He smiles.

—Mademoiselle, it is, um, how do you say eet. Over you all?

—All over me?

The smile makes his whole face seem different; it's quite strange. She feels that he could pass for two separate people, using the smile, and then not using it. Forgive me, he says in perfect English. I have decided not to toy with you. Usually, I give travelers something to remember France by. A kindly French waiter. But I'm from Devonshire.

—You're English?

—I was born there. My father brought me here when I was nine. He was in her majesty's foreign services. A widower after my unfortunately difficult arrival. He traveled extensively, of course, and when he came to live in Paris he brought me with him, where he married a Frenchwoman and died, and I stayed. Everyone here thinks I'm a very smart French boy who can speak English, and I let them.

—Why?

He holds his hands out, palms up.

—I am malleable. You have the most startling face. From the look of it, I can't decide whether you're going to laugh, or fight me.

—Is it your custom to speak so informally to women?

—Ah, I think you're going to fight me. So I'll remove myself. *Pardonnez-moi*, mademoiselle.

She watches him with the other customers in the place, and he brings her hot tea, along with a small glass of mulled wine. She doesn't like the taste of the wine, but drinks it anyway, for the experience. It goes almost immediately to her head. The sensation annoys her more than anything else. She's beginning to feel strangely outside the flow of events. Others come and go, one of them a crook-backed man wearing black, who glances at her and then glances back, apparently marking the color of her dress, also black. He walks with a terrible limp, and with him is a young woman whose arms look like those of a muscle-bound man. She wears her sleeves pulled up, puffed around the top of her biceps, and seems proud of the looks she earns from the other patrons. Another woman who wanders in has a badly deformed upper face, one eyebrow pushed down, as if she were a clay figure and the artist had tried to ruin his work. The lower eye socket is empty and dry-looking. Mary can't stop looking at her.

Finally it's time to go. The place is closing. Her English waiter comes to her and says that he has paid for her tea and wine, and when she protests, he touches her cheek and says:

—*Ma chère.*

She falters, realizing that she has never been touched that way by anyone—not even her mother or father. A touch meaning sex. The isolation in which she has lived all the years of her life glares at her, now, as if from a hellish dark corner in a dream. She straightens, bows slightly, realizing that this is no place for her, even as he takes her hand and leads her to the doorway.

—What are you doing? she says to him.

—I'm taking you home with me, ma petite.

—No, she tells him. You are doing no such thing.

—Tell me, then, where we should go. I only want to know you better, to talk to you.

She hesitates, then begins to walk away from him.

—I'm certain we can 'ave nothing to talk about, thank you. I shall not accompany you to any rooms.

—A walk, then, by the river?

She stops.

—It's such a beautiful night and there are people there.

—Well.

It comes to her that she would like to see what she can. Tomorrow there will be the Louvre, and the Bois de Boulogne, and the botanical gardens with Lucy. Walking mile upon mile and looking at paintings, sculptures—frozen shapes of people depicted living. In life.

—I am only being friendly, he says.

—I don't know your name.

—No, that's quite right, we haven't been properly introduced. My name is Philippe.

She stares at him. The smile changes his face again.

—Now it's customary, I believe, for you to tell me yours.

—Toulmin-Smith, she tells him. Lucy.

5

*S*OMEWHERE during the walk through the weirdly half-lighted streets, it comes to her that she has no idea of the time, possesses no timepiece, and though she has done a lot of reading about the path of the moon across the night sky and the relation of this motion to the passage of night itself, she can't quite place this Paris moon in a quadrant of a sky so often obscured by buildings and then by trees. She can still make out its reflected brightness on the water, but that's a shimmer across a subtly wavering space. He walks along at her side and seems content, as she has been—at least initially content—simply to look at everything. They reach the river, and stand for a few minutes at the stone ledge that overlooks it. Here, nobody seems to be with anyone else. Behind them, on the grass, a small, wiry man does handstands and tries to walk that way, failing over and over, and speaking angrily at himself in French. Several elderly people sit on benches, and a man in what looks like a priest's garb lies on his back, his hands folded over his chest, uttering something in Latin to the sky.

—You wish you hadn't come, Philippe says to her.

—No.

—Are you normally so quiet?

She laughs.

—No.

They walk on. The trees lining the bank give way to open grass, and a thoroughfare down which a coach and four passes. Several people crowd to the edge of the road on the other side, and then cross and walk down to a boarded sidewalk and another quay. There's a boat waiting there, lantern lit, with a paddle wheel in back and a deck on which there are tables set.

—Would you care to ride on the river? asks her companion.

—It's late, says Mary.

He takes her arm at the elbow, and she goes with him, down the small wooden planking to the boat. They get in with the others. She sees a woman with luminously white, almost translucent, skin that the moonlight seems to enhance, as if the face itself is made of that light. She sees an old man with two young women, who cling to him, and chatter at him in French. Several couples are seated on the bench opposite her. They murmur and laugh and flirt, and one man drunkenly presses himself against his lover, kissing her neck, opening his mouth awfully to kiss her mouth. Mary looks away, out at the silver trembling of the water, as Philippe pays the boat master, and takes his seat at her side. He puts his arm over her shoulder.

—No, she says.

—I mean no trespass, he says.

But he leaves his arm resting on the gunwale behind her. She looks at the riverbank gliding by in the ghostly, lambent air, like motion in a dream. She sees dimly lighted windows, and shadows moving on the banks and in the streets; she sees the heavy cathedral shapes, outlined by the incandescent sky, with its dim stars. There is a breeze, now, and someone is singing. Other voices rise to the song, and across from her the man is still breathing down into the girl's mouth, the two of them appearing to grapple with each other there in the dark. A mist has begun on this part of the river.

—They are in love, Philippe says.

She removes herself slightly, looking out at the iridescent surface of the water. She breathes the odor of wine, and of the river, which is dirty, and of the air of Paris, which is very much like the air of London. But the city itself looks ghost-haunted and beautiful in the spring night. The boat turns, and the moon is on the other side now. It illuminates the streets and buildings on this side. Mary watches it all, and the singing goes on. More voices join in.

—What are they singing? she asks.

—A love song. A song about lovers on a river in the night.

Philippe begins singing now, in a voice that fails to find the notes, and is therefore heard above all the others.

The boat lurches into the quay, and Philippe stands to help her out. She steps up on the pier, and walks with everyone to the riverbank.

—Thank you, she says to him. That was very pleasant.

—Come on, he says.

—I 'ave to go back now, she tells him.

When he takes hold of her arm again, she resists.

—We can ride again.

—No, I think not.

—What is it you need, then? Tell me and I'll pay you.

—Pay me?

He stares. She can just make out his eyes in the night. Oddly it reaches her, from some half-conscious part of her memory, that she has knowledge of something shameful her uncle Charles had let be known at the table once: that he and his fiancée had looked at obscene drawings he'd made of their copulation as he imagined it. She, Mary, has been skirting those very possibilities with this young man, exploring the territory. Her blood thrills at the nearness of it. She had let herself think of him as courting her. And now she recoils, thinking of the mean thing this flirtation is, what it really is.

—I do not wish to suggest, Philippe says. Don't misunderstand me.

—I understand you perfectly, Mary says. You wish to negotiate.

—No, he says. Forgive me. I like you. I hope to see you again. Tomorrow. I'll make up for it, for saying such a thing to you, and my name is actually Tristram.

—Tristram.

—I use the other name for fun.

Suddenly she has an acute sensation of what it all amounts to, men and women, the whole round of loves and counterfeits of love, paid and arranged and mediated, blessed by society and shunned by it or hidden in it. And she wants none of it, not even courtship, or marriage, wants nothing of the confinement that sex, and by extension marriage, are—or would be for her, since she has lived in that prison all her life, her parents' marriage. She's free, here, wandering the streets of Paris, and this young man has assumed that she's fallen, a prostitute. He's trying to compensate for it now, being probably not a particularly bad man, only someone who has misread the circumstances. She almost pities him, while he walks a little away from her and then comes back, striving for some sign of forgiveness from her. She can be anyone she wishes to be, here, alone. And she desires, with all her heart, to be above all the turmoil, those passions.

Until this moment she has thoughtlessly assumed her life would eventually conform to the lives of the young women she knew: someone would come into the house, brought by her father, and would make an offer. Her father would provide her with a dowry, and she would enter the married state. No. The idea makes her laugh. When Philippe/Tristram gingerly grasps her wrist, she pulls free, and turns from him, moving off in the bath of moon and lantern light, laughing, putting her hands to her mouth.

—Have I not explained? he says.

—In a word, she says, laughing, no.

He takes her by the arm again.

—I'm not accustomed to being laughed at in this way.

—If you don't take your 'and off me, I'll fetch you a slap in your face.

He drops his hand and steps back from her.

—I'm no rapist, mademoiselle.

—That's very fortunate for both of us, she tells him, not quite subsiding.

—*Bonsoir,* he says crisply, then turns on his heel and strides away from her.

She waits a moment, and then calls after him.

—Good night.

For perhaps an hour, she walks the streets of the city, partly seeking the hotel, but also simply looking at things. The nightlife in Paris is slowing down. It's getting on toward morning. She uses her sense of direction, and the lowering moon, to navigate her way to the end of the rue de la Paix. Some women stand in the doorway of a building on the corner, the edges of their gowns turned up. She knows what they are, and resists the temptation to walk over and speak to them. She's begun to worry that Lucy will wake and find her gone, and be frightened. She herself feels no fear at all, now, nor any sense of disorientation. It's as if she has undergone some elemental trial, and come through it in this new, habitable self. She stops a moment, and breathes the words: *I am extraordinary.* They please her, and she finds that she's ready to believe them, oddly more so than at any other time in her life. It is a distance, from the feeling that one is different from everyone to the discovery that one is extraordinary.

The street climbs away from the river, and she makes her return slowly, taking in the air, the fragrance or stench—sometimes changing from one to the other within the space of a few paces—of this strange, sleepless city.

She stops before the facade of the hotel and asks herself exactly what has happened. She wants to put it into some sort of order in her mind: she went for a walk in Paris; she stopped in a night café and walked down by the river and rode in a boat along its banks, and then wandered the streets; she met a young man who thought she was one of those gay women who were kept by fancy men, and she disabused him of this. And she understood, in the moment of knowing what he thought and finding it funny, that she must seek never to be overruled by sex, by the demands, or the allures, of sex. She breathes deeply, extends her arms to the quiet street, the part of the moon that's still visible above the silvered rooftops and shapes of trees in the far distance. She has never felt more free, more herself.

Paris shines for her.

In the hotel, she decides to ride the new invention, the electric elevator. She waits for a long time, but the man responsible for working it is not there. An elderly man sits reading behind the desk. She approaches him, then thinks better of it, and moves to the stairs and up. In the room, Lucy's snoring contentedly. Mary undresses, gets into bed, and pulls the blankets up under her chin. *I am extraordinary.*

PART 3

"So Quick Bright Things Come to Confusion"

—SHAKESPEARE: *A Midsummer Night's Dream*

THIRTEEN

1

$\mathcal{T}$HOUGH EVERYONE in the Galatierre household talked of the quickly vanishing weeks, for Lily the summer's progress seemed glacial. Thunderstorms came and went, but mostly it was blistering hours without a stirring of air, days that faded with red sky and humid stillness into sluggish nights whose stars seemed washed out, drained of all shimmer by the thick vapors of July and August. She and Tyler had bought a used Olds Cutlass through the dealership, and Tyler had been given a new demo, and so, apart from the fact that she was unfamiliar with the surrounding countryside, she was not housebound. On occasion, she took the Cutlass and drove the country farm roads, with the windows open and the wind blowing in on her and the radio playing loud. The land was inexpressibly beautiful, the air sweet with the heavy fragrance of wildflowers and honeysuckle. She liked the sound of her own voice, belting out the songs, the white lines of the highway seeming to keep time, coming in under the shining hood with its silver ornament.

In late July, she went into Oxford and read for the group at The Loft, and they liked her. She was helping with set design for now, twenty hours a week. They were planning to put on a bare-bones production of *The Merchant of Venice* in the fall. Because she would be showing by that time, she didn't try out for it. There would be a meeting late in the summer to decide what the two productions of the winter would be.

Most of the rest of her time she spent looking for a real job, and for a place she and Tyler and the new baby might live. Millicent was very thoughtful about her, and Sheri kept bringing her little gifts, mostly baby things.

Both young women went out and talked to real estate agents and people who had put ads in the paper about places to rent. Tyler was so busy at the dealership that the task of finding something was essentially

Lily's, and Sheri wanted to help. She didn't speak of her "platonic friend" again, and for this Lily was secretly grateful.

Very little of what they looked at appealed to Lily. There were several places inside the city limits, but most of these were small apartments that reminded her too much of the little room in Charlottesville.

Oxford was, after all, a college town.

Earlier, at the beginning of July, she and Sheri found a white clapboard Victorian, slightly run-down—it had been built in 1892—with a small porch and a finished basement, only five blocks from the dealership, and they returned to the Galatierre house with the conviction that this was the place. Tyler went with Lily to see it, and he agreed. Everyone seemed happy for the young couple. They all celebrated, and Nick set off some bottle rockets early in honor of their good fortune.

The night of the Fourth of July they went to the high school to watch the fireworks, and on the way home they saw flames licking up into the sky of the city, making a hectic red backdrop to everything. "Look at that," Buddy said. "That's bad, whatever it is." They had come to an intersection and were waiting for the light to change. Buddy left the car idling through two changes of the light while they watched the moving glow on the clouds.

"Buddy," said Millicent nervously, "let's go. This is awful."

"Light's red again, sugar."

They waited. They heard many sirens. The night smelled of ashes and smoke and burning. When the traffic signal changed, Buddy went down the side street, and then made a series of turns. The fire was so high that it was simply a matter of drawing closer to it. When he drove past the dealership, Millicent emitted a sigh of relief.

"That did cross my mind," she said.

Buddy nodded, and drove slowly on, and made another turn. To her horror, Lily recognized the street. "There it is," she said.

And Buddy stopped the car. Before them was a massive, furiously upward-rushing conflagration, a house, *the* house, the same one Lily and Tyler had decided to rent. It was completely engulfed. The roof had partially collapsed; the windows were all charred frames and licking fire. Tyler said, as if only now realizing it, "That's—oh my God. That's—" He didn't finish.

For a long time, no one said anything. They watched the movement of the firefighters hurrying back and forth in the wild intermittent radiance and darkness, the arterial pulsing of the emergency lights, the bending, heavy streams of water from the fire hoses disappearing into the flames.

"Now that's a freaking portent," Nick murmured. "God is watching."

"Somebody *wasn't* watching," Lily said, through her trembling.

"They're not gonna save much of that," said Buddy. He waited another moment, then pulled the car around and headed away. He glanced at Lily in the backseat. "I'm sorry about it, sweetie."

"You'll find something," said Millicent, reaching back to pat Lily's knee.

The next morning, over breakfast, Tyler and Nick spoke about fate, and how evident it was that Lily and Tyler were destined to remain right where they were. Though Lily understood that they were not serious, she felt the weight of the event anyway, and she let the idea of moving out of the Galatierre house rest for a time. Tyler went on as if it had never been a question; he was too busy at the dealership to think about much else.

He was gone most nights until late, and when he came home he seemed worried and tired, as she was worried and tired. She was finding the work at The Loft taxing, and she went over there less and less.

Tyler was overly solicitous of her. In every circumstance, he seemed less playful. And whenever they were with the rest of the family, it seemed to her that Nick was *too* playful, too ready to tease or make a joke or a sardonic remark. It made Lily vaguely restless and nervous, as if there were some matter of her knowledge of his marriage that had leaked to him, through Sheri, or through his study of Lily's face. She had trouble looking him in the eyes; and he seemed to be watching her. His jokes about the play wore on her goodwill, and made her seek to avoid him, without being obvious about it. Often, she took to finding some pretext to leave a room when he entered it, and she tried never to be alone with him.

Tyler unwittingly helped her in this: he didn't like to leave her alone, and would follow her through the house. She chided him about being too attentive, and he appeared injured by this, lowering his head like a boy who has been called out in school. So she found that she was, in turn, being more careful with him, as though both of them had become rather more delicate than either of them actually was. She attempted to be less watchful of his moods, to try giving him room for adjusting to everything.

It was during these weeks that she realized how strong her need for him was. One night, she had a nightmare that he was cold and distant, turning from her, and she woke in fright, gripping the blanket and trying to catch her breath. She lay close to him, luxuriating in the way he put his arms around her. He murmured something she couldn't distinguish, and then went back to sleep. She lay wide awake, imagining herself in England, a hundred years ago, the old, habitual way of riding over the dark.

It seemed to her that she missed him more in the days, and that when he came home, his weariness got in the way. They had settled into a kind of mutual companionability that made her think of middle-aged couples, and when she told him this he stooped and put one hand at his back, hobbling across the room like a very old man. "Can I get you something to chew, there, Maw?"

"I'm serious," she said. But she laughed.

On a Sunday morning in late September, he turned to her in bed and murmured her name, and they made love, making wordless concessions to the changes in her shape. She placed herself astride him, and moved so slowly that he reached up and held her face, gazing at her with an adoring expression, staring, quiet, almost still.

"Oh," he said. "Oh, Lily."

She lifted herself, so that only the tip of him was inside her, and she moved from one side to the other, then settled, slowly, slowly, on the full length of him, pressing down, then lifting again, still slow. She repeated the motion, talking to him the while, telling him that she loved him, that she loved *this* with him. This. When he came, he kept repeating her name, holding her by her shoulders and saying it. She slammed herself against him in the last pulses of his coming, and kept doing it, until she came, too, and during it all he kept saying her name.

"Oh, God," he said. "I love you, Lily. I love you so much." There seemed something almost mournful about the way he said it.

She said, "Are you all right?"

"Oh," he said. "Yes. Yes."

They lay together without moving for a long time, and he grew soft, was sliding out of her. "Don't go," she said.

He put his arms around her and held on. "I do love you."

She straightened, resting her hands on his shoulders. "You make it sound like there's been some question about it."

He blinked, reached up, and kissed her breast. "My upbringing, again," he said. "Remember? Me and happiness?"

"Well, believe it, baby," she murmured. "It's right here on top of you."

Then they were separate, and she could feel him pouring out of her.

He let his arms down, sighing, gazing up at her with a satiate impassiveness that now made her feel his difference from her. That was delicious, too. She lay over on her back, and saw the little imperfections in the ceiling.

Later, they went into town, to the square, and spent time looking in the shops that flanked the courthouse. In Square Books, they found a names book, bought it, and then strolled across to a small sidewalk café, where they ordered brunch, and looked through the book, trying to decide on a name for the baby. She suggested Mary if the baby was a girl, and he said, "Oh, God, no, I don't like that one. Anything but that. I had a terrible neighbor lady named Mary. My father actually went out with her a few times."

They found it odd that there were certain names, male and female, that both of them felt adamant about, and in each instance it was because they had known someone with that name, someone they hadn't liked, or someone who seemed less than attractive. There were several that both of them disliked for these reasons. And there were some that they agreed on, but tepidly. Each liked a few that the other didn't, and they could see how difficult it was going to be to choose. He liked Maxwell, if it was a boy. She was adamantly opposed to that. She liked Thomas; his fourth-grade teacher had been named Thomas, and he hated the idea. They talked and laughed and planned things, and Lily felt very happy.

She said so.

He shrugged, then reached over and moved a strand of her hair aside from her forehead. "I wonder if I'm made for happiness."

The rest of the afternoon he seemed a little distracted, even faintly remote, and when she tried to bridge the distance, suggesting with a look that they could go to bed again, he made a joke about being less of a man than she needed, and changed the subject. That evening, they went out with the family to dinner, and when they got home, and had retired for the night, he kissed her and said, "What a glorious day this was."

Yet as he drifted off to sleep, and lay over on his side, groaning softly with whatever he was dreaming, she had an unhappy sense that something had come between them. The shadows in the room seemed to take on life as lights were turned off in other windows of the house; the dark seemed to move, and the shadows crossed over her, like spirits, bearing the weight of trouble.

Was happiness so bound up with the knowledge that it was also ephemeral? And was it therefore always to be accompanied by the stubborn fear of its loss? Something wasn't right. And yet she believed that she had developed an unusual capacity to ruin her own good fortune with this anxiety, this expectation of something going wrong. It was Tyler who had said he didn't trust happiness. She couldn't find the answer to any of it, now, and so she berated herself for her morbid imagination, turning in the bed, sleepless and worried, she believed, over nothing.

∽

 $\mathcal{S}$ HE HAD EXPERIENCED few physical discomforts from the pregnancy once she was past the first trimester. Aside from a few small waves of nausea, she'd had no morning sickness. Her appetite was healthy; usually, and if she had no nightmares, she slept fairly well. She'd even managed to do a little more work on the play.

Often enough, she doubted it would ever be finished.

In the mornings, she looked at herself in the mirror, marveling at the roundness of her abdomen, and at the fact that she hadn't been able to trace its incremental swelling, no matter how hard she tried. That was herself in the mirror, and as her body had changed she found it impossible to remember its shape as it was before. She marveled at the excitement and fright that she experienced, and it seemed odd that the world could go on as it always had, with its entertainments and sufferings and appointments, while this tremendous thing was happening inside her. She had been told that by September she should feel some movement, and when she didn't, she worried about that. But her gynecologist assured her in his authoritative way that things were coming along quite normally. He turned out to be right, of course, though Lily worried anyway.

The movements, when they came, little flutters, delighted her, and made her feel involved more profoundly in life than she could find words for; it was like a great secret she possessed, separating her from the rest of the world. It was deeply defining, and calming, too, each time it happened to her. Yet at the same time, when she thought about its significance, it caused her to tremble, and to experience the nameless apprehension that comes to people facing something momentous and unknown.

2

You said once that you had never been in love with anyone, and no one had ever been in love with you. But you moved with men, rough men, who it is difficult to imagine were gentlemen in all circumstances. What was it about you that gave you the power of setting boundaries they wouldn't cross (while you were crossing boundaries no white man had ever ventured past)? It must have been more than Victorian dress and custom because those social boundaries were crossed routinely during that era. Your own father crossed them with your mother. In everything I've read, I've found only the smallest inklings of your true being—the things that made you what you were. Forward-looking, but always dressed in black; funereal, but thoroughly charming, witty, and unforgettably plucky. Plucky the way E. M. Forster meant it about Chekhov—that he was entering the world of the intelligent, the charming, and the plucky.

There were proprieties you paid rigid and absolute attention to, yet you were quite willing to deceive the British Museum authorities by maintaining that you were collecting fauna and looking for species—though you did bring an enormous number of things back with you—when what you were really after was a way into the African mind, into the world of fetish, and religious practices. You claimed not to have any kind of mind for writing, and yet you wrote some of the most beautiful descriptive passages ever rendered in English. Studying you and your contradictions, I ought to feel more comfortable with the contradictions in myself—the fact that I'm a silly little romantic fool when it comes to my husband. And then there's the contradiction of my feelings for this family, with whom I would like to stay, in exactly the same proportion and force as I would like, also, to leave. I've come to love them so, with all their complications and kindnesses. As these weeks have passed, I've found that I have less of myself to give my husband, who is carrying some worry I can't get him to express. Lately it's hard to concentrate on much of anything. I've spoken to Doris several times, and it's always about the stages of pregnancy, what she's doing in the house, what Scott and Peggy are up to. We never seem able to say anything about how we feel. I can't seem to express it to anyone.

I sense this eerie kinship with you, and maybe what I am experiencing most is a desire to be like you. To command my own demons as well as you clearly commanded yours. As it is, I find that in conjuring you as you might've been in your time, I'm constantly having to resist investing you with my own unresolved, and irresolvable, contradictions. I find it very hard to accept your belief that women should not have suffrage; that, doing what you did and going where you had to go and seeing everything you saw, you could still hold so fast to the assumptions of your time, assumptions that you yourself, with your life, exploded, or proved false. I admire your outspokenness, and am puzzled by the ways in which you still clung to the social norms. I think sometimes people took you seriously when you were joking, and others took you to be joking when you were serious. But you were determined and quite serious about the duties of a woman, and took the pains to fulfill them as you saw them, even after the journeys and the books, even after you were famous and Charley wasn't and he belittled your accomplishments by insisting that you continue to serve him, like any paid housekeeper. You lived in a closed world, a repression I can only imagine, assumptions about you that in today's light seem so cruelly designed to imprison you, and still you broke through to yourself; you went so far; you astonished everybody.

But I sense the facade of your chipper, amusing, discursive speech as a protective shell. And when I think of you, I feel stronger. I have such awful nightmares. I have gotten so big.

⌒⌒

*O*NE MORNING Lily, suffering a bad headache, labored up the stairs for a glass of milk. She found Nick sitting in the kitchen, talking on the telephone. Earlier, she'd fallen asleep, and had a terrible nightmare, and the feeling of it was still reverberating inside her. She had thought there was no one else in the house, and seeing Nick, had emitted a small gasp of surprise. Nick hung up the phone and said, "Hey. I had to come get a box of forms Buddy forgot to take with him this morning. I'm heading into town. Want to come along?"

"Thanks, anyway," she said. "I'm not feeling all that good." She averted her eyes, and moved across his field of vision. She almost asked him to stop staring. She had determined to pour a glass of ice water and go back downstairs.

"I'm thinking I'd like to help somehow with this play you're writing," he said.

She shrugged, and gave him a little smile. "I'm not writing it, lately. And I don't really feel much like teasing today, Nick."

"I'm serious." His own smile was almost sheepish.

She waited a moment. Evidently, he had no other comment to make. She had expected some sly remark, and when it wasn't forthcoming, she felt a little at sea.

"You were down there all morning," he said. "Writing."

She nodded.

"Do you have to write preparatory stuff? Sketches, things like that to get ready?"

She realized that he was serious. She said, "Right now I'm writing letters. Back there. To her. To Mary Kingsley."

"I don't mean it as a joke—but that sounds a little batty."

"Exactly. That's exactly it. But they help me think about her. It's like a journal, really—working notes, say. That sounds less batty, doesn't it?"

After a pause, he said, "It's still a little batty. But I think I know the feeling."

She turned to the refrigerator, and opened it. She had to hold her lower back with one hand, it hurt so much. "Where's Millicent?"

"Went into town for something. Rosa went with her. You all right?"

"A headache." She poured the milk and stood there drinking it while he watched. The quality of the light was watery here; it made her think of depths, labyrinthine murk, the dark that the residue of the nightmare had left. She turned and tried to smile.

"I hate back pain," he said.

"Right now," she said, "I hate headaches."

"You're not very comfortable around me," he broke forth abruptly. "Are you." There was something tentative in his tone; he had let his gaze drop to the floor.

"Nick," she said. "Stop being silly. You're family."

"Has Sheri told you anything about me?"

Lily shook her head, swallowing the milk. She felt everything Sheri had told her burning in her face.

"You're sure."

Putting the empty glass in the sink, she averted her eyes. "What would Sheri have told me?" The falsity of the response felt like a lash on her spirit.

"Well, I've had the feeling you've been a little jumpy around me from the first."

"I didn't know how to take you," she said. "I didn't grow up in a big family, Nick."

He cleared his throat, and looked down at his hands. "All that teasing I've done—well. And that first night. I have to admit it. I was crocked. I was trying—I guess I was trying to make friends. I thought if I could make you guys laugh."

She said, "You know how it is when everyone else has had something to drink and you haven't? That's how it is sometimes, with me. Even when nobody's had a drop. I don't know why. Or, I do, I guess. I just don't know how to change it or make it go away."

"Of course, I'd had a lot more than a drop, that night."

She nodded, smiling. "I believe that was noticed."

They were quiet for a time. Somewhere outside, crows sent up a racket.

"You haven't really answered me about Sheri," he said.

"Sheri didn't say anything, Nick. Really."

"She didn't tell you about the dirty movie episode? I can see it in your face, Lily."

She took a few seconds before answering. "That was so long ago."

"It was recent enough." He smiled guiltily. "Look, I just want us to be okay, you and me. That's all. I'd like it if you weren't thinking bad things about me. About the—the movie, well, I had a little boy's interest, for fun, for laughs, and it got twisted out of proportion. Really. Let me, for instance, let me tell you how this all figures into my life. I come from Biloxi. You know where that is?"

"You don't have to explain anything."

"No, now really. I want to explain this. You know where Biloxi is?"

"It's south. I saw signs for it when Tyler and I went to New Orleans that time."

"Biloxi is on the Gulf of Mexico. There's an air force base there—Keesler. Nice place. I grew up in that town. An—an only child. My parents—well, my parents. Hmmm. My parents are two of the most repressed, closed, unhappy people you ever saw. Closed and shut. You name it in culture and in life—they've shut it off. They don't even own a damn television. They never have owned one. They gave me a—shall we say—sheltered existence, growing up, and it took me a little while to realize that they were, and are, afraid. Deeply, spiritually, physically terrified of everything. And they don't even know it. They think the rest of the world is nuts—you know? And every last thing made by God or man was made to thwart their efforts to make me into a perfect sexless human being. Now the sexless part—that's Mom's thing. She's what you'd call, ah, prudish. I call her Medusa. And Dad, well, Dad just takes punishment. It's incredible. The two of them were awful when Sheri and I got married. This is Sheri we're talking about. Cheerleader, good grades, good home life. Nice girl from a good family. A little spoiled, but good-hearted, you know? They acted like she was Eva Braun. It was the goddamnedest thing you ever saw. And so ever since then, well, I've sometimes done things, you know, I'm sure, just to foil them. Piss them off. I mean, I certainly learned to look for ways of increasing their sense of the collapsing immoral world they live in, if you know what I'm getting at. I took to exploring things like that just to torment them. And I don't mean to say that my interest in the—uh, well, that particular movie—was entirely from that, or that it necessarily had anything directly to do with them. Though it did—Lily, it just did. And it wasn't really as pornographic as all that. It was a freaking *Playboy* video and I meant it as a joke and I was a little drunk and I thought, you know, what a good idea, Sheri and I can watch it, for laughs, and then we can talk about it in front of Medusa and Daddy. Only Sheri got nearly as upset as they would have, and that worried me a little bit and it got out of hand, because some part of me kept saying, 'Well, yeah, why not. Why should we be sexless?,' you know, and Sheri acted as if I'd asked her to *perform* in a video. And I'm still paying for it with her and that isn't what I deserve. Not that, I don't think. I mean I'm not as bad a guy as she—as she thinks I am. As she must have said I was. Because Sheri has a way of exaggerating."

Lily sought for something to say, and could only nod.

"You've noticed it." He thought a moment, then shook his head with what looked like appreciation. "She's something."

Lily nodded again.

"Anyway, the whole thing's ridiculous, because my quietly hopeless, sad parents and I aren't even on speaking terms now." He paused once more, then seemed to sigh some doubt away. "Look, I know I've teased a lot about you and your—your writing. And you deserve the truth. The thing is, I wanted to write. I did. And I think maybe a little bit of me might've wanted to discourage you." He folded his hands and looked at them. "No, I know it. I did."

She said, "Nick, what's going on, anyway?"

"I think Sheri's—I think my wife may be growing weary of me." His smile was pained, and sad. He looked at the floor, and then at his own hands again. "I was wondering if you'd noticed."

"No," Lily said, meaning that she did not wish to be put in the middle. But she left it there, understanding that he had taken it as a direct response to his question.

"Anyway, I'd like to see whatever you're working on—when you're ready to show it. I don't have much talent, but I *am* a pretty sharp reader. And I promise to be sympathetic."

"I would think sympathy's what's needed." She hadn't meant it as glibly as it sounded; she'd intended it as self-deprecating sarcasm. Reaching across the small space between them, she touched his wrist. "Joke," she added.

"Oh, right." He shook his head. "That's me, you know. Always with the jokes."

"I'd be happy for you to read it," she said. "If it ever gets close to being finished."

He rubbed the back of his neck. "I know it's hard to find time to work in this house. I'm thinking of writing letters to Miss Kingsley myself."

She laughed. "It is batty, isn't it? But at the very least it helps me remember what I've read. She wrote some letters to somebody, an anybody in the future, that are in some ways more revealing than her other letters, even to friends. So I thought I'd—" She paused, and shrugged. "Write back."

"This is nice," he said. "I like this. Talking to you."

"Nick," she said, "why haven't you and Sheri looked for a place of your own?"

He put his hands on the table, and then took them off again, and folded his arms. "Good question. But you see how it is, here. It's a big house and there's so many good things about being here. The fact is, Sheri doesn't want to move. And—and, well, we are saving for a place. I've been cut off, remember? We don't have a lot to show for my years in the oil magnate's sad house."

"I think we'll all remember these months as a sweet time," Lily told him. "Years from now. Don't you?"

He nodded. They were both silent. She rinsed the glass and put it in the dishwasher.

"I hope we can be good friends," he said.

"I'd like that," said Lily.

He stood. "And I don't mean this just as a ploy to help me with Sheri, either."

She couldn't help but think of people who unwittingly explained their own motives by denying them. But Nick was not so transparent as all that. There was a malleable light in his eyes, a kind of admission of need, that struck her. "There's not much I'd be able to do with Sheri, anyway," she told him.

"Oh, Sheri thinks the world of you, you know."

"I wonder what she's thinking, sometimes," said Lily. "But that's true of everybody, isn't it? Is there anything more mysterious than another person?"

"The feeling I get from her is—well, it's as if she doesn't respect or like me very much, and I wondered if it wasn't because I'm selling cars instead of writing poems or acting or something, I don't know. Writing for a newspaper maybe."

"You said you wanted to write."

He shrugged. "Well. I didn't know." Then he gave forth a little huffing laugh. "Still don't. I was always—from the time I was a little, little boy—always more in favor of just, you know, having a ball." Now she thought she saw something of the familiar self-mockery in his expression. She took her gaze away, out the window, and saw brightness on all the metal surfaces—the fence, the railing, the supporting braces on the side ladder—of the swimming pool. The reflected sun glittered in the little breeze-disturbed eddies of water there. "I don't mean to bother you with this," he went on. "It's just that you do spend a little time with her and—and she talks to you."

"She doesn't say all that much to me. Have you spoken to Millicent about it?"

"Oh, no. Oh, hell no. Are you kidding? According to Millicent that girl can do no wrong. If she thought there was anything—that I had anything less than slavish devotion—no, you don't really know Millicent."

"Millicent's been great to me," Lily said.

"Oh, she is," he hurried to say. "Of course that. But don't get in the way of her and Sheri. I'll tell you, I like it here, as I said, but sometimes I can't wait until we can move out. It's like I can't really get near her, here."

Lily couldn't help blurting out, "Well, Nick, you drink so much."

He left a pause. Then: "Yeah."

"I know she does, too."

"Everybody," he said, leaning on the counter and shaking his head.

"Everybody what?"

"Hmm?" He looked at her. "Oh—nothing." He sighed and ran one hand through his hair. "You know what? A part of me knows quite well that we haven't moved out of here because I don't want to let go of the nice life it affords us. The—the nice things and the drinks and the freedom from certain kinds of worry."

"Listen to what you just said," Lily told him. "Listen to what you're saying about yourself."

"That's what Sheri says. You sound a little like her now."

"It'll be all right," said Lily.

"Your hands are shaking," he said.

"I'm tired."

"Well, you should try and get some rest." He grinned, turning from her, shoving his hands down in his pockets. The sardonic demeanor and tone seemed to have come back, as if someone had flipped a switch. But as he left the room she realized that it wasn't irony, particularly, but discouragement that sounded in his voice and determined his expression. He walked through the other room and up the stairs, hands in his pockets, head down.

3

February 1893

Language is useless as bleating. This awful morning, after weeks of worrying about him, and tending to him, and withstanding his bad temper and his guilty sorrow over it all, I woke from a dream of him, an apologizing figure I didn't recognize but who, in the logic of the dream, was my father. I washed and dressed, feeling a terrible sense of foreboding, looking out at the gray light of the day, with its cold wind and its flattened columns of coal smoke over the trees, and wishing for summer. Later, walking upstairs in the silent house, I felt the weight of the silence, and I believe I knew full well what I would find. I had letters for him, and I knocked, and there was no answer. I had spent the night in Mother's room, reading by candlelight because of course I couldn't sleep. Before he went to bed he said that he felt better than he had in a long while. A shadow crossed in my mind as he spoke, a feeling that in some circles, I suppose, travels under the name of premonition. I put it down in myself, chided myself for my morbidity. And now there was this freighted morning, with its dimness and its gloomy thoughts. I was bringing the mail to him, trying to act as though nothing but my mind was amiss. I knocked on the door and, receiving no answer, I knew. I opened it with that feeling of breaking in on a profound privacy. There he lay, as still as any object in the gloom. I put my hand on his shoulder. His eyes were partly open, but they often were when he only slept. I shook him, saying his name, and that vibrant man who survived so many close scrapes and wandered the world on high seas and among primitives and in wilderness and hunting dangerous creatures, was gone to that bourn from which—oh, God! One knows the words! One bloody well knows the bloody sodding words! That wasn't my father there in the bed, that ghastly thing was not him, now, and it hardly needs repeating and rehearsing! As I have had to do over the past two days, with members of the family who would scarcely have anything to do with him, or us, when he was alive.

He went peacefully in his sleep. At least there is that.

I have had to tell Mother, who has lived all these years in dread of this very thing. She took it better than I supposed she would—almost fatalistically, though she hasn't stopped her crying since, and is so down that I fear for her, too. I fear for her anyhow, since she can have no part in the estate, and it all goes to Charley, who is not nearly capable of handling it and who is so grief struck that twice I have had to come near scolding him, reminding him of the responsibility that devolves on him now. There are acceptances Father gave out, charges for moneys he needed in his travels, and

there is a small inheritance, and these must be balanced and settled imme-
diately.

Today, the ladies from the Kingsley side of the family came, all in crepe
and bombazine, to pay their respects—and the passing bells rang, though it
is an accomplished thing. They sat in our parlor with their little black ker-
chiefs held in their laps, and spoke in low tones, an official condolence the
likes of which I can't bear for wanting to tell them exactly what I think of
all of them. Having taken it upon myself to arrange things, since Charley
is like a little lost boy, I have come upon letters of Father's, and encountered
his hardened feelings toward some of these people, who shut him out of their
circle because of his choice of a wife. Mother, for all her weakness and her
failing health, was faultlessly gracious to them. But she stood out so—as I
stand out—as soon as she opened her mouth to speak. They exchanged
glances; they are all so pious, and they were busy congratulating themselves
inwardly for being kind to her. It was in their faces, that damned satisfac-
tion in one's good deeds, the complacency, the confidence that the Lord
approves, and that they are safe from reproach. . . .

The talk wanders far afield. Mary watches the men—all of them from her
father's sphere of associations in the world: medical men, and scientists,
and the one adventurer, Mr. Ploworth, whom she has never seen. He
says he remembers her as a little girl, and her mother, in her flush-faced,
glaze-eyed grief, seems to recall him. He talks of the islands, and of the
plentiful game in the North American woods. He's a big, red-haired man
with a large, bushy mustache and a very heavy neck, on which a close-
trimmed beard seems merely to delineate the lower aspect of his round
chin; the beard stops, and the neck flesh goes on into the collar of his
shirt. He dips snuff, and sneezes, and his stubby hands manipulate the
snuff box with some difficulty. The cigar between his fingers appears
small and slender, for their roundness and size. Yet for all this, he looks
more large than fat—a solid wall of man, with powerful shoulders and
the florid face of a baker in a hot kitchen.

—I first met your father in the Canaries, you know, he says.
Wonderful chap. Quite oblivious to danger. We shot buffalo in America.

Mary serves tea, and is gracious. Charley hides his fear in brave talk
of making his own explorations, and writing his own books.

Cousin Lucy's talking about Tennyson, because someone else mentioned Gladstone, that horrible man. These remarks seem so casual and cruel, as though there is not a living, breathing someone named Gladstone who desires, as does everyone, a decent life, and happiness for his loved ones. It is all such drivel, this talk, and she wants to scream, resisting the urge with a little twinge of horror at herself. People have to observe the rituals.

Her mother sits so far down in her chair that it looks as if she's dissolving under the heavy black dress. People speak to her only briefly, and it's just as well, since she isn't capable of a conversation. But the way the other women of the family avoid her is hard to ignore. Charley elicits more stories from Mr. Ploworth, who is happy to oblige. They are smoking cigars, now, and two other men have joined them. Mr. Ploworth talks about being with George when he encountered his brother in the city of Chicago, in America. It seemed to him at the time that there had been some ill will between the brothers, but in Chicago, he says now, they made up.

—It did me such good to see how they were together, like old friends. I never had any brothers. He goes on, attending to Mary, watching her, and abruptly—she realizes it with a start—speaking directly to her.

—You ought to come riding with me, Miss Kingsley, I have an excellent pair of new horses I just bought at market. Arabians—very well trained. I have a wonderful mare for you. Fifteen hands high.

—I don't ride, says Mary.

—Oh, but surely you would want to learn. I understand that you've been very active in this business of educating yourself.

—Sir, I beg your pardon. I can't think of it. Thank you anyway.

—I had heard you were an intellectual adventurer. It doesn't extend to the physical?

He drew on his cigar and blew out the smoke.

—Not when it comes to riding, Mary says.

—Not afraid of gamecocks, though, I'm led to understand.

Mary turns to Charley, who can't return her gaze.

—I'm sorry to disappoint, sir. But I do not ride.

—Well, I should love the opportunity of teaching you.

—I don't wish to offend, Mary tells him. But I do not wish to ride your bleeding 'orse, Arabian or no. And there's an end to it.

Later, when everyone has gone, and she and Charley have put their mother to bed, they sit in the library among their father's things, and try to talk. Minutes pass in silence. They're tense with each other, and the silence seems to contain the terrible absence, his very voice, stilled forever. Yet here are his things, his papers and books, and letters—packets of his letters, which, over the past few days, Mary has read and reread.

—You know, Charley says abruptly, Ploworth was interested in you.

—Oh, she says. Please.

—He spoke to me. As head of the family now. He would like to know if he can call on you. He might even make an offer.

She opens an envelope and finds an acceptance her father had made out at some point during the past ten years of borrowing in order to travel. It's a canceled one—has been paid. She puts it back.

—Of course, the devil knows if he'll call after that squelching you gave him.

—I'm not interested, Charley. Please tell 'im, if my telling 'im didn't make it clear.

—An offer from a man like that is nothing to take lightly, sister.

She sits behind her father's desk and opens another envelope, which contains a blank sheet of paper and a ticket stub from some London show. She throws this away.

—Are you hearing me? Charley asks.

—I will not entertain a call from that man, or any man, Charley.

—You're already past the age . . .

She stands.

—Either go see to Mother, or go tend to your own affairs or remain where you are and *I'll* go, but do please leave off this plaguing of me.

—Forgive me, he says.

He's offended.

—I still must care for Mother, she tells him. And you.

—I was trying to be magnanimous on that score.

—Spare me.

He's silent for a time. Then he rises slowly, and goes to the window, parting the heavy drapes there to look out.

—She isn't long to be with us, I suppose you know.

—Charley, please don't talk of this. Not now.

—I don't know how long I'll be here, either.

—Are you speaking of *dying*?

He turns from the window, and folds his hands behind his back. He has his father's looks, but none of his father's energy, none of his charm or brightness of mind. It seems to her now that she has always understood that whatever George Kingsley possessed in the way of strength and intelligence he had bequeathed not to his son but to his daughter. She feels only concern for Charley, poor worried Charley, his mind turning in the conventional little circles: Mary is single, and there are no suitors, and there are, given her unconventional ways, not likely to be any suitors. She watches him pace to the other side of the room, thinking, brooding over this problem. Outside, a blustery wind blows; the fire in the grate flickers from a downdraft. It is the coldest night of the year. She knows he feels the dark closing in, because she feels it. This will be a terrible winter; and the spring will come late. She tries to reassure her brother, that she's quite happy to be where she is, as she is. The frivolity of courtship, of thinking about it and wasting hours hoping for someone to offer, or pay court, it all feels exactly the same to her as it felt in Paris, when she first realized her aversion to it. It leaves her with a cold sinking at heart, which she describes to Charley as an impatience, an unwillingness to lend herself to such games.

—Father has left us with enough so that I needn't worry about it, and I am relieved. You must believe me, I am relieved.

—Mary, he says, I'm so terribly panicky right now.

She answers in a whisper.

—Yes.

FOURTEEN

1

*T*HE BABY'S MOVING NOW. *It feels like the motion of the whole world—it is so immense to me, and yet secret. Poor Tyler's almost the last one to have felt it. Sheri did, and then Millicent. He made a joke about it. And of course the baby won't move when he's near. There's been a terrible earthquake in San Francisco. We were watching the World Series, and there was a sudden shimmer and the announcer said, "We're having an earth . . ." and the signal was cut off. We all sat there stunned. And on the news, later we saw the city burning. A long camera view showed an awful glow in the sky. I sat on the sofa, back hurting, half sick, unable to take my eyes away. We saw a picture of a collapsed highway overpass, and Buddy said, "My God, there's people in that mess." I started crying, and Tyler came over and held my hand, and the baby kicked. It felt like something climbing my rib cage, inside. I didn't say anything because this just wasn't the time. But I had to shift myself so it was less uncomfortable, and Tyler said, "Is it moving?" I shook my head and tried to stop crying.*

You, who spent the first thirty years of your life in seclusion, saw so much of death. People want to say that it was different for people in your time, that because life was more precarious, one adjusted rather quickly to the idea of mortality, and therefore it was in some ways less horrible. I don't believe it. People brought more courage to the world because the world required more courage—maybe that's true. I admire your bravery because I sense how prodigious your fear was, as mine is. And I have so much less, in terms of daily threats to existence, than you did, to be afraid of. I've never had to drive a leopard away from the door.

2

$\mathcal{I}$T SEEMED TO HER that people looked at her differently, and then there were occasions when no one seemed to notice at all. When she saw other pregnant women, she expected some exchange, some glance of commiseration or recognition, but they seemed particularly to be avoiding her gaze, as if the whole thing were an embarrassment they would rather not talk about. She had to stop working at The Loft, just as the stage sets were complete and rehearsals for *The Merchant of Venice* were starting. She went twice to watch these first rehearsals, and she was surprised by the quality of the acting. The whole thing depressed her now, because she could have no active part in it.

When hunting season began, the men all went north, to Tennessee, for deer. It was a fall day, with wind and a chilly mist, and when they returned with a deer strapped to the trunk of the car, they were like excited children, exhilarated and soaking wet. The deer was a large buck, "with an eight-point rack," Nick said proudly. Buddy and Tyler hauled the carcass into the utility room, to the left of the back door. Nick had been drinking beer, and merely watched them, with yet another can of it in his hand, sipping it and looking at Lily.

"You're not gonna stay out here for this," he said incredulously.

"Stay out here for what?" Lily asked. She had been fascinated by the size and bulk of the animal, and the struggle of the two men to move it. There was a heavy, sodden look to the long belly, as if it were a bag of something gelatinous but solid, and Lily was morbidly curious; the inanimateness of the thing, its lovely shape gone slack—she couldn't look away. The men chattered as they struggled, and there seemed something rather adolescent about it all—their loud voices, going on about the details of the afternoon, their breath on the frosty air. It was Buddy who had shot the deer.

Nick went into the house, and the other two hung the carcass up by its hind legs, at the fetlocks. Lily saw the dark, facetless, unseeing eyes, and the tongue lolling out of the mouth. She felt weirdly detached; though when the head moved as the men hoisted the animal even higher, something turned over in her stomach, above where the baby was. Nick came out of the house with a box of plastic garbage bags and some newspapers. The three of them worked together to spread the newspapers beneath the carcass.

Tyler looked at Lily and frowned. "Why don't you go on inside, honey."

"I'm fine," Lily told him, wrapping her arms around herself.

"I don't think you ought to see this in your condition," Nick said. You could hear the beer he had drunk in his voice. "It might turn you into a vegetarian."

"If this is going to be a regular thing, I guess I ought to get used to it."

Buddy looked over at her and seemed to think a moment, as if he were doubting the wisdom of letting her stay—or reading her doubts, which she was beginning to feel. He grinned sweetly. "This ain't pretty, darling, but it's clear. There's no mistaking what it is."

"You-all are so impressed with yourselves. It isn't as if you've killed a lion."

"Tallyho," Nick said. "The lady has a point."

"Okay," Tyler said. "But nobody's going to make fun or comment at all if you decide in a few seconds that you don't want to stay out here. Isn't that right, Nick?"

"Not me," Nick said.

Buddy brought a knife out of a small leather holster on his belt, and with an air of casual practicality, as if this were no different from opening a letter, stuck the blade into the soft white belly of the deer, and carved downward, opening the cavity. He reached in and pulled out what looked like a wet sack of dark fruit, and the blood followed, flowing onto the newspapers, where the pile of innards had flopped with a surprisingly loud slapping sound. There was an immediate strong odor, something akin to that of dirt basements, that took her breath away. At first she thought this was the smell of death, but almost in the same instant she realized that it was the smell of these organs, their natural odor, and she felt the violation of the animal's life all the more powerfully.

She turned from them at their work and made her way into the house, where she found Millicent and Sheri sitting at the kitchen table, drinking wine. They had let the day wane without turning on any lights yet. What was going on outside was visible through the glass doors. The women could see it from where they were sitting. Lily took her coat off and sat with her back to it, and thought of Mary Kingsley walking through the bush, in Africa, past rows of dead from a yellow fever outbreak in 1895.

Sheri said, "You're white as these walls, honey."

"I'm okay," Lily told her.

They watched as the skin was pulled from the fetlocks downward, and there was the final hollowing out of the rib cage. All three men worked efficiently and they talked through it, making jokes and drinking beer. When it was done, Buddy began cutting the meat away from the bone, and making fillets. It took only a little more than an hour. Then Buddy cut the head off and worked over that for a time. He swathed what remained of it in a green plastic bag, and took it out to the car. When it was all finished, they spent another hour wrapping the meat and putting it in the freezer out in the garage. They came into the house stained with blood, and with the dirt from the places they had wandered, hunting the creature they had just made into steaks and chops. The strange exhilaration was still with them, and they drank more beer and talked about the whole trip—the one stag that Tyler had missed, the tumble downhill that Nick had taken, after his second beer, which he had secreted away in his knapsack (that was how they came to know that he had brought the beers along). Buddy was unhappy about it at first, they said, but then relented and had one himself. Nick had packed eight cans in the sack.

"What will you do with the head?" Lily asked.

"That'll be stuffed and put on a wooden plaque for the wall," said Nick. "We'll take it out to the taxidermist's right after we eat—or Buddy will. It's his deer."

They all ate pasta for dinner, and Sheri joked about going out to the garage and getting some flesh to chew on. They began to talk about carnivorousness, and the fate of the eaten; it was odd. Sheri talked about a little boy who had climbed over a retaining wall at a zoo, and been attacked by a tiger; how the boy had called to his mother that it hurt while the tiger was eating his foot. Lily felt ill, and got up to leave the table. Tyler followed her to the head of the stairwell heading down.

"I'm sorry," he said, low, so the others couldn't hear him.

"Oh," she told him. "I'm okay. That last thing got me a little."

"Sheri's about as subtle as an ox sometimes."

Lily smiled at him. She leaned over and kissed his cheek. "Come to bed soon."

"I will." He touched her arm, squeezed it, the faintest pressure, then let go.

She started down the stairs with that feeling people sometimes have in the middle of a big change, the relieved, happy sense that whatever the change will bring is all quite blessedly beside the point, meaningless as a rainy day. She lay down on their bed and felt the baby move, and cried quietly for joy, even as, in her mind, she saw images of the knife tearing through the soft white fur of the killed deer.

3

She WAS CARRYING the baby low, and had gotten very big for being only six months gone. She had gained the weight too fast, and the gynecologist scolded her for it several times.

Sheri and Millicent had strongly recommended this gynecologist—the sort of recommendation that carried a press of obligation; they were his patients, too, and they both made claims for his charm and his qualities: a family man, with a wife and seven children, and now two grandchildren. A great doctor, they said. Lily couldn't do better.

All over the walls in his waiting room were pictures of the hundreds of babies he had delivered, with names and dates and sometimes with photos of the young people they had grown to be, and with letters to him as if he had kept in touch with all of them, and perhaps he had. There was a meticulousness about him, and a kind of cerebral capaciousness. Along with the usual magazines in his waiting room there were dozens of books on wildly disparate subjects: literature, history, politics, art, horticulture, geology, viticulture, even cooking. You had the sense, looking through them, that they had been carefully selected to yield a picture of the man. Tall, handsome, blond (sculpted-looking, Sheri had said), the doctor spoke with a German accent that always made Lily feel tense. He was stylish, tidy, resourceful, thorough, obviously intelligent, articulate—and tyrannical. His name was Rudy Volker Brauner, and it was wearying to have to keep appointments with him. To Lily, he seemed only faintly more concerned with medicine than with the shine of his shoes, or the strands of his impeccably combed hair. Yet his frowning attention to the details of her pregnancy seemed all-consuming, a part of his enormous grasp of everything.

"If I was casting a play," she told Tyler on the way to one appointment, "he'd be the head of the gestapo. I know that's unoriginal, but that's how I'd cast him. Even if there wasn't a part for someone in the gestapo."

They were scheduled to attend a preliminary Lamaze meeting afterward. A friend of Millicent taught the classes. Tyler drove. The day was not terribly hot, but the humidity had been climbing since first light, and the traffic was bad. It was the second week of November, and the few chilly days had given way to Indian summer. Nothing seemed to have changed; the summery weather held. They were in his demo, and they had the windows down because the air-conditioning, along with the new-car smell, made her woozy. Tyler suffered visibly, hair mussed, one arm on the sill of the window and the other draped over the top of the steering wheel. A single bead of sweat ran down the side of his face.

"Let's put the air on," she said.

"Are you uncomfortable?" he asked.

"I'm worried about *you*."

"I'm okay."

Earlier that morning, Dominic had telephoned from Knoxville, Tennessee, to say that he and Manny had stopped there, after driving all night. They would sleep for two hours and then head out again, and they would be in Oxford by evening. Dominic had said all this to Tyler, who joked with him about driving too fast and falling asleep at the wheel. "Just be careful," he said. Then he handed the phone to Lily, who nearly wept with happiness to hear his voice.

"How are you," she said to him. "Tell me how you are."

"I'm happy," he told her, "because I'm gonna get to see you and Tyler."

"We can't wait."

"Neither can we."

A moment later, he laughed. "Have we already run out of things to say?"

"I'm pregnant."

"I know."

"I'm so excited."

"What if it's a girl?" Dominic said. "What's the female equivalent of Dominic? You are naming this baby after me, right? Manny and I are going to live in New Orleans awhile."

"Oh, that's such good news."

"His great-aunt—well, they're not really related. I told you all this in my letter."

"Just hurry," she said to him. "We're all anxious to see you."

Now, she looked over at Tyler, so depleted-looking in the heat. Her own body, with its distended, rounded belly, appeared foreign to her. He had pulled into the parking garage, and they were slowly making their way to the top. No spaces. The tires squealed slightly with each turn. At last he found a place and pulled in—but he had pulled too close to the car on her side. She opened her door and realized in an instant that there was no way she would be able to get out. He had already left her there and was standing a few feet away, having paused to pull his shirt-tail up to wipe his face. She closed her door and waited, hearing him come slowly back to the driver's window. He looked in, his face gleaming. "Oh, hell."

He walked around to the back of the car, and then returned and got in, pulling his door shut with a slam. "I'm sorry," he said. "What an idiot." He started the car, and looked back. She touched his arm where he had put it on the seat back, and he stopped and looked at her.

"If I wasn't so fat, I could get out of a car."

After a little shake of his head, he continued backing out. "I should've looked at it, though."

The only other open space was out on the roof, in the blazing sun. The temperature here was at least fifteen degrees higher than it was down on the street or inside the garage. This was blacktop, and it soaked up the heat, sent it back at them in wavering lines that looked like the very coinage of delusion. They got out and crossed to an elevator, shielding their eyes from the brightness. Below them was the square, with its statue and its drooping trees and shops. It looked deserted. On the elevator he stared at his own reflection, a dull shape in the metal. Then he seemed to remember himself, and put his hand on her elbow. They went out and down the corridor, and she stepped close, winding her arm around his.

When they reached the brown door with its fake wood-grain sur-face, he patted her shoulder, and pushed the door open for her.

The office was crowded with women, several with small children. Two of them were extremely pregnant. No one looked at anyone else. Lily took a seat, and Tyler went to the magazine rack and bookcase and began rifling through what was there. The door to the inner offices opened, and a young nurse Lily didn't recognize said, "Lily Harrison?"

She stood and Tyler stepped up to enter with her.

"Just Mrs. Harrison right now," said the nurse. "We'll call you."

Tyler backed away and the door closed on him. The nurse, a wiry, small woman with dark freckles on her face and neck, and dark skin that had the leathery look of many hours outdoors, preceded Lily along the corridor, with its photos of babies and its degrees in frames. She led her to the scale and Lily got on it. The nurse adjusted the weights, whistling softly through crooked teeth, then wrote it down on her chart. As she took Lily's blood pressure, she said, "Still gaining more weight than we should. Are we drinking our water?"

"Yes," Lily said. "We are." She handed over her urine-sample bottle.

The nurse took it and showed her to one of the small cubicle examination rooms. In the room, Lily saw the aluminum sink, and the small swivel chair, the charts on the wall illustrating the stages of pregnancy. And here was the examination table, the sight of which always gave her an obscure feeling of dread, as though it were a device for some sort of institutionalized torture. She began to undress. "Sonogram today, right?"

"Yes," said the nurse. "You know the drill."

Dr. Brauner came into the room, looking like a banker: gray suit, white shirt, silver cuff links, spit-shined shoes. He had apparently just come in from the street. His hair was perfect. "Hello," he said to Lily. "Und how do vee feel this morning?"

"We feel fine," Lily said.

He was looking at her chart, along with the nurse. "Vee are ztill gaining a little too much veight."

"We're not eating," Lily said.

He handed the chart back to the nurse. "I vill be back shortly."

When he was gone the nurse asked her to finish removing her clothing. Lily looked at the other woman's name tag and saw that she was a medical student from the university hospital. "You're going to be a doctor," she said.

The other woman smiled at her as if to say, "Evidently." But she didn't speak. She nodded, and went back to looking at the paperwork.

"I really haven't broken the diet. I don't know where the extra weight is coming from."

"I think it's coming from a baby," said the other.

"Then there's no reason for him to scold me, is there."

4

A͎ꜰᴛᴇʀ ᴛʜᴇ ᴇxᴀᴍɪɴᴀᴛɪᴏɴ, the medical student went out to get Tyler, while Dr. Brauner began to set up the sonogram. Tyler came into the room looking sheepish and ill at ease, and the doctor shook his hand, turning his back on Lily to do it. For an interval she saw just the broad back in the white coat, and heard the two men talking—Brauner congratulating the father and talking about all the babies he had brought into the world, and Tyler making sounds of polite appreciation. When they faced her, she felt exposed, though she had a sheet covering her legs. Her belly was uncovered, and the medical student had begun spreading the cold jellylike substance on it. Tyler stared for a second, then turned his attention to the little television screen. Dr. Brauner moved the flat-headed instrument along Lily's belly until the image of the dark little chamber came clear in the screen, with its impossibly folded, faintly human shape.

"Sings look very healthy," Dr. Brauner said. He pointed out the hands and the head and the little eyes. "Very good."

"Jesus," Tyler said, low. "God."

"If you find zis beautiful, you are probably not far from wrong," said the doctor with a small, dry laugh.

Outside in the heat, waiting for the elevator to take them to the roof, Tyler said, "Lily—" and then stopped.

She turned to him. "What is it?"

"That—that was just—that was strange. Actually seeing the—seeing the baby like that."

A moment later, he said, "Do you want to go through with this Lamaze thing?"

"A part of me does, sure. But I'll skip it now if you want to. It's such a muggy day."

The elevator opened and they stepped in. "No," he said. "We'd better go. It'll just get back to everybody if we don't."

"So?"

He pushed the button for their floor and stepped back, leaning against the side and not looking at her. "I don't know. We should go."

"But really," she said. "So what if it gets back?"

"I don't want to hurt feelings."

"It'll hurt feelings?"

He made no answer. The elevator opened on a blast of heat, and they went out into the blinding light of noon, through the lines of heat rising from the black surface. The car was momentarily unusable, too hot to sit in. He started it and then stepped out and left it running, with the air conditioner on full blast.

"Honey," she said, "let's skip the Lamaze and go somewhere and get an ice-cream sundae. I don't have to go back to see Herr Himmler for two weeks."

His expression was faintly hangdog. It annoyed her unreasonably. "We should go to the meeting. It's just a meeting," he said.

"Let's not and say we did. If it gets back to the authorities, we'll deal with it then."

He said nothing else. He looked out over the roofs of Oxford, hands in his pockets. The muscles of his jaw clenched, and then relaxed. He moved to the driver's-side door of the car, got in behind the wheel, and waited for her. It took her some effort to get seated, and to get the door closed. The leather was still too hot to touch; it burned her legs, and she sat around and tried to lift them. For a few moments she was too busy trying to adjust herself out of discomfort to pay much attention to him, and it took a while to realize that he had spoken.

"I didn't hear you," she said.

He waited a beat. Then: "When was the last time you called home?"

"I don't know."

"Well—maybe this—maybe my family means more to me than yours does to you, but my mother made this appointment for us and I think we should keep it."

"All right." She gazed at him.

"Well," he said. "You made that sarcastic remark about the authorities."

"I was teasing. It was a joke. We'll go to the fucking Lamaze class."

They went down Old Taylor Road, and at the sharp right curve where the Faulkner house was, the tires squealed. Several people standing out in the sun, in the yard, tourists, turned to stare after the speeding car.

5

𝒯HE CLASS was meeting in a little white house down from Old Taylor Grocery, which was a restaurant. The house was set back off the road under a tall oak draped in kudzu. The oak provided cool shade. They crossed the root-broken ground to the sidewalk. He put a hand on her arm, and she put her head on his shoulder. "Forgive me?" she said.

"Nothing to forgive," he told her.

The windows of the little house were curtained, the shades half drawn, the whole facade suggesting a countenance with lidded eyes. Inside, a small round woman with features that made Lily think of those tiny heavy-furred, snub-nosed dogs, greeted them. She was the leader, and said her name, which Lily didn't catch, and had to ask for again. She said it again, but then a small dog, exactly like the ones Lily had thought of upon first seeing the woman, barked from the hallway, and once more the name was lost. Lily nodded as if she'd heard, and walked with Tyler holding her arm into the living room, preceded by the dog. As they stood in the room, the dog jumped at them and continued to bark.

"Nelly! Down!" the woman said, apologizing and smiling with that snub-nosed face, her eyes disappearing into the flesh around them, two small arcs of mascara. It came to Lily that she now knew the dog's name, but not the woman's. There were two other couples in the room, seated on blankets that had been spread out on the floor. The sofa and coffee table had been moved aside. Lily realized, the instant the woman asked her about it, that she had forgotten to bring a blanket with her.

"We have extra blankets," the woman said, turning in a tight, confused circle, one hand up to her head. "Now let me see." She hurried out of the room and down the corridor. The other couples sat staring.

Tyler said, "Hello."

The responses came back in a confusion of voices. The other men were both older than Tyler. One wore a waxed handlebar mustache that appeared false, as if it were attached by some glue above his lips. He had a sallow, pitted face and a wattle below his chin. He looked fifty. The other appeared rather ordinary in comparison, in his early forties perhaps, with large gray eyes and thinning hair, wearing wire-frame glasses and a white shirt with a pen holder in the pocket. He offered his hand to Tyler and said his name was Marty. The man with the mustache introduced himself by his last name: "Johnson." He took Tyler's hand and Lily saw the cords of muscle in his forearms, under thick blond hair. He sat back down and regarded her, looking directly at her middle as though she were goods or equipment. It made her feel naked. His wife was a willowy dark-haired woman with black eyes and a heart-shaped face, no more than thirty years old. She stared, too.

The other man was speaking to Tyler about this being his fourth time. This man's wife was very dark-skinned, with olive-shaped eyes, and when she spoke it was with an indeterminate accent. Lily thought she must be from some tropical country, but then as the blanket was brought and Tyler spread it out, she heard this woman tell Johnson's thin wife that she was from Alaska. Johnson's wife wore a sweatshirt with an arrow pointing to the bulge where her baby was. She folded her thin arms over this bulge, and talked about how she had always wanted to go to Alaska to live among the Eskimos.

"Really," said Marty's wife, without much interest.

At last they were all seated, and the woman with the snub nose introduced herself again. Lois. "Let's just go around the room and introduce ourselves."

Johnson spoke first, after clearing his throat to make clear his intention to begin. "We're here because Janice dragged me here." He indicated his wife. "This is Janice."

She laughed, clearly working at appreciating his attempt to be witty. Gazing at him, she said her name again, then nodded at him and said, "This is Tommy."

"I go by my last name," Johnson said. "Preceded by Mister." He went on to say, with a strange, significant glance at their hostess that while they had been waiting for the class to begin, they had gotten onto the subject of politics. In the tone of someone conducting a meeting, he announced that he had worked very hard for the election of Michael Dukakis. He had been quite disappointed in the election of somebody like George Bush to the lofty office of president, and he knew he did not look like a person who would vote Democratic, but there it was.

"Oh, Tommy," said his wife, "you don't have to tell everybody our business."

"Well, we were talking about it, for God's sake. Don't correct me all the time."

"Well," Lois said. "So you're Tommy Johnson, and you're Janice. Is this your first time doing Lamaze?"

"If you mean is this my first child, it's the first one I know about." Johnson looked at the others with a smug gleam, evidently waiting for them to appreciate the humor.

"This is our fourth," Marty quickly reiterated. Then he indicated his wife. "And this is my wife, Lucinda. I guess we should say whether or not we voted Democratic last fall."

"Hello, everyone," Lucinda said. "In case you're wondering about it, we did. Nobody in my family's ever voted Republican."

"Lucinda," Johnson said, after clearing his throat again, "are you an Eskimo?"

She seemed mildly embarrassed and confused. "My mother's Italian and my father's Irish."

"So you're not an Eskimo." He pronounced it Es-kee-mo, with an emphasis on the second syllable. "You said Italian-Irish. I just wanted to know if being from Alaska and all, if you're Eskimo. You have some kind of accent."

"No," she said. "Not Eskimo. My mother's Italian. I speak both languages."

"Really, well, that's a wonderful advantage," said Lois. "And now let's move to our next couple."

Tyler said his name and Lily's. Johnson stared at Lily again, as did his wife.

"And is this your first?" asked Lois.

"Our first. Yes."

"And what brings you to us?"

"A friend of my mother recommended you," Tyler said.

"Has she used the Lamaze method?"

"I wouldn't know, actually. My mother's Millicent Galatierre."

"Oh, of course. Forgive me, I should've remembered." She turned to Lily. "And you're the young writer whose father is a famous actor."

"Well," Lily said. "Not exactly, no." She could not quite take it in that Millicent had described her in this way. And she could tell from the look on Tyler's face that it was rather a surprise to him as well.

"No?" Lois said. "But, I—which part of that is a no?"

"I bet all of it," said Johnson, nudging his wife roughly and then laughing to himself. There was something almost prissy about the laugh, coming from the pit of his throat and kept in by the backs of the four fingers of his right hand.

"All of it is a no," Lily said. "Right. That's exactly right. I'm probably not a writer, and my father is not famous. He was in a couple of movies. Years ago."

The others showed interest now. Johnson's wife leaned forward slightly and asked what the titles were, and Marty's wife asked Tyler if Lily would sign an autograph.

Johnson cleared his throat again and said, "So what is this Lamaze going to be then?"

But the others hadn't heard him. Tyler was trying to explain that Lily's father was a professional actor with a steady job at a professional theater in Washington. Lois had begun to rummage around in a box of supplies she kept within reach. She pulled out a baby doll, a small towel, a book, and a plastic model, side view, of the uterus and the birth canal. "Well," she said. "I do think we should get started."

"I think we should all talk about what we do," Johnson said. "Get to know each other a little bit." His voice rose on this last, carrying with it an insistence that it be heard. The others stopped. "We don't know anything about each other yet. For instance, talking about authors, I happen to be an author. Everybody's making a fuss over Miss—I didn't catch your name, there, girlie."

Lily couldn't bring herself to utter a sound.

"Her name's Lily," said Lois.

"Lily," said Johnson, "that's right." It was as if he had sought the name in a lesson he was teaching and now that the name had been spoken, he was satisfied. "You've been getting all excited over Lily for being what I'd call an incipient author, and here I am a published author."

"No kidding," Marty's wife said.

Johnson sat there nodding with outsized gratification. "Published two books."

"He has," said his young wife.

"What are they?" Tyler asked him.

"They're, what you call it, history books."

"What history?"

Johnson actually affected a yawn. "I used to be a member of the Klan. That's Klan spelled with a K."

"Who published these books?" Marty's wife asked, with an edge of a challenge in her voice.

"I did," Johnson said.

"So they're privately published," said Lily.

"It was a regular New York publisher seeking authors," Johnson's wife said. "I got it out of a magazine."

"I did some bad things when I was young," Johnson told them importantly, folding his arms and nodding as if to accept their appreciation of the change he had made in himself.

Lily began to laugh. It rose up in her like a coughing spell, and she couldn't keep it down. She put her hands over her face and pretended to be coughing, but when she looked through her fingers at Johnson, she saw anger. "I'm sorry," she said. "I can't help it."

"Maybe you got a problem with meeting a real author. Have you ever published anything?"

"No," Lily said, "I haven't. Not a scrap."

"Well, then," said Janice. "What makes you call yourself an author?"

"I—I don't." Lily couldn't stop laughing. It worked its way up from the narrow column inside her body, and wouldn't be quelled by anything. She held her hands over her mouth and it forced its way out, a helpless giggling. And looking at Johnson and his wife, feeling their eyes on her when she was not looking at them, only made it worse.

"I think we should move on to talk about the class now," Lois nervously said.

"I don't know if I want to be in a class with somebody like that," said Janice, indicating Lily.

"I can't—can't—oh—can't help it," Lily said. "I don't mean—a-any—anything by it, really."

Tyler said, "She gets like that. It's the pregnancy." Then he, too, began to laugh.

"What the hell," Johnson said. "Couple of hyenas or something."

"Really," said Tyler. "I'm—I'm s-sure it's got nothing—nothing to do with you at all—not at all."

"Can't we all please get down to talking about the class?" Marty said, looking from one to the other of them.

But Lily was unable to curb her hysteria, and it became dizzying, so that she had to excuse herself and ask where the bathroom was. She made her way out of the room, and closed the bathroom door behind herself, then stood in that heavily perfume-scented space, still laughing. Finally she ran water, and, filling her hands, laved it over her face. Her mascara was coming down her cheeks, and she worked to get it off. The fact that she was wearing it at all was a concession to Sheri. Tyler knocked at the door. "Are you all right?" and she heard the mirth still in his voice. She couldn't wait to get outside and be alone with him.

After another minute, she opened the door and padded with him to the small living room. The others were all staring. Without sitting down on the blanket, she informed them that she wished to go home. She kept her eyes averted from Mr. Johnson and his mustache. "I have a headache," she said. "I'm so sorry I disrupted everything." Tyler took her arm and the two of them went together out into the end-of-summer heat, to the car. "My God," she said, laughing hysterically again, "do you—do you b-believe that?"

They got into the car and he started it, turned and backed out of the driveway, the tires making that small squealing sound on the asphalt, then gunned the engine as they pulled away.

"It's like a getaway car," she said. "Perfect—my God. Step on it."

"That was embarrassing," he said, still laughing. But there was something in his face. "I couldn't wait to get out of there."

She gained control of herself, and looked out at the passing countryside. She saw hills burned by the sun, a shade of combustible brown. Yet it was all steaming in the humidity. When she turned to him again he was still smiling, but there was that something shadowed in his eyes. "Me, too," she told him. "God. That's going to make a great story for dinner."

"Yes, but—now what'll we do about the class?"

She moved slightly in the seat, and turned to him. "Well, we can't go back."

"That's what I mean."

"So," she said, "I guess there won't be any Lamaze with Lois." She laughed again. "Sounds like a television program."

"Lily, we can't just drop it like that."

She said, "You're kidding, right?"

"Well, no. I mean, what will we do about it?"

"We'll forget about it, I hope. We'll tell it at dinner. Jesus, Tyler."

"I just said we can't do that. That would hurt feelings. There's going to be hurt feelings already because my mother recommended that lady to us. And we went in there and laughed at them."

"Oh, come on."

"No, you come on."

She stared at him for a moment in disbelief. Then she laughed again, shaking her head. "This is ridiculous. And I'm too hot and tired to talk about it anymore."

"You don't want to talk about it, so we drop the subject. Is that right?"

She looked out the windshield at the oncoming road. He was speeding again. "Slow down, will you, please?"

"I'm only going five miles over the limit," he said. "You told me to step on it."

"Please slow down," she told him. "I don't care what I said."

They went perilously close to the guardrail going around a bend in the road, and she put her hands to her face. He slowed a little, then began to pick up speed again. She said, "You can let me out anywhere along here."

There was no answer to this, only more speed. They were going close to eighty miles an hour now.

"Will you please slow the fuck down," she said.

To her surprise, he did so, a little too suddenly, pumping the brakes, and she realized that a police car had veered in behind him with lights pulsing.

"Son of a *bitch*," he said, pulling over.

6

THEY SAT IN SILENCE for a few seconds while the police car slowed and stopped behind them and the patrolman got out, then reached back into his car for his ticket pad and paper. The patrolman wore a flat-brimmed hat with the black strap shiny and perfectly arranged across the bottom of his face. He approached cautiously.

"This is partly your fault," Tyler said.

"Oh," she answered. "That's right. *I* was the one speeding. When will you grow your handlebar mustache? What the fuck is this, Tyler?"

"As a matter of fact, I think I actually *liked* the way that mustache looked."

"You probably liked Tommy Johnson, too."

"He voted for Dukakis."

"Oh, God," Lily said, laughing. "That qualifies him. I see, now."

The patrolman had written down the license-plate number, and now came to stand at the driver's-side window. He was a stooped, older man with a perfectly fitting starched shirt and wiry, dark-brown arms. He leaned in and looked at Lily out of gray eyes set back into leathery pouches of brown skin. Then he looked at Tyler and asked if there was an emergency.

"No," Tyler said.

"Driver's license and registration, please."

Tyler was already reaching past Lily to open the glove compartment. It wouldn't budge.

"New car," Lily said to the patrolman.

Tyler got it open at last, retrieved the registration, and handed it, with his license, to the patrolman, who held it open and copied information from it into the ticket pad. "You have any idea how fast you were going?" he said to Tyler.

"No, sir."

"I clocked you at more than seventy-five miles an hour."

Tyler said nothing.

"You got a pregnant lady in the car. She your wife?"

"I don't see what that has to do with anything," Tyler said. "That's my business."

"We're married," said Lily. "For now."

The policeman's face broke into a little grin on one side of his mouth, which he wiped away with a rough motion of the back of the hand that held the pencil.

"Just write the ticket," Tyler said. "There's no detective work required."

"I think you might benefit from a little advice, there, fella. Ain't no necessity for you to break bad with me. Not here, not under these circumstances. You can't win under these circumstances. Under these circumstances, no matter what you say, I win and you lose, see, because you broke the law and I clocked you."

Tyler said nothing.

"You owe me an apology."

"Okay," Tyler said.

"And you owe her an apology, too."

"This is not in your power," Tyler told him. "Give me the ticket."

"Well, you ought to take your family into consideration a little." The cop looked past Tyler to Lily. "You like going that fast?"

"No," Lily said. "I don't."

Again, he looked at Tyler. "I'm gonna cite you for speeding and for reckless driving."

"Okay, look, Officer, if you do that, I'll lose my job."

"You should've thought of that before you hit the gas, son."

Tyler sat back against the seat, and then gripped the wheel. It took a long time for the citations to be written out. The officer walked back to his car to do it. Lily and Tyler sat very still in the quiet. She could see the rage working in her husband's face and neck, the pulsing there.

The officer walked slowly back to the window and handed him the license and registration, and then the ticket, and said, "Nice and slow, now. Right?"

Tyler simply held the wheel and stared out.

"I said, 'Right?'"

"Right."

"Court date's written in that box on the upper left."

"Yes, sir."

"That's better." The cop leaned down and looked at Lily. "Good day, ma'am."

Tyler waited until the police car had pulled around them and was out of sight down the road. Then he started out, and nearly pulled in front of an oncoming truck. The truck driver blared his horn and came roaring by, and Lily screamed. After the truck had blown past, Tyler sat with his head drooping, still gripping the wheel. Finally he looked back, and with great care pulled out. They went just below the speed limit. Lily watched the side of his face, and tried to summon anything to say to him, a path back through the last few minutes. She couldn't even find something neutral to speak of.

He spoke first: "That was just terrific."

"Oh, Tyler—you're not really going to tell me that was my fault, too?"

He looked fiercely at her. "We'd still be at the Lamaze class."

"You're funny," she said. "Really. Hilarious."

"I guess you'll see how *funny* I am."

"What is that, a threat? Jesus, listen to you."

He said nothing. He was picking up speed again.

She said, "Sixty in a forty-five—you want to try for two in one day?"

He pulled the car over into the gravel by the side of the road, so that it fishtailed slightly, and the brakes made a terrible screeching sound. He got it stopped, turned in the seat, and fixed her with glittering, cold eyes. It was like the worst of her nightmares, the antipathy in his expression. He was getting hold of himself, and this was in a way more frightening than the rage he'd been in. "Look," she said. "We're both irritated and hot and miserable, and we just got a fucking speeding ticket. Let's wait until we can be civil again."

He faced front, gripping the wheel.

"We'll calm down and see how silly the whole thing is."

"We'll tell it at dinner," he said with a brittle, sardonic smile. He shook his head. "No. I can't do it. I just can't. I thought I could but I can't."

"Can't what?" she said.

He didn't answer, but sat there staring out.

"Tyler? What? What is this?"

Nothing.

She felt frightened; something awful was coming. But then the fright gave way to anger. She opened the car door, got out, and began to walk. The surface here was uneven and she wavered and nearly stumbled.

After a minute, he inched the car forward. "Will you get in?" he said.

She kept walking, looking straight ahead.

"I wonder," he said, "if you know what Buddy's insurance people are gonna say when they see this ticket for speeding and reckless driving in a fucking *demonstrator*."

She stopped, leaned against the guardrail, reached down and took off one shoe, then braced herself with her other hand and took off the other. She held them, walking along on the asphalt now, though it burned the bottoms of her feet, and made her have to move to the tall grass beside the road. The grass was too dry, here, and hurt almost as much as the asphalt. He kept inching the car along.

"We can do this all day," he said.

She didn't answer.

"Okay," he said, shouting at her. "I've got some news for you, sweetheart. A bright little piece of news." He pulled ahead, then accelerated so that the tires squealed, and went on, into the distance and around the long bend to the east.

For what seemed a long while she walked down the road and no other cars came. She crossed to the other side and passed a series of grass lawns, then crossed again, heading around the long bend. She heard a car somewhere in the distance, but it was hard to tell if it was ahead or behind. She stopped. A green Cadillac approached from the east, driven by an elderly woman. It went by, and she watched it go on. A minute or so behind it was Tyler in the demo. He went by her without looking, then made a U-turn and came back, slowing to where he had been as she'd stopped.

"You wanna hear the news?" His voice was ugly. There was a frightening, violently derisive edge to it.

She couldn't believe it, and she did not respond.

And now he shouted. A full, horrible scream: "The GODdamn baby isn't mine!" And he pulled away again, tires squealing, rear end fishtailing. She watched him go, and kept walking, rote movement, paying no attention now to what the asphalt was doing to her feet, her nylons, which had torn and were coming to pieces. Her mind was a blank wall, and this was just happening; she was merely going on in it, whatever this was. The road went up a slow incline, into the shade of some live oaks, and she sat under one of them to cool off. She pulled the shards of her nylons from her feet and looked out at the road. Beyond it, bordered by a wide prospect of wild grass and mounds of coal, was a railroad. A train went by over there, a freight. The whistle sounded. The smells of creosote and tar were on the air. She watched the traffic, and waited for something to come to her, some way of deciding what she should do. It seemed to her that he had said the most outlandish and terrible thing he could think of, and that it was rather sickly absurd, so childish as to indicate a kind of pathology. It might even have made her laugh, except for the awful expression of pent-up anger in his face.

7

$\mathscr{P}$RESENTLY, she got to her feet, and went along the road for another mile or so. She went past a yard where a family was having a picnic— babies on blankets and lying in mothers' laps, children running and shouting in the shade, men standing together over a fire. She breathed in the smell of charring meat, walking by, and they all gazed at her—she realized she must look quite funny, a pregnant lady with stockings torn off at the ankles, striding along the road alone, with her shoes in her hand. She hadn't even taken her purse with her.

A young man came over to the end of the yard as she reached it. "Is everything okay, ma'am?" he said.

She couldn't bring herself to speak. She smiled and nodded and went on. She saw him watching her when she reached the end of the next yard. She wanted to stop there, but decided that if she did he would see it as an indication and follow her, wanting to help. So she kept going, until she was well out of reach of the picnic. And when Tyler came from the other way, slowing as he neared, and then going ahead and making another U-turn, she decided to face him.

He pulled up and stopped with a scary disarrangement of the dirt and gravel by the roadside. "You want to talk about it?" he said.

"I don't know what there is to talk about," she said. "I laughed at Mr. Johnson and I thought *we* were laughing—"

"That isn't what I mean," he said. "Will you get in?"

She did so. She realized, with a shock, that she was crying.

"Do you understand now?" he said.

"No." Her purse was still on the front seat. She reached in it and brought out a handkerchief and wiped her eyes, her face.

"Did you hear what I said back there?" he demanded.

She nodded.

"And you don't under*stand* it?"

"No—I said *no*. I *don't* understand it. Jesus Christ."

He looked away, and then shook his head slightly. He seemed afflicted with a kind of sickening apprehension. There was no color at all in his face. "I was going to be a good guy and try to keep this from you. I love you and I was going to do it. I *was* doing it. But I saw that—I saw the—the sonogram. It did something to me, okay? I can't help it."

She stared.

"I mean, it's partly my fault. I should've told you at first. I mean, I tried to. I—I lied, all right? To begin with. It amounts to a lie. I kept it from you. I blame myself for that."

"Tyler, will you please tell me what you're talking about?"

His eyes trailed down to her abdomen. "That isn't my baby."

"What?"

"You heard me," he uttered under his breath, looking away.

"Tyler, what the fuck is this about? You don't want the baby?" She was crying, her nose running, she couldn't get all the moisture off her face, and he was a blur on the other side of tears.

"Okay, look," he said. "Listen. I'm only going to say this once."

She sobbed.

"Jesus Christ," he said.

"Tyler, please—what in God's name."

"You have to promise me you won't tell anyone. I'll support you and all that and I'll be a father to the kid, okay? As long as you don't say anything."

It crossed her mind again that this was pathology; he was having some sort of psychotic episode. She nodded in order to humor him.

"When I was seventeen, I got the mumps. Okay? I had a complication from it—orchitis. Do you know what that is?"

She shook her head.

"Well, it made me sterile. Okay?" He waited for this to sink in. "I can't get a woman pregnant. There's no way I could've made you that way." He suddenly leaned close. "Do you *get* it now, Lily?" Very slowly he sat back and rested his hands on the wheel, looking out at the houses on that side of the road. Suddenly he broke into tears, sobbing, holding his face in his hands.

She couldn't speak, couldn't find a way through everything that was coming at her in her mind. It was as if she stood in a violent wind, trying to open her eyes to it, trying to see everything that was veering toward her out of the dark. She took a breath, then stopped, and held it, and looked down at herself, her hands, her legs. When she raised her eyes to him again, she saw that he was still crying, though he'd let his hands down, sitting there with the tears running down his face, staring out the windshield.

"But—" she started. Nothing would come.

For a long time, neither of them said anything. Then he looked back, and carefully pulled out onto the road, going slow now. She heard him sniffle. "We can't go home like this."

She said, "Tyler—"

"Who was it, anyway?" he demanded abruptly.

She didn't answer. She was looking at the countryside, the blue sky. She saw a jet at the edge of a long, trailing wisp of cloud, and the cloud looked like a white rope, slung from the horizon, something spun out of control, from massive forces beyond the sky.

"Come on, you can tell me. Or was there more than one?"

"But—but there's—there has to be—some mistake," she told him. "Maybe the doctors are wrong."

"Oh, it's a *virgin* birth," he said. "Goddamn."

She didn't respond to this.

"I'd like to know who it was."

"There wasn't anyone," she said.

"Oh, come *onnnn*," he said, drawing out the last word on a shout.

She looked at him. "I didn't know you were coming to me, Tyler. I didn't think I'd ever see you anymore."

"*Jeeee*-sus Christ!" He had begun to speed up again.

"Well, it's true," she said, crying. "Please."

"Just tell me who it was, for Christ's sake."

"Nothing happened. I didn't—it didn't finish. Tyler, it couldn't be—there has to be some other explanation."

"Look," he said. "I want to know what his name was and I want to know when it happened and I want to know where it happened and why it happened and I want to know all of it right fucking now!"

She stared at him, sitting there with his eyes fixed on the road and his hands so tight on the wheel that his knuckles showed; his mouth was set in a narrow line of stipulation, anger, and expectation, his whole face one pinched, unhappy, priggish, crying mask, and something rose up inside her, a sudden rush of outraged resistance. "I'm not going to tell you," she said in a trembling voice. "You can go to hell."

He turned onto a narrow farm road, bordered on both sides by tall stalks of corn. He went for a mile or so, and then pulled off into a little grassy opening at the end of one field. There was a house off at the far end of the row, a run-down-looking clapboard place with a sagging porch and peeling paint along the window frames. She saw a truck parked in the yard and a small children's swing. Tyler was wiping his face with the backs of his hands.

"What're you going to do?" Lily asked him.

He said nothing. He turned the engine off and let his hands come to rest on the bottom of the steering wheel.

She sat with her arms folded over her heavy abdomen, waiting.

When he began to speak, it was with the measured tones of someone addressing a child. "I should've said something to you about the facts. It was wrong of me to keep it from you—"

"Which facts?" she said.

His tone was a commingling of rage and frustration, barely controlled. "The—the facts of the situation. The situation. The *situation*. I should've goddamnit said something to you about the fact that I was sterile. Okay? At the very beginning, when I was asking you if you wanted a baby and you said you didn't want to have children. *You* said you didn't want to have children and I decided not to mention the situation. Okay? It's a thing I've always been sensitive about. I should've said something and I didn't, and I'm sorry for that. Now. *You* didn't tell me something that was going on, and I think it's fair if I have a *little* curiosity as to *whose* kid I'm gonna be paying for and supporting."

"But don't you see? I didn't know it wasn't—I thought it was—" She stopped.

"I *know* what you thought!"

"Take me home," she said.

He shouted, "To Virginia?"

She gave no answer to this. She sat there not looking at him, and waited.

"Was it that—" He stopped, a low, burning ire in his voice now; it didn't even sound like him. He sighed. "Was it Dominic, for Christ's sake?"

She turned to him, and turned away again. It hadn't quite struck home yet that if all he'd said was true, indeed she must be carrying Dominic's child. The thought arrived in a strange, sourceless nonrecognition, a mute something wafting over the surface of a wall that was herself, and then was gone in the low, wrathful sound of Tyler's voice. "Was it my mother's house you wanted me to take you to? The one who screwed around on *her* husband?"

"You were *not* my husband when this happened," she said. He was so close now that she could smell the sour afternoon sweat of him, and the staleness of his breath. She believed that he might even harm her. She felt the ill will emanating toward her.

"Do you realize that you could be fucking HIV positive?"

"That's ridiculous. I'm not even going to dignify that with an answer."

"Is it so ridiculous? How do you know?"

"He was just finding out he was gay. It didn't—it didn't go well with me and I was his first. He's not HIV positive. Christ."

"'It didn't go well'? It didn't—you say it didn't go well? Goddamn, that's stretching things a little, isn't it? 'It didn't go well.'"

"I'm not going to talk to you about it. You're raving. You're so far out of line."

"What did you think of me, anyway?" he said.

"Please take me to the house, Tyler."

"Tell me what you thought of me."

"Oh," she began, then screamed, "Can't you leave it alone! Can't you please stop this!" And she was crying again, against the effort of her whole body not to.

He started the car and pulled out onto the road and went along at the speed limit. He closed the windows and put the air-conditioning on. Neither of them said anything for a period of slow, agonizing minutes. She cried in the cold air from the fan, and the sick feeling increased. He drove into Oxford, and turned into and out of neighborhood streets; it was as if he were giving her a tour of the town. He drove slowly past the dealership and on, out into the country again.

"So," he said. "What do we do?"

"I'll do whatever you want," she said. "Do you want to separate?"

"Oh, no. Oh, Jesus Christ. Believe it or not, I'm in love with you. Isn't that amazing? I think that is absolutely fucking amazing."

She said nothing.

"And you're in love with me," he said. "Right?"

The word came before she could call it back, and then she was struck by the fact that in that instant she had wanted to call it back. She said, "Yes." It was offered as if out of some fugitive wish for unattainable peace, and order—a desire that would seek some safety even in lies. But it was not a lie. It was truth that ached more deeply than she believed such pangs could go. "Yes," she told him, sobbing. Surprised at the mingling passions of sorrow and revulsion in her. "Yes."

8

They AGREED, with what seemed to Lily to be a dismal emotionless rationality, to do nothing about the situation until after the baby was born. Tyler looked at her with sad, disappointed boy's eyes and said that he loved her and that there were larger things to think about—there was this marriage, which he wanted very badly to make work, and there was the child, the family they would be. She thought of what it would take now simply to pack up and return to Virginia, to live with Doris until the baby came, and then after . . .

The prospect of the next months opened before her, and as they pulled past the broken gate and into the long drive leading to the Galatierres', and she saw the yellow house in the distance with its double porch and its columns, she had a kind of gelid resolve. They would find some way to weather this trouble. She glanced at him once more, saw the expression on his face, of a man steeling himself for something hard, and experienced an abrupt wave of panic that she could have ended up in this confusion, this intractable distress.

Sheri was on the porch with Millicent, Nick, and Roger, the contractor. The weight of their secrets, added to her own, nearly made her collapse. She would not be up to it, not in her exhausted state. They were all sitting there with a pitcher of something with ice in it between them. Nick was drinking a can of beer. "You met Roger yet?" he said, smiling.

Lily hesitated, and saw the quick motion Millicent made, sitting forward. "Actually, she did meet him, Nick. A few weeks ago."

"Hello again," Roger said. His eyes were not visible behind the dark glasses he wore. He extended his hand and Lily, feeling the effort, hardly able to lift her arm, took it.

"Good to see you," she managed.

"That friend of yours—Dominic—called," Nick said. "Where you guys been?"

"I've gotta talk to Buddy," Tyler said. "I got a ticket. Speeding and reckless driving."

Nick sipped the beer, then threw his head back and emptied the can. He crushed it and held it in his fist, nodding slowly. "That's trouble, pal. Buddy won't like that a bit." He stood.

"I'll talk to him alone," Tyler said.

"I'm gonna get another beer." Nick smiled, and staggered, and it was difficult to tell if he had done so accidentally or on purpose.

The two of them went in through the living room, and Lily started to move along the front of the porch, toward the side of the house, wanting to enter her room through the pool entrance.

"Have an iced tea," Sheri said.

"Yes, dear—sit with us," said Millicent.

Sensing that it might be interpreted in some worrisome way if she refused, Lily took one of the wicker chairs and sat down.

Sheri poured the tea and handed it to her. "So how'd Lamaze go?"

"I don't think it's for us."

"You're kidding. Everybody loves the hell out of it," Sheri said. "Everybody I talk to loves the absolute hell out of it."

"We didn't," said Lily.

"Not everyone takes to it," Millicent said.

Roger leaned back in his chair and rested one leg at the ankle, across the other. "We did that—Lamaze. That's the breathing thing, right?"

"Well, partly," Millicent said. She looked at Lily, and then looked away.

Roger drank from his glass of tea, concentrating on it.

"What the hell is the matter with everybody?" Sheri said.

"Sheri," said Millicent. "Please."

"You could cut the tension with a damn *knife*."

"I'm sure I don't know what you're talking about. Perhaps you ought to have something to relax this—this tension you feel."

"It's not *me*," said Sheri.

For a long moment, no one spoke.

"The Lamaze lady was nice," Lily put in.

Sheri regarded her with a curiosity that felt nearly prying. "You and Tyler have a fight or something? Your face is red. You okay, honey?"

"It's hot," Lily said. "We got a ticket." She drank the tea, which was too sweet and left a film on her teeth. She excused herself and went around to the pool.

Here was Buddy, floating on a big black inner tube, half in, half out of the shade of the house, holding a drink in one hand and a small plastic-tipped cigar in the other. "Hey," he said, with a sheepish grin. The line of shadow bisected his face and momentarily gave him the look of a clown. Gazing into the light where she stood, it was necessary to squint, and the network of wrinkles in the skin around his eyes gave her a moment of realizing how essentially good-humored he was. A man who was wholly gentle—a man who looked through you when you were suffering and knew what to say.

"You look a little beat up in this damn humidity, sweetheart, and even so, you're still one of the loveliest, fragrant women I've ever seen."

"You're prejudiced." She forced a smile, appreciating him.

"Everything okay, darlin'?" he said.

"Tyler and Nick went in to look for you," she got out. "You won't be happy with what Tyler has to tell you."

His face changed to concern. "Seriously, you all right?"

"Tyler got a speeding ticket."

He chuckled ruefully, shaking his head. When he spoke, there was a note of relief in his voice. "I'll chastise him severely."

She tried a joke. "I think he needs it."

"Well." He lifted the drink, smiling broadly, a happy man. "I guess he'll find me soon enough."

She started to enter the sliding door to her room.

"You sure you're okay?"

She stopped. He was all in the shade now. For a second, she was close to making some sort of declaration to him. *Oh, Buddy, talk to my husband.* Instead, she mustered a smile, and nodded.

"Why don't you fix yourself a drink of that oversweet lemonade Rosa made and join me. Best thing to do on a badly humid day is go ahead and get wet and stay that way."

"Maybe later, thanks."

He held the drink up.

FIFTEEN

1

DOMINIC AND MANNY arrived, like complications in a bad soap opera, a little more than an hour later. Lily heard the hubbub of the car and its horn and Sheri calling her. Tyler's voice was in it, too, full of counterfeit cheer. She got out of the bed where she had been half sleeping and quickly brushed her fingers through her hair, then went into the bathroom and ran water over her face. As she came out, Buddy was standing at the sliding door, his tall, wide shadow on the drapes. He tapped twice with the knuckle of one finger.

"You awake?"

She slid the door open and stepped out.

"You look great," he said. "It's amazing what a little rest and cool shade'll do."

"Thanks, Buddy." He stepped to one side and offered her his arm.

"You think they'll stay with us awhile?"

"I hope so," she said. She had an almost irresistible urge to tell him that the baby she was carrying was Dominic's. The strangeness of this knowledge went through her like a blast of cold air. She shivered, and he took hold of her arm above the elbow.

"Hey, really. *Are* you okay?"

She gazed into his questioning eyes, and the truth rose in her heart that of all the people her parents' age that she knew, she only felt completely at ease with him. She lifted her hand to his face. "Oh, Buddy," she said. "I'm so glad I got to know you."

"I think that's the best thing anybody's said to me in a long time."

She locked her arm in his, and leaned into him. "How many emotions do you think can mix in the same moment in a human heart?"

He smiled. "Probably all of them, don't you think?"

She almost began crying. It took a great effort to speak. "Well," she got out, "I must be feeling all of them now."

On the front porch of the house, Dominic stood, with one hand on the lower back of a small, dark, round-faced man, to whom he was introducing Tyler. Tyler shook the man's hand, then shook Dominic's. He introduced Sheri and his mother, and Roger Gault, and then he saw Buddy and Lily.

"This is my stepfather," he said. "And Lily." He nodded at her, his eyes just missing her.

Dominic shook hands with Buddy, then stepped back and folded his arms, regarding Lily. "You seem to have gained a little weight around the middle."

She longed to put her arms around his neck. She accepted his small, dry, chaste kiss on the side of her face, and couldn't, for the moment, find her voice.

"I won't break you if I give you a hug, will I?"

She could only shake her head. He stepped forward and very gingerly put his arms around her, barely touching. Lily closed her fingers on his bony shoulders and squeezed, feeling the tears come, and turning from them.

"Here," Buddy said, handing her a glass of iced tea. She saw Millicent and Roger gazing at her.

They got through the other introductions, everyone smiling and being kind and Manny extending his hand to each of them, saying, "Hello," in an oddly recited-sounding way. Nick carried the bags in. Buddy asked what they wanted to drink. Dominic turned to Manny and said, "Coke?"

"Yes. Thanks," Manny said, still smiling brightly. Nick called Rosa out, and she took drink orders from everyone, writing them down like a waitress. When she had gone, Buddy suggested that while the drinks were being prepared, Dominic and Manny should go to their room and change into bathing suits. "Let's have an old-fashioned pool party," he said, clapping his hands together.

Roger Gault said, "I've got to get going, Mr. Galatierre."

Buddy smiled at him. "How many times do I have to tell you to call me Buddy?"

"I'm sorry," Roger said. "Force of habit."

Buddy turned to Lily. "Roger designed and rebuilt our kitchen." He patted the other man on the back. "You sure you won't stay and swim?"

"I can't."

"Well, next time," said Buddy.

They all watched Roger get into his car and drive off. Buddy stood with his hands in his pockets, his weight shifting back and forth slightly. Then he turned to Manny and said, "How about you there? You feel like a pool party?"

"Yes—good," said Manny, as if he were hungry for something happy. His dark, prominent eyes shone. There was a faint Spanish lilt in his voice. He had gentle eyes, Lily thought; they seemed to emanate trust. His smile was bright—Lily had seldom seen teeth so white. And when he laughed, as he did now while Buddy made comments about the trappings of a Republican household—the swimming pool, the bottles of gin and vermouth, the owner with the avoirdupois and the opinions but no ideas—there was an almost frantic note in it.

Everyone went to their respective rooms to change into bathing suits. Lily had a maternity suit with a lacy panel across the front. She got into it, and then changed back into light jeans and a blouse. Tyler hadn't come back to the room, so she waited for him, sitting on the bed in the jeans, holding the ball of her belly. He came in and, opening his top drawer, brought out a pair of bathing trunks and unfolded them. He seemed not to have noticed her. After a pause, without looking her way, he said, "It's his baby, isn't it. Just to be definite. It's Dom's baby. The fag's—" He stopped, and shook his head. "Christ."

She said nothing.

He stopped, half out of his slacks, and stared at her. "Well?"

"What do you want me to say, Tyler?"

He shrugged. "The truth?"

"You wouldn't understand."

"Try me."

She stood, and moved to the door. "You know how there are people—you see them in the street, what they're wearing and how they seem, how their hair is cut and the music they're listening to and maybe the bumper sticker on their car, you know how they'll vote. You know who they voted for."

He simply returned her gaze.

"I just had one of those moments with you."

"You mean like the one you had with Mr. Johnson," he said quickly. "You could figure who he voted for, right?"

She opened the sliding door, but said nothing.

"And so you look at these people and make up your mind about them. Right? You know everything about them."

"I can't believe you still want to argue about the fucking Lamaze class," Lily told him.

"Hey, I'm defending myself," he said.

She went out to the pool area. Sheri and Millicent had already taken their places in the sun on the other side. She walked around to them and sat in a lawn chair.

"No bathing suit?" Sheri said.

"I think I'll spare everyone," said Lily. The sourness of her exchange with Tyler was still in her voice. She offered a smile, and Sheri smiled back.

"I think you look pretty as a picture."

"Rosa's making cocktails, I'm sure," Millicent said.

"This is the warmest November I can remember," Sheri went on. "I swear it could be July."

"It's supposed to be cold tomorrow," said her mother. "I think our Indian summer is about to end."

They were all quiet for a few moments.

"The boys're very nice," Sheri said warmly. "I like them both. Manny's so quiet, you almost get the feeling he's out of it or something. But he has such a sweet laugh. I think I remember Dominic in one of the plays at school."

"He played Bottom, the weaver, last spring in *A Midsummer Night's Dream*," Lily told her. "You'd left school by then."

"He didn't play Puck?" Tyler had come out, wearing black bathing trunks. He had a towel draped over one shoulder. "Puck, the fairy?"

"Tyler," said his mother.

He laughed low. "I bet Dom wouldn't mind the joke." He moved to the edge of the pool and put his legs in the water. "Cold."

Buddy came from the kitchen, pushing a tray with drinks on it. Rosa accompanied him. She was in a bathing suit as well. Light blue, and she looked stunning in it. She walked to the diving board, out to the end of it, and dropped, with almost no splash, into the water, moving like a dark shadow through it, coming up at the shallow end, then turning and lying back.

Buddy had begun passing out the drinks, standing over the cart. Nick emerged from the house, wearing a Hawaiian shirt open at the front, and a pair of white trunks and sandals. He was carrying a can of beer. "Anybody else want a beer?" he asked.

"I've got some on ice under the tray, here," said Buddy. "I'm like a flight attendant for the airlines, moving down the aisles offering libations. Who ordered what?"

"Iced tea," said Sheri. She had folded the back of her chair down and turned so that she was lying on her stomach.

"Iced tea it is," Buddy said.

Tyler edged off the side of the pool, and let himself down into the water, then propped himself on his folded arms on the edge, facing Lily, squinting into the sunlight.

"You should come in," he said. "It'd relax you."

She shook her head, looking at her own hands folding and unfolding over her belly.

Dominic appeared from the side of house, wearing green trunks that looked too big for him, and seeming even skinnier and sallower than Lily had remembered him. She caught herself trying not to stare. He walked down the pool steps and into the water up to his waist, then dipped and went under, coming up with his hair in his face. He stood and pushed it back, and then settled in again, arms out to balance himself. Lily had seen him look for her as soon as he stepped from the shadow of the house. Now he seemed content to move through the water.

Tyler took a scotch from Buddy and held it up as if to offer a toast to everyone. He drank from it, swallowed with satisfaction. "Aren't you going to have anything, honey?" he said. "Join the party?"

"I can't," she said. "You know that."

"Iced tea?" he said. "Lemonade? Grapefruit juice?"

There was something brittle and terrible about the whole exchange.

She watched the others, and tried to imagine how, or when, she would tell Dominic that he was the father of this baby she was carrying. Dominic flopped around in the water, talking to Rosa, and now Manny came out, wearing white trunks with silver-and-gray swordfish rising from fantastic blue-and-pearl waves printed on the legs. He accepted a glass of bourbon from Buddy, and then came over and sat in one of the canvas chairs next to Lily, who smiled hello.

Buddy had gotten into the water now, too, along with Sheri and Millicent.

"Very happy," Manny said.

She wanted to reassure him. "You are from Chile?"

He stared for an instant or two. Then, smiling quickly, with that nervous look: "Oh, yes. Chile."

She waited a moment. "And—do you like it in America?"

The smile was still urgent. "Yes."

"And how long have you lived here?"

The smile did not change. "Yes," Manny said.

"Manny has to be spoken to very slowly," Dominic said from the pool. "I thought I mentioned that in my letter. I know it's the old cliché of speaking loud and slow, but you know, actually it turns out to be necessary, at least in Manny's case."

"Very close," Manny said, nodding.

"Yes," said Lily. "Very."

"Yes."

"I am very much older."

She let her facial expression ask for her.

"Seventeen years." He pointed to his chest. "Thirty-nine."

"You don't look thirty-nine."

He understood this. "Thank you."

The others were all talking and moving around in the pool. Nick wanted to go out to hunt in the morning. "What about it, Buddy?" he said, pushing backward in the water.

"We've got company," Buddy said.

"Let's bring 'em along. I think the, er, nearly parturient Ms. Lily'll even let her hubby go again."

"Tyler does what he wants," Lily said with as little inflection as possible.

"What the hell is he talking about, anyway?" Sheri said. "What-urient?"

"It means Miss Lily's about to bring forth young," Nick said. "But I'm talking about the manly art of killing soft, furry creatures from a distance with a scope rifle."

"Shut up, Nick."

Buddy hoisted himself out on the aluminum ladder at the deep end, and poured himself another drink. Tyler kept floating along on his back, not speaking to anyone, really. Rosa and Dominic had begun to discuss movies. They clung to the side of the pool and sipped their drinks and argued—Dominic going on about how he hated Siskel and Ebert. "Wouldn't you love to see them stop for a minute and say, 'Of course, folks, you realize that most of this stuff we're talking about so portentously here is pure unadulterated class A shit.'"

"Art form of the century," Rosa said. "Isn't that right?"

"I know a guy thinks *commercials* are the art form of the century. Imagine the inside of *his* head."

"What will you do after New Orleans?" Lily asked Manny, speaking very slowly.

He seemed puzzled. But she could see that it was not over the language: he had understood the words. "We stay there. My aunt—my lady friend—"

"I'd like to come visit," Lily told him.

"Visit—yes."

Tyler had come to the edge of the pool nearest them. He folded his arms on the side and rested his chin on them. "You'd like to visit where?" he said.

She returned his cold, falsely cheerful gaze. "New Orleans."

"You've been to New Orleans."

"I'd like to go again."

"Well, then of course we'll do that," Tyler said.

Manny cleared his throat and sipped his drink, looking at each of them in turn. "New Orleans," he said. "Lots of place. Big, nice house. *Sì.* Yes. Burgundy and St. Philip. Wonderful with a garden. Flowers."

"I'll bet we walked by it that time," Tyler said. "What do you think, Lily?"

Manny said, "Yes."

Lily felt as if everything around her were closing in. Just now, in the too-bright light, it was easy enough to imagine that Dominic would be unhappy to be told that this child was his. She ran her hand lightly over her abdomen, and was momentarily light-headed.

"Why don't you change into your little maternity bathing suit and come on in," Tyler said from the pool. "The water's really nice."

"Nice," Manny said. He stood. Lily watched him move around to the steps and then walk into the water. Dominic swam to meet him, followed by Rosa. Sheri held on to Nick, and Millicent and Buddy walked in a small circle in the shallow end; Millicent lifted her head and kissed him. They murmured to each other, shutting out everything around them. Lily pulled her eyes away, trying not to think of it all as a lie.

Tyler was still resting his head on his arms, gazing at her. "Come on in," he said. He was trying to make up.

"Maybe later," she told him.

She got up, walked to the sliding doors, and entered the house. There was a terror gripping her now that she could feel this alienation and bitterness, and she went into the downstairs bathroom and washed her face, cupping the water in her hands and splashing it at herself, trying, in the pure sense shock of the cold water, to gain some control over her own mind. It seemed to her now that she would bear the baby and be alone, without help or love or solace from anyone. It was impossible to imagine Dominic being happy about the fact that in the single most humiliating experience of his young life he had engendered a child. But then, she worked to remind herself, he had kept the relationship with her, had remained her friend.

When she came out into the room again, Tyler was standing in front of the doorway, wrapped in a towel.

"You okay?" he said.

"Fine," she managed.

"Look, I'm sorry about all of it. I—I lost it and I'm sorry."

She waited for him to go on. He stood there gazing at her. "Sorry's a word," she said. "I'm sorry, too. But, Tyler, we've got trouble, now. Bad, bad trouble."

"You're gonna tell him."

"I don't know," she burst out. "I don't know what I'm going to do."

"I don't think we should ever tell anybody."

She sat down on the bed and folded her hands in her lap, feeling that her presence, her body, her solidness, were heavy, blocky, all bulk and weight, while he was almost air, almost spirit, standing there in his bathing suit with the towel draped over his lean shoulders.

"You're gonna tell," he said. "Aren't you."

2

*L*ATER, Buddy and Nick drove out and bought a lot of barbecue and side dishes, and lugged it all back in plastic bags, which they opened on the picnic table by the pool. Their repast went on into the night. There was more swimming, more drinking. Manny and Dominic got very drunk, and Dominic made everyone laugh by doing imitations of public figures; he was particularly adept at the new president. "Better than the *Saturday Night Live* guy," Buddy said.

At some point during the long evening, Dominic told Lily that Manny had once been a priest, had worked as a missionary in a quiet country parish in the mountains of Peru, and had left the order in 1984, though he still practiced his faith. "He can read English perfectly and he's not such a bad writer of it, either, though he misses some idioms. But the spoken word still gives him a lot of trouble. He keeps trying to get me to go with him to Mass."

"Why don't you?"

There was a sadness in his features—some grief had crossed his mind. "You know, for the life of me, I can't seem to figure out a reason. But I don't want to go, and that's a fact."

"Did he leave the priesthood because . . ." Lily stopped.

"Not really," Dom said. "No." He touched her wrist. "You needn't feel uneasy talking about it, Lily."

"No," she told him. "It's—there's—it's not that."

"You're Catholic, too, right?"

"I think my father was. I mean, he was raised Catholic. I know he was. I don't know what I'm saying here."

"Am I making you nervous?"

"Not quite," she said, feigning irony.

They were quiet for a space, watching the others.

She saw Tyler, off by himself, near the entrance to the porch, pacing slow, and smoking a small cigar. The baby kicked inside her—the other life. She moved slightly to accommodate the discomfort. "Oh," she said.

Dominic said, "May I?" and without waiting for permission, he put his hand very gently and tentatively on her abdomen. The baby moved there, and he looked at Lily. "Oh, my. I felt that. That was amazing."

"Yes." Lily could not imagine how she had gotten the word out.

He kept his hand there, waiting for another movement. Tyler walked over and stood staring at them both. Lily breathed in the cigar smoke.

"I just felt your baby move," Dominic said, without removing his hand.

"It's something," Tyler said, "isn't it." His voice was warm, but Lily saw in his eyes a sour, horrid, nearly malignant light.

She took Dominic's hand and sat forward. "I'll be back in a little bit." She patted the back of his wrist, and stood, and Tyler followed her to the entrance to the kitchen. At the door, he said, low, "Forgive me. I'm trying. Christ, that was bad."

She kept her eyes on him, opening the door, then stepped in and closed it on him. The kitchen was littered with paper plates and cups, napkins and plastic knives and forks on the counters, and piles of the leftover food that had been brought from the take-out place. It all looked congealed and stale now. She began to put things in trash bags, cleaning up, and in a moment the door opened. Nick, and Buddy. They were arm in arm, and Nick was telling the older man a joke, faltering and getting things wrong and trying to correct himself. At last Buddy stopped him and said, "Why don't you wait until you've really got it, okay?"

"Damn," said Nick, swaying with what he had drunk. "S'good one, too." He went out, and Buddy closed the door. Grinning conspiratorially at Lily, he shook his head.

"Nick's lit. He's not alone, of course."

She gave him a tolerant smile, though it took him in, too, or she meant it to. She hoped he understood.

"Must be tough to be the only one not drinking."

She was filling the dishwasher. She said, "I'm all right."

"Something's hurting you, kid, isn't it."

She looked at him—at the wrinkles around the eyes, which were only slightly glazed with what he'd had to drink. She felt a wave of hoping that Millicent was not cheating on him. He put his glass down and picked up a paper plate of food scraps and dropped it into one of the plastic bags she had been using for refuse.

"It's none of my business, of course."

"I'm all right," she said. "Really."

"Scared, maybe?"

She said nothing.

He finished putting the food in the bag, then set it down and looked at her. "When Millicent was pregnant with Sheri, she was as scared as I've ever seen anybody."

Lily stopped what she was doing.

"It's a natural thing. There'd be something the matter with you if you *weren't* scared."

She faced him, and her throat constricted. No words would come.

"Let's go in the living room and talk," he said. "Want to?" He moved toward her, and gently touched her elbow. "Come on," he said. "Just for a minute."

They went through the little hallway and into the wide space with the bear rug and the big window overlooking the prospect of the valley, the far river, and the overpass. It was all dark out there. The faint moving illuminations on the sky were the lights of cars heading to and from Oxford. Electric lights, which looked like the last burning vestiges of sunlight in haze. He sat on the sofa and extended an arm, evidently wanting her to sit within the circumference of it. She had taken the seat across from him before she realized this. It was too late to change positions now. He put his hands together, then wiped them over his forehead and hair. "Sometimes it's just good to get off by yourself," he said. "So if you want me to leave you here, I understand."

"No," she said. "I don't."

He looked around the room as if he had forgotten whatever he had planned to tell her, and was searching for something to say.

"I'm—I am nervous about it," Lily said.

He appeared almost relieved. "When I met Millicent, Tyler was something like four years old, as I guess you know." He tilted his head a little to one side, looking amused; she knew the look. Something that was a pleasure for him to think about had passed through the stream of his thoughts. "I'm not going to tell you *that* story. That's just a garden-variety love affair, you know. She was working for me, and married, and a mother. And she had this marriage that was smothering her. Well, it seems that now I *am* telling you about it."

"It's all right," Lily said. "Really, Buddy. It is."

"Anyway. Tyler's father had a bit of the tyrant in him. Used to give her grief over things you wouldn't waste five minutes on."

Lily felt abruptly as if the blood in the veins around her throat had thickened.

"He never let Tyler see it—I doubt Tyler ever saw anything like it. And the old man was really pretty good with Tyler. Well, he doted on him. You might even say he spoiled him a little."

Lily caught herself shaking her head. "No, he—he was rough on Tyler."

"You're thinking about the hunting story—the buckshot and the rabbit."

"That and other things."

Buddy shook his head and pondered this for a moment. "It's true, he didn't have a great deal of tolerance. And remember I'm talking about *before* I arrived on the scene.

"Anyway—yeah—well, it looked earlier this afternoon like Tyler's not used to being yelled at." Buddy smiled a forbearing smile, and shook his head. "He's a little old to be racing around Oxford in one of my demos."

"You yelled at him about it?"

"In a manner of speaking. I get too many of those kinds of tickets and I could lose my insurance. As it is, the rate's gonna go up now. I told him I would take it out of his pay next time it happened."

"We were arguing," Lily said. "Something happened at Lamaze." She recalled with an unpleasant little jolt to her nerves that the woman had been recommended by Millicent and Sheri. "It was probably my fault."

"He was driving, sweetie."

She was quiet.

"Anyway," he went on, "when we—when things developed as they did and Millicent was pregnant with Sheri, we sort of—both of us decided it was best to leave the boy with his father. Fact is, Tyler was his father's, really. From the beginning. All boy, as Millicent used to put it."

Lily merely echoed the phrase. "'All boy.'"

"At the beginning," Buddy went on, "we kept it all platonic and we were friends, you know, and we denied it for months, what was really happening to us. Months. And then when we went over the top—well, it was like a dam overflowing. There was no stopping us. It swept us completely along on the tide of itself."

Lily saw her father and Peggy, holding hands across the table in a restaurant.

"We never wanted to hurt a soul," Buddy went on. "You know? I mean—well, you're in love. You know how it is. Love makes you want to be kind. You want to believe so badly in the essential goodness and kindness of everyone. So you talk yourself into believing you can find a gentle way of getting everything into some kind of livable arrangement, and of course you don't stand a chance of accomplishing that without causing a terrific amount of pain, and you see the damage you're causing, and even then you don't feel much of the pain, really. You're too close to getting this matter accomplished that you know is going to make you so—so happy. That's the word, all right. *Happy*." The expression on his face was faintly nostalgic. He went on to talk about growing up in Tennessee, and about his parents, who still lived there and worked the same jobs— she was the reference librarian and he was the events manager at the Nashville Public Library. He'd grown up around books, he said, and in his family, among his uncles, aunts, and cousins, there had always been a big love of them. He had started out in the car business right out of college, working as a salesman, the same job Tyler was now doing, and he had been fortunate enough to make his way to general manager of a big dealership in Point Royal, Virginia. That was where he'd met Millicent. And the year they were married, with the help of four cousins, he'd borrowed enough money to open the present dealership. The move here had been a gamble that had aged him; he still felt old when he thought about those first couple of years. He went on to talk about Sheri as a little girl, the fright of his first days as a father. He was enjoying himself now, and the little wrinkles around his eyes deepened.

Lily kept thinking, *Here is a happy man,* and she felt fearful for his happiness. She remembered when her parents had seemed that way, and then she was visited by a wave of despair about the thing itself: happiness. She had spent so many nights as a little girl lying awake wondering about it; she had always known when she felt happy, but people used the word *happiness* as if it were a place, and she would wonder if she might never find it (all of this, the mix and flow of the memory of her childhood, was commingled with the image of Mr. Stapleton, standing at the door of Ronda's house with the back pocket of his pants sticking out). And now, here, this soft-hearted, graying man, Buddy Galatierre, was talking about the same hope and wish, his own longing, as a boy, for happiness. It so endeared him to her that she felt an impulse to go to him and sit down at his side and kiss his cheek. Now he said that he used to lie in bed in the dark and wonder about it, when he was a boy: would he be happy? Lily did not follow up on the impulse to move to his side, but she nodded, experiencing the feeling of having her thoughts read back to her.

He went on: "People think happiness is a country, a province, you know? And it isn't any such thing. It's good weather. Pretty weather. Climate. Inside, in the heart. It doesn't come from outside so much. And of course it's more complicated than that." He paused. "When you get people in love, and passions—all that. Kin and lovers. And requirements. It can get pretty confused."

"My parents seemed so happy," she said to him.

He smiled. "They probably were. For a long time they probably were."

For a moment, neither of them spoke. She was pulling at a thread on the tail of her blouse.

"I wish Millicent and I could've met in other circumstances," Buddy Galatierre said. "Because you know I was never the type of man who believed in wrecking marriages. I never would've believed I'd do a thing like that. But finally you don't question it. Happiness is what you feel when you don't have to ask yourself if you're happy. I know that's a bit shopworn, but it's also true."

She realized that she had been unraveling the thread of her blouse, and she stopped. Everything was connected; she saw the cloth of her blouse, absurdly, as a metaphor for her own falling-apart life. "God," she said, almost to herself.

"Well. That's all a long time ago now, of course. And you don't need me lecturing you. I'm sorry."

"Oh, don't apologize," she found the strength to say. "I feel better, thank you. You're a kindly, sweet, true gentleman. I'm so glad to be in your house."

"I'm happy to have you here. You and Tyler—and now this wonderful development about the baby."

Briefly, she had the eerie sense that he was referring to what she had discovered only this afternoon. For a lengthy moment, neither of them spoke. He gazed at the wall opposite him. She wondered, now, what he saw, what was going through his mind.

"I've got to call the insurance people on Monday. I'd rather they hear about this episode of the citation from me."

"I'm so sorry about it."

"It's funny," he said. "When Millicent and I fight, and she's driving? *She* speeds. I have to give in a lot to keep her from it."

"I hope Tyler's learned his lesson."

He gave her a long, gentle, evaluative look. "You sure you're all right now?"

"Oh, I'm—" She reached across and touched the back of his hand. "Yes."

He stood. "Let's go out and get something else cold to drink. Will you let me pour you an iced tea?"

She thanked him, and then let him lead her out to the pool area. Everyone had gone around to the front porch. They were seated in the wicker chairs there, sipping drinks and talking quietly.

"Here," Millicent said, rising. "I'll go get more chairs."

"I think I'm going to go to bed," Lily said. "I'm really very tired."

"We haven't had much of a chance to catch up with each other," Dominic said to her.

She smiled at him in the dark. "In the morning."

"Here's to all pregnant ladies," Tyler said.

Nick stirred, mumbling something of his approval, and then lifted Manny's hand, as if to offer Manny's salute as well. But Manny had gone to sleep, or passed out, in his chair. He stirred a little and laughed, then was still again. Nick got to his feet and said, "Is anyone familiar with th' custom droit du seigneur in ol' feudal Europe? Anybody?" He took a breath. "Th' custom was th' right of th' feudal lord to have sex-ee-al innercourse with th' vassal's bride on th' wedding night. See? Everybody get me? An' I wanted to say that on this peticular night, I do wush that's still a custom in these parts and I was feudal lord, and ol' Tyler there wuzza vassal. And it was wedding night for our sweet Ms. Lily, who looks like a renaissance darling with her lil' belly all rounded like a watermelon jus' ripe for harvest."

"Nick," Sheri said. "If you only knew what you were talking about."

"S'dirty," Nick said. "A very dirty thought about that pregnant lady standing there." He took a step toward her, then stopped and seemed about to try saluting her, but this cost him his balance, and he fell back into Buddy's arms. "I had an erotic dream about you, Ms. Lily," he said. "Having it right now."

"And you're going to be in so much trouble in the morning," Buddy said to him, straining to hold him up, and laughing.

"He's in trouble now," Sheri said. "Somebody drag him out of here."

"To you, beloved wife," Nick said, raising his hand as if he had a drink in it. "Sad-eyed lady of the—what is it anyway? Netherlands?"

Buddy pulled him to the other end of the porch.

"Gotta kill some deer in th'morn'n. Id'n that right?"

"For God's sake, put him to bed," said Sheri. She stood, unsteadily, and wrapped her arms around herself. "I'm cold. Is it me or has winter started?"

When the others had gone inside, Dominic and Tyler helped Manny to his feet. Manny sang softly to himself, nothing remotely like a melody. Tyler had him on one side and Dominic on the other.

"Thanks very good," Manny said, in an English that sounded less halting and uncertain. "I see lights, so nice—I—" He stopped, and then went limp.

Tyler looked across the drooping form and said to Dominic, "Your friend's not much of a drinker. I don't think he had but about two."

"The cheapest drunk there is," Dominic said. "He'll never go broke drinking."

The two men worked to get Manny through the doorway and along the hall to his room. They went in there and stayed for a few minutes. Lily stood in the light of the entrance to the kitchen. Rosa was there, making coffee.

"Somebody cleaned up in here," Rosa said.

Lily didn't answer her.

"And I'm drunk."

Tyler and Dominic came back from the bedroom, talking and laughing about Manny's drunken attempt to rise after they had put him on his bed. Rosa asked them if they wanted coffee.

"How about some eggs, Rosa?" Tyler said.

"The coffee's on, honey. And I'm goin' to bed."

"Alone?"

Rosa put one hand on her hip and gave him a withering look. "How would you like to spend time in a hospital?"

"Just teasing there, Rosa."

She looked at Lily and shook her head as if to elicit moral support, then turned and was gone from the room. Dominic poured coffee and held the pot toward Lily.

"No, thank you, Dom," she said. "I have to go to bed."

"She's sleeping for two," said Tyler with a quick, glancing smile. He nodded at Lily. "You go on ahead, sweetie. I'll be right along."

She went down the stairs, into their room, and sat on the bed, waiting for him. When he didn't come, she undressed, got into a nightgown, and curled under the sheets. Perhaps she slept. She didn't know. The dark seemed to be changing, but nothing really changed. Somewhere far off in the Mississippi night a train sent up its wail, a long moan that repeated itself, then faded.

Finally Tyler entered, and made himself ready for bed. He did not speak to her, and she pretended to be asleep.

3

$\mathcal{T}$OWARD DAWN, he stirred and got up, put on a pair of jeans, and stepped outside, by the pool. She lay half awake, waiting for him to come back. She'd awakened several times in the dark with heartburn and a nameless terror. Now she tried to go to sleep, and couldn't, and in a little while he came back, walked through the room and out, and upstairs, where others were now stirring. She heard Nick's laugh, and remembered that they were planning a trip north, to hunt deer. Tyler returned, closed the door quietly, apparently trying not to wake her. "I'm not asleep," she told him.

He went into the bathroom without answering. He was in there a long time. His coming back out brought her up from the sleep she had drifted down into in the quiet. He put on his jacket, standing by the bed, sighing. Then he sat down.

She said, "Are you all right?"

"Yeah." He lay down, slowly.

"Do you want to talk?"

"I don't know what else there is to say. I said I'm sorry I reacted the way I did. And I am sorry. But now it's—now we've—" He sighed again.

"I didn't know how much the anger was building up, Lily. I thought I was handling it."

"Did you say anything to him last night after I came down here?" she asked.

"Don't be silly."

"What'd you talk about?"

"New Orleans, a little."

He sat up and turned on the light, then rubbed his eyes, shifting around so that his feet touched the floor. His shadow on the wall was enormous; it made her feel crowded, outnumbered. "It's pretty serious, not telling a man a thing like that," he said.

"I didn't keep anything from you," she said. "I thought this baby was ours. Yours and mine."

"I meant us not telling him."

She felt suddenly as if she were being too hard on him. She moved in the bed, and touched his back.

He turned slightly to look at her. "How many times were you with him, Lily."

"I wasn't *with* him the way you think."

"What'd you do—use an applicator or something?"

She held her anger in. His tone had been simply, painfully bewildered. "It happened once. A couple of days before you came to me, at the dorm. It didn't work and he was miserable. It was sad and a little desperate and lonely and—I don't know, like a kind of clinging together. There wasn't anything romantic about it, and it didn't seem as sordid as it sounds, telling it. And I didn't think I would ever see you again."

"But you did it when you saw him the next time?"

"No!" she said, too loud. "I was never physically intimate with him after that first time. I said it happened once. That once. And I got pregnant from—from drippings, for God's sake. I mean we didn't even finish. He was figuring out that he's—what his sexuality is."

"Say it—he was figuring out he's gay."

"Gay, yes," she said. "All right. As far as I knew, you were not in my life when it happened."

"But you just jumped into bed with him. Out of friendship?"

"It wasn't like that, Tyler, and anyway I don't have to justify that to you. I told you, this was before you. Before *us*."

"How many other men have you been with, anyway?"

"How many women have *you* been with?"

"I asked you first." He actually smiled.

"I'm beginning to think I don't know you at all, not in the slightest," she said.

"Well," he said, "I know this is the eighties and we're all supposed to be so sexually liberated, even though there's a plague killing people by the thousands—but I do think I have a right to know how many people you had sex with before me. Were you promiscuous, for instance? Should I be worried about anything?"

"I had sex with the whole city of Charlottesville," she said. "I just went through the phone book and started with the *A*s and moved on through the *Z*s. I had sex with entire families, and in fact, while you slept on the train coming down here, I fucked the whole engineering crew, and all the passengers. You were asleep, so I didn't think you'd mind."

"Ha," he said. His mouth barely moved.

"Now, tell me your adventures," she said. "This is fun."

All the color went out of the flesh around his lips, and his eyes narrowed. "Oh, Christ. We're not going to get over this, are we?"

"Gee," she said. "Well, um, that's up to you, I think. Maybe the important thing to remember is that you don't have anything to say about this. This isn't Victorian England, for Christ's sake! This is my situation, and it happened before you came to me that day and I was so happy to see you. That's right, I remember it now. I was so happy to see you—and—and, oh, yes, I asked you how many lovers you'd had before I met you but, you know, I really don't care. And I expect the same from you."

"I was a virgin," he said.

She stared at him. Something about the overdignified cast of his facial expression, the way his chin jutted forward as he spoke, convinced her that what he had said was true. She was seized by the sour conviction that he felt cheated by the fact, and that he might want to exact some punishment for it from the world. His lips were so tightly drawn, and his eyes glittered with moral indignation and disapproval. "Well, I was, too, in effect," she told him.

"You were *pregnant,* for Christ's sake."

"I told you how it happened," she said.

After another pause, he said, "Jesus—what're we going to do."

"I'm going to have a baby, and then I'm going to raise it and love it." She was on the verge of tears again.

"Do you love me?" he said.

"I don't like you much right now, I can tell you that. But what do you think, Tyler? What would you say I feel about you given the last few months?"

He looked down at his hands. "Oh, God. I'm scared, Lily."

"I've never done anything like this," she said, beginning to cry. "I'm only twenty-two for Christ's sake. We've never—Tyler, I thought we were having our first child, starting our family—I thought you were nervous about being a father—"

He said nothing, nor did he move.

"Do you see? I wasn't ready for this—any of this. *You've* had longer to get used to it than me. You've known about it longer. I thought we were telling each other everything—"

He paced to the other side of the room again, then came back and sat down, and to her surprise, took her hands in his own. "Look. I'll be a good father. I will."

"Yes," she said, sobbing. "I know."

"Dominic's more your friend than mine. You know him better than I do. But I don't think this would make him happy—knowing it's—knowing this. And besides—oh, Christ. If he knows, everybody else will know." He squeezed her hands. "Everybody."

She kept her eyes down.

"You're sure you didn't have sex with anyone else."

"Yes, I'm *sure*," she said through her teeth.

"Well," he said. "I know—but it'd be easier if you had. You couldn't be sure it was his, then."

"Oh," she said, through her tears, and with a bitter, sobbing breath. "That would be just perfect, I can see *that*."

For a long time they sat there, without speaking and without moving. From time to time she sniffled. She noticed, after a few moments, that he had begun wringing his hands again.

At last, he took a deep breath, and shook his head. "We're going hunting. Imagine it. Buddy, Nick, and me. Nick tried to get Dominic and Manny interested but Manny's too hungover. Manny's been sick."

"Dominic isn't going either?"

"Listen, don't tell him," Tyler said.

"Tyler, please."

"I mean it. Say nothing. They'll go to New Orleans and that'll be that."

"I don't know if I can keep it from him for life. He's my friend. He's got a right to know, doesn't he?"

Tyler stood again, and moved with a tight, furious stride, arms showing veins and muscles, to the bookcase and back, his jaw working.

She had stopped crying, though her chest kept heaving with the sobs that had shaken her.

"Goddamn," he said. "Goddamnit all to hell."

In a dispirited faltering of her voice, she spoke: the words that came were exactly those she had uttered to her father's young wife, all those months ago, when she had felt so sure of her own sense of right and wrong. "Cheer up," she said, staring off at the dark of the window. "Maybe something will happen."

4

*L*ATER, she went upstairs and poured herself a bowl of cereal. None of the others seemed to have left their rooms yet. She went back downstairs, showered, and dressed, feeling an unexpected aversion now to seeing her reflection in the mirror. When she went back upstairs, she found Millicent and Rosa preparing to go into town. They asked if she wanted to go with them to Square Books, but she demurred. She waved good-bye to them, then went out and sat by the pool in the sun. There was a crispness in the air, but it had not turned cold, as Millicent had said it was supposed to. A thin cloud of steam rose from the water in the pool, which was glass smooth. There wasn't any wind. The sun was warm, and when you stepped into the shade you felt the difference. She pulled a footstool close, so she could prop up her legs.

Dominic came out of the house with a glass of orange juice for her. He sat down at her side. A moment passed, in which neither of them looked at the other.

He sighed, and made a clicking sound with his tongue. "Um,

Manny read somewhere that Bush sent a memo to the IRS telling them to crack down on back taxes, especially from the lower-middle class and the poor. Apparently the poor aren't paying enough taxes fast enough."

She made a sound she hoped he would take for agreement.

"What's the matter with you, kitty cat?"

"Nothing," she said.

"Maybe it's our collective hangover."

They were quiet for a few moments.

"Something's not right," he said. "Something's off center in this place." His gaze wandered over the house and the pool area. "Like, why're you and Tyler still living here? There must be some nice places in town."

She told him about the rental house that had gone up in flames, looking straight at him, feeling the weight of what she withheld from him like the weight of her body.

"Well, they're all wonderful and all that. But if it was me, I'd want to get off to myself. It must feel like you're waiting for your lives to start. I'd hate that." He tapped his knee with the flat of one hand, gazing off at the cloudless sky and the brilliant curves of the river in the distance. Some part of him was always moving. He was all energy. "Manny's—he's—positive. I guess I wrote you that."

"Yes."

Again, they were quiet.

"I met him at the house of a friend."

"He's got beautiful, kindly eyes. It's the first thing you notice about him."

Dominic leaned the chair back, and then let it fall forward again. "I think sometimes he'd talk better if the language barrier didn't provide him with a kind of cover. His writing's very cool. You wouldn't know from it that he wasn't from here."

"His aunt lives in New Orleans?"

He nodded. "Well. He calls her Aunt Violet. She's got a masters degree from somewhere. She's lived in New Orleans since the thirties. I tell you we're gonna stay there?"

"I think you told me over the phone."

"I thought I said we were going to see." Again, he leaned the chair back, only this time he stayed that way, clasping his hands behind his head. He looked toward the river. "Is that the Mississippi?"

"A branch of it, I think."

He turned to her. "I've never known you to be incurious. What's happened, anyway?"

Before she could realize the import of the question, she said, "Nothing."

He kept his eyes on hers.

"Dominic, *what*?"

"Something's different."

She waited.

"Are you happy about the baby?"

"Christ," Lily said. "What a question."

"That's cool," he said, and let the chair come forward, unclasping his hands. "Are you preoccupied about your book?"

She frowned.

"I mean, your play. Whatever. Mary Kingsley."

"I don't know what it's going to be," Lily said.

"Is that what's bothering you?"

At this moment, sitting there in the sun with him, with his pale eyes taking her in, she almost told him. The urge was so strong that she stood up, and walked to the border of the lawn.

He came with her, saying, "What? What?"

"Nothing's bothering me, Dominic—please," she said.

"Is it you and Tyler? You're not getting along. I saw it—anyone can see it."

She took his arm. "Were they talking about us?"

"Who?"

"Nick—Sheri. The others."

"Nobody said anything. *I* saw it. Okay? When I said anyone, I meant anyone of my superior sensitivity and insight."

"Dominic," she said. Then: "No. I—I can't talk to you about this." She moved away from him, back toward the house. Rosa and Manny had come out and taken two chairs in the sun. Lily walked past them and in, and Dominic followed.

"Jesus, there *is* something," he said. "Are you gonna tell me?"

She had the scary sensation that he knew everything, and simply wanted her to come across with it as a sign of their trust in each other as friends. "We had a fight," she said. "It's—it's nothing more than that." She told herself, moving away from him, down the stairs toward her basement room, that this was in some sense true enough, and that therefore she had not actually lied to him.

PART·4

Falling

SIXTEEN

1

That evening, two policemen drove up with the news that Buddy Galatierre had been killed. Millicent, Sheri, and Lily had been out on the porch, waiting for the men to return, and had all separately begun to worry as the sun went below the level of the trees to the west, and the air grew steadily colder. They had put sweaters on, and Lily was shivering, and still they had remained there in the failing light, waiting. Dominic sat with them and talked aimlessly about old television shows, trying to distract them from their anxiety. Finally he'd gone into the house to wake Manny from his long nap. After he was gone, Sheri had said, "I hope Nick doesn't have them out drinking somewhere."

Millicent was the first to see the police car. She gasped as the officers got out and approached. All three women stood. Lily recognized the taller of the two policemen as the older man who had issued the speeding ticket to Tyler. He was the one who gave the news, saying it in a flat, nerveless, but kindly voice, all business, "Mrs. Galatierre?"

"Me—that's me," Millicent said, as if she were pleading with them not to harm her.

"Ma'am—Mrs. Galatierre, I'm afraid it's your husband." He stopped, but only for a moment. "I'm afraid your husband's—" Again he stopped, and Millicent started to sink to her knees. Lily and Sheri caught her.

"I'm sorry," the policeman said.

Sheri began to wail. The two policemen helped carry Millicent inside, to the couch. Sheri stood at the door, her broken features registering only disbelief. "There's some *mistake*."

The officers were very considerate, and the older one explained to Lily that the other men were at the hospital where Mr. Galatierre had been taken. Tyler and Nick had brought him in. It was evidently a shooting accident. One of the rifles had gone off and the bullet had struck Mr.

Galatierre in the stomach. They were in the woods, far from help. They struggled to get him to the hospital in Memphis, but he had bled so badly from the wound that the emergency people couldn't save him. Nick and Tyler were with the police, there, now.

The younger one said, "Any time a firearm's involved—see, there's questions."

"We'll take you to the hospital," the older officer said. "I'm terribly sorry."

Dominic and Manny came out of the family room, entering the kitchen just as Lily started down to get her winter coat.

"Lily?" Dominic said.

And she broke down, unable to form words out of the spasms of weeping that came, while Dominic put his arms around her and held on, murmuring, "What's the matter? What is it? Lily, what's happened?"

They found Tyler in a little room off the hospital's main lobby, sitting at a desk, with two other police officers standing over him. Tyler had been crying, and he sat with his head in his hands. There was a tape recorder on the desk, the spools turning. Sheri asked tearfully for Nick, and was led down the hall toward another room. Lily went with her, because the two policemen were still interviewing Tyler. Nick sat in his room alone, staring off into disbelieving space. They saw him through the window in the door, but were not allowed, just yet, to enter. From somewhere a lean, dark man in a suit had appeared, holding a small pad of paper and requesting to speak with the women separately. He had prominent, almost swollen-looking cheekbones, and a widow's peak that gave him a sinister appearance, but his voice was very soft, his bearing completely sympathetic. He spoke to Millicent first. Lily and Sheri waited in the massive, open lobby, sitting on futonlike furniture of an absurdly bright blue color. Sheri was in shock. Someone had given her a sedative. She sat with her legs tightly together, holding a handkerchief in her small fists, as if to tear it apart. Tears streamed down her cheeks, but she said nothing, and didn't seem to hear what was said to her.

The older officer came back through the lobby. Lily asked, "Can you please tell me what's going on?"

"Ma'am, until we are absolutely certain of whatever made this an accident, we have a homicide."

She felt her legs falter under her.

"A man's been shot. We're trying to ascertain what happened. We have to file a report. Are you Harrison's wife?"

She nodded.

"It was his rifle."

"Oh, God," Lily said.

"Here," he said. He helped her back to where Sheri sat, hands still clenched in her lap, tears streaming down her face. When Lily sat down next to her, Sheri stirred, and then, seeing the officer, muttered, "I think he came down here to kill my father."

The officer said, "Excuse me—is it Sheri—Mrs. Green?"

She stared, bleary-eyed, at his face.

"Do you want to talk to me about anything?"

"He killed my father. He came here to do it," she said.

Lily touched her shoulder. "Sheri, please don't talk like that. You know how Tyler feels—"

"Uh, Mrs. Green, it was—apparently it was your husband who was holding the rifle when it went off."

"Nick?" Sheri sobbed. "Nick did it?" She looked at him, and then at Lily, and then sank into Lily's arms.

2

$\mathcal{T}$HE INTERVIEWS went on for more than two hours, and Nick and Tyler had been questioned in the hours before the women arrived at the hospital. Millicent seemed almost hollowed out, desiccated, and the sedatives she had been given made her so groggy that they admitted her for the night. The police officers were thorough, behaved with flawless courtesy, presiding over the elucidation of what was apparently no more than a ghastly accident, although they would not, for the present, rule out the possibility of there being some charge brought against Nick for failing to check the safety on the rifle.

The story, as well as could be made out, was that the three men had driven into the wilderness, and had walked a good three miles from the car. They had come upon signs of a bear, probably a black bear. They hadn't seen any deer—except, Nick said in a broken voice, a roadkill on the way—and because it was a bear and the tracks were fresh and they wanted to feel safe, they had their rifles ready. Nick asked to see Tyler's, and so Tyler had handed it to him. They traded. It was one of those casually juvenile things between men, Nick liking the new feeling of the other rifle. They came to a barbed-wire fence, and got ready to climb it, each of them checking that the safety on his rifle was engaged before starting over. Tyler and Buddy climbed it and jumped down, but something stirred in the brush nearby, just as Nick got ready to follow them. He took his safety off, and stood ready, while Tyler and Buddy waited, crouched and listening. They all waited for some time, almost fifteen minutes, talking low, and worrying about the bear, an attack, rabies. It was the woods, and the noise went on, then ceased, and then began again. This continued for another few minutes. And at last it stopped altogether. But the quiet became freighted with the presence of the bear, something watching them. They laughed about it, yet they were nervous. Nick started over the fence, hurrying because he had begun to imagine that the bear might rush him while he was suspended on the wires. The toe of his boot caught on the second one, and he fell, tearing the flesh under his arm. The rifle went off. A moment passed before either Nick or Tyler quite realized what had taken place.

Nick hadn't put the safety back on.

They hadn't been thinking right. The bear, if it was a bear, had occupied their minds. Now there was only the unspeakable fact that they couldn't call it back, retrace their steps and undo it. Go back there and be more careful, be so much more cautious.

On the way home, Lily drove. No one spoke. The night breezes were cold, and the starry sky seemed closer than before.

Rosa opened the front door when they arrived. She had been crying. She stood back for them to enter, and then disappeared to some other part of the house, to suffer her grief alone. Dominic and Manny were sitting in the kitchen, with that impotently sorrowful aspect of people on the periphery of a catastrophe. Sheri moved past them as if they were furniture and poured herself a large tumbler of whiskey. She drank long and slow from it. Though she already had tranquilizers in her system, nothing seemed to have any effect. She looked at the two men, and at Lily, but said nothing. As she started out of the kitchen, Dominic asked if there was anything he and Manny could do. "Oh, no, I'm sorry," she said. "Please—please excuse—me." Her voice broke. She went upstairs, sobbing, and they heard the door to the room she and Nick shared click quietly shut. Tyler wandered through the rooms of the house, lost, wide-eyed, a child in a nightmare sleepwalk. Nick lay facedown on the sofa in the living room, weeping.

"God," Manny said, wringing his hands.

"Lily," Dominic murmured, "I think Manny and I ought to leave."

She nodded, half remembering that there was something important that he should know. It was almost as if she might forget it. She went through the house, looking for Tyler. She found him in the wide living room, with its bear rug and its animal heads on the walls, and she remembered Buddy, only last night, walking her in here to calm her nerves by talking about how he had stumbled onto happiness. That seemed a whole lifetime ago. She watched Tyler pick up a picture in a stand-up frame and then set it down, and she saw the terror in his face when he turned to her.

"Oh, Jesus," he said, and began to cry. "Jesus." He pushed on, through to the next room, and the next, and then to the stairs, which he climbed, toward his mother's and Buddy's empty bedroom.

Lily followed. Tyler sat on the edge of the bed, and seemed about to slump over. Then he saw Lily standing in the doorway. "I can't believe it," he said. "I can't."

She went to his side and put one arm over his shoulder.

In the room, there were pictures of Sheri in all the stages of her growing up, and a few pictures of Tyler, apparently taken by whoever Buddy had paid to travel north to keep some kind of record, however sporadic, of Millicent's abandoned son.

"Lily, I wanted to hurt him. My whole life, I wanted to hurt him. Both of them. I think I made it happen, Lily. How could it have happened?"

"Shhh," she murmured. "Don't."

He sobbed, and held tight to her. "I never dreamed—Jesus. I got to liking him so much. I wanted to do what I could to hurt them both, Lily, growing up, I thought about it, went to sleep with it at night—they hurt me so much. My whole life. It's my fault. It's my fault. And I love them— I swear it, Lily. Oh, God, I swear it. When I got the reckless—the ticket, he was upset with me and he put his hand on my shoulder. I could see he was worried about me. Him. I never for five minutes got anything like that with my father. And I wanted it so much when I was small."

"Oh, baby," Lily said. "Let it go. Go on and let it go."

He was still talking through his sobs, but his words were not distinguishable now. He wept, and the minutes passed, and she held him, crying, too. She didn't know how long they remained like that. At length he subsided, and the exhaustion he felt, along with the drugs the doctors had given him, took effect. He drifted into a fitful sleep in her arms, in Buddy and Millicent's bed. And she held him for a long while before extricating herself, and making her way downstairs.

She'd heard movement there. Here was Nick Green, pouring himself a glass of bourbon, standing at the kitchen counter. His eyes were glazed over and raw-looking. "Can't sleep," he said.

"Don't have any more of it, Nick."

"The boys left."

"Dominic—"

He nodded before she could finish, and then took a long drink of the whiskey. It seemed to hurt him going down. He put the glass on the counter and gripped it with both hands, letting his head droop between his shoulders. A sound issued from the back of his throat, like a suppressed shriek. Then he breathed, straightened, and took another drink of the bourbon. She saw the blood on his shirtsleeve where he had been cut.

"Nick," she said.

Again, swallowing the whiskey seemed to hurt him. When he looked at her, his eyes had filled with tears again, but no tears fell. He sniffled, shook his head, and sighed. "They gave me stuff at the hospital. Nothing helps." He took another hard gulp, grimacing with the pain of it.

"Nick, don't. It was an accident."

He sobbed. "Oh, God, Lily. Jesus good Christ in heaven." She went to him, put her arms around him, weeping, too, again. The two of them stood there in the light of the kitchen, in the smell of alcohol and sweat and dirt.

At last, she moved to the other side of the room, to the doorway, where she held on to the frame and looked back at him. He hadn't moved from where he had been standing when she'd first entered. "The others are asleep," she said to him, sniffling.

He took another long pull of the whiskey.

"Go to bed, Nick. Please?"

"You kill a man," he said, "and they ask you a lot of questions about it, you know, and they want to know every angle, every little detail of the bullet and the bleeding and the dying right under your eyes—right under your eyes. Jesus." He sobbed, ran the heel of his palm across his left eye, half turning from her, sniffling again. "Ah. Christ. I'm sorry."

"I know," she told him.

He wasn't looking at her now, talking almost to himself. "And—and—God. They get you to repeat it—they're so considerate and nice through the whole thing, and you repeat it and you repeat it, and then they give you some medicine to help you sleep—" Now he did look at her again. He held his hands out, as a person does who has nothing to express but the most profound bewilderment. "And then they send you home."

3

𝒯HE FUNERAL was held in St. John's Episcopal Church that Wednesday. There was a large crowd, more than five hundred people, according to the funeral director, a Mr. Soburger, whose suit cuffs, Lily noticed, were threadbare. That seemed so incongruous—a funeral director with signs of wear in his clothing—though he was very quiet and dignified. Roger Gault stayed close to Millicent through it all. Sheri and Nick clung to each other.

The final judgment on the catastrophe was that it was an accident—avoidable, horrible—but an accident nevertheless. Two emergency-room doctors had spoken with the victim before he'd lapsed into unconsciousness, and poor Buddy had explained things exactly as Nick and Tyler had, the bear or whatever it was rustling in the underbrush, Nick falling on the fence and the gun going off. If Millicent was entertaining any ideas of pursuing the case further—a prominent lawyer had sent her a card inviting her to seek relief in a wrongful death suit—she said nothing. She let Nick embrace her, and indeed it looked as though Nick was the one in need of support.

The priest was a small, pale man with black eyes and a thin, bitter expression about the face—narrow lips, hollows in the cheeks, a long nose through which the cartilage showed white, as if the skin were stretched there. He spoke the words of the liturgy in a nearly offhand manner, standing in front of a colossal bank of flowers, one large section of which had been sent, jointly, by Lily's parents and Peggy. And then he delivered a homily about the salvation that awaits us all, his voice rising with his own satisfaction in the sound of it. Several friends and business associates of the deceased stood up to say something about Buddy. They kept repeating that he himself would never have wanted people eulogizing him. Buddy Galatierre was interested in other people—he had a real interest in you, in whoever the specific someone was that he was with, and while he had a famously bad memory for names, he remembered little details of your life, and wanted to know about them, to *talk* about them with you. And when you were with him you felt this. You felt more confident in the importance of the matters that concerned you because they concerned him. Lily wept, hearing this. Tyler, sitting next to her, reached over and put his hand on hers.

The eulogies went on. Rosa got up to say that the first day she'd worked for Buddy Galatierre she'd had an argument with him about politics, and that in the middle of it she'd had the amazing realization that he had made her feel that much at ease with him, that quickly. She lost her breath on the last word, weeping again. Two others followed her, with their stories.

The baby stirred in Lily's womb, like an awful, cruelly pedestrian reminder: life insisting on itself. She rejected the thought, the connection, and even so her mind wandered back in time, imagining the day Buddy Galatierre was born. All his life, this had awaited him. This gross misfiring of sense and expectation. She began to have gloomy thoughts about the baby—its unknown fate. Tyler squeezed her hand, and she realized that she had been moaning low, sobbing. Millicent looked back at her and nodded, her eyes swimming. Lily heard nothing else that was said. She looked at the other faces, and at the ribbed arches in the ceiling, the plain wooden cross above the altar. None of it made any impression on her now.

Everyone filed out into the sun, and the chill. The first truly cold day, windless and bright, a cloudless dark blue sky with a pale sliver of day moon showing in it. There seemed something cruelly fine about it, an intolerable merciless clarity in the air, as if the world were trumpeting at them its own magnificence, its indifference to human pain. They rode in the train of automobiles to the cemetery. Lily and Tyler were in the car behind the hearse, with Millicent, Sheri, Nick, and Rosa. Sheri sniffled, daubing her nose with a handkerchief, looking out the window at the country. Nick kept his arm around her, staring into space. The doctors had given him Xanax, to calm him. Millicent sat erect on the other side of Nick, watching the road ahead. Lily and Tyler were seated across from her with Rosa, who seemed to be holding herself together by tightly clasping her hands in her lap. They were all waiting for anything to do. It felt that way to Lily: a vast, helpless sorrow and futility, mingled with the desire to think of some practical way to be of use. Millicent said nothing. The only sounds were Sheri's small sighs and sobs. Lily had gained control of herself, and was fighting a battle with her mind to keep it on the matter at hand.

Millicent's gaze abruptly seemed to take her in, and to Lily's surprise she stirred, sighed, and then murmured, "I wish I'd said something sweet to him on that last morning." Her voice faltered.

"You said sweet things to him every day," Lily told her.

Tyler said, "He knew how you felt about him."

Millicent sniffled. "Thank you, son." She looked at Lily. "Thank you both."

The cemetery was surrounded by tall oaks, spreading their emptying branches to the air. The ground was littered with leaves, and even in this windless cold calm they dropped and fluttered to the ground. The shiny cars pulled into the complicated shadows next to the grave site, which had been covered with a green felt tarp. The mortician and his assistant, along with the pallbearers, including Nick and Tyler, drew the casket out of the back of the hearse and slowly advanced to the grave, where a brace with thick canvas belts had been placed. They set the casket on these belts. The hole in the ground over which it was suspended looked green, the tarp tucked into it, until you got close enough to see the black earth beneath. Lily saw this and felt her heart go. She managed, with great effort and concentration, to keep on her feet. There were chairs arranged along one side, and a few yards away there was a mound of earth, what had been dug from the hole.

"No," Millicent said. Nick and Tyler held her up. Sheri walked to the edge, looked down, then moved to one of the chairs and sat, holding the handkerchief to her mouth. Nick took the seat to her left, and reached over and took her free hand. Millicent sat to her right; Lily, Tyler, and Rosa took their places on the other side of Millicent. Others were arriving, walking quietly across the grass in their suits and fine dresses and coats, helping each other over the rough places in the ground. They were in the brightness of the sun, and then they drew close, passing into the sparse, leafy, intricate shade, which was faltering away little by little, by pieces. The priest—the same one from the church—stood waiting for them all to get into place. He held the prayer book, and he was shivering a little. The hush over everyone seemed to extend to the world. Lily saw two jet trails, high and far in the distance; no sound came from them. No breeze stirred. No birds sang. She heard only the faintest rustle and scrape of cloth on cloth, the muted thud of footsteps as the others arrived and took their places around the small clutch of people at the center. Lily breathed the odor of the dirt, and the fallen leaves.

"My brethren," the priest began. There were prayers from the Mass for the dead, final prayers. She heard very little of it. He threw some specks of water from a kind of wand, on the crowd, and on the casket, and he said more. The baby kept kicking her, and moving in her, and she couldn't help the feeling that there was some connection between it and this ceremony, the silenced, imagined shape of Buddy Galatierre in his casket. She wished for some cessation of thought, attempted to concentrate on the words of the priest, holding her hand over the place where the baby kept moving.

When the last words were said, Millicent and Sheri got up and moved to one side of the grave, and people began filing by to say something to them. Tyler murmured, "We belong there with them, come on." Rosa followed them. Nick, too, took his place alongside them, eyes fixed on the ground, a broken-down man. That was how he looked. It was hard to imagine that he would ever joke again, or be sardonic. That was all gone out of him and you could see it in his eyes, a desperate pressure to get out from under his own usual perceptions and personality, his own being, as though he now had to find some way to live down every witty thing he had ever said, every joke, every presentation of himself as the cool customer, the one with the acerbic wit and the irony.

They stood there in a row, in the cold, mottled shade, while the friends of Buddy Galatierre filed by them to express their sorrow, their condolences—the few empty, puny phrases that ten thousand years of human life and civilization have been able to muster for use on the occasion of the extinction of another human being.

4

$\mathscr{T}$HE FOLLOWING DAYS in the house were filled with tasks having to do with the arrangement or dispersal of Buddy Galatierre's personal effects—his clothes, his letters and papers, the records of his life—and Millicent, in a moment of awkward practicality, asked Lily if she thought Tyler would want Buddy's gun collection. Lily could scarcely muster the voice to say that she couldn't know, and then, seeing the distress in the other woman's face, quickly added that she would ask him.

On the Saturday after the funeral, in one of those macabre coincidences surrounding the loss of a loved one, the mounted head of the deer they had killed on the earlier hunt arrived, on its plaque, ready for display. At first they didn't know what it was, opening the large package and removing the protective Styrofoam pellets. When the nose was revealed, Nick uttered a small desperate sound and walked out of the house, away, toward the road. Sheri went after him. Lily and Tyler took the half-opened box down into the basement room, and then Tyler sat down on the bed and began to cry. Lily stood at his side, one hand lightly on his shoulder. When he looked up at her, she saw the need in his eyes, for just this, just what she could give, this hopeless solace. She sat down and embraced him, rocking slowly with him as if he were a child. They wept, and everywhere about them there was the silence of Buddy Galatierre being gone. A few minutes later, Tyler took the box with the deer's head in it and went out the sliding doors, to the car. He drove away, and when he returned, a little more than an hour later, he said, "I took care of it." Lily didn't ask what he had done, or where he had taken it.

The reading of the will took place in a white-walled room, on the second floor of a very old flagstone house that stood at the end of a blind street in Oxford. The house had been built back in the eighteenth century by a glass merchant named Dodley, and above the front door was a plaque listing the several owners since Dodley had sold it and gone back to England, in 1791. The latest owner of the house was Buddy's attorney and executor, John West, a ruddy, heavyset man with swollen-looking red eyes and a wild, heavy shock of dyed-black hair.

Millicent had asked everyone to accompany her, including Nick, to whom she had been especially thoughtful and kind. Nick seemed utterly changed. At the Galatierre house, he had spent hours sitting out on the porch, even when the weather turned still colder. He sat with his shoulders hunched, wearing a coat against the chill, smoking one cigarette after another, staring out at the road, the quickly shedding trees. When you spoke to him, he was slow to answer, but his responses indicated that he had heard; his smile was tentative, quite gentle, and marred by the stricken look in his eyes.

Sheri had begun to worry that he might do something to harm himself, and she began to show the strain. "What is he *thinking* about sitting out there like that?"

"Why don't you ask him?" said Tyler.

"I have," she said. "God. You don't think I have, Tyler?"

Lily had asked him, too. "Can I do anything?" she'd said from the door.

He looked over his shoulder at her, and there came that smile, so downhearted and hollow. "Oh, no, it's fine."

"What's going on?" she asked.

He had turned back to gazing out at the road and the trees. "Nothing."

"Nick," she said.

And now he did turn.

"It wasn't your fault."

He faced the road again, and took a draw on the cigarette. The last leaves were flying out of the trees, and a chilly rain began to fall, though there was blue sky in the distance. He didn't move, and finally she closed the door.

Buddy's will left control of the dealership, the house, all the surrounding land, and the largest percentage of the profits to Millicent and Sheri, and a small percentage of the profits to Millicent's son, Tyler, to be distributed as Millicent wished. Millicent explained to them all that this provision had been made almost ten years ago, at her request, and that it was all long before Nick had entered the family, or there was any hope that Tyler might actually come to Mississippi. "Now," she said, her voice choking with emotion, "here you are."

Tyler kissed her cheek.

When everything was signed and accepted, John West cleared his throat, stood from behind his big desk, and came around it to offer

Millicent a hug. Lily stood off to one side, and saw Nick take Sheri's hand. Sheri absentmindedly took it away, then seemed to realize what she had done and quickly turned to him, offering it back.

They all filed into the car, and Tyler drove them back to the house. He and Nick had some work at the dealership, and they left immediately to take care of that. Millicent went to her room, and closed the door, and for a while Sheri and Lily sat together in the living room with the big window looking out onto the low hills of the country, to the distant river and the highway, all of which was much more clearly visible now through the bare branches of the trees. Neither of them spoke for a long time, and to Lily it seemed that they were both waiting for something to change.

"I'm not seeing him anymore, if that's crossed your mind," Sheri broke out.

"Sheri, for God's sake."

"Well, I have to tell you." She sobbed, and held her hands to her face. "Lily, I didn't sin. Why do I feel like I sinned? It was just a friendship. I keep feeling mad at Nick."

Rosa arrived from the college, carrying some shopping bags full of books and a few items of clothing she had brought. "You-all ought to put some lights on," she said, going on through to the kitchen, carrying the bags.

"I'm so scared," Sheri murmured. "I'm afraid I made it happen. Because I wanted to commit adultery. I *wanted* to. It's a sin if you think about it in your heart."

"Stop thinking of yourself," Lily said, low. "You didn't make anything happen."

"Oh, God," the other said, beginning to weep again. "It's true, isn't it? I'm sorry. My poor father. My father, Lily."

"You're hurting," Lily put her arms around her. "We're all hurting."

"I'm—I can't stand it. I have to blame myself, or Nick."

The phone rang and startled them. They heard Rosa answer it, and in a moment she came to the entrance of the room. "It's your mama, Lily."

On the phone, Doris sounded breathless, her voice trembling. There was no news, everything was fine. She wanted to know how Lily and the baby were doing, how everyone was faring. Lily answered the question about herself and the baby, and left the other. Her mother didn't pursue it.

"Are you sure you're all right?" Lily asked. "You sound like you're shaking."

"I guess I am. I wish you were closer."

For the first time in a very long time, Lily wished it, too. She said, "I know, I feel the same."

Her mother breathed, the sigh of someone trying hard to imagine a neutral remark to make.

"It's a desolation here," Lily said. "I don't know how it's going to change."

"It will. It takes time."

Lily was silent. Behind her in the big room, Sheri coughed, and seemed to sob. Lily spoke low into the handset: "I've got to go now, Mom."

"Oh," Doris said with tears in her voice. "It's been a while since you called me that."

"I'm sorry," Lily said.

"Don't apologize for it. I'm going to come down in February, now— right? I want to be there that first week, after the baby comes."

"Yes," she said, although she didn't know, now, what would happen—what plans anyone would be able to make. She didn't go on to add that she and Tyler hadn't found a place to live, yet. She got off the phone and went back to sitting with Sheri.

It was difficult to put all of it together in her mind—the baby, her own unabated desire for finding a place to live, the worry over the trouble in her marriage, and even the relatively banal question of whether or not Tyler would continue at the dealership. Since the funeral he had been very considerate and kind, and quiet. They had not spoken of the baby except in the minor daily matters of accommodating themselves to her pregnancy; they had made love once, a few days after the funeral, and he had been surprisingly tender, holding her for a long while afterward. She had slept in his arms.

As Thanksgiving came and went, and the colder weather, and Christmas, the pressure for finding a place of their own increased. Lily couldn't help feeling her condition was a kind of daily affront to the other people in the house: to Tyler for his reasons, and to the others, each for their own—and for the fact that Buddy Galatierre was gone. Everyone was kind. Millicent brought her things for the baby when she went out; Sheri and Nick still were solicitous of her comfort, as was Rosa.

For Christmas, Tyler bought her a padded rocking chair, and a boxed set of delta blues. She got him a new sport coat, and several shirts, and the same boxed set of blues. They laughed about it with the others, and Millicent told of the time she was wrapping a digital clock for Buddy, and Sheri, only four years old, had walked up to her and said, "Mommy, you opened your gift," and it was then that Millicent realized that Buddy had also bought her a digital clock.

They didn't decorate the house front as it had always been when Buddy was alive; no one had the heart for it. Nick had bought a small tree, and they put it up and decorated it, with a forced, almost timid jollity. Millicent sat on the sofa, watching them all, and in a little while Lily joined her.

The morning after Christmas, it snowed. A light dust, rising and swirling in the wind. They stayed in the house, and kept to separate rooms most of the day. No one knew what to do for anyone else. Rosa wasn't there, having gone to New Orleans to spend time with a cousin. Lily wrote in her journal, and then began to prepare something for them all to eat.

In the waning light of that afternoon, there was a knock at the front door, and she heard Tyler say he would get it. She entered the living room in time to see Roger Gault standing in the square of fading light, with a checked jacket on and his cap in his hands, nodding slightly and smiling at Tyler and past Tyler, at her, and at Sheri, who had come in from the kitchen. He had a package under his arm. "Merry Christmas," he said.

Tyler repeated the phrase tonelessly, and moved aside for him to enter. Gault offered the package, a box of Godiva chocolate truffles, which Tyler took and then handed to Millicent when she came down the hall from the family room.

"We're a mess," said Mrs. Galatierre. "Why don't you call a person."

Lily watched her face, and was seized by a strong desire to get out of the suffocating closeness of the rooms of the house. Millicent held the box of truffles and thanked him, running one hand through her hair, tears streaming down her cheeks. Gault hadn't seen the tears, standing half turned from her, talking to Tyler about the snow, and the almost white Christmas they'd had—clumsy talk about weather, utterly without a single trace of anyone's true thoughts or feelings. At last, he saw that Millicent was weeping, and put one hand, quite gingerly, on her shoulder. "I'm so very sorry," he said, his face betraying his frustration with the hollow sound of the words. He was a man needlessly repeating himself, who knew it, and still could do nothing to stop it. Millicent excused herself and went up the stairs to her room. Sheri followed her.

"Well," said Gault, almost as if to himself. "I can't stay."

"It was kind of you to stop by," said Tyler.

Lily felt a stirring of deep affection for Tyler in that moment, watching him guide the other man to the door and shake his hand—Tyler seemed the one person who knew what was expected, what to do next in the circumstances.

When the door closed on Gault, Nick, who had entered the room from the kitchen, muttered, "Oh, God."

Lily turned to him, but there was nothing in his face. He had apparently spoken out of sheer exhaustion at the prospect of contending with the world out there, in the new situation.

The days leading up to New Year's Eve were perhaps the hardest of all. No one would let her help with anything, so Lily spent a lot of time alone, writing in the journal, or trying to read, anything to take her mind away from her grief. The house was too quiet, and when Tyler put music on—a CD of Christmas songs from various artists, and then an anthology of torch songs by Ella Fitzgerald—it seemed depressingly pointless and unsatisfactory. But no one said anything, and twice they all sat down to the same table for a meal while Chopin's *Nocturnes* played—Millicent's choice. Neighbors brought food and gifts, and so there was the need to maintain some sociability. Lily worked to relieve Rosa and Millicent of the weight of entertaining these guests, who spoke in confident, soft tones of the better place Buddy had gone to. They all meant well, and their kindness was part of the nightmare, and Lily was as certain of this as she was of the baby's insistent movements.

New Year's Eve, they watched television, and saw the bright ball descend, the sudden brilliant lights: *1990*. Millicent had wanted to see the year turn; and her soft look of disheartened acceptance when the others had excused themselves to go to bed made them all relent.

So they were all awake for it. They watched the television in silence.

There were the thousands of people in Times Square, celebrating amid the falling streamers and fake snow, the honking horns and the cacophony of music, the shouts and the laughter and the general hysteria. It seemed to Lily that the crowds were all exhibiting the kind of frenzied cheerfulness people assumed in the unspoken, even unimagined, presence of the inevitable, and the terrible.

Millicent decided to let Nick run the dealership; he had been doing a lot of it anyway, because Buddy had planned to retire early. Nick went off to work, as Buddy had, in his own demonstrator, and he usually stayed later than Tyler did. Tyler had gotten some time off, to help Lily find their own place at last.

They chose an old sharecropper's house out near Yellow Leaf Creek, the remnant of a farm that had been sold piecemeal to developers. An apartment complex was being built within sight of it—they wouldn't have found it if they hadn't gone to the complex in search of a place there. But they saw it and on impulse they stopped. There was a lockbox, and a sign with a telephone number. They drove to the nearby 7-Eleven and called the number. Tyler spoke to the agent while Lily waited in the car, her coat wrapped tightly around herself. He came back and got in, frowning.

"It's already taken," Lily said.

"Son of a bitch asked me if I was black. He said it was just for his information."

She sighed. "What did you tell him?"

This made him smile. "You know what Buddy said to me once—the first hunting trip? He said in the South, whites'll get close to a black man, but won't let him rise; and in the North, they'll let him rise, but not get close."

Lily said the name. "Buddy."

"You miss him, too, don't you?" Tyler said.

She nodded, but he wasn't looking at her now. He stared out at the brown field before them, eyes filling with tears, absorbed in his own thoughts.

SEVENTEEN

1

It is somehow consoling to think of you now, still tending to your mother, still going on in the new silence that is more than silence. It's like that here, in this house, where Tyler's mother and sister go about their daily tasks in the aftermath of everything, and the whole world is an increment quieter, with a quiet that follows you, a ghostlike, awful, reminding silence, the not-voice of the one who is gone. I sit here and scribble in this notebook, and the scratching sound of the pencil calms me, and I feel guilty for the consolation of it. It is, after all, only the consolation of any action in such terrible hours. I have been cooking for everyone—I just took it over when Rosa left, and nobody said anything. That first time I could feel them all trying not to hurt my feelings about the mess I made. I'm still making a mess, each time, though it's not as bad as the first—at least it's closer to being edible. I never learned how to do any of this, and am depending on the recipe books that, I've discovered, Buddy liked to collect. His presence is still so strong, in every room.

I wonder how it must have been for you, bearing your grief and the grief of your mother, and Charley, caring for him and his frailties, seeing him off to school, finding a way to supervise and help him in his studies, going through your father's library as the proprietor of it, really, since Charley's interest never really matched your own, and you must've sensed that. You took on new duties every day as a matter of course, and you never seemed to fail at anything. I am coming to see that the only thing I can do well is this scribbling. I can't even do relationships well—am such a clutch of hurts and sore places and worries about the future.

Mrs. Gainseville spends most of her time in the kitchen, or the parlor, and Mary has the disturbed sense that she is being avoided. Any day now, she will have to discharge the woman, and the woman doesn't wish to be discharged. Lucy Toulmin-Smith visits, and other friends, Violet Roy, and Molly Brown, and friends from the London Geographical Society whom Mary knows through her father. Lucy bothers her about her failure to let Mrs. Gainseville go.

—You won't be able to keep paying her and have any freedom of your own, Mary.

She never thinks of it. Or hasn't. She has found a way to go on, and her mother's needs have kept her busy enough.

Guillemard is a frequent caller these days. She's come to think of him as a dotty old character, absentminded and easily disturbed, almost skittish. But he is kind, he has been a true friend; he has wide knowledge, and his fondness for her is evident. When her mother calls from the upstairs room, he interrupts himself, and waits quietly for Mary to tend to the older woman, and when Mary returns, sometimes nearly an hour later, he acts as if there's been no interruption at all. He busies himself with her father's library. She finds him with an open book on his lap, and he behaves precisely as though this is a welcome interruption of an already settled afternoon of study.

Mary is grateful for all her father's friends, most of whom are her friends, too, now, and they all call on her. She's finding herself with more to do socially than she ever had to do when her father was alive. Yet there is a curious form of apathy seeping into her soul, even as to others she seems full of bravery, still managing to be humorous and charming, self-deprecatingly sardonic. Inside, something awful is moving toward the center, toward the heart of her. She feels it like a sifting downward, a nothingness that no sight or sound or pleasure quite reaches. There is for her now only the pure sensation of the moment.

Washing her mother's pale skin, with its pitiable lack of resilience—it is like dead flesh; it is even cold to the touch—she observes the phenomena of dissolution and cannot call up a single element of feeling beyond this very minute, and her in it. The rest of the world's a blank.

One morning as she opens the curtains of the room, letting in gray afternoon light, her mother speaks from the bed.

—Don't stand there like that.

Mary turns, and says:

—What?

Her mother stares from the bed, not quite seeing her:

—Get your father.

—Mother?

The older woman's face seems to have sunk around her eyes, which shine with a scary, glistening something, as if an intelligence other than her own had entered her body:

—I 'ave to tell your father something.

—Mother, don't.

—Quickly, child.

The sternness of the voice, its surprising strength, startles Mary, who moves quickly to her mother's side and takes the thin, cold hands into her own.

—Mother, it's me, she says. Father's gone.

—Where 'as he gone to this time?

Mary cannot lie to her; it would be somehow to admit what is happening right here, before her eyes. And in the act of denying this, she insists on the truth of that.

—Father died in February, Mother. Remember?

But the other woman is silent now, has lapsed into a strange, open-eyed state of suspension. She's breathing, but it's clear that she cannot speak. She's trying to make a word come, or words, and nothing comes but the smallest puffs of air, and the breathing that goes on, and Mary holds her hands, wanting to run out of the room to send for Guillemard, and fearing at the same time to let go, because the look on her mother's face says "Don't leave me" even as the poor woman seems to be growing angry at her inability to speak. Mary stays at her side until she grows quieter, though the eyes never close, and the small breathing goes on. She starts downstairs, is on the landing in the darkened hallway, when the thought comes to her that the end is near. Something rises in her mind, a terrible stirring, and she sends for Guillemard, and then moves through the rooms of the house putting things in order, or changing the order that already exists. She can't allow herself to think.

Guillemard arrives an hour later, riding up in his surrey, and getting down with some difficulty. He strides up the walk and in past Mary, who holds the door for him and cannot quite find the words to answer him when he speaks. He looks at her and then turns to the stairs, looks back at her, hesitates, and then starts up. She moves from room to room downstairs, unable to concentrate on anything. Then she ascends the stairs, slowly, and stands waiting in the tenebrous silence of the hall. She has no concept of how much time has passed. It passes. Ten minutes; fifty years. At last the door opens and Guillemard emerges. He sees her, and beckons. She rushes to him, and he murmurs:

—I'm afraid you must prepare yourself, Mary.

—Yes, she tells him. She almost goes on to say, Did you think I didn't know it?

—I do not believe she will last this night, Guillemard says.

After he's gone, the phrase becomes fixed in her mind: *this night.* She sits in the library among her father's books and tries not to allow it in her thoughts, and it asserts itself, growing in power with her resistance to it. *This night.*

Charley arrives from being out among members of the family, and the two of them keep the vigil. Sometime near midnight their mother stirs and mumbles something neither of them can make out. She seems in pain for a few moments, and they rise to stand close, believing this to be the last struggle, but she subsides, and appears to let down, as if whatever has disturbed her has dissipated, dissolved back into the recesses of her body, her dreams, all she had seen of dreams in the long years of ailing. She sleeps peacefully, though the sides of her mouth are pulled down, and Mary and Charley wait together. After a time, the needs of her body take over, and they have to disrobe her, wash and dress her again, and put her back to bed. Charley helps do this, with a grimace of horror on his face, but without complaint and without having to be asked or prompted. They are in it, now; they are all that will be left of this strange household. They do not speak. Mary bears her inward struggle not to think, not to allow words, not to see words, and the quiet of this old house begins to expand with the syllables, the language riding through her mind anyway—terrible, muffled, but still all utterance: *this night.* Her mother's breathing slows, and slows again, becomes labored. Yet her features betray no pain or anguish. The sides of the mouth have even relaxed, so that it is as if gravity has settled her here, sunk in this bed, asleep. Mary retreats to her own room, and buries her face in the blankets, crying, a dry, painful sobbing. *This night.* The two words are only a beginning, and some secret part of her knows it, and knows, too, what follows, what awful words follow. She gets up, and frantically occupies herself. She's in a kind of interior retreat. She goes down into the kitchen and makes tea, and then she rushes to the cellar and works the coal into the furnace, though the cold outside is that of early April, the late cool vestiges of the month of March. Finally she hurries out of the house and away from it in the fresh chill. She is aware that this is something she is repeating, that these small forays out away from the structure are a form of escape, a way of seeking breathable air, even though the air may be heavy with the acrid, stinging odor of coal smoke. She stands in the dampness, the dark, where it has rained, a thundershower that she hasn't even noticed. She can't bear her own mind. She turns and looks at the tall house and the lighted window of the room, the one room, and she's caught, she feels the inevitability of it, in spite of all her fright and all her attempts to escape the thinking of it, the thing comes anyway, seizes possession of her—complete, terrifying, the whole thought: *this night, at last I shall be free.* Somewhere in her soul, she accedes to it, welcomes it.

—No, she says, and realizes she has spoken aloud. She falls to her knees on the wet ground, in the darkness, the moonless quiet, and begins to weep.

2

*S*HE AND CHARLEY are both there for the very last, perhaps three hours after her flight out of the house. Her mother never regains consciousness. Her breathing simply continues to slow, and finally becomes so labored that they believe each in-suck of air must surely be the last. But it goes on that way for a long time, and when the last gasp does come, a deep breathing in that doesn't expel itself, they sit quite frozen in attitudes of expectation, as the quiet stretches and grows too long for any human pause, and then the death rattle begins.

—Well, Charley says. He sobs.

—It's over, says Mary. Will I call on everybody?

—No, Charley says. I'll do it. He stands, but then seems to falter. Mary reaches over and places her hand on his forehead.

—You're feverish, she tells him.

—I feel awful.

She washes her mother's body and prepares it for the undertaker, tying the jaw shut with a long scarf her father gave her when she turned sixteen. Charley has taken to his own bed. There is no one else to perform the task. Her mother's body, so light when she was alive and wasting in the bed, is heavier in death, unwieldy, eerily demanding. Mary looks at the hands, the long fingers, the folds of the neck, the hair, which never lost its sheen, even through the years of bedridden existence—the hair is still beautiful, like that of a young woman. Mary dresses her in one of the gowns she wore when she was indeed a young woman, and first in love with George Kingsley. It's a fine sky-blue garment, something her mother kept in a special box in the closet, and on occasion brought out to show Mary. She sometimes talked about putting it on to go to a dance with Mary's father, one last dance under the lights of Islington Hall, where they met. Where the handsome, dashing young adventurer first had the acquaintance of a servant girl, a cook, Mary Bailey, whose charms he found so alluring. In her mother's things there's an old daguerreotype of the two of them, George Kingsley standing behind the chair in which his young wife sits, with a baby that Mary knows must be herself. The gown her mother wears in the daguerreotype is the one she will wear into her grave. Mary fights back tears, thinking of it. But this is not her mother now, this inanimate thing whose arms she works into the sleeves of the dress.

When Mary Bailey Kingsley is laid out in her coffin, looking too deeply asleep, Mary kisses the cold cheek. It is the first of her actions with this body, this inanimate thing, that isn't designed to manage it in some way.

Members of her father's family come to call, to express their condolences, but they seem anxious to be gone. Mary and Charley and a few of their father's friends, and some aunts and uncles from the Bailey side of the family, are the only ones at the funeral. The bells toll, and they accompany their mother to the site of George Kingsley's grave. It's a chilly, cloudy day, with the threat of rain in the air, except that it feels, finally, too cold for rain. The clouds look bruised, swollen. The wind bites at their faces, and blows the coat and shirtfronts back.

Rest eternal.

Mary looks at the faces of the people standing with her, and feels strangely separate from all of them. She experiences the coffin and the hole in the ground, and the blustery wind, the biting cold, the rattle and jingle of the wagon wheels, all of it as a provocation to her senses, a kind of assault. Her brother sobs, holding his hands over his face. She hears none of the prayers, and nothing anyone says to her.

3

*T*IME SLOWS. She goes on in the house, taking care of everything, alone, mostly. Charley has finished without distinction at Cambridge and is home all day, now, in frail health, requiring her attention. She finds no taste of life in anything. The air grows warm and the trees on Mortimer Road begin to bloom. Birdsong is everywhere, and everywhere people move through their happy concerns, their moods that are determined by the fresh, sunny air and the return to bloom of the world. She goes out for walks with Lucy Toulmin-Smith and with other friends, and they all express their worry for her. She rebukes such worries, denying that anything has changed. But at night the quiet room where she tries to sleep is like a small compartment in hell.

Charley's grief has exacerbated an overly fastidious strain in him. He sits in the library at his father's big desk and holds forth in a tone she recalls quite well as being that of someone like Lord Dunraven—but that gentleman had a sort of imposing ruddiness and vigor about him, even with his recurring cough. Charley is pallid and lethargic, and when he talks of making a journey to the Far East, there is something almost too boyish in it, as if he were only elaborating a daydream, a sickly boy talking from a bed. He's all complaisance when she asks anything of him, but he is also increasingly rather sophistic and opinionated.

One evening, while sorting through some of her father's papers, she discovers her parents' marriage license, and her own birth certificate. Earlier, she was thinking she might try to make a book out of everything her father left. There isn't enough. It is becoming evident that he never expressed himself fully about anything, though she hasn't quite allowed herself this thought. She reads the marriage license: "George Kingsley, bachelor and of full age," and "Mary Bailey, spinster," both in residence at 30 Tavistock Terrace, Islington. "October 9, 1862." The date seems off, must be off, she thinks. She turns to her birth certificate, entertaining for a moment the thought of what it might have meant to be the first-born if she had been male. But something is nagging at her, and she stares at the piece of paper, and reads her birth date: "October 13, 1862." Again she stares at the marriage license, and *that* date. It is not a mistake; she realizes that all the dates are correct, repeated twice in each document.

Four days.

With trembling fingers, she puts the papers in the drawer of the desk and then sits down behind it, gazing at the wall of books. *Four days.* She feels all the more her own difference from the rest of the society she lives in, and very quickly, with revelatory strength, various matters of exclusion and casual slights from the Kingsley side of the family take on a significance they've never had before. The picture she has always had of her parents' life together changes, too, as if in a vision before her eyes: her father's long absences, the deeps of stillness that had existed in the rooms of the house when they were together; her mother's terror of losing him, even her long years of invalidism—everything about the two of them. It is all altered, or it shines forth in a terrible fresh way in the light of this new understanding.

Now, Charley's self-satisfied calm, his pompous holding forth, annoy her irrationally; and it is more than mere aggravation: there he sits, perfectly accounted for, the second child, on whom all the money has been spent for education, and she knows without quite admitting it to herself that the education is wasted on him; that she could have put it to such far better use.

I am extraordinary.

She rejects the thought; it is unattractive. She dutifully performs all that is expected of her, and begins gently to agitate about getting away. Everyone, even Charley, agrees that she needs a change of scene, some other climate and place. They're alarmed for her health, and especially her mental well-being.

—There is a wonderful spa at Baden-Baden, Charley says to her.

She rejects this.

—What do you propose, then? Guillemard asks.

They are sitting in the parlor with its window overlooking the wide, shady lawn in front, and the sparse horse traffic on Mortimer Road.

Beyond the road, there are more trees, and a grassy meadow where a cricket game is under way. Mary thinks of her father—how he loved to watch them, and to walk down to the river to attend to the rowers, the crewmen from Cambridge in their round of practices. Abruptly, the whole expanse seems oppressive and cloying. It comes to her that the whole island of England, all of Europe, depresses her immeasurably.

—I would like to go farther south. The Canaries.

Charley snorts, and clips the end of a cigar:

—Surely you're not serious.

—I think it could be arranged, says Guillemard. Mrs. Toulmin-Smith might be prevailed upon.

—I wish to go alone, Mary says.

Neither of the others speaks for a moment.

—I intend on going alone, Mary tells them.

Guillemard says:

—Well, I've learned by now not to argue with *that* tone in the voice of a Kingsley.

—It will have to wait until I leave for Singapore, Charley says.

Mary nods:

—Of course.

—The whole thing may be academic.

—Of course.

—Perhaps you should settle for someplace closer to home. There are several wonderful spas very nearby, actually. I've looked into it.

—The Canaries, Mary says.

Charley rises and leaves the room, sighing as if with exasperation. He climbs the stairs and the door to his bedroom closes.

Guillemard says:

—I think Charley is a bit at sea.

—Master Charley will have to come to terms with himself, Mary says. I'm certain that he will.

4

*H*E PUTS OFF sailing for the Far East until the end of June. Mary doesn't speak to him about it again, either. She waits, bides her time—it will become something at which she grows even more adept than twenty years of nursing her mother has already made her—and performs the services of a sister, preparing his meals and looking after his needs. She bears it all gracefully, including his progressively more arcane opinionizing, his verbal hairsplitting, his flourishes of bombastic rhetoric, and his evident assumption that every single thing his mind touches on is as he perceives it, without the possibility of question or contradiction. She learns, in fact, to keep her own opinions to herself, for the sake of peace between them, and she believes finally in his intentions, understanding that the best thing is not to press him about his plans: he must be allowed to think that they are all his idea. Occasionally she gives him small reminders of his Far East journey-to-be. She buys him a new compass, and a gauge for reading barometric pressure; she expresses the hope that they will be useful to him, but she never mentions the journey itself.

Finally, he settles on a time. He elicits the help of some friends of his father at the British Museum, and Mary also helps, packing for him, writing out lists for him to refer to, and booking passages ahead. At last he's on his way.

Watching his steamer pull slowly out of Liverpool, she rejoices, waving at him, and attempting to look sorrowful at his departure. The next day, she goes to Guillemard and with his help applies for passage to the Canaries.

She takes a passenger Castle liner out of Liverpool. Guillemard and several others, Lucy Toulmin-Smith, her cousin Lucy, and two friends of theirs see her off. It's a curiosity to some of them, Mary, so strange and reclusive, after all those years of hiding in books and in the requirements of her mother, walking up the gangplank in her skirts, with her parasol and a perfectly ridiculous hat. She waves to them all, and makes her way up, steps onto the deck with its tightly seamed planks and its stained, pitted surface. She goes to the railing and the smell of the harbor lifts to her nostrils—smoke and dead fish, brackish water lapping the supporting posts along the pier; old wood, the heavy stench of the streets of the city. She waves to everyone as the ropes are untied and the ship makes its slow shift toward the end of the harbor. They are under way. The land seems to be moving, and she feels herself to be stationary. She gazes at the dirt and bustle of Liverpool as it slides out of view—the coal stacks and the brick facades stained with soot. The city grows small, recedes into a brown line on the horizon, and sooner than she would have believed possible it is gone, swallowed by the constantly shifting surface of the ocean with its little crowns of foam. Standing on the deck, she has the sense that this is a kind of rehearsal.

All the way south, in the troubling waters of the Atlantic, she finds that she is suited to it; it is her father's blood, she believes. Others are ill, even the sailors. She sits on deck in her dark dress, and writes letters home to Lucy Toulmin-Smith and to Guillemard, and others. The words to describe what she sees come to her with a facility that surprises and delights her. And in the open air, in the free, far-distant waters, so far from anywhere, she begins to feel her spirits lift, the pall that has been over her dissipates like the morning mists over the sea.

5

THE CANARIES are a group of seven volcanic islands off the coast of northwest Africa. They were often used as ports of call for Greek and Roman ships, and for a short period after the fall of those empires, they were relatively free of outsiders. The story goes that they were rediscovered when a European vessel bound for France was blown by gale winds to the islands, and that when the vessel finally put in to port on the coast of France, the sailors spread the word about the lovely volcanic paradise to the south. In 1399, the Spanish came in conquest—five vessels landed at the second largest island, Lanzarote, and took the king and queen captive, along with nearly two hundred native islanders. But this possession lapsed, and again for many years the islands were left in peace, or rediscovered and then forgotten again. The French established a colony there, led by a man named Juan de Béthencourt, who introduced slavery, among other aspects of civilization of the time: he also built churches and brought in the first missionaries. But it was the Portuguese, along with some of the tribes of northern Africa, who first began to develop the slave trade that would flourish throughout the world for the next four hundred years.

The largest island in the chain is Tenerife, with its twelve-thousand-foot-high volcano, and this is what Mary first sees rising out of the ocean to the south. She has been at sea for seven days. She has spent hours in the nights, walking the deck, aware of the vast spaces all around the small vessel, and the limitless expanses above it. She watches the stars, and the changes in the sky as the morning approaches. She sleeps very little. It is too beautiful to let it go by her in sleep, this ocean, the great curve of the world, thousands of miles of water and sky. She stands at the railing, breathing deeply, taking in the salt air and the odor of the smoke from the stacks.

Finally, on this morning toward the middle of July, here is the amazing purplish peak of Tenerife rising out of the sea. Last night there was a squall, and several passengers were ill, and one sailor broke his leg working during the worst of the storm, trying to secure a lifeboat that had come loose in the pitch and yaw of the vessel in the turning waves. Mary, with her medical knowledge, assisted a shipboard doctor in setting the leg, and the doctor, a young, gruff, heavyset man with piercing dark eyes and a way of snorting when he talked, expressed his admiration for how well she had been trained in medicine.

—I've no formal training, Mary told him.

He shook his head, smiling. Then said:

—You trained yourself well.

Now, standing on deck again, sleepless, faintly shaky, she sees the mountain peak in its violet haze, lifting out of the green and bluish distances. It is odd to her that while Liverpool had receded so quickly upon her departure, this arrival seems to draw out—an eon of slow time, while the distant mountain remains essentially unchanged, as though all approach to it is illusory. She feels a pang of loneliness; there is no one to whom she can speak to tell what she's feeling now. The waters almost swallow Tenerife, and the sky reddens. Others come on deck. There is a game of dice being played against the pilot house—two sailors and a German clergyman, and his heavy wife. Jolly people, who never fail to smile at her as though she has just done something to please them.

Finally, the heights of Grand Canary rise out of the flat green expanse. She sits at the railing and looks through the bars, and writes in her notebook: *yellowish-red peaks, and how beautiful is the lovely, lustrous blue of the air which lies among their rocky crevices and swaths their softer sides. I believe that if I were to find some alchemy by which I could put it in a jar and take it back to Cambridge, it would come out as a fair blue-violet cloud in the gray air of Cambridge.*

6

THE LINER comes to port in Las Palmas, all white beaches and white villas, the mansions of wealthy Spaniards whose banana plantations give a faint yellow cast to the far sweep of the coast. The sand looks whiter than the foam in the waves. She allows her bags to be carried ashore by a tall, stooped man whose correct English delights her. She discerns that he disapproves of her cockney accent, and this makes her a trifle self-conscious, and at the same time rather gratifyingly defiant. He calls himself Marco, and when she asks for his surname, he says there is none. To herself, she calls him Polo. He accompanies her to what he calls the English Quarters, a white sandstone building that is near a strikingly ornate cathedral, with tall spires and minarets, too. He offers to show her the city. She refuses, politely. He scowls, looking pained, as if he suffers some physical ache or infirmity, though he is obviously very strong, carrying her bags into the open foyer of the English Quarters.

When she comes down from her room, perhaps an hour later, there's Marco, waiting for her. He puts down the book he was reading and comes to his feet. The book is *Tales of the Notorious Pirates*. She asks him what he thinks of it.

—I think it is rubbish, he says. And you?

—I very much liked it, she answers.

He says:

—You are very young.

—'ow old are you? She asks.

—I shall be fifty-six in November.

—And you've always lived here?

—No.

She waits for him to explain. He doesn't, and the urge to laugh comes upon her. She manages to keep this back.

—And where else've you lived?

—Persia, he says.

—Are you Persian?

—Spanish. But my family believes we are also descendants of the aboriginal people who once inhabited these islands.

She says:

—The Guanches.

He's unable to hide his own surprise.

—And where do you come to know about them?

—I liked to read, she tells him. When I was a child. And of course I still do.

She walks out of the building, and looks at the wide whiteness of the sandy beach in the near distance. People are lying there, or moving around in the water close to shore. To her left, bordering the horizon, is the jagged, tawny beginning of mountains, with patches of dark forest—pine and palm trees, mostly. There are Spanish goats in the street, and people in all sorts of different styles and colors of dress—Arabians and Europeans and Africans. A man in a white toga walks by and bows, smiling, showing, in the middle of his wiry black beard, with its stringy appendages down his chest, a cavernous mouth with no teeth. A dog snuffles along behind him.

—Would madam care to walk the beach? Marco says.

She looks at him, at the deep-set, lined eyes, the unhappy wrinkles around his mouth.

—Do you have family here, Marco?

He bows.

—Yes.

—Go see them. She starts away, toward the cathedral.

He steps around in front of her.

—I have done something to offend madam?

—Of course not.

—It is not permitted for a woman to be unescorted in Las Palmas, madam.

She has no reason to suspect the veracity of this information, and still she hesitates, regarding him. He shifts from foot to foot, not quite returning her gaze.

—And if I don't wish to be accompanied?

He makes no answer to this, but stares at the ground between them.

She starts toward the beach again, and he walks along at her side.

—Who of your family is here? she asks him.

He mutters:

—I am a widower. I have a brother.

—Here, on Gran Canaria?

He shakes his head. His bearing is now something akin to that of a shamed child. He keeps his head down, walking along, a look of distraction on his dark face, as if something distasteful has begun to plague his mind—some unsolved dilemma that he had forgotten about and now freshly recalls.

She senses that he feels chagrined at having to insist on being her companion. So she turns to him and says:

—Thank you for saving me from causing trouble.

—No, don't mention that. His tone is aggrieved.

—I do not wish to cause you discomfort.

—You have caused none. There is a small fee.

—I expected nothing less.

They walk on a few paces.

—I'm quite glad to 'ave your aid, she says.

He nods, almost dismissively; yet she can see that he's pleased.

On the beach, he procures a wide blanket and a canvas chair, and leads her to the water's edge. There are booths up and down the beach where people change into bathing clothes. She sits in the canvas chair and the sun beats down on the dark folds of her dress, but the air is cool. The wind plays with her light hair, blows strands of it across her face. She breathes the salt fragrance of the sea. Marco tells her about the man-made carved shallow pools for gathering salt, which is one of the substances for trade produced here. The unevenness of the coastline lends itself to these giant salt pans, as they're called. He talks about the banana plantations, and the many people who stop here in transit, from Africa to Europe, and back.

After she has had enough of the sun, she rises and he walks with her back to the English Quarters. She says:

—Tell me, Marco, are there French and Italian and African Quarters as well?

He finds this amusing.

—It is for all Europe, he tells her. It is only called the English Quarters. The English built it.

—Do you know who else is staying there now?

—Disraeli, he says.

She stops and turns to look at him, shading her eyes.

—Now?

—Last year.

They walk on. She says:

—I wondered who is staying there *now*.

—I will find out for you, he says.

At the Quarters, she thanks him, and then returns to her room. It is a small square place with windows on three sides. Each window looks out on something different: one gives her the wide emerald shoreline, fading to blue sea, and the brown rumor of Tenerife in the distance; another gives her the white sides of the buildings of Las Palmas, with blue angles of shade and bright gold shafts of sunlight and other windows, mostly curtained; and finally there is the view of wild palms and clear blue sky, rising landscape, with a scattering of other houses, and the far mountains. She spends time standing in each window, breathing the air, filling her lungs with it and tasting it on her tongue. There's an ache in her lower back, but she pays no attention to it at all.

She eats alone, in the privacy of her room—shellfish and fresh bread, and fruit. It is all luscious. She watches the sun set on the town, and when it's full dark and the bustle and noise has died down, she lets herself out and descends to the street. No one stops her, or speaks to her; the desk in the foyer is unattended. She walks back down to the beach, which is deserted, looking like the auroral beach of the world— Adam's beach, and Eve's. She walks along it, watching the waves crashing in, bigger than they were in the day, some of them reaching a height of six or seven feet. There's a brilliant moon, and a soft sea breeze.

Later, in the room, she sleeps like an infant, dreaming of waters.

7

IN THE MORNING, Marco waits for her, and she allows him to guide her down to the first floor, and the entrance to the central dining room.

—I have found out for you, he says, proudly. There is another English staying here. A gentleman recuperating from fever.

—Oh? I'm not interested in procuring any fevers, Marco.

—The fever is gone.

The dining room is large, with high ceilings and tall open windows. It affords a lovely view of the tan buildings of the town, and the sea. Sitting in one of the heavy, padded chairs on the street side of the room, smoking a small black cigar, is an emaciated man with very brown, pocked skin, heavy-lidded eyes, and bony, hollow cheeks. He nods at her and stands, with some difficulty.

—That is the gentleman, Marco says to her.

—Would you care to join me? the man says. He's holding a pewter mug, and he takes a swig of it as she approaches.

Mary offers her hand as a man would. This is a forwardness he's evidently not used to, though he quickly recovers himself, gives her hand a manly squeeze, and settles himself again. He tells her his name: Batty. She tells him hers, using only the surname, as he has done. She sits across from him, and Marco quietly removes himself. Batty watches him go without much interest; it is movement, and his tired eyes follow. After Marco is gone, Batty turns those eyes on Mary. He looks older than he is. Mary guesses him to be in his late forties.

—Kingsley, he says. Any relation to the author of *Water Babies*?

Surprised, she smiles.

—My uncle.

He nods, and then seems to wander off in his mind, smoking the black cigar, which is very strong-smelling, and reminds her of the ones her father brought straight from the Americas. But these, he tells her, are from England; he sends for them there. He's never been to the Americas. It's a pleasant thing to inhale the fragrance of the tobacco here, in the open-aired room. There are light muslin curtains bordering the windows, and they move with the slightest current of air from the beach. It's cool, and rather quiet for this hour of the morning. Mary mentions this, and wonders what the custom of the country is regarding the start of the day.

—Fishermen leave early, he says. I've noticed that. He takes another drink from the mug, and swallows with obvious satisfaction. She sees that the sclera of his eyes is yellowish, but then she doesn't want to look him directly in the eye.

—I would gladly provide you with something cool to drink, he says.

—What are you drinking?

—Oh, this. It's a concoction made of rum and banana juice. Would you like a drop?

She demurs.

After another long silence, he sits forward and regards her.

—You don't seem like the others who come down here from, shall we say, the home office.

—'ow long since you've been there? Mary asks him.

He turns the cigar slowly in his fingers, looking at the ash end of it. The sides of his head, near the temples, are skin on bone. A nerve pulses there.

—Ten years, he says. I've been spending my time in the bush. In West Africa. Do you know where Cameroon is?

She nods.

He sits back again, smoking:

—Something bit me. I don't even know what it was. A little sting on the side of my neck. And I almost died of it. Blisters, and fever, and delirium, and it all came on by little increments, chronically, you might say. And there was a touch of the coastal fever, of course.

—What were you doing in West Africa? she asks him.

He smiles cryptically.

—I was trading. I take a boat up the Gabon River, and stop along the way. We trade for exotic oils, fabrics, all sorts of goods that we bring back and sell on the open market. They take tobacco and sugar from us, and whatever else delights them.

She nods, and waits for him to continue.

—Well, it isn't a proper subject for talk, he says, low.

—On the contrary, she tells him.

—I'll wager you thought I might be a missionary.

—No, she says.

The smile widens.

—Well, and are you? he asks.

She shakes her head.

—I'm 'ere to take the air, she says. After years of being inside.

—You don't strike me as a hothouse flower.

Now she smiles.

—Tell me, what does a trader do in West Africa, besides trade?

—Not much else. We travel inland, and we do business with the bush tribes. They don't like missionaries, these tribesmen. They don't especially like any Europeans. And so one must be very careful and attentive. The Europeans have brought them servitude and kidnapping and disease and murder, and the missionaries have brought them religions they do not at all need or understand. Some bushmen will kill a European on sight.

—You've survived.

He nods, and the smoke forms a blue wreath around his head.

—Sometimes it has been a very doubtful matter. I've been fortunate. One keeps fairly close to the coastlines.

—Are you going back to England?

He nods.

—For a time, yes. But I'll never go back for long. I've got Africa in my blood now, missy.

He finishes the mug, and smacks his lips. Then he rises and starts to the other side of the room.

—More of this, he says to the man standing there. I'll bless you when I get to the gates of paradise.

8

*T*HAT AFTERNOON, a sandstorm comes from the sea. Batty tells her it has been blown here all the way from Africa—the great Sahara Desert. The sky turns a tawny color at the horizon. The color rises, the water itself changes hue, from rich blue-green to light brown. In close, toward shore, it turns the color of a hawk's wing, with the same dappled places, spots of lighter color, where the waves crest. But even the foam at the top of the waves begins to darken with it. The air is one wall of dust. People move through the streets of Las Palmas with rags across their faces, showing only the smallest slit for their eyes, in front of which they keep one hand, as if to block out bright light. Mary sees fear in their movements and in what she can make out of the expressions on their faces, and yet she feels only a kind of unselfconscious sense of wanting to *observe* everything without the prejudice of fear. It is not an affectation; she's only partially aware of it as a difference from how everyone else is undergoing the experience.

The sand blows down the little changing booths along the beach, and sends tiles flying from the roofs of the town. There is the terrible roar of the wind, punctuated by the sound of shattering glass, and cracking wood. Trees are bent over nearly to the ground, and several of them break, making an awful rending sound. At the height of the storm, no one at all is stirring. Mary looks across the square in front of the English Quarters, to the mosque there, and she sees women with children huddled against the white wall while the wind covers them with the tawny-colored sand, which is sifting over them so quickly that the women keep rising to shake it off, their backs to the wind.

Batty watches it all with her, drinking quinine water, lowering the rag from his face to do it, and trying not to cough. He has slept off the effects of the morning's excess, he tells her, and is now attempting to balance the salts in his blood. He believes everything about one's health has to do with the salts in the blood, and he likes to keep salt with him, so he can replenish himself. When he's recovering from the alcohol, he drinks quinine and licks salt from the palm of his own hand.

—This is not the proper subject for talk, he says. Forgive me.

—That's the second time you've said that. I'm not in the least offended, says Mary.

He bows, and takes another pull of the quinine.

—You flatter me, Miss Kingsley. I know I'm a rough, uncouth man.

—I've not found you so, Mary says.

—Well, of course. I was talking of polite behavior.

—Yes, Mary says. I understood what you meant. I'm not in possession of much in that vein, either.

Now, he seems at a loss. He reaches into the pocket of his khakis and pulls out a small leather pouch. The bottom of it is stained, and when he opens it she smells the fresh fragrance of drying tobacco.

—You'll get sand in it, she says, meaning it lightheartedly, like a joke. A gentle chiding of him, as she used to chide her father.

He closes it quickly after taking some of the tobacco and putting it in his mouth.

—It relieves the pain of a bad tooth, he says.

She watches him chew it, a big bulge in his gums.

—You know it came from the Americas, she tells him over the sound of the storm.

He nods, then spits appallingly out on the windblown walk. He seems ashamed, turning away from her.

She goes on watching the storm, the sweeping curtain of brown dust, and the people struggling in it. The sand gets in everywhere, collects on the windowsills and along the baseboards of the foyer and the dining room. It gathers in the folds of their clothes and in their hair, and even, Mary notices with a shock of fascination, under their fingernails.

She breathes into the moistened cloth of a scarf, and Batty tries to say something to her through his own tobacco-stained mask. She can't make it out. He holds out his hand, and in it there is a small island of collected sand, scintillate, like salt, only of the purest tan shade. She looks at it and then at his face. He pulls the rag down and says, smiling, out of the blackness of what he has been chewing:

—Yesterday, no doubt, this bit was slapped from the back of a camel in the bloody Sahara. Think of it.

She lowers her own mask so that he can see her pleasure at the thought.

—I am thinking of it, she says to him, nearly shouting.

The storm goes on for more than two hours, and there is a lot of destruction of trees and some buildings, but miraculously no one is killed or injured. Batty comes back from an excursion into the city with this news. He's drunk, and he has a friend, another trader, with him, also drunk. They both smell of the tobacco and the rum, and they stand before her, wavering, arm in arm, boys at play, except that she knows they have been in bad country together and seen things. They are not boys, but hardened men, in many ways damaged men. Batty introduces his friend, using only the surname: he is a Russian, Dolokov, a man who speaks perfect English, Batty tells her, and whose general ability with spoken languages, when sober, makes him very valuable to everyone: he knows dozens of dialects—Indian, African, and Asian. He can pick up a language the way some women can pick up the playing of a clavichord, and Batty knew such a woman when he lived in Suffolk, years ago. Batty goes on talking about this woman who could play the clavichord merely from having seen it played, and Dolokov watches him drunkenly, proudly, as if he is still the subject of the talk. He stands very tall and sticks his chest out. He can barely stand.

—Anyhow, no one was hurt by the storm, Batty says. These kinds of storms are rare here, but not so rare that they don't know what to do when they come.

—And we are now standing on African soil, Mary says.

He smiles, showing his bad teeth.

—That we are, Miss Kingsley. He sweeps with his foot the loose sand that has collected on the floor. His footsteps make a whisper in it. He walks unsteadily with his friend to the entrance of the room and turns to gaze at her.

—Tomorrow, she says, I'm anticipating that you'll enlighten me.

He says, smiling:

—As to what?

Mary smiles back.

—Trade, and Cameroon.

9

*S*HE WALKS OUT alone at night, and during the days, if she is not accompanied by Marco, she's generally with Batty and Dolokov. Twice they take a small boat with others, a trading vessel, across to the African coast. Batty knows the trading villages there from his first journeys away from England. The boat carries candles, saltpeter, iron bedsteads to the coast, and returns with monkeys, parrots, palm oil, snakes, canary birds, sheep, gold dust, ivory. There are also Africans on the journey back, men and women from different tribes. On the last trip, Mary goes aboard after the boat is weighted down with its cargo, and leaving Batty and Dolokov on deck, goes down to her cabin. She opens the small door, fatigued and wanting sleep, and finds that the cabin is occupied. Looking into the dimness, she sees four shapes, two on the small bunk, and two more, in blankets, on the floor.

—Excuse me, she says.

Silence. She knocks on the door, and is greeted with more silence. She bangs the door closed, opens it again, and waits. No stirring at all. She breathes the odor of alcohol, and of something else, sickness, she believes, a heavy, oversweet something that snatches at her breathing passages. They are drunk. Passed out from drink.

She makes her way topside, looking for the steward, who she finds retching over the gunwale into the water, in the throws of delirium tremens. He imagines there are insects crawling on him, and when she touches his shoulder he screams, flailing; she barely escapes being struck by him. Batty and Dolokov are nowhere to be seen. She walks through the several Africans standing on deck, and at length is able to distinguish the purser, a rail-thin gray man with a scraggly beard and a look of perpetual annoyance.

—Yes, he says. I know about the gentlemen in your cabin. Frightfully sorry about it. They're dead, you know.

Mary stares at him. Evidently he appreciates the shock value of what he's said.

—Yes, he goes on. It's quite usual. They all died within the last ten days.

—What killed them? Mary asks.

—Fever, I believe. One of them was either mauled to death or something got at him after his decease. Quite mangled on one side.

She keeps her composure, understanding that he wishes to upset her. He's one of those men who pretend an interest in the welfare of ladies while secretly enjoying the pains he might cause them. He has badly misread her, and she wants him to know it without having to announce it to him. So she gives him an impassive expression, as if nothing could be more familiar to her than a corpse monstrously half-eaten by a marauder, and says:

—I would like to know what I'm to do for a cabin.

—We'll be in Gran Canaria soon enough, miss. You don't want them lying about here on the deck, do you?

—Why couldn't you 'ave stored them in *your* cabin, then. Since you are the one that brought them on board.

He waits a moment, regarding her, then turns and orders one of the sailors to look sharp, tying up a line.

Mary remains on deck, among the half-naked members of tribes whose names she long ago memorized, finding ways to observe them without intruding, pretending an interest in the receding horizon line, the northwest coast of Africa.

10

$\mathscr{B}$ATTY AND DOLOKOV are often drunk. They smell of alcohol, and they like to tell stories about the life, as they call it. Batty, it turns out, knows little of the sciences, and less of history, or, for that matter, geography. He has only the roughest idea, for instance, where the Great Plains of the United States are, or where certain Asian countries fall on the map. He knows the coast of Africa, specifically the west coast. He calls himself a coaster. He numbers himself, with Dolokov, among a group of men, traders, all of them familiar with every inch of ground along that coastline—a stretch that in most respects, they tell Mary, is the worst and most dangerous, not to say uninhabitable, area of the world.

They talk of the various illnesses—brought on by nothing anyone can pinpoint; illnesses from the water or the food or the fetid air, or from attacks by insects—and they talk about the many species of killer, from lions, leopards, wild dogs, and boars to crocodiles, to little multicolored snakes whose bite can carry a person off in a matter of minutes. There are so many things in Africa that can snuff out a life, including hostile tribesmen, not to mention brigands and pirates and bandits. The whole of West Africa is badly administered by the European countries—it is the French who have the Congo, and whose presence there is most prevalent. But there are also the Dutch, who seem to want to make a religious colony wherever they go, the Germans, who are at least organized, the Spanish, who are totally inept, in their view, and the English, who are the worst of all.

Dolokov tells her in what is after all not perfect English—it is heavily Slavic sounding, and often idiomatically rather eccentric—about a man he knew whose talent involved sword swallowing. He had been to America and done it in traveling shows, and a few miles up the Congo he did it for some bushmen of indeterminate origin, tribesmen in wild paint, looking very excited and rather frightened, too—never a good combination among the native populations. The man swallowed the sword, and quickly three of the tribesmen rushed forward to thrust their spears where the sword had gone. They accomplished this after a fashion, in spite of the terrible choking sound the man made. They were quite surprised that he couldn't do the magic with their spears, and very crestfallen when, by dying, he went past their ability to question him about it.

—We almost died, Batty says. Because we were with him and could do nothing to draw him out of the state he'd gotten to with two spears and a sword stuck down his gullet. We buried him in the sand right at the edge of the ocean, near the entrance of the Gabon River.

Dolokov grows sullen and uncommunicative, drinking whiskey now, and recalling his friend the sword swallower. He passes out, and Batty hauls him to his room and puts him to bed, then returns, staggering with what he has had to drink. He lights a cigar and sits down, staring out at the moon over the ocean.

—Dolokov will never go back.

Mary says:

—I'm sorry about his friend.

—Oh, he was my friend, too. Wonderful card player. And he told good stories. Nothing like a good storyteller in the bush. Dolokov used to be very good, but then he got gloomy.

—He seems a good man.

—The best, Batty says. Once, we were on the river and a hippo rose. They're not meat eaters, hippos, but very ill-tempered, you know. Worse than a water buffalo. They'll kill a man out of sheer animal rage, merely for crossing their path. This hippo would've taken a hunk of my leg if it hadn't been for Dolokov. He stuck a five-pound box of ammunition in its mouth, and it withdrew, coughing. For all I know the beast swallowed the thing, a walking, water-floating explosion waiting to happen.

The talk is very entertaining, and she says things to make him tell her more. She wants to hear everything he knows, everything he's learned. But now he seems reluctant to go on, since to him it is mere complaining.

One afternoon, she slips out of the Quarters and evades Marco, walking down to the harbor in the blazing sun, through a crowd of tourists from America. At the harbor, she walks up to a big wooden stall and rents a canoe. The man in charge is black, enormous, wearing European clothes, including trousers that look like they could be used for a sail. His legs are so wide that he has to walk by what appears to be a steady, waddling, rearrangement of himself. He hands her the paddle and labors to the water's edge, holding the canoe under one arm as if it is nothing more than a parcel out of a mailbox.

—How long? he says in an amazing high tenor voice, almost like a boy's. He speaks each word with an intake of breath. He's winded.

There is the added amazement that he speaks English. She stares straight back into his muddy brown eyes and says:

—I don't know 'ow long.

—You're not dressed for it.

He hands her the paddle and struggles back up the beach. She climbs in and makes her way out into the shallow swells. The heat is daunting, and the canoe is difficult to manage at first. For a long while she has trouble keeping a steady course. But the repetition teaches her, and soon she's making good headway, paddling from first one side and then the other. The motion is so clocklike that she begins gaining speed. Below her the water's clear; she can see all the way to the bottom. At one point, she finds herself being kept pace with by a large stingray, moving like a live cape along the perfect whiteness of the sandy bottom. She paddles over to Lanzerote, then hauls the canoe ashore, dragging the weight of the drenched clothes she's wearing, the dark dress, and the several undergarments. She stands on the hot sand and wrings the hem of the dress, gathering it about her knees. The beach is deserted. She wanders toward a column of smoke in the distance, picking up specimens of sea and plant life as she goes. Perhaps a thousand yards up the beach, she finds a salt pan, and factory. She stands gazing at it for some time, then turns, deciding that she will seek no human company on this expedition.

Heading back, she sees only the uneven spars of sand going out into the pristine water, with its million shimmering facets and its sparkle.

In spite of every ugliness she has experienced, she can only think, *How beautiful the world is.*

Two days later, she makes another journey, this time over to the island of Gomera, to look at its volcano. It is another brilliant, cloudless, blazing-hot day. The saltwater in her clothes as she hauls the canoe onto the sand makes her want to sink down in it up to her shoulders. There is no one on this beach, either, and no column of smoke, and so she does just that. She lets the dress billow around her, still holding on to the canoe. The water is cold, and as refreshing as anything she has ever experienced. She stays in it for almost an hour, and then pulls the canoe onto the sand, and starts up the slope of the volcano. There are palm trees at the base of the slope, and barbed plants, and hip-high blades of yellow grass. And then this all gives way to bare lava, black as pitch. By the time she has made the crater, the sun has dried her clothes and she has wet them from the inside out, with her sweat. There are large salt stains on her cuffs and under her arms, and around the whole circumference of the hem of her dress. She looks into the crater, observing the many openings in the black rock from which little feathers of smoke issue forth. Perhaps an hour passes while she gazes into it, and moves slowly around the circumference of it. Finally she turns to gaze out at the sea, the lowering sun, and realizes, with a start, that she has stayed too long. There isn't even enough time to get back down to the beach before the sun sets. She has a moment of cold panic.

But it passes.

She strides back down to the beach in the falling dark, and after securing the canoe—hauling it still farther up onto the beach to account for the tide—she retreats into the darkness of the palms and finds a place under a ledge of stone, out of the bright moon that is rising, and protected from rain, if it rains. She makes herself as comfortable as possible by taking off her outer garment and folding it, for a damp pillow. She thinks about insects for a few moments, and snakes, other predators. But in fact nothing can penetrate the sleepiness she feels after the work of this day: another surprise; she expected to be frightened, to lie awake keeping a watch.

She wakes in the dawn, hurting on one side, and with a headache, but feeling otherwise rested and fresh. She has had the forethought to pack another day's dress, so she changes, stuffs the dirty clothes into her reticule, and makes her way back to the canoe. She goes back to Las Palmas, and feels strong enough to explore a little beyond the city, to the south. She takes a winding path, passing in and out of shade, reveling in the little breezes, until she reaches the border of one of the banana plantations. There are already people working in the distance, gleaming with sweat. They sing a chant, unbelievably close harmony, a marbling of voices that thrills her not only for its rich tones but for the exotic fact of it, so early in this fresh morning on earth.

She returns to the Quarters, and here is Marco, standing so tall in the open doorway, with his disapproval of her, like a weight on his shoulders.

—Good morning, she says.

—It is not good to go about unaccompanied.

—I will take it into consideration, she tells him.

For a moment, he doesn't move aside. She walks up close, and is ready to bump him if that is what it takes. But then Batty and Dolokov come down the street, singing, arm in arm. They falter on the steps, and then, supporting one another, with a lurching movement, are standing next to her.

—Welcome back, says Batty. Where've you been?

—I spent the night on Gomera. I slept under a rock.

Saying this fills her with an unexpected elation, and she sees that this is apparent to Batty. He smiles, and then he winks.

—I see you returned without being eaten by sharks.

—That is not good to sleep outside in the tropics, says Dolokov. As God is judge.

Batty turns to Marco and, wavering a little, smiling, he waves one hand at him and says:

—Don't stand there like a starchy old schoolmaster, Marco. I've a terrible thirst this morning. Dolokov and I have a terrible thirst this morning.

Marco turns and strides back into the recesses of the lobby.

Batty, supporting Dolokov entirely, now—Dolokov having passed out on his arm—tips an imaginary hat at Mary and says:

—Woman, where are they that accuse you? Go and sin no more.

11

ON ONE OF HER LAST evenings in the Canaries, a rainstorm comes in off the ocean, and she waits with Batty in the entrance of the cathedral for it to slacken. They came to look at the architecture of the building, and some of the statuary inside, Spanish paintings and icons, looking vaguely Byzantine. Dolokov is fighting a slight fever again, lying on his back and drinking quinine back at the Quarters.

They talk about Batty's experiences on the African rivers: he tells her that he saw a man taken by a crocodile, once, pulled out of a boat and dragged to the bottom of the river. The croc hauled this unfortunate trader and the boat for several hundred feet in the current of the river before the man's grip was broken, and it looked for a minute as if they were wrestling with the boat, trying to keep the boat from going under. There was something horribly human-looking about the croc's movements. It was a young one, not much larger than the man, who kept cursing it and calling it names. It truly seemed that the man was scolding the animal, yelling at it as you would a child, with exasperation and anger rather than the terror he must have felt. The croc finally pried him loose of the boat and took him to the bottom.

The whole thing happened in full view of a dozen Ajimba tribesmen, four other coasters, and Dolokov and Batty, all of whom were so dumbstruck by the suddenness of the attack that they made no sound at all, so that the man's struggling and shouting, his curses and his gasps for breath—and, at the very end, his gurgling utterance of the Hail Mary in Dutch—carried to them. None of them who saw it will ever forget it, or stop dreaming about it. When Batty was in the worst part of his fever, lying in a tent under mosquito netting on the beach at Cameroon, he imagined that the same croc had come from the water and was pushing inside the tent, its snout rooting under the ends of his feet. He screamed for more than an hour, and the image wouldn't leave him, even waking, and with the fever breaking. The Ajimbas brought a stout matronly German woman with medical training to him from one of the smaller missionary settlements inland, and she required that he drink goat's milk, which had made him sicker. But the Ajimbas took care of him, and watched over him in his madness. They tolerated it, even as they supposed it came from something in the trees, or from the currents of air blowing in from the top of the mountain, with its cap of snow, like a shroud. He spent a long time staring at the white peak of the mountain and several times he dreamed that he had gone there, wandered there on the air, a perfectly reasonable proposition in his delirium. He lost track of the German woman, who had rattled at him in the foreign tongue, only a fraction of which he understood.

—The only people I trust down there are the other traders, Batty tells Mary. The traders, and some of the tribesmen we trade with. I trust them, too. There's more cutthroat in an English schoolboy than in the whole continent of Africa, if you ask me. They treat everyone with honor and respect; they listen well, they learn quickly; but because they don't like the knowledge, or find it very useful for themselves, the Europeans think them inferior, or incapable. Half the time I do not know what an African is thinking, Miss Kingsley, but I almost always know that he is not *deviating*, if you know what I mean. I always know that he is not *dissembling*. He keeps a great deal of himself in reserve, but he does not dissemble. He believes in witchcraft and in a world animated by souls and spirits, and there is no time for dissembling, or for sophism, either. His life is brutal and short. His ways to *us* seem quite cruel—quite remorselessly savage, in fact. But then I don't imagine we look very gentle to him, with our guns that kill from a distance and our appetite for killing. The African has no time for refining his taste in ways of killing, or in music, and the arts, if you understand what I mean, and for this I think he pays a heavy price with the Europeans. But he is honorable and he expects nothing but the same from you.

—I should like to get to know them, Mary says.

Batty looks down at his knees, one of which has begun to ache and bother him. He's been rubbing it slow, grimacing now and again as his thumb passes over the tender place. It strikes Mary that he has taken her remark as a politeness of conversation, so she repeats it.

—Yes, he says. I heard you.

—But I don't think you quite understood me, she tells him.

—I've spoken generally, he says. I shouldn't have. There are several hundred cultures down there, you see. I don't think it serves to lump them together as I have just done. I apologize for it. I should have said that the Africans I know, from the few cultures I've been exposed to, are often as I described them. Because, you see, the unfortunate aspect of our situation there, Miss Kingsley, is our appalling lack of knowledge about them, any group of them and any individual from those groups. Most of the time, we haven't even taken the trouble of listening.

—I would like to change that, Mary says.

Once more, he appears to take this as a politeness born out of her sociability.

—That's quite admirable, he tells her.

—You're thinking of going back, she says.

He nods.

—Will you stay in touch with me?

He makes a gesture of futility.

—I have no means, Miss Kingsley. I'm ill.

—'ow do you think I mean this? she asks.

Now he seems puzzled.

—Why, I don't know.

—I would like to know more about the West Africans.

He nods again, and smiles.

—You are an interesting change from every other Englishwoman I have ever met, here or elsewhere, I'll say that much.

—I mean to know more about everything you've told me, she tells him.

—Perhaps you'll write a book, he says. Like Mr. Burton.

—Yes, she says. Quite.

He seems faintly troubled.

—I hope I haven't said something to offend?

—No, she tells him. You worry overmuch about that.

—You're a bit of a mystery to me, Kingsley. I wonder if this is something you've set about with some design.

—Being mysterious? No. I'm very plain, Mr. Batty, and my requirements are simple and direct. I've never possessed the ability to be otherwise.

He nods, almost approvingly. It's only his natural reserve that mutes his expression. She understands this without voicing it to herself.

—Shall we go back to the Quarters? he asks.

—You go on, she tells him. I believe I'll remain 'ere for a while.

—I'll wait for you, if you like.

She knows this is a formality, and decides not to cause him any discomfort; the habits formed while growing up in her house will not permit it. She walks back to the English Quarters with him, through the slow drizzle of the remainder of the storm.

At the entrance to the Quarters, he takes hold of her with surprising roughness, and kisses her on the mouth. His breath is heavy with the odor of the cigars, which she doesn't mind, but the contact of his body against hers, the solid, bone and stubbled-flesh otherness of it, disturbs her, and she puts the heels of her palms against his shoulders, pushing him away. He lets go and steps back, and seems immediately contrite and chagrined, shuffling before her like a little boy caught out of school.

—I think you're a lovely young woman, Miss Kingsley, he says. Forgive me.

She feels faintly ill, and her heart is pounding. She forces a smile and says:

—You've paid me a great compliment.

He says nothing, stands there, sheepish. It's almost funny. She has an abrupt urge to laugh, and has to fight it back.

—At least I think you 'ave, she says.

He gives her a strange analytic look, as though he's trying to decide the next plan of action—a stratagem to gain something from her that she realizes, with a little pang at her heart, is out of her power to give. She likes him, though; she's quite fond of him.

—You are, he says. You are. A beautiful young woman.

—I can't speak of these things now.

—I've never been a gentleman, you know. I don't know what the social graces call for. I know that you have lovely skin and that I'd like to touch it. I wanted to walk over and touch you the first instant I saw you, when that silly bugger brought you to me.

He stops himself, and then seems to draw inward, as if he has received a blow to his chest.

—Forgive that, he says.

She understands that his talk is what he will do instead of anything she might have to resist. He will indeed behave like a gentleman. She reaches over and touches his arm and says:

—Thank you.

—You won't take a lover on your southern journey, he says.

It is almost a question.

—I came 'ere to get away from love, she hears herself say.

At first the words seem merely something to tell him in order to establish once more the boundaries between them. But then it strikes her that this is a literal statement of the truth: her journey has been a kind of defection. He looks so hangdog, standing here before her. She says:

—It's only been in these last few weeks that I've felt I could draw in enough air to breathe.

—I hope I haven't ruined the friendliness between us, he says.

—Nothing of the kind, she tells him.

He shifts slightly, looking at her, and then taking his eyes away.

—I take it as a kindness, she tells him. And I don't even know your proper name.

—James Henley, he tells her. I suppose I must satisfy myself with being your friend.

She smiles. This doesn't seem to require an answer. They enter the Quarters, and she makes her way to the stairs and up to the corridor and the gas-lit space of the entrance of her room, where Marco sits dozing.

—Marco, she says.

He stirs, is startled, and then embarrassed, wiping the sleep from his eyes.

—Well? Mary asks.

—I have learned that you walk out at night. A woman must not walk out at night alone in Las Palmas. It is my job.

—I was not alone, she says.

He bows.

—And I don't wish to 'ave my door guarded, thank you.

—I thought madam was inside. I was prepared to accompany her.

—You poor man, she tells him. You may leave.

He bows again, with an exaggerated dignity that annoys her, though she manages not to show it.

—Good night, madam, he says, and then moves with his slow, gliding gait along the corridor, his shadow following him on the wall.

12

She SPENDS the last few days exploring the islands with Batty, and continuing to question him about his time in Africa. They make the journey to the Salinas del Rio at Lanzerote, where she had gone alone in the canoe; and they stand at Roque Nublo, two giant rocks standing at the top of a brown mountain, with its spectacular view of other mountains, and the sea beyond. They visit the factories, and the shops, and Mary speaks to the merchants, the plantation owners and their workers. She goes with Batty over to Tenerife, and the other islands. They scale to the top of Pazo de los Nieves and gaze at the opposite mountain shrouded with low, still clouds. They visit Laplaya Veneguera, with its white cottages scattered among long-needled pines and palms, the pine trees so tall and skinny that their spiny tops look as though they have been attached by some giant hand reaching down out of the clouds.

There are a lot of clouds now, rolling in low across the ocean. The undersides are ash-colored, but it doesn't rain. The days are dry, and mostly windless, though an occasional sea breeze comes to them, a fugitive stirring of the tropical air, smelling of the bananas from the plantations nearby. Batty seems finally to be recovering what must have been enormous energy and strength. His friend Dolokov has been delirious for two days and is now resting, pale as death, but gaining strength again, slowly. He has his appetite back; he can sit up. This siege appears to be over. Batty tells her that there will be others, that poor Dolokov never quite comes all the way back, and that he, Batty, is prepared to suppose the poor man's troubles have more to do with his drinking than with the malaria or the other afflictions he has brought with him out of the bush.

—I've tried to tell him, Batty says. But he's past hearing it, I suppose.

Batty climbs the steep, volcanic hills without getting winded, though the veins stand out on his forehead. Talking about poor Dolokov has made him realize his own recovered strength. He begins to talk about not returning to England.

—You know, Kingsley, I believed I wasn't long for this world when I arrived here. I don't wish to live in England, but I would prefer dying there when the time comes.

—You're a long way from dying, she says.

Neither of them requires anything of the other. Mary has never been happier.

When, after almost two months, she boards a steamer bound for Liverpool, under a gray, lowering sky, she feels an oppression that seems to take the pleasure and taste out of the days she has spent here. It feels like waste, a desolation and a ruin. She understands that this is purely a childish wish not to have the time here come to an end, not to have to return to her life on Mortimer Road, and the gray day here looks like the gray days in London, where the choking, acrid fog makes the air all but unbreathable. Batty hasn't come to see her off; he has business in the town, preparing his own journey back to Cameroon. Marco stands on the end of the pier and waves dutifully at her. Strange, gloomy Marco, with his downcast features and his dignity, which he maintains with a kind of doggedness that threatens every moment to strip him of any semblance of it. She waves back at him, but does not smile, for she knows this is not expected and would not be welcomed.

The captain of this steamer is a thin, blond, wiry man of rather surprisingly short stature. He's not quite as tall as Mary. He wears muttonchop sideburns, and, were it not for the wrinkles surrounding his steely blue eyes, one might suppose him to be not much past boyhood. His name is Edgars, and he is nearly sixty years old. His voice is gravelly and his manner rough. The men who serve under him do so smartly, without question or hesitation. They are clearly afraid of him. Mary finds this rather comical—these big, muscular sailors scurrying about in terror of their little captain.

He invites her in his hoarse, basso voice to the stern, to watch the islands recede. She stands with several other passengers—two Dutchmen and a German, a Frenchwoman with her two daughters, and a few islanders, Muslims apparently, on their way to Spain. The cloud-capped peaks of Grand Canary dissolve all too quickly into the general grayness, and no one says anything. Mary has a momentary sense that the islands are actually disappearing. She experiences, for a few moments, that fear people feel when leaving a place they have loved—the fear that they will never see it again, that something will happen to take it away from them.

Later, alone on the deck, pacing from side to side in the pitch and yaw of the vessel in the choppy water, she thinks of Africa. The word repeats itself in her mind, *Africa, Africa*. A gloriously musical and mellifluous word.

Africa. A fine idea. She looks out at the vast expanse of ocean, at the foamy wake trailing off into the dark folds of the water, and thinks of how it would be to go there. A perfectly wonderful notion. Why not? There are aspects of her growing up that might be said to have been preparations for such a journey. *Africa*. It is not expected behavior, she knows; it will be frowned upon by some. There is no telling what Charley will say—not to mention the other members of the family, on both sides.

It is a fine idea, nevertheless. Something to occupy her thoughts. Something to think about in the nights, when she lies awake, feeling the lifting and settling of the ship in its passage through the waves, hearing the moans of the German woman and her children, all of whom are seasick. She murmurs the names of places to herself, those words uttered with so much relish by Batty and Dolokov: *Cameroon; Agonjo; Remboue; Sierra Leone; Ogooué; Gabon*. Such a strange, blood-stirring combination of sounds.

Finally, she drifts off to sleep, no longer feeling low or depressed, but anticipating the battles she will have to fight, one way or another, to get her way, to force the world to give her what she wants, the freedom she craves.

13

Soot-tarnished Liverpool bakes in the sun on the afternoon she arrives. The few scattered clouds are the color of ashes. The air is laden with the smell of coal, and it is unbearably hot; everything droops. The drays pulling a refuse wagon along the street leading away from the harbor have their heads down, as if the heat of the sun has weight and substance. She takes a coach to Cambridge, and finds that Charley has returned from Asia. He's been back two days, he says, and has plans to edit their father's papers. This is something she had started on her own, with no help from him, and she keeps to herself the exasperation she feels at his obvious belief that it is his idea, his project. He spends hours in the hot days, sitting in the shade of the back porch, reading through the letters and diary entries and articles, and occasionally he makes a note to himself. He keeps a flat board across his legs, to write on, and from the doorway of the kitchen he looks like an invalid, sitting there with the boxes of paper at his feet, and the pages he's reading laid out before him on the board.

She writes two letters to Batty, and then tears them up. She keeps the house; she is essentially Charley's housekeeper and cook. No one from the Kingsley family visits. She seldom sees any of her former friends—even Guillemard has kept away, busy with his own concerns. The old oppression begins to work in her again, and she has fearful nights of wakefulness, lying on her back, arms at her sides, trying to empty her mind.

When, a little more than a week after her return, Charley announces that he wishes to live in London proper, she secretly rejoices. It occurs to her that she has begun to keep her own thoughts and feelings from him, because in his complacent and dilettantish way he will say things that undermine her. He isn't even aware that he does it. There are times when his calm, magisterial gaze enrages her, and his conventional way of viewing everything makes her want to shock him with a curse, or throw something at him. She enters a room where he is, and he lifts his head, so open-faced, so happy, so satisfied and stupid that her strongest impulse is to shout at him. He hasn't even got the gumption to notice that she's rather testy and short with him.

He does go into London and chooses a place for them—a small flat on Addison Road, near the Uxbridge Road Station, the kind of place that everyone in the family and all the friends will certainly perceive as reduced circumstances. The neighborhood is close, crowded, row upon row of two-story houses with uniform stone stairs and a look about them, with their curtained windows, of a group of drowsy faces staring at the street. She organizes the move, and spends hard, sad, grieving days dispensing with her parents' belongings, everything that defined them and everything that still calls them up for her: clothing and hairbrushes and combs; cards and charms; her father's pipes, and humidor, and shoes. She manages to get rid of all of it, giving some to charity, and throwing the rest away—the debris of a long and, she understands it now, hopelessly unhappy marriage.

At the Addison Road flat, Charley collates papers and makes notes, and talks vaguely about getting off somewhere again—perhaps back to the Far East. It strikes Mary that they haven't really spoken at all about their mutual adventures. She knows nothing of what he may have done or seen in Asia.

One evening, when Guillemard has come for a visit, and she hears them talking about the bad roads in Singapore, she asks him if he kept any records of what he saw or heard or learned. She has poured brandy for them both, and they are sipping it, smoking cigars and relaxing, legs crossed, in opposite chairs in the small parlor, which Mary has had to use at night for a study.

—I mean to write all of it down someday, Charley says. A study of, well, Eastern religious practices, let us say. No, actually, I would like to do a study of Eastern thought—Chinese thought, to be specific. How their philosophical history affects their cultural growth. The . . . the assumptions of the common man, for instance. Something of that nature, I believe. Quite strange goings-on with the Buddhists, you know.

Guillemard clears his throat.

—I had thought you would write a biography of your father, as you said you wanted to do.

—I haven't given that up, either. That is a very strong possibility.

—I 'ope you'll be off soon, Mary tells Charley. I think I would like to make another journey myself.

Charley seems amused, but says nothing.

—You're a Kingsley, says Guillemard.

—Where would one hope to go in your circumstances? Charley says.

—I want to go south again, she tells him. But farther.

—A lot of luck you'd have these days. A spinster with no real means of support and no experience. And your education, being what it is, Mary, the, how shall we say, informal nature of it . . . well.

She keeps silent, while he puffs on the cigar, and breathes out the smoke, watching with great satisfaction as it coils ceilingward.

—I suppose you might accompany me, if you like, he says.

She waits for him to reveal his plan, because it is expected that she do so.

He smokes the cigar and leans back, crossing his legs at the ankle.

—I think Peking will yield up some useful information.

—When will you go? Mary asks.

—That is undecided at the moment.

She waits again.

—You wouldn't care to accompany me?

—No, I would not.

—Well, I didn't imagine you would.

She pulls air into her lungs and then, sighing, says:

—I am going south.

—Where south?

—Africa.

She nods. She hears the word and inwardly some element of her makeup presents her with the vastness of the place. *Africa*. Yes, she tells her brother. Africa.

14

*N*OTHING IN LIFE quite equals the waiting of the following weeks and months—after the black horses with the high black feathers, and the black mantled coaches, after the bombazine and the perfumes and the murmured

pieties, after the words of the priest and the burials, and the long accom-
modations to brother and aunts and uncles, after the selling off of goods
and the removal of the accumulation of two lives, after the sale of furniture
and a house, and the move to Addison Road, after the service to her
brother and the talk talk talk as to what he will decide to do, what he will
choose to spend resources on, after days and weeks of seeking the information she needs and the acceptance she craves and the means to proceed,
she is finally on her way out of the world she has known all her young life—
and even as the day approaches for her deliverance, she is cruelly plagued
by the sense that she's running away, that her use to all the people around
her is circumscribed by her very nature. Her own anxiousness to put the
thousand miles between herself and anyone she knows is distressing to her.
The last night in London is sleepless, as so many recent nights have been.
Charley's gone, the house is empty. For a long time she replays in her mind
the stories she's been told, by everyone she knows, of the terrors of West
Africa. A doctor with whom she's acquainted, not through her father but
through Guillemard, actually repeated the story Batty told, of the man
being pulled from the boat by a croc. There were several small variances
from Batty's story—the croc, for instance, was described in the doctor's
story as being twice the size of the boat, never mind the man; and the man
was reported as having been English, a missionary on his way to Fernando
Pó—but the similarities were striking enough for Mary to wonder at it, and
in the night she goes over both stories, deciding gloomily that they are both
true, and that one stands a very good chance of being eaten by a croc in
West Africa.

Finally, giving up on sleep, she rises and walks downstairs to the little room where most of her father's books are stored. These, she realizes, have always been her means of travel, her taste of the distant places
her father saw; but they have also been her solace and her companions.
She moves among them, paging through one and then another, putting
each up to her face to breathe the fragrance of it. She opens *The Pursuit
of Knowledge Under Difficulties*. For some reason, holding this one in
her hands, with its pages that she herself cut when she was fourteen
years old, she begins to find it difficult to breathe. She gasps, twice, and
then realizes that she is sobbing. She stands there among the thousands
of volumes, crying, holding the book open, in the quiet that is broken
only by the sound of her weeping.

In the morning, Guillemard sees her off, this time on a cargo vessel, *The Lagos*. She has lugged her portmanteau, without help, aboard, and she stands at the precariously low railing, supporting herself on a black umbrella, and shouldering a black reticule made out of fustian. She has also carried aboard a long waterproof sack, into which she has put books, blankets, even a pair of Charley's trousers, in case a dress becomes too cumbersome for safety.

The crew of *The Lagos* are calling to each other and singing little ditties, and the captain, a man named Murray, whose eyes seem crowned with heavy black brushes, and whose mustache is a steely gray, solid-looking, as if carved out of some thistlelike growth, stands at the helm and shouts orders for the loading of more cargo, though the ship is loaded down, sitting low in the filthy water, and covered with the accumulated muck of years in the sea lanes.

It seems to Mary that they will never get under way. Standing in the hot August sun, she recalls that it's been a year since her return from the Canaries. For a moment, she thinks idly about how recent that seems, and yet how slow this waiting is, for the last of the cargo to be brought aboard. There is an elastic element to Time, and it grieves her: how much it had seemed to stand still all those years at Highgate, and Bexley Heath, and Mortimer Road.

The sun dips behind a screen of yellow clouds, fog, the coal fires of the dock. For a moment, there are no shadows anywhere, everything showing forth in a flat, gray light. But then the sun pours through a chink, and the cloud cover breaks open wide, to blue, blue sky. Somewhere in her soul there is the temptation to take this as a sign. She rejects it; what will happen will happen, and as if to reinforce this thought, the world presents her with a vision of wet, dark rats crawling amid the refuse at the edge of the dock. A malodorous vapor rises from there—rotting vegetables and fruit; rancid meat.

Finally, *The Lagos* is under way, rocking and shifting down the Mersey and through the Crosby Channel, toward the open sea. There is a wind now—she hears Captain Murray say to one of his mates that it's blowing at a good twenty knots. The waves roll under them, shaking the ship, lifting it and letting it drop with an enormous crashing sound, and then lifting it again, repeating the same swell and fall, over and over. The ship is laden so that she's making through the waves up to her plimsoll line, and Mary rides with her, basking in the sun and salt air, until Captain Murray decides it's best for her to retire to her cabin.

15

*P*ICTURE:

A cabin room of a ship at sea, and the sea is rough. It is night. There is the sound of men singing—drunken, raucous singing. In this cabin is a young woman, two months shy of her thirty-first birthday. She has a book, which she manages, somehow in this noise and shaking, this great swaying, to keep reading, even as the light keeps shifting from the swinging lantern above her. The world all around seems to be breaking apart with commotion and clamor, shrieks and laughter—the singing, the moan and protest of the boards of the ship, the bending joists and beams, holding everything together in the pitching and rolling of the sea. In the midst of this tumult, there is, for her, a profound silence—the whole of life seems to have descended to this stillness, this strange, inner not-sound of the moments after death. Feeling the rush of waters along the sides of the vessel she is in, heading for a frightening and dangerous country, she thinks of her dead father and mother, and has a sudden terrifying sense of how alone she is; and she has a premonition, too: she will die at sea. It comes to her with a bottomless chill, which stops her breath. At some point during her reverie, she has lain down, and now she sits bolt upright, puts the book aside, clasps her hands tight in her lap, and rocks slowly back and forth, trying to gather her strength, striving for the courage she will need. She recalls lying in the calm, sea-scented, cool dark of Gomera, alone, under the ledge of volcanic rock. She thinks of that long night and the easy sleep that came upon her, the sense of well-being when she woke, even with the aches of having slept on the ground, in damp clothes. Why should this pitching vessel, manned by professional sailors, be more frightening than that should have been, and wasn't?

Nevertheless, the fear takes possession of her, and what she sees, in spite of herself, is the dim alcohol-smelling cabin of the small coast steamer, with its four wrapped shapes in it, those dead men. It is as if she's seeing this for the first time, as if some psychological screen had protected her from the actuality of the vision until now. She knows it is her fear that gives her this sense, and that it is not true. She knows it's the storm, the violence of the waves on the other side of the wood, that makes every thought seem to harrow her soul, but she can't blot any of it out, can't get the image from her mind of those four trussed shapes, elongated white shapes, that she should have known in the first instant were corpses. Her own horror tosses her, as the ship is tossed in the whining blasts of windswept rain.

Finally, she rests against the pillows piled at her back, her hands still clasped. Perhaps she drowses a little. She opens her eyes, feels the rocking of the ship, then does drift off, in a swoon of horror, a dread fall through darkness. She sees her brother in an open carriage, wearing a black cravat and holding an earthen jar, and something about his face tells her he's dead. She comes awake with a cry, and gets off the bed, drops to her knees, then lies down on the hard floor, curling her legs up. She has never known such terror. She puts her hands over her head, crying, and the roar of the ship changes—a clatter, a shattering. The ship must be sinking; there is a sound like an explosion, oddly mingled with something utterly incongruous: musical notes, struck simultaneously. Not sequential melody, but a percussive ringing, as if several hands were attempting at the same time to hit the same group of notes. The explosion comes again, and again there is the sound of the struck notes. Then there is more glass shattering, more thudding of wood and steel, and, still again, the curious, jangled, several notes struck together. She half believes this is a terrible dream, the last dream before death. Slowly, because it is intolerable to remain where she is, she brings herself to her feet, wipes her eyes, and moves to the door of her cabin. Outside, water sloshes back and forth on the deck, and she sees no one. The sky is black, and there's a sheet of rain out of the blackness, the sea tumbling over the gunwale and crashing down on the surface of the deck, all foam. She closes the door and quickly gets into her camisole and dress, her boots, which she laces while sitting on the floor of the cabin. Her fear is roiling in her, climbing the back of her neck, but she sees water running through the bottom of the doorway, and decides that the ship has hit something in the ocean and is sinking. She cannot feel anything now but the urgency to get out of the cabin and see what is happening, and once more there's the sound of the eerily discordant, banging mass of musical notes. She gets to her feet, having twice to brace herself on all fours for the rolling of the ship, and moves to the door, which she opens again, looking out at the tumultuous night, the surging, angry sea, which is even darker, swept by fierce wind and rain. When the pitch of the deck is away from her cabin, she takes advantage of this and allows herself to be half-thrown to the opposite side, and the entrance to the saloon, the door of which gives way with the force of her coming against it. She nearly tumbles into the confusion and destruction of the place, and then scarcely misses being crushed by something large and solid and black, rolling toward her. She ducks and it hits the door frame, and there is the same tuneless clatter of notes, and the ship wrenches the other way, so that the thing rolls from her, to the other side of the saloon, where it slams against an overturned table and the wall, from which a lantern hangs precariously by a partly broken chain. The light plunges crazily on the walls and ceiling, jerks with each blow of what Mary now sees is a piano sprung from its moorings and being tossed by the motions of the ship. She starts toward it, and is hit, and stunned, by something flying through the air. She topples over, and again has to dodge the onrush of the piano, and when she rises again, a little dazed, she sees a young woman in the white uniform of a stewardess standing against the wall to her left, hands flat against the surface, eyes wide with fright. The piano has struck a shelf, and bottles of beer are rolling on the floor, along with containers of sauce, and one tin of fruit. Mary rushes to where the piano has lodged momentarily under the swinging lantern, and with all her strength pushes against it.

—Come on, she shouts to the other young woman. Grab 'old of it.

The stewardess braces, then lurches in Mary's direction as the ship begins to roll again, and all the weight of the piano shifts. They are both holding it now, pushing with every ounce of strength they have, trying to keep their feet planted, until the ship rolls back, and the weight is less, the piano resting against the inner hull, under the wildly swinging light. The other woman begins to shout for help, and the ocean starts tipping things back in the other direction, the piano growing heavy again, nearly insupportable.

—I can't, the stewardess says. I can't hold it.

—Yes, you can, Mary tells her. But she believes she's losing her own grip.

Finally, another pair of hands takes hold, and then more, and the two women are surrounded by sailors, Captain Murray among them.

—Save what ye can of the ale, Captain Murray shouts.

And soon there are several men working in the room, expertly balancing themselves with the unsteady footing, as the ship pitches to and fro. Mary supports herself in the entrance of the cabin, watching them, and a sailor she hasn't spoken to before looks at her, tilting his head curiously, and then seeming to show concern.

—Yeh're wounded, miss.

The stewardess, a girl with very red hair and large blotchy freckles on her face, steps up and puts a soft white cloth on Mary's cheek.

Mary sees blood on the cloth, and touches her own fingers to the place on her cheek.

—It's a cut, the girl says. And then she indicates a small crescent-shaped wound on the side of her arm. Me, too, mum.

There's a strange light in her eyes. Mary can't quite discern what it might mean. More than a moment passes before she can take her own gaze away.

—You took it upon yerself, the stewardess says. Where did yeh get the gumption?

Mary realizes it is admiration in the girl's eyes. The knowledge of this confuses her for a few seconds. Then it pleases her so much that she experiences a surge of affection for the other. It's almost elderly, though she cannot be more than four or five years her senior.

—We did it together, she says to the girl. The two of us.

—I'd still be cringing against the wall if you hadn't come in, the girl says.

Mary smiles, wiping the blood from her own face with the cloth.

—And if you 'adn't come to my aid, I'd still be dodging that piano.

The girl laughs. But then she contains herself and straightens, brushing the front of her dress, because Captain Murray has approached them from the opposite wall. He taps the girl on her shoulder.

—Work to do, he says. A lot of cleaning up.

—Yes, sir, Cap'n.

He turns to Mary.

—You seem to have saved the day. I don't know that that thing might not've gone through the hull. He reaches into the pocket of his shirt and brings out a silk handkerchief, which he touches to the side of her face. For an awkward moment the two of them seem to be taking turns stanching the blood, which still issues forth steadily from the cut. He steps closer and takes her by the chin, excusing himself, once again touching the cloth to the place.

—It's not deep, he says. It won't scar.

She breathes the several odors that emanate from him: talcum, pomade, tobacco, and whiskey; it all combines to cause an obscurely agreeable sensation in her, as if she were in a room of home. She looks into his gray eyes, meaning to express her satisfaction in him, in his presence. It occurs to her that she likes him, exactly as she once liked Mr. C. F. Varley the electrical engineer, and Guillemard, in his way. And Batty. There is no sex in this liking, even as she appreciates the tactile sensation of his fingers holding her chin. It is a pure, creaturely feeling of contact, and a memory of rooms when her father was in them, the charms there, the talk and the happy excitement of anticipation, the adventures he would relate, the places she would hear of, as he held forth, smoking, one leg crossed over the other, a man who had been all over the world.

—Thank you, she says to Captain Murray.

—I believe I am the one in your debt, Miss Kingsley.

When she returns to her cabin, she closes the door and looks at the place where, earlier, she lay in such terror of her own solitary little life in the immense, turning world. Without quite voicing it to herself, she understands now, finally, that the one hedge against this fear (the fear on the periphery of which she has lived since she was a very small girl), the one weapon available to her for battling it and keeping it at bay is action, even if the action is nothing more than movement from one place to another.

EIGHTEEN

1

Dear Lily and Tyler,

We're settled in at 1123 Burgundy Street, right in the middle of the Quarter. Miss Violet Beaumont has been driving us around in her pickup truck. The three of us make quite a picture, I'm sure. She's taken us to some of the best places, off-the-wall places nobody else seems to know about—a wonderful barbecue place no bigger than a living room, run by a black family named Rachambois. Very nice folks, quite at home—they live upstairs—and they made us feel at home.

I wanted to tell you both that I can't begin to express my sorrow over what happened, and how awful it was leaving the house that way, when you-all were suffering so. But it seemed for the best—Manny especially felt that the last thing you-all needed was to have us to worry about. That following day, and for the three days after, we thought long and hard about coming back for the service. Buddy was so kind to us. But we had already been there a couple of days and it seemed that it would've only added to everything for poor Millicent, who can't think about herself and would have therefore been worried about us. It simply felt like it would have been an intrusion. So Manny sent the flowers and I hope they expressed something of our sorrow.

We think of you-all, every day, and we hope you'll keep in touch. I've got a job at another bookstore, not as good as the one in Charlottesville, but the pay is good, and Manny is looking for something in the newer part of the city, though he's being quite well taken care of, as I am, by Aunt Violet, who is, as my father used to say, something else—and I'd love for you both to meet her. Lily, Aunt Violet could be Mary Kingsley, or someone so much like her that you'd feel you knew her in the flesh. Aunt Violet has never been married. She's done exactly what she wanted to do all her long life, although until she was nearly twenty-eight she did nothing but care for her sick father, who had her when he was already old, and fought alongside Stonewall Jackson in the

Shenandoah Valley. He was in his seventies when she was born and lived to be a hundred and three. The guy was thirty-five years old, Lily, when the Civil War began. Imagine it. He lived through it, achieved the rank of major, retired at the end of the war, and moved to Louisiana to start up a dry-goods business. There's a picture of him on the mantel. He looks like George Bernard Shaw—long white beard and a lot of white hair. He had a talent for making money and for surviving horrendous mistakes. Aunt Violet has thousands of Confederate dollars in a trunk in the attic—his hedge against the day when it would all turn around and the Yankees would collapse. He had hordes of women, and outlived most of them, and then when he began to sink, waited eighteen years to complete the job. Aunt Violet cared for him through all that time, and when he died she up and went to Japan, where she lived for three years. She's been around the world (she taught high school here for nearly five decades, using most of her summers for travel—she even spent some time in West Africa, and knows some things about Mary K.). She was fascinated to hear of your interest in her.

How is the pregnancy; and how's the job going for Tyler, and are you both getting back to some kind of normal life? I don't mean that question to sound glib, or unfeeling. I do have the sense, though, that Buddy would not want anyone spending too much time moping around, even for him. My father, when he was still comfortable with me, once said, upon the death of a cousin of mine, "You honor his life by living your life as fully as possible." I know it sounds like greeting-card stuff, but I think it's true. I feel the truth of it.

Please write when you can. And think of driving down for a visit. We would both so love for you-all to meet Aunt Violet. Maybe soon after the baby comes?

Both of you call us the minute there's news, or if you get an urge to head down this way. The number's enclosed. I remember so fondly Tyler telling me about the impulse honeymoon you both had down here—and what a lovely time it was. How awful it would have been to have planned it. How marvelously surprising it had turned out to be.

Those are the kinds of surprises I love. So think of surprising us. Aunt Violet says to plan on surprising us (wicked grin). That's Aunt Violet.

Love,
Dominic

Dear Dominic,

It was so good to hear from you. Aunt Violet sounds wonderful. Can't write much now—contractions. They're called Braxton Hicks, and are not significant, except that they're uncomfortable.

We are all getting along here. Tyler and I have found a place. Millicent seems better, and Nick's natural humor seems to be returning, though slowly. He goes to work and comes home. I've never seen anyone work so hard. He is the most considerate and kindly person now. He hardly ever jokes, and when he says anything at all that might be construed as such, it's always at his own expense. And it was always, now that I think of it, mostly at his own expense. I feel so sorry for him sometimes— he just seems lost. He reads—the Bible, lately, and Shakespeare. He serves Sheri as if she's a queen, and she's like a frightened little girl a lot of the time. Nick takes care of everyone, it seems, and I've been learning how to cook. The house is very quiet. Tyler and I keep to ourselves, and sometimes I see in Tyler the pain he's carrying. He keeps it all bottled up. I'm planning for the baby mostly by myself (not a complaint—really! Ha!), and I feel most of the time like a kind of spiritual nurse, except those times when I need comforting myself. We are all working to comfort each other—to get used to the difference: Buddy not here.

Well, this must be short. I have to write my parents, in their separate houses. And I wonder now, with a kind of hard pressure in my chest, how I could've been so unhinged by their separation, as if that were the worst thing that could happen. How selfish I've been. I blamed my father—who is human, and flawed, like the rest of us—for not being who I thought he was. I'll try to write again soon. And I'll call you—or someone will—when the baby arrives.

Love,

Lily

P.S. Tyler says "Hey."

Lily and Sheri were sitting in the living room of the little rented house, with its view out the small picture window of the giant red edifice being constructed an acre away: girders and stairs and wood framed into skeletal squares of imaginary living space. You could actually make out something of what the layout of these apartments was going to be, but at this stage of construction it might as easily have been a ruin. Several bulldozers were sitting idle in the foreground, their insectile shapes suggesting giants of some uncataloged genus or order, with their extended squarish metal arms and bucketlike fronts. There were large sections of ground disturbed around them, piles of dark earth, where preparations were under way to build a lane in from the main road. It had snowed the night before, and patches of it still lay on the dry grass, melting away in the chilly sun. Sheri had come unexpectedly for a morning visit, and the place was a mess. There was still unpacking to do. In boxes along one wall was Tyler's hunting gear—all of which he had decided to discard or give away. On the table, cups of coffee and tea were scattered, on either side of a small box of chocolate doughnuts Sheri had brought with her. The two women had spent the last few minutes striving, with meaningless chatter, to get through the awkwardness they both felt. Lily had put the radio on and they had listened to the weather, and spoke about that a little. Sheri went on for a few minutes about things at the house—Millicent walking around in a daze, but managing to keep up with the order of things and with some of the aspects of running the dealership; Nick showing consideration, and other qualities—patience and solicitude and strength—that she hadn't known he possessed. This was said with an air of offhandedness, which Lily suspected was an attempt to fend off questions about him. She wished the other woman would leave her alone, finally. She was tired. The baby had kicked all night and kept her up. She had so much work to do.

Now Sheri asked, "Is everything all right with you?"

"I'm uncomfortable—you know. I'm so big."

The silence that followed seemed to gain solidity with the few seconds of its duration; in another moment it might be impossible to break. They gazed out the window at the construction. A few flakes of snow spiraled down from the mostly clear sky, and made an odd moment of contrast, this little flurry from one rolling cloud that had already broken up beyond the sun-bathed hills to the east.

"I was so wrong about everything," Sheri muttered. "I thought Tyler might want to hurt them. It made me suspicious."

Moments before Sheri had arrived, Lily and Tyler had spent a cold hour over breakfast, Tyler's breakfast, anyway, barely speaking. In the days since the move, they had both been surprised by the force with which their trouble returned to them, the same trouble that, in the face of Buddy's death, had seemed rather small and unimportant—even petty. It was depressing to discover that the tension between them hadn't really gone away at all, or even changed as a result of their mutual grief; it had simply been momentarily pushed aside. The small kindnesses, the holding on, the tender apprehension and anxiousness, and the days of a sort of shy dependence on each other had given way with the passage of time, and they were where they had been before: in the complication and confusion of knowing the baby was not Tyler's.

Because it was in her nature to see things empathetically, she understood what he felt. At his heart's core, he was a little boy whose mother had abandoned him, and in a way, everything else about him was predicated on that. This morning, she had tried to reach through the silence by attempting to talk about it all. But he had wanted no part of it. He turned her questions back with a baleful look, refusing to discuss it, denying that anything was wrong, and accusing her of trying to stir things up. She told him that she'd awakened in the middle of the previous night with an awful scare at the pit of her stomach and the realization, as if it had been shown to her in a dream, of how wrong it would be to keep her child's paternity from Dominic. It was wrong, and she felt it all the more as the time for the baby's delivery approached. She believed that keeping to the lie, basing their lives on this falsehood, would surely poison everything else, as it had already begun to do. Tyler shouted at her that it was her lie that had poisoned things, and then stormed out of the house and sped away. She sat crying in the living room with its boxes and curtain rods and newspaper-wrapped dishes. The baby climbed her rib cage and made her gasp. Finally she put herself to work getting some things in order. The sight of Sheri's car pulling into the driveway gave her mingled feelings of dismay and relief.

Now Sheri broke a doughnut in two and dipped the end in her coffee. "Roger Gault came by this morning." She bit into the doughnut, a large bite so that her cheeks bulged, and sat there chewing it while Lily waited. Then she shrugged, as if throwing off some doubt that had assailed her, and sat forward to dip the doughnut again. "I think he's gonna do some work on the house."

"There was something Buddy wanted done," Lily said. "Wasn't there?"

"I don't like him," Sheri said. "It just dawned on me this morning that I don't like him a little bit."

"Why do you think you feel that way?" Lily asked her.

Sheri's eyes narrowed. "You sound like a *psychiatrist*." After another long pause, she shook her head and muttered: "I don't know. Everything's weird, if you ask me. I've started seeing David again."

"David?"

"Okay—right. I never told you his name."

Lily was silent.

"He wanted to meet for lunch, and I said yes. I've seen him twice. Nick—Nick doesn't come near me anymore."

"I don't want to hear this," Lily told her. "I really don't."

"I'm sorry. I wasn't going to tell you. I don't mean it the way it sounds. It's just—to tell things. Like you and Dominic. I mean, if I can't even talk to you, my best friend—"

This occasioned a long, painful silence.

"I thought we told each other things."

Lily felt pinned under the other woman's steady, sorrowing gaze, and for a moment wondered what Tyler might have said to his half sister about this pregnancy. She couldn't be entirely certain about anything, now. "We can talk about anything but your marriage," she said. "Please?"

Sheri gave forth a desperate little laugh. "That doesn't leave much. I guess we can talk about the baby."

"You mean this one?" Lily said, putting her hands on the tight ball of her abdomen.

Sheri sat back and folded her hands in her lap and sighed, without speaking. She fidgeted, then seemed to relent. "Nick takes care of the house just like Daddy used to—the grounds and the pool and the business. He's steadier than he ever was before. This gentle, tender, sweet guy, and it's not *Nick*. It's not the one I married. I don't think I've heard him laugh—really laugh, like he used to, that high, loud, old belly laugh—once since all this—since it happened."

Lily said, "We all need time," and felt the inadequacy of it. She almost apologized.

Sheri began to cry. This appeared to surprise her, and she looked around as if seeking some reason for it. Finally she straightened, grabbed her purse, and reached in, rummaging, sniffling. "Jesus Christ," she said. "I'm a mess."

Lily went into the other room and brought back a box of tissues. Sheri took one and put it to her eyes. "You don't need me leaning on you, honey. Forgive it."

They were both quiet, then, gazing out at the confusion of machines and the half-finished structure across the way—someone was working over there now, a big round man in a brown jacket that looked as though it was coated with dust. And there was dark dust rising all around him as he turned the earth, hacking away at it with a pickax.

The telephone startled them both. Lily got up, with some difficulty, and felt the waddling motion she made, moving to the other side of the room to answer it. It was Tyler.

"Hey," he said. "It's me."

She said, "Hey."

Silence.

He sighed. "I'm calling to tell you I'm sorry about this morning."

"Sheri's here," said Lily. "She came in right after you left."

"Did she see me speeding away?"

She looked over at Sheri. "He wants to know if you saw him speeding away from here."

"Oh, great," Tyler said in her ear as Sheri shook her head and frowned.

"No, she didn't see you."

"You've got your mind made up, haven't you," Tyler said.

Again she looked over at her sister-in-law. "He's telling me that I've got my mind made up. I don't know for sure whether he means the fight we had before you got here or our general trouble."

Sheri said, "General trouble?"

Lily addressed her husband. "Did you hear what Sheri said?"

"What're you trying to do, Lily? I told you I was sorry."

"I'm sorry, too," she said to him.

There was another silence.

"I wish you hadn't brought Sheri into it," he said.

"Well," said Lily.

"Why'd you do that?" he went on. "You know how I feel about that."

"I thought it was funny," Lily said. "I thought I'd try a little joking around. I thought I'd try something, you know?"

"Are we that bad?"

She didn't answer this.

"You want to argue now? With Sheri sitting there?"

She said to Sheri, "He wants to know if I want to argue with you sitting there."

Tyler hung up.

Sheri had stood. "I have to go."

"He hung up," Lily said, and put the receiver in its cradle.

"I thought you'd *apologized*. God. What did you mean 'general trouble'?"

"I was baiting him," Lily said. "You know."

Sheri shook her head and shouldered her purse. "This is the most awful winter."

2

$\mathcal{L}$ILY SAW HER OFF, then went to work in the house, limited in her movements by her size and by the continual drag on her energy from carrying the baby. When the phone rang again, she almost didn't answer it, but she thought of her mother, and her father and Peggy, and she picked up the receiver. It was Tyler again.

"I said I was sorry," he said.

"I'm sorry, too."

"Is Sheri still there?"

"She left right after you hung up."

"I suppose you told her that I hung up on you."

"I can't remember," Lily said, "whether I did or not." And in that instant, it was true. She searched for the recollection, and recovered it. She said, "Now that I think of it—yes, I did tell her."

He said nothing.

"I think we should tell each other things," Lily said. "I'm tired of all the secrets."

He sighed deeply.

"I'm tired of lying," she said.

"Well, isn't that just perfect. *You're* tired of lying."

"I am, yes."

"Well, maybe I'm tired of it, too." This was said with a sigh of exhaustion.

She waited for him to go on. It was a long time.

"What're you doing, just now?" he asked.

"I was putting things away."

"I wish I could be there to help."

She experienced a few seconds' surprise, wondering at his tenacity, the element of his character that made him resist giving in to his darker impulses, even, sometimes, in the heat of an argument. She felt a little stirring of admiration for him. She strove for a lighter tone. "I'd work your hands to the bone."

"I'd be doing something," he said.

The sadness in his voice made her wish to reassure him, if she could. "It doesn't have to work out wrong, Tyler." She took a breath, and then: "When do you think you'll be able to get home?"

"I'm not staying past closing."

"Would you like me to bring you something to eat?"

"You've got enough to do there."

They ended on these notes—gestures of consideration. He was, after all, a gentle-hearted young man whose desire for goodness and peace was genuine. She understood this about him. He wanted, at heart, to be a kindly man. He worried over it, and so few people ever gave that much thought.

She sat by the phone crying, quietly, while the light changed at the window and other men came to the building site outside, moving around with what looked like aimless wandering, the big yellow tractors rumbling back and forth across the desolation they had made.

3

SHE SPENT TWO HOURS writing every day; the results were less than pleasing, and gave her little sense of progress or accomplishment. So she returned to the reading. She had sent away for more books, and there was the university. On days when she felt good enough to make the trip—her swollen ankles pained her; it was uncomfortable being on her feet—she would drive into town and spend part of a morning in the library. She brought books home and she made notes on index cards, trying to keep in mind what she was learning about the Victorians: the way of thinking, the cultural traditions and assumptions, the values, anything she suspicioned might tell her something about how someone like Mary Kingsley could come from a society so fixed in its attitudes toward women and in its expectations concerning the relations between the sexes.

Most nights, Tyler came in from work and opened a book and sat staring at the pages, drinking beer, while she made dinner. He was reading philosophy, and the Bible. Frequently enough, he made dinner, and on occasion he came into the small kitchen and sat talking with her. They had settled into this routine. Their trouble had moved to another stage—a kind of mutual looking away. Even so, there were moments when she was tempted to believe that things would smooth out, and they would be a real couple again.

He was trying so hard. He had anxieties about his health now—a new development. The slightest ache or pain upset him, ruined his outlook for days at a time. "You want to know what's wrong with me?" he said. "Every single thought I have leads to something negative. Each impulse makes me think of the uselessness of everything. I'm selling cars as fast as anybody over there, I've finally got the hang of the business, I'm making money, and I'm constantly carrying around this feeling that it's completely absurd, all of it. I keep thinking that if someone were to describe me to somebody else, or if I was a character in a movie or a book, I'd be the car salesman, you know? That's what would be in the heading for dialogue: car salesman. That's how I'd be designated. I hate that. Just hate it. And I like the job. I meet different people every day and no two days are alike. The pay's good. I get to drive a new car. I like the guys I'm doing it with. But it's this other thing—this feeling that I hate. This conviction, down in my bones—that I'm reduced by the goddamn stereotype." He shook his head and seemed to consider a moment, as if he were searching for the right word. But then she saw that he had been seeking the resolve to say something else. "But that's only a small part of it," he went on. "Nothing makes any sense now, or has any taste. It all looks like make work, something to occupy the mind until it's canceled out. Like it was canceled out for Buddy. Like that. It's all just marking time for that. I keep looking for some answer in the books, and I can't find anything."

"It's part of your grief," she said. "We're all feeling it."

"Maybe. I don't think so—I've felt it before. I used to call it my dead time."

"But that's always passed, hasn't it?"

"It's not passing this time. I feel—dead. Down inside. People look like species—I can't explain it."

One night, toward dawn, he awoke with an alarming, unreal yell. She shook him, saying his name, and holding tight to him until he had come out of it, and he lay there in her arms, trembling.

"Can you talk about it? Tell me, Tyler."

He shook his head, breathing so deeply that his throat began to rasp with it. And then he did speak: "Oh, God," he said. "I was with Buddy and Nick somewhere. Not the trip, not when he died. We were in a room looking around. A big officelike room I've never been in. The three of us. But then Buddy was bleeding bad and he—he was talking to us, telling us what to do. It was the accident all over again." He took a deep, wheezing breath and held tighter to her. "Lily, he was already dead, and he was talking to us."

"It was a dream," she told him.

"No, you don't understand. I'm talking about *then*. When it happened. He was dying, not an hour to go, and he was talking to us. We were carrying him and he said, 'Not that way,' when we started down this path. So we went the other way and he made this sound like a laugh, and said, 'Not that it'll make any difference.' And then he told Nick not to blame himself. He said that. And—and in this dream, I knew that was next. Buddy was bleeding and we were in this gray room and I knew it, and I couldn't stop screaming."

She held him, rocked him slowly. The baby was moving. Neither of them marked it, quite; it was the character of this night, the air that surrounded them—the dismal predawn—and the two of them holding on to each other in the gloom.

"I'm sorry, Lily," he said abruptly.

She kissed the side of his face, and they remained that way for a long time, until he went back to sleep, stirring sporadically, with a jolt, as though something in his dreams had startled him. Finally he was asleep.

4

*S*HE HAD MANAGED to get the house in some kind of order, and on weekends he had helped—he got rid of all the mementos of his once-enthusiasm for hunting; he had put pictures up, hung curtains, all those things she wasn't supposed to do. He worked hard, and he seemed almost happy. At intervals, his natural appetite for life would shine through, and she felt close to him again. But there was always the fact of the pregnancy. It was clear that this, more than anything else, discouraged him. There was a forlorn softness in him about it. He never mentioned Dominic, and she had begun to hope that Dominic wouldn't write again, or call. She knew this was wrong, and felt that at some point she would have to tell him the truth. And of course Tyler understood this, too. Doubtless it was part of what depressed him.

"Maybe I'm getting screwy," he would say. "I can't feel anything."

They clung together frequently in the long nights, when neither of them could sleep, or he had experienced another nightmare, another attack of terror, or she herself had dreamed something awful and awakened in the silence, staring into the dark and making the effort to compose for herself the reasonableness of her waking existence, the reading about Mary Kingsley, the letters to her, that were for some reason so consoling and calming. Sometimes, after a nightmare, her breathing—the little catches in her breath as she fought the panic that wanted to descend on her there in the dark—would wake Tyler, and he would be sweet, understanding, asking if she wanted to talk. In several such instances he massaged her legs and ankles to remove an ache or a cramp, then put his arms around her and held her, as she had held him after his nightmares. She wondered at the fact that they were most intimate during these periods of dark, and fear. They did not make love. They were like children, scared by something for which they had no words. He kept poring over the books—Kierkegaard and Spinoza, Hegel and Pascal, several of the Christian mystics, even Aquinas. It was as if he were studying for an examination. But in the nights he seemed bereft of everything, and no word or expression seemed to affect the place where he felt the emptiness. "They don't know," he said to her, looking up from a thick tome about the history of western thought. "It's all noise."

Lily traveled out into the terrain of chain stores and neon lights and housing developments, the riot of clashing, gaudy colors and garish cartoon shapes, clown faces, broken signs, boarded-up windows and empty lots that lined the highway, and felt as though her spirit had been dampened, put to sleep, awfully, and that the only thing that cut through any of it was the idea of this child she was carrying, though she was also aware of the inevitable fate that awaited the child, too. The whole matter between the child's birth and his or her eventual end seemed cheapened, tarnished by the vulgarity of the buildings, the hideous look of late-twentieth-century America, and even, finally, the shape of the hills themselves in the distance, the yellowed grass showing through bare trees. When she was in this mood, it all looked like the sick scenery of the world, with its catastrophes, holocausts, and assassinations. Tyler's dark mind-set was having an effect on her that she deplored, and she couldn't find a way out of it—certainly not with Sheri or Millicent or Nick, or her own family, or, really, with anyone who knew what they had all so recently been through.

5

Tonight, Tyler would be late, and she thought of calling Sheri, but then decided against it. She had periodically wondered if her connection to Sheri and Millicent and Nick were not slowly moving toward atrophy. And then Sheri and Millicent would surprise her by showing up in an afternoon, or calling her to ask if she would come to dinner. When she thought about it, she realized that she herself seldom if ever called them. She looked out the window again, and tried to think of something else. She sat at her table with all the notes and her writing, and attempted to work. But she felt headachy, and she couldn't concentrate.

Finally, she got her coat on and waddled out to the car. There was an intermittent, warm southerly breeze, tree branches clicking and agitating in the sudden little eddies of wind. The clicking sounded like someone tapping out a code. The grass had gone brown, and looked like straw in places, and the wet patches were black as pitch. Except for a lowering escarpment of charcoal-colored clouds to the west, broken in places, but solid-looking where they were darkest, the sky was blue. Perhaps there would be another storm. She wedged in behind the wheel of the car and started it, and drove through the disheartening muddle of chain stores and gas stations, toward the Galatierre house. By the time she saw the two-tiered porch, she was fairly well discouraged. The big house felt like sanctuary, and perhaps it had been a bad idea after all to move into the little place out by Yellow Leaf Creek.

Rosa answered the door, wearing an apron and holding a wooden mixing spoon. "Oh," she said. "Hi." She stepped back, holding the door, and spoke to the room. "Look who's here."

Millicent and Sheri were in the living room, sitting on opposite ends of the sofa. They were drinking wine, and the television was on. There was Nelson Mandela, leading a large crowd through the streets of Pretoria. Millicent had muted the sound. "Have you eaten?" she said.

"No."

"Rosa's leaving us," said Sheri. "This is a farewell dinner. Impromptu. Rosa just told us. I tried to call you but you must've been on the way here."

Millicent stood and offered to take Lily's coat.

Sheri poured more wine for herself and drank half the glass down, then lay her head back on the cushions of the sofa, holding the wine upright on her abdomen. "You look so beautiful pregnant," she said.

"I don't feel beautiful." Lily sat in the wing chair across from her. She saw Millicent waver slightly as she came back from the hallway, and realized that both women were already on their way to being drunk. She wished she hadn't come. Millicent arranged herself on the sofa and picked up her glass of wine. "Rosa will bring you whatever you want to drink. Rosa's insisting on serving this farewell dinner. Her last gesture, as she calls it, in this house."

"We're having chicken. I don't know what kind. Not cordon bleu. Of that we're what you might call fairly certain."

They both drank, not looking at each other, or at Lily. Rosa was moving around in the kitchen. The quiet was oppressive.

Lily looked at the room. Millicent had taken down more of the pictures on the walls, and all of the big game trophies. There were bare places where these things had been, and darker shapes where the paint hadn't been faded by sunlight from the windows.

"The boys're working late again," Sheri said.

"Poor Nick," said Millicent, almost to herself.

For what felt like a long while, no one said anything. Rosa came in from the kitchen and handed Lily a glass of milk. "If you don't want it, leave it," she said. "It's supposed to be good for you."

"Where are you going?" Lily asked her.

"Back in the kitchen."

"No, I mean—"

"Oh." Rosa laughed. "School. I'm leaving to go to school."

"I thought you were in school."

"This is more school. And they're giving me money. And it's in California. Bakersfield."

"You'll be close to your father."

"You remembered that."

"Yes," Lily said. "Of course I did."

"Dinner will be ready in about ten minutes," said Rosa, speaking generally, to the room.

When the other two said nothing, she shrugged and returned to the kitchen.

On the television now, a woman in a bright red dress was standing in front of a green map of the lower South, pointing out weather patterns, cold air dipping down from the north again.

"Shit," Sheri said abruptly.

"What is it?" Lily asked. "I shouldn't have come."

"No," Millicent said impatiently. "It isn't you. I know you're pregnant, dear, but try not to assume everything is about *you* all the time."

Lily felt wounded by this, and almost got up to leave.

Sheri said, "Mother, here, has just been trying to talk me into getting pregnant, for Nick. She thinks my getting pregnant will bring him back from the edge of the abyss. And make me happy, too. And I've just been telling Mother that I think it would be nice if we let a couple of days go by without Roger Gault being over. In the middle of this, Rosa tells us she's quitting and that this is her last night. It's been a really pleasant evening so far. You can't *imagine* how happy we are to see you. At least *I* am, anyway."

Rosa stood in the entrance of the room. "If he's coming, he better get here soon."

Millicent said, "We get the message, Rosa, thank you."

There was another silence. It went on, and neither Millicent nor Sheri seemed to feel the awkwardness of it. Indeed, they were behaving as if each of them was alone.

Lily stood. "I'm tired. I think I'll go home and go to bed."

Millicent didn't look up. "Don't let Sheri chase you away, dear. We are glad to see you."

"I do believe I *said* as much," Sheri put in. Then she looked over at Lily. "Don't let Millicent drive you away, honey."

Millicent poured more of the wine, the last of the bottle, and then set it down with a loud thump. The scene was becoming pathological. Any moment one of them would begin to scream.

The doorbell rang into this silence with the shocking suddenness of a bolt of lightning. Sheri actually cried out. Millicent stood and moved unsteadily toward the door, but Rosa had come out of the kitchen and opened it, and ushered in Roger Gault. He bowed to Rosa, who took his jacket, and then he took Millicent by the hands and bowed again. He looked faintly absurd, Lily thought, and couldn't decide why. He wore corduroy slacks, a white flannel shirt with the sleeves rolled up to the elbows; a pair of brown Docksiders shoes. Perhaps it was that he was so consciously attired in the clothes that the college boys were wearing now. He was someone trying to appear younger than he was. He came into the room and gently shook Lily's hand (she had a momentary sense that he might bend to kiss it, and was relieved when he did not), and kissed Sheri on the forehead. Sheri had sat forward, and now she got up and went toward the kitchen.

"Need some more *wine*," she said.

"We're getting a little tipsy," Millicent said to her. "Aren't we?"

"I believe that is one word for it," said Sheri.

Millicent sat next to Roger on the sofa. "Sometimes," she said, "my daughter makes me ill."

Lily sat back down in the chair, her hands folded tightly on her lap. She wanted to leave, but felt how awkward that would be, and so she waited, while Sheri came faltering into the room with another bottle of red wine. She poured herself a glass, then handed the bottle to her mother. "Pinot noir is the drink of the evening," she said to Roger. "Unless you're pregnant, which of course I *ain't*, and it looks like I might stay that way. And it looks like poor Lily here will stay pregnant the rest of her life."

"Feels like it," Lily said, because they were all looking at her, and she couldn't stand up to leave.

"To Lily," Sheri said, and swallowed most of what she had poured.

Millicent asked Roger what he wanted to drink, and in the instant that it took him to decide, Lily felt everything go running out of her, a prodigious rushing of fluid pouring down, soaking her dress, and the chair she was sitting in. It was as if an overwhelming need to urinate had come over her in the instant that the ability to control the muscles of her body lapsed.

She went weak, and was momentarily dizzy. "Oh," she said. "Oh, God."

Millicent had stood, looking at the floor around the chair. She attempted to set the glass of wine down and knocked it over, and that was pouring, too. On the floor around Lily's chair was a widening pool of water, streaked with blood. Lily stood, holding on to the arms of the chair, and Sheri said, "Oh, honey, your water's broken."

For a few shaking moments everything dissolved in confusion. Lily simply stood there while it poured out of her. She felt no cramp or contraction; yet everything was changing inside, and she could feel that. Rosa had come out of the kitchen, spoon in hand, and then had gone back. Sheri was putting Lily's coat over her shoulders and talking at her, as was Roger Gault. Millicent spoke to all of them, telling them to calm down. "Someone—Sheri—go call Tyler and Nick."

But Sheri was still holding on to Lily, holding her up now, as Lily began to sink down, the light going away for an instant and then coming back. "I'm all right," Lily said. "I'm fine."

They all moved toward the door, and Rosa was there, opening it. "I called Tyler. They'll be on the way to the hospital."

Outside, in the cold, Lily felt the chill of being wet on her hips and legs, and Sheri pulled the coat tight around her, evidently feeling her shivering. "I've got you, honey," Sheri said. "Don't be scared."

They got into Millicent's station wagon, Lily in front.

"I'm making a mess of the car," Lily said.

"Don't worry about the damn car."

A fine rain was falling, a thin, misty cold, and there were low, heavy clouds visible in the light from the open door. The clouds were trailing down almost to the ground in the field opposite the house. For some reason Lily thought of ghosts. The car doors were closing. She didn't even know who else was in the car with her. She saw that Millicent was driving. She put her head back on the seat and closed her eyes, and the first hard contraction hit her. It came in a fierce wave, a band of searing pain across her lower abdomen. She tried to speak, to bring any sound out of her throat. This was the beginning of it all, she knew, this thing that she had so often put off thinking about, this thing itself, a baby coming, something she had no power to revoke. She had fallen into the habit of thinking beyond this transaction with the world, to the time when it would be past, when the baby would be there and the anguish of its coming would be already lived through. The realization of this truth about it filled her with terror exactly as it caused her soul to exult; she felt the excitement in the middle of the fear like the kernel of something inside a larger whole. Then she herself was the husk, containing something phenomenal and terrifying.

She was being pulled along, and the contraction hauled her out of herself, out of any thought at all but the tightness of her abdomen, the breath-stopping pain. She tried to remember what she had read of the breathing exercises, but nothing would come to her in any sequence she could recognize. In her mind, she saw the men at the construction site: the tractors, the ragged ground where they had been tearing at the earth; she would be torn that way. And now a series of images presented themselves to her mind: she saw the hills as they had looked from the window of the train south; she saw Buddy Galatierre holding his glass up in the pool, in shade and sun; she saw the ripped soft white belly of the deer.

Millicent was steering the car, both hands tight on the wheel. "Hurry," Lily said, or thought she said. Her mind closed on an image of something flickering in the distance, a flame. She opened her eyes and looked into the vanishing perspective of the road ahead and saw the flame. She closed her eyes and still saw it. The contraction had eased, and she could breathe again.

"Hold on, sweetie," Millicent said.

"Did anybody call the doctor?" Sheri asked.

"I did." Rosa's voice.

Lily turned in the seat and saw that Rosa and Sheri and Roger Gault were in the back. They were all looking at her with amazement and fright.

The hospital was in a row of white buildings a few blocks south of the football stadium. Millicent pulled into the emergency entrance and stopped. The others were out of the car quickly. Roger ran in. Millicent opened Lily's door, and reached in to help her bring her legs around, taking her by the knees. Again, Lily felt everything become vague, as if she were falling out of light toward some vast darkness. And then two men in white stood nearby with a wheelchair, and they came to take hold of her. As she moved toward the chair, another contraction came, hard and insistent. She said, "Oh, something's wrong."

"We've got you," one of the men said.

She saw that he had a space between his teeth and that he was blond. His glasses showed her the lights of the entrance, and shapes moving in those lights. None of it quite registered as experience. It was all dream and flow, half sleep and wide awake at the same time. The other man held her by her elbow and guided her to the chair, and now a nurse had come out of the double doors, just as the contraction eased off. Lily had the unreasonable sense that this nurse's appearance had brought about the release from pain, and she looked upon the other woman—a heavy, dark, round-featured woman with bulging eyes and fat cheeks—with a form of abject love, like the love of a pet for the person who feeds it. She strove to keep her eyes on the nurse, who had walked around the chair and was pushing her toward the doorway, where the two young men had moved to stand. She had lost sight of Millicent and Sheri and the others. The corridor of the emergency room was too bright; she saw pictures of fields and hills on the walls, and she saw a room where people sat reading magazines and watching television. One person had a cast on his leg, a man who looked to be a hundred years old. The nurse kept pushing her along in the chair, through a set of double doors and on, past wide wooden doors and people in white uniforms walking the other way. And here was Sheri, walking beside her. "Mother's giving them the pertinent information," she said. "How do you feel?"

Lily made a face, but couldn't speak. She thought another contraction was coming, but then it eased off, and she held tight to the arms of the chair. Before her, another set of double doors opened, leading to an area of what looked like office doors, in a lobby, with a lighted station under a low roof. Another nurse came out from behind the counter there and said, "Hello," walking before them around the station to another corridor, another set of double doors. Lily had the sensation of being spirited away, in a maze of rooms and hallways, and she worried about Tyler: how would Tyler find her?

There was no pain now, but only the discomfort of the wetness where she was sitting. She tried to shift her weight, and then remembered the baby. She said, "The baby's coming." No one answered her.

The new corridor contained three open rooms, the second of which she was wheeled into. She saw a bed, a sink, a strange gray apparatus. Sheri spoke to the nurse, and then looked at Lily and smiled. She was still in the doorway, had stepped aside to let the nurse leave.

"Feel okay?" she said.

Lily nodded, holding on to the arms of the wheelchair. A nurse came in and laid a gown on the bed, then handed her a bag in which to put her clothes. "Put the gown on," she said. Sheri helped her out of her clothes and into the gown, and then into the bed. She propped her with pillows, and raised the bed up a little, so that Lily could lie almost sitting up. Next to the bed was an array of equipment, a television monitor in the middle of all of it. The nurse came back. Everything seemed to be speeding now, a blur, and there were the several smells—perfume and soap and garlic and tobacco; starch and toothpaste, mint and sweat. She did not, for the moment, know where her own body left off and all of these sensations began—how much of it was imagined, and how much of it was real. The nurse, a frizzy-haired girlish young woman with square-framed glasses, told her to slow her breathing. "You don't want to hyperventilate, sweetie."

Lily tried to slow down. She had lost sight of Sheri. There were two nurses, now, and one of them was taking her blood pressure. The other said, "This will stick just a little." Lily hardly felt it. A pinch. She looked at her own hand, the back of which the nurse was taping. There was an IV attached, and she followed with her eyes the winding path of the tube up into the bottle above her. The first nurse had lifted her gown and was holding a stethoscope to her stomach. The stethoscope was cold. Lily watched it all, and was in a zone somewhere far away, waiting for the next wave of pain. But nothing happened. The nurses put small sensors on her abdomen, and she could look at the monitor and see her own, and the baby's, heartbeat. The machine made a small rhythmical beeping sound.

From somewhere she heard the snap of something, a rubbery squeal, and she thought of the soles of their shoes. The frizzy-haired nurse reached in and examined her, and abruptly there was a new level to the pain. There seemed something quite aggressive and unfriendly about it. Lily released a small cry, and held her breath.

"You're at four centimeters," the nurse said. "Is this your first?"

"Yes," Lily managed.

"Scared?" asked the round-cheeked one.

She nodded. "Very."

The nurse reached down and patted her free hand. "Well, it'll be over and you won't remember a thing and you'll have a nice healthy baby."

She began to cry. There was no sob, no convulsion of crying, but the tears streamed down her cheeks, and the nurses said soothing little things, "Hang in there" and "You can do it," as if she were an athlete in the middle of a competition. They left her for a few moments, and then Sheri came back. Sheri saw that Lily was crying, and she stood close, gingerly wiping the tears from her cheeks with a napkin. Lily took hold of her hand.

Another contraction started, a little hard wave, but then subsided. She braced herself, took her hand away from the other woman, waiting.

Dr. Brauner strolled in. "Hello."

Sheri stepped back.

"Vee'll be just a minute here," he said to her. "Are you zuh coach?"

"She didn't do Lamaze, Doc," Sheri said. "I'm with her until her husband gets here."

"If you vill excuse us," he said.

Sheri left, and he turned toward Lily, smiling. "You are going to do fine." He took a rubber glove from a dispenser of them on the small table, snapped it onto his hand, lifted the gown with his other hand, and examined her. "A little vay to go." He snapped the glove off, moved to a small cylindrical can, stepped on a pedal that opened it, and dropped the glove in.

Another contraction began. It seemed to move across her whole lower body, coming from somewhere near the end of her spine. Dr. Brauner stepped around to face her, and watched it happen. She gripped the sides of the bed, and a cry came out of her. Dr. Brauner said, "Vee are going to gif you a little zumzing for zuh pain. But you haf to go a little longer."

Lily couldn't speak. There was just the confusion of the room, the doctor and nurse moving in it, the insistent beeping, and the pain of the contraction, which went on, and on, and wouldn't stop. Wouldn't stop, wouldn't stop.

And now, very slowly, it started easing off. The relief made her begin crying again. The doctor was gone, and Sheri had come back into the room. Lily looked at her and heard herself ask where Tyler was.

"They're on their way, honey."

In another room, a woman screamed once, a long shriek that trailed off into sobbing.

"Jesus Christ," Sheri said. "What a place. *This'd* be the place to encourage people to practice birth control. They should bring high school field trips here."

"Oh, for God's sake, Sheri, please shut up."

The sobbing in the other room had given way to loud gasping and panting. There was quick movement in the hallway. Lily saw the nurses go by the door, pulling a gurney with someone on it, another woman, her face lifted from the pillow and her mouth open on another scream.

Lily lay very still. The pillows behind her felt like stones pressing against her back, and abruptly, as this discomfort made itself known to her, she realized that she had a gigantic thirst. She looked over at Sheri, and attempted to speak. Sheri leaned in. "Tell me, honey."

"Can I have some water?"

Sheri looked around the room, then stepped out, and Lily was alone. There was just the beeping now, and her own breathing, which was thick with the pain, and with the dryness of her mouth. She did not know how much time passed. She trembled and was cold, and in the next moment felt as if the room was too hot.

Presently, Sheri came back. She had a small terry-cloth rag, which she ran water into, and then put against Lily's lips. Lily sucked at it, she got almost nothing, and it tasted like the rag.

"That's what they told me to do," Sheri said, almost crying. "I'm sorry."

Lily lay her head back, and closed her eyes.

The next contraction was less terrible, and shorter in duration. It came sometime after she had felt herself drift toward sleep, almost half an hour after the doctor had left them the last time. Sheri reported this, standing by the bed and continually checking her watch. The minutes went by. After another long wait, Dr. Brauner returned. He had a pair of half glasses on. "How are vee progressing?" he said. He bowed at Sheri and gave her a look over the top of the glasses. She stepped out of the room, and then he examined Lily again.

"It ought to be zoon." He dropped the rubber glove into the cylindrical can, smiled at her, and walked out. She looked at the empty doorway. Sheri didn't come in. On the wall, the clock kept time; the second hand made several revolutions and she watched it. She lifted herself slightly in the bed, trying to adjust the pillows at her back, where all the pain seemed to be gathering.

Sheri came back in, and Lily saw the look of frustration and upset on her face. "You don't have to stay."

"Don't be silly. Look, you're not getting rid of me, honey. I'm not going anywhere."

"Where are they?" said Lily, feeling another contraction start. But it quickly stopped, and was nothing, and she was simply lying here in the long pain and discomfort, the awful pangs in her lower back. She asked for the wet rag again, and put her mouth on it. So little water came.

She closed her eyes, and then opened them again. Her sister-in-law had gone. It was past nine o'clock. The fact appalled her. Had she really been here two hours? Had she been asleep?

Two hours. She closed her eyes once more, and felt the contraction start. It was worse than anything had been before. It took all the other discomforts and pains and made them small, made them nothing, and it kept getting worse, making new and awful increments of itself, one wave that grew stronger and stronger, and she gave forth a shout, opened her mouth and blew the sound of her agony out, pushed it out, crying and shouting, and the pain seemed to fold over itself and expand, she wasn't even at the top of it yet and she knew it, and a dread rushed through her, a sense of the power of it to break her, even to kill her if it went on—as it went on, and on, and grew still stronger, and stronger yet before it let go, so slightly, and then let her hurtle, in a kind of terrible slow motion, down the precipice of its sharp sides. It ended, and she lay there, sweating, only vaguely aware of Dr. Brauner and a nurse, moving her, pulling her to her side, telling her to lie very still, and putting something hurtful into the middle of her back, and then turning her again, arranging the pillows under her like blocks of hard stone, under the long, throbbing bruise of her body.

The next contraction obliterated everything else. And there was no relief anywhere, and when it subsided, another started, and after a long, leaden hour of exhaustion and anguish, a pressure began, a terrific urge to bear down, to push everything out of herself, to be through with everything. Dr. Brauner was there; Sheri was there; the nurse; then the doctor again. And they were wheeling her down the corridor, everything was going away, and she wanted so badly to go home—desired, with something akin to a sexual ache, to get up from the gurney and walk out of the hospital and be taken home to her own bed. But then she felt only the urge to bear down, and push the baby out, push out from the dreadful hurt in her back; and she was pushing, feeling this tremendous pressure and need, the unbridgeable necessity of groaning the thing out of herself, expelling it, gaining release. She did not know now who was around her; there were several moving shapes, and the doctor's voice was saying for her not to push yet, not yet, not quite yet. The pain had gone into some zone of completion—it was itself, unabated, but she had borne it so long now that it no longer quite mattered. It was as though it waited, still strong, still fierce, but defeated, too, beaten because she had not been broken by it after all, and it no longer mattered. What mattered now was the urge to push out. She was in the room and the doctor was standing between her legs, and the pressure was so strong it nearly went beyond the pain, into a kind of exquisiteness, and he was saying for her to push now, push, "Like you're going to zuh bathroom," he said. "Come on," and at last, in one shaking heave of herself, there was release, it was out, the baby was out and she knew it. She had lifted her head, and she let it drop back on the pillow, and then tried to lift it again, then lay back and was gone, was in the Galatierre house, *morning, and no one is awake yet, and I'll get up now and go out, and I'll try not to wake a soul, because I like the solitary freshness of the early mornings, in this house that is not my house, in my new marriage; and which way will I walk if I walk out today? Somewhere in the sun. Somewhere toward the beautiful river with its gleam of sun, and I am a new wife, in love, oh, happy love, love that is trustworthy and good and here is happiness, a lovely sunny day in the heart*

"It's a girl." A nurse's voice.

Lily couldn't raise herself. The doctor lay the baby on her abdomen, a bloody, blue knot of limbs and head. It looked formless, at first. But then it emitted a cry, and the mouth opened. Lily saw the face, the pressed features, blood-streaked, and the hair, which was black, and surprisingly thick. "My little girl," she said, crying.

"What's her name?" asked the doctor.

"Oh," Lily said. "Mary. I want to call her Mary. Mary."

6

*N*IGHT.

The long hours of the rest of the night, and she dreamed that the doctor stood and pushed on her abdomen, producing another hard contraction, and then there was an emptying, a deeper relief. And she saw him bending, concentrating, with a hooked needle and thread, and there was a slight sticking sensation, the needle going in and out of her. She watched the practiced hands of the nurses as the baby was removed from her and taken to a small clear-plastic bassinet, where they washed her and cleared her mouth and throat, and they said she was pinking right up. She was precisely where she should be on all measurements. They took Lily to the recovery room, a big open space with curtains on metal racks in the ceiling, which were pulled around to form a cloth partition. There, after a time, they brought Mary in to her, wrapped in a soft hospital blanket, so that Lily could nurse her. The sensation was so strangely calming, the small clutching mouth. It hurt; she hadn't expected that to hurt, too, but it did, a small stab of pressure on the nipple. The round-faced nurse said that no one could get over the pretty black hair. Lily gazed down at the face, with its astonishing miniature eyebrows, and the working mouth. The eyes opened. Mary's eyes, blue as an evening sky. They looked at Lily, and then the unreal membrane of the lids closed over them, the long lashes—lovely, tiny, dark lashes.

"She's taking right to it," the nurse said.

Lily read the name tag: "Kathleen Montera, RN." "Thank you, Ms. Montera."

The nurse smiled. "We got rushed tonight. This is my friend Kathleen's uniform blouse. This is her name tag. We live together. My name's Ann."

"Thank you, Ann." Lily wanted to say, "I love you, Ann." Instead, she just repeated the words: "Thank you."

"Oh, you're quite welcome."

It came to her that the memory of this woman coming from the double doors of the emergency room seemed so far away now—the distant past. It felt like an age. She wanted to say something about it, but held the words back. Mary had begun to build up a cry, had let go of the nipple, and here were her gums, and her little shaking tongue, and the big sound she made. She was here.

Lily said, "Hello, little girl." She tried to move her to the other breast, but the mouth wouldn't settle, wouldn't take it.

"She's beautiful," said Ann the nurse.

Lily looked at her, and remembered Sheri, her family. "Is anyone—?" But the nurse had crossed to another part of the room. Another nurse— one she hadn't seen before—came in and took Mary away. Lily had a moment of realizing that she was alone, and she began to cry quietly, thinking—without wanting to—of Tyler and Dominic, and Buddy Galatierre, the unchanged predicaments of her life, which she must return to now, and with a baby to care for.

In a little while, Ann came to wheel her to her own room. She saw the long corridor again, and went through double doors opening automatically on their approach. And all the while, as she watched the doors sliding by on either side of her, she was thinking, "It's over. It's over. It's done."

Outside her hospital room, Sheri stood waiting, and here was Tyler, sitting in one of the plastic chairs, elbows resting on knees, hands clasped. When he saw her he came to his feet and ran his hands through his hair.

"Have you seen her?" Lily asked him.

"Not yet."

"Go look at her."

"I will."

"Seven pounds, nine ounces," the nurse said to him. "Perfect."

In the room, she lay propped up, and looked at Tyler. "Where's Nick and Millicent?"

"Downstairs in the cafeteria."

"I'll leave you two alone," Sheri said. She came close and kissed the side of Lily's face, patted her gently on the shoulder. "'Bye, sweetie. You did a beautiful job."

Lily reached for her hand and squeezed it. "Thanks," she said.

Sheri made a dismissive gesture, tears running down her cheeks. She glanced at her half brother, then turned and left the room. Tyler hadn't moved from where he stood, near the foot of the bed. He seemed confused. It was evident that he had no notion of what might now be expected of him.

"Her name is Mary," Lily told him.

"That's fine. That's good."

"Come here?"

He moved to her side, and she reached for him. It was a gingerly embrace, as though he were afraid of hurting her. Then he stood back again.

"Where were you?" Lily asked him.

He shifted on his feet slightly, and scratched the back of his neck. "Nowhere."

"I missed you."

He said nothing.

She reached and touched his wrist, then let her hand drop back to the bed. The room was so quiet. From somewhere far down the corridor, they could hear a baby crying. A pair of nurses went by the door, and then an orderly pushing a gurney, one wheel of which made an odd squeaking sound. That trailed away.

"I couldn't do it, Lily. Couldn't face it. I'm sorry. I couldn't watch you have another man's—have that—that baby, I—" He halted. His voice broke. "I love you."

"What did you tell them?"

He stared.

"Your mother. Your sister. Nick. What did you say to them?"

"I didn't say anything. They think I'm squeamish. Weak—weak stomach." Now he couldn't return her gaze.

"Go," Lily told him.

"What?"

"Please leave me alone."

"Lily, I can't do that."

"Do it," she said. "I don't want you here."

He didn't move.

She said, "I'll scream."

"Stop this," he said. "I called your mother. She's flying down. I'm going to pick her up at the airport at nine o'clock in the morning."

She turned her head, and closed her eyes.

"She's so excited for you—she—she said to give you her love."

"Well, that's *someone's* love."

"Stop it."

"I'm very tired now, Tyler."

"I even called Dominic."

Without turning, she said, "What did you say?"

"I told him you had the baby."

"And that's all?"

"Christ, Lily."

"What did he say?"

"Oh, you know—how happy they are for us." His voice broke.

"I have to sleep now," Lily said.

She felt him come close. His lips brushed her ear, and then he was gone. She waited a long time before she opened her eyes to look at the room again. It was decorated with all the forlorn warmth of institutional places: a picture on the wall of a flower field; cream-colored drapes on the window; a table, a lamp, a dresser, a television suspended from metal bars attached to the ceiling. In the blank television screen she saw the room, and herself in it, in the bed. The sight of it sickened her, and she wished for her baby, ached to hold her baby. Perhaps she cried some more, but then a deep miasma settled over her, coming on in a hazy melting, and she resisted it at first, recalling that something was troubling her, something was badly out of balance. She looked at the clock on the wall, and couldn't read it for the blurring of her sight. Squinting, feeling the tears run out of her eyes, she marked that it was after two o'clock in the morning. The baby had been born before midnight. She murmured the name: "Mary." Then she let go, still crying softly, drifting off into the thick, eerily delectable drowse that closed everything down, even her sadness.

Periodically, she was awakened by nurses, coming in to take her blood pressure and her temperature. They were different nurses. Their actions seemed almost haphazard, as if Lily were not a person but some element of an experiment they weren't particularly interested in. She woke each time, but it was all such a fog, and her tiredness allowed her to sink back so that it all became merely the pattern of this sleep.

Until this moment, waking from a dream of Dr. Brauner. It had been the deepest sleep; yet it hadn't refreshed her at all. She ached, and her heart hurt. She wanted to hold the baby again, just as a part of her wanted nothing of the sort. The conflicting emotions gave her a sense of impending exhaustion, and then she thought of Tyler, her mother arriving, the little house in Yellow Leaf Creek. Everything there was to do, that she lacked the energy or the will to do. She wanted to go home again, not to anyplace in Mississippi, but to Virginia, and her parents' house as it had been when she was growing up, and people were what they seemed to be, and if you wanted something to change you simply asked for it. She lay there awake, in the waning hours of the night, trembling, dreading the dawn, and the light, the coming day.

PART·5

The Thing with Feathers

NINETEEN

1

August 1893

I wonder where you are or will be as you read this. As you no doubt must know, there, in the unimaginable future, parts of the world I live in consider the written word to be a witch's spell, black magic. And the fact that this communication can take place at all, between a dead woman of the time of Queen Victoria and—well, whoever you shall be, whenever you shall be, even, I have to admit, if you shall be—is a miraculous thing, nothing less than a braid woven over time and across the abyss itself, carrying me to you. I must tell you that here I am perceived as something of a crank, and that while I seem quite undaunted and even in some way morbidly fascinated with the awful facts of existence in equatorial French Africa as it has been reported to me by the other passengers on this ship, my jaunty demeanor is a hedge against climbing terror—the kind that leaps up your spine and douses you in a spiritual cold bath. No one, if I can help it, will know this, of course, but you. Obviously, I write this in the humble aspiration that somehow these particular letters of mine will make their way down the generations to you, and in full knowledge that the likelihood, the overwhelming chance, is that they will disappear with me.

I am sailing for the West African coast. I have a commission, through my friend Guillemard, to collect species of fish and insects from the rivers of that region. Guillemard, apart from his confidence in my genes, is fairly certain, I can guess—and fairly gloomy about that certainty I can hope— that he's seen the last of me. I intend to collect species, but I am of course far more interested in fetish—the whys and wherefores of existence for human types on the surface of the earth.

Weather here is not kind, so far. Fast, raining breezes that flatten the columns of smoke that come from the stacks. This ship has sails, too, for softer weather. I have seen little of anyone, since we are all confined to our cabins while the seas remain so rough. What an odd combination of my parents I seem to be. My father's lust for travel coupled with my mother's retiring soul, people will say. I mean it in the opposite sense: my father, when it came to being with anyone, was retiring; my mother knew all the corners of intimacy. She will no doubt be seen as having overindulged in her own delicateness of health, or even to have brought it about. I was witness to the bravery of her days; I saw the cheerfulness with which she bore her suffering. And her suffering was real and perhaps you in your day will have a name for it. Heavy, daily pain wears down the humanity in us. And even so, she found the strength to be witty and a good companion. I saw the gift she had for being close—to me, to Charley, and to Father as well. That intimacy terrified my father, as it now terrifies me. The inclination to hide, and the wish to run out, are always warring in me, and I am beginning to believe that the bravery I have been able to muster to contend with my own nature and with the world come not from Father at all, but from Mother.

Mark that.

∽

The weather continues to be bad. Even the young stewardess with whom she fought the renegade piano, as Mary calls it, seems to have disappeared into the workings of the ship. She takes some of her meals with Captain Murray, but spends most of her time in her cabin, reading.

When the stormy sea begins to calm, and the sun comes out, heavy clouds billowing into the stratosphere turning a snowy color, other passengers start appearing at Captain Murray's table. There are two men, very used-looking and wrinkled about the eyes, whom Murray introduces as old coasters—traders from the West African coast. Another man is with them, and is returning for what will make his fifth year. Mary asks the others how long they have been going to the Congo—the older one, a man named Conklin, says he's making his seventh journey, and that he has spent the better part of twenty-five years there. He turns to his comrade, and says:

—Deerforth, here, is close to fifteen years.

—Seventeen, says Deerforth. Get it right, will you.

—We are veterans, Conklin goes on. Something of an anomaly, actually. I trust you know the meaning of the word *anomaly.*

Mary tells him, with an edge of irritability, that she does.

—Forgive me for assuming anything to the contrary, he says.

She nods and gives him a pleasant smile.

—Do you 'appen to know a man named James 'enley Batty? she asks.

—Batty?

—She's talking about old Cap, says Deerforth.

—And a Russian gentleman named Dolokov, says Mary.

Conklin nods, frowning, as if it is all coming back to him from distant memory, and says:

—We do know them.

He turns to the others, still frowning, and now scratching the back of his head.

—I thought Batty went back to England, he says.

—That's where she knows him, says Deerforth.

—I met them both on Gran Canaria, says Mary. Las Palmas.

The biggest coaster, a man with a Dutch- or German-sounding name that Mary didn't catch, looks from one to the other of them, but says nothing.

—I thought Batty might've died of the sleeping sickness, Deerforth says.

—No, Mary says. He's quite well. And he said, last year when I saw him, that he was heading back to the Gabon.

There are several other passengers at the table, a young Methodist making his first journey to Africa, going down to serve in the missions in Sierra Leone; and his wife, a sour-looking but actually quite agreeable woman, with a mellifluous voice and a soft, self-deprecating manner, who watches over her husband as if he is a child (and he does appear rather childlike). A third passenger is a man on his way to Fernando Pó, also on government service. Still others are on various expeditions of religious mercy or business—a trader, a salt merchant, the family of a missionary already in Sierra Leone.

—That Batty, says Conklin. He's tough as nails. He once fought a whole gang of Mpongwes, hand to hand, over a silk scarf they wanted that he didn't wish to give them. They put a gash in his upper leg and they broke his arm. But they knew they were wrestling with the old biblical Jacob, though they were no angels. I think he killed two of them.

—You saw this? Mary asks him.

He glances at her, and then looks down at the food on his plate.

—Well, I was in the vicinity.

Deerforth and the other coaster laugh, hard, and soon the whole table is laughing, though clearly some of them do not know what they are laughing at. Captain Murray, seated at the head of the table, sips red wine from a metal cup, and smacks his lips. Evidently the laughter has added to his enjoyment of the meal.

Mary watches him as the three coasters begin to talk about the dangers of the African bush, all the easy ways to fall into suffering and death.

—My father had a ranch in America, he interrupts them. Cattle. There are mountains in Montana that rival the Alps. And the spring there is as lovely as anywhere on earth.

Mr. Conklin asks the young Methodist, whose name is Withers, if he has brought any dress clothes with him.

—Why, yes, of course.

—Very good, says Conklin. You'll need them for the funerals. You have the service quite memorized, do you?

Mr. Withers looks doubtfully at the others, then back at Mr. Conklin, obviously worried that this is a joke being played at his expense. It occurs to Mary, watching him, that his experience of life has led him to expect such things: a stranger making him look foolish. But he straightens, and having fought the interior battle with his own suspicions, he smiles, and says:

—Well, not quite. There is a text, you know.

—You won't need it after the first week, says Conklin. Then he turns to Deerforth: —I wouldn't imagine it'll take him long to learn the service, do you?

Deerforth nods, smiling:

—No more than two weeks anyway.

—Do you know, Conklin says, my dress trousers did not get moldy once during last rainy season.

—Get along, says Deerforth. You can't hang a thing up for twenty-four hours without its being fit to graze a cow on.

Another of the passengers, the gentleman on his way to Fernando Pó, says:

—Do you get anything else but fever down there?

Conklin sits back and thinks about this for a moment. The others are all watching him. Captain Murray clears his throat and starts to speak. But Conklin breaks in:

—Myself, I don't have time for the fevers, as a general rule, but I've known some fellows to get the kraw kraw.

Mr. Withers turns an odd shade of gray. He places his napkin on the table and looks down at the captain:

—What is . . . excuse me. What is kraw kraw?

—Well, of course, says Deerforth, and begins counting off on his fingers. There's the Portuguese itch, abscesses, and ulcers, Guinea worm, and the smallpox.

—Yes, says Conklin, as though it pains him to think that these diseases were not prevalent in his part of the coast. They are mostly on the southwest coast.

—I once seen a man pinned to the ground by lances, says Deerforth. And his private parts removed, if you'll all excuse me for the reference to such things. Just to paint the picture, as it were. Six tall lances stuck right through him by, I think it was, members of the Fang, who are quite terrifying, a new tribe that has begun to show itself in the coastal areas. They're from the darkest interior, you know, migrating toward civilization. Cannibals, they are, and I understand they like to take your sexual organs. This chap had stolen something from them, I believe, or done something that they perceived to be stealing from them. You can never tell with these people, and when they take offense, apparently they tend to want to take your organs in return. Although it's also true that they don't really need a reason. It's all witchcraft. The whole world's populated with witches and evil spirits. Overpopulated, if you ask me.

—I would like to know more about this, Mary says.

—Witchcraft?

—The African beliefs.

—They'll teach you all right, says Deerforth. They'll put you on spits and cook you.

Conklin looks up and down the table, and as Captain Murray makes an attempt to turn the conversation to the peaceful pursuit of cattle farming in the Americas, begins talking about the insects:

—When they attack, you absolutely cannot fight back. You must remove yourself. That is the only recourse you have. If they decide to occupy your sleeping place, you have to get up and find some other. You can't even take anything with you, for they always have it in mind to spread themselves out. If you take anything along, you're only providing a means of transport for more of them.

Deerforth holds out his left hand, to show them a scar that runs along the palm, up into the wrist. He says:

—That was done by a beetle of some kind. Never saw the like.

—There's a species of red ant, says Conklin, that can strip a person down to his bones in less than a minute.

Deerforth indicates the coaster with the Dutch-German-sounding name, and says:

—This chap almost lost his head.

Everyone stares, one of the women actually leaning forward from her seat to get a better look at him. The man with the Dutch-German-sounding name is powerfully built, with wrists the size of Captain Murray's upper arms, and huge hands, a massive chest. He's heavy around the neck, thickly muscled there, and his head is enormous, with a high double crown of wiry hair, black as pitch. His face is globular—a protuberant nose; large, ruddy cheeks, thick brow, and squarish, stubbled chin. His lips are almost swollen-looking, the lower one hanging a little. He rarely utters a sound. There's something almost prehistoric about him. It is evident that, in this instance, he knows Deerforth is speaking of him, and his passive face, the lack of any reaction from him, makes Deerforth hesitate.

Conklin looks up and down the table again, as if to make sure of their rapt attention. He nods, looking across at Mary, and says:

—Kurschstler, here, looked like a prize to some group of Fang. Well, that is, they wanted his head. They thought it might make a nice trophy. They liked the brow, you might say. Thought it might convey special powers.

—They shot him in the legs, says Deerforth. They didn't want to ruin the prize.

—He fought them off.

Kurschstler looks briefly at the captain, then concentrates on his food.

—Does he never speak? asks Mr. Withers.

—He's a quiet sort, Conklin says. Unless you rile him.

—Don't rile him, says Deerforth.

—And what tends to rile him? Mary asks.

Deerforth cracks the shell of a walnut, and says:

—Well, I'm inclined to believe trying to take his head riles him. What's your opinion on the subject, Conklin?

—Yes, says Conklin, laughing. As I recall, that was a riling influence on our friend.

The others do not laugh now. They merely regard the big Dutch-German coaster, who continues to brood over his food, eating slowly, looking neither to the left nor the right, now.

2

At LAS PALMAS, several of the passengers say good-bye to Mary, clearly believing that she's disembarking there for good. She goes ashore for a few hours, hoping to catch sight of Marco. At the English Quarters, she finds Dolokov, sitting in a chair outside against the tan wall, smoking a pipe. At first, Dolokov looks better than she remembers him, but when he stands at her approach, reaching for his scruffy black hat and removing it, she sees that he's very drunk. Close up, his eyes are darkly bloodshot.

—Hello, Mary says to him. Do you remember me?

He squints at her, holding the hat at his chest. Finally he nods, but there's no conviction in it.

Mary asks if he has seen Marco.

—No, miss.

—And has Batty gone back to the coast?

—Oh, yes, miss. He's gone for the coast, miss.

She steps to one side of him, glancing into the lobby. There is a tall brown man on the far side, under a drooping palm plant, standing with his back to her, and as she has the sense that this might be Marco, she realizes she doesn't want to see him again. She bows at the Russian, who holds his hat out as if to offer it to her, and then she turns and starts back toward the harbor.

Dolokov hurries, drunkenly, to catch up.

—I will walk with you, miss.

—There's no need, sir.

—I do remember you, he says. Miss Kingsley.

She stops, turns, shading her eyes with one hand, and regards him in the brightness. She smells the liquor on him; it seems to be coming from his very pores. He stands there unsteadily, gazing at her with an expression on his face that is close to pleading.

—I'm glad, she says.

—I have not much long to live, he says in his heavy accent. I have just found this out. Gravid liver.

She casts about for something to say.

—I hope you would take pity on me, he continues, it is little to ask.

He reaches into his shirt pocket and brings out a small packet of letters, wrapped in a dark blue ribbon.

—There is friend of mine in Soho, a woman.

—I'm not going to London, says Mary. I may not ever see it again.

He puts the packet into her free hand, and closes her fingers over it with his own.

—You will deliver them, please.

—I'm not going there, Mr. Dolokov.

—Please. I ask you, as God is judge.

She stares into the blood-engorged and yellow eyes, and finally she nods, and puts the packet into her reticule.

—It will be months before I return, she says. You understand me, I hope.

He nods, and seems about to weep. This startles her, even with the knowledge he has given her of his unfortunate state. His eyes are moist, his lips tremble so faintly that she can't be sure.

—It is good for my seeing you, he says in a shaky voice.

—Yes, good, says Mary.

—You will not read them?

—No.

—Is all right, you read them. It cannot make difference, as God is judge.

—I will deliver them unopened, Mary tells him.

He nods, he has understood. He says:

—Is no difference. I have lost her, I am sure.

Then he turns and starts back to the Quarters.

—Just a moment, Mary says.

He stops, and looks back at her.

—Do you know Conklin?

There is nothing in his look.
—Deerforth? Kurschstler?
Nothing.
—Good-bye, she says.
—Yes, he says. Good-bye.

3

As THE LAGOS sails from the Canaries, she stands on deck, watching the islands drift below the horizon, to the north. She's aware of the strangeness of it, the ship heading southward, taking her farther than she has ever been from home—if there were such a thing anymore. No one else is on deck for a time. The waves tumble over themselves, beautifully crested swells of dark water, and in a little while she can see some porpoises riding along in the wake of the ship, playing in it, a whole school of them. Everything about them suggests delight in their circumstances.

She follows them, walks to the stern to see them better, and when they disappear she spends an hour continuing to watch for them. The big coaster, Kurschstler, strides past her, heavy hands clasped at his back. He looks out to sea, barely noticing her.

But at dinner, as she steps into the galley and takes her seat at Captain Murray's table, the others stare at her. For once their talk—even that of Conklin and Deerforth—is stilted and sporadic. For the most part, they eat in silence. It seems that there is now a rather concerted effort not to look her in the eye.

Deerforth clears his throat and addresses her:

—We thought you were headed for the Canaries.

—No, Mary tells him. I'm for Sierra Leone. She gazes down the table at Captain Murray, who, glancing back at her, occupies himself with his meal, cutting a strip of salt pork into small pieces.

The others look at each other, and then return to their own meals. The reticence continues. It's as if they are all trying to process the information.

Conklin speaks briefly about the rainy season in the tropics, and then about the great mountain peak in Cameroon, a desire he has always had to climb to the top of it—what a view it must provide of the coast and the sea.

—You stand in terrible heat below, he says, and there on the peak of that mountain is a crown of snow.

—Sometimes the bloody thing's covered with clouds, Deerforth says.

Captain Murray scowls at him. The others, fixing him in their gaze, offer their own version of opprobrium.

—I only said you can't see the top for the clouds.

They all go back to eating in silence. Mary understands that this strangeness has something to do with her presence, and is too tired to worry much about it. She eats her dinner and retires to her cabin to read.

The evening is quiet, calm, cool. In the late night she wanders the deck again, gazing out at the moonlit swells. She has her old trouble sleeping.

The following morning, Captain Murray calls everyone on deck for Sunday service. Withers is too seasick to lead them, so one of the ship's mates, a young man named Quilby, begins to read from the Bible. He keeps stumbling over the words. Everyone stands quietly while he makes this faltering effort, and intermittently they keep sending furtive looks Mary's way.

At last, Captain Murray says:

—Would you care to lead us?

—Excuse me? says Mary.

—Would you care to lead us, mum?

—No, thank you.

They stare at her. The crew, the other passengers. It is as if she has been abruptly set down here among them from the very top of the sky. They are not even bothering to hide their curiosity now.

She returns to her cabin, deciding to keep out of view for the day. In a little while, Captain Murray knocks on her door. She opens it a crack and peers at him.

—I assume I have upset everyone somehow, she says.

—I neglected to mention to anyone that you had booked for the coast. They all assumed you were getting off in Las Palmas.

—Well, I don't understand what I should do now to reassure them.

—They assumed, and—well, I assumed—you were on a missionary journey. That you were a missionary.

She says nothing.

—A religious, he tells her.

—I am not, Mary says, looking directly back into his eyes.

He smiles, and then laughs softly, shaking his head.

—We must have looked amusing to you this morning.

—I was perplexed, she says.

—So were we, mum. So were we.

They are both laughing as he moves along the deck and she reenters her cabin and shuts the door.

4

*T*HE REST OF HER JOURNEY down the world is mostly pleasant, the weather very calm, the sky a pageant of towering cloud shapes. For hours she and two of the older children of the missionary's family imagine animals and the faces of people in the changing convolutions of cumulus. Mary finds one rather large shape that resembles her brother in profile. She watches, bemused, without mentioning it to the children, as it slowly dissolves in its progress across the western edge of the sky.

They pass Almadia Reef, and the wreckage of what Conklin calls the doomed ship. He uses the phrase almost as though wanting to be ironical about it. There is a gleam in his eyes as he tells poor Withers about it, and about the hundred lost passengers. It is the *Port Douglas*, which foundered and broke up a year ago. Mary stands port side and watches it recede, two spars, and the jagged end of a mast, which juts from the moving water like a black stick.

They sail on, down to Cape Verde, off the coast of Senegal. Here, the weather changes for the worse: it is the wet season in West Africa, and everything is enveloped in mist and rain. For days they proceed with extreme caution in the blinding fog. Now and then another ship emerges from the obscurity, is visible for a few moments, and then is gone again, as if it had all been imagined, or was the product of some supernatural vision, a ghost ship.

The hours pass in a strange, languid fashion, as if this shroud of mist were permanent, the time onboard all that will ever be any more of life. She takes lessons from Captain Murray's men—in navigation and seamanship and sailing and Kru English. At night she walks the deck alone, amazed by the thickness of the fog. She cannot even see the other side of the deck, and, looking up, there is nothing but blackness obscured by heavy, misting rain. When she manages to sleep, she sleeps deeply, without dreams. And when she wakes, in spite of everything, she feels refreshed and happy. The steady, slow rocking of the ship is like a narcotic to her, and she witnesses its bad effects on the others with some measure of pride and amusement. She tends to the sick in their cabins—there are two cases of malaria and several of seasickness. She sees to them with the practiced hand of having cared all those years for her mother. It seems to her that, though sleep doesn't come easily, when it does come she sleeps so well that the sleep itself is an indulgence she can choose or ignore— many nights she's up until the fog begins to pale, and the gray hues begin to appear in the blankness of it.

One morning toward the end of August, the sky clears. She stays awake to watch it happen, the heavy continent of clouds sliding away from the moon, like a vision of the epochal changes of history, a magnificent unveiling of silvery light and sparkle, the stars again, as though reborn, or washed new. The sunrise is spectacular, light blazing over a low, blue escarpment of clouds and retreating haze, burning through on its way to noon.

She goes to sleep that dawn, only to awaken to a foul smell so pervasive and strong that it forms a clot at the base of her throat. She rises and dresses, drawing in air through her open mouth, and makes her way out on the deck, where the air is even heavier with it. The second mate, a Scotsman named Corliss, who has helped her with Kru English, says:

—Hello, Miss Kingsley.

—Hello, Mary says, and her vexed look seems to amuse him.

—Do ye know what ye smell? he says. Ye smell Africa.

She gazes out at the eastern horizon, and sees nothing but the line of blue ocean and the softer blue sky, with its scattering of hoary clouds.

—I don't understand, she says.

He doesn't answer, smoking the stub end of his cigar, which is something he seems always to have with him, as if it were one cigar that he is perpetually refurbishing by some mysterious means. There's something secretive and foreboding about him, though he has been friendly enough to her.

—It's close, he says.

As she watches with him, the ocean gives up two rounded promontorylike islands that turn out to be connected—it is the coast. And the odor is so strong now that it stings her lungs.

—What is it? she says. My God.

Corliss blows smoke into the malodorous wind, and coughs, then turns to her:

—Death.

—You won't frighten me, says Mary. You can't. I've seen death.

—I wasn't trying to frighten ye, mum. There's large areas of this coastline that carry rottenness on the wind. Swamps, stagnant water, dead masses of fish, and fowl, and every other thing that can die and leave the stink of itself behind. Bogs made of nothing but the slime of dead animals decaying with such speed that the only thing they do leave is their stench, because there ain't enough time for the scavengers to eat it. And it all travels on the air. *Mal-aria.* Bad air, ye see? That's where the word comes from.

Conklin and Deerforth walk by, holding handkerchiefs to their faces. Conklin removes his rag and smiles at her:

—Home, he says.

Mary faces into the wind and manages to keep herself in that stance, looking off to the expanse of brown and sick green that is the coast. They are tacking south at a fast pace now, helped along by trade winds. She watches the land change from rounded hilltops and low mountains to rocky cliffs, and back to soft hills again. She can see trees now, or at least a color that suggests them. Conklin and Deerforth are talking with Corliss about the rapids of the Ogowe.

—Nothing could be more beautiful and nothing could be more deadly, says Deerforth.

—I would say the swamps at the mouth of the Gabon are deadlier, Conklin says. Those marshes. God knows how many poor souls, black and white, have slipped down in that mud and disappeared. It grabs you—the damn stuff is alive.

He leans over so that Mary can see him seeking her gaze. With a broad smile, he continues:

—A woman in a dress now. That would provide the marsh with quite a hold. Quite an advantage.

—I'll be careful not to give it the chance, Mary says, smiling at him.

Corliss, throwing his cigar overboard in a gesture of exasperation, suddenly breaks forth:

—Ye're a damn fool to try this place. It kills. It will almost certainly kill *you*.

For a long while, no one says anything.

—I almost got taken by the marsh mud once, says Conklin. Gentlest tug, you know, and then, very fast, mind you, it became rather insistent. If I hadn't had a good purchase on my boat and a pair of kindly hearted Fulani tribesmen, I might not be here.

—I would like to know what ye think you'll accomplish down here, Corliss says to Mary.

—Leave her be, says Conklin.

Corliss ignores him, and doesn't take his eyes from Mary:

—I'm waiting for your answer.

—I'm in search of specimens, she says. I'm in possession of the means to support myself in this. Your job is to provide me with transport. I appreciate your working with me about the language, but that doesn't mean I'm obliged to follow your advice.

—Yeh're a fool, he says, chomping down on a fresh cigar, which is bitten half off, and looks like the old one. And Murray is as much a fool for taking you up on this. And we'll be transporting a box with you in it on a return trip.

He lights the stubby cigar, and blows the smoke, staring through it at her.

—Bugger, Mary says, and moves away. She hears Conklin laugh appreciatively as she enters her cabin. He shouts after her:

—After me own heart, dear lady.

She closes the door and in that narrow space with its hard bed and its battened lamp she feels suffocated, near collapse. It surprises her. The fumes from land have settled in the little cabin, a thick, invisible mantle through which she moves, gagging. She sits on the bed and finds herself thinking of death. Before her are the twin shapes of her knees under the black dress she wears, and she realizes that her knees are trembling. Her whole body quakes, and perhaps this is fever.

She's here. She's come all this way. Africa is out there in the sinking sun, sweating and pouring its damps and fetid humors into the air. How could a country emit such an odor? And is it possible that this is nothing but Corliss and the others trying to frighten her? Is it something emitted from the hold of the ship?

She stands. It's quite clear that they have great affection for her, these men, and that Corliss is truly concerned for her welfare. The thought causes her to experience something like a wave of mingled rage and gratitude: in spite of their affection, they still do not see her as an equal.

This, she realizes—and she phrases it to herself—would be scanned: she has always felt that her duty lay in service to her mother, father, and brother, and that her place in the scheme of things is dictated by her sex. Yet the short history of her life includes this journey, this exotic flight from home, from the little flat above Addison Road with its doorway letting out onto the street in front and its tall, leaded windows, its boxes of unopened correspondence and books. It occurs to her in the stinking gloom of the cabin that she must remember to express quite openly her beliefs about the place of women in society; that she must claim, for herself—in order to gain the cooperation she will need from all sides, from missionaries as well as coasters and traders—that she is only a woman. She believes this; it is available to her as an article of faith, though some hard little corner of her soul understands its use to her, too.

She goes back out on deck in time to see a soaring wall of dark clouds approaching from the east. These clouds reach up into the top of the sky. At the base of them is a greenish light, and a ghostly calm. The sea is mirror-flat. The rank air has gone utterly still. Conklin, Deerforth, Withers, Corliss, and Captain Murray, too, are all at the gunwale, gazing at the spectacle. Mary sees lightning forking down from the base of the cloud wall.

—A tornado, Conklin says to her. Watch.

She does. The sky appears momentarily stationary, a towering, solid mass. But then she sees that it's moving. It is all ferocious motion. The whole black expanse of it seems to stride toward them. An enormous, churning finger comes dreadfully down out of the bottom of it, exactly as a green rush of ocean water rises to meet its bottom-most edge. The whole thing becomes a spiral, and then there are several giant spirals staggering together across the ocean, coiling and bending and trailing strands of lightning. One funnel towers over them, sending sheets of rain in a terrible horizontal blast. They wait it out, watch it lurch on to the west, the funnel itself disappearing in a crashing of waves and lightning and hail. And when it is gone, a steamy calm settles on the sea. Another thick haze forms, still smelling of the fetid marshes in the distance. *The*

Lagos must slow down, for there is not twelve feet of water visible in front of them, and there is always the danger that they'll founder on the rocks that lie offshore. Mary's wet through to the skin, and so is everyone else. The ship has taken on a lot of water. Some sailors are bailing, and she moves along the deck to help. No one stops her. It's as though she's one of them, so much a part of their daily life that they scarcely notice her anymore.

Captain Murray steps out of the mist and they stop working to gaze at him, at the shape of him coming forward, as if materializing. He claps his hands together and says:

—We'll drop anchor here, mates. Sierra Leone is out there, but so is Carpenter Rock. I don't want us to suffer the fate of the *Port Douglas*, to name only one of the unfortunate multitude. There's a lighthouse on Carpenter Rock, but it has rather irregular habits, if you know what I mean. We'll put to shore as soon as the fog lifts. Miss Kingsley, you must be exhausted. You were out on deck all night last night, were you not?

—I was, she says.

—You should be ready for the rigors that face you, he says. And I'll have nothing else to say on the matter. My second mate is worried.

—Tell Corliss I thank 'im for the concern.

—Oh? That is not what Corliss tells me you do.

—I ask for indulgence from Corliss, then.

Captain Murray nods, smiling, then turns and disappears back into the fog. The others are staring at her.

—Well? she says. Is there something else?

They all go back to work. They continue for another hour or so, and after a few minutes' talk and storytelling, everyone, except Mary, returns to his cabin. Mary is alone, walking the clouded, damp boards of the ship. Corliss comes out of his cabin and walks over to her. She waits for him to speak. And the will to do so is apparently something he has to struggle for.

—Forgive me, he gets out at last.

—There is nothing to forgive, sir.

—Well, then, I shall forgive you, since yeh asked for it.

—Thank you, she says.

He turns on his heels and walks away from her. The sound of his cabin door closing makes her feel oddly abandoned, and she makes her way to her own cabin, where she closes herself in with the knowledge that in the morning she will set foot on the African coast.

It's a long night. If she sleeps, it's no longer restful, is so fitful as to seem mere hallucination—a falling off into some zone of disconnected images that bring her jolting back to consciousness, aware only of her wish for sleep, and of its refusal to come. She is too excited to sleep. At dawn, she dresses and goes out on deck, to see that the fog has lifted. There is a startling clarity to the air now, a vividness it could not have possessed before the fog. Landward are the green mountains of Sierra Leone, with the sun rising behind them. Here is Freetown Harbor, just as she had imagined it all those years ago, as a girl, reading Charles Johnson's century-old book: *A General History of Robberies and Murders of the Notorious Pirates.*

Captain Murray comes from the other end of the deck, smoking his long pipe and wearing a jaunty straw hat.

—This used to be a refuge, you know, for freed slaves. They came from the West Indies and from Canada, and from American ships we intercepted. A lot of their children still live here.

—Creoles, Mary says. I know.

Murray nods, puffing on the pipe, which gives no smoke, his eyes narrow with amusement.

—Is that so precocious? Mary asks him.

—Young woman, you make me proud of the English.

This sort of expression is not characteristic of him, and she senses his momentary unease at having spoken. She turns to practical matters:

—When can we go ashore?

—Almost immediately, he says, hitting the pipe bowl on the palm of his hand.

5

*T*HEY GO ASHORE together in a small rowboat, propelled by two of the sailors. The sea is quiet and calm, and the sky looks bluer than it could ever have been before. Her heart is beating fast, and she has to draw breath in small gasps.

—I must tell you, Captain Murray says, that I looked forward with no small degree of horror to the prospect of having a single passenger lady to take down the coast.

She nods at him as if to say that it is unnecessary for him to go on. But he gathers himself and continues:

—I haven't minded at all. And I will not soon forget you, either.

—Nor I you, Mary tells him.

Freetown looks like a confused collection of shambled ruins amid vines and flowers and unbelievably lush vegetation. The houses, whose walls are bleached by rain and sun, are jammed together under what looks like one pieced-together expanse of corrugated tin roof. There are doors off their hinges, and windows with sagging frames, sagging porches, and falling-down wooden stoops, all of it so close together as to make an impossible screen of dilapidation to the eye: she can't distinguish one building from another along the main thoroughfare, which is full of potholes and dung. It is hard to imagine anything but the most crushing deprivation here, and yet the street is festive-seeming, crowded with people, blacks and whites, wearing all the colors of the rainbow. Beyond the tangle of roofs are the mountains, green and fading at their heights to a soft blue. The air here, for all the ramshackle disorder around her, is surprisingly pleasant; it smells of flowers and fruits and, delectably, of meat. She discovers, to her delight, that it is market day. The whole city is bustling with commerce— there are open markets out on the side streets, and wall-less ones, white-stone pavilions, in the main street itself. She gazes upon the abundance all around, every conceivable kind of vegetable, dozens of exotic forms she can't even recognize—wild lettuces, yellow oranges, several different kinds of tomato; a profusion of many different sea foods and game, vibrant fruits, chains of beads, and an uncountable number of other commodities: kola nuts, vivid Berlin wools, pumpkins, alligator pears, pineapples, monkey skins, snails, and antelope horns, old iron. The midnight-black women behind the tables on which all these riches lie are dressed in bright colors, silk-print cloth, and they have lovely braids in their tight hair. The noise is deafening, human voices, thousands of them. People walk by her, men and women, larger than she can believe, some of them without much clothing, some of them with elaborate scars and marks on their faces and along their arms. Captain Murray tells her that the ones in the long Muslim gowns are Fulani. There are also some Creoles to be seen—one of them dressed in the clothes of a Cheapside banker, with top hat and cane, and spats. A young bare-breasted woman with a brilliant cloth wrapped around her middle strolls by with a tray of smoked fish on her head. Mary gazes at the sculpted flesh of the girl's shoulders and the perfect shape of her breasts, the astonishing smoothness of the skin. Following this woman comes another, with a small woven basket, her thin, shapely arm languidly holding it in place atop a long-faced, thickly braided head. And here is still another, with more smoked fish, her stride almost dancelike, strolling by. They are all equally beautiful and carved-looking in the heat, their dark flesh gleaming as though polished. The street is also home to a lot of stray chickens, goats, and sheep, who wander in and out of the clutches of people, avoiding being tripped over or walked on. Now and then a cur dog snaps at them, or jumps at something one of the passersby might hold out, a morsel of meat or a scrap of bread. The dogs look starved and dirty and half wild. There is a constant undercurrent of their barking and whining.

At the first crossing road is St. George's Cathedral, whose stone sides are stained and weathered in some places and bleached white in others. Five fat turkey vultures skulk along the edge of the facade roof. Their ugly red wattles appear blood-engorged, swinging as they turn their heads to observe the commotion below.

Mary and the captain move through the crowded market, the smells of smoked meat and fruits and flowers, and the inevitable fleeting breath of foulness or decay, to the office of a British trading agent Captain Murray knows. The man's name is Demby. The building is badly run down—but she has the sense, entering it, that the ruin is not from any sort of neglect, that Freetown itself is not a neglected or tumbledown place so much as it is a place built where nature refuses to allow much permanence. It is a tract of ground that nature is continually reclaiming. Mary, noticing the wooden wedge built into the door frame to keep it closed, has the realization that the city is in a pitched battle to keep itself standing in the extreme elements of the country. The fact that it is here at all is a testament to ingenious human will.

There's a small courtyard just inside the door, and in it an ostrich stands, fantastic, almost otherworldly, imperious-seeming, gazing at her and at Captain Murray as if from the heights of snobbery. It walks a few paces away, the clawed feet sounding like a pair of leather shoes on the gravel. Demby comes from an open doorway in shirt sleeves and a vest, his shirt coming out of his striped pants at the belt. He's a small man, with compact features, dark, thick, unruly hair graying at the temples. There's a distinctive thinning pattern just at the center of his high forehead, as if someone had scooped the hair out with a spoon. His smile is comical because of missing teeth on one side, and when he smiles, as he does, approaching them, his sharp nose crinkles charmingly.

—Captain, he says.

Captain Murray introduces Mary and briefly explains her mission, or, as he puts it, her "purposes."

Demby seems unsurprised by the news, perfectly at ease with it.

—There's plenty to do here in the way of collecting specimens. The insects alone will provide you with a very large collection. There are things in this place, Miss Kingsley, for which there is no European name.

—I'm also interested in the populations, and in religious practices. Fetish.

She's aware that Captain Murray has given her a look, she can see this out of the corner of her eyes. She concentrates on Demby.

—I would like to go to the interior.

Again, Demby seems unaffected by the news. He nods thoughtfully, steps to one side and then back, hand on his chin.

—I'm trying to think who is free to guide you. There are several Fulani, but lately they're a bit skittish. Some of the tribes from the interior are migrating this way, and they're quite primitive. Do you know of a tribe called the Fan, or Fang?

—Very little, Mary says.

—Cannibals.

—I believe I had heard that.

—Apparently they make it a regular part of the diet. The other tribes are quite frightened of them.

—So frightened that they won't serve as guides to the country?

—Some. I'm afraid so.

They stroll out into the sunny courtyard. The heat of the day is building up, and there is a thin vapor rising from the pond at the center. As they walk, followed by Captain Murray, the ostrich walks with them at a little distance, as if looking them over.

—I should say, someone will volunteer if the funds are available.

—They are limited, Mary says. Of course.

—That's understood.

—I say, Captain Murray breaks in. I've a powerful thirst in this heat. Demby turns to him:

—I've got just the thing for you, my friend.

—Well, I was hoping.

They all cross to the entrance of the office, the ostrich crossing with them, again sounding exactly like another human walker. When they step in, the ostrich follows, and Mary moves against the wall, away from it.

—Oh, says Demby, don't you worry about Patrick there. He has his freedom of the place.

Captain Murray has come face-to-face with the ostrich, whose small head tips slightly to one side, sizing him up.

—What a strange feeling, he says. What's it doing here, Demby, deciding which bits of me it wants to eat?

—Quite friendly, really, nothing to worry about, says the other, paying no attention. He pours two glasses of whiskey, and then reaches into a tin box that is sweating profusely along its sides, and chips off a few pieces of ice. He hands one glass to the captain and sips from his own, regarding Mary.

—No, thank you, she says, smiling.

—I should have given you the chance to say so before these drinks were poured, he says, perhaps you'll forgive me.

Captain Murray walks away from the ostrich, which follows for a step or two, and then seems to lose interest, turning its reptilian-seeming head, with its odd hairs sticking up like wires and its large moist black eyes, in Mary's direction. She stares back at it while the two men talk. For a space she doesn't quite hear what is said, the big bird's bill having come nearly close enough to kiss. She can smell its breath, a grainy, acrid odor. The head moves down the length of her body and back, twice nosing gingerly into the dark cloth of her dress. Then it comes back to face her, staring coldly, evaluatively, like a magistrate inspecting a subordinate. Mary hears the name Batty, and turns, with care, away from the ostrich.

—Excuse me, Mr. Demby, did you say Batty?

—I did.

—James 'enley Batty?

—Oh, forgive me, I thought it was Henry.

—Then you know him.

—Yes. He's known by almost everyone here.

—Is 'e in Freetown, then? Mary asks.

Demby seems confused. He glances at Captain Murray, and then back at Mary again:

—I haven't seen him for two years, I believe. He brought this whiskey, Miss Kingsley.

—I know 'im, says Mary. 'e's a friend.

They are both staring at her.

—I met 'im when I was on 'oliday in the Canaries. Last year.

After a pause, Demby nods and turns to Captain Murray:

—Yes, well, I did understand he had gone north. I thought he was going back to England, actually.

—Batty went back to the coast, Mary says. To this part of the world, somewhere.

They are staring at her. It occurs to her that they both now believe they have hit upon the thing that explains her and this journey of hers, this desire to head to the interior. Romance. She feels the urge to disabuse them, and realizes that in the act of denying that she is seeking not to explore the West African country but to find Batty, she will only further convince them of it. No. She watches them exchange a look, sipping their whiskey, and she decides to remain silent. The ostrich steps close and noses at her dress again. The two men go on talking, as if they are alone in the room. And very carefully, surreptitiously, Mary reaches into the tangle of feathers at the ostrich's tail, grabs one, and yanks it. The bird rushes from her, flapping its useless wings, and barrels into Mr. Demby, who spills his drink and falls backward, yelling. The shout frightens the bird, and pecking twice at Demby, it manages to hit poor Murray on the forehead. Murray drops his glass of whiskey and sinks slowly to his knees, stunned. The bird knocks over a chair and a table, and finally bolts out the entrance and into the yard, still flapping its wings.

—Good God, says Demby. What got into him? He's never shown the slightest sign of a violent nature.

Mary has come to the captain's aid, using a handkerchief she took from Demby's vest pocket to stanch the blood. It is only a little scratch, but it bleeds profusely, and she takes some time tending to it.

—Do you have any iodine? she asks Demby.

—I have some carbolic acid.

He walks to the other side of the room and opens a sideboard, where she sees packages of bandages and bottles of liquor together. The carbolic acid is in a dark bottle, and he brings it over with a gauze pad. She applies the antiseptic to Murray's wound, and together they get him up and into a chair. He shakes his head and says:

—What happened?

Demby shrugs, and gazes out into the courtyard, where the bird is still walking around as if looking for some place to get out and take flight.

—Something set Patrick off.

—The animal was very interested in my apparel, Mary tells them. Perhaps something in the cloth set 'im off.

Captain Murray is pale, and shaken. Demby gives him another whiskey, and he swallows it down quickly. The two of them pour still more of it, and this time Demby offers it to Mary, who demurs. They all watch the bird strutting in the courtyard, walking in a small circle and slowly beginning to seem less frantic. It drinks from the little pond, and stands very still for a long time, not even moving its head.

Demby and Captain Murray begin to talk about some missionaries they know who have recently survived a bout of yellow fever. Several of their converts died, and there was a general scare. The rainy season has washed much of the fear and panic away from the townspeople. Mary strolls out to the wall surrounding the yard and looks over it at the street. She sees another Creole, this one dressed in the finest European gown, long trailing hem and basting across the front, just at the chest line. The wearer is a very diminutive elderly man with a beaded scar across his forehead. He carries a parasol, and marches by without looking either to the left or to the right, like a soldier in a parade. Mary watches him disappear amid the hundred other faces of the street. She looks back into the office of the agent, and sees that he and Captain Murray are pouring more of the whiskey, deep in discussion. She makes her way around to the doorway leading out of the courtyard, and steps into the stream of walking people. A heavy, brightly adorned white woman coughs at her, and shoves by, followed by two Africans who appear to be carrying her belongings. Another European, a gentleman with side-whiskers and an enormous round belly, rides by on a hammock that is borne on the drooping shoulders of four black men, all of them quite young, and all of them struggling under the considerable weight of the man.

Mary follows along for a few feet, and when she comes to a side street, she takes it, into the hot shade, the refuse and the relative stillness. There is no one here. She walks along, gazing at the stone walls on either side of her, with their bleached places and their stains of weather and salt air. This side street gives off onto still another one, narrower and thinner. She's thinking of Paris, and feels the difference, like relief, that there isn't a fifty-year-old matron waiting for her in a hotel room. She makes her way to the end of this newest alley, and comes to a small sunny courtyard. It is almost too hot to breathe. Stepping from the shade, she moves toward a tall boothlike structure, in the window of which there is a very ugly dog. The dog screams at her, opens its mouth and emits a sound unlike any dog, and then jumps up into the window. Mary sees, to her horror, that this dog is clothed in a small shirt and that he has thick, manlike thighs and long, long forelegs that are not canine but simian. She sees a pair of long-fingered hands at the end of the forelegs. The animal screams again, and bares a set of very long canine teeth, and Mary turns to hurry away from there, holding up her skirt, breaking finally into a run, because the thing screams once more and has evidently decided to pursue her. She comes to the opening of another alley and starts into it, still running, when quite without any warning the ground gives way beneath her, is simply gone out from under her feet. She's airborne, not flying forward as she would be if she had stumbled on something, but falling, collapsing through space in a hail of dirt and hay and stones and refuse. She lands with a painful thud in a soft pile of something, and sees dark surrounding walls, shafts of light pouring through where she has come from, dust rising in it. In the obscurity, she can make out several African faces, men and woman, who gaze at her in pure amazement.

—Hello, she says, managing to sound the *H*.

One of them looks at the others, and then back at her, beginning to smile:

—You lady all right, you be healthy one time.

—I'm quite all right, she says. She covers her legs with her skirts and looks at everyone. They begin to laugh. It is soft and tentative at first, but she smiles at them, and soon they are howling with it. They are cotton workers, tying bundles of it for shipment. The roof has rotted through just in time for Mary's passage over it. They help her to her feet, and even help brush her off, which she allows, studying the concern and concentration in their faces.

—Fulani? she asks.

—Temnes, one says.

Another steps forward and shoulders the first aside:

—Mendes.

—Pleased to make your acquaintance, Mary says. Is that your name?

—He tribe, Ma, says the first. No got name long time for Europes.

—Well, she says. My name is Mary Kingsley, and I have to get back up there.

They all follow her gesture, and look up into the light coming from the ceiling. It turns out that the collapsing ceiling has taken the stairwell with it. They are all going to need the help of people up in the street to get out. They shout and throw things up through the hole and finally some people come to stare down at them. With much wrangling and yelling and arguing back and forth in the different languages, they manage to get someone to bring a length of railway tie, with which they can rig a pulley apparatus, much like the thing they had been using to hoist the bundles of cotton up. One by one, they are all lifted from the hole. Mary insists on being the last. When she is brought to street level, the large gathered crowd applauds her, some making a clicking sound with their mouths, some smacking their lips, others whistling, still others hitting their hands together in a flat, clumsy motion that doesn't resemble the European method of simply clapping the palms together. She acknowledges the applause, gathering her dusty petticoats about her, brushing the dust from the front of her dress, and trying to push through them to get to the main thoroughfare again. It seems important to recover some element of inconspicuousness, though she cannot decide why. She feels caught out in their gaze, and in the talk that goes on all around her as she makes her way through them, to the street.

Here, she is momentarily confused. Which way to turn? She must find Captain Murray again, for there is still the necessity of going to the customs house to procure a bill of health for traveling to Fernando Pó and Cameroon. The flow of the street seems all one way, and she recalls that she had walked against this flow to get here—yet it seems to her that she had come from the right in her flight from the monkey. She sets herself, takes a deep breath, decides, and heads against the flow of the traffic. Perhaps two blocks on she sees the entrance to the courtyard, and there is Captain Murray, framed in the opening, looking up and down the street, a small bandage on his head and his expression that of a man who is deeply perplexed.

She approaches him, glad to give him the relief of her return. But he looks at her as if she has never left, as if her presence is vaguely annoying to him.

—You had better get inside, he says, barely noticing her. He's staring off into the distance, beyond the roofs across the street. She follows his gaze, and sees a dark cloud coming down off the mountain. More rain, she thinks. Then he does look at her.

—Well, missy, you're about to have a firsthand experience of the changeability of this place. His words are slightly slurred by the whiskey he's drunk.

—An uncle of mine liked whiskey, she says. I'm not unused to its effects.

—No, he says, with obvious impatience, indicating the darkening sky. I'm talking about that.

She watches it move, blown by a wind she doesn't feel.

—A storm? she says.

—Aye, the likes of which you've never seen. And no one else here has, either. There hasn't been one here in a generation, and you've arrived just in time for it. There might even be some who will think you brought it with you.

She looks back at the cloud, and realizes, with a jolt at her heart, that it is made of insects. The first scattered ones are arriving—big, awfully buzzing wings, and long legs. Locusts, a swarm as big as the tornado she saw earlier. She steps with Captain Murray back into the courtyard, and they rush to the office, where Demby has already begun trying to close up the windows. Nothing works to keep them out. The swarm comes over the town and turns the sky black, and the noise of it, the deafening roar of the millions of wings, the appalling aggregate minute hectic agitation of the cloud itself—crawling insects on every surface, in every corner and quarter, every inch of ground and building, every branch of every tree, every leaf—is enough to make her fear for her sanity. She wants to run mad, and she looks at the two men, who are bending in it all, flailing, without sound. They seem as bewildered and helpless as she feels, but they are moving toward another door, the entrance to Demby's private rooms. Demby is staggering toward there and Murray is following. She tries to follow, too. The locusts are in her dress and her hair, and while she swings her arms through them, they manage to settle on her flesh. They do not sting, but their legs are a terrible irritant, and she is frightened that they will get into her mouth and choke her. They're on her face. She strikes them from her face and neck, and finally moves to the base of the wall, where she pulls her dress over her head. She notices that they retreat in the dark of the folded cloth; they throng around her, and then away. The roaring goes on. She thinks of the sandstorm in Gran Canaria, and gradually comes to realize that this is something to be weathered, like that. So she waits it all out, and after what seems a very long time, the whole cloud moves off, toward the sea.

All around her are dead and dying insects, and the few left behind are drunkenly lobbing themselves at walls and window.

Demby is against the opposite wall, with his coat held over his head. He looks out from it, at her, and smiles.

—Quite a welcome, mum.

She stands, slapping the insects from her front, and removing several from her collar, and from inside her blouse.

—I thought we were done for, Demby says.

Captain Murray stands from his shelter, under the table by the entrance to Demby's rooms. He removes one of the insects from his hair and drops it with a look of disgust and exasperation.

—I've seen these swarms twice now. Damned bloody awful business. Makes you want to go mad.

—I thought I might, Mary tells him.

He seems pleased by the confidence. He straightens, tugs at his waistcoat, and says:

—No harm done. They don't sting, thank God.

—Almost all of the insects of Africa sting, Demby says. A good three quarters of them anyway. And the rest of them either bite, or fix onto you in some way that you'd rather they didn't. These locusts belong to the last category.

—Well, miss, Captain Murray says. Have you had enough of Africa yet?

6

*T*HEY RETURN to *The Lagos* in the late afternoon. Mary has gotten her bills of health and the letters she will need to travel in the country. Captain Murray keeps a respectful silence all the way back. The locusts have gone, leaving a blue sky with pile upon pile of smudged clouds, a spectacular billowing mass, with sun breaking through the crevasses in its sides. Onboard *The Lagos*, there's a delegation from Freetown already present. Captain Murray finds his first mate, Conklin, and Deerforth arguing with four Hausa policemen and a large black woman in a bright print wrap, whose hair is arranged in coils at the very top of her head. The woman turns to Murray when he steps onboard and, with arms folded across her massive chest, announces, in a deep alto voice full of outrage and pride and righteous indignation, that she is William Shakespeare, laundress.

—Forgive me, says Captain Murray. I didn't quite understand you.

—I be William Shakespeare, laundress, she says, as if he could not be more obtuse.

Mary steps forward and in Kru English tries to ascertain what the lady wants, believing that it might be something requiring some delicacy, woman to woman. The four policemen simply stand there, as though waiting for some command from Shakespeare while hoping there will be none. Mary thinks there is something faintly reluctant about them; they keep exchanging glances while Shakespeare vents her anger. What she is seeking is the redress of an old grievance. She wants to arrest the ship's second mate, who left Freetown last year without paying his laundry bill.

—They want Corliss, Mary says, trying not to laugh.

—Yes, says Captain Murray, I understood it.

He steps forward and explains that this second mate is not the one who served on *The Lagos* last year, and as he speaks, Conklin brings Corliss to them, having gone to fetch him as the woman raged about what she wanted. Captain Murray takes Corliss by the arm and indicates him to Shakespeare.

—All time this be second mate now.

The woman stares at Corliss, and then fixes her stern gaze on each of the others in turn. Mary is impressed with her brilliant black eyes, the fearsome cast of her face. The expression remains outraged and furious. She looks Corliss up and down, and then with a harrumph that in its tone might be that of a London lady displeased with service at a country inn, turns and makes her way to the gunwale and down the ladder to the dinghy she came out on. From the dinghy, she shouts at the four police-men, who shout back at her in a language Mary doesn't understand.

—They're going to stay and have some whiskey, says Captain Murray. With the crew.

The policemen move off, toward the other end of the deck, while Shakespeare's oaths come at them from the water.

—Well, Captain Murray says. You've had your first day in Africa. What do you think?

—I hope every day will not be so eventful, Mary tells him. But she is exhilarated and it's clear that he knows this. His eyes are amused, and he smiles, taking out his long pipe and his tobacco.

—Care for a smoke? he says.

It is like a joke between them. She watches him stuff the pipe and light it, and puff with great satisfaction on it, blowing smoke.

—I think you enjoy tobacco almost as much as my father did, she tells him.

Now he seems serious.

—*Would* you care for some?

—Do you have cigars? she asks.

Without taking his eyes from her, he leans slightly to one side and calls Corliss to him. Corliss steps up, looking sharp, evidently still relieved over the fact that he is not the man William Shakespeare was after.

—Go to my cabin and bring me my box of cigars. We'll all have one.

Corliss glances at Mary, but doesn't speak. He hurries away. Mary and the captain wait, listening to the talk among the Hausa policemen and the crew while they drink their whiskey.

—I don't suppose you'd like a whiskey, too, says the captain. I dare say you've earned one.

—And what did you do to earn yours? she says, smiling warmly.

—Ah, I stand where I have been put, he says. In my place.

Corliss returns with the box, and Murray takes it from him and opens it, offering first to Corliss, who takes one, and then to Mary.

When Mary takes hers, Corliss glowers disapprovingly. The captain closes the cigar box and hands it to Corliss, lights both Corliss's and Mary's cigars, then takes the box back and tucks it under his arm, puffing on his pipe and gazing at them as if he has just created them through an act of imagination. Mary takes in a little of the smoke, and blows it out with some force. She feels the urge to cough, but holds it back. The flavor of the cigar is not nearly as good as the smell of it, but she says nothing. She has breathed enough cigar smoke in her young life not to be entirely overwhelmed by it, and so for a time the three of them stand there smoking. Other passengers walk by, including the Dutch trader, who seems rather sullen not to have been offered a smoke. So Captain Murray offers him one, which he refuses, with a kind of dour shrug, as if to say that it is too late now to spare his feelings. He walks on, his big hands thrust deep in the pockets of his trousers.

Corliss keeps glowering at Mary.

—My father smoked them, she says.

—And he let yeh smoke them?

—I didn't say that.

He bites down on the end of his, and leans on the gunwale, looking out at Freetown. The sun is on the other side of *The Lagos* now, and it is brilliant in the strands of his red hair, with its gray streaks. Captain Murray says:

—And your mother?

—No, she says.

For several minutes, they do not speak. The sun sets behind them, and casts the long shadow of the ship on the harbor.

Corliss asks, with some hesitation, almost with shyness, about her parents, her home life. She talks a little about her father's travels, and about having the refuge of his library, growing up with his books, especially the travel books. She finds herself telling them more than she has told anyone else, more even than she told Batty during her stay in the Canaries. She's not confiding in them, really; it's more as if she's regaling them, as if she's discovering, in the act of using it, a gift for reporting things: she embellishes and exaggerates and colors as she goes—talking of seeing the news article about the massacre at Little Big Horn only days after reading in a letter that her father was on his way to join General Custer, and the long wait for news of him; describing the explosion she caused in the backyard at Highgate; recounting the story of the cow in the lane, and the various difficulties she once faced raising game-cocks in a quiet neighborhood in Bexley Heath. She makes it all funny, and they are both laughing, Captain Murray sending his whooping laugh out over the water. Mary realizes that she's in control; she has them both completely in thrall. It's a palatable feeling. Finally she stops, and she has to resist the urge to apologize for going on for so long. Something tells her she should seek to make some excuse for her domi-nance of the conversation. But she faces them, smoking her cigar, and she marks their expressions of unmixed fascination.

Corliss smiles widely, and simply waits.

—Well, Mary says. Perhaps I'll write it all down one day.

—On the contrary, says Captain Murray, I hope you'll continue to talk about it. I don't remember when I've been more pleasantly enter-tained.

Is there a note of condescension in his voice? She decides not to permit herself the thought, and with a slight bow she tosses her cigar overboard and turns to leave them.

—We'll be under way in a few moments, he says.

The Lagos steams south again an hour later, after a pair of crewmen ferry the drunken Hausa policemen back to the harbor. Mary can't get the taste of the cigar out of her mouth; it sickens her slightly.

It is still there in the morning when she awakens, and dresses, and makes her way out to the deck to look at what she can see of the coast they are gliding past: Banana Island, and Liberia's "Grain Coast." The sky drains of color, and once again *The Lagos* is shrouded in mist, a fog more damp than anything they have yet gone through.

—I can't get the taste of that cigar out of my mouth, she tells Corliss.

—Nor I mine, he says, with an ameliorative smile. But he has another between his teeth, and he chomps down on it, blowing smoke.

—You are a good man, she says, with a small sense of wonder at hav-ing done so; she had not known this was coming.

—I am trying, indeed, he says.

—I don't know your first name.

—David, he says.

She nods at this, and a moment passes. It is as if they are both mulling over the name. Then she looks at him and says:

—Thank you, David.

She passes the day in her cabin, writing in her journal, and writing letters, too, to far-flung friends, including an unknown someone she knows she will never live to see. At the evening meal, just after Withers says the grace, she is listening to Captain Murray talk about having to slaughter a horse in Montana when she realizes that the Dutch trader, Kurschstler, has been patiently waiting to pass her a plate of yams, holding them toward her without speaking, his bulbous dark eyes burning with displeasure. She glances beyond him at Withers, and sees the look of consternation on his face.

—I'm so sorry. 'ow long 'ave you been waiting for me to take those?

He says nothing, but shoves a forkful of meat in his mouth and chews, looking down at his plate.

Conklin sends a smirk her way, as if to explain that it is nothing new. She passes the plate and sits squarely around, so that she can see Kurschstler out of the corner of her eye. The others are all talking about the next stop, Liberia, which is where many of them will disembark. Conklin tells about a fever that killed eleven of thirteen white people in Bonny, where the oil rivers are, as they are called, the transport rivers for palm oil from the interior.

—Terrible country, Conklin says. Stagnant water and mangrove swamps, mile upon mile of it, breeding death. While they were burying one missionary, his clerk got stinking on rum and fell into the grave. Nobody saw him do it because they were preoccupied with the coffin, which they then lowered on him, and if the poor sod hadn't waked up and screamed they'd've put the ground over him, too, no doubt.

Mary waits while more food is passed around, and she sees Corliss watching her. She frowns slightly, turning her head a little to one side as if to ask him what he wants, when abruptly, and with a kind of urgency, he nods. She smiles, nodding back, and when he nods again, she realizes that Kurschstler is once more waiting to pass her a plate, this time of biscuits. She takes it from him and says:

—Oh, yes, thank you, sir. Frightfully sorry.

At this, Corliss begins to laugh. Everyone looks at him, though Kurschstler simply keeps on with his meal, chomping down on the biscuit he has taken from the plate. Corliss puts a handkerchief over his mouth, and continues to laugh.

—I would like to know what is so funny, Withers says.

His wife, with her sour look and gentle disposition, begins to laugh, too, now, though she says she hasn't the slightest idea why.

—Africa does this to people, Conklin says to Mary. I've seen it. It's the proximity of death.

—Oh, is it, Mary says.

Corliss goes on laughing all the harder, and soon others join him, including Captain Murray.

—Yes, Mary says to Conklin, the old coaster, I'm sure it is the proximity of death.

7

September 1893

This late afternoon, I am writing you from a clear day. Coming south, during the worst of the enveloping mists, I wondered why humans didn't start specializing branchiae, as that would have been the proper breathing apparatus for such an atmosphere. For the first time, I have seen the African coast as it has always looked, untouched by Europe, or any other influence, the pure wild place itself that looks, upon first glimpse, as though it is one eternal sameness, and you can automatically believe that nothing else but this sort of world, past, present, or future, can ever have existed: and that cities and mountains are but the memories of dreams. I know night and day and seasons pass over these things, like reflections in a mirror, without altering the mirror frame; but nothing comes that ever stills the wildlife, or the thunder of the surf.

I had begun this journey with the sense that I should be very careful of the coasters, the traders, about whom the missionaries usually have something bad to say. But I have not found this to be so. I have been very glad of the company of men like Conklin and Deerforth, and Captain Murray, and I have found the Witherses, for all the kindnesses of Mrs. Withers, rather more difficult to be with. I think that may be temperamental on my part—God knows Father was always impatient with them, too. But the traders are trustworthy—at least these are. And I certainly found James Henley Batty to be so.

Today, we put in at Liberia, and at the sound of drums and a great upheaval I looked over the side of our little ship and saw hundreds of canoes freighted with black men, paddling toward us. Coastal tribes are familiar with Europeans, of course, and according to Captain Murray they are good and honest workers, too. But these were chanting some dire-sounding dirge as they came on, and it seemed for all the world to me as if this were a war party. I stepped back from the rail, and saw that Captain Murray and Conklin and Corliss stood quite calmly watching them all approach. This calmed me, though I still stood back. They came to us at the waterline and scaled up our sides and boarded us, so many and with so much noise I retreated to my cabin, where I found three of them looking through my portmanteau. I said, "Stop that." And one of them smiled at me. A tall boy, really, with wide intelligent dark mischievous eyes, who said back to me: "Stop dat." So I repeated it, and made signals for them to leave off going through my things. I saw their naked legs and upper thighs, their buttocks, and I admired the lovely shapes of their arms, their perfectly formed heads. They were all quite young. One of them actually had put an undergarment of mine on his head. He pulled the sides of his mouth aside and made a face at the others. They were speaking Kru English, I could tell, but at a rate too fast for me to be able to tell much. "Go away one time," I said, loud. "Now go quick-quick." The tallest one came toward me with a threatening motion, frowning deeply, one of my lace camisoles draped over his neck. He growled, meaning to frighten me, and I would be false to you if I said he was not entirely successful. So I picked up a broom in the corner and swung it at him, clouting him across the side of his head, just above the ear. He looked quite surprised and disheartened for a moment, and then dropped my camisole on the floor, no longer wanting anything that belonged to his sudden nemesis, who I am sure he now thought was a witch. He moved past me out onto the deck, holding his hands above his head and looking properly chastened. The others followed him, furtively peeking back at me, with something of the aghast expressions we give to people who exhibit primitive behaviors in polite society. There were several standing around Captain Murray, engaged in excited conversation—or what looked like that, until I realized that there was nothing at all being discussed. They were telling stories; they were all very glad to see each other.

I closed myself into my cabin, in a foul mood, feeling that I had failed my own best hopes for myself in this place. But later, at dinner, they were all still on the ship, and the one I had struck with the broom smiled sheepishly at me from the other end of the long table Captain Murray had fashioned out of the luggage trunks of his passengers.

They were all very noisy all night, drinking various intoxicating substances, singing and beating on anything that would make an echo, and I sat at the other end of the boat, behind a pile of paraffin tins in boxes, with a line over the side, fishing. No success. But it was calming. I felt a little like a pouting child, until Corliss joined me.

 —The loudest laugh of the evening, he said to me, was when the young chief told of the witch hitting him with a broom. He was speaking figuratively, too, Miss Kingsley, because Africans do not believe in that kind of witch.

 He laughed, telling me this, and I laughed along with him.

 I am in Africa. Soon I will be walking inland, heading to places unknown.

8

*I*N THE CLEAR WEATHER of a morning at sea, she stands at the railing and watches the coastline glide by. There is the changing hue of the ocean toward land, the green fading to a bright blue and then to a lighter green, and there is the pristine shore, with its white sand, the white beach leading to a dark-green solid wall of forest; and beyond the forest, the wide sky, ribbed with cumulus that is breaking up. The sun pours through it all. Mile upon mile she watches as this seemingly unchanging view goes on, trailing on behind them to the north, remaining constant before her eyes, the same sea, beach, forest, and sky. But the sky is always shifting, of course, revealing new shapes and masses and colors, new continents of air. The hours pass. The sun makes its journey across the world and turns the water darker along the line of the coast, turns the white of the sand there whiter still, and lights the green wall, gives it a new shade of green, turning the sky above it the color of dark wine. The stars come out. She has spent most of the day here, watching it all happen. She has never been happier. Corliss joins her on deck, with his stub of a cigar in the corner of his mouth. They say nothing to each other, standing side by side watching the changeless coast. She feels no constraint with him at all, nor any sense of expectations on his part. When a school of dolphin comes by them, leaping high and seeming in pursuit of each other, he says:

 —I never tire of watching them.

 —No, she says. I'm the same.

Later, they stop on the Gold Coast, at Accra. Mary and Corliss go ashore in a dinghy. They pass the port by water, and enter a lagoon, water so calm and smooth that the small disturbance of the dinghy makes lovely waves in it. All along the shore are thick mangrove roots standing high out of the water, wound with vines and wild flowers. It is actually rather cool, here on the water. At one tight inlet of the lagoon, she sees something long and strangely the color of the clay banks. It doesn't move, but there are ridges and horns on it, and she recognizes with a start the big sacklike belly: crocodile. She points to it, and Corliss nods, and in a few feet they see two more of them.

—I never understood how big, she says, low.

—I've seen bigger, says Corliss. Twice that size and more.

They stop at a Kru village, and find that a Kru man has just this week been taken by one of the crocs. Mary watches as they act it out and explain to Corliss, who looks back out at the lagoon as if expecting the poor man to rise from there and ask for help. The crocs take a man and dive with him to the bottom, without killing him. They roll slowly in the mud and water of the bottom of the lagoon, until the man drowns. And, the Kru say, they cry as they do this. They weep, as though they are sad about what they are doing.

Corliss does a little trading while she observes. She has brought a few things in her portmanteau, combs and small bracelets and some soaps, which she offers. The Kru accept everything graciously, with wide white smiles and eyes that take her in and *in*.

By the time they leave the village and begin the journey to the mouth of the lagoon, it is evening. The light is failing and a fog settles over them. Corliss is standing, using the pole to move them along. Everywhere there is the uproar and song of Africa, and now and again they hear splashes in the water. Mary thinks of the crocs, and keeps a close watch as the visible world sinks into the mist and disappears. Soon they are moving through a cloud so thick that their direction is uncertain. Corliss pauses, and listens. Screeches from the mangroves, bird calls, the whir of insects, the water lapping the sides of the dinghy, the cough of something off in the dense growth, a leopard or a lion. Corliss waits, and then begins to push on the pole again, and there's a thudding sound, and abruptly he drops down into the boat, heavy on her lap, his left hand making a strange nerve-jumping motion. She looks down at him, prepared to fend off an advance, almost shouting, and she's horror-struck to see that there's blood everywhere. Corliss has hit something, or something has hit him. She looks back in the dimness and can just make out the low-hanging branch of a mangrove tree dissolving into the mist.

—Oh, David, she says. David?

Nothing. The dinghy continues its motion in the water, carried by the current toward the sea. She touches his face, and she can feel blood soaking through her dress. The darkness is almost complete. She waits, and the blood washes down into her stockings; insects settle on her face and neck, and on his face. The alarms of night go up from the tangled mangroves, and there are the crocs to think about. She can tell that Corliss is breathing, but is beginning to believe that his wound must be fatal. There's so much blood—surely he's bled more than a man can do and stay alive. But Corliss keeps breathing. He's utterly still otherwise, and she can make out that his eyes are partly open; it looks like death. She puts her fingers to his jugular, and feels the pulse there, and the minutes pass, and then time beyond minutes or hours begins to go by. She will never rise from this flat expanse of water bordered by twisted roots and crossed by monsters. The dinghy bumps against something and slows, and then glides muddily to a stop. The water level has gone down; she knows the muck they are in. The odor of it rises to her nostrils, mixed with the smell of blood. The boat is mired, has come to a stop in the middle of the river.

It takes all her learning, everything she has ever taught herself, to keep from flying into a panic. She holds Corliss's head bleeding in her lap, and the hours stretch into generations. She experiences discomforts she could never have imagined—itches and aches and cramps and the torturous path of a single bead of sweat, taking an excruciating age to trickle down her back. She checks Corliss from time to time, finding no change: shallow breath, half-open, dazed, dead-looking eyes, regular pulse.

Slowly, and then more suddenly than she can stand, she is aware of movement in the boggy surrounding gloom. Something is approaching them in the dark, sliding along, stage by stage in the malarial slag. She hears the footfalls, small, flat, sliding thumps of the mire. It is pitch-dark. She peers in the direction of the noise, believes for a hopeful moment that it is something making its way past her, but then she's soaked in the terrifying knowledge that it is indeed approaching. She hears its breath. It moves into the near dimness right before her, a croc, at least eight feet long, and coming straight for them, with purpose.

—Corliss, she murmurs. Corliss, please wake up.

But Corliss is still deeply submerged in his knocked-out state. As soundlessly as she can, without thinking, in a kind of pure, dead terror, mindless as blinking at an object hurled at her face, she reaches around Corliss's heavy shoulder and manages to grasp the end of one of the oars. She pulls it toward her, startled at the scraping sound it makes in the bottom of the boat. The croc pauses at the sound, and waits. Mary scrapes the oar again, until its butt end hits the stern of the dinghy. But the new sound hasn't changed the croc's mind. It slaps the mud, waddling forward, and Mary knows how much speed they can muster when they decide at last to make the attack. She lifts the oar with one hand, the end of it slanting down, too long for her to gain the leverage necessary to raise it. But she can now grasp what she has of it with the other hand, and with all her strength she lifts it, holding it ponderously and uncertainly above her head. The croc moves to one side, and around the craft. She knows they are not dumb. This one is circling, to be surer of things. For a few seconds she loses sight of it beyond the bow of the dinghy. But then it emerges on the other side, and turns, starting right for that side of the bow. It hits the side, shakes the whole thing; Mary thinks she hears wood cracking. She moves slightly, and poor Corliss's head sinks from her lap, and thumps into the bottom of the boat. Now she has gotten to one knee, and here are the prehistoric-looking feet, with their heavy black claws gripping the side of the bow, the long head rising, straining; the thing wants to get to her, and will climb over the side to do so. She stands, wobbling, holding the oar high, and brings it down with tremendous force—and misses. The oar hits the wood, and sends a nerve pain all the way up to her shoulders. The dinghy is tipping now with the weight of the croc, and Corliss's body comes against her left leg, nearly knocking her over. She gains her feet again, grips the oar again—the croc has gotten both front legs into the boat now, and its tail is whipping back and forth and smacking the muddy surface of the bog, achieving the balance necessary, any second now, to haul its entire body in. Once more Mary raises the oar, holds it precariously, staggering in the shaking and agitation, the shifting of Corliss's weight, and the pitching and yawing caused by the weight of the crocodile on the bow and brings the shaft down with all her strength. This time it is true. It comes down directly on the animal's snout. She quickly lifts the oar again, and again brings it down, where it lands somewhere between the protruding eyes. The animal whips and snaps and lunges, she thinks out of rage, and she has lifted the oar to strike again, but sees that it is trying very hard to get off the fulcrum it is balanced on—the dinghy's gunnel. She fetches it one more blow, then uses the oar like a prod, pushing under its thick jaw, until it falls off and is flailing across the murky surface into the recesses of the dark and the undergrowth.

Mary stands there, out of breath, holding the oar like a spear, crouched in the dinghy over the fallen body of Corliss. She catches her breath, holds it in, wanting to be certain nothing else is coming toward them in the blackness. It takes her a very long time to relax enough to sit down, and to raise Corliss's blood-spattered head into her own blood-soaked lap again. She keeps the oar very near, at an angle at which she's confident she'll be able to raise it again if need be, though the muscles of her arms and back throb with such searing pain that it is hard to believe she could have the strength.

She waits in dread of another attack, begins to hear things, begins fearing that she's imagining the sounds. But there are so many sounds, and none of them are human. The dark wears on into more dark. The sky is timeless black. Morning will never come. She thinks of the living room in the little house on Addison Road. She recalls the friendly, happy times learning chemistry from Varley, the walks with her father; She thinks of Lucy Toulmin-Smith, and the warm Paris night, the starry, moon-bright dark over the Seine. It all comes to her with a tantalizing clarity, and she makes an effort to put it away, understanding the need for vigilance. At some point, in the endless waiting, another croc approaches, from the same direction as the first. It comes close, and she grasps the oar, but then it glides off into the blackness, and its motion is the first indication she has that the water is rising. It made splashing noises, quite close, slithering, then swimming away. She knows the water will rise. She has spent such a long time waiting for it that now it seems to be hurrying. It has begun to happen.

—David? Please. For the sake of God. For Jesus sake, wake up.

No stirring. Very slowly, almost imperceptibly, the boat lifts with the water's rising, and begins to turn. At length, it is free of the bog, and moving. Yet the darkness is still so complete that she can't begin to tell in which direction. In this blind, facetless night, with no stars and no moon to use for reference, for all she knows the current is taking them away from the port, away from *The Lagos*.

The fight she has had to make has left her parched and starving. She has nothing to eat or drink—at least nothing she can easily reach, and she left her medical kit behind. She curses herself for this, and realizes that she cannot even hear herself talk, the forest and sky are so filled with sound. She feels swallowed up. They are moving, she has fought off the crocodile, but the night has covered them. In her exhaustion, she's becoming certain that it will never give them up while they live; twenty thousand years from now a scientist will uncover the two of them from the primordial slime, and believe their fossilized remains to be a great discovery.

At last, out of the fog, the big shape of the city emerges, and the pier, and farther on, *The Lagos*, with its masts looking like gibbets in the haze. Corliss stirs in her lap.

—What happened? he says. Where are we? My head.

—Lie still, Mary tells him. You were a lot of 'elp getting back.

—I have such a terrible headache.

—You're blessed then, with one ache.

—I'm sorry.

—Couldn't be 'elped, she says. Don't add contrition to injury. Do you know your name and mine?

—I think yeh're Mary Kingsley, the conqueror of Leviathan.

—You were awake for that?

—I remember it coming up over the gunnel and then my head took another smack and I thought I was a goner for sure.

—I was forced to drop you, Mary says. Sorry.

The others help her with him, and she stands on the deck while someone Conklin has brought onboard for shipping farther south, a Scotsman named McNab, tends to him. McNab is a doctor, and is sick— has been sick with fever, and dysentery. The bloody flux, he calls it, winking at everyone. He observes the blood on Mary's dress, and then seems to realize Mary herself.

—Good Lord, what're ye doing here, young miss? It's a wonder ye didn't faint dead away.

—Careful, sir. Or *you* will, from the looks of you.

He addresses Captain Murray:

—I do hate spirited women, Captain. Especially ones with cockney accents.

After he wraps Corliss's wound—which, he says, is superficial, though the fact that he was knocked unconscious must be attended to—he asks for something to drink. Captain Murray invites him into the cabin for a cup of rum or whiskey. Mary accompanies them, and again McNab looks askance at her.

—I spent four months in Cabinda with a barrister, he says. A black. Big heavyset buck, he was. Black as pitch. Married to a plucky lady like yourself. A little white lady from Yorkshire or thereabouts. Terrible accent, like yours.

—A white lady, Captain Murray says.

—Ye should've seen her fawn on him. He must be a stallion in the bed, for her to be so appreciative. Ye never saw the like. Hanging on his arm and looking all moony-eyed at him. Her big black lover man.

—Stop it, Mary says.

—But you're a gutsy lady, are ye not? Surely, traveling among the blacks, it's nothing new to ye.

—I don't wish to 'ave it spoken of.

—Are we prudes now? And in Africa, no less.

Captain Murray pours rum and says:

—The lady you're addressing is not a prude, sir. And I know you've been ill, but I require some respect from you.

—I have all the respect in the world for the ladies, including the lady that's humping her black every night and singing in the high Yorkshire tones of her homeland. Singing with the joy of the satiated, if ye know what I mean.

Mary takes hold of Captain Murray's wrist as he appears to be about to swipe at the man. She smiles and nods slowly, and says:

—I must go change out of this dress. The blood'll be drawing insects.

In her cabin, she removes the dress and her undergarments, and stands before the mirror. Corliss's blood is on her legs and feet. She feels the soft shifting of the ship, and is abruptly sick at heart. The doctor's talk about the lady from Yorkshire and her black has upset her, and she's a little surprised at herself. There was a heart-deep reaction, almost a physical queasiness at the thought of sex between the races. She has already seen so much, and the bodies of the Africans, the sculpted musculature and the amazing unblemished skin of the youths—it has all inspired admiration from her. Indeed, she has discovered a strange preference for them in herself, like the preference a person might have for one kind of sculpture over another in an art gallery. Until now, there has been no direct convergence of her intellectual appreciation and the physical draw of her own being, her own fleshly appetites; and she finds the possibility, for the moment, unspeakable.

Thoughts wind inside thoughts, and all her tortured nights in England return in an instant—all the sleepless hours while her young womanly body changed and urged and grew. For a few seconds, the whole of the world seems freighted with this awful sense of the body, of needs and foods and waste and sweat and the damps and odors of being alive.

The ship pitches on this little half acre of the sea.

9

THE LAGOS puts in at Bonny in the late afternoon, and the sunlight on the water looks too pristine to be the cause of such terrible odors, which drift on the tide and the wind, from the mangrove swamps. She goes ashore with Captain Murray, and they have tea with the British agent there, a man named Boler, who says he never heard of James Batty. The air is heavy with a malarial damp, and Boler explains that the city is in a bad way with sleeping sickness and smallpox. He's a florid, heavy man, with a thin gray mustache and a clean pate, and spots that look unhealthy. He chuffs and coughs and complains, and slaps at mosquitoes, and then he tells a story of *two* clerks who, at the burial of their superior, got drunk and fell into his grave . . . and the coffin was lowered onto them. Mary looks at Captain Murray for some sign that he remembers the story, but he merely sips his tea and seems amused all over again at the macabre farce of it all. Boler goes on to say that the two clerks succumbed the very next day to the fever and were lowered into their own graves for real.

—I am so used to it all, Boler says. I think it may be the end of every-thing. The cradle of the world's death.

They leave him and return to the ship, and in the morning, they steam south, away from the fetid air of the oil-river swamps. They sail on, down the coast, toward Portuguese Angola and Saint Paul de Loanda. Corliss is groggy for a day or so, and he wears his white crown. Dr. McNab is ill, spending most of his time at the railing, retching into the ship's wake. Because he's no good to anyone in his condition, Conklin and Captain Murray are preoccupied with Mrs. Withers, who has come down with fever and is quietly raving, sitting in a deck chair with a towel wrapped around her neck and with her hair wild in the breeze. Conklin dabs her forehead with a damp cloth, and Corliss keeps putting her blankets back over her. Her eyes are unseeing, and her head lolls from side to side. Poor Withers stands by, helpless, offering prayers to the roiling clouds. There are storms all around them, but it all sails past, thunderheads bunching on the horizon to the west, and billowing off into the distance. Mrs. Withers grows worse. They begin to fear for her life. But the fever breaks toward evening, and she's sick, getting rid of the bad humors, Corliss says, which do exist on this coast. He says this last in the tone of a man tired of repeating the words.

By morning she's better, and Mary can see this instantly in the careful arrangement of the other woman's hair and dress. Mrs. Withers has gone to the trouble of grooming herself for the society of others, weary and shaken as she is—she's almost hollowed out, her eyes sunk deep in their sockets and the bones in her cheeks showing. At dinner, she eats lightly, carefully, and they all watch her in spite of themselves. Withers is like a child in his gratitude, and he wants very badly to go back to England. Africa has frightened him out of his will, and his good intentions.

—Don't be silly, dear, his wife says to him in her weakened voice. We can't go back now. You wanted this so much.

Corliss shakes his head, staring at his salt fish. Mary waits for him to make eye contact, and when he does she communicates with a small smile: Mrs. Withers has made her point.

She continues to make it, all the way to Saint Paul de Loanda, the last stop of *The Lagos*.

—I'd love to return to England, darling. But this was what you wanted. I would not dream of getting in the way of your hopes and your ambitions.

—I *want* to go back, Withers says.

—I wouldn't hear of it. I'll be fine. You must be allowed to seek your goals, dear.

—My goal is to go back to England.

—Nonsense. I won't speak of it. Our die is cast.

They disembark at Saint Paul de Loanda, and at the dock Withers takes Mary's hands and wishes her Godspeed. His suffering is so apparent that it's all Mary can do to keep from embracing him. Mrs. Withers gives a heroic nod of her head, and walks away on her husband's arm.

—Well, Corliss says. Where are you off to now?

—I've a letter of introduction to the consul, and I'll stay at one of the 'otels. I'm in possession of some funds.

—There are no hotels here.

—It says in this consular report that there are three of them.

—The report is wrong.

—Then I'll stay with the consul.

Corliss smiles, folds his arms, and gazes at her. His tall shadow is on her, the sun blazing at his shoulders.

—And from here?

—North. By land. Cabinda, the Congo Free State, Congo Français, Cameroon.

—I have great faith in yer ability, Mary. And yet I fear I'll never see ye again.

She reaches up and touches the bandage on his head:

—You almost didn't.

TWENTY

1

February 25, 1990

Mary. Mary. *In the Hebrew:* Miriam. *Sea of bitterness. Bitter sea. The world thinks: virgin; the world thinks: true and pure and strong.*

Your namesake doesn't sleep very much.

I've taken to putting her in the bed with us and falling asleep while she nurses. When she gets tired of one breast, and wants the other, she wakes me up, grousing and complaining. She's got a temper, which I must say I like. She looks like me, everyone says. She has my hair, and blue eyes and a stubborn little red mouth. I don't see the resemblance, really, to anyone. She's herself. Complete. A person who will live most of her life in the next century, and how strange to think of that. I remember my grandparents, who were born in the first part of this century—my grandfather came into the world only nine years after you left it. My father's great-aunt Mayfield was born twelve years before you died, and so for those years you were contemporaries. And, for instance, most people are not quite aware of the fact that Abraham Lincoln was seventeen years old when Thomas Jefferson died, which means that they were, for that span of time, contemporaries, and that Lincoln must have been conscious of the elder statesman, as a young, bookish, ambitious boy with an unimaginable future. All of this amazes me, and I have no words to express why, except to say that the knowledge of it brings you closer, so that you are not just a figure in the books. And a child fixes one's attention irrevocably on the future. . . .

The baby keeps me up at night, and I sleep when I can during the day. Doris hovers near, so glad to be of use. I have let her take over.

Scene: Blank stage again. Guillemard fumbling with his papers, followed by light, crosses to stage left, seems to be looking for something in the papers. He finds it:

GUILLEMARD

Ah, here we are. Now. She wrote two books. This was later, after West Africa—in those brief seven years God would give her. She never stopped wanting to go back there, by the way. She was never at home here anymore.

Mary comes to the edge of the light, behind him, like a memory.

MARY

I was never really at home anywhere, was I? Even in Africa, I was always going to the next place. Don't mislead anyone.

Guillemard has paused, but doesn't look back.

MARY

Go on. I want to see how you've exaggerated me in the African scenes.

GUILLEMARD

With a shrug. As she recedes into the dark. He clears his throat, glances to one side, then continues.

The books brought her fame rivaling that of her uncle Charles, *The Water Babies* author. The fame was work, more than she ever could have dreamed of. And in trying to meet all the demands on her time and still answer the passions of her heart, well, it taxed that heart. Did I mention she had a congenital heart weakness? No? Almost nobody knew that, as almost nobody really knew her. Not even the silly man with whom she was in love toward the end. In the most revealing of all her letters, to this very chap, whose name was Robert Nathan, who was rather a mama's boy and whom she no doubt frightened nearly out of his wits—

Comes downstage and sits on the edge, shifts the pages for a beat, then rests them on one leg and sighs.

She wrote to him that when her parents died, she considered that her usefulness in the world was at an end, and she went down to West Africa to die. An assertion that, given her behavior during her travels, seems rather odd. But she wasn't inclined much toward duplicity, either, so there it is. She was, finally, a puzzle. Even friends, to whom she confessed her spiritual and physical exhaustion in those days after the first book appeared and made her a public figure, even they found her an enigma when they didn't assume they understood her too well. She was in constant demand as a speaker and lecturer, and plagued with the needs of everyone else in her family, on both sides, so many people requiring her care: nursing the dying, arranging funerals, paying debts for those members of the Kingsley side of the family who'd had little enough to do with her when she was merely the angular daughter of someone who had married beneath his station, as the saying, I believe, still goes. No, before she became the renowned Mary H. Kingsley, they left her alone. She did not, shall we say, return the favor. She was sick with loneliness and despair through it all, and the lady never flagged once.

He stands, folds his arms, and clears his throat. He's moved by the memory.

Not once.

Enter a woman of the time. One of Mary's many friends. She's older, and she wishes to disagree.

WOMAN
She made me laugh. You mustn't talk only about the sadness she knew, or the heartbreak. We all have our share of that. She was as funny as anyone I ever knew. She could do every single worldly accent known to man, and everyone else's voice. The very voice itself. She did a very believable version of you, Guillemard. It was really quite hilarious, and not mean. Just—well, mischievously accurate. And she made such fun of herself all the time. You have to find a way to convey this. There was great sadness, but she never allowed herself to indulge in it.

Guillemard turns to her.

GUILLEMARD
Madam, if you wish to add anything, I suggest you wait your turn.

☙

*D*ORIS SLEPT in the living room, having made the sofa up like a bed with her books stacked beside it. The end table was littered with paper plates and cups, magazines, and more books. Tyler came home late each weeknight, and would sneak in when Lily was asleep with the baby at her side. Carefully he would pick the baby up and put her in the bassinet. Lily only half-awakened, and even so, in what had become the perpetually wakeful, disquieted region of her consciousness, she noted his tenderness with the child, and in the mornings she protected his rest, letting him sleep until just before time for him to go.

It was a strain on them both having Doris there, helpful as she was with the baby.

Lily was still very sore, and she tired easily. There were the things she had been told to expect—the pain when Mary nursed, for instance; it was quite surprising in its intensity, like a form of punishment for having brought a child into the world. Sometimes Lily thought of it that way, and attributed it to the fact that she felt so low and oversensitive all the time. She kept having to wade through this pervasive fatigue.

Sheri and Millicent were anxious to get to know Doris, and of course they wished also to help with the baby. Often they dropped by in the afternoon. Doris was faintly ill at ease with them, largely because of what she knew of their recent bereavement. She told Lily that she couldn't make herself relax. They were both so serious about helping. Sheri made a joke now and then, but there was something painfully half-hearted about it. Something soft and almost timid shone in her eyes as she spoke. Lily saw it, and tried to produce something gentle or reassuring to say. What she wished to avoid was any hint of personal interest: she had no inclination for revelations concerning the secret life Sheri or anyone else was leading, or not leading. She felt low about it, as if she had failed them all.

She was too tired to think, most of the time.

The nights went on with the cycle of waking and feeding and trying to sleep, and waking and feeding again.

Lily thought of her mother's stories about her first years with Scott—how they had stayed for short periods with his parents or hers, trying to get started. The truest characteristic of those times, the dominant feeling, was impermanence: a sense of always being-on-the-way-somewhere, a form of waiting for the circumstances to change—nothing settled, nothing established; a living-through, until things calmed down.

That was how Lily felt now. Something was undone, unfinished, and it weighed on her all the time.

The construction site across the way—with its earthmovers sitting idle and its walls that enclosed nothing, its iron staircases going nowhere—only added to her sense of transience, here. Some mornings, she sat with the baby asleep in the bassinet, and a pad of paper on her lap, trying to write lines for her play, while the men went along the level of the brick walls, adding to them almost imperceptibly as the sun went up in the sky and reached noon. Mary awoke several times, and would nurse with an almost desperate concentration, biting down, so that Lily had to lean forward and try to loosen the grip of the little mouth slightly, just to relieve the pain. This never failed to cause temper in the baby, and a fussy, mewling inability to get back to nursing.

The child's dark eyes, looking back at her, seemed to be intuiting something. It made her anxious, as if there were some divination coming from the universe that would see through all her doubts and worries.

But then there would be those instances when the baby smiled, or closed the perfect eyes and went to sleep on her chest. The milky smell of the child's breath, the perfect little mouth blowing out with each exhalation, and the small sighs uttered in sleep. Such peace. Lily wondered what the baby must be dreaming—what were the possible dreams of an infant?

One late morning near the end of the first week, Lily was alone with the baby when Millicent called, to ask after her. They spoke for a few minutes about the baby, and nursing, and Millicent recalled when Tyler was born. Something changed in her voice, remembering herself in those days, before Buddy. "Well," she said, finally. "I guess there's a lot to think about over there."

Lily was too startled to speak for a moment. Finally she said, "Think about?"

"Well, you know. If Tyler quits the dealership."

"Tyler's talking about quitting?"

"He's—he's kept it from you?"

"Since when?" Lily demanded.

"He's been talking to Nick about joining the army."

Lily couldn't speak for a moment.

"I'm sorry, I thought he'd've told you that."

"No," she got out. "He hasn't mentioned it to me."

"Well—you know how men—you know how they talk about these things."

Later, she sat in the living room nursing the baby, gazing out at the men working on the apartment building. They were bricklayers, and a wall was going up by increments. Her mother was ironing something, standing with the ironing board in front of the television. The sound was on low, so as not to disturb the baby.

"Honey," Doris said. "What's wrong here?"

"I'm tired and sore," Lily told her. "I wasn't ready for how long it would take to feel normal again."

"There's something between you and Tyler. I can sense it. You're so—civil to each other."

Lily shook her head and smiled sardonically. "Really."

Her mother walked across the room, and said, almost under her breath, "It's none of my business."

They spent the rest of the evening without saying much to each other. Lily changed the baby and put her to bed. Her mother roasted a chicken and prepared rice and carrots, and they ate quietly in front of the small portable television. No one called. They did the dishes together, and watched television. The wind blew and shook the windows and Doris remarked that it was surprisingly cold for this far south.

"I'm sorry," Lily said to her.

Doris yawned. "No need to apologize about the weather."

"I wasn't talking about the weather."

"I haven't got the slightest idea what you're talking about." She stood. "I'm going to bed."

Lily waited a few moments, then wheeled the bassinet into the bedroom, and got into bed herself with the baby at her side. Doris came to the door, wearing her nightgown.

"Do you need me to change the baby?"

"No, I just did. She's fine."

"I think Mary looks like your father a little, don't you?"

"I can't tell who she looks like," Lily said.

Doris folded her hands over her chest, a gesture that Lily had come to recognize as a kind of tick, a motion produced by nervousness or anxiety. "They seem very happy, you know. They went through Peggy's losing the baby and Scott was there for her in ways he never was for me."

"You were there for each other," Lily said. "I saw it. I grew up with it."

Doris's expression was tolerant. "We were really rather average."

"No."

"I think you've embroidered it a little in your mind."

"Stop it," Lily said. "I don't want to talk about it. The more I think of all of it the more confused I get."

"It *is* confusing. I'm fifty years old and seeing someone and I don't really know any more than I did when I first started going with your father. When Peggy and I talk, we don't quite remember that we're almost thirty years apart."

"You're seeing someone?" Lily asked.

Doris smiled out of one side of her mouth. "Friendliness."

"I wonder if Scott ever forgets the age difference," Lily said with a dry little smirk.

"That was unkind. It was especially unkind to me."

"I'm sorry," Lily said, beginning to cry. "I'm—I'm such a mess."

Doris hurried to embrace her. "It's just the blues, sweetie. It'll pass."

"No—Tyler's been talking to Nick about quitting the dealership and joining the army."

Doris seemed to be waiting for more.

"He hasn't said anything to me."

"Maybe it's just talk, Lily."

"You don't understand."

"I'm trying to."

"No—I don't mean that—oh, never mind. You're right, it's probably nothing."

"At least give the man a chance to explain. I did learn that much."

Lily kissed her cheek, and hugged her tight.

The baby stirred and fussed, then settled again into her heavy sleep.

The quiet that followed seemed freighted with something indeterminate and shadowy, like the residue of a nightmare upon waking. Lily felt it, and wondered if her mother did, too.

"Well," said Doris, kissing her forehead. "Good night." She moved to the door.

"I love you," Lily said.

"Oh, I love you, too, darling."

Perhaps an hour later, when Tyler came in, she was awake. One of the problems of having Doris in the next room was that they could never really let go in a quarrel. Their very conversations, if intended to be private, had to be carried on in a whisper. Lily felt the difficulty of bringing up his plans, fearing that she might begin screaming at him. Something about his very consideration of her fed her anger. She lay still in the dimness while he moved the baby to the bassinet, and put his sport coat and pants on the chair under the window. He went into the bathroom to brush his teeth. She heard the water run. She knew that it would be better not to say anything to him until Doris flew away. But rage battered at her chest from the inside, her heart thrashing, pounding under her breastbone. He came out of the bathroom, got into the bed, leaned over, and, lightly, so as not to wake her, kissed her cheek, then lay with his back to her.

She was going to be awake all night. It was impossible to remain quiet. "Tyler," she murmured.

He was already asleep.

Turning over in the bed, she stared at him for a few seconds. Then she struck the blade of his shoulder, a dull thud with the heel of her palm. He jerked awake, emitting a whimpering sound, like a wordless question, and then sat upright, looking around him. "Lily, what the hell?"

"You can't sleep, yet. Not yet, damn you."

She reached past him and turned the light on, realizing with a little inward throb that he had winced at the motion.

"What the hell is this?" he said, low. "Are you crazy?"

She sat back with her arms folded. "When were you going to tell me?"

"Tell you what? And keep your voice down."

"Are you joining the army?"

He didn't answer right away. He ran his hands through his hair and looked at the door, then rubbed his eyes. "Jesus, this isn't the time for it, Lily."

"So you are."

He let his hands fall to his lap. "I've thought about it. Yes, maybe."

"When were you going to tell me?"

"I don't know—maybe never. What the hell does it matter? You don't want me here anyway, right?"

"What made you decide *that*?"

"Oh, come on."

"Explain," Lily said.

They were both whispering, and now they heard a sound. Doris had gotten up. She went into the bathroom out in the hallway, and coughed. That door closed.

"Jesus Christ," Tyler said. "I love you, and I even love the baby. I do. But you keep putting things on me."

"Oh, like your plan to go into the army without telling me?" She said this in a normal speaking voice that, because of the circumstances, sounded louder. They both listened for her mother, and heard nothing.

He whispered, "That's not what I'm talking about."

"Why do you want to go into the army?" she demanded.

He paused, and seemed to consider the question. "I can't stand it here anymore."

"Here? With me?"

"Not you. The *town*. Come on, Lily. Look what happened to me in this place."

She felt abruptly sorry. Yet she kept her expression blank, simply looking back at him. "You said it was because of the way I made you feel."

"Some of it is, yeah," he said. "That's some of it, sure."

The baby stirred, and began to cry. They heard Doris come out of the hall bathroom. She knocked on their door. "Lily, do you need me to do anything?"

"No," Lily called.

Tyler took the baby from the bassinet and gave her to Lily, gingerly placing her in Lily's arms, even as he muttered: "I just can't seem to see any reason to go on."

"Do you mean us?" she asked, abruptly frightened.

The expression on his face was so broken that she almost reached up to touch his cheek. "I mean the whole thing," he said. "The whole nine yards. My fucking life."

She put Mary to her breast and waited for him to say more.

"I'm making a pot of money at the dealership. Business is good. Nick tallies it all and writes out the checks, and I put it in the bank, and there's nothing I want to do with it. We could move out of here tomorrow and have a really nice house and the idea of it makes me sick to my stomach."

"It's depression," she said. "I know—I have it, too."

"There's another stop past that, Lily."

"And you're claiming that for yourself."

"Okay, if that's the way you want to put it."

The quiet in which they passed the next few minutes was not as tense as it might have been were it not for the baby. Lily washed and changed her, and nursed her a little more, lying on one side. He dispensed with the dirty diaper, and brought a fresh nightgown for her. When it was all finished, they lay still, hearing the little sounds Mary made, sucking and breathing and swallowing.

"I keep thinking we can get past this," Tyler said. "I keep hoping for it."

2

March 5, 1990
Hello,

I know it's been a while. To be honest, I didn't know what I'd say, or how to begin after time went on a little. I said what we felt in the first letter, and then it seemed (still does, a bit) like it was wrong to presume you had reached the point of being interested in what I'm doing down here, in this very exotically beautiful city. It's Mardi Gras, now. I have never seen anything like it. New Orleans has never built up much of a theater scene, local or otherwise, and Mardi Gras is the reason. It's the social event of the year, and with all the resources going into something that's basically interactive theater, there isn't much left for other kinds.

The best time to come down here during Mardi Gras is what is called Fat Tuesday—the day before Ash Wednesday, and it's the final debauch before repentance. There are social groups, or clubs—really high society, some of them—called krewes (it's just a glorified way to spell "crews") who stage parades throughout the festival. On the weekend before Fat Tuesday, some of the biggest krewes parade; they have names like Bacchus, Orpheus, Endymion. On Fat Tuesday itself, Zulu and Rex are the two big ones to catch. Zulu is mostly black. They throw coconuts and spears into the crowd along with the traditional beads, doubloons, stuffed animals, etc. If you get a gold coconut, you're really cool. The chief of Rex becomes the king of Mardi Gras. The Zulu chief and Rex meet at the river, and that is the symbolic meeting of white and black in New Orleans. Incidentally, because there has been a lot of pressure this year for all the krewes (most of them are comprised of white Christians) to admit minorities, some of the bigger ones are refusing to march. But Ms. Beaumont says the feeling down here at this time of year is always so festive, it's hard to imagine this will have much of an effect. Certainly the thousands of people who come to see Mardi Gras won't miss anything, what with all the high school marching bands that turn up. There are a LOT of high schools in New Orleans, and most of them are Catholic. They turn out with majorettes, dancing teams, cheerleaders. The most popular band is from St. Augustine Catholic High, which everyone calls Saint Aug. Ms. Beaumont taught there for years before she retired.

Maybe you could get a job teaching here if you ever decide to move down this way. I know you and Tyler liked it here.

I also know that this letter is not really giving you much news about us. That's because we're not really doing a lot in the way of newsworthy things. I'm working in the bookstore. Manny's looking for work (again), and Ms. Beaumont is, well, mothering us both. Manny's been very patient with my adjustment to the environs. I think I'm suffering from a kind of sensory overload. But I like it, I do like it. We are right in the Quarter, you know, and the noise is sometimes hard to believe. But there are some amazing clubs down the street, people playing jazz the way it was meant to be played. Blues, too.

Speaking of blues, I don't get blue except when I think I might not see you two for a long time. And I wonder how things are going with the baby— Tyler, you were so vague and exhausted-sounding when you called about it. Understandably, of course. A typical father, and all. I had hung up before I realized that you hadn't said how much the baby weighed, or what you had named her. And I would've called, but was afraid to disturb you. Wake you both up in exactly the minute that you're getting your first real sleep in weeks. You're parents now, and that seems weird, thinking about it. Something I'll never be, I know now. But I'm happier than I've been in a long time. Manny and I are suited to each other in ways I could never have predicted. I'm presently teaching him how to cuss in English, and he's returning the favor in Spanish. It's a way of laughing and relaxing a little before dinner in the evenings. Spanish is full of wonderful curses and insults. And English, as you know, is probably the richest language on earth for those things. So the interchange makes us laugh pretty hard. It makes Ms. Beaumont laugh, too. She supplied an insult the other night when a pizza-delivery guy got short with her. He was really quite rude. So Ms. Beaumont handed him a twenty-dollar tip, then smiled, and when he thanked her, with this surprised and, well, slightly contrite look on his face, she said, "Yeah, well, now why don't you just go fall through your asshole and hang yourself, cher" (she calls everybody that; it's Cajun, though she's not Cajun; she's just lived here so long—and she wants me to call her Aunt Violet and I'm trying)—anyway, Aunt Violet Beaumont said that to him, and then he said "What?" and she smiled real sweet and said, "I shit in your mother's organs of increase," and closed the door. It took us a second to realize what had happened, and I don't know if the pizza guy ever figured it out. He stood there a long time, I guess trying to figure if this little old lady said what he thought she said and if she was really a witch. She said it so sweetly. I laughed until I thought my heart might stop.

I would so love for you two (well, now you three) to get to know Ms. Beaumont. She's the most wonderful amazing shrewd dear lady. I hope somehow it works out that you and Tyler decide to come this way. I miss you both and it would be nice to see the baby.

Well, Manny's home from his job search. Ms. Beaumont's making fish sticks and fries for dinner (nothing gourmet about it either—the fish sticks are Mrs. Paul's; the French fries came in a big bag in the freezer section of Food Lion), so I'll close. Please write when you can, or call if you can't write. We'd love to have news of you.

Love,
Dom

March 10, 1990
Dear Dom,

I'm sorry it's been so long, and this will have to be short. It was nice to hear from you. Doris is here, helping with the baby, and Tyler is working until nine every night. I'm still sore, and tired, and a little down, which they tell me is to be expected (I feel so helpless). The baby's name is Mary, and she's very healthy and normal. She came in at seven pounds, nine ounces, twenty inches long. Pretty blue eyes and dark hair, like mine. Everyone says she looks like me (ha). We would love to come see you but don't know when, as Tyler is working six days a week at the dealership. And of course there's the baby, who so far has been good, with a little trouble sleeping at night. Ms. Beaumont (or Aunt Violet) sounds wonderful and we would love to meet her

She could not bring herself to finish the letter, since it felt so much like lying, *was* lying, so she filled out a card, one of those announcements people send upon the birth of a child, and wrote, in her own hand across the bottom, "We miss you, more later," and sent that. She dropped it into the mailbox with a feeling of deceit and wrongdoing that made her chest hurt. Doris watched her from the picture window, framed there in the sun, squinting into the light. Lily went back along the walk to the front door and in, and started through to the kitchen.

"What was that, sweetie?"

"I was mailing a card."

"But the look on your face."

"Doris, please."

"No, you looked—it looked like you were flipping the switch on the electric chair or something. I never saw such a look of distaste and—well, guilt. You looked guilty."

"Dominic wrote me such a nice newsy letter, that's all. And I sent him that card. I ought to write him a letter, and I'm too tired."

"Don't be so hard on yourself."

"I'll try not to," Lily said.

Doris took a step toward her. "It's been my experience that people tend to get fixated on small things when something much bigger is bothering them."

It struck Lily that she had been fixated on the one big thing. It seemed to her now that her mother had often had a way of stumbling onto the truth by wayward means. She shook her head, and then kept shaking it, not from exasperation now, but with simple denial. "I don't understand."

"There's something not right in this house. And I think it's me. I'm afraid I've overstayed my welcome."

"No," Lily said. "Now, stop that. I'd like to quit worrying about what everybody's going through. We have the baby to think about. I'm tired, that's all."

3

THEY DROVE DORIS to the airport in Memphis at the end of that week. The sky clouded over, threatening rain, and Doris joked about her irrational fear of flying in clouds and amid storms, her face betraying how serious the fear was. Lily changed the subject, talking about a visit to Virginia. As they said their good-byes, Doris extracted a promise that they would come north as soon as the baby could safely make the trip. Tyler liked the idea of going back to Virginia, and started agitating for it on the way home from the airport. They could afford to take the time, he said. There wasn't anything in particular keeping them in Mississippi. Lily didn't want to go until she had gotten into some routine with Mary, who still did not sleep through the night, and was often colicky and difficult. They had been to the pediatrician twice because she wasn't keeping her milk down and had developed a low-grade fever. These things ebbed, and then came back, and then ebbed again. The doctor assured them that there was nothing to worry about. But Lily worried anyway. She did not want to go north anytime soon.

They hadn't said anymore about Tyler's plans to quit the dealership and join the army, and she went through the days hoping the thing would go away. But it was always at the back of her mind.

She did not want him to leave and she was ambivalent and filled with anxiety about what might happen if he stayed, what life was going to be like now, with the baby, and Doris gone away. Matters kept growing more complicated. Occasionally she would stop and think about her marriage objectively, the way a sociologist looks at the makeup of a town. It seemed a strange, rudderless thing, drifting from minute to confusing minute: they were a couple with a new child; he went off to work every morning and came home every night; she prepared breakfast, usually, and on the rare nights when he was home from the dealership, he cooked dinner; they used endearments for each other, like other couples; they talked about his day at work, her day at home; they kissed good night, and good morning; he helped with changing diapers and doing the grocery shopping. To anyone else, they looked fine. And yet she kept waking in the dark, trembling with fright, not able to recall what she had dreamed, and with a feeling so essentially wrong in her bones that she had to resist the urge to wake him and begin to say it all out: the thing that she was resisting, now, because there *was* this baby to think of, and she was in this marriage, and she still loved her husband. This was the element that heightened her anxiety most: she did not want to lose her husband, and on a visceral level, under the stream of thought and doubt and the little irritations, she felt everything slipping. So she found herself trying not to think at all. For weeks she was all reaction, getting through the time of healing, and adjusting to the new baby.

She did make several more attempts to form some kind of answer to Dominic's letter but it had been impossible to think what to say. *Dear Dominic, things are fine here. We're getting used to having a baby*

One afternoon she came very close to calling him. She dialed information for New Orleans, got Violet Beaumont's number, and wrote it down. She stood at the phone table for a long time, gazing at the number. But then Mary, crying from her bassinet, supplied her with a distraction that precluded making the call. And later, when she came to thinking about it again, it seemed rather pointless: she would only put herself in the position of having to do more lying.

Tyler never mentioned Dominic. Once, when she talked about him, and about New Orleans, he said, "Like to go down there again someday."

Tonight, he came home and sat on the couch, holding the baby up and cooing at her. Lily opened a beer for him.

"Thanks," he said.

"I almost called Violet Beaumont today."

"Violet who?"

"Dom's—the lady Dom and Manny are staying with."

He stood and put Mary down, and kissed her, and put his hand down in the middle of her stomach and moved her back and forth softly. "Little pitcher," he murmured.

Then he went past Lily, into the kitchen, to the refrigerator. She followed.

"Do you think we could go down there?"

"One day. Sure." He had the refrigerator door open, and stood gazing into it. "What should we do for dinner?" he said. "Did you eat?"

"Tyler, I was asking you something."

"I said 'One day. Sure.' Did you eat already?"

"Yes."

He took a brick of cheese from the refrigerator and closed the door. "Right now I think we should be talking about going to Virginia for a visit. Your father and Peggy have never seen the baby."

"The baby's not up to a road trip."

He had brought a knife out of the utensil drawer and was slicing the cheese. She had the feeling he was purposely not looking at her. "You were just talking about driving to New Orleans," he said, in a forced casual tone.

"That's a matter of half a day. That's not all the way to Virginia."

"So, we'll take it slow. Three or four half days of driving. We'll stop in some nice motels and get room service." He put the knife down, then put a slice of the cheese in his mouth, and stood there chewing. There was almost a breeziness about his demeanor. He held another slice of the cheese, leaning against the counter. "For that matter, we have the money to fly."

She felt curiously sullen, and she strove to keep her voice even and strong. "Look, why're you so anxious to go to Virginia?"

"Why're you so anxious to go to New Orleans?" His eyes widened the smallest increment, but he smiled. "Oh, of course."

"No, that is not it," Lily said. "No one has to say anything."

"Well, but somebody would, wouldn't she?"

"That's not fair."

"I'm not trying to be fair. I'm trying to protect my family."

She watched him take another slice of the cheese.

"I'd like, dear wifey, to go to Virginia," he said. "I'd like to move away from this part of the country. I don't like it with him living so close.

If I join the army, maybe we'll wind up in Germany or somewhere far away. I'd like that."

Lily stared at him.

"In the meantime, why don't we fly to Virginia? Take an airplane, the three of us."

"You don't want Dominic to find out," she said. "Ever."

"The way I look at it," he said without looking up, "I paid for the baby, and I'm supporting her and you. I'm doing the job of the father and in all respects other than biology I *am* the father. I should've told you what the situation was with me before we were married and you should've told me what—what had gone on with you. But we want a family and we are a family and Dominic, forgive me, is gay and has no desire to have a family and never wanted children and is at peace with it, and I think we are perfectly within our rights—"

She started to interrupt him: "I can't believe—"

But he spoke over her, raising his voice. "All right, it's perfectly within *my* rights, okay? Perfectly within my rights to require that what we know about this child is never revealed to anyone. Not to *anyone*, Lily. Not ever."

She turned from him and walked into the living room, where the baby was asleep in the bassinet. He followed her to the entrance of the room and stood there, watching her take Mary from her place and sit down to begin nursing her.

"Do we understand each other at last?" he said.

She did not respond.

"I require an answer," he said.

"Fuck off," she told him.

He went back into the kitchen, and was silent for a long time. Once or twice she heard him shift his weight. At last he went into the bedroom and closed the door. When the baby had finished nursing, Lily put her down, went into the kitchen, and opened a can of tuna fish. She mixed it with mayonnaise and put it on toast, and carried her plate into the living room. She ate quietly, sitting on the couch, rocking the bassinet now and again. The little protests the baby made were the only sounds.

In the bedroom, he had gotten under the blanket and was asleep. She got in, too, and lay there waiting for him to say something. But he was evidently asleep, and in a little while she was, too. She woke in the night from one of her fright dreams and saw that he was up, pacing in the hallway. By his shadow it was apparent that he was agitated, his fists clenching and unclenching; it was as if he were having an argument with himself. She thought of getting up and going to him, but then she remembered how the evening had gone, and she stayed where she was.

Everything, in those hard minutes, felt like a desolation.

In a while he came back to the bed and got in, and settled himself. For a long time she was certain that each was aware of the other's wakefulness. Neither of them uttered a sound.

4

*H*E WAS GONE before the baby stirred, at first light. Lily walked with Mary on her arm through the house, and she looked out the picture window at the silver-limned lawn and trees, the Olds in the driveway, the shadowy hulk of the partially built apartment house. It rather amazed her to see it all so unchanged. Then she reflected that finally nothing had really changed. This was merely the bad feeling of the night.

She called his office at the dealership, but there wasn't any answer.

Later in the morning, she got the baby dressed warmly, put her in the car seat, and drove into the city. It was a gray, breezy day with a hint of the coming spring in it. The wind had a balmy fragrance, though it still carried the chill of winter rain.

She spent an hour in the library, and then drove back to the little house. No one called; no one came by. She fed Mary and put her down, and then tried to write a little. It was almost impossible to concentrate. Across the way, construction on the apartment building was in full swing with the warmer weather, and there was the incessant roaring of a gas generator, the rhythmic, metallic clank of a pile driver. In the kitchen, fixing herself some crackers and cheese, she saw that he had taken some ground beef out of the freezer, so she knew he would be home in the early evening. She put music on, The Police, and tried to clean a little. The only thing to do was to observe the usual motions, get through the day. Finally she sat on the sofa in the light of the big window and read in Mary Kingsley's book about West Africa.

Tyler came home just before dark. He walked up to the door and in, and past her to the kitchen, where he started to prepare dinner, cutting celery and tomatoes, breaking up a head of lettuce. She went to the entrance of the kitchen and watched him for a time, but said nothing. He took the ground beef out of the refrigerator and began making patties. He made three.

"I'm not hungry," she said.

He put one of the patties away, slapped it into the unformed mass in the package, wrapped it, and put it back.

"Tyler," she said.

He made no answer. He set a fire under the skillet and started grilling the burgers, standing with his back to her.

"All right," she said, and went back into the living room. She put the television on. She was sitting there staring at it when he came in with a book under his arm, the plate of burgers, a bag of potato chips, and a beer. He sat on the couch at the other end, put the book down, and the plate, then tore open the bag of potato chips. Some of the chips fell to the floor. He picked them up and set them on the table. Then he reached over and turned the television off, flipped the book open to its marked place, and began to eat one of the burgers while he read. The book was an anthology of philosophers: *From Socrates to Sartre*. She had put it in the bookshelf in the hallway that afternoon, having picked it up from the floor on his side of the bed.

He turned a page, and took another big bite of the burger.

"Tyler, this is childish," she said. "It won't solve anything."

Silence.

She stood and moved to the television, then changed her mind and sat in the chair opposite him. "Tyler."

"You talking to me?" he said.

Now she was quiet.

He took a bite of the burger, and stared at the open book, chewing. She could hear the little breathing through his nose as he chewed, and he kept jamming the big sandwich into his face, taking it down greedily and with a kind of inattention, as if this were simply to remove a pang, and not for the slightest pleasure.

"Tyler, listen—" she began.

He looked up at her with an expression so fierce that it stopped her.

"I'm eating right now. I have to feel relaxed to eat. I don't want any upset when I eat. If you've got something to say, say it later. Or better yet, write it. Yeah," he went on, plainly happy with himself for thinking of this, talking loud and openmouthed, so that she saw the half-chewed food on his tongue. "I like that idea. That's fuck'n perfect. Write it down. I'll read it when I get a chance. When in my busy workday I have some opportunity to stop and think, or spend five goddamn minutes."

She said, "Since when is my writing an area of irritation to you?"

"Did I say that?" he fairly shouted at her. "I don't—you know, actually, I don't remember saying that. I think I didn't say it. But then, what the hell do I know? Maybe I did. And if I did, well, Jesus Christ in a wheelbarrow, please forgive me, because if there's one thing I don't want to do, it's express any irritation with you about anything, anything at all."

"The baby," Lily said. "Will you please—the baby."

"Oh, right. The baby. Jesus Christ, I forgot the baby. How could I— me, the father of record—how could I forget the baby." This was said at the level of a scream.

And the baby began to cry, a startled, frightened sound. Lily stood, crying herself, and reached into the bassinet. "Are you proud now?" she said.

He was quiet for a moment. But then he picked up the book and threw it across the room. It slammed against the wall and brought down a picture in its frame—a print Lily had bought of Monet's blue cathedrals. He got up and stalked into the kitchen. She heard water running, and dishes clattering in the sink. Mary cried and trembled in her arms, looking in the direction of the entrance to the kitchen. Lily went back to the bedroom and got into bed, cradling the infant, who still howled and complained and shook, the smallest quaking, deep down. Lily was weeping, too.

Finally, the tumult in the other room stopped. The television was on, another kind of ruckus. Lily fell asleep to the sound of it, while Mary nursed.

She woke to the motion of his hands under her arm, moving her aside so he could lift the baby. She screamed, "Don't you touch her!" And the baby started crying again.

He stood there, a dark, looming shape with the light of the hallway behind him. She pulled Mary toward her, and waited for him to do whatever he had it in him to do.

He remained still a few moments, and then he moved through the house, an almost casual striding, to the front door and out. He did not slam it. She got up in time to see him drive away in the demo. He went fast, tires squealing, the taillights disappearing down the road, and he was gone in the darkness.

She nursed Mary, and then watched her sleep. It was too late to call anyone. Too late to go anywhere. She listened to the small breathing, the little stirrings and moans, and was afraid. The night seemed borderless; she couldn't imagine that the sun shone anywhere. Finally she drifted off to a gray, edgy slumber, filled with dread and foreboding. She woke to the sound of him moving unsteadily through the rooms. He came to the entrance of the bedroom. She heard his breathing, there, and she lay perfectly still and quiet. He stood for a long time, then lurched away and went into the living room and turned the television on. She listened to it for an hour or so before falling off to sleep again.

Mary woke her toward dawn, trying to work up a cry. She sat up and held the baby, nursing her, and when she had finished with that, she changed her and lay back down. But Mary didn't want to sleep now. In the other room, the television played. Lily got out of the bed and walked in there. Tyler was sitting on the couch with his head back, mouth open, deeply asleep. There were two bottles of beer on the coffee table in front of him. She turned the television off, and started out of the room.

"I was watching that."

She went back and turned it on.

"Thank you."

In the bedroom, she got dressed, and changed Mary again. There was no sound from the living room. For a time she sat on the bed, fully dressed, holding the baby, who gazed up at her with eyes that seemed to contain all the fathomless knowledge of the universe.

Tyler was up and moving around now, coughing, clearing his throat, sighing. She stood, took a deep breath, gathered all her courage, and walked into the living room. He was by the open window, disheveled, running his hands through his hair. She lay the baby down on the couch, brought her suitcase out of the closet, and began putting things into it: clothes from her bedroom bureau, some of the things Millicent and Doris and others had bought for the baby.

"Where're you going," he said. There was no inflection in it at all.

"I don't know," she told him. "Out of here."

"I'm going. There's no reason for you to go."

She looked at him.

"I have to go to work," he said. "Remember?" He stared. There wasn't anything in his face. His eyes, though red and irritated, looked dead—the flat gaze of a doll. "I can see how you mean it."

She went on working: stacking blouses and dresses she hadn't worn since she had begun to show; gathering all her work on the play, all her letters, and some books, it was all going in.

"You gonna carry that, and the baby?"

"I'll manage."

Taking a step toward her, he grasped her elbow. It wasn't rough, but she pulled away as if he had attempted to strike her. "Look, I'm sorry," he said. "I'm sorry, Lily. I let my temper get the best of me. It won't happen again."

"Do you think it's just this one instance?" she said.

His face seemed to go soft. He looked down, and then off, out the window, and she saw that tears had come from his eyes and made their way down his cheek. "I'm sorry for everything." He sniffled. "Could you give me a chance, here. I've never had to deal with anything like this before."

"It's new to me, too," she said.

"Look, we—we had this—this one fight. I wasn't there—all right—I wasn't there when you had the baby. I chickened out. I'm sorry for it."

She sat down on the couch and put her hands to her face. For an instant, he wasn't even there, and it was just Lily, the baby, and her sorrow.

"I've been so low," he went on. "I've let it get to me."

"Please, go on to work," she managed. "You'll be late to work."

He came to where she sat and knelt in front of her. "Tell me you won't leave while I'm gone. Please don't leave, Lily. I love you. I love Mary. I'm—I was just trying to protect that—my—what I'm—what I've been working for. My family. None of it—nothing of anything makes the slightest bit of sense to me but this, Lily. I swear. You—you got to talking about New Orleans and I felt threatened. My mother left when I was five fucking years old. Can you imagine what that does to a person? I got scared it was going to happen to me again. I don't—I can't have it happen to me again. I couldn't help myself, Lily, please." He put his head down in her lap and wept. She touched his hair, a caressing motion, trying to soothe him. It came to her that in a way he was still that little boy who had been abandoned by his mother, and he was faced now with something for which he could find no action or answer, no solution but more anguish—a tribulation yielding nothing but continual increase of itself, compounding and broadening even as he wrestled with it. She realized that she was feeling sorry for him, and very gently she pushed him away, took his shoulders, pushing, so that he straightened, with his tear-streaked boy's face, that ruggedly fine-looking face, and regarded her.

"You have to get to work," she said. "You'll be late for work."

"Promise you won't leave me."

"I promise, Tyler. Please."

He got to his feet. "I'm so sorry."

She couldn't think of anything to tell him.

"I love you," he said.

Gazing up at him, she murmured, "I love you, too." She stood and put her arms around him.

"I'll do better," he said into her ear. "I mean it. You'll see."

5

Spring came with heavy rains and gloomy gray days and winds. There was flooding on the delta, and the construction on the apartment house had come to a standstill. In the last week of March, Sheri told everyone that she thought she might be pregnant. Millicent planned a party, which was to be outside, around the pool. But it rained all that day, and everyone congregated inside. Millicent had hired three musicians from New Orleans, a guitarist, a fiddler, and a bass player, to entertain. The fiddle player was a young, bronze-colored man, quite beautiful to look at. While he played the fiddle, the baby, suspended in her carrier, facing front over Lily's abdomen, made wonderful delighted screeching sounds, fascinated and wide-eyed. Lily watched the top of the small bobbing head with its new silky black hair, and she saw the others as they laughed and murmured together about the enchantment in her child's face. Millicent said the baby could claim responsibility for the party's success.

It was at the end of this party that Millicent announced her intention of marrying Roger Gault. The wedding would take place in the fall. The next day, Sheri called Lily, crying, to say that she was not pregnant after all.

"I'll tell you, honey, I was happy, and then I was scared, and it all seemed so wide and pretty, like a good dream, and now it's just—it turns out it was just—nothing. Nothing."

"It'll happen," Lily told her.

"I don't think Nick's been near me more than twice since January."

"He's just so sad."

"So am I." Sheri sobbed. "I miss my father. I wish none of it happened. I miss the way Nick used to be."

"I know," Lily told her. "He's trying to find his way. It must be so awful for him."

"I saw David last week."

Lily held the receiver against the side of her face and gazed at the sleeping form of her baby.

"It was just to talk to somebody who isn't weighted down with this—this suffering."

She kept silent, listening to the small sobbing on the other end.

"I'm sorry," Sheri said.

"Don't," she said. "Really, Sheri—please. The baby's awake."

"I don't know what to do. I'm only human. I don't know what Nick expects."

"Sheri, the baby—"

"I know, I know. The baby."

"I'm sure it'll be all right." As she spoke these words, Lily felt a sinking at heart, for the empty sound they made.

"I don't know why I told you," Sheri said. "You've got enough to worry about."

"No one will know from me," Lily answered.

Again, she heard the muffled sounds of the other woman's attempt to gain control of herself. A moment later, Sheri sighed, apologized, and said good-bye.

6

1893

I have made my way from Cabinda to Kacongo—King Leopold of Belgium's province—and on, until I can now say I have seen the territory. In Kacongo, the sleeping sickness and smallpox are ravaging the populace. I saw entire communities wiped out by what the Africans call the spotted death. That is bad enough, but then there are so many people—and so many of them children—in the dreadful final stages of the sleeping sickness, lethargic, without a shred of energy or will left, as if doped, looking at you with the lidded, unseeing gaze of death. And there are the lepers—awful to contemplate, human shapes in these lumpish and terrible masses of flesh. They are shunned in Africa as elsewhere, but there is a different reason for it. The Africans believe the lepers are under the spell of witchcraft; they have no idea of contagion, and nothing in their way of looking upon the world has made them ready to believe even the suggestion that these ills might have another cause, something in nature that can be outwitted, or worked with, in order to gain some relief. They suffer, and their suffering makes a terrible kind of sense to them.

In one of the smaller villages, I found five awful things stuck on sticks, in a cloud of noisy flies. This was in the very middle of the village. I stepped closer and realized quickly that these were organs—human livers and lungs. When I sought, with a distinct edge of fright, to know the reason, the guide, who had come from this village and had accompanied me through several others first, informed me that these objects were the witches that had been found inside witch doctors who had died of the spotted death. Later that same week, a woman of the village died of what I could ascertain in an autopsy was a simple aneurysm of the abdominal aortic artery; but I was told by the villagers that she had witched herself.

—She no sick, I was told. Then she go die one time. She done witch herself.

According to the best experts in this village, she had been eaten by her own familiar from the inside.

From Kacongo, as I say, I went on, stopping in villages and trading with the people, and doing some of my own wandering and collecting. My portmanteau grows almost too heavy for even the bearers to carry. I went on foot when I could, shunning the hammock that so many Europeans seem to delight in using. I think one would feel silly being carted about by others, like a fool king. I walked, and insisted on doing mostly for myself. And in my wanderings I met several Fjort, who seemed proud and quite happy and frankly to enjoy staring at me. I must report that in several ports of call I was quizzed as to my lack of a husband. I took to saying that Husband would join me later, even to some of the Europeans I met. It was simpler that way, though no less vexing for being necessary. At the Congo River, I was reunited with The Lagos, *and we steamed up to Matadi. We passed through the swirl of fast waters and raving river called Hell's Cauldron, and on the high hillsides they were burning the bush, the flames licking higher than I could ever have believed possible from those peaks, into the heavens, with a boiling black cloud. I had read of this part of the river in Stanley's accounts, and he did not do it justice, nor, I suppose, can I. As night fell we watched the wild, throbbing glow, such a terrible shade of red, on the dark sky.*

At Matadi, we rode the Congo Free State Railway, much to our fright, for it is always a risky proposition. Apparently, even in this climate, where one pays so heavily for the smallest mistake or miscalculation, riding this railway is one of the most dangerous of occupations. Aside from one harrowing hour when we were parked above a precipice of several hundred feet while a few lighthearted lunatics repaired a rail that had come loose, we had an uneventful journey. McNab and Captain Murray and I made this trip, cheerfully signing papers that relieved the railway of any responsibility for our lives.

I am heading home now.

I have walked in Africa, and I have sat in a canoe aground in an African river, waiting to be harvested by crocodiles. I have collected specimens for the British Museum, and acted as a scientist in all circumstances, even those of extremity and terror. When the terror comes, it manifests itself with a coppery taste on my tongue. When I receive that sensation and that taste, I know it's time to act. And so I act. Or react. As I have quickly learned, sometimes it is best simply to react. Any motion, toward or from, lessens the paralyzing effects of the terror. That is science.

On one of my last nights in the bush, I went walking, keeping to the path and feeling the strong sensation of the danger one is always in at night in such places, and thrilling to it. I wanted to test the quality of light on the river from a height of a few feet into the trees. But there was a path. I had gone some way down it when I came upon several Africans in some kind of ritual costume: animal skins and beads and chains of lion's teeth. I was immediately aware of that taste in my mouth as I turned around and strove to make a hasty and soundless retreat, since if this was what I suspected it was—that is, a secret society—I knew that the chances were very good that I would have walked my last in the African, or any other, forest.

Secret societies do not relish visits from strangers, especially of the female variety, and they treat intrusions with a quick death—or, in some instances, a not-so-quick death. So I scrambled as quietly as I could in the other direction from these gentlemen. But I was followed and accosted, and made to walk with them deeper into the bush; two of them held me by my arms, walking on either side of me. "Gentle firmness" is the phrase that best explains how I was held. I did not protest. Silence, I intuited, was required. One of them uttered commands, in whispers. I was unable to make much sense of it. Then they began to emit the strangest noises, sounds that I knew had to have come from their throats but which had an inhuman quality: clicks and clucks and barks, whooping howls and whines. When this ceased, we were the only quiet in the whole of night. We came to a clearing, and were still. I was held still, and remained so, and after a long, excruciatingly slow passage, monkeys came from the trees to look at these curious shapes in the darkness, and were then captured. I came to realize that I had been drafted by a company of monkey hunters. Their mode of operation was to appear bizarre to the monkeys, to excite their curiosity. And of course I was very much the most bizarre thing these men had ever seen. They were quite kind to me after they'd made their catch. It was as though I were their mascot now, and I feared they might want to keep me.

Soon I will be boarding another ship—the SS La Rochelle, *bound for Britain. I almost said home, friend.*

∽

In Libreville, in the Congo Français, she finds herself among English-speaking people for the first time in months—she revels in the sounds, and makes an effort to get others to talk, merely to talk at her, so she can bask in the comfort of it: her own language. She has been moving among Africans, Dutch, French, and Portuguese, and finding a way to communicate with them. It is only when she is again among the English that the mental strain of all that becomes apparent to her. It is as if some part of her consciousness has been at a sort of rigid attention for so long that relaxing the muscles provides her with a sensation of profound rest at last. She finds herself thanking people for the smallest things, sometimes for a simple gesture of speech, a hello, or a wish that she have a good morning.

The SS *La Rochelle* steams north to Cameroon, with its white-capped mountain showing from a far distance. They speak German in Cameroon, and she goes ashore with the captain, a man named Harrison, whose narrow features and high-pitched voice and drawing-room manner toward her she finds unnerving. The air is warm, wind-less, and blue in the distances, without the slightest haze. A clarity that gives her a small ache at her heart, because she knows that in England now the winter is coming on.

In port, she sees a nun approaching others coming from the vessel, with a look of disquiet and worry on her face. The nun's cheeks are pit-ted and scarred, and her eyes appear to be drained of all color. Coming closer, Mary sees that they are a pale blue, and that one of them is blind. There is a membranous something, also blue, over the iris. The nun turns to her, and says:

—English?

—Yes, Mary says.

—Missionary?

She shakes her head, and starts to move past the other woman, but something in the blue eyes stops her.

—I have some knowledge of medicine, Mary tells her.

—We have sickness nearby. A settlement. Fever.

Captain Harrison is standing a few feet away, but he has heard them. He gives the nun a small bow and then faces Mary.

—We'll be in port for a couple of weeks, Miss Kingsley.

—Lead on, Mary says to the nun.

The way is more arduous, and is farther than the nun had indicated. They climb for a few hundred feet away from the harbor, into deeper and deeper forest. Mary is short of breath. The air has grown hotter, and more densely moist. Eventually, after many stops to rest and after being joined by another, younger nun who nevertheless takes the climb with more trouble than any of them, they descend for an exhausting period, swatting at thousands of flying insects, and mosquitoes, and at last emerge into a flat, open plain, a clearing that stretches widely away to the south, and is bordered on one side by a tributary of the Congo River. The settlement is not much more than a few rows of thatch-roofed huts built on stilts. The sick are lying in these huts, separated by yards of matted earth and by the ladders necessary for egress and entrance from one to the other. There are twenty-three men, ages varying from twenty to fifty-one, each of them quite ill, racked with fever and dysentery-like symptoms. Lying on a cot alone in one hut, is Deerforth. Mary says his name, and he doesn't recognize it, or her. He's raving. He hallucinates snakes crawling all over him. She holds him down with the help of the blue-eyed nun. It dawns on Mary that she hasn't even remembered to ask the other woman's name.

She orders all of the victims to be moved to the central building, which is large enough to house them, and contains some supplies of quinine and other agents with which to fight fevers. The movement of the sick allows the nuns to keep a better watch on them, and to remove the dead with more safety and efficiency. Two of the men die in the first night. Mary keeps a vigil by Deerforth's bed. His fever is so high that she fears for his life every minute. But the hours pass, and he drowses, mutters, moans, going on. She keeps putting a cool, damp cloth on his forehead, and in only seconds the cloth is hot, a clammy heat in it. She keeps putting it back in the water and replacing it. By morning, he begins gasping for air. She calls for the nuns, and stands by his bedside, exhausted, while a nun administers the last rites.

—Deerforth, Mary says. We saw each other again. I'm 'ere. You are not dying, Deerforth, and you are not alone. Talk to me. I wonder where you went after we landed in Saint Paul de Loanda. I would like you to tell me now. Please tell me.

—I fear it'll be soon, the nun says. God have mercy.

—Shut up, Mary says. Please.

She sits on the bed and takes his hand. It is burning. She feels the heat in his blood, and now she begins, quietly, to weep.

—Deerforth.

The nun drenches a rag in water and places it, again, on his forehead. He begins to thrash, and suddenly his eyes open wide.

—Ah, he says. God.

Then he lies back and is quite awfully still.

After a time, Mary reaches up to close his eyes, still weeping. The nun watches her.

—Did you know him well?

Mary doesn't answer.

—Who was he?

—A friend, Mary says, low.

—Someone close.

—Yes. No. I didn't know him well.

—Such a terrible effort it takes to pass on, the nun says. One's body doesn't want to let go of the spirit.

—Leave us, says Mary. Please.

The nun goes out. And in the silence, Mary crosses Deerforth's hands, and wraps his jaw shut in the soggy rag that she had been using to cool his forehead. She prepares him for the grave, working alone in the silence—or in the only silence that ever obtains in a place like Africa. She sobs through the whole process, remembering her father and mother, and wondering at the tremendous mystery of it. Life seems so savagely not what the polite society of her growing up had ever suggested it was.

Before the week is out, four more men die of the fever. She and the nuns take turns keeping bedside vigils, and digging graves. The insects are unbearable, and Mary has taken to calling the house Centipede Villa. The others, the nuns, and two others, doctors, who have come from the port to help, all marvel at her strength, her refusal to rest, and her bravery. They use the word, and to her face.

—I have never been in the company of someone truly brave, says one of the doctors, a man with the rough look of a veteran coaster, and the bearing of a sad, tired, elderly curate. He is indeed a priest; his health is precarious, and has been for more than a decade. He has recurring fevers, and there is a jaundiced something in his eyes. The bones of his skull are visible in his face and forehead. His name is Empson. The nuns, of course, call him Father. He has a way of staring at Mary, as if he can't quite believe his eyes. He tells her that he had been on the verge of losing his faith, and that finding her has changed his life.

Mary deflects this with a joke about the heat and the constant sodden conditions and the biting insects. Only this morning, she killed a scorpion.

—I say it simply and in all truth, he tells her. I have never been with a truly brave human being, anywhere. I have been with fools and idiots and braggarts and killers, but never anyone truly brave. The experience has shaken me.

Mary lifts her shoulders slightly, not quite a shrug. It is night; there are groans coming from the trees, animal sighs and growls. A monkey screams, shrill as a woman. Mary kills a centipede, and sweeps it from the table. She begins to tell him about her first day in Africa, being chased by the dog-faced monkey and falling through the ceiling of a cotton-processing factory. She attempts to make him laugh, but he only stares, solemnly, almost lugubriously, a man gazing upon an ideal in which he had long ago ceased to believe. That is the expression on his face.

—Dr. Empson, you're making me uneasy, she says.

—Forgive me.

A little more than a week later, the fever has passed, those who live are leaving or are well enough to talk about it, and the dead are buried. The storm of illness is over. She packs her things, pays a visit to the displaced earth where she knows Deerforth is buried, and then, saying good-bye to the doctors and the nuns, she heads alone back to the port at Cameroon, and the SS *La Rochelle*. It will be Christmas soon. There's a fine soft rain falling, and it soaks her to the skin. She trudges along, with a sense of herself as coming to the end of this journey, and wanting it not to end. The thought of England is strangely without effect for her; she feels nothing about it. That small, wintry island, with its cities and its empire, and the whole broad, blood-soaked continent of Europe take on a sort of unreality for her, as if it were all something hinted at in dreams, unattainable and finally undesirable, too.

She doesn't want to leave.

The SS *La Rochelle* steams north to Calabar, and the offices of the British Niger Coast protectorate. While the ship takes on tons of palm oil for the journey back to what Captain Harrison calls The Home Island, Mary goes through everything she has gathered and packed, her specimens in their jars of preserving fluid, her collections of charms and beads, and carved figures. She rewrites her catalog of artifacts, and composes a few letters. It is still difficult to believe that she is going back to England. The minutes draw out, and she can almost believe this is the rest of the life she will lead.

In the evening, she takes the dinghy with Captain Harrison, and two others, into port. Calabar is soaking under a fine rain. She makes her way to the offices of the protectorate, and Captain Harrison is gallant, walking along beside her, holding an umbrella over her, and talking about the savages, as he calls them, that they encounter in the streets.

Mary receives his alarmed consideration of her in tolerant silence. The offices are housed in the center of a high-walled courtyard. Captain Harrison introduces her to a man named MacDonald, the head administrator of the protectorate. He's a tall, barrel-chested man with a graying beard, trimmed so close to his face that it appears from a distance to be coloration rather than whiskers.

—I have heard of you already, Miss Kingsley, he says in a rich baritone. I know Captain Murray of *The Lagos*. I saw him only last week.

—How is Captain Murray? she asks.

—He's bound for England. I expect he's reached the Canaries by now. He spoke of you with great wonderment.

—As you see, I'm hardly a wonder of any kind.

—Consider it an opinion, then, which I'm reluctant to contradict.

Mary nods, smiling. This is the sort of talk she habitually dismisses, and is always annoyed by, since it singles her out for being a woman in the circumstance, and her qualities as therefore appreciable only because of this: no man, undergoing the same things she has undergone, is ever considered anything at all but average. Yet this Mr. MacDonald has such a light of humor and even irony in his eyes; it is as if he's perfectly aware of her feelings, and is speaking for the benefit of Captain Harrison. It is like a joke between them. She says:

—If you find me so wonderful, I suppose it should be no surprise to you that I am determined to return to Africa as soon as possible. I 'ave only begun, 'ere.

—Just so. We must stay in touch, he says. I'll make an introduction for you to my wife, in England. Lady MacDonald. Well, Ethel is her name. Awful name, Ethel, but a marvelous woman. You'll find her very agreeable.

—I've no doubt of it.

They have tea, and Captain Harrison talks about the failed efforts of missionaries to inculcate Christian values into the savages. In his mind, the prospect is fruitless, doomed to failure from the start. He favors trade, yet sees it only in terms of plunder for the Empire. He has no interest in preserving anything of the life he encounters in these rivers and estuaries; it all looks benighted to him, a region of hellish vapors and feral people. He wants ever so badly to get back to The Home Island.

MacDonald gives Mary a rueful look, sipping his tea and waiting for Captain Harrison to finish talking.

—The Home Island, he says. I haven't heard it called that in a while.

—Yes, well. I'll be glad when my services are rendered, and I no longer have to make the voyage down here. I'm not ashamed to confess that I've reached the end of my tolerance for it all. What I wouldn't give for an English winter.

Later, as they are taking leave, MacDonald gives Mary a piece of paper with an address on it.

—This is where you will find my lady, he says. I trust that you will be great friends.

—I already feel your trust is not misplaced.

He stands back and appears to rock on his heels, a gesture of gladness in her, almost like a swagger.

—I feel I have made a wonderful new friend.

—Well, Mary says, that speaks of a generous spirit.

She and Captain Harrison stride down the wet street, past lantern-burning windows, and she looks back once to the entrance of the courtyard, where MacDonald stands watching. He waves, and she waves back.

—Good man, says Captain Harrison. I have always liked him.

—Yes, Mary says, deciding to ignore the tone of condescension in his voice, as if his imprimatur is necessary for her to form any opinion. But perhaps she's being too hard on him. In truth, there is an aspect to certain English attitudes about Africa that angers her; she sees so much of it now from the point of view of the Africans. She cannot help this, nor does she wish to help it. She embraces it.

Gazing out at the drifting coastline of the strange and mysterious and beautiful continent, retracing the exotic cities and ports north, she begins to plan how she will accomplish the task of convincing the museum, or Guillemard, whoever can supply her with means, that she must return, must come back to this wild coast and go deeper, deeper in.

7

There is a story that you drove a leopard away from the centipede villa, in the middle of a night when you had, for some brief period of surcease from the vigils over the sick, fallen asleep. You threw a gourd full of limewater at it and scared it off. This sort of thing happened all the time, apparently, and you just went about doing what you set out to do, and you seem in your writings to be paying no particular attention to the astounding nature of such behavior. The almost offhand way you report these things, the humor you seem to have no trouble finding in them, leaves me cold, quite frankly. I don't suppose there is anything else you could have done, and you were probably very uneasy telling these heroics on yourself, and so by default, your attitude must tend to shrug it all off. It leaves such a hard example for me, though. I can't find the bravery you had in such unfair abundance. And it is only when I have the time to reflect that you are controlling your fear, that there is no true bravery without fear—it is only when I think of this that I can come back to my fascination and love of you, for what you did. For everything you did—even, in some strange, endearing way, your mistakes.

I wonder what you would make of this play I'm trying to construct out of your life. Such a brief life, and yet you crowded so much into those last seven years. And in fact, when one considers the long process of your self-education, it becomes obvious enough that you crowded a lot of a kind of living into the whole thirty-seven.

The raw spring rains gave way to a burning sun, and humidity. Tyler bought a window air conditioner, and began again, gingerly, to agitate for a trip north. He brought it up like teasing, and Lily teased back. They had received no more letters from New Orleans, and Doris called almost every day, wanting to know how they were doing. Lily could answer with some truthfulness that they were doing fine. When Nick and Sheri came to visit, or Lily and Tyler went to visit them, there was always so much unspoken between them that Lily felt it as tension: apart from what she knew about the marriage from Sheri, there was the fact of the shared nightmare the two men had been through. And then, too, Tyler and Nick saw each other all day at the dealership. They would talk about the day's work, and then grow quiet, and they would begin to seem faintly restive, though Nick was unfailingly kind to Lily, and attentive to the baby. The visits grew farther and farther apart. Sheri and Millicent still stopped by in the days, frequently just as Lily had gotten the baby to sleep and was planning a nap. But she was always happy to see them. Withal, several days could pass in which Lily would feel almost comfortable, nearly content, in the middle of things with her baby and her work, and with the people who filled her life. Then, without warning, the waking in the nights would come, the sense of a sort of primal violation: a badness, a shadow that haunted her.

There had been no more pathological scenes with Tyler, and mostly the tensions that arose were allowed to dissipate reasonably. They were considerate of each other, and they could take pleasure in the baby's fast-developing personality: certain things brought a lovely, open, half-moon-eyed smile to the little round face, and on occasion her bright voice would come forth, a trill that charmed them both. They had exquisite moments watching the child.

Their lovemaking had begun again; it was quiet, and rather surprisingly tender. The first time, Lily initiated it. They were sitting on the couch, reading in the quiet, with the baby asleep between them. She reached over and touched his wrist. "I've missed you."

"I've missed you, too."

She waited.

"Do you think we could?"

She took him by the hand and led him into the bedroom. He was tentative, and very careful of her, and she discovered that she could forget herself, and take pleasure in him. Afterward, they lay in each other's arms.

He sighed. "I have such regrets."

"Don't," she said.

"I mean in the way I've treated you through this."

"Let's not talk about it. Not now."

"I think I've lost my sense of timing."

They were quiet for a few moments. And he sighed again.

"Tyler, don't."

"No, I was thinking about work."

"Well, don't."

"You're right." He leaned up on one elbow to look at her. "I think you're such a beautiful woman." The words sounded wrong, in that tone—it was almost forlorn. He shook his head. "I haven't deserved you."

She pulled him down to kiss her.

This time, things went less well. His movements hurt her a little, and she held tight to him, feeling the straining in his back and sides. She had a moment of being too conscious of him as separate from her, and then she worked to make this an aspect of the gratification of him there in the bed with her. This time it was purely sex, and she knew it and felt guilty for it as he pulled out of her and lay over on his back, sighing, not with regret, but with satiation. "That was good," he murmured.

"Yes."

"You know," he said, "the odd thing is that I didn't really miss it after Mary came. Those first weeks I don't think I even thought of it. And when we were—weren't getting along, it didn't enter my mind. I mean, I couldn't think of you that way. It's only been in the last few weeks that I've thought of it and I wondered if you were, too."

"I was," Lily said.

He kissed her and she smiled into his kiss.

"I hate it when we're not getting along," he said.

She nodded, and was at a loss for something else to tell him. The truth was that there was only one reason they had fought, and that reason, for all the adjustments and careful gestures toward affection and companionship, had not gone away. She wondered if he really supposed the problem was solved, or lived past, behind them. Yes. His behavior showed it: he believed, or at least he wanted to behave as if, they had reached life on the other side of the trouble. And she knew that when she brought it up again, if she did so, the trouble would begin all over again.

"Tell me how things're going with the play," he said.

"Oh, right now I'm only studying. Not writing much. Well, not as much as I'd like. It's going all right, though."

He said, "Well, how's the studying coming along?"

"I've got this problem—you know. This baby."

"Mary, a problem?"

She knew he wished to tease with her, hoped to be lighthearted as they had just come close to being. She couldn't muster the feeling. It felt wrong, like a lie they might tell each other. When the baby stirred in the other room, she was relieved, and hoped he hadn't perceived it. But Tyler was not dense, and he spent the rest of that evening off to himself, turning the pages of his books.

8

 Tyler DECIDED that he wanted to go to Europe in the fall, sometime after Millicent's wedding. He'd started saving money for it, he said. They might live in Italy for a few years. Rome. Why not? Lily could use it for her writing. Mary could learn to speak two languages, growing up. He hadn't spoken about the army at all in the past weeks, and while the new plan was disconcerting, it was nevertheless something he brought home with him, that he discussed openly with her. Over these months with the baby, watching her go through the small increments of growth, Lily had come to realize how much she was fitted to this task, and how rewarding it was for her. She liked being needed so completely, though she believed the feeling was probably common to the state of having a child. But there was something else, too, something quite physical, including the faintly sour odor of the baby's breath near her face in the nights, when the child lay at her side to nurse. Tyler, sleeping soundly on the other side of the bed—oblivious to this pleasure she received, and separated from it, too—seemed obscurely peripheral, for all his efforts to involve himself.

He had taken charge of the four o'clock feedings, using formula that the pediatrician had suggested to them. He was working so hard. At the dealership, Nick and he seemed to have formed a zone of comfort between them, though there were nights when Tyler appeared rather sorrowfully tense, and would mutter that work was on his mind whenever he caught her watching him. She understood that the longer the truth of Mary's paternity was kept from the others, the harder things would be when the time came to reveal it. And it would have to be revealed sooner or later. Yet she couldn't find the way to broach the subject. It was something the two of them avoided with all the self-consciousness of a person trying to keep from noticing a scar, or a bad lisp.

He came home with talk about Rome. He had picked up some brochures at a travel agency, and he brought some books from the library.

She was surprised by how much the idea appealed to her.

The little milestones came and went through the days: Mary rolled over on her own; she lifted her head and came to a wobbly all fours; she ate rice cereal and strained peaches, Lily spooning it carefully into her mouth and catching it as it came back out and down the dimpled chin. Tyler helped with this, a long and patient operation, getting the little jar of strained food down. The mess was comical. They had it all over them, and Tyler washed the high chair they had put her in, a beatific smile on his face. Lily noted this as she nursed Mary, and some of what the child had gotten on her mouth was on Lily's nipple. The little mouth worked so perfectly. Tyler came and watched, and when he said how miraculous it all was, his voice faltered. In the mornings, now, they listened to the child's babblings and lip sounds, a form of singing.

Lily kept her forebodings to herself.

Sometimes, it was all like a game they were involved in, a pretend game that children might play. The unreality of it was never far from her thoughts.

9

May 6, 1990
Dear ones,

Just wondering how you-all are. The spring by the water here has been a soaked affair. You pour yourself a glass of anything cold and the glass drips on you, forms a puddle around itself on the table. I've never seen such humidity, and the air conditioner Aunt Violet has only cools a little radius around it. So we three sit there in the evenings and several times we have sat in chairs sleeping there, too. At night I lay a sheet and pillows on the cool wooden floor between the upstairs rooms—Aunt Violet's and ours—and sleep there, for the little cross breeze. And it's only May, for God's sake.

Manny's working as a short-order cook in one of the joints in the Quarter. Nothing fancy. He makes eggs and bacon and hamburgers, that sort of thing. Turkey melts. It's a chain, and stuck right in the middle of these world-class establishments. You wouldn't think it could survive, but they are constantly busy and Manny comes home exhausted, discouraged, and in a bad mood, though he's mostly pretty cool with it. It's a job, and it helps pay the bills. When he's down, Mrs. Beaumont and I are understanding, but then it's been so hot in the days that sometimes we're not in all that much of a good mood either. I'm still working in the bookstore. We don't have a lot of time to socialize, though we do a little. I see some people I met in a writing group I joined, and they are all fine people, and they treat me wonderfully. But I don't really confide in any of them, the way you and I used to, Lily, when we were students and so sure of everything. I'm still a little at sea, I guess. I'm beginning to wonder if I like it here.

I like Aunt Violet. I still end up calling her Mrs. Beaumont to her face, of course. My Southern upbringing. She keeps telling me to call her Violet. And she can say it so coquettishly, you'd swear she was flirting with me. Even knowing what I am. And, for that matter, what she is.

Does it sound strange, having it all said out that way? Even as a joke? It looks odd on paper, I admit.

Aunt Violet has a thing she says to us, every morning when we leave for work: "Widen the province of love, boys." I know that that's at the level of an over-the-top homily, but it sends us off with a kind of exuberance. It does. We've talked about it. There's something settling and consoling about it. "Widen the province of love."

She lives it.

She heads out each morning to visit her friends in the nursing homes of the area. She's got so many; she's gone all day. And she talks sadly about how they're dying off. She says she's older than everybody she knows, now. Manny gets so tired of his job that he hints about wanting to go back north, and she becomes frightened. You can see it in her face. She doesn't want us to leave her here, says she's gotten used to us, but of course it's more than just being used to us. She clings to us both, really, without quite coming out with it. She's so solicitous of us and so full of stories—there's something a little frenetic about it, as if she's afraid to let a pause become silence, terrified of the space of quiet where one of us might decide to leave, and say so. It's actually as though she's afraid of the words, like words have the power to affect temporal reality: say it, and it becomes so, no matter how impossible or unlikely.

This last week we had a real scare with her. She walked downstairs about an hour after going up to bed and didn't know either of us, kept calling us by the name of some boy she knew long ago, when she was a little girl. This boy went off and died in the First World War, Manny said. We got her into her silk robe and took her in her truck to the emergency room of Saint Thomas Hospital. She sat there in that white light looking so forlorn and lost and sad. It made me shake. It scared me farther down than I have ever been scared. Like cold, bony ghost fingers on my spine and clutching at the pit of my stomach.

The doctors came and looked her over and talked to her. By this time she'd recovered some—she could recognize Manny, and after a little while, me. They said her blood pressure was a little high, but nothing unusual for someone her age. Her heart rate was good, all her vital signs were in the normal range. The doctor said it could have been a cerebral episode, a little stroke, such as happens often in the elderly. He said he would prescribe some blood thinner, but the side effects might be worse than the cure with someone so old. She seemed fine, by then, and he said it was probably best just to keep an eye on her for a time, and let her go on with her life, which has obviously been so rich and long, and she was clearly so fortunate to have two young men like Manny and me to care for her. We took her home and all of us sat in the little column of cold from the window air conditioner and talked. She told us about living in Ireland until the age of nine, and then coming to the United States. Of meeting the boy who went off and died in France, in 1914, before America was even involved in the war. She was sixteen years old when she waved good-bye to him, and she had thought she was desperately-and-for-all-her-life in love. She told us she's still in love with him, in her way, and she's never found another man who interested her like that. There have been many female friends, she said, and smiled that smile. But she wished she could have had children. She kept her connection to so many of her students, but a lot of them are gone, now, too—and the many others seldom write or get in touch. She has let some of them go, and blames herself for not keeping up. And as she was going on about all this, she began talking about finding some way to start over with everything. She told us this, crying, and it wasn't sad crying, either, it was scared crying. Panicked crying. But then, very slowly, she calmed down, and her natural cheer came back. Her very large appetite for life. Do you believe—she wanted to go out into the Quarter and get some gumbo. It became a thing, like a quest. She had a craving, at almost five o'clock in the morning, to get some gumbo and pie, and whiskey, and to listen to some jazz. I watched her all that night, and still felt my own fear, even as *she seemed to get back to normal. She was still riding over what she's riding over and the fact that she was being brave didn't take away the dark, even a little.*

I envy you and Tyler, having Mary. I have lately become so terrified of being alone. Manny is fine, and Aunt Violet just seems to go on, and still I have this horror that it can't continue much longer, and I think of you two, and every other friend I have, as if you are all beacons in my dark. Forgive this. I might not even send it. It's just that I haven't heard from you and I wonder if something I said or did has alienated you both.

Well, enough of that. You're both busy with being new parents. I was stupid and self-indulgent to mention it. I'm happy to hold a one-way conversation for a time, until you two get your lives settled and are fully adjusted to the change. And when you are adjusted to it, please remember that Aunt Violet and Manny and I would love to have you down for a visit, so we can see the baby and make a fuss over her. Aunt Violet talks of nothing else since we told her about you. Really.

Oh, I hope you like the enclosed beads. I caught them from the Zulus, during Mardi Gras. Quite an accomplishment for a first-time spectator, Mrs. Beaumont says. They're for Mary, when she's old enough.

Love,
Dom

The anniversary of their marriage was approaching. Millicent, who kept good track of dates, and was always sending cards and little gifts to far-flung family and friends, called Lily and said she wanted to have a small dinner party for them that Friday, from which they could leave to spend a few hours away. Millicent would take care of the baby, and she would also reserve a room for them in a hotel in town. "I know you're nursing and you won't want to be gone the whole night, but a few hours away might be so sweet."

"Yes," Lily said. "I'd like that."

When she told Tyler about it, she felt nervous, and it must've shown on her face. He stifled a little laugh and said, "Okay, sure."

That night, Wednesday, two days before the planned party and night out together, he found the letter from Dominic.

He had come in late from the dealership, his jacket off, and big circles of sweat under his arms, his white shirt already unbuttoned down to the midline of his chest. He took the shirt off, and draped it over the chair in front of her dressing table. A notebook she had been keeping with work on her play fell from the dresser as he moved by it, and the letter dropped out of the notebook. She saw what it was, and couldn't move to pick it up before he bent and retrieved it, and held it, staring down at it in the dim light, in his undershirt. He stared for a long time, then put it on her dresser. His face betrayed no emotion at all, but when he spoke his voice was edgy—a barely controlled, brimming-with-rage voice. "You had any others from him?"

"No," she said.

"This didn't just get here today."

"I didn't want to show it to you. I was worried about it."

"Oh?" Now he seemed about to smile.

"We've been—things have been—" She halted, couldn't say it out to him.

"I see."

"Tyler," she said, "I didn't want to have it between us this weekend. I would've shown it to you eventually."

"Thoughtful of you," he said.

She followed him into the living room, where he flopped down on the couch and reached over to turn the television on. There were rumblings of trouble in the Middle East, and hints that the Soviet Union was about to go through some sort of upheaval. The networks were working the stories. He kept flicking from one to the other of them.

"I've tried to answer him, Tyler. I can't."

"Good. Maybe he'll drop us."

She sat down at his side and put her hand on his thigh. "Honey—"

"Lily," he said, "you don't want to get into this with me."

She sat there while he watched the reports. On the television were scenes of crowded streets, people waving flags, angry faces open-mouthed with screams, anti-American slogans. Saddam Hussein strutted on a balcony. Tyler sat watching, arms folded. Finally he turned to her and said, "Look, I thought we'd ironed this out."

"We haven't ironed anything out. We're marking time, both of us—"

He turned the television off. "Okay, now do you want to tell me what you mean by that? Are you unhappy?"

"We're both unhappy," she said. "Look at us."

"I am not unhappy. I am *very* happy, in fact. Happier than I have ever been in my whole waste of a life. I was looking forward to an anniversary dinner at my mother's house and an evening in a hotel with you. My lover. My dear wife."

"I didn't want this to ruin it. And if I'd shown it to you, it would've, Tyler. Can't you see that?"

"How about if you just threw it away and didn't mention it at all, ever? That never occurred to you?"

"I just told you what I was thinking."

"Well, you were wrong."

"Can't we talk it out?"

"Okay," he said, with a murderous calmness, "talk."

"I love you."

"That's a relief."

"I do. And I understand how you feel about everything—I do. But, Tyler, I keep getting this terrible feeling that we're violating some law of nature—"

"No, it's Dominic who's violating laws of *nature*, Lily."

"I can't believe you could *say* a thing like that. Do you know how stupid you sound?"

"Stupid? Really?"

"When will you start on your fucking handlebar mustache?" She wrenched herself away from him and went into the bedroom. The baby was asleep, the tiny fingers of one hand visible above the line of the blanket. She moved to the bed. He had come behind her, and when he put his arms around her middle it startled her into a small cry of alarm.

"I'm sorry," he murmured. "That was awful, what I said. *And* stupid. I can't believe I said it. And I hope we can forget about Mr. Johnson and his handlbar mustache."

She turned in his arms. "But you must—a part of you must believe it, Tyler. It must be something of what you actually feel."

"Yes," he said. "Okay."

She left a pause.

"I'm not going to pretend I've totally beat down the culture I grew up in, Lily. Because I haven't, and neither have you."

Again, she was silent.

"I was lashing out, okay? I reached for anything. You reached and brought up Mr. Johnson and his mustache."

She lay her head on his chest. The sheltering feel of it was troublingly counter to the emotional turmoil inside her. He ran his hand down her back, and when the baby sneezed, they both stood apart and gazed at her. Without taking her eyes from the small, still shape, Lily said, "The trouble is that I don't believe we can keep it secret, and you do."

"Yes," he said.

"You're willing to keep it from her, and from everyone—and from Dominic—forever."

"I don't see what it would hurt, yes."

"I'd like to keep the secret," she said, still without looking at him. "Part of me would. But I don't think we can. I think it poisons everything."

"You've already decided to tell him."

"No."

"Well, then what is this about?"

She had no answer.

"Can't it wait?"

"That's what we've been doing."

"That's been all right," he said. "Hasn't it?"

"It's poisoning everything."

"You know what I'm afraid of, Lily? I'm afraid you're going to take the baby and go live with Dominic. That's what has me scared. It's got me doing and saying things to drive you right to it, too."

Now she did lift her eyes to him. There was an element of his personality that was objective, that faced straight into his own failings. In the light, he was beautiful, even in this stress; his eyes shone, and his skin looked darker against the white of the undershirt; the fine musculature of his arms gleamed.

"I'm not in love with Dominic," she said.

"Then—" He couldn't finish. His voice caught. "I don't want to lose her or you or this family."

"That won't happen," she told him.

He put his arms around her again and for a long time they simply stood there, casting their double shadow on the sleeping child.

"It won't change anything between us if we tell the truth," Lily said. "And I think it might save us."

He was silent.

"Do you see?"

And he let go. "It's just that—well, Lily, it—we lied. There'll be *that*."

"But how?"

He shook his head. "Oh, come *on*. You're not that obtuse."

"It happened by accident, before we were together."

"But we lied. All this time. Lily—we lied to my family. This family. We lied to—to Buddy, for God's sake. Everybody. Jesus. Don't you see?"

"I see. I see it clearly, Tyler. But it's the lie that's hurting us."

"Oh, right. Christ. And the truth will set us free."

"Yes," Lily said. "Yes. We won't have to worry about it anymore. We won't have it scarring all the places between us anymore."

"Scarring," he said, incredulously.

She kept still.

"What if Dominic wants something like visiting rights?"

"He can have them."

Now they were both silent.

Presently, she said, "Can't he?"

"I don't—I can't do this. It can't—we can't—I won't—Oh, Christ, forget it."

"No, Tyler. Say it. At last we're really talking about it."

The baby, as if to remind them, sneezed again, and lifted her head, waking, sending up a small whimper.

"Can't you—" He stopped himself. "Look. You want me to see. I see, okay? Can't *you* see what a terrible admission this is for me, to have to admit a thing like that to *everyone*? Jesus Christ."

She had no words to answer him. The truth was that she did see it, and there was nothing she could call up to say. No words would come. The baby had lifted her head again, wobbling. She put part of her left hand, two fingers, into her mouth, and began sucking on them, whining low.

"Christ," he said. "I don't know what I'm likely to do."

She stared at him. "What do you mean by that?"

His eyes narrowed. He seemed to peer at her from a distance, standing two feet away. "I'm trying to tell you how it is. What I'm going through here." He held his arms out in a gesture of surrender. "I'm describing the territory."

"I can't live this way," she said.

The baby started crying. Lily picked her up and sat down on the bed to nurse her. She needed changing, too. He stood and watched, hands in his pockets, saying nothing. She attended to the baby, seeing him in her peripheral vision, a blur, and finally he moved out of the doorway, muttering something low.

"What?" she said.

He paused. "Nothing. I wish things were different."

"So do I," she told him.

He went into the other room, and the rest of the evening they were apart, walls between them. She nursed Mary and fell asleep, and later he came in and moved Mary to the bassinet, and got into bed. Neither of them spoke.

10

$\mathcal{T}$HE ANNIVERSARY DINNER was more relaxing than she had imagined it would be. Nick and Sheri were more affectionate with each other than they had seemed in a while. Nick held the baby and made faces, to which the baby responded with bright smiles. Roger Gault was there, and he offered a solemn toast: "To the memory of Brendan Galatierre." In the long quiet that followed, they all touched glasses. Sheri's eyes brimmed with tears and she put her head on Nick's shoulder. Roger had brought music from an Australian singer, and they listened to her as they ate. The singer used odd synthesized sounds, but her voice was quite magically strange and beautiful. Tyler seemed interested without quite being involved. Lily watched him, and when she put her arms around him, he returned the affection. The others were preoccupied with the baby, though there were toasts to the couple on their anniversary. Thunderclouds rolled in from the east, blotting out daylight. Nobody went outside. When dinner was finished, Lily and Tyler were expelled by everyone, playfully, with teasing remarks about how the local hotel clerk would react when he saw the couple's address at check-in. They got into the Oldsmobile under the threatening sky and drove to the end of the entrance road. As they turned past the broken gate, onto the highway, Tyler honked the horn. Everyone was waving from the Galatierre porch.

Lily put her hand out the window and waved back. When the house passed out of her view, she turned in the seat and looked at her husband, who held the wheel with both hands and seemed rather emptily placid. He said nothing. The sky grew darker, and some heavy raindrops fell, spattering on the window. He put the wipers on, and the rain stopped. The sky was black, but there wasn't any more rain, and the wipers continued to sweep across the windshield, squeaking each time.

"Why're you keeping the wipers on?" Lily asked.

He said, "Oh. That was stupid of me," and turned them off.

After a time, she reached over and touched his arm, and he glanced her way. "Sweet party."

She unbuckled herself, moved over to the middle of the seat, and lay her head on his shoulder. Perhaps a full minute went by. She saw the buildings of the square. "Honey?" she said.

"We're almost there," he told her.

He pulled into the parking lot of the Hilton, found a place, and maneuvered into it. Then he turned the ignition off, sighed, paused a second, patting the top of her hand. They were quiet, sitting close. Lights went back and forth in the road, and altered the dark inside of the car. Finally he opened the door and she stirred, and got out. He carried her overnight case and his own, walking in to the front desk. When he signed for the room, she hung back a little, and then the two of them got on the elevator, and the door closed. The quiet was oppressive, yet she could think of nothing to say. He pushed the button for the seventh floor. The elevator had a window overlooking the main lobby, and she watched the objects and people grow smaller, feeling the increasing height a little unpleasantly. She took hold of his arm. The elevator opened and they separated again, going down the hall, their footsteps muffled by the thick carpet. The room was large and sunny, with a desk, two king-sized beds, and a television in a big armoire whose doors stood open. He set the bags on the desk and flopped down on the first bed, folding his hands on his chest. She sat on the other bed, picked up the remote from the night table, and flicked the television on. A commercial: two women talking about feminine hygiene. She flicked to another channel, and another, and still another. People were in situations of conflict and folly, to the accompaniment of music or laugh tracks, or both. On one channel two men were chasing another through city streets. It was a movie she thought she recognized.

"I think I saw this," she said.

Nothing.

She turned to look at him. He was lying there watching the television. "Do you want to watch this?" she asked.

"I guess."

"We don't have to watch anything, do we?"

His gaze went from the television to her, and then back to the television.

"Tyler, it's our anniversary."

He said, "You're the one who turned the television on."

She turned it off. The silence shook her. She stood, and unbuttoned her blouse. "You're right."

He watched her undress.

"Well?" she said when she had dropped her skirt and stepped out of it.

He sat up, kicked his shoes off, unbuckled his belt, unzipped his pants, lifted enough to pull them off, then was sitting again. He had taken his undershorts off with the pants. He unbuttoned his shirt, staring at her. She turned from him as she dropped her slip and panties, not wanting him to see in such glaring light the stretch marks Mary had caused. Finally they were in the bed together and he was kissing her with a kind of cold, mechanical expertise—it was like expertise, calculated, skilled, unfelt. At first she responded, and then she couldn't, and when he rolled over onto her and thrust himself inside, she moved to get it over with fast, accomplished it, keeping her face turned from him, her arms tight around his neck. He relaxed, let his weight down on her, then removed himself, lying on his back again, saying nothing. She waited. He sat up, leaned over her and kissed her breasts, licked and sucked, and for a little while the tactile goodness of it aroused her. She reached for him, took hold of his prick, ran her hands up and down the shaft, and this time he lay back, waiting for her to rise and straddle him. She did so, and he moaned softly, eyes closed. Once more she worked to get it over with fast, but then he had taken her shoulders, and his hands ran down to her lower back, stopping her.

"Wait."

She was very still, though she continued to contract and relax the muscles around her perineum.

"Now," he said, urging her. "Now, oh, yes. Now."

She rose and settled back down, rose again, settled again. She moved her hips back and forth, and he came, and then she herself was close. He had stopped, was merely lying under her, and at last she gave it up, pretended to have satisfied herself, feeling the lie in it and wishing it were otherwise, not for this moment but for all the hours and days ahead. She lay over on her back and sighed, and they were both quiet.

"Good?" he said.

"Yes."

"Wasn't very tender on my part."

"Tyler, don't."

"Working out on each other."

She said nothing.

"Horizontal athletics."

"Stop it."

He leaned over her and picked up the remote and turned on the television. News. She went into the bathroom and drew a bath, and sat in the warm water trying not to cry.

When she finished the bath, and came out, she put her panties on, and her bra, and sat on her bed. He was watching the television. She regarded him, where he lay, relaxed, watching the television.

She stood and pulled on her skirt. "We ought to get back soon."

"It hasn't even been an hour, has it? Let's watch a movie or something and then make love again."

She joined him, and he put his arm around her. She was nestled there, one hand on his bare chest, her fingers lightly playing with the hair. A sadness coursed through her, so fierce that she nearly sobbed. He breathed, and kept flicking through the choices on the television, and at last he settled on an old Alec Guinness/Stanley Holloway film about a pair of amiable gold thieves. She held on, kissed his shoulder, and they watched. Near the end, as the inevitable failure happened and the likable thieves were caught, she experienced a loathing for all the authorities and the net of laws that had caught them. Tyler fell asleep.

When he awakened, perhaps an hour later (she might have drifted a little, too), he turned in the bed and put his mouth on hers, then trailed down her body until he had parted her legs and was licking her there, parting the lips and sucking them into his mouth and then releasing them, putting his tongue inside her, and then running it up the length of the opening. It felt wonderful, and she lay back and sighed, letting the warmth of her lover wash over her. After a time, he moved in the bed and, lying on his side, brought his lower body level with her head. She took him into her mouth while he licked, and held him, moving only slightly. He tasted of sourness, and salty sweat, and smelled of their sex. Finally he stopped licking her and lay back so she could suck. She did so for a little while, then let him rise over her, where he supported himself on his arms and said, "Put me in you." Taking hold of him, she guided him in, and he was so excited that he caught her hand between his pelvic bone and her own. She got her hand out, and he pushed in with jarring force, once, twice, pulling almost all the way out before ramming himself at her again. When he came, he squeezed her shoulders, arched in the bed, head back, and then he let his head drop forward, relaxed, still supporting himself on his hands. When he removed himself, he said, "You were finished, weren't you?"

She couldn't catch her breath. "Yes."

She made herself lie over close to him, nestling at his shoulder as she had before. The television was still on. Someone talking about the heat and the air quality, and a hazardous-materials accident out on the interstate to Memphis. The world to her just now seemed a calamitous place, full of noise and madness.

Tyler turned the television off. "Do you know what I am?" he said. "I am an immediate soul. I'm a person whose life is lived in immediacy. Do you know what that means?"

"*Should* I know what it means?"

"It means that I have no self," he said. "I have only the semblance of a self. I am something included along with 'the other' in the compass of the temporal and the worldly."

"Tyler, I'm not a philosopher and I don't read philosophy."

"You ought to. That's direct from Kierkegaard. And it's a truth about me. I live by how all others around me live, and therefore experience nothing other than their immediacy. I have no authentic self, and am in despair, though my defining it makes it comic."

"I don't understand," Lily said.

"Makes it absurd," he went on. "So even my striving becomes nothing but a comic dumb show, like the pantomime act of a puppet on a string."

"Oh, give me a break," she said. "That's a lot of self-congratulatory shit."

"I'm only describing what it looks like from the point of view of Kierkegaard."

"But what are you telling me? That you're depressed?"

"Do you see it, then? Even in the act of *saying* it, I have no being, since I'm taking most of it from Kierkegaard."

"Tyler, what's the point? *Are* you depressed?"

He seemed to consider this, and then shook his head. "That's not the thing itself. Your next question will be what am I depressed *about*? I'm so far gone from that. The word has no meaning where I am."

"And where are you?"

His smile seemed genuine. "I'm here with you."

"You *know* how I mean the question, Tyler."

"I don't have an answer for you, though," he said. "I'm still trying to figure it all out myself."

"Okay," Lily said. She got out of the bed and went into the bathroom, where she ran water and took a shower this time. When she got out, he had dressed and was sitting on the bed, watching *Jeopardy*.

"We'd better get back," he said tonelessly.

11

100 ADDISON ROAD, in the cold and damp of a day in January. Winds sweep down coal ash and the dust of chimneys, swirling. The sky is the color of iron, and the swollen folds of dark cloud at its edge move with a sluggish, chilly sullenness, letting so little of the sun's light through that one can't tell if it is almost day or almost night. In the street outside, horse-drawn carriages go by, curtains closed, the riders bundled in black to just below the eyes, or in the dark colors that soak up whatever heat there is. The clatter of horses' hooves makes an unfamiliar sound for one who has walked hundreds of miles in forests and spent months on water.

Now and then a lone dog skulks by, and once or twice someone may walk past, some gentleman on a walking errand, also bundled to the eyes against the chill. At intervals, one may see people come past on the new-fangled mode of city transportation, a bicycle. It is so curious and so strange-looking that other pedestrians stop to watch.

The day she takes a coach to Soho to deliver Dolokov's packet of letters, there is a chilly mist, which seems to rise from the ground. A dreary, English winter afternoon. She sits unhappily in the gloom of the closed coach, and looks through a chink in the heavy curtain, at the wet streets, holding the packet of letters in her lap. The coach goes by what is apparently an accident involving a bicycle. She observes this with a certain sour, amused vexation—and wonders about the import of the letters. She hasn't looked at them; she promised not to. The name on the outside of the packet, above the address, is Jane Darnsley. The coach pulls in front of a tall stone house, with a closed gate and shuttered windows. It reminds her of Highgate. She expects to hear the chatter of gamecocks in the yard as the coachman gets down and opens the door for her. A murk is over the city. The air stings with its cargo of industrial grime and garbage. She enters the gate, and goes up to the door, clutching the packet. The door opens a crack before she gets to it—the denizens of this house have heard the coach, and have seen her coming. A very tall shadow stands in the doorway, with the dim glow of firelight behind it. A hand comes out of the shadow, white as bleached bone, and makes a beckoning motion. The shadow turns, and moves into the house, and Mary enters it. Not a word is spoken. She follows the figure down a corridor and to the left, into the room where the firelight comes from. The figure turns, and is revealed to be a man with a grotesquely long face, long nose, long ears—his features are exaggerated in the way of a carnival mirror. His eyes are bottomless; you can't see the whites of them.

There is a couch in the room, on which is seated a very heavy woman in white lace with ivory combs in her hair.

—We received your communication, she says to Mary.

—Are you Miss Darnsley?

—Miss Darnsley is dead.

—Jane Darnsley?

The woman nods solemnly, and the man utters a syllable of pain or sorrow.

—The same. Dead, the woman murmurs.

For a moment, no one says anything more. The tall man moves to the fire and begins tending to it.

—I am her mother.

—I'm so terribly sorry, Mary says.

The man begins to emit a sound, a low keening. Mary doesn't realize at first that it is a human sound.

—The letters were written to her by her Russian friend?

—Well, I've not looked at them. But I assume so, yes.

—You are certain you have not looked at them?

—No. Mary hands them over.

The woman turns heavily on the couch and reaches with the packet of letters toward the tall man, who takes it and looks at it for a few moments, holding it in both long-fingered hands. Then he turns and thrusts it into the fire.

—What are you doing? Mary says. What in the world.

—He was evil, the woman says. He's a foreign devil who put ideas into her head.

Mary stands there, looking at the woman and then at the man, and then at the packet of Dolokov's letters, curling into flame, darkening and collapsing to ash.

—Leave us, the woman says. Go back to your devil, and tell him she's dead. She drank poison and died choking on her own filth. Tell him that. Tell him what he did.

—Mr. Dolokov is probably dead 'imself, by now, Mary says. You might've communicated your feelings to me by return post. I could've burned them myself.

—Leave us, the other says.

Mary lets herself out in the sound of the man's weeping.

The coachman is waiting for her, standing by the open door.

—Take me 'ome, she says.

Then she stops and thinks to correct herself.

—Take me back to Addison Road.

12

*T*HE TEMPERATURE in their apartment is a tropical eighty-six degrees. That is how she keeps it these days. She has had a malarial episode, a bout of fever that will recur, now, periodically, the rest of her life—coast fever, she calls it—and the leaden cold scene outside the windows, even now that she has recovered from her illness, chills her to the marrow of her thin bones. She has put mementos around the flat—charms, amulets, masks, chains of beads, woven cloth, bracelets, one dried leather shield, painted in twilight colors, the image of a woman with exaggerated breasts and the heavy trunklike legs of a crocodile. At the entrance to the flat there is a three-foot-tall statue carved from wood, stained with dried blood, and riddled with nails that are blood-colored with rust. The face is agape in either horror or ferociousness—it's hard, Mary says, to tell which.

This violent-looking figure causes a small sound of alarm to rise in the throat of a visitor whom Charley brings to the flat one evening in February 1894. They trudge up the stairs together, Charley leading, talking, and in typical fashion neglecting to mention the unusual nature of the decor. Mary is prepared to dislike the visitor, since in the past weeks she has had to collect all of her family spirit to keep from flying off the handle with Charley. Charley has reverted to his old, lofty indolence, depending on Mary for everything while holding forth as if the matters he deigns to speak of are raised in stature by his attention. To put it quite plainly, he's spoiled: a child who never learned that one has to work at being interesting, that one cannot expect the world to give up its riches without the expense of spirit.

—Mary, he says, stepping up into the flat. Meet the head of the Royal Niger Company. I thought you ought to meet him. Sir George Goldie.

She's familiar with the name. In Africa, she had dealings with several traders from the company. The Royal Niger Company plies the interior, and though their concerns are more with the inland water routes, there is friction between them and MacDonald's Coastal Oil Protectorate. It was Goldie, she knows, who organized the several different concerns of the region into the Royal Niger Company, which maximized efficiency in trade and went some to keep from ruining the ability of the African tribes to continue producing palm oil and the other commodities the Empire expected to take from the continent. Goldie was knighted as a result of this. Now he stands before her in a waistcoat and holding his hat, a wide-brimmed fedora, she notices, far from fashionable. He bows, never taking his eyes from her. His eyes are the color of distance on the ocean—a pelagic dark blue suggesting depths. He takes her in.

—Well? Charley says.

Mary and Goldie begin to speak at the same time, and then stop. They each try to encourage the other to go on, and in the process again speak at the same time. Mary puts her fingers to her lips and nods at him.

—I bring greetings from James Henley Batty, he says. But this is not what he started to say, and Mary indicates this with a nod, and an encouraging smile.

—I send them back to him, she says, after a pause. You were saying?

He hesitates, with a charming attention to the brim of his hat.

—I was going to say that the gentleman at the entrance of this flat is quite formidable indeed.

—A gift, she says. From a Fang witch doctor, retired.

She pronounces it Fong, as the tribal chieftains do. He smiles, appreciating her dry tone.

—You have been among them? he asks.

—Some. I would like to travel farther up the Ogowe, where I understand there are others. The kind who 'ave not seen Europeans.

—They're purported to be rather unpredictable, not to say terrifying.

—Exactly, she says. I've received the same information.

—My sister is in a rather anxious hurry to get herself killed, Charley says, with a sour little smirk.

—I'm very happy to meet you, says Goldie to Mary.

—And I you, Mary says.

Charley stirs, as if coming to himself after a period of daydreaming. He claps his hands together.

—Well, Mary. We'd like a sip of brandy apiece. And two cigars, if you will. They're in the sideboard.

Mary sets out to accomplish this task while the two men talk. Mostly it's Charley who talks. Charley met Goldie after seeing him lecture earlier in the evening. Goldie's subject was the failure of the royal administration of territories—this mostly having to do with meddling in the cultural life of the people where meddling was not called for, of refusing to understand them, or to give them the credit of supposing aspects of their culture to be something they might wish to protect.

—I admire that business about behaving as if the savages are all waiting to run from their own history and traditions, Charley says. Although one must admit that the assumption carries a good deal of power. That is, acting in that way seems to convince the savages of just that. I understand they convert in droves to Christianity. And one understands it, hearing about some of the fetish practices.

—Well, says Goldie. But if you ruin the economy and the structure of the place, there isn't much left to trade for, is there?

Charley hasn't heard him.

—It's exceptional, that just as you were ending your talk I had the thought that it would do my sister a service to bring her into your acquaintance. And here we are.

Mary pours the brandy, and then moves to the other side of the room. The men talk for a few minutes about the evening's lecture. Their exclusion of her rankles, though she observes that Goldie is uneasy, and keeps glancing her way. Charley asks for more brandy, and she gets it for him. Goldie watches, and politely accepts more himself. Charley drinks his rather quickly, and asks for more. When she sets the bottle by him, he gives her a disapproving look, so she takes it back to the sideboard. For a few moments, the only sound is the contented smacking of Charley's lips as he drinks his brandy. But then he lights his cigar and begins spouting his opinions to Goldie, droning on in his cocksure way about the responsibility of the white man in the world of darkness and despair. It is all borrowed, badly, from Kipling. Goldie tries gingerly to disagree, but then seems to relent, with a gentle grin. Mary decides that there is a supple kind of appeal about him, an acceptance: he won't be contentious here. He exhibits a willingness merely to provide a sounding board.

—I say, Mary, it's so awfully hot in here, Charley says abruptly, pulling at his collar.

—I 'adn't noticed, she says.

Charley turns to Goldie.

—As you no doubt see, my sister learned to talk from our poor mother. Goldie looks at her.

—James Henley Batty can't speak highly enough of you, Miss Kingsley.

—Oh, Charley says, she's quite a substantial character. Do you know she's writing a bloody book about Africa? And as if that weren't enough, old Macmillan is going to publish it. He was our uncle Charles's publisher. My namesake. You are no doubt familiar with the book *Water Babies?*

—I'm afraid not, says Goldie, staring at Mary, clearly relieved at the chance to move the conversation to another plane. Tell me about your book, Miss Kingsley.

—I'm afraid, she says, it's not much more than a knockabout farce. But I am aspiring to do something more serious, soon, in terms of anthropology, along the lines of Ellis, and Sir Alfred Lyall, or the Germans, Baumann and Buckholtz, or Kohler.

—I know Ellis, says Goldie, smiling as if out of chagrin at not knowing the others.

—Mary speaks German fluently, says Charley. This is very good brandy.

Goldie nods distractedly at him.

Mary says:

—I plan to return to West Africa as soon as possible. I've spoken to the people at the British Museum. I've got support and the means, and I'm going down there again.

—I may be off to Singapore soon, says Charley.

Mary is returning Goldie's frank gaze.

—I would like to go down to West Africa and stay. I feel adrift in London.

—It's in your blood, then, Goldie says. As it's in mine.

—Mary lost weight, down there, Charley says. And she's been sick because of it. She brought some sickness back with her from the wretched place. There's nothing but sickness down there, I'm led to understand. It's misguided to want to return, Mary. You already have a book out of it.

—Notes and letters, she says. I mean to do a thoroughgoing study.

She addresses Goldie:

—I'm quite taken with the African mind. They see the world more clearly, I think. I 'ad a conversation with a witch doctor one middle of the night after 'elping him with a sick man. I used our medicine and he performed some incantations and uttered some spells. It was just a case of some kind of mild food poisoning, and nothing, really. An 'our out of the night. But we talked almost all night afterward. The man was a very proficient speaker of English, and 'e explained to me what 'e was about. I felt I could've been speaking with Spinoza. That view of the world, you know, as animate and soul-haunted.

—I can't say I've ever had that feeling, says Goldie. About the world.

Charley says:

—Tell her what you told us in your lecture tonight about the death rate in Cameroon last year.

—I already know it, Mary says. I know that statistic.

Goldie leans toward her, the faintest motion, looking into her eyes, as if trying to read her feelings. But he speaks to Charley.

—Your sister is quite rare, Mr. Kingsley.

Annoyed at being spoken about in this way, and oddly unsettled in her mind by his forthright gaze, Mary rises and pours still more brandy. This time she pours a glass for herself. Charley protests, but in a slovenly, half-drunk manner, without force. He drinks more of his own, and puffs on his cigar.

—There's Father's work to finish, don't forget, he says to Mary.

Goldie glances at the daguerreotype in the oval frame above the desk on the other side of the room.

—Is that your father?

—That's Father when he was a younger man, says Charley.

Goldie nods absently.

—I should like you to meet my wife, he says to Mary.

She receives this comment with a polite nod, feeling the flush of embarrassment in her cheeks. It astonishes her to realize that she has been drawn to him in exactly the idiotic romantic way of a girl on a summer picnic with an eligible someone. She gets to her feet and moves to the sideboard, where she retrieves the brandy and pours more into her brother's glass, as well as her own. She's certain now, from his faintly crestfallen demeanor, that Charley looked upon Goldie in this light all along, as a perfect match for his sister: doubtless, it is the reason Charley brought him here. Charley drinks most of his brandy in one pull, looking a little like a trader on a barge, ringed with the cigar smoke, lounging in his chair, swirling the remainder of the drink and staring at the amber trembling of it in his glass.

—We'll have to look forward to the pleasure, he says. And so much time has gone by that the comment seems oddly out of place, as though he is carrying on a conversation the other two can't hear.

Goldie keeps his gaze on Mary.

—My wife's name is Mathilda, he says. And, like you, she's a bit of a nonconformist.

—Nonconformist? Charley says.

—You'll admit, Goldie continues gazing at Mary. You'll allow, I mean, that your recent journey to Africa, and your plans to go back there, are not in the pale of normal experience for a woman of your age and station?

—I don't conceive of it that way, says Mary.

—No, and neither has Mathilda, about anything she has done. I'm certain you will adore one another.

—We'll look forward to the pleasure, Charley says again, aimlessly, sipping the last of his brandy. He holds the glass out to Mary, who moves to the sideboard to refill it. She puts her own glass down, unfinished, and asks Goldie if he would like more. He demurs. When she hands the glass to Charley, he lifts it as if to offer a toast, and then appears to change his mind. He takes a small swallow of it, and then breathes a long sigh. It's clear to Mary, and certainly it is also evident to Goldie, that her brother is getting drunk.

Goldie and Mary both begin speaking at the same instant again, and Mary sits down in her wing chair, smiling at him, her fingers to her lips once more.

—No, he says. You, this time.

—I wondered where you saw Batty.

Goldie thinks a moment. Then:

—Oh, you mean tonight. He was at tonight's meeting.

—I spoke to the gentleman, says Charley.

—Batty is in England? Mary says.

—He sails for Sierra Leone tomorrow morning, says Goldie. I had finished my talk, and he approached me. We had some dealings in Africa a few years ago. Good man, Batty. I spoke to him a little, tonight, and then Charley here introduced himself to me. Batty heard Charley speaking about you, and he stepped in to say that he hoped we would carry his good wishes to you.

—I would like to've seen 'im, says Mary. I very much enjoyed Batty's company in the Canaries, two years ago.

—Sent his greetings, Charley says, drunkenly.

—Well, I should be going, says Goldie, rising from his chair.

Mary has a moment of realizing how tall he is.

—I 'ope to see you again, she says.

They both notice, in the same moment, the increment of quiet in the room, and they turn to see that Charley has fallen asleep.

—Well, says Goldie.

The expression on his handsome face is almost ameliorative, as if to apologize for Charley's behavior.

Mary goes to the head of the stairs with him, and he bows at the fierce figure full of nails on the landing.

—I hope you continue to keep out evil spirits, he says to it.

She watches him descend the stairs, and at the bottom he turns, and tips his hat. She waves, as if this were some long expedition he is embarking on. He opens the door and there is the jangle and uproar of the street. Again he looks back.

—It isn't Africa, he says. Is it.

—No, says Mary. I'll 'ave to change that.

He smiles, a nearly conspiratorial smile.

—If I can help, he says.

TWENTY-ONE

1

I wonder how you did it all. Taking care of feckless Charley. Collating your father's writings for Macmillan to publish in a book; working to get Charley to do the memoir of his father, which would finish the project, and all the while sitting up in the late nights, in the stifling hours, fighting sleep and working on your own journal of the first trip to the coast. I think of you discovering your power to evoke in language what you saw and heard. A natural writer, a born writer, everyone said. Yet you were reluctant. You hesitated and caviled, even when Macmillan, having seen the pages of The Bites of Benin, *wanted to publish, and not only to capitalize on the lady explorer, not only for the novelty, but because the prose was so vivid and true. Was it that you were so serious about the work, not the writing but the exploration, the quest, that you refused to let him do it that way? I can't understand why you would want to publish it anonymously if you published it at all, unless it was to take away what you had come to feel was the stigma of being a woman.*

What must it have been, waiting that winter and spring and summer in England, for the chance to go back to what you were now calling your home?

I have discovered the strong sense that I myself, and my little daughter, have no real home. I don't feel at home anywhere anymore, and the world I recognize as mine seems to be receding all the time into some background I don't understand. This came to me recently, while I was standing in the small kitchen of the house, stirring a glass of chocolate milk for myself. I was looking out the window above the sink, at the line of trees, and the yards with other houses, beyond the field in back of this house, and it came to me like a blow to the stomach that I am not home here; that this is not my home, and nor is anyplace else. I'm occupied with the baby, and I do an adequate job of keeping this house where we act out life, and I spend time on this frail attempt at a play. But I never feel at home.

Over the next few weeks, Tyler drew down into himself, while remaining, to others in the family and among friends, outwardly unchanged. When she told him, one morning as he was eating breakfast, that she wanted to write Dominic about a visit to New Orleans, he stared at her for a long moment and then shrugged and went on eating. He left for work without saying anything. Yet he remained civil. She could do as she wished, he told her that evening; she would anyway. When she asked if he was angry with her, he said, "No," with an air of being surprised that she should think so.

He never spoke impatiently to her or argued with her, really; he was cooperative, staid, and finally dull-seeming. It was maddening. He paid attention to the baby, and he was in every way a dutiful family man, still going to work in the mornings and coming home. She was tempted to try saying things to him, to draw him out, to break through his apparent apathy. But then she told herself there was no sense in starting a fight. He was making his own peace with the situation, and she convinced herself that one day soon he would suggest that they go to New Orleans as if the whole thing were his idea. She trusted his intelligence, and if worry for him still nagged at her, she was willing to grasp at the possibility that this was how he adjusted to things.

It occurred to her during one of her sleepless passes in the middle of the night that she really didn't know him very well. She lay there trying to catalog what she did know about him: she knew that he was meticulous in some ways and slovenly in others; she knew there was a curious strain of mistrust in him about people, having to do, she was certain, with the central fact of his growing up, that his mother had abandoned him; she knew he had once liked to hunt, that he was an avid—lately he had been an obsessive—reader, and that for all his growing erudition there was a modest something in his makeup that prevented him from airing what he knew in company. She knew that while he was not quick-tempered, when he did get angry he tended to rage, and his rage could be towering, even frightening. And she knew he was immature. She was familiar with the songs he liked and the kinds of movies he had enjoyed, what movie actors and directors he preferred or trusted. She had knowledge of what some of his favorite foods were. She had been privy to some of his nightmares. She understood that he was mostly decent, and that he loved her. Yet all of these things added up to a kind of blur, finally. And while he lay sleeping at her side, moaning with whatever his dreams were, she had to beat back the overwhelming feeling that he was a stranger.

Everything settled into an inertia.

It dismayed her how little anyone could see of it. The two of them spent some time with his mother and Roger Gault, at his mother's invitation. They went out to dinner a couple of times. No one seemed even vaguely aware that a change had come, that Tyler was this hollowed-out someone, barely there.

They spent a weekend afternoon at the Galatierre house, sunning by the pool (Lily tried the baby in the water; the baby took to it, letting out a high-pitched squeal that made everyone laugh). And they met Sheri and Nick at Old Taylor Grocery, for fried catfish. Everybody seemed perfectly at ease with them both. Yet there were all too numerous times when Tyler, at her side, was nevertheless elsewhere, when she would say something to him and he wouldn't hear it, and after she repeated it, sometimes slightly louder, he would turn, and seem to discover her there in the room with him, others in the room with him, and he would say, "I'm sorry. Could you say that again?"

In the society of his mother, his distraction was even worse. He seemed to be observing Millicent from some dizzying height, scarcely able to control his own equilibrium. There was something like wonder in his gaze. Yet his mother never appeared to notice it.

When he and Lily were alone, coming away from the afternoon by the pool, he spoke of Millicent in a detached way, as if she were merely an interesting outsider, a woman with a kind of inscrutability about her, whose motivations were hard to read. He told Lily that he believed Millicent was a woman whose soul contained unexplored caverns of ice; that she was one of those people who moved through life with charm and apparent elegance, but who were capable of huge selfishness.

"Isn't that true of most of us?" Lily said.

He never spoke of Dominic. They never spoke of it. He spent hours alone, in one room or another of the little house, reading or seeming to read. Several times she passed the entrance of a room to see him sitting with the book open on his lap, staring at the opposite wall, or at the floor. It was growing more and more difficult to be easy and relaxed with him, though he appeared oblivious to this. And he was gone a lot, too. It was undeniably true that there were practical day-to-day reasons for the widening distance between them.

His appetite had fallen off, and he wasn't sleeping very well. Neither of them was. She would wake with her own nightmares to see that he was out of the bed and in some other part of the house. Twice she found him sleeping on the sofa in the living room. Another night she got up just in time to see him come walking back to the house from the construction site, his shadow on the moonlit grass.

He said he'd hoped a walk might make him sleepy.

"I'm not sleepy either," she said.

"Ah." He smiled. "The life of the guilty."

"What if we just tell Dominic?"

"And tell him how we figured it out, too. Oh, nothing humiliating in that."

She had no answer for this.

"You know what this is like?" he said. "No matter which way I turn, there's hell. That's what the doctors I think call an irreconcilable conflict. What that really connotes is a *trap*."

"Don't," she said. "We're capable people. We can figure something out."

"You know what I'd like to figure out? I'd like to figure out a way not to have it between us all the time. I'd like to figure out a way not to have to talk about it or think about it or look at it or hear about it. I'd like a year of complete *quiet* about it. That is among the things I would like." He got into bed. The thought went through her mind like a breath of doom that it was as if they had aged forty years.

The next morning he fixed coffee for himself, and went out the door to work. He kissed her on the cheek, leaned down and touched his lips to the top of the baby's head. Lily watched him walk out to the car, get in, and drive away.

By nightfall, when he returned, she knew, he would be off in himself somewhere, wanting quiet, claiming exhaustion. He would be apathetic and drowsy, staring at the pages of his books and nodding off, a man who has searched for some kind of meaning and found only the niggling and inescapable demands of the body.

She was working on the play in earnest, spending almost every morning on it while the baby napped or babbled in her playpen. She had decided to try it from the last hours of Mary Kingsley's life: the scene in Simon's Town, South Africa, as she's fighting delirium from yellow fever, contracted from one of the soldiers she'd been nursing, a casualty of the Boer War. Mary on a makeshift cot, feverish, dreaming of going back again to her beloved West Africa, and of all the adventures. Scenes from her life could be played out on another area of the stage, as memory and hallucination. She had spent so much time in and around theaters, watching her father and the others put it all together. It had appeared so uncomplicated and good, like a kind of charitable operation, struggling to make a play. An entertainment for strangers. She had never dreamed how hard it could be, nor had she ever suspected what pleasures there were to be had from the complexity and the labor of solving its difficulties, bringing it about. She showed nothing of the work to anyone. And each morning, reading through it again before going on with it, she was freshly heartened and even excited.

2

On THE FOURTH OF JULY, the family gathered for a cookout. The big surprise for everyone was that Rosa had come for a visit from her new home in California. She was there when Tyler and Lily arrived, sitting in one of the canvas chairs on the porch with a glass of iced tea in her hand. She stood and walked over to them as they extricated Mary from her car seat. Rosa kissed the baby, and made a soft, cooing sound, then walked with them up onto the porch and stood quietly by while Millicent greeted them. Tyler embraced his mother, or took her embrace, and accepted her offer of a glass of wine.

It was a bright, still, cloudless, scorching day, as the last several days had been, and all the grass had begun to whiten with the sun; it had a crisp and cooked feeling underfoot. A thin cloud of dust rose with every footfall. In the house, Nick and Sheri were seated on the sofa in the living room, in the air-conditioning, drinking orange juice out of wine glasses. Lily put Mary down in the bassinet Millicent kept now for those times when Lily visited, and took a seat next to Sheri. Tyler went into the kitchen with Rosa, to get his wine. Lily heard them talking with Roger Gault—light chatter about the wine, and the hot weather.

Nick leaned across his wife, toward Lily. "You look like you could use one of these." He held up his glass. "It's a mimosa—champagne and orange juice." His speech was faintly slurred.

Lily saw how much the look of the house had been transformed. She still felt ambushed by it—the hunting trophies all gone, and most of the pictures of Buddy and Millicent in their diverse travels. She surveyed the room. The big window behind them showed the thick-grown green prospect it had shown when she'd first arrived here, more than a year ago now. She listened to Tyler's voice in the kitchen, and saw Sheri sip her orange juice, wondering at her own sense of displacement.

Nick said, "Business is so good, we may expand."

Neither of the women answered him.

"I know Buddy was against it. But we're gonna lose a lot of profit in taxes if we *don't* expand."

Sheri stood. "I don't feel like talking business now. I'm sorry, Nick. Excuse me."

"I'll stop," Nick said. But she had headed into the kitchen, and was already making a fuss over Roger Gault's loud Hawaiian shirt.

Nick cleared his throat, and took a long drink of the mimosa, then glanced over at Lily. "Things're a little edgy."

Lily said nothing for a beat or two. The talk in the kitchen was louder, opposing voices, arguing about the possibility of the reunification of Germany, as though this were high-level deliberations of the diplomatic corps. Lily heard a note of fatigue in Tyler's voice, and realized it was boredom. The same boredom he had begun to show about nearly everything. She sighed, and then leaned up to look into the bassinet at Mary, who lay quite peacefully asleep.

"How's Tyler at home?" Nick said. "If that isn't prying."

She returned his look.

"He's not doing much of the work anymore. He was really gung ho in the beginning. Even after Buddy—after the accident. He seemed anxious to do well. He did extra things. He was good, too. Customers took to him. Now he stays there all day and does literally nothing much. He doesn't use the phone. When people come in, he takes forever to notice them. It's like he's in a daze. People react to that. We've—we've been losing sales."

"Have you talked to him about it?"

"A little. He apologizes, says he'll do better. Say's he's got some things on his mind. You know the drill."

"Well, Tyler's going through everything, Nick. Like you."

"Then you think it's because of what happened."

"Yes." As she spoke, she received the sensation of having lied to him. She could not look at him.

"He wants out," Nick said. "He wants to get as far away from here as he can and he wants to take you and the baby with him."

"I know," Lily said. "We've talked about it—the army. Germany. Rome."

"We wouldn't want to lose you, Lily. You've been one of the ones who understood everything. I don't think I'd like the change. I *know* Sheri wouldn't."

She felt suddenly as if she might begin to cry. "We'll—we'll always be in touch, Nick."

"Yeah." He sighed and took another sip of the drink. The others had all gone out to the pool, and now the whole house was quiet. He tapped his fingers on the rim of the glass, and when Mary began to fret, he put the glass down and stood to lean over her. "Do you mind?" he said.

"Of course not."

He reached down and with great care brought the baby, with her blanket, out of the bassinet, and held her, cradled, gazing with a kind of sad wonder at the small, round face. He rocked his arms slightly, and then looked at Lily, his dark eyes moist, an expression of mystified happiness in his features, as if his own emotion were some profound puzzle he couldn't understand or explain. Lily's heart went out to him, for what his sorrow had wrought in him. He handed the child to her and cleared his throat again, putting his hands in the back pockets of his slacks and turning a little, looking toward the window with its view of the fields, the far river, and the overpass.

"I can't imagine this for me."

Sheri called them both, from the kitchen door. "Bring the baby out here. There's plenty of shade. And Mary can swim a little if she won't nap or nurse."

Nick picked up the bassinet. "I'm sure things'll be okay with Tyler. He just needs to get his brightness back."

"'Brightness,'" said Lily. "I've never heard the word used quite that way."

"Millicent used to say it to Sheri all the time when she was a little girl. Sheri says it to me. She—she says it a lot to me." He gave forth a small, self-deprecating laugh, shaking his head again. "You know I still wonder if your sister-in-law has it in her to forgive me."

3

*A*FTER THE SUN dipped below the trees and the sky grew gray, the fireworks started. There were two public displays visible from the back of the house, and at all the widely separated houses of the neighborhood there were others, rockets, little explosions, Roman candles, streaking shafts of brightness, trailing fires, expanding blooms of red, white, and blue, rivaling the heavy, booming showers in the distance. The explosions rose in the sluggish air and fell to earth, the ashes already falling even as they blazed so brilliantly. In the distance, they looked strangely fatal, troublingly feeble in their rising. They gave Lily an unpleasant consciousness of the pull of gravity. She hadn't known she was so tired. She held Mary close, with one hand alongside her head, to shield her ears from the noise.

Finally, Millicent asked if she couldn't take the baby inside with her. She'd had enough of the show, and the smell of the smoke and gunpowder was bothering her. Lily went with her, and she noticed that Tyler wasn't with the others. She strode down the hallway, to the upstairs bathroom, and found the door open, the light off. So she went along that part of the house, which opened onto the den, with its empty places on the walls, and then down the steps toward their old room. There she saw Tyler sitting on the stripped bed, the bare mattress, holding one of Buddy's rifles across his lap. He was staring at it, running one hand gingerly along the polished stock.

"Tyler?" she said.

And he looked up, startled. "Oh—yeah."

"What—what're you doing?"

He stood, and set the rifle against the wall. "Nothing."

"What were you doing?"

"I was—I was looking at one of Buddy's hunting rifles." He walked over to her and simply waited, gazing into her eyes as if he thought she had come to tell him something.

There was an explosion, from right outside the sliding door, that made them both jump. She said, "Tyler—" and could find nothing to say.

His face was blank. "I was looking at a rifle. Okay?"

She felt the tears come. But when she reached for him, he backed away.

"Everybody's gonna wonder where we are," he said. "We don't live here anymore."

"Tyler, tell me what to do."

Now, he looked almost weary. "I don't have any idea what you're talking about. It's the Fourth of July and about time we went home."

She moved toward the sliding door. "Why did you come down here?"

"I don't know. Old times? Do I have to explain everything I do?"

She walked around him and up the stairs, though she made sure he was behind her. And her unease, the pervasive gloom that had become so general and that she had endured for so long as to begin almost not to notice it, renewed itself.

She held Mary, and said the good-byes, took the kisses, good wishes, little jokes, smiles, and admonitions to be careful going home, and she went out and spent the cautious time getting Mary into the car seat, safe, everything in order, Tyler having loaded the playpen and the bag of bottles, diapers and formula, the teething ring and the binky, everything put away. He got in behind the wheel, started the car, gazed at the others standing on the porch, and when they waved, he waved, as Lily waved—all this accomplished in a kind of haze, and she sat in the car and watched him while he drove them home. She saw his impassive face in the silence. When they arrived at the little house, she got Mary out of the seat and went in, and put her down, changing her, getting her arranged in the bassinet. He was elsewhere, in the quiet rooms. She sat on her side of their bed waiting for him, and when he didn't come in, she went in search of him, moving almost stealthily through the house. She found him sitting in the easy chair by the door, his head back, mouth open.

"Tyler?" she said.

He started. "Oh," he said. "I fell asleep."

"Honey, can we talk about tonight?"

Again, his eyes showed no emotion at all. "Lily, I didn't like the fireworks."

"I'm just going to say this," she said. But she couldn't get her breath.

"You want to go to New Orleans, don't you."

"Tyler, I have to know what you were doing with that—that—what's happening, please." She had begun to cry again. She stood there, trembling.

"What I was doing with what, Lily?" He hadn't moved.

"Are you thinking of—" Again, she couldn't breathe the words out. "We can work things out, Tyler."

"Jesus," he muttered. "Go to bed, will you? Christ."

"We won't ever tell anyone. Okay? No one will ever know."

At this, he smiled. She thought she had never seen anything so terrible as that open, ruthless grin, that boy's grimace, all teeth, a smile from the bottom of hell, involving only the mouth. "But *we* know, princess."

"Stop this," she said. "You're scaring me."

"Go to bed."

She strained for the courage to ask him to come with her. She could feel herself working it. "Let's both go," was what she found the will to say.

"I'm not sleepy." He still stared, still had that awful grin on his face.

She struggled for a more casual tone. "I'm not sleepy either. I wasn't talking about sleep." But her voice shook, and she couldn't control her breathing. "Tyler, let's go see someone. Let's get in the car and go back to the house—"

He held up one hand. "You're panicking."

"No, I'm—I think we ought to go back to the house."

"*This* is our house."

"Yes," she said. It was little more than a breath.

"This is the house of the little Harrison family."

She could say nothing. She felt his eyes on her, but she was looking at the floor now, waiting for him to say something else, or do something else.

He stood slowly, as if the effort of it ached and smarted in his bones, the motion of an older man, someone tired and sore. He walked across the room and when he reached her, he paused, but only for a second, then went on into the hall, toward the bedroom. She followed. He took his shirt off, and stood over the bassinet, where the baby had moved to one side, sleeping so peacefully.

She put her hand on his shoulder, and when he didn't respond, she took it away. "We'll never tell a soul," she said.

He shook his head, but said nothing.

"I mean it, Tyler."

He had walked around to the other side of the bed and sat down to remove his sandals. "I didn't like the fireworks," he said, without looking back at her. "Did they bother you? All those sounds, like gunshots." He stood and removed his pants, draped them on the chair in the corner, and then got in under the cover sheet, pulling it to his chin and folding his hands over his chest. He closed his eyes.

"I didn't think of that, Tyler. It must've—it must've been awful for you. I didn't see any—I didn't see what it must have done to Nick."

"Nick didn't seem to mind. I think Nick's gone beyond minding anything. Nick gets a little drunk really early in the day and then maintains it into the nights, and nobody seems the slightest bit aware of it. Least of all his customers."

She got out of her clothes and into her nightgown quickly, and when they were lying side by side, he took a breath, as if steeling himself, and hauled himself up onto his elbow, leaning over to kiss her on the cheek. It was a strange, cold kiss. He lay over on his side, and she turned the light off, closed her eyes, knowing she wouldn't sleep. He was very quiet, not moving; he didn't even seem to be breathing. The whole night had grown silent as death. In a few moments, he began to snore. The baby was making small noises, sighing, and giving forth little sleep gasps and sobs, stirring, then settling into stillness again. Lily was the only one awake. She lay in the dark, seeing the image of her husband sitting on the bare mattress in the downstairs room, with the rifle across his lap.

4

$\mathcal{S}$HE WOKE with a start in the light of morning, with Mary playing and babbling next to her, and Tyler gone. It was after nine o'clock, a dismal, hazy day. In the kitchen she found a half-eaten pear and a glass with milk in the bottom of it. There was no note. The house had the feel of a place just vacated by someone who lived alone. She called the dealership and asked for him, and waited a few minutes. When he didn't come to the phone, she hung up and dialed again, and asked for Nick. Once more, she waited, and she was about to hang up when Nick came on the line. She said, "Nick—I need to talk to Tyler."

"He's not here, Lily. I'll tell him you called when he gets here."

"He hasn't been there?"

"No."

She began to cry. She did not know how she kept from sobbing. "When he comes—if he comes—will you tell him to call me at his mother's?"

"Lily, what's wrong? Why hasn't he come in?"

"He left before sunup, Nick."

"Did you call Millicent?"

"I'm going over there," she told him.

"I'll have him call you there if he comes in. I'll *make* him call you."

She fed and dressed Mary, then got dressed herself. The sky threatened storms, big black thunderheads lowering to the east, at the treeline. Heavy, lightning-laden clouds so thick they looked as though they would topple the trees in the foreground. She put Mary in the car seat and drove to the Galatierre house. The rain began before she arrived, gusting in wind and blown leaves. For a few minutes, she sat in the car waiting for it to subside. She glimpsed Sheri in one of the windows at the front of the house. Sheri waved. A moment later, Millicent came out with an umbrella, and helped her get the baby into the house.

Sheri was dressed for work, but hadn't gone. She wasn't feeling well. She kissed Lily on the cheek, and then went out of the room.

Millicent said, "She had too much to drink last night after you-all left. She's hungover and she ought to be ashamed of herself."

Lily held back her panic.

Rosa came from the kitchen, and for half a second Lily thought the other woman had gone to work for Millicent again. But Rosa was carrying her own cup of coffee, and she sat on the sofa and took a polite sip of it. The baby made a small fluting sound from the back of her throat, and Millicent said something soft to her that Lily didn't hear. She waited for Rosa to speak to her, and wished she weren't there. Rosa blew across the surface of the coffee, and then sipped loudly from it. "Sheri and I are supposed to go into town," she said. "I guess that's off now. It's bad out there. And it's bad in here. Remind me never to get drunk."

"Rosa," said Lily. "I—I have to talk to Millicent. Do you mind?"

Rosa put her coffee down and looked from one to the other of them with frank curiosity. It was Rosa's way with everything, and there was nothing personal in it; she might've been gazing at a pair of birds on a branch. She picked up her coffee and went back to the kitchen door. Before she closed it, she looked back in and said, "I'm going into town when this lets up. Tell Sheri for me?"

Millicent said she would, her voice brittle with uncertainty.

When they were alone, she turned to Lily and said, "I hope there's nothing wrong? You look upset."

Lily realized, as she drew in air to begin, that she couldn't speak freely. She felt hamstrung. It was hard to muster any words at all. Her throat caught. She was fighting back tears. She said, "I'm—oh, there's nothing. It's just—"

Millicent waited for her to go on.

"Nothing. Never mind."

"Something's wrong," Millicent said, pushing a strand of hair from the side of her face. "Are you two having some trouble?"

"I don't know," Lily said, and as she spoke, the frustrations of the past weeks rushed in on her. She sat down on the sofa and wept, her hands to her face. She was aware of the other woman moving around in the room, and soon Millicent was sitting next to her, gathering her into an embrace.

"It's the baby," Millicent said. "Remember, I said they have trouble adjusting to the responsibility sometimes."

"It's not that," Lily said. But she could not bring herself to go on. She was painfully conscious of the confining fact that further revelations would lead inevitably to the central, unsayable one. And it seemed now, even in her unhappiness, that to tell the other woman about the scene with Tyler and the rifle would be to give in to her own hysteria, to let her anxieties get the better of her at Millicent's expense. She wanted urgently to believe that her mind had run away with her.

Millicent gave her a handkerchief, and waited for her to compose herself. "Can you talk about it?"

Lily knew that to say it out would mean the saying out of everything; she should never have allowed herself to speak at all.

"Nick told us that he's noticed a little apathetic something—well, a distance."

She nodded.

"Men, and their inability to express how they feel."

"He tells me how he feels. He says he doesn't feel anything."

"For you?"

"For anyone. Anything. The world—all of it."

"Well, he's still thinking about what happened. They're both going to have trouble for the rest of their lives. Tyler and Nick."

Lily nodded.

"Can't the two of you talk about it?"

"We're—we're not—it's all—oh, I shouldn't have said anything. It's just a bad morning."

"What is it that you can't say to him?"

She couldn't return Millicent's gaze. She pulled the handkerchief nervously through her fingers.

"Nick was going to have Tyler call here when he got to the dealership."

Millicent was silent. There was thunder outside, now, breaking across the top of the sky, flashes from far off.

"It's me," Millicent said, "isn't it."

Lily said, "What?"

"It's me—what I did all those years ago."

"No," Lily said, almost impatiently, even as it struck her as containing an element of the truth.

There was a clap of thunder that made them both jump.

"I have a bad feeling," Millicent said. "A chill. I wish we—I wish this would go away. From the beginning, I felt it was better if we all went along and got used to each other and nobody thought too much about it."

Another thunderclap struck, after a bright flash. The rain ran down the big window, and then beat against it in a gust of wind. It was coming down in sheets, and the tops of the trees in the distance were waving back and forth, a chaotic perturbation, a titanic agitation.

Millicent sighed. "So—what do you want me to do? You want me to explain to him that I'm a fault-riddled human being who fell in love with someone not her husband and got pregnant by him and couldn't see any other way out? Because that's what happened, and there really wasn't any other way out, because if I had taken—if I had hauled my son away with me, we would've had to be running—would've spent all our lives running away from Tyler's father. Do you know what Tyler's father was like?"

"Tyler has said some things about him," Lily told her.

"I'd like to hear what Tyler says about him. I would. But let me tell you about Geoffrey Harrison. First and foremost, he was always quite exacting about what belonged to him. Guns, cars, property of every kind, appliances, a parcel of land and the sticks thereon, as we used to say. *Everything*. And of course he thought I belonged to him, too. And I think that if I had stayed, carrying Buddy's child, and Geoffrey'd had to deal with that fact every day of his life, eventually he might've killed me."

Lily stared, and she could feel the blood leaving her face.

"Oh, not that way—not in the way you're thinking, although Tyler's father, along with being possessive, was a violent, frightening man who didn't suffer restrictions on his choices very well. No, he wouldn't have done anything like that, no physical violence—he'd have killed me with *noble behavior*. He'd have killed me with *forgiving* me and letting me *know* I was forgiven every single solitary little minute of my life. And poor Sheri—he would have punished her with *kindliness*, while finding ways of letting her know that of course he didn't *begrudge* her anything. It would've been in everything he ever did with her, and everything he ever said to her, too. Because Geoffrey had the sort of rehearsed benevolence that always somehow allows the reasons for it through, even as it's happening, you know? An upright, religious, helpful man who couldn't manage one lone act of unconscious generosity if his soul depended on it. Do you know what he did when he found out I had fallen in love with Buddy? He took me aside, in our room, asked me to kneel down with him and *pray*. Which I did, since I was only twenty-three and quite horrified by what had happened to me. So we knelt there in our little bedroom and said a Hail Mary, and then he looked at me and said he forgave me. He *forgave* me. I was confused and partly relieved—I had seen his violent side—and at the same time filled with the knowledge that I had to get away from him. That I had to get as far away from him as I could. For my own life. And I also knew that if I took Tyler with me, I would have both Tyler and Geoffrey to contend with—that Geoffrey would've followed me to the ends of the earth, and Tyler would've been so unhappy and wanting to go back all the time. Because Tyler was really his child. Tyler belonged to him in the most complete way, even as an infant. He was always Daddy's boy. And so, I left him. Left *them*. I didn't really have a choice in the matter. And through the years, with Buddy's help, I kept up with Tyler as best I could. The reports were that he was happy with his father, that the two of them had a special bond. It broke my heart not to have him with me, but at that age, he didn't want to be with his mother. He wanted his daddy and the woods and the games and the roughhouse play. The boy had his own fishing rod and tackle by the time he was four."

"He wanted you, too," Lily said.

The other woman stiffened slightly. "That's a revision. If he's told you that, he's telling you something he revised. And maybe he doesn't—maybe he isn't aware of the fact himself. I mean, he was only five. But he would've pined for his father."

"I'm afraid," Lily broke out.

"I am, too," said Millicent. "Welcome to parenthood."

Lily wiped the tears from her cheeks with the handkerchief.

"Look," Millicent said. "There's some trouble between you two, as a couple—and you're not telling me all of it. I understand if it's private, but I can't very well give you advice without knowing more than that he's—that you're having a bad morning."

They both looked at Mary where she slept on her stomach, in the bassinet. The gray, rainy light from the window gave a faint bluish cast to her hands and face.

"He has his father in him," Millicent went on, "I've seen that a little. I have seen that. Geoffrey wasn't exactly conscious of it all, you know—but that man was capable of the most *vicious* sweetness. That's the only way I can describe it. He was very successful at containing his anger about something, but it would come out anyway in acts of noble mercy, gestures of his—his enduring tolerance of you, his willingness to overlook your many weaknesses. It drove me nearly insane." She sighed.

"Then I met Buddy, who had a wonderful way of being—you know how he was—he had a way of being, well, uncomplicatedly interested in me. At first, he was just friendly. That's the truth. A nice man with a kind of—I don't know—a—a kindly sincerity about him. I'd been far more comfortable in his company for such a long time before I realized what it was. I could—*breathe* with him. I could be myself, with all my little strangenesses, and faults, and peccadilloes, and with Buddy they didn't *require* forgiving, any more than a summer shower requires it. I can't tell you how much that meant—realizing that. I was young, remember, and it was a little like finding out something wasn't so that I'd *thought* was so for the whole world. You could be with someone without feeling guilty for all the little ways you fell short of perfection. Anyway, one day I was on my way to see Buddy, filled with happy anticipation, and it came to me that I wanted to be with him all the time. We hadn't even kissed yet. And I might as well tell you that it was me who initiated things, no matter how Buddy ever told the story. And I realized I wanted him at almost the same instant as I realized that nothing I could do, or try to make myself do, would stop me from going after him. It was like being in deep water and seeing the one lifeline. To me, there wasn't any choice."

Sheri had come from the entrance of the kitchen. She said, "Ah, the famous deep-water lifeline story."

"Well, darling," Millicent said, "you might hate the story, but be thankful it happened because you wouldn't be here if it hadn't."

"I didn't mean it the way it sounded, Mother. I'm just sick. As a matter of fact, I like the story. A lot. I like to hear it."

"Rosa said to tell you she was going into town when things let up."

"They haven't let up, and she's sitting in here with me. I've been trying to get some saltines down and talking to her between upchucks. This hangover stuff reeks."

"Maybe you'll think of it the next time you want to overindulge."

"I'll keep some of what I throw up next time, to remind me."

"As usual, Sheri has gone over the line."

Sheri turned and went back into the kitchen, letting the door swing shut behind her.

Millicent looked at Lily. "Let's not say anything to Sheri for a time. I don't want to worry her. She has her own problems right now, of course."

"No—right."

"Do you want me to try and talk to Tyler?"

Lily didn't know how to answer her.

"I don't know what I'd say."

Lily was at a loss. "No," she said, finally. "Please. Don't say anything."

Millicent sighed. "I'm sure it's nothing to worry about. His father used to get in these mysterious moods and once or twice I was worried about him, now that I think of it. Sometimes—I believe that sometimes poor Geoffrey wasn't really happy unless he was suffering. Suffering impressed him. There was something about it that made him feel as if the world had been *righted* again, set back on its normal track. That man wasn't made for prosperity. Nothing upset him like success. Black Irish—you know. I think he was proud of it. Anyway. You might think of getting pregnant again. I've known women who had a good deal of success getting back the attention and the involvement of a husband that way."

Lily kept still while her mother-in-law went over to adjust the blanket on the baby's shoulders. The baby was sleeping soundly. Sheri moved in the kitchen, dishes clattering. The rain had let up now, though thunder still brawled somewhere in the distance. Lily got up to leave. She felt hopeless and sick, and her eyes were edged with tears, which she wiped away with the back of her hand. Millicent was standing there gazing at her.

"You'll tell me what else there is, when you can," Millicent said. "I'm not taking it lightly, even though I may seem to."

Lily caught herself shaking her head out of pure helpless defeat. She went over to the phone and dialed the dealership. The receptionist's voice was deep, rasping with cigarettes. She said there was a meeting of the sales force. "I'd like to speak to Tyler Harrison," Lily told her. "It's important."

"One minute," said the voice.

She waited a long time. Finally Nick's voice came through. "I didn't get to talk to him. He took a new demo and he told one of the other salesmen he was going home."

"Home?"

"Jeez, Lily, I'm sorry. I didn't even see him."

"Nick—" Her voice broke.

"He's probably at your place."

She couldn't speak.

"Millicent and Sheri are there, aren't they? You can't talk."

"Millicent's here with me. Yes. I mean, I'm at Millicent's."

"Well, the salesman said he seemed okay. Why don't you go back to the house. He's there."

"How long?" Lily asked.

"Fifteen minutes—twenty-five. He's at home."

"Thanks, Nick."

When she hung up, she saw that Millicent had crossed the room, and was standing in the watery light from the big window, back turned, mostly shadow.

"He's at home," Lily said.

"I know," Millicent said, as if the trouble were solved. "Why don't you leave Mary here?"

5

*T*YLER WASN'T AT HOME. And he hadn't been home.

The house was as she had left it. She walked through the rooms, searching for any indication that he had been there. She waited at the picture window, looking out on the rain and the road, expecting him to pull in. At last she called the dealership again.

Nick said, "Maybe he was going to Millicent's."

She tried to call Millicent's, but there was no answer. She tried several times. Finally she drove back. The rain had picked up again, a heavy downpour, and when she got to the entrance of the long driveway, she saw that his car was not there. She stopped, peering through the pelting rain at the veranda, the double porch, the windows. It was possible that Millicent could see her here, and would be worried. She pulled in, and made her way to the door, her arms over her head. The rain was beating down, thousands of minute splashes on the black surface of the drive. Millicent opened the door as she reached it.

"What?" she said.

Lily stepped inside, dripping wet. She heard Mary crying in the other room.

"Sheri's rocking her," Millicent said. "For heaven's sake, what is it?"

"I don't know," said Lily. "He's not at home. I thought he'd come here. I tried to call."

"The phone's out. This storm." Alarm, or the strain of resisting it, showed in Millicent's face now. "Look—we don't know that anything's happened," she said. "Right?" And when Lily didn't answer her, she said, again, "Right?"

"Yes," Lily got out.

"Then let's not jump to conclusions. He's probably getting something to eat."

She nodded. The storm swung rain in at them, and there was a bolt of lightning and more thunder. The lightning forked across the whole raining sky and then left a kind of imprint of itself before disappearing.

"Do you want to come in and wait it out?" Millicent said.

"I'll be at home," said Lily. "I'll—I'll go wait for him there."

In the car, she watched the windshield wipers displace the rain, and saw the smallest sliver of sunlight in the fog- and rain-heavy horizon. At the house she went in and busied herself folding laundry, and then trying to work. But it was impossible to give any real attention to anything. The rain let up again, became a drizzle, and then a moving mist, and finally it stopped. The sun came out, pouring through a crevice in the big, massed, angry clouds beyond the trees. The crevice widened, and blue sky showed through. Every surface shimmered and sparkled with sunlight, in beads of water. The house was as quiet as thought. Nothing stirred. She waited, and listened, and the day changed to a bright, sunny, cloud-billowing breezy calm, pile upon pile of snowy canyons, making moving shadows on the whole curve of the earth and over the trees. In the sky to the east was a stupendous pair of honeyed yellow bows spanning the entire horizon, with the air between the parallel curves showing the color of a deep bruise. She watched it, and remarked it as something to say to him when he pulled in; they could both be amazed by the rainbow, and in their amazement they could forget that they were coming apart. It was a childish little fantasy that she clung to, waiting for him.

But he didn't come. He wasn't at the dealership. He didn't go to his mother's house, or to the house of a friend. The sun sank below the level of the hills, and the night drew down, clear and moon-bright. Lily drove to the Galatierre house to bring Mary home. Millicent, Sheri, Rosa, and Nick were all waiting for word. It was too early to call the police. It hadn't been long enough, Nick said. Rosa thought she had seen Tyler in town, making the turn out of the square. She couldn't be absolutely certain, but it had looked like Tyler, and he had seemed perfectly at ease, one arm resting in the frame of the open car window. She'd honked and waved, but had rounded the bend before she could see whether he had seen her, or responded. So they all waited.

And no word came.

By the middle of the next afternoon, they had gotten the police involved. Lily and Nick rode into town and filled out forms at the police station. And the following day, two officers came to the house. They questioned Lily about her husband's habits, about his problems, what might cause him to leave and not come back. They were not rude, and yet she felt the questions as rude and invasive, and of course she couldn't spell it out for them—what she knew to be the reason for everything.

6

PART OF THE HELPLESSNESS born out of the disappearance of a person is a dread that runs so deep into the psyche that the psyche recoils from it, clinging to the possibility of a return, of some sort of harmless explanation, or, if the absence becomes prolonged, of a miraculous recovery. This dread becomes indurated and leaden as despair, and causes all the symptoms of grief, because it contains the ever-growing suspicion, resisted with all the energy of the mind and heart, that the one who is missing will never be found.

By the third day, they were all expecting the worst.

Lily, between bouts of worry and anxiety, was seized by waves of anger at Tyler, a kind of floating rage, beyond reason. The anger rose up in her gullet like a fit of nausea.

Because she couldn't do otherwise, she took the baby over to the Galatierre house in the morning, and waited with everyone. Millicent greeted her with a desperate, dazed look, though she cooed at the baby and flitted about the living room making things ready for her—putting a gate across the entrances to the kitchen and the downstairs, and laying toys around on the soft carpet. Rosa came in from the kitchen with breakfast on a tray.

"I don't know what I thought I could eat," Millicent said, and began to weep. Rosa took the tray back into the kitchen.

"Where's Sheri?" Lily asked.

Millicent seemed bewildered. "Sheri?"

"Went to work," Rosa said from the kitchen doorway. "Nick's at the police station."

"Oh, God," Millicent said, wringing her hands. "God."

Toward the middle of the morning, Nick called. The police had located the car Tyler had driven away from the dealership. It was parked by the river, under the overpass. It had been driven off the road and down the embankment. The keys were in the ignition. Apparently it had been left running; it was out of gas. There was no sign of Tyler.

"Lily," he said, in a broken voice. "The police are talking about dragging the river."

Lily wept, holding the handset tight, unable to believe any of it.

"Lily?" said Nick on the other end of the line. "That doesn't necessarily mean anything. He's not in the river, Lily."

She couldn't speak for a moment.

"I know it, Lily."

7

THEY ALL WAITED for more news. They lived through the hours, the hideous waiting, fearful of thought itself, anything that might lead them to contemplating the unimaginable, answerless future, with its long blank. Lily kept waiting for some change, and the pressure to reveal what the crux of Tyler's trouble had been was becoming all but unbearable. Yet she refrained; there was always the chance that he would come home. And she understood, too, that a component of this desire to unburden herself was selfish: it would be such a relief to get it all out at last, the truth, no matter the results. Moreover, she saw how Millicent was suffering, and was fairly certain that the knowledge of Tyler's rage and despair over patrimony would relieve the older woman's sense of being the proximate cause of this desolation. Yet in the instant of having this thought, a disagreeable little turn of her mind told her that in very important ways Millicent *was* the reason for it all. If she hadn't abandoned Tyler in his infancy, perhaps he would have been stronger. There were also signs—little comments about Tyler's happiness, or the lack of it, in the marriage; a certain grudging tone with Lily—that Millicent held Lily responsible. And so Lily felt the resolve rise in her: if Tyler *was* in the river, she would bear their secret to the grave for him.

She understood full well the trap she was in: it had been only three days. Tyler might simply be trying to punish her, and if she told them everything and he returned, things might end up even worse. Mixed with her fear that he had harmed himself was her continuing wrath, a stubborn feeling that he was doing it all with purpose, and out of malice.

They were in the kitchen, sitting at the table. Rosa had prepared spiced shrimp, and a salad, but no one had eaten much. Outside, the afternoon sun blazed on the pool, the trees, and the lawn. There was no wind. The sky was a perfect merciless unblemished blue.

"He talked about joining the army," Millicent said. "Can't we call the army?"

"Can a person just walk up and join the army?" Nick wanted to know. "Abandon a car and join the army?"

Sheri said, "Why're you asking us?"

He gave her an exasperated look, but said nothing. She returned a penitent and supplicating expression, and he rose and went to the phone. They all listened to him request the number of the nearest army recruitment center from the information operator. He disconnected, punched in the numbers, and waited. Roger Gault was seated next to Millicent, and he held her hand. Lily couldn't look at them, couldn't look at anyone. She was feeding strained pears to Mary, who spat them out, making little screeches, slapping the high chair's miniature table surface with both chubby hands.

Nick spoke in a murmurous tone, like someone in a funeral parlor, but they could hear him. "Is this the army recruitment center? Yes, I was wondering—if you don't mind. I wondered—if you had a record of someone enlisting in the army, if there was a way to see that record." In the pause, Mary emitted a happy cry, and put her hands together, fingers clasped tightly, so that she had to pull hard to unclasp them. This delighted her, and she did it again, as Nick's voice came to them: "Well, actually, it could be a police inquiry—a—a missing-person inquiry."

"Oh, God," Millicent said.

"No, this is an adult," Nick said into the phone. "Twenty—uh, hold on a second." He leaned into the room. "How old is Tyler?"

"He's twenty-eight," Lily said.

Nick repeated the number to the person on the other end.

"Oh," said Millicent. It was almost a random sound.

"I see." Nick's voice. "Well, what would be necessary in order for someone to enlist?"

"He's not in the army," Sheri said. "*Jesus*."

They heard Nick again: "Thank you. You've been very helpful." He hung the phone up, and walked in to them. "All they need is to make sure there's no police record. And they don't have to check with the family of an adult male who decides to enter the army."

"He's not in the *army*, Nick. He left his car by the *river*."

Millicent stood and faced her daughter. "You *stop* talking like that, Sheri. You *stop* it right now."

"I'm sorry," said Sheri, lowering her head. Millicent moved to embrace her, and then they were both crying, holding each other, while Nick and Roger attempted to calm them. In the middle of this, the baby's bright sounds took on the feeling of unspeakable contrast, and Lily was constrained to try quieting her. Finally she lifted her from the high chair and went into the living room. Nick followed her. She set Mary down on the sofa and began to change her diaper, and he went up to her and took her by the elbow. "Lily." His face was ashen, his eyes shaded and circled by lack of sleep and worry. "Is there anything—" He halted.

"We were having trouble," she murmured.

"I know he was having trouble about what happened with Buddy."

"Yes."

He appeared to be expecting her to go on, and when she didn't, he sat on the sofa, next to where the baby lay. The baby was still making bright cooing noises and flailing her fat arms as Lily changed her. The diaper was only wet. Lily put it in a plastic bag and Nick handed her a fresh diaper.

"We were having trouble," Lily repeated.

"What kind of trouble?"

"Trouble, Nick. The kind married people have." She hadn't meant him to, but it was manifest that he took this to be a reference to his relationship with Sheri. He shook his head, and dropped his gaze. She let it stand. There was an inertia down in her heart, now, a soul weariness, that drew all the strength out of her will. She no longer felt that she could decide anything; she was all reactions, watching him take hold of Mary's hand and put his thumb in the middle of the little palm. Mary's fingers closed around the thumb.

8

*O*N THE EIGHTH DAY, a call came through from a marine recruiter in New Orleans. He was calling at the request of the Oxford Police Department to say that Tyler C. Harrison was in basic training at Parris Island. The police had uncovered a form requisitioning any criminal record for the individual, as the recruiter put it. He'd already sent word to the commanding officer of the training unit that Harrison's family wished him to contact them. But he was twenty-eight years old and an adult, and, as long as there was no abandonment, nor any neglected familial responsibility or emergency, they could not do more than make certain that he received the message.

Millicent, who took the call, thanked them, and then collapsed. Sheri was standing right there, and helped her to the sofa, where she lay in a befuddled trance made out of a combination of sorrow and relief. Lily, who had been feeding the baby, stood with the others around the couch where Millicent spent herself in tears and cries of anguish. "I did this. This is my doing," Millicent said. "I'm being punished."

Lily shook her head and was silent. The waiting had been so hard on everyone that the new situation took a long, strange hour to sink in. They moved through the house and got through dinner and the evening, with Millicent muttering from the couch, and the television rattling out stories about the ongoing crisis in the Middle East, like a vague something unfolding in the background, something inside the noise of the television itself, interior and of its construction, like a malfunctioning part of the machine. The television was always on, and was always so much the same as not to be noticeable, quite. It was the drone of other voices, something to fill the silences between the gloomy inmates of the house. Lily had gone back and forth between the two places—the little cottage in Yellow Leaf Creek, and here. That eighth night she'd spent at the Galatierre house, in the room she had shared with her husband. The wait was to be different, now, though it would still be waiting: now, they were all waiting for Tyler to contact them, to phone, or write a letter, or send a card. Something. But the days passed, and there was talk of war, as if the world had conspired with him to take him irrevocably away. Perhaps even to kill him.

No word came.

Lily went home, and kept, as well as she could, to the routine of her days. It was life now, and there wasn't anything else for it. She went over to the Galatierre house each morning, for an hour or so. Rosa was there, too, having settled in for the rest of the summer, a houseguest. Everyone was being careful of Lily now, because her husband had abandoned her, and their child.

Nothing could be more frustrating than the feeling that people were only making minute scratches across the surface of the real dilemma.

She went on trying to write. The play was progressing, but in stops and starts; twice she had torn it down to begin again. And her concentration was divided all the time by the thought of Tyler, off on his self-destructive flight from her, even as she angrily sought not to consider him at all. And she *was* angry, when she examined her true emotions about it. She hadn't expressed this to any of the others.

What she couldn't decide was when, or how, or if, she might unfetter herself of the secret history.

One Saturday toward the end of August, Nick came to see her. "I was wondering if I could take you out to lunch," he said.

She had already eaten a sandwich, but she went with him to the café on the square. It was a sunny, unpleasantly muggy noon, a blue haze obscuring everything in the distance. He seemed even more pensive than usual, staring at the menu. The waiter was a boy, with fair skin and his hair cut so close he had only stubble on his scalp. Nick ordered a chicken sandwich, and then asked Lily what she wanted.

"Iced tea," she said to the waiter.

After the waiter left, Nick took a breath, leaning back in his chair and looking down at his own hands on the table. "I've had a call from Tyler."

Lily waited for him to continue.

"We had a long talk."

"About me?" she asked.

His gaze only brushed past her, then seemed to wander about the room. There were other people in the café, and he nodded at someone who had evidently recognized him. "About everything," he said, low.

"Tell me."

"He told me everything, Lily."

She looked at him.

"He doesn't want to come home."

"He told you that."

"In so many words."

"And?"

He sat forward. "Well, he wants to know what you're gonna do."

"Does he think I'll divorce him?"

"I don't know."

"Well, what did he say, Nick?"

"He said he wants to know what you'll do."

"As in?"

Nick shrugged. "I guess divorce."

"What else did he say."

"Well, that—that you and he were a mistake."

"Go on."

"Lily, I said he told me all of it."

She felt the pain rise under her heart, that it had come. It was here. The feeling was truly as if she had only been waiting for it to be final, even as she had hoped for some answer. She let the tears come, did not move to wipe them from her eyes; they welled up and rolled down her cheeks. He reached across the table and took her hand.

"I wish it was anybody but me having to tell you this."

"Who else knows now?"

"Nobody," he said with an edge of incredulity. "You couldn't think I'd say anything to anybody else."

"But Tyler told you." She sniffled. And now she began wiping the tears away.

"He—he wants to know what you're gonna do."

"He can't call and ask me himself?"

Nick looked down. "He says he doesn't—that he can't talk to you again."

"Oh, really." She felt this along the nerves of her face, like a slap.

Nick said, "He's nuts, if you ask me. Completely crackers."

"Even knowing what you know?"

"Yes." His gaze was direct.

"He doesn't want to see me or the baby."

Nick nodded. "I could tell it hurt him. But yes. He seemed especially adamant about that—the baby."

"Well—that's complete, then." She sobbed. "That's that."

"I'm sorry, Lily. I'm so sorry."

"No," she said, waving this away. "Really."

"If it means anything—he has no desire to have anything to do with his mother or Sheri, either. Or me, for that matter. He wants to sever all ties. That's his phrase. 'All ties.'"

Lily regarded him. There was a grave, wounded expression on his face, and he ran one hand across his forehead, as if to soothe a pain there. She said, "Tell Tyler I'm going down to New Orleans." Until the moment the words had come from her, she hadn't known this was what she would do. Now, having said them out loud, nothing else seemed possible, or right.

"Well, as I said, he's not coming back here. He's determined about that."

"I haven't expected that he'd come back." She was trying to gain control of herself, fighting the tears with everything she had.

"I'm so miserably sorry about this," Nick said. "I feel like a bastard. He wanted to dissolve his interest in the dealership. That's the only reason he called me."

"I know," said Lily. "It's okay. I know."

The waiter brought the sandwich, and the drinks. Lily's hand shook, lifting the glass, and Nick reached over again to take hold of her wrist, a sympathetically steadying touch. "I wish things were different."

"No," she said. "It's all right. I'm fine. I am." But she couldn't stop the tears.

"He wasn't up to you, Lily, wasn't worthy of you."

The others in the café were noticing them. She held a handkerchief to her face, and turned a little, sobbing, trying to keep herself from making a sound.

Nick took a small bite of the sandwich and then set it down on the plate. He touched her wrist again, and then drew his hand away. "Lily, I made him set part of the money aside for you now—separate from whatever comes out of the divorce. I got that done. It's not a lot, but it'll tide you over."

She couldn't speak. It seemed to her now that everything before this had been dreamlike, a progress of trials from which she believed she could emerge wiser, stronger, braced for the next set of difficulties but essentially unchanged, her life fundamentally as it had been. "I want you to tell Sheri and Millicent," she said. "I'm going to spare myself that one."

He nodded. "He'd like you to sue for the divorce."

"I want it mutual," she said. "Grounds of incompatibility or something like that."

"He said you could say he abandoned you."

"No," Lily said. "Mutual incompatibility. There is such a thing, right?"

"I think there is."

"Then that's what I want."

"I'll make sure he understands it."

"I'd like you to help me sublet the house."

"I will. I'll manage it."

"You're my closest friend here, now," she told him. "And I would've thought that so unlikely once."

He set his gaze elsewhere, and she saw the moistness in the bottom lids of his eyes.

"Nick," she said.

He turned to her.

"How soon can you get me the money?"

TWENTY-TWO

1

$\mathcal{T}$HE SPRING and summer months in London are filled with social responsibility. It is as if Mary's presence, after the time away, is a catalyst for family members and new acquaintances to concoct ways to trespass on her time. No one means to impose upon her, and she knows this, and yet she feels the intrusion, and must therefore expend the effort not to be rude or neglectful of anybody. She has made the acquaintance of Ethel MacDonald and Mathilda Goldie, and there are daily communications from Macmillan about her book, which she has begun to decide she wishes not to pursue, feeling unready yet to express what she will finally have to say about it all. A cousin, also named Mary, has published two novels under an assumed name, and when this cousin sees the pages of *The Bites of Benin* she speaks of descriptive power, and tone. Mary reads her cousin's novels and feels too unprofessional as a writer, though she finds her cousin's subject matter painfully frivolous. She communicates to Macmillan that she definitely wishes not to pursue publication, and supposes therefore that the matter is at an end.

But there are money worries, and Charley maintains his languorous ways, talking idly of the Far East and his study of religious practices there, usually going on about it as though it is an accomplished fact. Nothing comes of any of it; and nothing comes of his proposed memoir about their father, either. Mary confides in Mathilda Goldie, who is exactly what her husband claimed she would be: a maverick, with ideas of her own about almost everything. Mathilda thinks she should ignore Charley, and make her own plans. The two women spend afternoons together, sometimes joined by Lady MacDonald, and old friends from Cambridge. Charley remarks that Mary is like someone daydreaming a lot of the time, but the fact is she's planning her return to Africa. When it becomes clear that Lady MacDonald must go down to join her husband in Calabar, Mary decides that the two of them must travel together.

But then Lady MacDonald is delayed indefinitely. There are matters she must attend to in London, and in any case Charley continues to dally, putting off his own journey. There is so much tension in the flat that Mary spends many afternoons in the reading room of the British Museum, poring over the work of the great scholars of anthropology.

One afternoon in late October, she's coming out of the venerable old building, and she sees Gladstone, only seven months removed from his last, and disastrous, stint as prime minister, making his way in. He wears a long black coat. His side hair is long and unkempt under the crown of a straw hat. He's accompanied by three young gentlemen of apparent military rank, and he walks very slowly, stooped, using a knobby cane, and looking every bit of eighty-five. He glances her way. She looks into the piercing old eyes, and he looks back.

—Young woman, he says.

—Sir, says Mary.

Then he's gone inside, the door closing on him.

She goes home with the excitement of a girl, and a little of the feeling of having seen a ghost. Charley is lounging on the couch, under the bright window, as she climbs to the top of the stairs into the flat.

—I saw Gladstone, she tells him.

Charley's reading a newspaper, and doesn't look up from it.

—I'm hungry, he says.

There is a char woman and a cook, both of whom she desires to dismiss, to save money. He won't hear of it. And it incenses her that he lacks even the energy to request his meals from them. He leaves that, and everything else, to Mary.

—That's fine, she says now. That's very well indeed. You're 'ungry. I'm Mary.

He looks up from the paper.

—Excuse me?

—Nothing, she says.

—Sound your aitches, can't you? My God, that's annoying.

She goes into the small kitchen, where the cook, a Mrs. Starrett, is already preparing tea. Mrs. Starrett is a squarish, heavy-featured woman whose family disowned her for having married an Irish Catholic. In the evenings, she tends toward garrulousness, and likes to tell Mary of the sacrifices she has made for the love of her husband. Her good-natured belief that Mary is headed down the wrong path by not immediately seeking a husband is, of course, manifest.

—I 'eard, mum, Mrs. Starrett says. The master's 'ungry.

—Thank you, says Mary.

She goes up the little stoop into her study, where her father's notes and papers are stacked and boxed, and maps of various rivers and estuaries of the African coastline are hung. She works on her notes a little, though she has resolved not to publish the book. Her studies have demonstrated to her the superficial nature of the knowledge she gathered on that first stay in Africa. Her earlier modesty about it with Goldie, she realizes, is justified. She possesses enough detachment to know this.

So she will go back. And it is more than simply wanting to. It is a requirement, almost a duty, not a little because she's convinced that if she stays in London she might go out of her mind. Charley comes bumping up the stairs, having found something in the newspaper to amuse him, and wanting her to hear it. Someone has speculated that the never-caught Cheapside murderer might be a member of the royal family.

Mary watches him read this little tidbit, his eyes bright with glee, wide with a boy's pleasure in macabre speculation. She loves him, loves even the irresponsible idleness that is so much a part of his being. She no longer feels maternal toward him, if she ever did, yet she does experience the wish to protect his fragile sense of the world as a place existing for his entertainment. This understanding of him is almost visceral, wordless: Charley is not capable of viewing things straight on, but must always see through the prism of his appetite for diversions.

—Imagine the queen reading this, he says. She'll have apoplexy.

—I don't imagine she'll see it, says Mary.

—What are you doing? he demands.

—I'm looking over some maps of the coastline. I'm studying navigational charts. I'm collating Father's notes on religious practices among the aboriginal tribes of America and comparing them to what I observed in Africa. What are *you* doing, brother?

He stares for a few seconds, completely unaware of the irony in her question.

—I'm getting ready to eat, he says.

2

*T*HERE ARE THINGS to do to prepare, not the least of which is procuring enough funds to scrape by. At the British Museum, she visits with an anthropologist named Gunther, whose book on the species of fish in Africa she has read, and who is impressed with the samples she has collected. He kindly provides her with some tools of the trade—jars and utensils that are better, more advanced in design, than the crude ones she has used. She knows more now, what to pack, what to say to those whose goodwill she must have to succeed. It's fortunate that Lady MacDonald desires to be accompanied on her own journey to rejoin her husband at the oil protectorate.

The months between August and December pass in a flurry of study and activity, and even so she feels banked, held back, imprisoned by all the requirements at 100 Addison Road and by her growing number of acquaintances. At last, Charley has left on his lark, back to Asia, and she can close up the house and make her own plans. Christmas week she and Lady MacDonald take the train down to Liverpool, through a driving wind and rain. In Liverpool, the *Batanga*, a large vessel bound for the African coast, specifically Sierra Leone and Calabar, is at anchor until the weather clears. The storm is pounding in from the sea, a gale, lashing the shore and the town. They leave the train in an icy, needle-thin, pelting rain, and make their way to a little inn to wait it out.

Ethel MacDonald is the model governor's wife. She cannot understand Mary's desire to get into the bush, and hasn't quite taken it seriously. They are devoted to each other, though there is this decided difference between them concerning what there is to do and see in Africa—and Lady MacDonald's attitudes are somewhat restricted: she sees the African as a kind of bright animal, and the Mohammedans, black or white, as infidels. She believes in the purposes of the Christian missionaries, and expects that Africa should be exploited for the uses of the Empire. Mary shares this last belief to some extent, but sees it more as an exchange between equals, at least where trade is concerned. These differences between them are overcome by the small but important matter of their mutual temper: they amuse each other; their affection is real. Ethel MacDonald possesses no trace of the dogmatic. She's tolerant of foreign points of view, and Mary makes her laugh.

Indeed, she told Mary in their first days of knowing each other that it is Mary's dry, often wildly self-deprecating sense of humor that she finds most appealing. Mary has a gift for startling exaggeration. Ethel MacDonald once expressed the conviction that if Mary could put it all into writing, she could make a lot of people very happy.

—I have tried to write and failed, Mary told her.

They check into a room to wait out the storm. Mary feels as if the boat might slip away in the dark, though she knows this is a child's anxiety; they have booked passage. There are others waiting at this same inn for the storm to pass. She gets into her bed and stares at the glimmer of light on the ceiling, from a guttering street lamp out in the rain. The rain rattles the window, and something knocks repetitively against the casement. It is impossible to muster the assurance that it is not a person seeking to gain entrance. Lady MacDonald has piled blankets and pillows on herself, and is wearing a sleeping cap with little bows tied all around the circumference of it. She looks like a big infant, nestled in the heavy bed. Mary thinks of Lucy Toulmin-Smith, and of Paris.

—Have you ever been to Paris?

—Every summer when I was a girl, Ethel MacDonald says. You?

—Once.

—Did you fall in love with it?

—No. I liked it.

—You *liked* it. Paris.

—I was with someone older. A friend, who wanted me to see the sights. So I didn't get to see the sights.

Lady Ethel MacDonald laughs softly, and the laughter grows louder, until she begins to cough. The coughing goes on for a few seconds, and at last she settles deeper under her heavy blankets, puts her hands to her face, and with a small sigh of satisfaction, subsides. Mary can't sleep, and so she waits for the wind and rain to stop, and for light to come to the window.

The change is so slow that she almost misses it. She drifts for a very few minutes just before dawn. But she's wide awake and watching as the shadows come to the objects in the room, and to the thick violet and crimson folds of Lady MacDonald's bedclothes. They rise with first light and dress, and have tea and biscuits in the dining room of the inn. Several other passengers are there, none of whom Mary recognizes, though she knows the types: two missionaries and their wives, a government official, a military man.

The dock is crowded, and noisy, and every surface drips with the night's rain. The smell of the dockside is of the rain and the rotting vegetables and dead flesh of fish and fowl in crates once bound for markets, but ruined now by the storm. There is continual shouting and uproar. The cargo is being loaded, walked across on planks, carried and dragged by shore men, and sailors. Mary walks up the gangway ahead of Ethel, and comes face to face with Captain John Murray.

He has seen her first, and is smiling—an expression so uncharacteristic of him that two of his crewmen have stopped their work to gaze at him in amazement. It is *their* wondering faces that cause Mary to pause, and to see the captain, standing on the deck with his arms folded, waiting for her.

—Oh, she says, dropping her reticule, throwing her arms wide as if to embrace him.

But she stops short, and folds her arms, tilting her head to one side, elated.

—What good fortune, she says to him.

He's beaming with uncontainable delight.

—Miss Kingsley, he says, I see you have survived London.

3

Dear Doris,

I have sublet the house, and made my farewells to Sheri and the others, and tomorrow I set out for New Orleans. Tyler and I are over. I would not be at all surprised if I never set eyes on him again. He's somewhere in Georgia now, with a marine unit, going through officers' school. If we were characters in a movie, the country would go to war and he would go off and disappear into the flames of battle. What will probably happen is that he'll settle somewhere far away, meet someone and marry again, and live out a quiet life with someone he trusts. I wish him that. Even as I wish something could turn everything around for us and we could be innocent and happy again, like the children we were. I know I sound jaded and so pretentiously "mature" and you're probably cringing. But the hard fact of the matter is that I still feel something for him and don't really know how to qualify it or explain it. I'm only twenty-two. I think I still do love him—that hasn't changed. So I miss him—or I miss him as he was before everything flew apart in recrimination and suspicion, and the weeks of each of us wondering what the other one was feeling, and Mary at the heart of it, nobody's fault, really, and needing uncomplicated love.

I wanted Tyler's trust. I felt I had to try regaining it. I didn't think about you or Scott or Peggy and it never entered my mind what it would mean to you to find out what had happened—it was always, as I told you on the phone, what it would mean here, with Tyler and Millicent and Sheri and Nick, and with Buddy gone that way, all of them nursing their sorrows, and poor Dominic down in New Orleans, so terrified of being alone, and I had the knowledge that he has a child he doesn't even know about. His child. That fact, which would not be swallowed, or absorbed, or ignored, would not let me rest. It divided Tyler and me—it was the only thing that divided us, and maybe (probably) given time, other things would have.

And I still haven't told Dominic.

He's said over the phone that he's got a room for me and the baby, and I'm going down there, really, to see what's next. I'll stay with him and Manny and Aunt Violet Beaumont, in that row house in the Quarter.

I thought Daddy's offer of work at the theater was sweet, even though I know he would have twisted arms to get it for me, and probably put himself on the enemies list of several people. But I really don't want to take advantage of his work or his position. In a few weeks, believe it or not, I may have a completed play about Mary Kingsley (well, it's about bravery, imagine that, me writing a play about bravery), and if and when that happens I expect to submit it to theaters without using his name, and he'll just have to understand that. I told him he wouldn't have accepted for himself, when he was my age, outside help of the kind that he's offering me.

What I mostly want you both to understand is that I'm all right. I'm hurting because my marriage is dissolving and I wish it wasn't. I'm having to pick up with a seven-month-old baby and go to a town I've only been in once in my life. But I feel that's better than staying here, or going back to Virginia, just now. I think this is what I have to do. When I phoned Dom to tell him what had happened to us, he offered before I had the opportunity to ask. The conversation was very hard, and very strange, because he tried at first to reassure me that Tyler would come home, that these things happen in early marriage and Tyler was still trying to adjust to the loss of Buddy, and to being a new father. All that. All the things I told myself in the beginning. I managed at last to convince him that the marriage was over by claiming that I wanted an end to it. Well, I wanted an end to something. And Dominic is the father of this baby and I have to find some gentle way of letting him know this, and then seeing what his wishes are regarding that fact. I plan to let him know that I have no expectations of him; it's only that I can't let the knowledge of it be kept from him. So I'm not coming to Virginia, and I don't know when I will. Maybe I'll be able to save enough of this money Tyler sent from his part of the dealership to make a trip up there for the holidays. I don't want to be brought back, though, Doris, and you'll just have to make Scott understand that. When I come home, I want it to be on my own dime.

Mary is beginning to say things now—"Ma-ma." "Da-da." "No." She says no a lot. To any phrase that ends with the inflection of a question. So Nick will say to her, "Mary, you believe in the ineluctable modality of the visible, right?" And Mary will say, "No." Sometimes even shaking her head. It makes everyone take a second look. He'll lean close to her little glowering face and say, "Mary, you do believe in the dictatorship of the proletariat, don't you?" And she'll already be shaking her head. "No."

Nick has been so helpful, and has been in the awful position of having to serve as the middleman between Tyler and the rest of the family. Tyler will not speak to his mother or his half sister, will only call Nick at the dealership, and has let it be known that when he clears all his ties with the business and with me, he plans to get as far away from all of us as he can. Nick has been so helpful, and I feel so sorry for him, carrying what he's carrying, and having to be the man in the middle of this.

It seems to me that when Buddy went, all my need for this family ebbed out of me, without my quite knowing it was happening. It's possible that Buddy softened everyone's hard edges. He held everything together.

I don't know what else to tell you. I love you. I'm still working on my play, almost every day now, at least two hours a day. Mary grows in leaps and bounds. I've sold or given to Goodwill what little furniture we had, and I gave away most of the records and books. I'm all packed (Nick and Sheri helped), and in the morning I'm getting into the Oldsmobile and heading south to the Gulf, and new quarters. Another life. Of course we'll be talking before you get this.

Love,
Lily

I've so presumptuously imagined you heading off to another world—a journey at least as drastic as a modern flight to the moon—and here I am, waiting for sunrise, and my little trip south, to live for a time with the father of my child, who has no idea of the truth, and I'm so frightened that I can hardly hold the pen.

It seems to me that your life may be explicable as a private struggle to search out some answer about existence; about—as you put it once—the nature of God. You possessed the sense of the world as a created thing and a mystery. It seems to me that your journey began in a private quest for answers to that mystery, and ended in the public quest that it became, almost without your realizing it. You were a person of such magnetism, you bound so many people to you—Lucy Toulmin-Smith, Varley, Corliss, Captain Murray, the MacDonalds, Batty, and the Goldies, and all the others, missionaries as well as traders, members of the government, and all the Africans, and you were always the same. They all have provided in their own way their accounts of you, and the one fact that emerges is the consistency of who you were with all of them: energetic, determined, funny, self-critical, assertive, opinionated without being doctrinaire, loyal, gentle, interesting, intrepid—they all speak of your apparent lack of fear, of the fact that you never showed it to anyone. No, what I mean to say is, that because you never showed your fear to anyone, they believed that you did not feel it or experience it. They attributed to you a fearlessness that in my mind devalues the bravery you did possess. And it was bravery.

I would like to have some of that bravery now. I'm not going to wild places, but I have a child with me, and the intricacy of another person, the responsibility of another person, of that other life in the world whose being is from my body and blood—well, that is a wilderness, too. Going out into the world, and making your way amid the forests of expectation and definition—that's an exploration, too, isn't it?

When I write about you now, it's as if you murmur in my ear. I see you standing at my shoulder, hands on hips, a look of mild and tolerant, perhaps even humorous, impatience on your face. Get on, get on, I hear you say.

Writing these small entries to you—people will say that's a conceit. For me, it's a beautiful mystery.

The morning was steely-colored, an almost unearthly gray, and so humid that her blouse clung to her within seconds. Nick drove up at first light, with a package of Danishes and two cups of coffee.

"The coffee was Sheri and Millicent's idea. Millicent wants you to stay alert."

"Thank them for me," Lily said. Then: "I'll send them a card."

He nodded, but said nothing. She sipped her coffee, feeling the need to go, get away. Briefly, she had the intuition that she was causing the whole family to suffer, each in some separate way, though they were collectively striving for concern and trying to help. It was so strange, now—now that they knew the baby was no kin of theirs, and now that Tyler was gone. Things had been friendly, but in a brittle way, cordial, and not like real friendship at all. There was something rehearsed about it, nervous and on edge, except where Nick was concerned. He seemed to understand what notes to strike, and in any case had proved himself to be her friend, apart from the Galatierre household. She felt that.

They were standing in the kitchen, with its cabinets open and empty. Mary played on the floor, waving a rattle back and forth and then trying to dismantle it, sitting up straight. They watched her for a few moments. The whole morning seemed illusory.

"Millicent wanted me to repeat for her that she hopes you'll stay in touch," he said.

"Of course," said Lily. "Tell her I repeated that I will."

"Tyler's adamant. It's crazy."

She felt the stab of knowing her marriage was over; it was as much fear, now, as sorrow.

"If there's anything that I can do, you know."

She put one hand on his elbow. "I know."

He drank the last of his coffee and then crushed the cup in his fist. "Well, I've got to get to work. I'm supposed to tell you to be careful and good to yourself," he said, looking down.

She had the feeling that he longed to disclose something, and a stirring in her soul urged her to move past the moment, talk through it. She said: "I'll write you when I get down to New Orleans. I'll keep you posted."

He hesitated, then appeared to back down from whatever he had determined earlier to say or do. He started away, then stopped, turned, knelt to take Mary's dimpled hand and kiss it, and, standing again, put his arms very gingerly around Lily. "You take care," he said, at the bottom of his throat.

Her own voice caught. "I will." She kissed his cheek.

"Well," he said, letting go of her, backing away. "I hope we—I hope to see you soon."

"Yes," she told him.

"You won't lose touch."

"No." She smiled, and wiped her eyes.

He made his way through the grayness to the car, got in, gazed through the windshield at her, without gesturing, then started it and backed out, looking over his shoulder. Having backed into the road, he glanced her way once more, without waving, and was gone. She lifted one hand, but he hadn't looked back.

She stooped, crying a little, and picked the baby up. She felt quite alone and abruptly very afraid. "You ready for this, girlie?" she said to Mary.

The child looked at her with the perpetual questioning that was always in the small face, and said, "No."

Lily laughed, in the middle of her tears, carrying her out to the Oldsmobile, then put her in the car seat in back. The humidity had soaked through everything. She got in behind the wheel, opened the windows, and started the ignition. Each of these motions required effort, it seemed. And each of them was irrevocable, a step away that could not be retracted. She was really doing this.

The apartment building across the way was almost finished. There were flags flapping in the soaked breeze, in the dullness of the drifting haze and murk. Fog was everywhere this glowering morning. It lay thick and quite still over the whole town, though as she drove out onto Highway 55 South, she saw the slightest tinge of a carmine glow in the dense, sodden screen of it to the east—the sun about to burn through. She put the radio on, and Mary slept in the car seat. She sang along with the radio songs, mostly old rock songs from when she was in high school, back in 1986 and '87. She felt oddly as if she were again there, a teenage girl, on an adventure. There was the trouble, of course, the heartache she had been through, and when she thought of Tyler the anger and hurt rose to her mind from the injured places; it was all unabated. Yet she felt this release, this thrill. She glanced back at Mary sleeping in the car seat and marveled at the fact that she was a woman with a child, a mother. It was always as if she had not yet fully realized it, was only now seeing the magnitude of it, though the realization itself was familiar. The road ahead emerged from the folds of mist, and was mostly empty. And as the fog lifted—or as she drove out of it, she couldn't tell which—she sang louder, with an exhilarating sensation of being free, of escaping into breathable air.

4

THREE HOURS from New Orleans, in the little town of Harker's Bend, Mississippi, she stopped for something to eat. She carried the baby in the car seat into a truck stop called Dorsey's, and set her, still lying in the car seat, on the table in a booth. Mary was half awake, opening her eyes and then closing them again, complaining softly, and then settling back.

The waitress was a lean, pale young woman with long straight black hair and cloudy blue eyes. When she turned them in Lily's direction, Lily saw a pronounced flaw in the iris of the left one, and a deeper recession of the eye itself in its socket.

"I've got four myself," the waitress said. "My husband says that's the best way, leaving them in the car seat like that, and I think so, too. He works for the highway department at night, so he's got them during the day."

Lily nodded.

"What's your husband do?"

After the slightest delay, she answered: "Sells cars."

"Must be nice. They get new cars to drive around, right? I had a brother-in-law who sold Lincolns."

She ordered scrambled eggs for Mary and a sandwich for herself. And while waiting for these things to be brought to her, she thought about the fact that she had felt the need to lie about her husband. Something in the waitress's expression had made Lily sense that saying the truth would be awkward, or would make the other feel awkward. She was so weary of untruth. She came close to calling the waitress back.

Instead she waited, and kept still, watching Mary begin to wake up.

The waitress brought the food, and said nothing else. Lily couldn't help looking at the one strangely caved-in eye. There was a husband, and people forgave each other their mutual imperfections in love.

She caught herself crying a little, eating her sandwich and feeding the eggs to the baby, who wasn't interested in them, and thinking about Buddy Galatierre, Tyler, the events of the past weeks. Two men came in and ordered Cokes and sat drinking, talking low. They kept looking over at Lily and the baby. The taller of the two tipped his hat, and smiled.

"Are you all right, Miss?"

"Yes, thank you."

Everyone was so kind. She hadn't expected this desolate sense of aloneness; the fact of it surprised and demoralized her. She paid the waitress, then lifted Mary in her seat and made her way, sniffling, to the car.

In New Orleans, she would have to face this; she would have to contend with the efforts of others to care for her. And she was not nearly prepared for any of it. She knew she was a long way from being over what had already happened. She was going to need time to recuperate, time to gain back some sense of the life she had been trying, and failing so miserably, to lead. Going into Violet Beaumont's house in this wounded and distressed and panicky condition seemed a selfish thing to have agreed to, and it occurred to her, heading south, that she had known that was so, had made her decision to go there in the full knowledge of the self-centeredness of it: she could not be very good company in this state of mind. And while Dominic, even in the circumstances, was making a big fuss over the fact that she was coming, he also knew what her feelings were. She was one of the walking wounded, and her stay in New Orleans would be a convalescence more than it could be anything else. And it was, of course, entirely possible that, where Dominic was concerned, she was bringing bad news—trouble, complexity he could not want, responsibility he would hate.

By the time she pulled into New Orleans, thunderstorms had rolled in from the west and gone on. The rain had missed her, but the streets were wet, shimmering with sunlight. She took the exit ramp toward Canal Street, past a graveyard full of enormous, washed-looking stone mausoleums, like a crowded complex of ornate city buildings, Gothic cornices and facades in vague profusion. She pulled into an Exxon station. There was a warm wind, and the thunder cracked, far off. She saw a tremendous tendril of lightning strike across from one cloud bank to another in the distance. Here was brilliant sunlight, and sharp shadows in the cemetery's sprawling miniature city on the other side of the overpass. She thought of Mary Kingsley on a steamer in the middle of the ocean, with her belongings in a portmanteau, and her whole existence dependent on the rough strangers around her.

She was in the self-serve island. She backed up, and pulled the car around to the pump marked "Full serve," and one of the men sloshed through the puddles in the lot and around the front of the car to stand at her window. Everything depended on knowing where to be. This struck her as being quite funny, much funnier than she might ever be able to explain. She had begun to laugh. It was like an attack of nerves. His size and shape alarmed her, and she felt panic, even as the laughing erupted from her throat. She rolled the window down and then couldn't speak right away.

"I'm sorry," she said, striving to gain control. "Can you fill it up?"

He didn't speak. Mary began to fuss, and Lily, still trying to stop laughing—and feeling at the same time as though she were beginning to weep—reached back to give the child a rattle, her hand trembling. The baby held it, pulled at it, and dropped it. The rattle fell to the floor of the backseat and Lily felt this as a catastrophe; her mind raced. She was having trouble drawing in air. Off in the scoured Southern sky she saw skyscrapers, and the torn shapes of clouds scudding across in front of them. She endeavored to catch her breath, and keep from passing out.

The man came to the window to collect for the gas. She couldn't find the money in her pockets or in her purse; her fingers wouldn't work. At last she found it, and passed it through the window to him. She spent a few seconds looking at Dominic's directions, trying to collect herself.

"You want anything else?" the attendant asked her. "You need directions?"

"I've got it," Lily said. "Thank you."

He went back into the building. She put the car in gear and drove on, into the wet streets, the cataracts of water running in the gutters and drain spouts, and the distant rattle of thunder, her heart pounding, a headache coming on, and panic racing through her. The baby was fuss-ing now, and crying. She couldn't read the street signs, or find where to look for them at some intersections. It felt like sheer accident when she reached Canal Street. She took it, and began watching the signs for the crossing streets. The sidewalks were crowded. Restaurants with tall windows that looked open to the air lined the street, and on every porch and balcony there were dozens of plants, palm leaves and flowers in profusion, all of them dripping with the recent rain. She saw row upon row of double porches, with the look of lace in the woodwork. There were beautiful churches, and Victorian fronts with chairs ranged across the verandas. She couldn't remember if she and Tyler had walked this part of the Quarter.

Tyler.

She slowed, holding tight to the wheel and peering through the glare of the windshield in the racket Mary was making. It was crying, and then it was play, and then it was crying again. She, too, had begun to weep. Cars behind her were honking their horns.

"All right," she said, as if anyone but Mary could hear her. "Jesus."

She pulled over to the curb and let the cars go by her. People turned their faces to glare, or to smile gratitude, or simply to see, but she scarcely looked back. They came past, and she saw it all in the corner of her eye. When there was an opening, and she had gotten her breath, wiped her face, and, using the rearview mirror, wiped the mascara from her cheeks, and patted new makeup around her eyes, she pulled the car back into traffic and went along slowly, almost benumbed now, reading the street signs and seeing little else on either side of her.

By the time she pulled up in front of Violet Beaumont's tall house, on the corner of Burgundy and St. Phillip, the whole sky was sunny, cloudless. The thunder was far off, now. She got out of the car and was removing Mary from the backseat when Dominic came out onto the porch and called to her. "*Cher*," he said, in a bad imitation of a Cajun accent. He came down and wrapped his arms around her, and she felt herself crying into his shoulder. It was only a moment, but he held tight, patting her shoulderblades. Manny had come down, too, and was getting Mary out of the car seat, cooing at her and murmuring her name. "So happy to see you, little one," he said.

"Let me see her," said Dominic, letting go of Lily, who stood there, drying her eyes, and watched them make a fuss over the baby.

They insisted that she go ahead into the house with the baby, while they unpacked the car, so she went ahead up the steps and into the foyer of the house, where she waited for them. Somewhere in the rooms she heard the strains of jazz. She was reluctant to look very far, and kept her attention on the street. For some reason, she felt that it wouldn't be appropriate to go exploring the place by herself, and besides, the panic was coming back. Quite suddenly all of this felt like a horrendous mistake.

In the living room, someone coughed, and she knew Violet Beaumont was just on the other side of the wall. She wanted to walk in there and ask the old woman to hold her. It was absurd.

Dominic came up the stairs with a suitcase and a box of her books.

"Go on in," he said. "Aunt Vi's napping."

"I'm awake," came a rich alto voice. "Come in."

Dominic put the suitcase and the box of books down in the hallway, then walked her, with Mary, into the room and presented Violet Beaumont; it was almost a gesture of unveiling.

Lily set the car seat on the floor and reached to shake the thin proffered hand. Aunt Violet had the softest grip, surprisingly firm, but light, too, a friendly pressure. She was lined in every part of her face, neck, and upper chest, her lower arms and hands—deep lines, like cracks in an old painting, and her skin was the color of arid ground. The eyes were light brown, and the hair was wispy and white, parted in the middle and framing the rather handsome features. Doubtless, this woman had been very startlingly beautiful when she was young, and she was quite striking now. She looked at Manny, coming into the room with more boxes. "That's my spiritual nephew," she said. "You've met?"

"Yes," said Lily.

Violet Beaumont turned her brown eyes on the baby in her car seat. "Pretty child."

"Can't get over it," said Dominic.

"I don't—I don't know how long we're staying," Lily said.

"A thoughtful child," said Violet.

Lily smiled at this, uncertain as to the level of irony in it. The old woman had a wry little grin on her face.

"You might not be staying?" said Dominic.

"I just don't know for sure if I'll be able to stay," Lily told him.

The old woman waved this away. "Me, too, *cher*. Me, too. Been like that since I was thirty years old, more than sixty years ago."

The baby sent up a sudden cry, and began to fuss.

"Life just got more complicated," Violet Beaumont said, winking at them.

5

That EVENING, they all went to a small Cajun place called Daddy's. It was little more than a square room with tables covered with checked tablecloths, and a glass counter through which you could see plastic containers of the gumbo and crawfish and other foods that were prepared on the premises. Daddy's was owned and run entirely by the black family named Rachambois, and there were pictures on the walls of famous jazz musicians who had been patrons. The pictures were signed with flourishes of affection for Daddy Rachambois, who, Dominic explained, had died only the year before. His son was running the place, now. Their waitress was a lovely, tall, cinnamon-hued woman with tight, burnished black curls and long nails the color of blood. Aunt Violet introduced her as one of Daddy's nieces. Violet called her by name: Felicia. Felicia took their orders, and leaned down to look at the baby.

"Such a prutty chile."

The baby made a smacking sound with her lips and then said, "No."

They all laughed. It was a lovely moment, with this stranger, who went on to say that she had a nephew, not one year old yet, who could walk. They chatted for a moment about precocious children. Lily noticed that Violet Beaumont's movements were rather startlingly fluid and graceful for someone almost ninety-two.

But she was beginning to see that a long stay with Dominic and what was now his family might not be workable, after all. Manny and Dominic both worked all day; Violet had her rounds to make in the Quarter. What little money Lily had wouldn't last long, and she didn't want to impose on anyone—not her parents, and certainly not these good people, who seemed to be scraping by as it was.

But there was still the problem of telling Dominic what she had come to tell him. She looked across the table at him, and felt lost.

The conversation went on. Violet introduced Lily as a friend who had come from Oxford and was new to the Big Easy.

"You love it here already?" Felicia asked.

Lily nodded.

"You all right? You look a little pale."

"She's got the jitters, *cher*," Violet Beaumont said. "I know them when I see them."

"New surroundings."

Violet nodded.

"Well, don't you worry," Felicia said, smiling brightly at Lily. "You're with friends here. And you have that prutty chile to love."

"Thanks," Lily said. "Yes."

A moment later, Manny walked over to see what was on the jukebox to play, and Aunt Violet strolled across to the counter to say hello to Daddy Rachambois's son. Dom and Lily were alone at the table. He leaned across the table and said, "It's gonna be okay, Lily. You'll see."

The baby made a sound, laughed and made it again, playing with her hands.

"I have to find a baby-sitter and a job," Lily said.

He leaned close. "I won't dwell on it—but I can't believe it about you and Tyler."

"You told me that," Lily said. "Over the phone."

"I still can't believe it. I mean, there's no chance of any change?"

"Nothing'll change, Dom. It's over. I'm alone with the baby and I'm afraid we're on your hands for the time being."

"That's okay with us." He smiled, and nodded as if to emphasize the remark.

She drew in a breath to tell him—and couldn't. Not here, not in company. She looked at the baby and spoke a few soft endearments. Mary was getting cranky. Violet came back to the table and, before she sat down, tottered a second; the slightest pause, but it drew everyone's attention.

"I'm not dead yet, *cher*," she said to Dominic, who had come to his feet.

She sat down and gazed across the table at Lily. "You look so sorrowful."

"I'm a little tired."

"Divorce," said Dominic. "I bet that can sap your energy."

"Nobody ever gets married planning to make unhappiness," said Violet. "Everybody thinks it's the glorious beginning of being happy, even knowing how much disaster there is out there."

Dom kept his gaze on Lily. "It was Buddy's death that did it, wasn't it."

"Partly," Lily said, realizing, perhaps for the first time, just how hard it was going to be to tell him the whole truth.

"Dominic," Aunt Violet said, "can't you see she doesn't want to talk about it now?"

He kissed Violet's leathery cheek, and sat back. Manny rejoined them. He had a pleasant, almost serene expression on his face. Aunt Violet began describing her history with Daddy's. She had been coming here for fifty years. She had known Daddy, and she had known Daddy's father, who first opened the place, under the name Tap House, back in 1925. Prohibition was in full swing, and you couldn't get into Tap House unless you knew someone, or were expressly invited by Daddy's father. Billie Holiday had sung here, once, early in her career. Aunt Violet had seen her. Aunt Violet had seen almost everything, she said. Or she felt like it, anyway. She knew Manny through his mother, Inez, who had come to this country with her two younger sisters to get away from an abusive father and two fierce, troublemaking brothers, in 1949. She didn't speak a word of English, and went to work for Violet just after Violet's retirement from teaching school that year. But Violet had met her before this, back in 1946, on a stay in Santiago during one of her summer trips. Crossing the street in front of her hotel, she had dropped her valise, and papers had fallen out. The girl had helped her collect the ones that blew away, and Violet insisted on buying her dinner at the hotel. The two struck up a friendship, and saw one another several other times over the next two weeks. As Violet was getting ready to leave the country, Inez showed up outside the hotel with two ragged looking-toddlers, her sisters, and asked Violet with tearful passion to hide them both away and take them with her to America; she wished for them to escape their moody and violent father. The self-sacrifice in this touched Violet so deeply that she sought a way to bring all three of them with her. It was, of course, out of the question. Violet and Inez exchanged addresses and promised tearfully, upon Violet's departure, to correspond. But no letters were exchanged, and Inez became a tender and aching memory.

Until three years later, when Inez showed up on her doorstep. Her younger sisters had remained behind, but were being raised by an aunt, now, after her father's demise from alcohol. It turned out that Inez had never wavered from her intention to seek her American friend, as soon as she was of age.

It was Violet's godson, Chandler Boudreaux, who got Inez pregnant with Manuel. Chandler intended to marry her (she was nineteen), and he would have provided for her as best he could. But he had developed a bad cocaine problem in the army, and one night, late, several weeks before the planned wedding, he had massive coronary failure after ingesting an enormous hit of the stuff. The autopsy showed that his heart had burst.

Violet took mother and child in with her, and for the first few years of Manny's life, they had it pretty good. His mother went to work for the city, and still kept Violet's house, for which Violet still paid her. Violet spoke fluent Spanish, and she taught the boy some English, though Inez and the boy were not interested in becoming fluent. The household spoke Spanish, sometimes for weeks at a time.

Since, by then, the few members of Violet's family who remained would not speak to her—"For indiscretions," she said, "mostly having to do with not satisfying their expectations"—there was no help to be gotten from anywhere, and she was on a pension, so she went back to teaching for a few more years, to help pay the bills. Life was simple, and mostly happy.

But then Manny's mother fell in love again, this time with someone in her office—a Chilean man who had come to school at Tulane. When Manny was six, his mother and stepfather took him off to live in Chile. Manny had kept in touch over the years, writing her in English when he had time, and sending her little postcards dashed off in Spanish. When he was grown, and his mother was gone (she died in an automobile accident at the age of fifty-one), and his stepfather had found it sufficiently hideous that he was a homosexual, and therefore had disowned him, he began to think of coming back to America. He settled at first in Virginia, where he had a distant cousin, and where he met Dominic. All along, he had wanted to go down to the city of his birth.

"And here he is," Violet said. "A consolation for my last days."

"I am a booby prize," said Manny, in what Lily noted was a surer tone.

Evidently, his time with Dominic had improved his capacity for English speech. The improvement was subtle—she hadn't marked it until this moment, mostly because Manny was so naturally phlegmatic. He went on, now, indicating Dominic: "I brought the door prize with me, too."

"Ta-da," said Dominic. "If you reach a certain age, young gay men will come live with you, for free."

"Look at this baby," Violet said, playing with Mary's hand. "She'll grow up and make strong men slit their throats."

The waitress brought the food on a large tray, and for a few minutes they all spoke at once, trying to get everything distributed. The songs Manny had chosen were playing loud on the jukebox; they had to shout to be heard. The food was spicy, and tasted wonderful.

When dinner was over, they strolled home along the busy street, amid the various peppery fragrances of the restaurants, through conflicting strains of music—zydeco, and blues and jazz from several different clubs. Dominic carried the baby.

By the time they got back to the house, the sky was threatening more rain. They went inside, and Lily was shown to her quarters, up the stairs and to the left. It was a large, high-ceilinged room. There was a double bed, at the foot of which stood a large cedar chest. Next to the bed was a nightstand with a small reading light and a row of books. To the left of the entrance, a bureau stood beside a tall, wood-framed window overlooking the street corner below. A full-length mirror hung on the door-side wall, suggesting still another window. In the opposite wall there was a set of French doors leading out onto the upstairs veranda. Lily saw palm leaves there, and hanging plants. Dominic had borrowed a crib from a neighbor for the baby. Lily put her down, and tucked the soft blanket over her shoulders.

"I didn't dream Mary could've gotten so big since February," Dominic said.

"She likes the new bed," Lily said. Then: "Dom."

"Yeah?"

She heard Violet laboring up the stairs. She said, "This seems one of the better rooms in the house. I'm afraid we're putting you all out."

"It's Ms. Beaumont's old room. It can get a little noisy in the mornings—you'll see. She has the best room, believe me. This is a nice big house."

Aunt Violet came into the room and crossed to the French doors. "Look," she said. "Come out here and see."

Lily hesitated.

"The child's asleep. She's happy."

Lily followed her out onto the veranda. There were wicker chairs, and a settee, and a wooden rocker. Violet settled into the rocker, and gestured for Lily to sit next to her. A faint fragrance of indefinable spice was on the air, and thunder sounded far off, a low drumming. The only light came from the windows of the room behind them, soft gold, and Lily had an unwanted moment of remembering the balcony of the apartment in Charlottesville, her first few moments with Tyler. On the street below them, people hurried by against the threat of rain, and cars moved past, tires swishing through the puddles already in the pavement. The whole Quarter was alive, and a stupendous cup of liquefied light went up into the lowering twilight clouds, the freshening wind.

"I had to sell my truck," Violet said.

"You kept running into things," said Dominic.

"Still—I did hate to let it go."

He nudged Lily. "Truck was a '36 Ford. Should've seen it. The bottom carriage of it was in a fossilized state."

"It ran," Violet said.

"It dropped fragments. Following you was like navigating a spaceship through an asteroid belt."

"It ran," Violet repeated, in exactly the same tone.

"Ms. Beaumont got two tickets the last week she drove her truck—one for going too fast, and the second for going too slow. And it was the same cop, on the same road."

"Young man couldn't make up his mind, *cher.*"

Somewhere in the distance, they heard a crowd cheer. The sound rose and was so clear you could distinguish individual voices, then faded and was like a whisper; and finally was gone altogether.

"Amateur baseball," said Dominic.

"Could be the racehorses," Violet put in.

"We're too far away for that."

In the following silence between them, they all listened for the crowd, but there was only the busy clamor of traffic.

"You know something?" Aunt Violet said, touching Lily on the arm and then taking her cool, dry hand away. "When I was a girl, I met some-body who spent some time with this Mary Kingsley you're writing the book about."

"It's a play," Dominic said.

"It's writing. It will end in a book. They publish plays in books?"

"They do," said Lily, admiring her.

"There."

"You knew someone who knew her?"

"Somebody came to the school I was in, and he lectured about Africa. You know what year? 1913. This man talked to us about an explorer, a woman, Mary Kingsley. This middle-aged man, and he's long gone now of course. I remembered the name Kingsley. Such a strong-sounding name. This man knew her, and he knew some others. There was an English missionary named Mary Slessor."

"Mary Kingsley knew her," Lily said. "They were friends. They spent a lot of time together at Mary Slessor's mission house at Okyon, on Mary's second trip to West Africa. They sat up talking through the night, just the two of them. So far from England."

"This man knew them both."

Lily sat back and let this soak in.

"Women had no rights then, you see? Couldn't even vote. But in Africa, it was worse. Men had many wives. A woman was expected to be in the married state. There was no visible function for them otherwise. Their sexual organs were cut; they were mutilated. If a woman had twins, it was death. For both babies and sometimes for her, too. This man said when he met Mary Slessor and Mary Kingsley, they were pro-tecting a woman who'd had twins. The woman, and the one twin that survived. She was a slave, this young woman, of the Eboe tribe, an expensive slave—and maybe you haven't learned yet that slavery was a widespread thing in those districts, back then, thirty years after it ended, in blood, *here*. You know? Anyway, *cher*, she belonged to this woman who had treated her kindly. According to this gentleman, the slaves in that part of Calabar were all treated well. But when this woman had her twins, all her things were taken from her and she was driven away—they would've killed the babies if it wasn't for Miss Slessor, and, as it was, one of them died because he had to be hidden by being stuffed into a basket under the first one. And then in the village, after the mother had gone, the ground where she walked was dug up and raked over by the rest of the tribe. This gentleman told us all this, and I never forgot it.

"He was writing a book about these African explorers, see—but, well, if he wrote it, I never saw it. But recently I read her books, Miss Kingsley's books. And there's a reference to that episode in her first travel book. Of course a lot of people read that book, and he could have, too, you know. The books were best-sellers. It's possible he read the same passage and was trading on it. But he had the look of a true man—rough and ruddy, and solid as a rock. And his face got a kind of light in it when he talked about Mary Kingsley. You know what they called her in Africa, *cher*? They called her Only Me. The natives. Cannibal sorts. Witch doctors and warriors. She'd walk into their villages and introduce herself that way. 'It's only me,' she'd say—see? So they called her that. Only Me."

"I think I remember seeing something about that in my reading," Lily said kindly.

Violet nodded. "Anyway, I believe this man who came to my school to lecture, all those years ago, knew her. He said she was the most stubborn type of woman and not someone to cross. He claimed he knew her well. Talked about her like you and me talking about Dominic, here. Her nature. He said big men were cowed by her when she got her anger up. But mostly she got people to do for her because they didn't know what to make of her. They didn't know what to make of her, *cher,* and never did really know her. I was fourteen years old, maybe. And I never forgot that, all these years. That they didn't really know her at all. I said to myself, how could that be? How is it that men take risks for her? Follow her places they are afraid to go. They did that—blacks and whites. Somebody who called herself Only Me."

Lily said, "I've been writing letters to her." It had come out before she realized she would say it. "Well—it's like a—a journal. It—it helps me to think about her as living—helps me to write about her."

Aunt Violet didn't respond. She stared out at the roofs of the Quarter, and rocked slowly, the smallest motion.

After a moment, Dominic said, "She takes little naps."

They were quiet. The several different kinds of music came to them on the heavy air, along with the sound of traffic on the next street. Someone shouted from over there, and someone else, farther away, shouted back.

Violet stirred, and coughed, then started again: "That's what it is, *cher*. You get yourself dressed and walk out in the world and see what you can see in it. Whatever comes, you keep your dignity as best you can and your humor, too."

Dominic stood and stretched his arms out, yawning, then sighed and said: "I'm going to bed and try to sleep. At long last, we have a cool night."

"You're a savage boy, all appetites."

Lily stifled a yawn.

Aunt Violet reached across and took her wrist. "Don't you go."

Dominic leaned down to kiss the old woman's cheek, then touched Lily's shoulder, and kissed her as well. "We'll work on getting you settled in the morning."

Lily thanked him. He went into the house, and through the room to the hallway, and when he was gone, she turned to see that Aunt Violet had nodded off again. The streets had rather abruptly become very quiet. She sat there, growing sleepy herself, watching the quality of light change in the sky. The rain had passed over, and there were holes in the cloud cover, one great scalloped edge of the cloud bank shining with moonlight, iridescent as mother-of-pearl. You could still hear thunder in the far distance, and now and again lightning flickered at the darker edge of the horizon.

"*Cher*," Aunt Violet said. "What're you doing coming down here?"

The question startled Lily, who found that she had no voice to answer it.

"I've been all around the world, you know. And I get to falling asleep. But I don't miss much."

"I—my marriage—Dominic and I—"

"I know the story."

Lily shifted in the chair. "Well, then—I don't understand."

"There's something you're bringing with you to tell."

"Yes." It felt good to confess it. She breathed out, staring, amazed.

"And when you're ready, you'll tell."

Lily was quiet, and a moment later realized that Aunt Violet had nodded off again. She waited, and after a time she cleared her throat, faked a cough.

The other woman stirred, and leaned forward to look down at the street. "Something else about that Mary Kingsley, *cher*. She faced the lions and leopards and savages and went up the dark rivers nobody'd ever seen before, you know, but she was afraid of love. I knew that way back when I first heard anything about her. And I can't say why I knew. But I did. I knew she took care of her mother and she got to thinking that was love, and she ran away from it as soon as she could and nothing was ever gonna bring her back. No, sir. That scared her so bad she went running in the world, like her father."

"But she cared for people—nursed them through fevers. She died caring for the sick. For wounded prisoners, in the Boer War. They weren't even of her country."

"That wasn't anybody she loved, though. See? That was general. And when her time came, she didn't want anybody around. She demanded to be left alone. Wanted to die alone, like an animal."

"As in nature," Lily said. "As it was in some of the tribes she moved with."

"But she never went over to that. She wore her drawing-room dresses on the hottest days. She always insisted on her English habits—the tea and the reading and the talk. No, *cher*, you can only solve the mystery of that lady by thinking of love. She was scared, down in her heart, of it. Nothing else came close to scaring her as bad as that. It's not hard to understand, either, when you look at what she had growing up, and where she was when she grew up. When you see her qualities against the things she was beating back all the time in herself, you can maybe see where the real bravery was. Stubborn, determined, brave, funny, all that. Funny. The self-mocking jokes. All the time, you know? Intensely smart, too; smarter than just about everybody she ever came in contact with. Wily smart, *cher*. The kind of smart that made other people think something she wanted from them was *their* idea. And the Africans called her Only Me, because she never once took herself too seriously. Not in print and not in life. So you think of that, and then think of love, think of being an English spinster in 1895 paddling up the rapids of the Ogowe River, and her guide saying, 'You no husband-ma?' And she saying, 'No, no husband,' and he saying, 'Where husband-ma?' and she answering it again. Over and over. Bad manners to complain, see? So you make a joke."

They were quiet. Violet sat there with closed eyes. But then she opened them and yawned. "You direct your attention out in the world. What do you have to complain about, *cher*?"

"Nothing," Lily said. "I'm not complaining."

The old woman lay her head back. She sighed and the corners of her creased mouth curled into a smile. "I'm a complainer from way back. Always have been."

They watched the lustrous edge of the cloud bank recede in the sky, revealing the bright moon, the faded sparkle of stars.

"You've studied Mary Kingsley, too," Lily said.

Aunt Violet looked at her. "I'm ninety-two. Except for a boy I knew who went away and died, I have never been in love with anyone and no one has ever been in love with me."

For a strange moment, Lily felt as though she were in the presence of Mary Kingsley herself. Her breath caught.

Aunt Violet said, "Are you going to stay here with us, *cher*?"

"I—I don't know."

She tried to stand. "Be a good girl and help me."

Lily quickly got to her feet and grasped the other woman by her bone-thin elbows. There was a tremor in Aunt Violet's hands now, which made her seem to be straining all the muscles of her wrists and fingers. "Think of it," she said. "I once spoke to a gentleman in whose eyes Mary Kingsley was reflected. The actual woman herself, in the flesh. I think he must have been a little in love with her, too. But I think a lot of men were in one way or another, and I wonder what kept them from acting on it. This man was going to write a book." Her left hand went up to her brow to move a strand of hair from it. "Well, he said he was. I guess I told you that." They moved through Lily's room and out into the hall. Aunt Violet then indicated the doorway at the far end, opposite the stairs. Her step was a little wobbly. Lily guided her to the room. Aunt Violet grasped the door frame, then turned and thanked her.

"No," Lily said. "Thank *you*."

The old face with its many lines receded into the shadow of the darkened room. Lily saw the bony fingers, holding the door open. "You'll tell us tomorrow what you're bringing to us?"

"Pardon?"

"Bon chance, *cher*," said Violet. "Tomorrow." And she closed the door.

6

$\mathcal{I}$N THE MIDDLE OF THE NIGHT, the baby woke up and wanted to play. Lily took her into the bed with her, and held her, and they both went back to sleep. In the morning, she woke first, got herself dressed, changed Mary, and went downstairs. It was already very hot and sticky. Manny was sitting in the living room by the small air conditioner, reading a newspaper. He stood as she entered the room, and bowed sweetly.

"Good morning."

Mary was striving to get down, so Lily put her on the floor, where she crawled to the bookcase and pulled herself up. Manny removed several small statuettes from the lamp table there, placing them high up on the bookshelf. The baby held on to the bookcase, wobbling but remaining on her feet. Lily took the chair on the other side of the air conditioner.

The room contained a settee, a long, low cherry table on which were stacked many magazines and books, an easy chair, a lowboy, and two soft chairs on opposite ends of a pair of tall windows that looked out on the street. In the window farthest from Lily's chair, the little air conditioner was set, so that if you sat back, you couldn't see the person sitting in the other corner. Along the wall beyond the entrance from the hall was a floor-to-ceiling bookshelf, and on the wall opposite that was a dry fireplace, sealed, Manny told her now—observing her interest in the room—long before Violet bought the house in 1938. This room opened out, through oak doors on a sliding track, into the dining room, where an outlandish life-sized statue of the Virgin stood in one corner, beyond a heavy oak table and chairs, a sideboard, and a curio cabinet full of more figures of the Virgin. Aunt Violet was a collector of statues of the Virgin Mary. She had them from every country and in every style and size. The life-sized one was a sad, aged-looking figure, the Virgin as she must have been at about the time of her son's death, staring with blind eyes at the room, stone cheeks with believable stone tears. Lily thought there was something grotesque about it.

The dining room gave off onto the kitchen, through a small space that crossed the front hallway. The baby had let herself down and crawled through the dining room, into the kitchen and back down the hallway, with Manny and Lily following. When she reached the living room again, she pulled herself to a standing position using the first chair, and then sat down suddenly, and crawled toward the entrance of the dining room again.

Manny said, "Such a fall would put me in the hospital." His accent was charmingly slight now.

"They don't have as far to fall," Lily said.

"No," he said. Then: "Yes."

Lily lifted the baby to her feet, and stood holding her that way, by the upper arms.

"Are you hungry?" he asked. "Coffee?"

"I'll have some coffee, yes."

He went into the kitchen and poured her a cup, and brought it out to her. She was contending with the baby's curiosity about everything in the room, which was overpopulated with artifacts and figurines, glass bric-a-brac, and gimcrack plaster icons.

"Your aunt Violet is everything Dominic said she is and more," Lily murmured over the coffee. "I don't think I've ever met anyone like her."

"I can't theenk of a soul," Manny said. "I am so scared for her."

"But she seems so strong and healthy."

"Yes. True."

They watched the baby.

"I wouldn't have said she was more than sixty-five."

"A doctor told her that," said Manny. "That she didn't look a day past sixty-five. Last year. She took eet as an insult."

Before Lily had finished her coffee, Dominic and Aunt Violet came down. Manny patted the top of the baby's blonde head and then left for work. Dominic cooked cereal for Aunt Violet, who seemed too sleepy and tired for talk. She smiled at Lily and appeared to tolerate the baby, offering Mary little pieces of her toast, as if she were a puppy. Mary crawled around in the kitchen and then in the dining room, shrieking her merriment, delighting in the sounds themselves, and repeating them, merely to hear the echoes in the high-ceilinged rooms.

The morning passed with the adults attending to her, and talking quietly. Dominic wanted to tell Lily about the city, and the Quarter; Violet corrected him once or twice, and then said something about the Persian Gulf, and the war that was threatened. She and Dominic got into a mild argument about whether or not the Iraqis would back down, and what it would mean if they didn't. The air in the rooms grew heavier and heavier with the heat, and the little air conditioner labored away in the living room window. They all moved, without having to speak about it, to proximity with its feeble suspiration of cooler air. Once or twice, Lily caught Violet staring at her, as if trying to divine what she might be thinking about or withholding from the conversation. But the conversation never got personal or intimate. They might have been amiable strangers on a station platform. Dominic played with Mary for a time, and then she grew cranky, so Lily took her upstairs to the crib, and a nap. The room was tropical. She patted the baby's bottom, and waited for her to drift to sleep. After this was accomplished, she thought of changing into something lighter than her jeans and blouse. She straightened up, and turned to find that Dominic was standing in the doorway.

"I was thinking maybe we ought to move the crib downstairs. Where it's a little cooler, anyway."

"She's asleep," Lily said.

It was just the two of them in the room. Violet's voice came to them from the kitchen below, talking to someone on the telephone.

"I have something to tell you," Lily said.

Dominic smiled. "It's fine. You don't have to worry about—I mean I know—"

She broke in: "No, you *don't* know."

He waited.

"Dom, this is big. This is—it's big."

"Okay," he said.

"I'm—I'm so sorry for—I should've told you from the beginning—when I knew—" She halted, looking into his eyes. Then: "Listen—I'm just going to tell you this, okay? Mary's—Mary's not Tyler's child."

He stared uncomprehendingly at her.

"Tyler couldn't have fathered Mary. Tyler's been sterile since he was seventeen."

Dominic nodded slowly, looked at the floor and then back at her. "So that's why the split up."

"Yes."

"That's—I'm—he should've—"

It was clear to Lily that he still didn't understand it all fully. She said, "Dom, I wasn't with anyone else."

He kept nodding, trying to put it together in his mind.

"Do you see what I'm telling you?"

Now he frowned. "Wait a minute—"

She reached to take his hand. It was as if she meant to steady him. "That's right," she told him. "There was the time you and—you and I— and there was Tyler. I was never with anyone else."

"Mary's—"

Lily squeezed his hand. "I should've told you as soon as I knew."

"Jesus Christ," he said, moving to the bed. "I—Christ." He stared at the empty doorway, his face registering only disbelief.

"I didn't even know at first," she said. "Tyler didn't tell me he was sterile—he—he didn't tell me about it. He kept it to himself for the longest time."

"I can't—I mean, Christ," Dominic said. "You're—you're saying this baby—that I'm—I'm the father of this baby?"

"Yes."

"But—we didn't even—we never—" He paused, shaking his head, stupefied.

"Tyler didn't want us to tell anyone, ever, and it's what finally broke it for us."

He stood, took a deep breath, and faced her. "Man. I'm not up to this at all."

She said nothing, watching him pace the room.

"Jesus Christ. I'm so far from being up to this."

"Who ever feels up to it?"

He stopped. "Don't say that shit to me. What're you gonna do, break into song? That's the glory of love? It didn't even work for us, and we got a *baby* out of it? Jesus, it's as if God said, 'Well, okay, this is the instance when you finally come to figure what your nature is, and oh, by the way, along with this humiliating disaster with your female friend, and even though thousands of hetero people try for years to get pregnant, I'm gonna let you-all get that way on a couple of dribbles and some tears and a limp prick." He caught himself and held out one hand. "Sorry."

Then he was pacing again.

"But, Lily—I mean—damn."

"Would you rather I hadn't told you?"

He pondered this, still moving back and forth in his agitated state. "I can't believe it, that's all. What did you do, perform a fertility dance after I left that night?"

"It happened," she said. "I didn't do anything. Nobody's at fault here for the fact of it happening, Dom."

He paused, finally, bent over and put his hands on his knees, and breathed. "Goddamn. I'm—I can't get my breath."

"We'll leave whenever you want us to," she said. "I didn't come here to trouble you. I thought you had the right to know."

"I'm feeling a little sick to my stomach."

"I didn't think you'd react this way."

"What'd you think I'd do? Oh, by the way, Lily, I forgot to mention, Aunt Violet is your real mother. How does that make you feel?"

She couldn't answer this.

He began pacing again, back and forth in front of the doors leading out onto the balcony. "My God, my God."

"Dom—"

"How long have you known this?" he asked.

"I was still pregnant with her when Tyler told me."

He threw his hands up. "Jee-sus Christ. So, when we went there to visit—you both knew then?"

She nodded, sniffling.

"I thought there was some trouble between you and Tyler."

"There was. I wanted to tell you and he didn't. He'd told me about it and we were fighting it all out."

"Oh, God*damn*."

A moment later, from the bottom of the stairs, Aunt Violet's voice came to them. "What're you two talking about up there? I'm getting lonely."

He went to the doorway and called down, "We'll be there in a little bit." Then he closed the door and crossed to the bed again, where he sat down and put his hands to his head. "All the feeling's going out of my hands. I can't breathe."

"Are you all right?" Lily said, realizing as she spoke that the question was absurd.

"Oh, I'm just keen," he said. "I like dry mouth and clammy palms and terror racing through all the extremities of my body. It's invigorating, like waiting out those last exciting seconds before a firing squad."

"I said I wasn't here to ask anything. It's not like *you* had to do anything, you know? I'm the one that carried her and had her and I just said I don't expect anything. And I don't."

"That's not the point. I expect it of myself. Jesus."

"Look," Lily said, barely able to control her voice. "You can be mad that I didn't tell you sooner—I was trying to hold my marriage together." She sobbed, then took a deep breath and went on. "But you can get mad for that. You can, and I'll understand it. You *cannot* be mad about the fact of the baby. There isn't any, any, any room for that kind of anger. Not ever."

He was shaking his head, still disbelieving. "A child. A *child. My* child."

"*Our* child," Lily corrected. "And watch your mouth about her."

"Well, and we're the perfect couple. Between the two of us we could raise a battalion of neurotics."

"I'm not asking you to raise anyone—Dom. I thought you had the right to know. And that's all I thought."

He stood again. "Look, I know I'm supposed to be happy and say not to worry about anything, but I *am* worried about it all, and I'm not happy. I'm not *unhappy*, either, you know. I'm—well, I'm, let's see, mortally afraid. There isn't all that much room for happiness when you're terrified as bad as this."

"I'm not here to ask you about happiness, and I'm not here to take it away from you, either. For Christ's sweet sake, have you been listening to me?"

He touched her shoulder, then let his hand drop to his side. "I'm sorry. Jesus—this is just so scary to me."

"Don't you think I'm scared, too?"

He thought a moment. It was as though he were seeking a way to unravel some secret wellspring of choices in the predicament. But when he spoke, it was only to exclaim again that he was frightened. There was a look of wild-eyed invention on his face. "What the fuck will we tell Mary when she's of age? 'That's right, honey, your father's gay, and you were engendered by a faltering, failed, debased, humbling attempt to screw for consolation and recreation? Your parents are a pair of consenting incompatibles?'"

"Oh, that's wonderful. Oh, you're making everything so much better, Dom. What personal courage and character you're showing. Maybe Tyler was right."

"I'm in shock. I'm rattling around in little pieces in my chest."

"Shoulder it," Lily said thinly.

His smile was ironic, and desperate, and grieving, too. "You mean get in touch with my feminine side?"

"Oh, God. *Tyler* handled it better than you are."

"I meant it as a joke."

"I'm not laughing."

"That registered. No more jokes. Okay? Give me a little slack here." She was quiet for a moment.

Presently he moved to the bed again, and sat down, his hands folded in his lap. "Really. You know, Lily. What will we tell her?"

She simply returned his gaze.

"Our daughter," he said.

"You and I were friends," Lily said. "Are friends." After a pause, she added, "We *are* friends, right?"

He said, "You feel the need to ask?"

"A little, maybe."

"We're friends," he said, with a perplexed, smiling frown.

"Then I guess that's what we'll tell Mary. We're friends. It happened. Some married heterosexuals don't have friendship. Some of them spend a lifetime looking for it."

He said nothing.

"In the end, Tyler and I didn't have that."

"And he wanted to keep it from me for good."

She nodded.

"I can understand it. I really can. I can understand why he would."

"You wish I had kept it from you," Lily said. "Don't you."

He shook his head, staring at the floor. The gesture was not in reaction to her; it rose out of whatever he was thinking.

She walked over and stood before him. "What do you think, Dominic? Do you think I came here to get you to do your duty by me and marry me? Do you think I wanted you to act as my child's father? I wanted you to know something that everything in my whole being told me was your right to know. I lost my husband and my marriage because I couldn't bring myself to keep that from you. But I never once thought anything *else* would come of you knowing it. I just believe it's your right—and Mary's right—to know a thing like that."

He kept nodding, but she could see that he was off somewhere in himself.

"Grow up a little," she said. "Can't you?"

He stood again, and moved to the door. "I can always depend on you to lecture me whenever I stray from the path of righteousness. Or words to that effect."

"Are you going to tell Manny and Violet about it?"

He thought a moment, but said nothing.

"Do you want me to tell them?"

"No. They wouldn't believe you." He smiled, shaking his head. "I still can't believe—can't put it together in my mind that *that*—that little pathetic performance—what happened between us that mortifying evening—could've gotten you pregnant. I can't believe anything about this. This is the single weirdest conversation I've ever had in my life."

She was silent.

"A little sex between friends. And the operative word is *little*."

"Don't demean it," Lily said.

"Well, but it was so farcical."

"Okay," Lily said crisply.

"Don't be mad."

"I'm not."

"Promise?"

"We're not in Psych 101, Dom."

He started to leave, then turned. "I keep thinking there's something else you expect me to say."

"There's nothing else I expect you to say."

"Well," he said. "And—you're still my friend. But then, no—we're not exactly friends, now, are we? Not exactly. We're—oh, what's that word. I used to hear it spoken a lot when I was younger and getting the shit kicked out of me. How's it go? Begins with the letter *p*. Parents. Isn't that it? I feel reasonably certain the word is *parents*." He shook his head again, then opened the door and started down the hall, to the stairs. She followed. Violet was sitting in the window seat in the living room, eyes closed, nodding off in the small exhalation of the air conditioner. When Dominic entered the room, she looked up.

"Hey, Aunt Violet," Dominic said to her. "Guess what?"

7

Dear Doris,

I'm sitting out on this veranda overlooking Burgundy Street. Pronounced, Aunt Violet says, BurGUNDY Street. Mary's asleep in her crib. It's sunny and hot—not so humid, for once. We've been here three weeks, and I've been looking for work, and for someone to watch the baby. A nice girl who comes over from the school nearby and tends to Violet's needs has been helping out with Mary. Her name is Amy. And since Violet still goes out to the nursing homes around here to visit friends, I've paid Amy to come on those days as well. She doesn't mind it, but she's only eighteen, has just left high school, and I'd like to find someone a little more experienced.

I went on something like fourteen interviews for jobs, all of them nothing remotely like anything I want to do, and it didn't matter because no one was interested. So Violet prevailed upon the people at St. Augustine to let me substitute teach there on the strength of my all-but-conferred degree, and I have the money you and Scott sent, in spite of my asking you not to. (Thank you.) I do still have some left, you know, from the settlement, if that's what it can be called, with Tyler.

It's not so strange, I suppose, that I've been dreaming about him. In the dreams we're happy and I'm lighter, somehow. I don't mean weighing less, either, quite. I mean I'm the same size, and all that. But it's as if gravity is different for me. Yet when I move in the dream, I move slowly— not slow motion, but more creaky, as if I'm very old and lighter than a leaf. I think of Tyler in the days; I wonder where he is and what he's doing, and I keep expecting that he'll come back from this silliness and we'll go ahead and try to make a family. But that's daydreaming. No—it's more like a kind of woolgathering. Because thinking about it calmly, I wouldn't take him back if he asked me. I do feel the old longing for him sometimes, but then once, recently, feeling it, I had the realization that what I was missing was the husband I had before anger and sorrow arrived, and I don't really blame him for it because he's just scared, faced for the first time in his life with something for which nothing in his experience has prepared him, and for which he's had no models or examples to look at and emulate. I don't mean that to sound as twenties-wizened as, reading it over, it sounds. Tyler himself said something like it. It's just that now I am, after all, a divorced woman with a child. And I live with two gay men and an elderly lady, and at least twice a week—and sometimes several days a week—I teach English and history classes at St. Augustine Catholic High School. The students there are always glad to see me, and they're also, for the most part, hardworking and intelligent. I like being with them, and that's something. The nuns are quite well read and have a serenity I envy—well, most of them do. There are a couple of newer ones who seem quite tense and uneasy with life.

Dominic spends a lot of time with Mary. Everyone in the house has been wonderful about it. But he and I are now carrying the burden of parents—the weight of it, I guess. Nothing is as carefree as it was between us when we were school friends, and since we're not involved in the way of a married couple, there's a very odd kind of negotiated feeling about it all, nothing like the old times when he used to make me laugh, and I could tell him things. Now when we're together in company and we have Mary between us, there's the natural sense of our being a couple, and of course we aren't. We're—some kind of friends; or, we're in some complicated zone of friendship, and the fact is that a strain has been put on it all. We have fallen to bickering once or twice—but it's been so uncomfortably blistering here, and I have to say that might have contributed to it. Dominic took time off from work to look for a good day care center, and then we decided not to go that route. We've been interviewing baby-sitters, and in the meantime Amy helps out. She's a nice person, Amy—though a little fast for my comfort. A different boy picks her up every day it seems, and she's always talking about how much this or that one means to her—always talking about what beloved friends they are—yet she dresses for them, looks half the time like a hooker. Though she wears a cross on a small gold necklace, and talks about church, and once I came home to find her trying to teach Mary how to say Jesus. Another time I found her asleep with Mary curled up on her chest, and Mary clearly loves her, is always very excited and happy to see her.

Dominic helps feed Mary, and walks the floor with her when she's restless, and rocks her to sleep every night. He's even changed her diaper a couple of times. She's still a little leery of him, sometimes, staring that way she has when she's trying to decide whether or not she's happy. But she's *getting more at ease all the time. When he picks her up, she no longer tries to pull away from him toward me or Amy.*

In the evenings, we sit in the living room, all of us—even Amy some-times—and watch her play. It's like watching a TV comedy special. There have been moments when I've had the sense that we're a family, odd as we are. Yesterday, Saturday, we went to the river to a café to eat dinner and listen to some jazz, and people looked at us with frank curiosity, trying, I'm sure, to figure out the dynamics. Even in a place like New Orleans— there's Manny and Dom, obviously together, and Aunt Violet, and then the baby and me.

I don't know how much longer I'll stay here, and we don't talk about it. It's almost as if we're all avoiding it as a subject. I'm writing every day, and feel as if I'm making headway. But there are still so many areas where I'm at sea about it all. I would like to finish what I've started, and get it out of my hands. But there have been good days when I really do feel I'm getting there. I was pleasantly surprised when I first sat down to it after all the confusion of the move here and getting into some sort of routine again.

The baby is learning to say things, and starting to pull herself up. In the mornings, she stands in the crib and holds her hands out to me and says Ma-ma. I love waking up to it.

I haven't heard much from Sheri or Millicent or Nick since I left Oxford. Nick sent some money out of what Tyler paid him, and put a little note in saying he hoped things were all right. I still have not received divorce papers, and don't know if I should worry right now about putting them through myself. Dominic says I should wait. Tyler might decide to come back. Dominic says he lives in the expectation that he'll turn up here. He doesn't believe Tyler is the type simply to let go, like that.

Sheri called twice, both times wanting me to turn around and come back. Sheri, when we talked, said Millicent is still inconsolable, and that Rosa went back to the coast. Sheri's unhappy, in a sad, half-offended way, about all of it. They've heard nothing from Tyler, and she said even Nick has stopped hearing from him. With this stupid situation in the Middle East, Millicent is convinced that we'll go to war with Iraq and Tyler will be sent over there to be killed. Sheri said the whole thing's ridiculous, but I think she's worrying about it, too. There's some point of pride with her where Tyler's concerned. It was always there, even before all the trouble. As

I said, I don't know how much longer I'll be here, and just maybe I'll be heading back to Virginia before very long. I don't know and I don't believe Dominic knows how we'll settle things at last concerning the baby. But there's a definite feeling of the temporary about us—a feeling I have become so used to that I sometimes fail to notice it. Aunt Violet talks about all of us being in transit, the whole household on our way to some other place. Yet Dom seems so good with Mary, and dotes on her. And she responds to him. He keeps telling me he's afraid he's not up to it.

Anyway.

I'll call you soon. I'd like to hear your voice. Please give Daddy my love, and Peggy, too. And take some for yourself. You know.

Love,

Lily

⚭

Night. Alone.

I've been working on the play about you, and arguing with Aunt Violet, who says perhaps it is on some level possible to explain you as an exaggerated case of sexual hysteria. I think you would laugh at this. I have pointed out your early childhood interest in explorers and exploring and in the study of human spiritual beliefs. I've reminded her of your private study of Spinoza and Goethe, of your pantheism, your lifelong curiosity about the manifestations of human faith and the definitive questions of the meaning of things. I have spoken to her of your lineage, and of the example of your father. She nods, and gives me a tolerant smile, and then mentions the fact that at the turn of the century it was considered neurotic for a woman to experience, or wish to experience, orgasm. And that in such a climate an extraordinary, healthy, passionate intelligence, if it felt the pressure to break out, would either self-destruct, or run. She says you ran. She's perfectly admiring of you in saying it, and talks about your toughness and valor. Though she insists that valor doesn't depend on events or extraordinary people for its presence in the world; extraordinary people only serve as the dazzling illustrations of it over time: for most women, it was brave enough to raise their families and bear their crushed passions in secret.

She confesses that at some level she's describing her own experience. But she can't be moved in her distinctions concerning yours. . . .

I have to go to work. I'm a teacher now.

⚭

The heat of September and October gave way to a softer kind of warmth, the breath of the cerulean Gulf. Hurricane season had come and gone. Storms washed in from the sea, but nothing worse than a squall, a few somber days of rain. She taught classes and came back to the house to care for Mary. In the late afternoons, she sat out on the veranda in the barbed shade of the palm plants and wrote. Sometimes she simply watched the traffic on the street, and what she could see of the lime-colored river between the houses on the other side. There were many nights when, sleepless, she sat out there, as if presiding over the restless and always agitating city, with its cries and hubbub and songs, its continual uproar of human voices.

Dominic brought her books from the store, and in the mornings, Manny always had coffee for her. Aunt Violet found things to do away from the house, though it was growing more complicated for her to get around. She had friends in various homes, private and institutional. When she walked, her pace was quick, or looked in some way hurried, even if she took it more slowly. And it was true that on the infrequent occasions Lily accompanied her, Lily had some trouble keeping up. Violet was fond of walking to the river, to sit on a bench and watch the traffic gliding along there. She would talk about the history of it all—the big steamboats that had plied the "Old Man" north, and the terrible floods of the Mississippi delta back in the twenties and thirties. She liked to think about how the muddy-looking water came all the way from Minnesota, down the curve of the planet, stretching that far, dividing the continent. "Think of it, *cher*, you're looking at water that washed out of Lake Itasca in northern Minnesota. It's like looking at me and realizing you're looking at the nineteenth century. Well—the last year of it, any-way." She smiled wryly. "I'm old as the river and I'll never die. Don't I sound like a fictional character? The wise old lady from the novel about the wise old lady."

Lily watched her stare out at the smoothly coursing water. The deeply lined face was far more interesting than the muddy flow along the banks. Lily only wanted her to go on talking. But then Violet would nod, and close her eyes, breathing so shallowly that it was difficult to tell if she was breathing at all. If the younger woman touched her shoulder, she'd stir, and give a chiding glance. "Not yet, *cher*. I'm still here."

"I wish you'd stop talking like that," Lily said.

After a time, Violet would rise, and hike back up the bank, and on through the busy confusion of the Quarter to Burgundy Street. Now and again she would stop at one of the small shops, or cafés, or she would buy food and sandwiches at Central Grocery (mufalettas, a delicacy of the region) that Lily would carry back. When Violet went alone, if it was raining or the weather was too humid, she took cabs, and there were particular adjustments necessary to get her into the backseat.

In some daily instances, she appeared a little confused—especially about having a child in her house, but this was momentary, never lasting longer than a few seconds. When she was home, she drifted into her naps more frequently, it seemed, though Dominic said it ebbed and flowed—she had good weeks and bad weeks.

She was not the kind of simple, positive soul with a youthful vitality and serene wisdom that people took her for: in the evenings she sat on the veranda outside Lily's room, and Lily's company was required in these hours. Indeed, the presence of everyone in the house was required. She would ramble on about the old days, the old city as she had known it when she was a girl, talking easily, with the slight pauses that told them she had dropped off for an interval. She would wake with a little shudder, and rock back and forth, as if animated by her own surprise at having drifted away. She would watch the night come, napping off and on in this fashion. She had a large fund of stories about people she had known and places she had been, and she liked to talk about them. Stories of violence and mayhem interested her enormously; it had been a subject of long study when she was younger. She had a sophisticated understanding about most of the important battles of the last two centuries. In her room, she kept a police scanner and a radio so she could monitor the crimes of the city. The subject fascinated her. Outlaws had her grudging allegiance.

"Mary Kingsley was an outlaw," she said. "We have to widen the definition of the word, don't we, with her. An outlaw in bombazine and lace."

"I'm trying to understand her more as an exemplary person," said Lily.

"That's precious."

"No."

"Of course it is. Who cares about that?"

"You do. We all do. If we pretend to civilized life."

"You're young."

"Well."

"Civilization is overrated, *cher*. There are instances where it wrecked everything."

"I know, I know," Lily said, unable to keep back the note of weariness at the thought. "Every civilization is built on a crime. I've heard and read all that. I'm interested in the particulars."

"Laudable," Aunt Violet said.

"Mary was obsessed with the nature of consciousness—searching for explanations of ultimate matters."

"Again, laudable."

"I'm boring you," Lily said.

"No."

There was an aspect of Violet's makeup that urged her to challenge whoever she was with. It took a few weeks for Lily to realize that the other woman had a horror of being thought of in the stereotypical ways most of the people with whom she came in contact did think of her. She was so old; and everyone assumed that this meant that she was religious, and too rickety as a personality to withstand conflict, or change, or the changes in the culture of the times. Her hatred of being thought prudish made her decidedly blunt on matters of sex, and to friends of hers and Dominic's, she was careful to explain that the baby was an accident, and what the real situation was between Dominic and Lily.

"Dom's gay as a wren," she would say, grinning out of one side of her mouth. "And this girl is not. But they had this baby together. We don't know what the baby will turn out to be." Dominic feigned mild amusement about it, but Lily could see that he was silently irritated. She couldn't bring herself to ask him directly what he felt. The fact was, the two of them were skirting their feelings with steady, vigilant determination when it came to the baby.

In the first week of November, Mary caught a bad cold that subsequently turned into a fever. After the second day, the fever spiked alarmingly, and Lily and Dominic were told to bathe her in cool water in the bathtub. It was the flu. There were many cases in the city. Lily and Dominic took turns with the baby, but no one slept very well, and then Violet came down with it, too. Violet grew starkly pale, and was delirious.

They put her on the sofa in the living room, and Manny tended to her as best he could. Dominic and Lily sat up with Mary, who pitched and tossed on the blanket they had laid out on Lily's bed. Mary's fever had gone down some, but she still had a terrible croupy cough and no appetite.

"The flu usually doesn't do well down here," Dominic said. "It doesn't like humidity. It shouldn't be so severe."

Lily was exhausted, and everything grated on her nerves. She had been seized by a desolate fear that she had brought her child here to grow ill and die. It was impossible to muster any belief in health, or in a future: they would stay this way, witnessing the suffering of her child, who had no understanding of it, and no ability to express where and how it hurt. Dominic's remark about the flu only exacerbated Lily's sense of aloneness in this predicament. There was an element of complaint in it, as if the fever were the baby's fault. She said, "Go get some sleep, why don't you."

"I'm okay."

They were quiet. They could hear the low rambling Aunt Violet was doing in her delirium, downstairs, a steady stream of half-enunciated words and phrases.

"It's too much," Dominic said abruptly.

Lily turned to him. "Go on to bed."

"No—I mean this—this responsibility. I've never been so scared. I hate it."

She was silent. The baby coughed, deep and awful-sounding, then cried some. Lily reached across the bed and patted her back, the crying slowed and stopped, and she was asleep again.

"Jesus," Dominic said.

"Dom, please leave us alone."

He seemed affronted at the suggestion. "How can you say that?"

"I just mean go get some sleep."

"I can't sleep."

"Well, take a walk, then. Go get some fresh air."

"It's the middle of the night, Lily. I'm not going out."

She was conscious of his hands knotting in and out of themselves in his lap. He coughed and sniffled; perhaps he was coming down with it now. "Lily," he said. "I love you."

She stretched out her arm and patted the back of his hands.

"Let's get married."

"Oh, Dom," she said.

"I can't help it," he told her. "I've been thinking about it. This country—this place—what kind of life can she have?"

"I don't want to talk about this now. Please."

He sat there fretting.

The baby coughed again, a bad spell this time that necessitated Lily's lifting her and holding up the little arms. Mary coughed so deeply that the crying she tried to do would not come, and when at last the coughing ceased, the crying brought on another fit. Lily held her, feeling the heat in her skin, the small convulsions of her chest. Every breath seemed labored and wheezing, noisy with rheum.

"I can't stand it," Dominic said.

"Well, then leave," Lily told him. "Get out. Christ."

He appeared stricken. He stood and moved to the door, where he hesitated and seemed about to say something. But the baby was in a coughing fit, and Lily was attending to that, so he left them there and banged down the stairs. She paced, holding the baby until she fell back to feverish half-sleep. Then she put her down again on the blanket. The fever was still there, but the cough was loose, now, phlegmy, a good sign. It was breaking up; the tightness in the little chest was giving way, the breathing seemed slightly easier. Lily sat down again and rocked, waiting, watching.

Dominic came back up and stood in the frame of the doorway. She found it hard not to think of him as being like Tyler in this respect: no tolerance at all for the kinds of trouble parental love brought, the kinds of nurturing it required. The messiness of living upset him. And maybe it was something that upset any man. She was too tired to examine the thought; it seemed true enough.

"I'm sorry," he said, coming into the room. He sat down next to her, and folded his hands tightly between his knees.

"She's better," Lily said.

"She doesn't sound better."

"Yes, as a matter of fact, she does."

"I hate it."

"I think we've established that, Dom. She's not having any fun, either."

He seemed surprised, straightening a little, frowning. "I mean I hate it that she's having to go through this."

"It's a little flu," Lily said. "She'll be all right."

"People have died of flu, Lily. Lots of them. Millions."

"Oh, for God's sake, nobody's dying."

He said "Forgive me. I'm scared—okay? Please."

It occurred to Lily that he had merely expressed out loud her own fears in this bad, long, ominous-feeling night.

He stood and began to pace. "Violet's in another world," he said.

"She's the one we have to worry about," Lily told him.

This turned out to be true. Mary was markedly better in the morning, and improved rapidly from then on. Violet's flu turned to pneumonia, and she had to be hospitalized. Manny was beside himself. He didn't sleep, and in the few hours he was home, he couldn't sit still. He moved from room to room, ashen-faced, nursing his fear. His mind kept running ahead, and he would stop and gaze at one of Aunt Violet's statues of the Virgin and begin to quail and sob.

Because the baby had so recently been ill, they couldn't take her out, so Lily stayed behind in the house when the two men drove to the hospital to be with Violet. The vigil over the old woman was therefore all going on at a remove from Lily, who received progress reports each day like bulletins from another part of the same battlefield. By this time, she herself was down with flu—a mild case, headache and cough and fever. But there was the baby to care for, and she couldn't rest or do anything to doctor herself.

It wasn't until the week of Thanksgiving that Violet came home.

Her improvement had been so slow and she was so frail that secondary problems developed, all of which required more time in the hospital, and occasioned more agonized imaginings and suppositions by poor Manny, who could not be calmed or comforted. Dominic told Lily that on several nights he simply held the other man, that they were like two children huddled against the blast of a terrible storm.

Thanksgiving was quiet. Manny brought home a cooked turkey breast from Central Grocery, and Dominic put the dinner together—boiled noodles and gravy, canned string beans and cranberry sauce. Nobody had much appetite. Aunt Violet said the prayer, a simple "Thank you," her gaze lifting slightly to the high, carved ceiling.

Dominic cut the turkey. They were all coughing now, the tail end of the siege, as Violet called it. The color had come back to her face, and when Mary grew fussy, she brushed one thin finger gingerly across the left side of the small round face and said, "Look at the bounce in that cheek. This child is healthy again. You can always tell by the bounce in the cheek."

After dinner, they sat in the living room for a couple of hours, but no one felt much like talk. Aunt Violet put the little portable television on and watched a movie. Dominic read; Manny napped. Lily helped the baby move from one area of the room to the other—Mary was beginning to want to take steps. Lily stood her up, and walked with her gently across the living room floor and back again. The others watched.

"I'm scared," Aunt Violet said suddenly. "Oh, Lord, am I scared."

They all gazed at her.

"Tell us," Dominic said.

"Nothing to tell. I just had this awful scare come over me."

"Can I get you something?" Lily asked.

Violet shook her head.

"What are you afraid of?" Manny said.

Violet turned to him. "Don't be an idiot, *cher*."

Lily bent down, lifted Mary, and held her, feeling the cloud of worry about Violet, but reveling in the coolness of the little forehead, the arms.

"Your name is Lily," Violet said to her.

Lily nodded.

"I couldn't remember it for the life of me."

"You've been sick," Lily told her.

"Couldn't call it up. I was watching you and the baby and I couldn't remember your name to save my soul."

"I get that sometimes," Manny said.

"Not this, *cher*. Not like this."

They were all quiet for a moment.

"Hold my hand," Violet said, reaching for Lily.

Lily moved to the chair next to her, sat down, with Mary on one knee, and took the extended aged slender hand. The fingers were surprisingly warm. "Better?" Lily said.

Violet smiled. "No. But I can withstand it now."

PART·6

The Shores of Home

TWENTY-THREE

1

The River of Lost Souls, the early missionaries called it. They used this great equatorial river to travel inland, where violence and fever and death awaited them among the exotic peoples they saw as benighted and in need of the word of Christ. They brought it with them, possessed of the hopes of zealotry, the bravery and belief of their time and place: they were fishers of men, as the words of Jesus had called the apostles to be. But along with their zeal and their goodwill they brought European varieties of sickness that hadn't reached this part of the world. A place that, aside from a few tentative and then rather quickly forgotten incursions of the Portuguese—who named the area (they called it *Gabao*, which translates as "hooded cape")—had been free of any other influence for centuries. With the new influx of Europeans, whole tribes were decimated by illnesses that barely affected the white visitors; conversely, there were sicknesses in this tropical tangle that no European had been exposed to, and many of them died as well.

With few exceptions, the Europeans also brought an unwillingness to understand the people they were giving everything of themselves to save, or serve. They found the Africans repugnant and considered them inferior. The misunderstandings were of course reciprocal, and in all too many instances, disastrous. Back in the 1860s, when Mary was a little girl, traders began using the river, building way stations for the traffic in palm oil, ivory, and rubber; and for transporting rum and guns and powder, beads and charms and calico to the natives upriver, although there had been one kind of trade or another going on up and down its banks long before Europeans found their way here—longer still before the French expeditions, led by the explorer Brazza, came in conquest, back in 1880.

The Ogowe courses from the Congo Plateau more than seven hundred miles to the Atlantic. Three major tributaries lead into it. In recent years a tribe has begun to displace other tribes on the river, coming from the uncharted—at least by Europeans, and by this time most Europeanized Africans—lands north and east of the Ogowe. These are the Fang, or Fan, and everyone fears them. They are purported to be cannibals (the word itself, Mary knows from her father's papers and from her reading, comes from the Caribbean, and is the bastardized form of the word *Caribel*, used by the people of that region of the world whose custom was the partaking of human flesh). The few Fan that Mary has seen in her travels seem more directly dignified and powerful than other Africans, even though these also have been, to some extent, Europeanized. It seems to her that she can only really study the beliefs of these people by going among them where they have not yet been exposed so much to Europeans, and the European influence.

She's staying at the governor's house in Calabar, with Lady MacDonald. There is an epidemic of typhoid, and so her services have been required—long nights of sitting with delirious men and women and children. Even in exhaustion, she stands at a window overlooking the town, where for days she has been nursing these patients and in many cases helping them die, and thinks about getting away, going south to the Gabon, and the great river. She imagines finding her way to the country of the Fang, and walking among them, new.

2

July 19, 1895

I've written several brave letters home, and have managed to sound in good spirits, intrepid and entirely free of dire imaginings. Nothing, no amount of reading, could have prepared me for the harshness of the life all around me here, and nothing could have forearmed me as a witness to the failures of the various systems of European supervision of these lands and these divided tribes. I have had to use all my powers of persuasion to get the official governments to allow me to progress at all, and in each instance, even with the help of people like Captain Murray and the MacDonalds, I have had to deplete my already depleted funds to gain what little access I have been able to accomplish. First, I had to go through this typhoid crisis in Calabar, and there was a terrible outbreak of violence in the neighboring town of Brass, so Lord MacDonald's presence there was required. He left shortly after Lady

Mac and I arrived. The violence has to do with conflict between independent traders, or "middle men" as we have called them, and George Goldie's Royal Niger Trading Company. Goldie's men had been preventing the middle men of Brass to trade on the Niger, and a smallpox epidemic broke out. The Brassmen, starving and sick and unable to support themselves except by trade, and prevented from doing so by the Royal Niger Trading Company, sacked the company headquarters in Akassa and put everyone to the sword. Lord MacDonald is off to find some solution, and is of course at odds with George Goldie, whose company men and women were so terribly slaughtered and, in some cases, eaten. I'm fond of both men. I would like to get out and away from all of this, since I can't involve myself one way or another. Poor Ethel tries to be effective here, but cannot understand my fascination with the people, and continually finds fault with me for my language. It is all friendly; even to some extent meant as good-natured teasing. I have for some time had the habit—I may even have gotten it as far back as Cambridge—of using the Lord's name in vain. What is worse, according to Ethel, is my use of the term Allah as an expression of emphasis or alarm. I have, it seems to me, used both for some time: Jesus, and Allah, in the same way—both as a prayer, and an exclamation. Ethel finds this upsetting, and so along with curbing my urge to wander about and see what I can see, I am forced to watch my tongue, like a child in church.

Here in Calabar, I have made the acquaintance of a woman the natives call The Mother of All the Peoples. Mary Slessor has been in Africa for twenty years and is a fine woman. We spent several evenings together, talking of this country and its people. She knows them well. There will be more to tell you about her, I'm sure. For the present, I'm dazzled, and I have the gift of being able to make her laugh. She's the only person I have spoken to directly about my plans to leave the Europeanized areas of the country and see these people in a purer state.

Very soon now, I am going to have the men and the wherewithal to start on a journey up the Ogowe River. And the country of the much-feared tribes of the interior. We'll go beyond the trade routes, though we intend to trade. There is no reason to believe we can't do that in any part of this astonishingly extreme continent. I am going to the heart of Gabon.

∞

Toward the end of June, she hires four Ajoumbas (also called Ajimbas, and Ajumbas) to go with her to explore the lower part of the Ogowe River (also called the Ogooue, and the Ogawe). She is finding out that names of places, and things, and even of people are spelled and often even pronounced differently, depending on where she is and who she's with. The four Ajoumbas have names so similar-sounding in their language that she dubs them according to their features: Gray Shirt is the leader of them. The others are: Singlet, for the English jersey undershirt he wears and for his Irish accent and manner; Pagan, who is blacker than the others, the deepest blue-black, with wide whites in his eyes and black round irises that look like glossy stones; and finally a thin, elderly man she first calls the Earl of Kent, but then, noting the worry in his features at the many syllables, decides simply to call Silent. The names please them; it is as if she has shown them some sign of her admiration and respect for them. Gray Shirt and Singlet are Christians; Pagan and Silent are fervent believers in witchcraft and magic.

They depart in a long canoe, with Mary seated in the center and two men each in front and in back of her. In the bottom of the canoe is her portmanteau and several bags of goods to trade. She is wearing the usual dark dress, with high collar, and long sleeves, and white lace on the cuffs. She sits erect in the canoe and observes the changing splendors of the banks on either side: colors inside colors, the richest jade hues, limned with gold that looks as though it could have dropped intact from the blazing sun that comes brokenly through the thick branches overhead. Her anxieties and her impatience have begun to wear off. All the sounds of the bush come to her like warnings of their advance along the glassy brown surface. She breathes the odor of the men—a strong, pungent smell that exhilarates her, as does the redolence of mangrove marsh and the dung of crocodiles on either side, mingled with the heavy fragrance of wildflowers whose lavender heads angle out from the banks like soft bells caught in the act of swinging.

They stop at the village of Arevooma, the home of Gray Shirt, who insists that she stay in his house. The house has a veranda, and is comfortably appointed: there are chairs and a small table, and a calico tablecloth. She drinks tea here, masked from the other members of the tribe by another calico cloth—a courtesy that Gray Shirt extends to her. Before her tea is done, to her surprise, a man she had briefly known in Calabar shows up. This is a Christian convert named Ndaka, who has come to attend to the affairs of his dead brother. Ndaka is an heroically ugly man, with jagged teeth and the braided scars of fetish, and his features are so bulbous and unmatched as to suggest that his face was put together from several others. Yet she remembers that she liked him in Calabar, that he was very helpful during the epidemic. He has come to Gray Shirt's house with a lantern to fetch her for the service he intends to say over the body of his brother, who, he informs her, with a small, sad, disapproving frown, was a pagan. It has taken all his powers of persuasion to convince the other members of his family not to treat the brother's death as an element of having been witched, but to allow Ndaka to perform a Christian service over him.

She has a broiling headache, and is worried that she's in for a bout of West Coast fever, but she accompanies him. The service is held in front of the brother's house, and the lanterns draw thousands of biting and stinging insects. The Mpongwe and Igalwa sing English hymns, loudly, in a more terribly pitched screech than anyone in an English church ever heard, High Church hymns, while the gathered crowd slaps at insects and moves with increasing discomfort in the bug-clouded light.

At last, she is led by Ndaka into the brother's house, which is even more magnificent than Gray Shirt's. There's a plaited bamboo floor that seems to give slightly with one's weight, and she crosses it with an increasing sensation that she's about to fall through. Having already experienced this before in Africa, she says to Ndaka:

—What is below this house?

—Nothing, ma, he says with a smile. It will hold you all steady.

—Will it hold all of us?

—All one time, ma.

At length, she makes her way back to Gray Shirt's house, and is shown into a clean room with mirror and dressing table and great calabashes—gourds made from the tree of that name—full of some pungent-smelling liquid. She brings one to her nose and breathes the aroma; it stings her nostrils. She puts her little finger into it and touches that to the edge of her lips. Most poisons in Africa have powerful odors, and if they have no odor—as some do not—they sting inordinately on the skin. Moreover, it makes little sense for a rich man like Gray Shirt to keep poison in such quantity in his sleeping quarters. This is liquor of some kind. She sips it, and receives the burn of it, not without pleasure. It goes down easily, and she has another before she prepares herself for sleep. The bed is spread over with mosquito netting, and is covered with calico and chintz, and soft pillows. Were it not for the sounds outside, and the constant haranguing buzz of the insects, she might be in an English inn, somewhere near the sea. But the night is sleepless and long. The headache lost some of its searing power with the sips of Gray Shirt's liquor, so she tries some more of it. But this time the stuff exacerbates things, and the headache grows much worse; it makes her nauseous. She paces a little, and fights off the urge to be sick, and she tries to read by the guttering candle: Gunther's book on bird species. But it's impossible.

Dawn takes an age to arrive. At first light, she gets up to go out for a turn. A walk into the surrounding bush is inviting to her. She steps out on Gray Shirt's veranda, and sees Conklin standing in the center of the village with two other white men, his hands on his hips, two long-barreled pistols crossed in his belt, a bush hat on, and a whip curled over one shoulder. He carries a bag, and there are several Ajoumbas coming up from the river, bearing boxes of goods and calabash gourds, no doubt of whiskey or rum. He's here to trade.

—Conklin, she says. You old coaster.

The sun isn't fully risen. He turns and squints at her.

—Hello, he says. Who the devil am I addressing?

—You are addressing Miss Mary Henrietta Kingsley, she says, sounding the *H*.

He considers a moment. Evidently her name has not come through to him as the name of someone he knows. He takes a few steps forward, head tilted, staring.

—What the devil?

—Do you have a smoke, Conklin?

And a broad smile comes across his whiskered face. He strides toward her, hand outstretched.

—Why, my God, it's Miss Kingsley. Kingsley, of course. From *The Lagos*. What in blazes are you doing in this godforsaken place?

She takes his hand, and sees, even in this dimness, that he is either just over, or just about to come down with, fever: his eyes are shadowed and the irises look unhealthily jaundiced.

—I'm studying fish and fetish, she says. And trading some.

—Damn foolery hanging about a place like this.

—Well, 'ere we are.

He turns and indicates the dim gray course of the river in the low light.

—That river took two of my men yesterday. Bloody fever. And one of them drowned. Fell off the gunnel in a sick fever and was waterlogged before we got him back in the boat. He's down there waiting for a decent burial.

—I saw Deerforth, Mary says.

Conklin merely stares back at her.

—I was with him when he died of the fever.

The other's face changes only slightly—a kind of sinking in the cheeks, making them look even more emaciated than they are.

—I don't think he recognized me, Mary says.

—Yes, well. That's how you die here. Alone. Unless you're in the company of a snake or a leopard. Or a bloodthirsty savage.

He looks at the ground, and then adjusts one of the pistols in his belt. The two other men who are with him are instructing the Ajoumbas about where to place the boxes of goods. One of them indicates the long canoe at moor on the bank, and the wrapped bundle in it.

—Where are you headed, Miss Kingsley, if you don't object to my asking.

—The country of the Fang.

—I'll take that lightly, he says. Even you wouldn't be so reckless.

—You may take it any way you wish, sir.

She can't articulate for herself, in the little amount of time between his words and her response, why it angers her so. She registers the surprise in his features, and the slow dawning of her seriousness and offense. He nods, and tips his hat, and looks beyond her at the house from which she has come.

—I meant no disrespect of you, he says. Surely you know that by now.

—I was so sorry about Deerforth. I'm sorry to be the one to tell you.

—I had a suspicion, Conklin says, when the poor chap didn't show up on Corsica Island. We were supposed to meet there.

They are silent for a few seconds. Somewhere off in the bush a leopard makes a long, terrible, coughing guttural roar.

—You really are going to the Fang?

—Yes, Mary says.

—Did you hear about Withers? he asks.

—No. Did he go back to England?

Conklin spits at the ground and then moves his boot across it in the dirt, turning from her to watch his men and the Africans putting the bags of goods down on the side of the path leading into the village. The sun is just reaching the tops of the giant redwoods on the other side of the river. Two of the Africans—one of them, Mary sees, is Gray Shirt—are carrying the wrapped body up from the canoe.

—Did he take his wife back to England? she asks Conklin.

Conklin gives her a rueful look, then shakes his head.

—They think he bludgeoned her, and then took his own life. Well, he took his own life, all right. He put the bloody pistol in his mouth and shot through the top of his own head. They found her beaten senseless with a cane. She survived. She sailed for England under the care of a nurse hired by her family. She wouldn't say who it was beat her that way. But there were no other likely suspects. He thought he'd done the job on her and then he did it proper on himself. And she woke up.

—Where did this take place? Mary asks.

—They never left Saint Paul de Loanda. He lost his mission rather quickly—drinking rum to calm his nerves. Afraid of losing his bloody wife to the fevers. Or the insects. Or the snakes. Then he was just afraid.

She says nothing. Some others in the village are stirring. Soon there will be a rush of people coming out and down to the bank to dispense with the body, and to begin trading with the newcomers.

—I saw them once more after *The Lagos*, you know. I was in Saint Paul de Loanda getting up supplies for a little trading up this very river. They were standing in the square at the marketplace, having a terrible row. I walked up to them and when they recognized me they became two gentle, loving, considerate souls, filled with the most killing consideration of each other and wondering whatever happened to the lovely Miss Kingsley.

—I have survived, Mary says.

—You look none the worse for wear.

—There is some sort of liquor in Gray . . . in the 'ouse. Would you care for something this early in the morning?

He smiles, then tips his hat again.

—All we need are Corliss's cigars.

—Do you 'ave any word of Corliss? she asks.

—Nothing. Not a word or a whisper. Haven't seen him since *The Lagos.*

They start up to Gray Shirt's house and walk up the steps of the veranda. Several people from the village are already in the path, among them Gray Shirt himself. She waves at him and indicates Conklin.

—Very good one time, says Gray Shirt, smiling with his amazing white teeth.

But then he frowns and points back in the direction of the river.

—Dis body bad palaver for town. Dey feel it, ma. I think dese men have to must take it downriver wid dem.

—We'll bury it downriver, Conklin says. Christ.

—Hab mercy, sa.

—Thank you, Gray Shirt, Mary tells him, and watches as he turns to direct the others to carry the wrapped corpse back down to the river-bank. Conklin stands at her side.

—I'm beginning to get sick of it here, he says.

—You look a bit feverish.

—I've been fighting it this whole trip.

Inside the house, in the closeness, she breathes the sweat and faintly rum-stale, tobacco odor of him, and is strangely happy. The news has been bad—Withers dead; she has had to tell him about poor Deerforth. There is a cadaver by the riverbank waiting to be consigned to the water. Yet she feels a stir of exaltation, handing him the calabash she drank from last night. He holds it to his nose, then sips it and closes his eyes tight, swallowing.

—It's some liquor made from bananas. Very strong. And very bloody good.

Now he takes a long drink of it.

—Ahh. Very, *very* good indeed.

—Is Kurschstler with you? she says. I forgot to ask.

He just holds the gourd to his mouth and is swallowing a large draft of the liquor, so that it washes in two small rivulets down either side of his mouth. He brings the gourd down, and runs the back of his hand across his lips, eyes closed tight again, for the sting of swallowing. Then he straightens and looks at her as if she's far off. He blinks again and smiles.

—You know, you are really quite a strikingly beautiful woman.

—'ere, she says. Let me 'ave it.

Evidently he thinks she's going to drink from it, and when she puts it back in its place he frowns, and steps back a little, looking at the room.

—What's your host's name?

—I asked you about Kurschstler, she says.

He waves this away, moving sullenly to the other side of the room and gazing for a moment into the mirror there. Then, in a low, almost capitulating tone:

—Kurschstler's dead, too.

—Tell me.

—Something bit him. It attacked his face while he was asleep. He woke up to the stinging and screamed. We never saw what it was. He had three stings on his cheek. Small ones. Little points of discolored blood. The Africans called it a name I'd never heard. Their name for it. Or what I could bloody well make of their bloody name for it. You can't tell with the Negroes. They could've meant some sort of magic, or spell. But it started with three small rashes on the stung places, like a little rawness in the skin. But those rashes connected into one rash, across his cheek, and he washed it every day and it kept growing and getting more angry-looking and he kept washing it and then one day he went mad, and he stayed that way for a long time—almost a bloody month. Mad, screaming, with this dreadful place widening all the time on his face. It turned his skin to a leathery, festering mess. And then one morning he was dead. A man lying dead with his mouth wide open on a scream that had been going on for twenty-three days.

Mary looks out the window of Gray Shirt's house, at the white men standing with their goods and the dark people of the village, men, women, and children gathering around them. In the distance, the body of the unfortunate man who drowned is lying next to the lapping waters of the bank. There's an irremediable pang at her heart, looking at them all under the rising sun, these precarious souls crowding around a lot of boxes filled with baubles and material goods, and beyond them the person who is beyond all these sounds and passions and excitements. She turns to Conklin.

—We leave this morning, she says.

—I wonder if you've heard me at all, says Conklin.

—Yes.

A moment later, she draws up the courage to ask about James Henley Batty, and Captain Murray, and the others. Mary Slessor, and the MacDonalds, whom she has just been with.

—Batty's fine, last I heard he was still in England.

—No. He left for Sierra Leone before I left for 'ere.

—Well, I haven't seen him.

—And the others?

—I heard MacDonald has recently been in a mess at Akassa. A lot of damned killing and shooting and cutting up of people. I also heard that he's about to be assigned to go to India. You probably know more about all that than I do. I'd heard you were in Calabar with Lady Mac.

—No, Mary says. I left there. Against her kind wishes.

—Captain Murray has another vessel.

—Yes, I traveled on it.

—Well, if you know, why in bloody hell did you ask about him?

—I thought you might've seen 'im since.

—I don't know anyone named Slessor, he says. Another woman, is she?

Mary nods.

—More craziness, he mutters.

—I'm very sorry about Kurschstler, she says.

—You knew Dolokov, didn't you?

—Yes. Slightly. I delivered some letters 'e wrote to someone in London. Or I tried to deliver them.

—Well, he's dead, too. Drink, and the consumption.

—I think I knew that, Mary says.

Conklin looks at her, and then at the calabash gourds on the table next to where she stands. He wipes one hand across his mouth.

—Even knowing Dolokov's fate, just now, I'd like another touch of that banana liquor.

She offers him the gourd, and watches him swallow.

—Damn country's going to kill us all, he mutters.

It strikes her that in some ways, now, she is fresher, more vigorous than he is. And she had looked upon him as such a hardened, strong part of the mysteries of the place. She says:

—You're really thinking of shipping to England?

He shakes his head slowly, as though giving the thought every consideration; but when he speaks, his tone is that of mild puzzlement.

—No, he says. You?

3

THE FOLLOWING MORNING she and Gray Shirt, and the other three of her original party, along with three members of Conklin's group, depart for the uncharted reaches of the Ogowe. The new members of the group include two Europeanized Fang and a Mpongwe named Obanjo, who also calls himself Captain Johnson, and speaks a slightly idiosyncratic, though perfectly accented English. They are all in two long canoes, Mary in the first one with Pagan, Silence, Singlet, and Gray Shirt. She offered a guarantee to Conklin for the other canoe and the use of three of his party, using a voucher from Hatton & Cookson. Conklin accepted it. This counts as an exorbitant expense, since very few remain in her reticule. She left Conklin with only partially feigned irascibility.

—I wonder what you would've charged a man for these things. Or if indeed there would've been any charge.

—Maybe if you run out of Hatton and Cookson gold, you'll have to stop this foolery and do something to save your life, he said.

—Rot, she said in return.

—I still think you are an astonishingly, strikingly beautiful woman.

—I should've given you more of the banana liquor, she said. Enough to send you off. I'd feel better now.

—I might've had less restraint, lady.

—I'm not amused, she said.

He tipped his hat and smiled a crooked smile, bowing, as a gentleman would seeing a lady into a surrey in London.

—Perhaps I'll see you on the river, madam.

Now, the two canoes glide along, and the growing tension of the men with her is testimony to how far they are getting from the protection of European flags or authority. For long intervals, no one speaks. The vegetation on either side closes in on them. They pass the burned remains of an abandoned trading post, the charred boards torn from the frame and left in a pile partially in the water, which releases a fetid odor, fused with the smell of wood ash.

A few miles farther along, the current speeds up, and the banks recede, until it looks almost as though they have entered a lake. There are sandbars and islands of trees and mangrove stands and marsh grass, looking like cruel blades jutting from the mire at the edge. They see crocs sunning themselves on the banks, and moving through the heavy green water, like pieces of a sunk barque on a tide, the surface parting with their motion, forming a widening V of ripples, a thin, nearly translucent wake. Above them the sky is blue-white, with thin, hazy wisps of cloud high up. The vision of it is stunning after the long passages in the foliate gloom of the trees.

Gray Shirt calls this part of the river Lake Ncovi. Mary notices that the oars are no longer fouled with mud and sand, but have been washed clean in this deeper water, the drops melting from the end of the oar blades like liquid silver as they are lifted and then put back under, pulling the canoes along. The two canoes are headed north/northeast, now. A little to the left, over the clefts of low mountains in the distance and the near darkness of the trees, the sun begins to sink, causing the whole sky to glimmer with new colors, new shades of the rainbow—such clarity of hue and tint that the whole prospect of the prodigious, accepting distances before them is transformed, as if it has never before been quite visible to human eyes. Mary looks at the others in her party, and notes that they are not even quite aware of this matchless beauty.

As the light fades, they come into a region of loneness, and of something else. The sky is indigo, without a trace of a cloud or a star or the moon. There is still wide space all around them, yet a kind of pall hangs in the air. Mary has an image of the forests on the shoreline leading into some region of death and decay. She looks at the others, who all seem to have noticed the change in the air; they are looking around them, paddling more slowly. They pass one small island and Gray Shirt says, abruptly:

—I smell them blood.

This, Mary knows, is the African equivalent of a European saying that he has just felt someone pass over his grave. It's a morbid remark, expressing his fear and unease. Everyone else berates him in several languages, and he stares ahead, tight-lipped, having made his observation. Mary finds herself admiring his steadfast pessimism.

They head for a second, larger island, and as they come near, a big village becomes visible in the sinking grayness, scattered among the trees at the summit. The beach is a crescent-shaped sandy cove, bordered by a small cliff, along which a wide path ascends into the first trees. Something is going on in the village—a tumult comes from there, shouting and singing and the heavy unison of many tom-toms. The two canoes come close to the bank, and beach among the rocks. Each of the men brings out his pistol, checks that it is loaded and that the safety is off. Mary calls forward the two Fang she had lured away from Conklin for the promise of Hatton & Cookson vouchers and money. Though Gray Shirt and Pagan say they have a pair of friends in this village, she wants these pure Fang to see their fellows, even in their rather un-Fanglike appearance and demeanor. Obanjo/Captain Johnson wishes not to leave the canoes, and refuses to do so, because it is clear, now, that the village is aware of their arrival. Down the path alongside the small cliff, running, armed with guns and spears and clubs, come forty or fifty very fierce-looking men, all of them shouting and whooping and making threatening gestures. Very quickly the whole beach is crowded with them, standing in a half circle around the visitors, who are backed against the edge of the river. The villagers grow very quiet now, wielding knives as well as guns. A fight is imminent, and it will be short work, too. Mary stands forward, partially aware that the strangeness of her dress and appearance might buy some time. She makes signs that she wishes to trade, and she gestures for her two Fang guides to begin speaking. They say nothing. They are as frightened as Obanjo/Captain Johnson, who cowers in the canoe, nowhere in sight, really, understanding, no doubt, that if he is seen, he will be perceived as cowering, and will be treated accordingly.

Gray Shirt and Pagan step quickly forward, arms extended straight out from their bodies to show that they are not armed, and they say the name of the Fang villager they believe resides here.

—Kiva, Gray Shirt says, echoed by his companion. Kiva.

The Fang begin speaking to each other, some trying to be heard over others, so that it is abruptly rather like a town meeting.

Silence steps close to Mary and says:

—It would be bad palaver if Kiva no live for this place.

—I wish you would go back to living up to your name, Mary tells him.

Finally, after what seems a horribly long interval, Pagan recognizes Kiva, and rushes toward him, speaking quickly, offering such heartfelt affection that everyone is embarrassed. In the next instant, Gray Shirt recognizes another man, a friend of his own, and one more scene of overwrought warmth unfolds. There is prickly, careful friendship all around now, and Pagan introduces Kiva to Mary, followed by Gray Shirt doing the same with his friend. Gray Shirt's friend puts his big dark hands in the air on either side of Mary's elbows, as though he is about to take hold of her and lift her up. But he doesn't touch her, and his smile, though baldly curious, reassures her that he means no harm. Finally the village men circle Mary and her party, and herd them along in a wave of naked brown humanity up the path to the village. At sight of Mary, women and children at first seem curious enough to approach, but then shy away; some scatter to the protection of their huts.

Unlike most African villages, this one has crossing streets. Mary is taken with the others to the central house, where immediately the trade talk begins. Now she's glad of the two Fang members of the party, who are being petted and coddled by children, and even admired by some of the young boys and girls. But it is Gray Shirt who does most of the talking. He tells them that ma wants three members of this village to guide her overland to the Remboue River. They all have what the natives call a palaver over it. What will Mary's party give for the privilege of having these guides along? Mary is aware that without these guides, they may never find the way across to the other river, but she keeps from showing this. She offers some Hatton & Cookson money, a few tins of food and tea, some rum, using Gray Shirt almost exclusively as her interpreter. At one point, the chief Fang gestures as if to catch Gray Shirt's words and throw them to the dirt floor of the house.

Mary stands her ground, calmly restating what she's willing to give, and rejecting what fails to interest her. She has been told by her Europeanized Fang that a palaver with these people can last for weeks. She does not have weeks. She doesn't want to stay here at all, in fact. The village is in a terrible state of disarray and neglect; there are the remains of an elephant or hippo or manatee lying nearby, sending off a suffocating stench, and buzzing so loudly with flies and other insects that, in the dark, one might believe the carcass itself is making the sound. There are bird droppings and other, smaller carcasses hanging from strands of woven grass in the surrounding trees.

Mary keeps tranquilly repeating what she will give and, at last, the friends of Pagan and Gray Shirt, along with a third man, agree to take part in the journey. They say they know a way to the village of Efoua, whose inhabitants have never seen a European at all, but who have forged a wide path down to the Remboue. The deal is struck. And after the fact, several others seem willing to volunteer for the journey. The Ajoumbas are nervous, and say so, about having more than the two other Fang along, for they know stories about Fang killing black traders who happen into their country, eating parts of them and then smoking the rest for later feasts.

So the friends of Gray Shirt and Pagan—their names are Kiva and Fika—and the third one, Wiki, are taken on as guides. This settled, a celebration begins. Mary sends Pagan down to the canoes to fetch Obanjo/Captain Johnson, who strides up to her and says, in a hearty imitation of a drawing room voice:

—Thanks, p'raps, for your gracious excellency.

—You are quite welcome, sir, Mary tells him. P'raps.

—I was p'raps certain of a bad outcome, madam.

—I sensed that you were.

He bows at the waist, without ever taking his sincere and contrite and shamed eyes from her.

—I thank ye once again.

—Do not trouble yourself, she says.

He moves off and finds someone with a calabash full of rum, from which he takes a very long drink. Then he turns and bows.

—Strictest mod'ration, he says. P'raps.

She nods and tries to give him her most compliant smile: he may, tonight, after that scare, get as drunk as he pleases. Were it not for the fact that she is going to be asking him to be taking further risks, she might have told him how frightened she herself was for that very long twenty minutes.

As the leader of the expedition, she is given the best house in the village—Kiva's—and finds it all but intolerable. She lies on the makeshift bed of bark and straw, in the reek of the place, and waits for all the noise outside to die down. When it has grown quiet enough, for long enough—and she has no sense of having fallen off to sleep even for a moment—she gets up and steps out onto the village street, in the malodorous air of the buzzing carcass in its cloud of feeding insects. Two frighteningly large and heavy-winged vultures rise from it sluggishly as she appears in the dimness of the street, a darker figure on the dark. She makes her way alone down the path to the river, and steps into the water, feeling the chill of it, walking in up to her knees, climbing into the farthest canoe. She paddles out into the current of the river, and away from the island. The air is cool now, though still oppressive with putrefaction, the choking smell of offal. The water makes the softest rippling sound as she glides out, and in the crepuscular dimness she can see the faintest shadow of the other island. She heads for it, working easily in the still water, gliding along. The sky above her is chalky with stars, so bright they make a glitter on the smooth surface. As she nears the smaller island, she hears several splashes on the shore and supposes them to be crocs, so she presses on to the right, circling that side, until she can see what looks like a beach.

It is a group of hippos feeding, their movements in the shallow surf making it white. She skirts this, turns the canoe—with some difficulty— and heads back to the larger island, certain that this exercise will help her sleep when she returns. As she comes around the smaller island, she sees three lights, bright as lanterns, and with as wide a circumference of illumination, moving erratically near the shore. Thinking this is surely some species of flying fish—they seem to be skimming the surface of the river—she paddles quickly toward them, striving for quiet, but hurrying nevertheless. As she approaches them, they spread out, seem actually to circle her, hovering just over the surface. She can turn and try to close on any one of them, but will be leaving the other two behind to do so, and they seem to know it; they seem aware, remaining quite still, suspended at their distance, observing her. She glides slowly, as if to go between two of them, and they spread out as though to let her pass, and when she turns again and attempts to close on one of them, they all circle her again. She stops, and coasts, and they fly away, low across the night-sparkling dark water, quickly outdistancing her, and almost as quickly moving out of sight, except for the last one, which stops, suspended again just out of the water, then comes racing scarily back, seems bent on ramming her, or stinging her, this round, gold illumination the size of a china plate. It stops with a suddenness she takes to be unearthly, seems to wait, and then with something like a wavering dance of some sort of mischief, showing her how little she has to do with any of its movements, sinks suddenly and soundlessly into the water, just next to her canoe, carrying its illumination with it, showing moving fish and nettles and forms of water life, plant and animal, like brief images in a fever dream of light and shadow, until it disappears in the bottomless darkness.

She paddles back to the larger island, watching all the time for more of them. But nothing comes. In the village, she sits outside Kiva's house, opens a bottle of red wine Conklin gave her, and drinks it down. It tastes like wet stones, and is not very warming; it has no effect at all on her. She has the sudden realization, tinged with fear, that she is soon going to be thirty-two years old. And for perhaps the last time in her life, she wonders, with her old hard objectivity about herself, what could have possessed her to want to make this life out of her life, this living from the living she was doing in England, a girl with so little experience of anything.

In the morning, she tells Gray Shirt what she saw on the waters of the Ogowe, without mentioning that she had been out there in a canoe. He tells the Fang about it, and they smile at her.

—Akom, Kiva says. Devil Bush.

4

July 1895
Somewhere between the Ogowe and Remboue Rivers:

I have been up the Ogowe, in the rapids of it, fighting through them, periodically jumping for the bank when the rocks loomed too close, and being therefore by turns drenched and then dried in the blazing sun. Along with the others I am accompanied now by three Fang from M'fetta, the first pure Fang village we visited. At the end of the river trip, the group of us labored over ground on which no European, male or female, has set foot. Yet I felt strangely as though all this was familiar and I had lived it before. I felt as if I had come to the farthest reaches of my life, and all of it really had been a sort of flight, to alight at last on my own ground, the ground on which I was born to live.

The Africans have a song about it—a plaint, when someone dies.

—Come back, *it says.* Hi, hi, don't you hear? Come back. Come back. See here. This is your place.

I understand it so well, now, though I am of course still far from comprehending the mind and spirit of these strange, unpredictably resourceful, powerful human beings.

Their humanity is available to me in every gesture and in every sign, every motion of their eyes, the expressions on their faces, their tears and laughter and worries and loyalty and humor. Yet so much of the time they are eerily "other" to me. And if they are so to me, they must be and are of course infinitely so to other Europeans.

I imagine you in some future, with a finer instrument of understanding than my own—someone to whom my questions must seem as childish as the questions of so many of my friends and acquaintances among the Africans.

All of this stems from the complex of the African's beliefs about the physical, natural, and spirit worlds. Because everything in Africa is haunted with life; everything is spirit. And the spirits are seldom benign ones—nothing, to the African, is random.

In many tribes, even death, every death, is explicable in terms of witching, of ill will. The God who made everything in the universe is not personally involved in it; he keeps his distance. But there are a host of lesser spirits, or souls, who must be pled with or placated, and, as with the Greeks—and there are strong similarities—these lesser spirits are involved with human beings and behave very much like human beings. Each person is believed to have three souls, and only the first one is the animate being one sees or speaks to. The other two souls are always there, and indeed the Africans build little huts to offer shelter for one, called the Bush soul. You may see these small structures on the sides of the paths near the villages along the Ogowe. There is also a soul that a person possesses that he can use to cause harm to another—he can "witch" that person.

Ill will, in Africa, has power.

When a man dies, his slaves and friends and everyone he knew and all the members of his family, including his wives, come under suspicion of witchcraft; and there are rituals devised by the witch doctors to reveal the guilty party. I know of one instance where a man's death from fever resulted in the deaths of four other people—the witch doctor stalked down the village street slapping a straw basket lid on and taking it off and slapping it on again, and saying the names of everyone in the huts, one by one, and when the lid did not come exactly over the lip of the basket with one swipe, as it did not seven times, the unfortunate individuals whose names were called in each instance were then hauled out of their huts and forced to swallow a terrible substance made from tree bark, a poison that killed two of them outright, caused three of them to vomit—which was interpreted as meaning that their souls rejected the evil spirit and therefore exonerated them—and did nothing to the other two (apparently the poison weakens with exposure to the air). These two who did not vomit were roasted slow over a fire, until at last, as an act of screamed-for mercy, their throats were cut. The terror of this practice is rife all over the Congo, and in several instances has caused tribes to be practically wiped out. It is all in the hands of the witch doctors, and they are a force unto themselves, identified from earliest youth, and singled out for training. And beyond dealing with witchcraft they have various remedies for rheumatism and other human maladies. I saw a witch doctor treat a man with a broken arm by means of shoving a bamboo stick into the wound, and then tying the broken bone to it and wrapping it in palm leaves soaked in some substance that smelled of cacao. Not long after this, I saw the injured gentleman, and the skin was healed, but the arm itself was withering rapidly from the inside. Yet I have also seen wounds and festering sores, and one bad snakebite, healed in a matter of a few hours with the use of certain concoctions put together by the witch doctor.

But in a place where so many things can kill you, the obvious terror is in supposing every death to be the effect of witchcraft.

Here, even if a person is taken by a crocodile or a lion, the animal is thought to have been witched by someone else, and the round of rituals seeking the culprit begins. In other words, in this place that Europeans see as having no respect for life, there is such deep respect for it that every death is perceived as murder, *and therefore every death must be avenged. Every death. And of course there are the souls everywhere: the Africans worship while pounding grain into powder, or while hunting antelope, or eating. I have seen the medicine men ingest something from a wooden bowl, and begin to foam and froth at the mouth, their eyes becoming unnaturally bright, and yet they are lucid, and rather scarily acute, their senses seem enhanced, as if they had taken on the nerves of the animals they hunt—and they look* into *you; they understand what you say, even when you speak your own language, or another (I have spoken German to these men and found myself to be communicating with them).*

I'm so frightened all the time. I ride over a titanic loneliness, and am all too painfully aware of my strangeness to everyone. My only defense for it is this exterior of proper decorum and bravado; the calm of the lady in her own drawing room. My curiosity is like a drug. If I find nothing to exercise it with, I feel dead.

☙

One week later, at Egaja, Congo Français:

I write Lady MacDonald, I write Lucy, and friends in Cambridge, and Gunther, and Guillemard, and all the other acquaintances and friends, and then I write you, so much farther away than anyone, and yet the one of all of them with whom I can be entirely myself. You, who can never answer. And of course we have established this. I cannot bring myself, even so, even given the nature of these letters, which will be silent until they stand up and speak to someone—I can't bring myself to think of you as many. Perhaps several—or many—pairs of eyes will see me here, but there is one pair of eyes I take to my heart. I imagine you, one person, among however many.

We have been collecting and trading in several Fang villages along the path to the Remboue. Among the pleasures of the stay was that I had word of Corliss through one of the Fang minstrel singers we encountered. It came about quite by accident. We were watching him perform (the African minstrel is an astoundingly gifted storyteller/musician, whose one function in life is to tell stories. These are not, as you might expect, lore, or the history of any given tribe or people; they are not religious or admonitory or inspirational or cautionary, but are simply stories for the sake of the stories, filled with magic and mystery, usually violent and always at least as entertaining as much of the popular literature that I used to read—one must barter with these men first, of course, since everything on the continent is based on trade. One must ask for a given story from a cache of them that each one keeps, often represented by the various charms and objects that dangle from their bodies). At any rate, in the middle of one medium-priced tale that the others had decided upon, Obanjo/Captain Johnson, my African who is more English than the English, turned to me and said:

—Corliss, madam.

At first I didn't understand him. But he repeated it, and I nodded at him.

—You understood, p'raps? This gentleman speaks of you and a person of the male gender by the appellation of Corliss.

—Yes, I said.

—Corliss is in this story. The big captain demised a crocodile with a machete. This man says he heard it from Corliss. You p'raps understood this?

Again, I told him I had.

—Corliss was in the small boat trapped by mud in the river, p'raps.

He demised the big croc in his little boat while protecting the damsel of great distress, p'raps. A jolly good story.

—Oh, so, that is true, then, I said, thinking of the boasting boy in Corliss that I hadn't known was there. But then of course I wanted to know how it was that the minstrel knew Corliss, and of my association with Corliss. I suddenly missed David Corliss with a physical ache, and had to lower my eyes.

—I sabe Corliss, the minstrel said. He talk about you all one time.

Which means that he talks about me nearly incessantly, since in Africa the English expression for anything ongoing and continuous is all one time.

My heart quickened like a little girl's, to think of David Corliss talking about me. A silly little girl at an afternoon tea with a young suitor. I was quite ridiculous to myself, and even so I quickly assayed to discover news of him. But Obanjo informed me, in his inimitable way, that the minstrel had no news. Only more stories and songs, about other heroes.

One of the sorrows of this wandering existence I'm now leading is that I'm always passing in and out of lives. The conversation with Conklin shook me at a level I was unprepared to think about, or decide about. In any case, it becomes quite easy to believe that I will end my life in this country. I am filled with wonder every minute, even so. In a place not far from here, a missionary named Robert Nassau and I spent a wonderful evening discussing fetish. He's one of the few of his type who allows these people their culture; he's become quite expert at their religious beliefs, and is happy merely to serve them in practical ways. I mentioned Mary Slessor to him and was pleasantly surprised to find that he knows her well, that the two of them have been corresponding for years. I think, like her, he's more African than European, and as a result lives among them as a brother. He maintains his faith (he also has chided me for my increasing use of the Lord's name, and the name of Allah when in moments of surprise or consternation), and of course he still believes that these people can only be saved by Christianity; yet he keeps from proselytizing them to what I will call the usual harmful effect. There is nothing so heartrending as seeing a converted African in pain, suffering and seeking some solace from the silent God. Nobody to blame for his grief, no culprit with which to exorcize the anguish by exacting revenge. Their world is alive with souls, as I've said, and the souls are very active and filled with sound and fury, since they exist in every moving thing and, in some cases, in the whole visible and invisible world. These converted Africans have not the solace of supposing a spirit to be displeased with them or ill-disposed toward them; no, they have the curse of Deuteronomy, and the silence.

Silence.

There is no other silence here. When a person becomes ill, there is a horrific wailing from the members of the family, and I am sure a clinging fear that one might be perceived as having caused the illness. Among the tribes of the Niger delta, when a woman dies who has a child of six months old or more, they believe she'll come back for the child, and they perform a ritual of holding the child before her dead form, making it cry out and telling her that it will follow soon, and backing away slowly until others of the family or tribe rush in and cover the body with plantain leaves, thus shielding the mother's eyes so she may not see the direction in which the child has been taken away. If the child is younger than six months, she is simply thrown into the bush to die, as twins are thrown away to die—and sometimes, among some tribes, the mothers of twins.

When I was staying with Mary Slessor in Okyon, near Calabar, I saw a lovely child, aged four, whose mother had died at her birth. The others in the compound called her Wonder Child, *and I later found that this was because she had survived several days lying alone in the bush. When her mother died having her, this child was, according to the custom, simply thrown away. In a place where famine is common and food is by turns scarce or nonexistent given the extremes of weather and changes in fortune, this custom actually is not quite as dreadful as it sounds. Anyhow, some of the others who regularly go back and forth from Mary Slessor's compound to the market heard the child crying in the bush, weak little sobbing cries. She was barely alive. The leopards and snakes and other predators had missed her, somehow, as had the killing insects, though ants and flies had swarmed over her eyes and nose and mouth, and into her ears; they had eaten into the nasal cavity and through part of the upper lip. But she survived, and, happily, is not badly scarred. The mark on her upper lip gives her a questioning look that absolutely increases her charm. If I do come to write and finish a book, I would like to express something of this kind of missionary—Miss Slessor and her work, and the work of several I have known like her, are examples of the rare instance when Christian ideals are practiced rather than preached.*

The problem with the African mind is not its simplicity, because it is not simple. The trouble with African culture is that it is so determined by belief. If there is a hypocrite in these tribes, I have not met him yet. It is true that in some tribes a man accused of committing witchery against another can designate a slave to die for him, or pay to have someone else undergo the ordeal of poison, which in almost every case, as I have described it, ends in the death of the person involved. But fetish is so fervently believed as to animate the world—and the Africans are nearly absolute in their observance of their religion. Everything has a soul, and the soul doesn't leave after a thing dies; it remains for a period of weeks or months, which is why in some of the tribes the bodies of the dead are kept aboveground, and in some instances in plain sight. More so than in any society I know about or have read about, the whole of existence is governed by magic, by spells and witchcraft. It involves death, and it is brutal, though I hasten to add that if one were suddenly plunked down in the middle of a High Church ceremony in Kensington, without previous knowledge of the development of the religion and customs that lead to it—if one looked from a distance of cultural estrangement at the various forms of punishment in English law and at our wars of religion, our own conversion by sword, the crusades and pogroms and historical slaughters, political, religious, or simply inexplicable, as in the recent case of the Cheapside Ripper, one begins to understand that criminals exist in every society and that horrors exist there as well, and people attempt to build workable relations with their fellows as best they can under the specific circumstances. A great deal of African fetish makes a terrible kind of logical sense, given the extreme place in which these people must scrape out an existence; understanding, too, that while it is stalked by leopards, and driver ants, and snakes, and crocodiles; while its other earthly inhabitants can kill you more efficiently than just about anywhere else on earth, it is also the most spectacularly, wondrously, spirit-liftingly beautiful country. A country one loves, and carries into every other place one ever travels. In any case, I have come to like these people. I admire them. Especially the most fierce and feared of them, the Fang (others here call them Fan—the name rhymes with sawn, or long, not ran or sang). They have taken me in. We have tea.

⟋⟍

Two days later. Village of Esoon.
I went for an excursion with several Fang, some men and a few of their wives (polygamy is practiced in Africa for what I have come to believe is good and sufficient reason, given, as I have already said, the demands of the climate and the work that there is to do merely to stay alive).
    But this isn't what I have to set down here.
    There was a crowd of us, on a pleasant afternoon outing, talking as best we could. I'd had five days of waiting and trading and resting and collecting, and I'd decided to go on a stroll with others instead of going alone. So we all headed out from the village, breathing the dry, hot air and taking pleasure in what little breezes stirred, like cool caresses. I was reveling in

the lovely wall of forest surrounding us on three sides, and thinking, even then, of being so far out of the pale of the society I knew in England. Over the past weeks, I have often stopped to appreciate my surroundings in just this fashion, wanting merely to savor it; I am here, I have come all this way and I am here.

Above us shone a lucent, tranquil sky, without a single blemish in it. We had entered the tall blade grass, dry and prickly, sharp as knives, and were on a wide path through it, walking abreast, and there was a lot of laughing and chattering back and forth (one never quite hears about the humor of these people—I have divined something of the sharp and superbly subtle shades of it, even understanding as little as I do; the world is a threatening, haunted place, and still the human laughter rises, a song to the astral foment of the sky).

This was a perfect day, bright and breezy, and we were strolling, like a group of parishioners looking for a good place to have a picnic, when something came streaking from the forest wall, bursting from that great, shadowy, verdurous gloom like a bolt of lightning—it did not, at first, seem that it could be made of anything but a bolt of insubstantial electricity. But it was a leopard. It plunged across my path within three feet of me and leapt upon one of our party, a tall young man named Talouga. He had just repeated an English word, "dress," and was proud of himself. I had recited for him one of his words; it was a game we played. The leopard hit him with such force and suddenness that he was on the ground and in a cloud of dust before we quite knew what had happened. There was a horrible personal look to it, man and leopard locked in that grisly embrace. One of the other men had a machete, and we all tried, without success, to get the leopard interested in us. We shouted and flailed at it and swung the machete, but the leopard held tight to Talouga's throat, and pulled him away from us, looking at us as if to question why we were so interested in this meal he had captured. Talouga's feet dragged the dust and we chased after—it was only a matter of five or ten yards—flailing away and screaming, and the entire time the animal's attitude seemed to be that of puzzlement about why we were tormenting him. The man with the machete was someone who had told me his name was Joe and that he had been converted to Christianity. Joe kept calling for Christ and then for Allah to help him, screaming in a tone deeper than terror—there was something horribly incantatory about it—and swinging wildly with the machete. He hit the leopard several times, blood-spattering blows on its neck and shoulders and in the middle of its back; but to no avail. Poor Talouga kept making a drowning, gurgling sound, and then fell ominously silent. We managed at length to drive the leopard away from him, and Joe killed it with one last blow of the machete. The cat's mouth had opened a killing gash in Talouga's neck, severing his jugular vein and probably breaking some of the bones there, too. His lower body, while he was still struggling with his hands and arms, had gone quite limp before the thing was over.

For several aghast moments we stood around the body, the women crying, the other men beating the grass and waving sticks. They were fearful of another attack, I'm sure, as I was. We looked at the forest, as if it had coughed this up at us—or I suppose it was me that looked at it in this fashion.

For the rest of that day, the witch doctor, a lugubrious, lanky, ugly man with sharpened teeth and a long, pointed chin that made his face, from certain angles, look like a blade, went among the members of the tribe banging a drum with the flat of his hand, and shouting names. I could do nothing but watch, and wasn't at all certain that I myself would not be the prime target and sign of a witch. But my animus is too strong for this one—the fact is, he's frightened of me. So frightened that he glanced my way every time he started to name a person as having witched the leopard into killing poor Talouga, and my frowns kept him from naming anyone. It so happened that earlier that same morning an old woman who had borne twins long ago and had been shunned by the others had died of fever, and the witch doctor took this opportunity, observing my concerned and disapproving countenance, to ascribe the death of Talouga to her. He did so not out of any duplicity, mind you, but out of honest fear of my magic.

I have come so far from my father's library.

As they travel across the forbidding tracks of swamp and forest, they encounter more Fang who have never set eyes on a European. Many of them show a polite fascination with her hair. They approach and try to touch her, gingerly, and with wonder. Yet it is also quite clear that they find her ugly, the whiteness of her skin seems horrendous to them. She sees a kind of pity in the eyes of the women, and there is the feeling that they're all regarding her the way people look at a person in terrible misfortune, attempting to stare without seeming to.

In one village, she's given the chieftain's hut, and being more weary than she can believe, she sets about getting herself ready for bed, standing in the light of a tallow candle whose guttering mingles with a rank smell, which she assumes is caused by the closeness of that cramped little space. She has gotten her blouse untied and is about to remove it when she finds that the villagers are peeking at her from every chink in the side walls of the hut. So she buttons the blouse again, and curls up in her boots and dress, and sleeps as best she can. The dark settles around her, the sounds of the village grow still and there is just the raucous forest night. No physical comfort obtains in places like this and sleep comes like a coma, usually, from the bottom of exhaustion. But she can't sleep. She's assailed by the increasing odor, a dreadful stench, like a thick layer of bad air, cumbrous, descending over her in a smothering blanket. At last, she sits up and begins to explore, wondering if something has gotten in under the walls and floor and died there. But the odor is coming from above her head, and is unmistakably something rotting. Coming to her booted feet, she reaches up to retrieve several small bags hanging from the ceiling, and is nearly overcome by the odor's denseness. Whatever is causing the smell is in these bags. She takes them down very carefully, opens them one by one, and pours out their contents on the table. Lumps of some foul-smelling substance, too dark to distinguish as anything but feculence. Upon closer inspection, she recognizes, with a muted gasp, that amid these fragments is a human hand, quite freshly cut off, and she realizes that these other bits are also of human origin: four eyeballs, black as pitch but eyeballs nonetheless, three big toes, two ears, and several other parts she can't take the time to identify. The hand horrifies her more than the rest—not only because it is fresh, but because it's a part of the body that acts rather than being acted upon. The ear, the eye, are so much a part of the structures they belong to that one can miss what they are, seeing them this way; but there is no mistaking a hand. The shape of it, the uses of it, arise powerfully in your mind when you see it separated from the body.

She supposes this cache to have something to do with the notorious cannibalistic habits of the Fang, and quickly puts everything back, gagging as she does so. With a violent hurling of herself she flees the hut, out into the center of the village. Everyone is asleep. All around her are the sounds of the bush at night. She stands there stifling her own urge to gag, sputtering and coughing into her fist. At last, the fit subsides and she can breathe again. There can be no question of returning to the hut. In keeping with her habit of exploring alone, she makes her way down a smooth path to a small stream that several of the women had earlier shown her. How wonderful it will be to bathe the stench from her clothes and body. She's only a hundred or so meters from the village. A way they travel every day. It is probably safe. She's almost too tired to care, one way or the other. But she moves with stealth, and is wary, stopping several times to listen.

In the darkness, the moonless black, she gets out of her clothes as quickly and silently as possible, folding them as she goes and setting them on the bank. Then she turns, and by slow stages, worrying about what she can't see all the time, enters the cold water. The chill of it wakes her completely. But as she goes under and comes up, paddling in a wide motion with her arms, gliding on her belly and feeling the weight of her drenched hair on her back, she experiences the sense of being pleasurably renewed. She pushes along and then turns and floats, watching the faintest pearly tracings of clouds in the starless dark. She remains in the water for a cleansing hour, and then has to spend the better part of another hour trying to dry herself with her own cummerbund. But she has taken her hair down and wet it good and wrung it out, and she's more refreshed than she has felt in days.

The thought comes to her: *I do not want to go back to England. Even with what I have seen and heard. I do not want to go back. Not ever.*

It is almost as if someone else has spoken. She starts up the path to the village, and in her mind she sheds the damp clothes and her own skin; she becomes a woman of this place, someone returning from a dream of another world. *I wish never . . .*

5

THE FOLLOWING MORNING, as they are getting ready to set off, the chieftain whose hut she had slept in wants badly for her to have something special. She realizes that he wishes to trade some more.

When she and the others first arrived, in order to make it quite clear that she was there for trade (and not as an invader, or as a part of their purported diet) she gave him, in exchange for some balls of rubber, a favorite red scarf—a gift from Lucy Toulmin-Smith, that she had taken with her to Paris. He prized this, and wore it all through the evening, and he wore it in the pale dawn when he walked up from one of the other

huts and questioned her, with a bemused, tolerant expression of com-
passion, about why she was outside his hut, sleeping on her blankets,
rather than inside.

—Out of them night, he said.

—Please, your name, she said.

He uttered something in Fang, that for the second time, she missed.
She decided not to press it. They stood together and she indicated the
beauty of the sky and the pleasantness of the surroundings as her reason
for sleeping outside the hut.

Now, he seems to want the whole village turned upside down to find
the one thing he feels she should have.

But it has been misplaced, apparently. She and her group stand
waiting. They have their packs on, and are sweating in the hot, dry, risen
sun.

Obanjo, who is traveling under his African name on this particular
leg of the journey, says:

—This is indubitably something he has been in possession of for
some lengthy long time, madam.

—I don't know what I have left to give him for it, Mary says. Is it a
religious object, do you think?

—I have, on the other hand, p'raps, no way of confirming such.

They wait. Mary goes over in her mind what she has so far been able
to discover about fetish, and perhaps this will be something to add to it,
some juju that the chief can explain to her, and that she can therefore
add to her collection.

The precious item is at last brought to her in several layers of sack-
cloth, folded many times. She believes she's about to be shown something of immeasurable value in her quest for knowledge about the spiri-
tuality of these people. The chief stands there gazing at her with all the
anticipatory emotion of a child on a birthday while she unfolds the last
part of the cloth—and uncovers an ordinary straight razor, the kind that
any English gentleman would use. The look on her face betrays her disappointment. He's seen this. He appears momentarily crestfallen, even
embarrassed. It is a profoundly unpleasant thing to witness embarrassment in someone so fiercely proud and dignified. She reaches into her
portmanteau and hands over to him a belt that she has little use for, and
that he can have little use for, and she behaves as though this is of great

value. He's instantly delighted, and the two of them go into his hut, with its horrible ornaments hanging from the ceiling (what is it about daylight and the air of daylight that keeps the odor somewhat abated in these places?), for tea. Tea. In the day and a half that she has been with them, she has taught them to drink tea, and they all love it. So they have tea together, Mary and her friend the chief of this Fang village. She's uncertain that the value he placed on the old straight razor is not akin to the value she places on her belt. They are, after all, traders together in the same enterprise of give and take. But neither of them speaks of it again. They have a pleasant tea together, and part as friends.

She trudges with the others up the slow incline of a wide expanse, climbing to a height and then making the slow descent, and then climbing again, all of this in the hot dimness, the verdant dark; above them, the sun sluices through thousands of tiny interstices of leaf and branch, and the trail closes off. They have to use the machetes. Mary keeps up with them, wearing her dark dress, keeping her increasing exhaustion and discomfort to herself. Near the base of a gigantic rock that looks as though it could have been dropped from the sky, they encounter a cobra, perhaps twelve feet long, the fanning black hood opening with an alarming and impressive fullness as its body coils and rises. They all shy back from it, keeping a distance. It's as if the cobra wishes to block their path, stop their already slow progress across the trackless marshy breadth of the field before them. Mary asks for a machete and is refused. Pagan takes aim with a pistol. But the snake lowers its head, slithers into an opening at the base of the rock, and is gone. They all wait for a time, listening, and then very carefully they skirt the area, entering the wild grass and chopping their way with the machetes. Mary, too, wields one before it is all over. Her palms blister, and the joints of her fingers seize up, so that for periods of time she can't close her hands to make fists, can't open them, or grip anything. Adjusting her collar in the heat amounts to flapping her limp hands against it, the hands trembling so badly, the ends of the fingers numb to the touch. She endures it, tries to think beyond it, pushing on, aware of the others watching her.

They come to the brow of the last hill, overlooking the many-shaded viridity of the final stretch of uncultivated land before the Remboue River. Beyond the river basin are more hills, rising in the blue-hazy distance of the late morning, wreathed in wisps of thin fog, and littered with outcroppings of white stone that look like parts of the same creamy substance, some aspect of the center of the mountain itself pushing through the crust of earth. All of this under the bluest sky—a sky so richly blue, unlike any English sky, in any weather of the year.

I do not want to go back. I do not wish ever to go back.

6

SHE CAN'T SAY EXACTLY when it came to her to leave all her research, her work on fish and fetish and specimens of flora and fauna, to take a small group of men—"my men," she has come to call them, whoever they happen to be, and of whatever kind—and climb to the peak of Mount Cameroon, Mungo Mah Lobeh, as the Africans call it: *Throne of Thunder.*

When, back from Congo Français and the Fang, she sees it again from the deck of *The Niger,* a German trading vessel which has brought her north to the Cameroon River, some obscure region of her soul is prepared to believe that the will to climb it stems from the first time she ever saw it, sailing south on the 1893 trip, half-frightened and in breath-stealing wonder at its height and strength, a massive, craggy fastness of innumerable shadow shapes and colors, the peak disappearing into a screen of plum-colored twilight clouds, and its rocky west face spotted with deep glooms of green and brown.

From the deck of *The Niger,* she resolves to make the attempt, and immediately sets about trying to convince Obanjo and the others to accompany her. Obanjo tells her he's not interested in climbing any mountains, nor in any new expeditions, at least for a time. He wants to sit on a veranda somewhere, smoke an English pipe, drink French brandy, and watch the sun go down over the sea. No one else on *The Niger* is even slightly interested.

This is the luxury ship of the southwest coast, and she and her party are among Bible readers and tribal members, African traders from the Fjort and the Ajoumbas; and she's discovering that Africans are generally unwilling to face the cold air of the higher altitudes. Some of the Africans stare at her as if the last stage of her madness has set in—these are the ones who consider her as fairly lunatic in the first place.

The Cameroon Mountain has two peaks. The smaller of them, only a little under six thousand feet, is a sheer cliff. The Throne of Thunder is more than twice that high, and no woman, African or European, has ever climbed it, as far as anyone knows. Very few men have climbed it. Several have ascended to the peak from the west. No one has scaled it from the east. If she reaches the top, she'll see the African coast from the point of view of the sky itself. She'll stand on one of the highest peaks of the continent. She feels the rush of her own will, and imagines the feeling, the soaring pride and pleasure, to look upon the country she has been traveling, the country she has been exploring and living in, from the height of the sailing clouds.

The Niger makes a brief stop at Corsica, and she prepares to go into port to trade for some supplies for the climb. There's little that she has left to trade, but she loads her reticule with English soap and a few samples of fetish she's collected, along with the razor given her by the Fang chieftain. The sun is bright and hot and the humidity is terrible; it will be rainy season soon enough. The smell of the oil rivers is heavy on the air, and mosquitoes form dark clouds of themselves in the swells of the harbor water. In port, there has been an attack of driver ants, and people are roiling about in the streets. At one hut, a man and a woman are screaming as if in great grief, and their gestures convince her that they have left something of immeasurable value inside the hut. She looks in and sees an infant covered in driver ants. No feature of the child is visible through the millions of dreadfully eating insects. She throws herself into the furiously busy mass of them and hauls the baby, still completely enveloped in ants, out into the open air, getting bitten several times in the process. The baby is quite heavy and dead feeling, cold. Mary watches in horror as the child's mother seizes it and pushes it immediately into a trough of water, holding it under. Both she and her husband give Mary grateful, though vaguely suspicious, looks. Mary stands there and soon she's demanding that they bring the baby up. They speak Kru, and they understand her, and even so they stare at her with bewilderment.

—No, ma, says the man at last. Dis no baby, ma.

And he holds it up out of the water. The ants have drowned, and fallen off. It is no baby, but a fair-sized ham. The man gives her a nod, and then begins to laugh, as does the woman. Soon others join in, and she recognizes the timbre of one laugh, turning in the crowd, in the talk that she knows perfectly well is about this farce she has played out over the ham. She turns, and sees James Henley Batty, standing with two Fulanis, looking ten pounds heavier than when she saw him last, and a lot hairier—but it is James. She walks up to him and abruptly feels the pain of realizing that he hasn't recognized her. There is no recognition at all in his face.

—James Batty, she says.

He speaks through his laughter.

—Miss Kingsley.

—You didn't seem to recognize me.

—I could never forget you, Miss Kingsley.

His breath reeks of rum and tobacco, and he hasn't shaved for days. She steps back a little, and he turns in a small circle before her, as if to allow her to examine him fully. When he faces her again, he says:

—You have been well, I trust? I hear all sorts of things about you.

—I've written you, Mary says. Care of Goldie's company. I've met Goldie. I saw 'im the night *you* saw 'im, in London.

—Just so. I sent my greetings, as I recall. I was about to head down to Sierra Leone.

—Goldie delivered the message. I would like to 'ave seen you myself.

He bows at the waist.

—Here I am.

He escorts her to the market pavilion, which is all but deserted as a result of the driver ants. He tells her that there's trouble brewing in South Africa, and that he's going back to England for good.

—Ever get the feeling you can see the future? he says.

—Only when my expectations are dire, she tells him, and realizes that this is the truth. She almost comments on the strangeness of it.

—Well, I know what's coming to this place, he says. This whole, poor, beautiful, bloody continent. It's like an enormous pie, and all the big boys want a piece of it, and I can't stay here and watch 'em carve it up in these people's blood. I never wanted to share a bath with these blokes, mind you, but I like them. I like trading with them. I like the back and forth and the sly little tricks and the games and the humor. And their biggest trouble is they trust the bastards who're going to take it all away. Bloody Bible-reading bastards.

—They'll fight, Mary says. The ones I have met will fight.

—They're too divided up into factions themselves. Too many separate tribes. And the big boys know it, too. These chaps don't have an empire for nothing.

—Still, they will resist.

He nods, looking off, musing, and wavering slightly with what he's had to drink.

—Then they're bigger fools for that. It'll be their blood. The ones on the coastline, they've learned to adapt, and speak the language. It's already their dignity. Now it'll be their blood.

—You are in a darker mood than usual, Mary says.

—But the trouble in South Africa isn't the blacks. It's the whites. Dutch and French Huguenots. Boers.

—Yes, I know of them.

He smiles, and shakes his head slightly.

—Afrikaners, she says.

—Yes, he says. Well, war is brewing. Transvaal and the Orange Free State against the crown. Gold has been discovered in the Transvaal, Miss Kingsley. The whole crowd of buggers will be killing each other over it soon enough.

—I can't be as discouraged as all that, says Mary.

—Well, one of us is right. I hope it's you.

They are quiet for an interval. He waits while she tries to trade two bars of soap for a water canteen. The woman she's trading with is coal black, and tall, with large flaring nostrils and sensuous, heavy lips. Mary finally offers the razor, and the woman takes it, and gives her the canteen.

—You no want ham? she says, smiling with those enormously fleshy lips.

—No, Mary says with exaggerated dignity.

Batty laughs. Both he and the tall woman have a good laugh together over the whole affair, and they speak of it in a language Mary can't quite translate fast enough. She knows they are talking about the look on her face, hurling herself out of the hut with the "baby" in her arms.

—So, Batty says, gaining control of himself. Where are you off to, now?

—I'm going to climb Mount Cameroon.

He stares at her for the amount of time it takes to understand that she hasn't spoken facetiously.

—The east face of it, she says.

Solemnly he raises one hand over her head, then makes a sign of the cross, and intones the Latin: *In nomine patrias et filie et spiritu sancti, amen.*

She smiles at him and nods.

—Even for you, he says.

—I don't understand.

—It's too big a thing, Miss Kingsley. Even for you.

—I suppose I'll find that out.

—Pride goeth before a fall.

He accompanies her back to the harbor. Their conversation, in this last hour, is very stilted and formal; they speak of the various societies in England, and mutual friends: poor Dolokov, with his packet of love letters and his gravid liver; Goldie and his wife; the MacDonalds, whom he knows only slightly. She tells him how good she has felt in the company of Mrs. Goldie, and he relates, with a certain stiffness, his plan to go to work for the Geographical Society in some capacity or other. His plans, he says, are vague at present, certainly nothing as definite as climbing a bloody mountain on the most inhospitable coast in the world.

He stands on the sweating boards of the dock, waving sadly at her as the ship pulls away.

—Who dat be, ma? Gray Shirt asks her.

She looks back at her friend, who is still waving.

—Dat be my first friend outside, she says.

—Good man all one time, ma.

—Yes, Mary tells him, feeling abruptly, and to her enormous surprise, that she might begin to cry. Good man all one time.

She stays there on the deck of *The Niger* with Gray Shirt, and in a while the folds of cloud to the east unveil the massive shape of Mount Cameroon.

—I'm going up there, she says to Gray Shirt. No matter what any of you say. I will see this place where we're presently standing, this spot on the ocean, from up there.

He nods at her as if to say that he believes she means it, but there is a quality of tolerance in it, too.

—Will you come with me? she asks. Please.

She has the shaken sense that it is the first time she has ever used that word with another human being. Surely this isn't so. She stands there seeking to recall some other occasion.

Gray Shirt shakes his head.

—No chance, ma.

7

She's forced to gather an entirely new group of men in Victoria, and the effort depletes her energy and resources so much that on the day of her scheduled departure she wakes in the predawn with a terrible migraine. But something else is bothering her, some element of the last few days on *The Niger*, and her brief time with Batty. Can she have been so lonely, all these weeks and months? There was such a sharp pang when Gray Shirt said no—an ache, deep down. And later, when he took his gear and lifted one dark hand to wave good-bye to her, she felt the same hard knot of pain below her chest bone. It seems to her that she is always saying good-bye.

Her whole life is a farewell of a kind.

The mission house in Victoria, where she has been given a room, is run by the Wesleyans, and its pastor is a man named Dennis Kemp. He has a burnished look, ruddy skin and high brow, with soft green eyes and auburn hair swept back on either side of his head. She first encounters him that morning when, blue and downhearted and suffering her migraine, she comes out on the veranda to get her new chief guide to wake the others, for the assault on the mountain. The new chief guide is a Christianized Fulani who calls himself Thomas, after Aquinas, whom he's reading slowly in German. He speaks English as well, and several of the African dialects. With her, and with the men under his charge, he's rather imperious and even surly at times.

She tells him to get the others ready, and he goes off without a word, so that she wonders if he heard her.

—Thomas? she says.

—I go do it, ma.

Kemp walks up to her from the other side of the entrance, having come around the building, following the progress of several young boys carrying wood. He sees her, and bows.

—Miss Kingsley.

She bows in response, wondering if he can see the crease she feels in her own forehead.

He introduces himself, then turns to follow the progress of the boys again. They're crossing the road, and heading up a side street, each with his own handful of wood. The light is a flat, dim gray; it is still more night than morning, and everything is streaming with mist.

—You're becoming rather a legend, you know, Miss Kingsley. One hears tales about you from every quarter. Especially one hears of your low opinion of missionaries.

—I 'aven't any reply to that, she says.

—I mean no offense.

—Nor I. And I take none.

He smiles, and she has the thought that this must be his best gesture, the winning gesture he possesses, like a gift, to disarm anybody: a beautiful, transforming expression; it alters everything about him. His face becomes very much like a guiltless boy's face.

—I'm sorry I wasn't here to greet you on your arrival last night.

—I spent most of yesterday trying to put a party of men together for an expedition. She indicates the shape of the Cameroon peaks in the distance.

—Yes, that got around, too.

—Well, you're well informed. She starts down the steps, and has to pause, holding on to the wooden rail.

—Are you all right?

She puts one hand to her head.

—Here, he says. And before she can do anything about it, he has grasped her by her arms, and is guiding her back up onto the veranda. There are four wooden chairs ranged across the front, and with his help—her legs won't support her—she sits down in the first one, a rocker, whose initial swaying with her feels like a part of her swooning. His strength is surprising. She closes her eyes, realizing that it's been a long, long time since she has felt the touch of another person. She can't recall how long. She thinks the word *please*, and she puts her hands to her eyes, making an attempt to remember life before she left it for these journeys. It seems abruptly very important to remember. But then she's drifting away inside, feels the memory of a child's embrace in Calabar;

the handshake of the captain of *The Niger*. The nerves of her skin contract, it is so real. But then everything is melting in the sense of failing consciousness and fever. Quite suddenly she's awake, he's holding her upright in the chair, and she can't find the memory of the last time she was held in this way, supported by anyone, or so close in proximity to a grown man. It is all very alarming.

He sits down in the chair next to hers, and for a few minutes says nothing. Her men are stirring in the yard, making ready, Thomas standing with his hands on his hips, watching. People are coming out into the streets. The day is starting, light coming to the edges of things, the easternmost sky turning the color of a glowing coal. Kemp remains at her side, perfectly quiet, as if they've both simply come out here to observe the preparations, and the sunrise.

—Thank you, she says. You're very kind. I'm feeling somewhat better now.

—You're ashen, if you'll forgive my saying so.

She doesn't respond to this.

—I think you should put this off for a day or two, he says.

From somewhere, as always, she draws the strength to rise. Stabbing pains seem to come from the very center of her brain. She blinks, and finds herself sitting down again. She hears him instructing Thomas to tell the men to put things back, to wait, and she hears Thomas doing that, in the tone of a man who knew all along it would happen. But she lacks the energy to protest.

After a time, Kemp helps her inside, and up the stairs to the entrance of her room. He says he'll have some water brought to her, and asks if there is anything else she might need. There is a doctor in the mission house.

—I could have him here in a minute. I'm sure he's not awake yet.

They are standing in the upstairs hall, at the open door of her room. The hall is long and dim and the wood is polished and she's aware of paintings ranked along the one wall, of men in vested suits, with large mustaches and the dignified air of rectitude.

—No, she says. I'll be fine.

—Can I bring you anything else?

—You've been most kind.

In the room she lies down, without undressing, and falls into a dismal, aching sleep. She wakes in a sweat, moisture gathering uncomfortably in the hollow of her neck. At her bedside is a washbasin with cool water standing in it. She sits up, and with a tremor in her hands soaks a rag, which she wrings out, and then uses to wipe her forehead and face, her neck and upper chest. The light at the window is blinding. The sun seems too close, burning just beyond the parched branches of the palms.

She dresses and makes her way downstairs, out to the shade of the porch, where she finds Kemp, sitting in the same chair he occupied the night before. The rocker that he helped her to last evening is free, but is the first chair from the door, and is rocking slightly. She has the feeling that he's just this second switched to the other. He's fanning himself and drinking tea out of a calabash, and he glances at her with what appears to be studied casualness.

—Miss Kingsley, he says. You're better, I trust?

She takes the rocker, and the seat is warm. He's watching for her reaction. She glides back a little and swings forward, rocking.

—I thought you should have the rocker.

—I make no claim to it, she says, and gives him a slight nod. She feels the blood running to her face, and looks away. This absurd shyness has come over her; it has all but robbed her of speech.

—I have been sitting here thinking about you, he says.

—I do feel much better, she tells him.

—I was imagining what life will be for you when you get back to England.

She lets this go by.

He goes on to talk about England, and how much he misses it. He likes Africa, but is often homesick; he wonders if she ever feels the same.

—I only felt it when I was in England, she says.

—You mean to say, don't you, that you've only ever felt it for Africa.

—Yes.

—We are very different, then, aren't we?

This doesn't seem to require an answer.

—Still, I believe we are both here with the intent of helping these people raise themselves.

—I'm not entirely sure they need raising. In some very important instances, I think they most require us to leave them alone.

—They'll take you to task for that kind of thinking in England.

—No one will notice me in England.

They spend the rest of the afternoon talking in a slow, desultory way, with long, somehow restful-seeming pauses, about the country and its customs and people. Her earlier nervousness is gone. She begins to feel confident of him, sensing that he isn't holding back, and isn't making any judgments about her, either. He knows a little about the secret societies, and the part the societies play in perpetuating aspects of belief in witchcraft, spells, and magic. He believes these are problems that must be worked through in order to bring Christianity to the area; and of course in his eyes there can be no doubt about the importance of that. She disagrees with him on almost everything, and yet she finds that he's reachable when she explains things clearly enough. At least he's willing to make the effort of understanding.

—If there is going to be conversion, she tells him, I believe the Muslim religion is more suited to their way of life. I believe the transition would be less difficult.

—Is difficulty to be the only measure?

—I mean less bloody.

—Still, the question remains. Is that to be the only measure?

—As it is not in the rest of European society, I suppose it can't be the only measure 'ere, either.

—Quite so. I take your point.

They dine together with several other members of the mission—a young doctor whose sallow features give him the look of long ill-health, a Europeanized Fjort with a missing front tooth and a bad scar across the center of his mouth where he was struck by a sword in a fight with a German sailor, ten years ago, and two older men, ordained ministers who have been in Africa since the late eighties, and seem rather hardened to it. The talk has been about the various failures and the few successes in the administration of the country, particularly the cruelty and repression in the Belgian Congo. One of the ministers, a tall, freckled, rather heroically handsome gentleman in his mid-forties, whose cleric's collar is loose on his thin neck, uses the word *nigger* to describe the Africans, and Kemp gently corrects him. Later, the man utters a remark about someone belonging to the mission congregation, who hasn't attended services on recent Sundays, and was seen only this morning with a charm tied to his wrist, a leather pouch with some grisly thing in it.

—I must say, they do slide back if you let them, he says, given half the chance. These nigger practices are so deeply ingrained.

—What is the man's name? Mary says.

—I beg your pardon?

—I asked for the man's name, the man you're telling us about. She looks across the table at him and waits.

—I believe his Christian name is John.

—And belonging to which tribe?

—What did you say?

—Do you know which tribe?

—I beg your pardon? Tribe?

—I wonder what tribe the man you speak of belongs to. Mendes? Mpongwes? Fjort? Fulani? Ajoumbas? Fang?

He looks down the table at Kemp, and then back at Mary.

—Well, I wouldn't know. It would be presumptuous of me to guess. I mean, they're all pretty much the same, aren't they?

—Since you are reluctant to presume, sir, would you do likewise over a German or a Dutchman, or a man from Yorkshire as opposed, say, to a man from Dublin? *They're* all pretty much the same, too.

The other looked at Kemp again.

—See here, Kemp. What is the meaning of this?

—Miss Kingsley is an advocate, says Kemp.

—I don't wish to offend you, Mary says to him. I only point out that truly aiding these people is not possible unless one comes to know them on their own ground, on *their* terms. At the very minimum that means seeing them first *as* people.

—Oh, so I'm to be expected to go running about in the bush with them, is that it? Well, no thank you. No thank you indeed. I'm not of that school. And, if you'll forgive me for putting it bluntly, neither has this mission been of that particular school. At least not until your arrival, young woman. And I will also add, if you'll forgive me, that I do not like being spoken to in this lecturing way by someone from your, well, your class.

—A commoner, then. I didn't know I was speaking beyond my station.

—I mean age, as well, madam.

—Miss Kingsley's experience gives her the authority to teach us, Kemp says. Don't you agree, Martin?

—I do not agree, says Martin. No, I do not. And there it is.

—I meant no offense, Mary says.

He stands and folds his napkin, and with great dignity pulls down the front of his vest.

—Perhaps if you'll excuse me.

He crosses the room, stands for a moment at the large opening into the foyer that leads out to the veranda. He reaches into his coat pocket and retrieves a pipe and puts it into his mouth with a kind of emphasis, and then is gone.

Everyone else is quiet for a moment.

—You know, Kemp addresses Mary, he's a good man, Martin. He truly is. Believe it or not, he'll think long and hard on what you've said. And he'll pray on it, too. But he won't, in the end, change his mind.

8

THE FOLLOWING MORNING, with her newly assembled crew, she begins the expedition to climb the east face of Mount Cameroon. The day is an unmitigated disaster. A cold rain besets them all the way on the road inland from Victoria to the first base camp, a place called Buana, which seems at the tag end of things, since the road ends here. It is a mission camp, run by two African gentlemen. She spends a sleepless night there, among a party of Africans and others who are taking part in a sort of traveling seminar on the Bible. She retreats to her room with another headache. There are tiny square paintings in the room, inspirational scenes, and on the table by her bed is a daguerreotype of a man and a woman, staring severely at her in the wavering light of the lantern.

She turns the picture around.

In the next dawn, the rain comes with a gray, misty force. They are late starting, but they make the next camp, a government station. The official there, a man named Liebert, asks her to stay in his house, an unfinished frame, with shutterless windows and a lot of propped boards against the walls. No real shelter in the sense that she can have no sort of privacy, here.

The weather continues unabated, chilly and misty and miserable, and the day passes slowly, with Mary suffering still another migraine. Herr Liebert is kindly, and very curious, and he wants to talk. They speak slowly in German, and then he tries laboriously to get a few phrases of English out. She can see that it has meant much to him to have the conversation with her in his own language. But she doesn't want to talk now, and she tells him, at last, quite gently but directly, that she must retire.

—I have bored you, he says.

It strikes her that she's tired of the company of men, and then she realizes that it is simply that she is tired. Tired and sick, and the rigors of the day have so drained her that she knows she won't sleep. She asks him if he has any liquor.

—Wine, he tells her, looking doubtful.

—I would like some, if you can spare it.

—*Ja,* of course. Yes.

It is a variety of French wine he has had shipped to him from friends. He opens the bottle and pours liberally from it, and apparently considers that this means more talk. His features betray a kind of endearing relief: he hasn't bored her after all. She wonders if in the society from which he comes, back in Europe, he has worried about this as well. The fact is, she hasn't really found him to be so dull. He has been perfectly agreeable and thoughtful. She sips the wine without tasting it, quite, drinks the glass down a little faster than she would if she were in London, and asks for another. He pours it, looking at the glass and then at her and then at the glass again. She drinks that, and he talks. Mostly now, he wishes to delineate the qualities of the wine, and he makes up long phrases in his language to do so. She holds her glass up and nods, and asks for more, speaking in her own cockney, and with a thicker flavor in it, that she is only partly aware of.

—'ere, let's 'ave sum more a' that, shall we, Cap'n?

So he pours more of it. And she clinks her glass against his, and holds the rim of her own against her upper lip. Africa is setting up its racket all around and the rain keeps coming, a steady, cold drenching, and she's warm inside at last, even in her damp and muddy clothes. At length, she rises, and can feel the effects of the wine.

—Good night, Cap'n, she says.

She can feel his eyes on her as she crosses to the entrance of the house and leans for a moment on the door frame—not from the wine, but from the exhaustion she feels. She looks back at him.

—*Gute Nacht,* he says.

In her open-windowed room, alone, she sits on the bed and emits one loud hiccup. This makes her laugh. She lies down, brings her booted feet up onto the bed, listening to the drumming of the rain. In only a moment, she's deeply asleep.

9

*I*N THE MORNING, she discovers that several of her original party, including Thomas, have gone in the night back to Victoria. Only two, another Fulani named Kefalla, and the headman, remain. The headman is a Fjort, named Bum. Herr Liebert is anxious to help, and he commissions three men who work for him at the station to accompany her—a Liberian named Xenia, a Europeanized Mpongwes named Sasu, and a man she calls Tomorrow, whose tribe is uncertain, and whose language is unrecognizable. Herr Liebert also gives her a foldable camp bed, an ingenious gadget invented for the military by a friend of his from Düsseldorf, who assumed that Liebert would be sleeping outside in Africa. It takes some ingeniousness getting it into her portmanteau along with her books and other supplies. The whole process and the hours she spent with Herr Liebert begin to seem comical to her. She has to strain to keep from laughing. He's so earnest, so eager to help, and so obviously worried about her, too. And his gallantry takes the form of a kind of ramrod-stiff politeness, tinged with discouragement.

They are late getting started, and Kefalla troubles himself to remind her that it is Sunday. She knows from his tone that he wishes her to mark this and take the day to rest. She ignores the tone, and replies that she understands what day it is.

The rain continues, and progress is slow. They reach the timberline of the mountain in early evening, and set up camp. Mary goes on a little, into the hour before dark, to gain some sense of the rock face ahead of them. She's gone only a few minutes—but by the time she returns, the men are half drunk on the rum she packed for medicinal purposes, and for all of them to be able to warm themselves against the cold. Only Kefalla has refrained from having any, and he's remonstrating with the others. The weather worsens by the minute; there is nothing anyone can do to keep dry.

—We want to go down, ma, Kefalla says.

She has learned by now that he always uses the imperial *we* when speaking of what he wants. In his bearing he is much like Thomas was, and she has to work to individuate the two men.

—We will go down after we have reached the summit, she tells him.

—We don't see the land, too much rain one time, sabe?

—I sabe, she says. Good night, Kefalla.

He turns from her with a frustrated shake of the head, and begins opening a tin of pork fat, muttering to himself.

10

KEFALLA PROVES RIGHT about the view from the top of the mountain.

She climbs to it alone, in a snowy, freezing mist, and, reaching the pinnacle, turns in a circle and looks at nothing but whiteness, the raw elements themselves, as if she has come upon them in their primal, continual argument with each other. She has left the two remaining members of her party—Kefalla and Xenia—behind at the last base camp. The expedition, from the start, was plagued by delays and disagreements and desertions. Twice she had to send down to Herr Liebert for more supplies. The men grew sullen and quick to temper; there were several near fights. Through it all, she commanded their reluctant obedience, but in the end, after one gloriously sunny day of climbing in which she paused several times and saw tremendous vistas of the coast from the three-quarters height of the mountain, the weather closed in again, forcing things. Kefalla and Xenia went on with her to the last base camp, and from there refused to go farther, forcing her to press on in the driving rain and snow, alone to the top.

The one sunny day gave her the sunburn that she suffers from now, staggering in the bad weather at the peak, alone.

Alone.

This young woman. Alone at the pinnacle of one of the highest mountains on the continent of Africa. She. Mary Henrietta Kingsley, a bookish, once-reclusive English spinster with no formal education, just thirty-two years old, from Highgate, Cambridge and Addison Road, London. Having traveled here by way of the African river tribes, through unmapped country and among people no white man or woman has ever seen, in the bush, and at river's edge. And here she is.

Well.

And she admits to herself that she expected to feel something more than what she does feel: there is exhilaration, yes, but it's mingled with disappointment, too, a simultaneous draining out of emotion; there is an emptiness at the heart of it, a sense of its lack of utility in her life: she can't *use* it for anything, this arduous ascent to a barren mountaintop.

She leaves a small paper card, her calling card. She can only spend a minute or two looking around; it's too cold to stay very long. There are other artifacts on the ground, left by other Europeans, but by no other woman. Her face is so badly sunburned, the wind stings her cheeks—how odd to feel the heat of sun in this cold—her lips cracked and bleeding and dry, her left cheek abraded from a blister that got pulled away in the night when her sleeping bag stuck to it.

She knows the little calling card will dissolve in the wet and sifting cold, and she can't bring herself to care. After one last revolution in the blinding cold and snow, she starts the slow descent.

TWENTY-FOUR

1

PROLOGUE

Scene: The Royal Colonial Office of the British Empire. The walls are only suggested by frames. A map on the left, a globe downstage. A desk at stage right, flanked by flags, under a portrait of Queen Victoria. Across from the desk is a single ladderback chair, in which Mary Kingsley is seated. Behind the desk is the colonial secretary, Lord Chamberlain. He looks exactly as one would expect the colonial secretary to look.

LORD CHAMBERLAIN

I am one of the many who have read your book, Miss Kingsley. I very much admired it. I found it marvelously entertaining and instructive. I'm not unaware of your influence. I even attended a lecture you gave at the Women's Geological Society. That's why I sent for you, of course. I'm hoping you'll listen to reason.

MARY

I've been entertaining the same 'opes about you, sir.

Pause.

Excuse me. H-hopes.

LORD CHAMBERLAIN

Are you quite comfortable?

MARY

Shifts slightly, looking around her.

Quite. This is a pleasant office.

LORD CHAMBERLAIN

Well, I rather like to consider that this is like the center of the web, Miss Kingsley, and I'm the spider who only waits for others to come to him.

MARY

I shall try diligently to keep that in mind, sir.

LORD CHAMBERLAIN

Clearing his throat, all business now.

As you no doubt know, Miss Kingsley, for some time now the crown has not been realizing enough revenues from West Africa. The protectorate is in disarray, the trade wars have made everything worse. There is precedent in all English law for the use of taxes to raise revenue. It was felt that a tax on each hut in the protectorate would raise the necessary revenue to aid in bringing some benefit to the very people you wish to help.

MARY

I do not wish to 'elp—

She pauses, clears her throat.

I do not wish to help the people of West Africa. I wish to see them left alone as much as possible, while continuing to trade with them. The treaty we made with the West African chiefs guarantees them their property.

LORD CHAMBERLAIN

With some frustration.

It's been said so many times—no one is taking away any property. There is nothing in the statute that refers to taking any property. If the Africans can be brought to an understanding of Christianity, why can't they be shown that this is nothing more than a tax. It's merely a tax.

MARY

Patiently.

In the African mind, to ask for money in that fashion is to seize the item you wish to tax. They own their 'uts. Huts. They built them. A tax on a man's h-hut takes it away. By *their* law, and by every tenet of their religions and their institutions and their customs, paying a tax to anyone *means* they no longer can claim ownership. They're fighting you for their very h-homes, sir. And that is the cause of all the violence and you will not turn them. It will only get worse.

LORD CHAMBERLAIN

With an air of wishing to placate her.

You are a formidable opponent. You have power, Miss Kingsley, and I wonder if you've thought how that power could be put to use for your queen.

MARY

I've no power at all. I am a deliverer of entertaining lectures about the exotic continent. I wrote a book that provided me with some unaccustomed wealth and then proceeded to make it all that much more difficult to get where I wish to be—which is Africa. I've no time to myself, and no private life as it is. I certainly 'ave no desire to be a politician. I am merely trying to save the crown and the people of West Africa from further violence. You will 'ave . . . excuse me. You will h-have war over the h-hut tax. Nothing will stop it. You must rescind the tax immediately.

LORD CHAMBERLAIN

With foreboding resignation, the sigh that comes of power about to be exercised to deadly extent.

The Empire has fought wars before.

MARY

That is what I was afraid you would say, sir. If you are willing for war to break out, if you accept war, then we've nothing left to say to each other.

LORD CHAMBERLAIN

Rising from behind the desk.

Well, perhaps we'll talk more on the subject. At any rate, it was a privilege to meet the only woman who ever stood on the peak of Mount Cameroon. Tell me, what was the view like from up there? Must've been magnificent.

MARY

Sadly.

I saw a lovely green land about to be bathed in blood. I saw my . . . place. If I write you about this tax, will you read it?

LORD CHAMBERLAIN

I shall look forward to it with great anticipation. I would prefer you write to me, though, rather than the newspapers and journals, if you know what I mean.

MARY

Also rising now. They shake hands across the desk.

I know exactly what you mean and I shall write you, sir, *and* the newspapers. I intend to be quite outspoken about this folly.

LORD CHAMBERLAIN

As is your privilege. You have done great service for Englishwomen, Miss Kingsley, and I daresay, for women around the world.

MARY

Wearily, dropping his hand.

I never 'ad any ambition to do anything of the kind. I merely went about my business. Can you not see me outside of all that, as a person with knowledge of the place you're trying to administer, and doing such a bad job of it in the bargain?

LORD CHAMBERLAIN

Coldly, politely.

I shall take what you have said under advisement. Good day, madam.

Lights down, spotlight on Mary as she walks to stage center, then comes downstage and crosses slowly to stage left, along the lip, addressing us.

MARY

When they buried me at sea, off the coast of South Africa, only a little more than three years later, the strangest thing happened. My coffin wouldn't sink. It floated away from the ship, which was called *The Thrush*, and some men had to get into a dinghy and chase me down, fix anchors to the brass handles, and try me again. It took them most of the afternoon. Imagine that. I was still sailing the seas, even in death. I was wandering away.

Shakes her head, crossing to stage right again.

My two books have disappeared, mostly. The history books forget. I wasn't for the feminists, or for suffrage. I did what was expected of me before I did anything else. That was the time and place where I lived. But don't let them tell you I wasn't in love. I was in love, once.

She moves to the empty chair, and stands for a beat, looking at the desk, and at the picture of the queen. Then she takes the chair and sits, facing us.

His name was Robert Nathan, and in 1897 he sent me a letter that I took to be an overture. I knew nothing of such things, of course, though I was always being consulted by my friends, who wanted my advice on their own amours. We were friendly. He kept seeming to come my way, and then withdrawing—or perhaps I interpreted some things. I was only thirty-six, and then thirty-seven. Old by the standards of my time, of course, for a single lady. And my public persona was more or less established. The last night I was in England, after a terrible round of lectures and work and supporting family and keeping up with needy friends, and looking after my poor feckless brother Charley—

A note of bitterness comes into her voice.

—on whom all the money had been spent for an education—

She shrugs, then stands and puts the chair back. She walks behind the desk, still talking, and sits in Lord Chamberlain's chair.

—after all of that, and after being thwarted again and again in my desire to return to my beloved adopted country—well, I had volunteered to go down to South Africa, where a dirty little war was starting up. I wanted to be of use. But that last night, the night before I left England for good, I wrote and asked Robert Nathan to come visit me. I waited alone for him, in terror. The heart has nothing to do with politics. I kept thinking of being on the river with Corliss and fighting off the croc, and how much more frightening *this* was, this waiting for a man I thought might love me. And of course, Mr. Nathan never came. It was to him, in a long, rambling letter, that I had bared my true soul. Well, I did that. I was in a shy, terrible kind of hopeless love, the kind that cannot declare itself and yet does, with every gesture. Nothing hurts so bad as those gestures being ignored. As they were. Poor Nathan, living quietly with his mum when he could have had the love of a woman like me. But I flatter myself into thinking he missed *me*. Now, it hardly matters.

She rises from the desk, lets her fingers trail across it as she comes around it, and then on, to the lip of the stage.

I came down to Cape Town, in South Africa to die. The ostensible purpose for the journey, as I have indicated, was to be of some kind of help as a nurse. The Boer War. The whites, you see, were slaughtering each other for their own reasons. Factions, I believe they are still called, were warring. This wasn't because of a primitive thing like witchcraft, or spells; no, it was civilized; it was territory and empire. But the boys were dying in huge numbers and of course they were dying just as dead. I was asked to nurse Boer prisoners with typhoid and enteric fever and measles, too. I helped them die and I tied their jaws together, and when I began to die myself, I knew it. I asked them to leave me alone, wanted, finally, at the end, to be alone. I suppose it was partly embarrassment. But it was my journey to make, and as I'd already made so many alone, already wandered out alone so many times and in so many places, it seemed right and just. So I made the request, and it was granted, at least until I was beyond knowing, as they say. My heart stopped peacefully; its beating grew slow and weak, and then just—stopped. I was asleep. The place I died in is called The Palace. Think of it. I died young. There is, really, only a little to tell.

She stops, and indicates the stage behind her.

Here, see for yourself.

Lights fade.

2

*O*NE SOFT, unseasonably warm, breezy morning in December, only days before Christmas, Lily finished the play. She was sitting out on the veranda, writing through one of the baby's naps, and she worked out a scene showing a fever hallucination of Mary Kingsley's, involving the peak of Mount Cameroon. Mary going on alone to the peak, a white windy mist of snow and cold, leaving her calling card, like a visitor to an English parlor on Mortimer Street. Mary, denied the panoramic view of her beloved country, by that country's weather in that great height, more than thirteen thousand feet above the sea. That seemed the place to stop the action, and move, with a shifting of props and actors, from the top of the mountain to a procession bearing her up the catwalk of a ship, as the curtain closes. Lily had already suggested the years of celebrity in London, after *Travels in West Africa* became a best-seller; it was in the action of the play as it alternated back and forth through scenes of Mary Kingsley's brief, but crowded, life. The playwright had constructed everything around her heroine's last moments in The Palace Hospital in Simon's Town, South Africa, when Mary lay dying and knew it, and longed hopelessly for her beloved West Coast. The struggle of writing the play, of working out its problems, had been to find some means of suggesting the truest quality of the woman as she had been in her time and with her own attitudes, and to portray her courage. Lily didn't want to make the historical figure into a modern mouthpiece; nor did she wish to be too literal about the life.

When, later that day, she tried to write another letter to her dead friend, she found that she couldn't. She considered that perhaps now that the play was finished, there wasn't anything left to tell her.

I have been telling you, in some strange way, your own story. . .

Dominic came home in a good mood, and she gave it to him to read.

He took it to his room, while she prepared something for dinner. Violet was gone to one of the nursing homes in another parish, and Manny would be back late from the restaurant. He was on a search for other employment, having decided that he hated the restaurant business. There were two openings nearby: one for a janitor in a nearby school, the other for a motel clerk. He had interviews for both positions.

Lily cooked soup from a can, and then opened some applesauce, and made hot dogs. She put Mary in the high chair, cut a hot dog into small bites, and fed them to the child, who warbled and ran her tongue in and out of her mouth, making noise with it, clapping her hands and laughing at nothing.

"Good hot dogs," Lily said to her. "Right?"

"No."

She called to Dominic that the food was ready. Briefly, she felt married again—it was an odd moment. She hadn't heard from Nick in weeks. She thought of calling him with the news that she had finished, then was tempted to get in touch with Sheri and Millicent; but that smacked of manipulation, and finally she reflected that her Oxford life was over. Even so, Nick came into her mind several times a day.

Now, looking out the window at the alley behind the house, she saw some men and women standing in a garden, having drinks, and something seemed to separate and drift loose in her heart.

Dominic came down, and sat at the table. "Don't ask me," he said. "I'm not through reading."

So they said little during the meal. She kept watching his face. He ate quickly, and went back upstairs. She washed Mary's face and hands and then took her out of the high chair, and let her wander in the downstairs rooms. Mary's fascination with the statue of the Virgin in the dining room was undiminished, and now she could pull herself up to stand, using the thick stone base for support. She would look up at the carved features and make sounds that seemed to demand a response; and when no response came, she grew all the more gleefully adamant.

Manny arrived, with the news that he had gotten offers for both jobs. He had taken the motel job, though it meant he would be gone some nights. It was lower pay than the janitor position, but more than the restaurant, and he was amenable to the work—he would have some time to read. He sat in the living room with Mary on his lap, talking about the worry over being gone at night, getting used to that kind of schedule, and then his eyes welled up.

"You know," he said, "Aunt Violet has money for me when she—when she goes. I weel not starve. We won't starve. I'm so frightened of losing her. The trouble ees I am terrified of losing her and she ees going to be ninety-two." He wiped his eyes with the backs of his hands, and looked at Lily. "Forgive me."

"No." She reached across and touched his wrist. "I understand."

"Eet's very hard."

"I know."

For a time, they were quiet. He blew his nose and sniffled, and when Mary crawled to the place on the floor at his feet and used his legs to stand, he smiled at her, and touched her cheek. "No," Mary said, as if that were the final utterance.

Manny made faces for her, and when she grew tired of this and got down to crawl to the other side of the room, he asked how Lily's day had gone.

"I think I finished my play," she told him.

For a moment they watched Mary crawl toward the dining room, and the statue of the Virgin. "Shouldn't we be celebrating?" he said, getting up to retrieve Mary, who protested at having been stopped.

"Dom's reading it right now."

They were quiet, as if waiting for word from Dominic. The house made its groaning-wood sounds as the temperature dropped outside. They heard a car, and Manny went to the door, then out and down the stairs to help Aunt Violet in. She entered the room with a huffing, and looked at Lily. "Cab fare," she said.

Lily stood.

"I've got it," Manny said. He went down to the street to pay the cabby.

Aunt Violet sat in one of the wing chairs by the window and watched him. Then she turned to Lily. "I forgot it, *cher*. Had no money for the return trip."

"Manny got the motel clerk's job," Lily said.

The other woman nodded.

"I think I finished my play."

Violet smiled. "Then we all have to celebrate."

Manny came in and closed the door. "It's getting cold."

"I want to celebrate, tonight," Violet said to him. "You got a job. This child finished her play."

Lily said, "Dom still hasn't finished reading it. Maybe there's nothing to celebrate about the play."

Violet closed her eyes for a moment, then opened them again and looked at Lily. "You know the poor girl had a perforated bowel, from the typhoid. They operated on her, and her poor heart began to give out. Thirty-seven years old. I was born the year before she died. I got so many more years out of it than she did, I had all the advantages, and I didn't do shit compared to her."

"You taught all those children," Lily said. "You gave that to life. You've done fine."

"I wasn't seeking pity, *cher.*"

"No pity," Lily told her.

"Everything I do is the last thing I do, until I do it again." Violet laughed softly. "I'm almost entirely spirit, now. And I'm making you nervous."

Dominic came down, carrying the pages of the play in one hand. He set them in Lily's lap, and stood over her, arms folded. "I love it."

"Oh, do you really, Dom?"

He reached down, took the play from her lap and set it on the table, then took her hands and pulled her to her feet. "It's beautiful, and it says as much about you as it says about her."

"Then we celebrate," said Manny. "Money is no object."

"We don't have money for anything," said Violet, "but whatever we need."

She started to stand, and couldn't. "Help me get up," she said to the two men, who quickly moved to her side. They lifted her by her forearms, and after she was standing, her legs momentarily wouldn't support her. But then she got her balance, tottering slightly, until Manny had fetched a cane for her. She used the cane, turning slowly to the door.

"Daddy's," she said.

Outside, stars sparkled in perfect clarity on one side of a prodigious coastline of luminous cloud, smooth as a sandy shoreline. The moon was just behind the cloud, which was advancing, almost perceptibly. By midnight the whole sky would be overcast with it. They got into the Oldsmobile and drove to Daddy's. They had a waitress they didn't know, and Daddy's relatives were off somewhere, probably on their way north, Violet said. They had family in Chicago, and on Christmas they often made the trip.

Manny ordered wine, and when it was poured, Dom held up his glass. "Here's to Lily and the play," he said.

Violet said, "And to Manny's new job."

"Amen," said Dom.

They all drank. Lily felt rather weirdly out of it, though she tried hard not to show this to the others. She looked around the room at the little groups of people, families and friends, eating, or just finished with eating. It came to her that she missed her mother and father. And Peggy, too.

"I think I'll go to Virginia to celebrate New Year's with my parents," she said.

"Virginia's cold," Violet said. "This time of year."

"Do you want company?" Dom asked.

"I think I'll just take Mary and go," Lily said. And when she saw the look of distress on Dominic's face, she added, "For the holidays."

He held his glass up again. "To all holidays, wherever they are."

Violet leaned toward the baby and said, "You want to celebrate, too? Don't you?" The baby smiled and gave forth a delighted little cry.

Lily touched Dominic's sleeve, and pulled the cloth, so that he turned to her. "I'm so happy, Dom. And you really liked it?"

He nodded, and took her hands. "No, I loved it." He leaned over and kissed her cheek. "Can I come with you? Just for the holidays?"

This surprised her, and, in fact, she had been thinking about being on the road again, just her and the baby. She touched the side of his face and said, "Sure."

But he had seen her surprise. "You go," he said warmly, squeezing her hand. "We've got you and Mary for Christmas."

3

THE SOUTH AFRICAN SKY is purple and streaked with heavy clouds, a twilight sky, over a chain of beautiful mountains, stretching the whole length of the horizon. Mary steps out of The Palace Hospital and sits weakly on a hard-backed chair on the veranda. Off in the low hills in the near distance, she hears gunfire. The sun is behind the building, so its long shade extends all the way to the gate, with its crossed beams and its bronze latch. There's a bicycle propped incongruously against it. Off to her right, some of the roofs of Simon's Town are visible.

The air is growing chilly. The nights here are always cold, no matter the time of the year. In the hospital are several hundred wounded soldiers, boys, really. Boer prisoners who have been wounded or are sick and dying. So many of them die. She has seen so much death now, and is so exhausted and feverish, she's almost numb to it.

Almost.

A number of new nurses arrived this afternoon, and one of them joins her now, a young woman from London society, who is formally trained, and belongs to the Wesleyan missionary group.

—I can't bring myself to feel Christian toward them, this nurse says, sitting beside her with a sigh. She pauses a moment, then sits forward and regards Mary:

—I'm sorry. We haven't been properly introduced.

—Mary Kingsley.

—Margaret Lowes.

They shake hands, and then Miss Lowes draws back.

—You have fever.

Mary shrugs. They are silent, and more gunfire sounds in the hills.

—You're quite warm.

Now, Mary nods.

—Have you lived here long? Miss Lowes asks.

—No.

She sighs again.

—Mary Kingsley. That's a nice name. Somehow familiar-sounding. Have we met before?

—No.

Another minute later, a second nurse comes out, also from the Wesleyans. She sits on the other side of Miss Lowes and speaks familiarly with her about the horrors inside. Miss Lowes says:

—Have you met Miss Kingsley?

—I haven't had the pleasure. Hello, my name is Chalmers.

Mary nods at her.

—How long have you been here? Miss Lowes asks.

Just now, both women appear to be dissolving before her eyes. The light wavers, and out in the sinking sun the mountains shift, and then shift again. She gathers herself, fixes her eyes on the two women, and sees them assemble into their respective shapes, staring at her with concern, and not a little fear.

—I'm just so tired, she tells them.

—I do hope we can be given the chance to work with our own boys, says Miss Lowes. These chaps are so dirty.

—Miss Kingsley, have you always been a nurse? I mean, you aren't with the Wesleyans.

—I've been 'ere for a month. I came from London.

—Oh, you did. And what did you do in London?

Mary stares at them. Then she smiles, or thinks she does.

—I kept 'ouse.

—You show such skill, such a knowledge of medicine, for being a housekeeper, Miss Lowes says. Wherever did you learn it?

—Reading in my father's library.

—But the practical skills.

—That is practice, Mary says. You learn 'ow by doing it over and over.

—But how did you come to leave your household?

—I wasn't needed anymore.

—Cashiered, were you? How awful.

—I volunteered to come 'ere, Miss Lowes.

—And how perfectly fine of you.

Miss Chalmers clears her throat, her little fist over her lips. Then she sits forward and says:

—I noticed that you had a great familiarity with the bodies of these awful young men. I believe it is most Christian of you. It's all I can do to go near them.

—Are you originally from London? Miss Lowes asks. That is, do you make your home there?

—Not quite, says Mary.

—You've been worked awfully hard, haven't you. I'm so glad we've come.

—I 'aven't got much sleep, Mary says. Red wine only 'elps a little.

—Evidently not schooled in London, Miss Chalmers murmurs to Miss Lowes, who makes an effort to cover this with a cough.

—Well, you should try to rest now.

—Yes, says Miss Chalmers. You do look as if you feel ill.

—It's nothing, Mary says, though she knows enough to understand exactly what is happening to her.

—We'll hold things down, says Miss Lowes.

—If I can only sit 'ere and rest a bit. I'll be able to work on a little.

—Perfectly wonderful of you.

Mary closes her eyes, and the other two begin to chatter about the hardships that await them. They are naively excited about it all, these well-trained young women who have so far seen only a smooth sea passage and a barracks room lined with beds in which men they do not consider their own lie suffering, or dying. They seem so young, these two. Babies. They go on about the people they left behind in London, and it is evident to Mary that neither of them has the slightest idea about her, or about Africa, or about the carnage all around them.

She tries to rise, but can't. They do not notice this. They go on talking, and she feels herself drift toward delirium, sees rivers, men, dark faces, women and running children and masks, the fierce animal eyes of some lost night, Batty and Dolokov and Guillemard, her mother and father, the shadows moving toward her and then receding, the night sky gliding over, and the swells of the boundless, storm-tossed sea. She opens her eyes and looks at the fantastically altering shape of the world, and she knows this is her last fever. The gunfire comes across the undulant green plain leading to the hills, the softening shapes of the mountains.

4

December 2, 1990
Lily,

As must be painfully obvious, I've decided to make one last communication with you, to let you know what my plans are and to set some things in motion, too. I want you to know that I bear you no ill will. I mean that. I hope you're happy now, and if you're not, I hope you find happiness.

When I left you that morning and headed for the dealership, I was as close to doing something really pathological as I hope I ever get. You were right to worry about it, and I was thinking exactly what you were afraid I was thinking that time at the July Fourth party, when you found me with Buddy's rifle. The truth is, I had started thinking about it a lot by then. At any rate, I drove the car down to the river and sat on the bank for a long time, trying to figure out some course of action. I couldn't stand anything any longer, the whole pressure of keeping up appearances about something that had been ruined for me for good. It was finished between us and I knew it, even if you didn't, because no matter how hard I tried I couldn't get the facts out of my head, couldn't shake the anger all of it caused every time I thought of it, and you were right, we were only marking time, faking it, and it was just killing me. I acted like the good father as best I could, and I mean I really tried. But it wasn't there, and nothing had any taste for me anymore and the future looked even worse to me, looked like it was only going to go on getting worse.

When I decided to leave, to take up my own life elsewhere—when it hit me that I had, really, nothing but the accident of blood keeping me in Oxford, and that I could spare myself the trouble of worrying what Sheri and my mother and Roger and Rosa and all of them would know, and what all of your family would know, just by getting out, taking up my life somewhere far away; when I realized how much it hurt me to have to be there where Buddy died and with those people whose faces and voices and every gesture reminded me of it; when I realized, in short, that I could leave, that nothing was keeping me from leaving—well, I felt like a man who has had a tooth pulled after a long period of suffering and worrying over it. The tooth has been his only concern for so long that he forgets what life can be like without pain, and when it's out, and the pain's gone, the relief is like nothing words can describe.

I had already been thinking of committing an irrevocable act, merely to spare myself the humiliation. And I came to the knowledge that the act could consist of simply leaving everything, and everyone.

It's easier than you might imagine.

I wish things could've been better for us. I wish we had both been better at it all. But we weren't. Neither one of us was. If that sounds bitter, it is not meant to. The fact is, now that it is out and everybody knows about it, I'm finding it easier to live with, and I admit that I wonder how it would be if we tried to work things out. If we were to think about finding some ground on which to meet and find some way back to each other.

I'm living like a single man, now. But I wanted you to know I've not begun the divorce process, though a lawyer has advised me to under the circumstances of my having left the way I did. The lawyer's advice was to behave as if there would be an attempt at vindictiveness on the other side. I haven't followed his advice, of course. I miss you. I miss you both terribly. I just couldn't stand it thinking about how it would be when Mary was told who her father really was, and how she'd look at me then, and I know that's selfish, but I couldn't help it. I see now that nothing was as bad as my imagining of it, and the one thing I've learned out of all this is that there is not a thing you can do intellectually to change a feeling once it happens to you. But you can change an outcome. I do believe that. You can find a way to make up for your failings, and go on.

As you'll see by the postmark, I'm stationed in Texas—officer training school. Talk here is all about the Persian Gulf. I don't think it'll add up to much, and even if it does, I'll be here, still, in training. I am finding out how much I was made for this kind of life, where everything is in its place and one doesn't have to be questioning everything all the time, and maybe I should've stayed in premed. Anyway, this war would have to end up being a protracted struggle for me to be involved in it. So there's no need to worry. I acted precipitately when I severed ties with the people in Oxford, including Nick, with whom relations had been very difficult for a long time, even before Buddy died, but especially afterward. He was very helpful through the process of my separation from the family, and now I'm hoping to elicit his help in arranging some sort of connection with them again, after all. I do not feel that I did anything to apologize for, since I was acting in faith, and in pain. But I think I deserve some benefit of the doubt, and maybe you might feel the same way.

I wish you and Mary could see me here, in this element, where I'm not afraid all the time and worrying what people are thinking about me. I know I haven't been the best husband to you, Lily, but I hoped that after all the dust settles, we might find our way to some sort of life again.

I forgive you. Love,
Tyler

December 18, 1990
Dear Tyler,

I am happy to think that you are relieved of your toothache. I don't think I want to see you now, or ever again. Judging from your recent letter, I have only to go on fearing the next time something difficult comes along, and the next trouble you feel must be dealt with by leaving without a single word as to what you've planned or where you're going. And it's inspiring to see how far you're willing to go to forgive my depredations. No, Tyler. It won't ever be that easy, and I don't know where you got the idea it was or could be. I can truthfully say I feel quite fortunate to have been through this last four months

∞

She tore the page out of the pad and crumpled it in her fist. She wanted nothing from Tyler, now. The rage that she felt she put down to pride, and she would make the effort to let that go. Something of the anger would always remain, she knew, but it would eventually be manageable, as an old wound becomes manageable. One can adjust, and work on the problem. She told herself this, but nothing quite soothed her.

She was sitting in the wing chair by the living room window, with a pad of paper on her lap, trying not to cry. Aunt Violet had observed her writing the letter, and had labored into the kitchen to make herself some coffee. When she came back, Lily had wadded the page up and dropped it into the trash can beside her chair, and she was wiping her eyes with the backs of her hands.

"I've spent most of the last thirty years worrying about one thing," Violet said, carefully placing herself in her chair by the other window. "Dying." She laughed, as if surprised by her own admission.

The two women were now in opposite corners of the room, with the tall, sunny windows between them. They were facing the entrance to the dining room, which was just beyond the bath of sun coming through the windows. Lily closed her eyes for a moment and felt the craving for some sleep. It had been a long, tossing night of bad dreams and worries. The baby had coughed several times, and seemed congested again. Lily feared another bout of flu. But in the morning Mary was herself, overactive and cranky, and then bright and comical by turns. Even her temper was heart-pleasing, and made for laughter.

Now she was asleep in the crib upstairs.

Violet sipped her coffee, holding the saucer under the cup. Then she placed it all on the lamp table at her side, and leaned back. "What a strange household we make."

Lily saw the other woman's bony knees, and the threadbare sleeves of her dark blue dress, with the small white polka dots. This morning she looked too gaunt, depleted and pallid around the eyes, and her breathing was laborious, as if the effort of talking might harm her.

"You don't have to entertain me, Violet. I'm writing a letter."

"Am I disturbing you?"

"Oh, no."

"I thought you were writing the play some more."

"No, it's done—for now, anyway."

"But I'm disturbing you."

"You're not disturbing me. I just didn't want you to think you had to entertain me."

"I never thought that, *cher*. I said: 'What a strange household.'"

No response occurred to Lily, so she left a pause.

The other woman regarded her. "Did you say something?"

"No."

"I thought you said something."

Lily kept still, having smiled at her and nodded. She looked at the pad she held on her lap, and realized that she wasn't going to write anything just now. Violet was observing her with a discerning, narrow gaze; it might even have been scheming. She said, "What is it?"

"You look worried, *cher*."

"I was just writing my—my soon-to-be ex-husband."

"You're at the start, *cher*. Don't be so down in the mouth, if you can help it. You know the worst—most unhappy time in all the years I've had? My twenties. And I've spent the rest of my life wondering what I could've been so unhappy about back then. I was in love, I was out of love. I was always in a panic, running from one extreme to the next. Always making myself miserable."

"I'm all right," Lily said. "Really." But she sniffled, and was angry with herself for it.

"I hate to see a young person unhappy," Violet said. "You finished your play and it has made you sad."

"I'm not sad."

"People ask me if I have any regrets," Violet went on, apparently veering off to another subject. "I say I wish I had learned to stop doing math, all the time. All that counting and subtracting and figuring, based on the arbitrary thing—when it stops. When any of us stops. It's a stop. We stop. Counting takes away some joy."

"I don't count," Lily said.

"No, I wasn't talking about you, *cher*. I wasn't sitting here trying to give you a lesson. I said that about being down in the mouth, but that was for *my* benefit. I want lighter company."

Presently, Lily said, "You've been an inspiration to me."

"I never liked hortatory speeches, *cher*. I crave interesting talk. Cheer me up. So I can stop *counting* all the time."

Lilly sought vainly for something else to say. But now Violet had nodded off, her head lolling forward, her skin-and-bone hands, with the blue veins roped across the backs of them, gripping the chair arms.

Lily waited. The room was so quiet. Somewhere out on the street, a dog barked and yelped. The sunlight changed, a cloud passing over, and the room was gray for a few seconds, before the light returned, beams of it, full of dust rising in a slanting rush.

Violet lifted her head and then reached for more coffee. She took a sip, and looked over at Lily. "What're we waiting for, *cher*?" Her smile was almost a leer. "You and me."

"Mary's going to be waking up soon," Lily said.

"Waking and sleeping. Yes. A lot of that."

She stood. "Can I get you something, Aunt Violet?"

The old woman considered this, then shook her head slowly. "No."

"Mary will cheer us both up," Lily told her.

"It's the afternoon nap," said Violet. "Mary will be very cranky."

This had indeed been the pattern, and the child proved to be true to form. She sat in the middle of the living room floor and whined and cried, and nothing Lily did would placate her. Violet sat in the chair, sipping cold coffee and drifting in and out of sleep. But then, toward evening, she seemed to perk up. She went into the kitchen and began to put together some gumbo. Since she had been forced to stop driving, she had begun to get into various dishes, cooking. It had been a thing that fascinated her when she was younger, she said, only fifty. The spicy fragrance of the gumbo filled the downstairs rooms. Dominic came home and went in to help out, after picking Mary up and dancing around the living room with her, singing about Santa Claus. Lily couldn't bring herself to share in the festive mood, still thinking about the letter from Tyler. When Manny came in from the restaurant, he was also out of sorts, and so at dinner he and Lily were of one mood, while Dominic and Violet were lighthearted, faintly intolerant of their dour companions. They communicated this through the things they said to Mary in her high chair, and the remarks they made between them—Violet leading the way by saying that in all her many years she had hardly ever had a dinner so good, and it was Christmas, another of her many Christmases, and how wonderful it would be if the whole world could have such enjoyment, every single minute. Dominic talked about how much he liked the play, and said she should title it *The Shores of Home*, since the title *Hello to the Cannibals* suggested something rather more lighthearted than the story of the tragic early death of a great explorer and travel writer, who, at least in Lily's portrait of her, was lonely for a man, and who, at the end, fell in love with a homosexual and was rebuffed. "Anyway," he went on, "there're the people in Oxford, of course—since they've already expressed interest in it."

"Wait a minute," Lily said. "That's not what the play is about."

"Well, in a way it is. I mean, what's all that stuff in the prologue about: 'Don't let them tell you I wasn't in love,' or words to that effect. That announces it, doesn't it?"

"That's not how I meant the play," Lily said. "I meant it to be about how she used what life gave her and went out and saw what she could see. I meant it to be about bravery. The different kinds of bravery. She had it for everything that ever happened to her."

"Okay," Dominic said. "And she had it for the fact that no man ever loved her, too."

"What're you saying?"

"I'm saying that's there. It's in the play as you wrote it."

Lily shook her head, and for a moment, no one said anything.

"Don't be upset with me," Dom went on, laughing softly. "I love it. I think it works on every level, the ones you say and the ones I say."

Lily sighed. "I'm in a bad mood. I had a letter from Tyler today."

Dominic's smile disappeared. The others simply stared at her as she told them the rest of it.

"Are you going back to him?" Dominic asked.

She frowned and gave him an incredulous look.

"You're going to tell me you don't feel the slightest pull?"

"I know what I'm going to do," Lily told him, "and what I'm not going to do. I don't want anything from Tyler."

"Can I see the letter?"

"I threw it away."

"Where? The trash hasn't been emptied, has it?"

"Leave it alone, Dom. It's just a lot of self-excusing bullshit. Really."

Violet said, "She was moping around all afternoon."

Lily turned to her. "It's still *all right* with me, Aunt Violet."

"Okay, *cher*. I'm sorry to interfere."

"I'd like to see the letter," Dominic said.

Lily put her fork down. "What difference does it make, Dom? I told you what it says. I'm not even going to respond to it."

"You're still in love with him."

"Oh, for God's sake, what difference would *that* make? Even if it was true?"

"It makes a difference to me."

"Why? Why does it make any difference to you? How could it make any difference to you at all, Dominic?"

"Both of you—that's enough now," Violet put in.

Dominic stood. "I only wanted you not to be suffering it," he said. "I wasn't looking for comparisons."

"Now, I haven't the slightest idea what you're talking about," Lily said. "What in the world are you talking about? Comparisons—what is that?"

"Forget it," he said. And started to move from the table.

She stood and caught his arm. "No, tell me. I want to know what you meant." As she spoke, she was aware of motion to her right, and a sudden banging. Manny had begun beating the end of his fork against the table.

"Stop it, stop it, stop it." His voice was even, the words clipped, calm. But the banging upset Mary, who began to cry. Lily went over to her and lifted her out of the chair. Manny went on, "I hate this day. I hate this day."

"All right," said Dominic. "It's cool. We're having a discussion. Let's everybody calm down."

"This is not a good day," Manny said. "This is a bad day."

They all sat down, Lily holding Mary on her lap.

"I was fired today," Manny said. "My job ees over. The manager found out about my—about the positive—the HIV."

Dominic seemed rather visibly relieved. He sighed and shook his head, and then strove to appear concerned. "You've already got the other job. Start early. We'll be all right," he said. "Christ, don't scare me like that. I thought you were going to tell us that—well, just think before you say a thing like that: 'This is a bad day.' Jesus, Manny."

The baby had come to a standing position on Lily's thighs now, facing her, the unsure baby feet pressing and shifting the small weight into Lily's bones, reaching beyond Lily's shoulder for the statuette on the counter. She turned the baby and held her up, then set her in her lap again, wrestling with her, because Mary wanted down. Looking across at the others from this straining, she said, "Mary and I have to find some other place to live."

"No," Dominic said. "That's just not so."

Manny shook his head. "I don't want anyone to leave."

Aunt Violet sat back and folded her hands in her lap. "Everyone finish eating. The wolf hasn't broken the door down. We're all right."

"No one has to leave," said Dominic. "We'll work it out. That's my child, too."

"No one's contesting that," Lily said.

"Well, you can't make a decision like that—you and Mary leaving. You can't just decide that like it's only the two of you and I'm not involved."

"I didn't mean it that way," Lily told him.

"Both of you be still," said Violet. "Before you say things you don't mean."

"No one has to leave," said Manny. "Please."

The baby began to complain and cry, and so Lily set her down and watched her crawl to the other side of the room. They all watched.

"Manny," Violet said. "You have a job to go to."

Manny said, "What if they find it out from the restaurant about me?"

"It's a motel clerk's job," Dom said. "It couldn't matter to them."

5

$\mathscr{T}$HE FOLLOWING MORNING, Violet and Manny took a cab somewhere. Amy took Mary, while Lily and Dominic went off to work. The morning was gray and misting, the color of dashed hopes. They didn't say much. Dominic was still smarting over the night before, and Lily was beginning to have thoughts she knew to be unworthy of her: that all men were alike; they were all possessive and selfish in the same way, all involved in their children only as aspects of ego. She thought of her own father, with his midlife affair and his marriage to a girl half his age. A girl. That's all Peggy was. And they were having a child. Scott would be fifty by the time a child was born. He would have to live as long as Violet to be able to give that child a parent as other children are accustomed to parents. It was selfish and the whole country had given over to it: the entire culture was built on greed and avarice, not so much for money, but for ease and power, or the illusion of power, or for pure empty sensation. She was occupied by these thoughts when she dropped Dominic at the bookstore, and they exchanged a few words about how he would get home. He would get a ride from one of his co-workers.

"Fine," she said, feeling priggish and dismal.

"Are you still upset?" he asked.

After a pause, she said, "No." And she felt like crying.

She drove the Olds through what was now a downpour, passing the cemeteries with their teeming blocks of heavy stone, packed-together granite mausoleums and statues and towers, all gray with a watery, stained grayness, as if tarnished by the rain. She thought of George Kingsley, traveling the globe to keep from fulfilling his responsibilities to his wife and two children. Her disaffection had settled into a kind of imponderable gloom, in which it was impossible to have a positive thought. The play was finished and nothing would come of it, and all the work on it had been wasted.

At the school, she was greeted with a crisis involving four students who had gotten into a fight, and the fight had racial overtones—two of the boys were black and two were white; there was still a lot of tension in some parts of the city over the previous winter's protests about the krewes and Mardi Gras. Lily didn't understand it all fully, but she had seen enough racial tension to know that this would not yield to talk. She was placed in charge of resolving the matter—calling parents to apprise them of the situation, and speaking to the four boys who were involved.

The morning's work took all the energy she had. There were students decorating the classrooms, and the bulletin boards in the hallways, for parents' day; the school chorus was preparing a concert. Their rehearsing sounded in the bricks and mortar and beams of the old building, and there was no escaping it: Christmas cheer. The song they were working so hard to perfect, using a complicated descant and a polyphonic arrangement of many harmonies, was "We Wish You a Merry Christmas." The song rang in Lily's ears and embedded itself in her thoughts, adding to her dejection.

She drove back to Burgundy Street with the radio blasting jazz, and nothing would erase the song from her mind. Her usual parking space was taken, and she had to pull around the corner to St. Philip Street and go halfway up the block. She got out of the car in the rain—it was still coming down, a steady, straight, windless screen—and hurried to the corner and up to the entrance of the house, getting soaked and feeling all the more fractious as a result. She was muttering curses as she climbed the front steps of the house.

And almost ran into Nick.

He was standing at the door, having apparently just rung the bell. And he had seen her hurrying toward him on the street. "Hey," he said, with a casualness that seemed faintly rehearsed. "I thought that was you."

She couldn't speak for a moment. She was very glad to see his face. She stood back a little and could only say, "Nick."

"I rang the bell," he said, indicating the door.

"The baby-sitter's here somewhere with Mary."

He smiled. "Are you locked out?"

She came to herself. "No, of course not." She reached in for her key, and opened the door, pushing in ahead of him. Water spilled from the folds of their coats onto the hard wood floor of the hall. She called for Amy, and led the way into the living room.

Amy came from the upstairs, where she had put Mary down for her nap. She was introduced, and then softly excused herself. She had work to do at home. Lily walked her to the door, thanking her, and helped her into her coat. She watched Amy walk away down the streaming, rainy sidewalk, holding her umbrella. Nick was still standing in the living room with his coat on.

"Hey, take your coat off," she said. "Stay awhile."

"I can't stay very long. I just thought I'd—you know—" He looked at her. "Stop by." The falseness of the note he struck rendered the moment nearly absurd. She drew in a breath to ask what he was doing in New Orleans, and saw how much this would contribute to the already considerable awkwardness of the moment. In the next instant, she decided that a joke was the only possible response.

"You just happened to be in the neighborhood."

"I—I took a day, you know." He shrugged, and it was as if she had caught him out in some way; the look on his face was so sheepish.

She took the step toward him: "I'm so happy to see you."

He looked down, muttering, "Well, you know. Thought I'd—come by." Then, seeing the place on the carpet where his coat had dripped, he murmured, "Jesus."

"Here," she said, reaching for the coat as he took it off.

She hung their coats on the coat tree in the hall, and was momentarily grateful for the pause to think.

He still stood in the living room, in the gray light of the windows.

"I finished the play," she said, reentering the room.

"Oh—hey, that's great. That's good news."

"Dominic's read it, and says he loves it."

Nick smiled. "No prejudice there."

It was a glimpse of the old Nick, she thought. But then he shifted his weight and looked very uncomfortable, even regretful, as if he wished to call the words back.

"I'm not going to send it to my father."

"No?"

"I haven't decided where, yet."

"You don't want to put him on the spot."

"You've grasped it." She smiled. "Do you still want to read it?"

His expression lightened. "Yes. Very much."

"What if it's awful?"

He grinned, shaking his head. "I'll deal with it." The rainy light from the tall front windows gave the room a painterly look—soft contrasts, coupled with a muting of the colors, Nick standing there.

"Actually the rules are these: you have to like it, you have to say you like it, and you have to mean it."

"I accept the rules with an open heart," he said.

There was something downcast about him, and she took another step toward him, noticing, with a mild sense of chagrin, that he took a small stride backward. "Nick," she said. "What is it? Is everything all right?"

"Sure," he answered, nodding automatically. "Sure."

The silence stretched between them. She started into the kitchen, saying that she wanted some coffee, and asking if he would have a cup. He said, "Sure," and followed her, and took a seat at the table. He looked around at this room with the same placid expression, not incurious, but polite, mildly observant, more a kind of nervous movement of his gaze away from her. He tapped his fingers on the smooth surface.

"Nick, have you got some kind of news?"

His face didn't change. "I had to come down here to see about expanding the dealership. There's a Mazda dealer looking to sell out."

"So you'd—you'd have one here?"

"Maybe. I haven't looked at it yet. It's Millicent's—Millicent wanted us to look at it. She and Roger have begun to take more of an interest in things." He emitted a small laugh, out of one side of his mouth, and when he spoke it was more to himself than to Lily. "And I was the one who wanted to expand."

"Would you move down here?"

"To tell you the truth, I'm leaving the business."

She was attending to the coffee. She stopped and looked at him. "What are you going to do?"

He shook his head. "I'm not sure. I'm looking around, I guess. I haven't said anything to the others."

"Will you stay in Oxford?" She had still not gone back to what she was doing.

Again, he shrugged. "Maybe, I don't know."

She poured water into the coffeemaker, spooned the ground coffee into the top, then turned it on. He had put his hands up to support his chin, and was simply staring at the tabletop.

"You seem down," she said.

"I'm okay."

"Are you?"

He looked away. "I've been better."

She waited for him to go on, but he said nothing.

"How's Sheri?" she managed.

"Let's see—how's Sheri. It turns out that Sheri is seeing somebody. Sheri is looking for herself, I guess you'd say. And she's figured out that the best way she can be a good wife to me is to see other people. It's the nineties, you know. She spends all her time lately with this one person. A shrink, this guy. Lots of inner-child crap. Have you ever looked at the list of 'rights' those people say everybody has? It ought to be called the inner Hitler. But before Dr. Freud Lite, as I'll call him, there was a professor. I don't know." He drew an invisible circle on the table with one finger, avoiding Lily's gaze. "She's—she's performing stupendous feats of rationalization and mental gymnastics to have her way, and still have me and all the trappings that tell her she's not out of her fucking mind. This shrink is married, by the way."

Lily attended to the coffee.

"And that's how Sheri is. But then you already know most of this."

She looked at him. "I hated it, Nick. And I told her so."

He frowned now, folding his hands, as if about to recite something. "In fact, I wasn't going to say anything at all about it. To tell you the truth, I hoped it wouldn't come up. I wanted to see you. My friend. That's all."

Neither of them said anything for a beat.

"Do you—are you angry with me for not telling you about it?" Lily asked.

He pondered this, without taking his eyes away. Then he looked down as he spoke. "No." A second later, still looking down, he added, "To be absolutely truthful with myself, I haven't been completely faithful to Sheri, either."

Lily allowed him the space to continue.

"I mean I wasn't physically unfaithful."

"She said she wasn't either—"

He interrupted her. "It was you, Lily." His voice was almost too low to be heard. "I spent an awful lot of time, from the beginning, thinking about you."

She sat down across from him, and put her hands on the table. He wasn't quite looking at her. "From the beginning?"

"From the first minute, yes."

She stood and set about getting cups and saucers from the cabinet, and found herself talking of the house itself, its high ceilings and the old radiator along the wall. She poured coffee into two cups, took them over to the table, set them down, and took the seat across from him again. The rain was running steadily on the windows, creating a wavering, liquid look on his face, like the shadows of melting.

"Anyway," he said. "I've moved into an apartment."

She was silent.

"It was getting ridiculous living in that house as it was. Every brick—every corner of it, every hall and window and angle, even with all the trophies and the pictures down, it all reminded me of—kept calling everything up."

She felt something now that went beyond the sympathy she had felt for him since Buddy's death, or even the gratitude she had harbored during her last days in Oxford. Something about the sharp curve of his eyebrows rendered him present in a new way, as if an aspect of his being had unexpectedly been laid bare for her, and she was seeing the man alone, isolated from everything she had known about him or thought about him. She came close to reaching across the table to offer him her hand.

She said, "When I was a little girl, I used to say a prayer at night. 'Bless everyone I've laid eyes on, and everyone they've laid eyes on.' I don't even know where I got it, or learned it. But I used to say it every night. And then when I was fourteen, the night of my fourteenth birthday, something happened—a man who was supposed to be responsible for me put his hands on me in a way I knew was wrong, and he went all to pieces, and for me things—the world—went to pieces. And I couldn't say that prayer anymore. It had no meaning, you know. But I still like it, the sound of it. I like it more every day, these days."

"Say it again?" he said.

She repeated it. Then said, "It's silly, I know."

"It's wonderful, Lily. And if you think about it, it's what we pray for that says the most about us. I think of my mother praying for a spade in a damn bridge game, you know?"

She laughed. And then they were both laughing.

"Dom and Violet and Manny will all be home soon," she said. "Why don't you stay?"

"I really have to get back," he said. He started to say something else, but then stopped. His features drew into a discouraged frown.

"Nick," she said, "what is it?"

"Hey, hell—nothing."

"I'd like to see you again."

He shifted in the chair, looking beyond her for a second, and then bringing his gaze directly on her. "Well, we'll do that—stay in touch. Sure." He held both hands out, a gesture of openness. "I'm gonna read the play."

"Nick," she said.

"I don't want you to think—" He halted. "I didn't come down here to take advantage of you."

"Is that what you're doing?"

He leaned slightly toward her. "Look. I know we're both—we've both been through it. And—but I want to be truthful with you. I'd be lying to you if I said I haven't had you on my mind."

"I've been thinking about you, too," Lily said.

He stood, and she stood, too. For what seemed a paralyzingly long time neither of them moved. At last he strode down the long hall. His coat was hanging on the coat tree there, and he put it on. She had followed him. When he turned, he said, "I'd still like to see you." And his soft smile contained something of the old self-mockery. "Next time I'm in the neighborhood."

"Oh, the play," Lily said. "Wait here." She turned and headed up the stairs, into her room, where she checked on Mary. Still sleeping, one hand up by her mouth with the thumb cupped into the fist. The pages were on the nightstand. She collected them, looked at Mary once more, and then hurried back to the stairs. It came to her that she wanted Nick to see Mary. So she stopped at the landing, turned, and went back up to the room. She put the play in the drawer of the nightstand, and called downstairs.

"Come up and see Mary."

"Oh, the baby. Sure."

He came up to the room, and they stood over the crib. "Beautiful," he said.

She went to the nightstand and opened the drawer, feeling how absurd this little charade had been. Handing him the pages, she said, "I just thought—you might—I wanted you to see her."

"She's beautiful," he murmured.

They both stood there.

"How's Dom doing with it?"

She hesitated. "It's—it was a little tough at first. But he's great with her now."

"Must've been strange, telling him."

"You could say that." She laughed.

"So you're a family."

"A household, Aunt Violet calls it."

"I'd like to meet her."

She touched his sleeve. "Then stay. They'll be home in a little while."

"I really can't."

There seemed nothing in the world left to say. Then he held up the play and said, "When I've read this, I'll come down and I'll see them then."

Slowly, they left the room, and went down the stairs to the door, Nick leading the way. At the door he paused again, hand on the knob.

"I do want to see you," Lily said.

He stepped closer and put his arms around her, and she kissed his cheek. He held her quite tight, the side of his face against hers. She smelled the rain in his hair and felt the rough, damp cloth of his coat. After a moment he backed away. She looked at him, feeling the tears come.

"Sometime when it's not about them," he said.

"I don't care about it, Nick."

"I know." He reached up and took the tear from her cheek with a soft touch of his thumb. "I'll come see you again. Soon."

"Promise?" she said.

He nodded, his expression nearly solemn. Opening the door, he stepped out on the stoop. "Don't go anywhere I can't find you."

He went down the stoop and along the sidewalk to his car. She didn't realize until he had driven down the street and turned, and gone out of sight, that the rain had stopped. There was just a smoky haze on the city now. Dominic and Violet and Manny would be home soon, the other members of this household, this family. She did not know what would happen with Nick, or where anything would be in a month, a year, two years, ten years. She didn't know what the outcome of the finished play would be, and for now, she didn't want to think about it. She felt ready for anything—whatever it might be.

She sat by the window looking out on the street. Nothing to do just now, nothing requiring her attention. How wonderful it would be to stitch together a real family. She thought of Buddy Galatierre, who had always behaved as if he had stumbled onto happiness. Manny and Violet would be home soon, as would Dominic, her friend, who was turning out to be a father. She would be cheerful with him when he arrived; she would let him see how glad she was of him.

A little later, she lifted herself from the chair, realizing that she was physically quite tired, her legs aching, her hips sore. She thought of her spiritual companion of the past eight years, saw her on a pitching, yawing troop ship in the South Atlantic Ocean, a public figure in the brown uniform of an army nurse, treating sick sailors and soldiers, a still-young woman in the middle of heartbreak and exhaustion and all the physical hardships, far from anything she might call home, concentrating her attentions and her gifts on these boys, many of whom were already dying. Mary had gone out in the world and made her way, asking no special favors, requiring only that she be allowed to proceed as she wished; she had never been more nor less than herself. Taking a book from the table before her, Lily opened to Mary's picture, looked into the beautiful dark eyes, so matter-of-factly courageous. *Another human soul is also a wilderness, and the exploration of that requires courage, too.* It was as though she could hear Mary saying it, and in that moment, there was a stirring upstairs. Lily made her way there, climbing the long staircase, legs aching almost pleasantly, to her room in this house, where Mary Kingsley's namesake had awakened, and was standing in her crib, singing.

—Broad Run, Virginia, 1997–2002

AUTHOR'S NOTE

I wanted in particular to write about friendship, and about the affections we form for those who have gone before us. Some of what Mary Kingsley is known to have done is here, all of it in a form that is transmuted by fancy—Keats's deceiving elf. Moreover, and most important, it should be noted that I imagined a very large number of things for which there is no record. For instance, Mary's letters to an imagined someone in the future, her modern "correspondent," are the product of my imagination, as are many of the people Mary comes into contact with. Even those whose names come down to us from the time are, of course, imagined as they appear here. The fact is, I have presumed upon Mary Kingsley with the liberty of the novelist, but with great respect and affection for her, along with the growing admiration one experiences when examining her extraordinary life, and her uncanny ability to form lasting friendships while remaining a mystery to everyone. More than anything, of course, I wanted to tell a good story. Those who wish to read about the factual and historical Mary Kingsley should consult Katherine Frank's beautifully written *A Voyager Out,* or Cecil Howard's *Mary Kingsley.* There is also *The Life of Mary Kingsley,* by Stephen Gwynn, who knew her; and Kathleen Wallace's novel *This Is Your Home.* Or you might read Mary's own *Travels in West Africa,* and *West African Studies,* and finally Catherine Alexander's *One Dry Season: In the Footsteps of Mary Kingsley.* These books were an immense help to me in the construction of the novel, and I hereby acknowledge my debt to all of them.

—RB